PRAISE FOR THE ADVENTURES OF DUKE LAGRANGE SERIES

I0741388

A raucous new kind of action hero—Flash Gordon, Jack Burton, and Buckaroo Banzai got nothing on Duke LaGrange.

MARCUS MULLER, COMIC ARTIST (KING
OF THE UNKNOWN)

For goofy grown up pulp readers and sci-fi geeks, it's as much fun as a Pan-Galactic Gargle Blaster.

FRANK R. SJODIN, PULP AUTHOR AND
2017 AUDIO VERSE AWARD WINNER

[W]itty, fast-paced...[an] imaginative style of writing.

READERS' FAVORITE

PRAISE FROM READERS LIKE YOU!

PRAISE FROM READERS LIKE YOU!

THE ADVENTURES OF DUKE LAGRANGE OMNIBUS

VOLUME I (BOOKS I-III)

JAY KEY

STAR WHEEL
BOOKS

THE ADVENTURES OF DUKE LAGRANGE OMNIBUS BY JAY KEY. PUBLISHED BY STAR WHEEL BOOKS. © 2019 JAY KEY. © 2019 STAR WHEEL BOOKS. WWW.STARWHEELBOOKS.COM

FOR INFORMATION ABOUT SPECIAL DISCOUNTS AVAILABLE FOR BULK PURCHASES OR MEDIA COVERAGE, CONTACT PUBLISHER@STARWHEELBOOKS.COM.

INDIVIDUAL BOOKS EDITED BY TIM MAJOR. INDIVIDUAL BOOKS PROOFREAD BY SASHA GROSSMAN. COVER ILLUSTRATION BY MARCUS MULLER. BOOK FORMATTING BY VELLUM. USED BY PERMISSION. ALL RIGHTS RESERVED.

ISBN 978-1-7333472-1-1 (PAPERBACK) ISBN 978-1-7333472-0-4 (E-BOOK) ISBN 978-1-7333472-2-8 (HARDCOVER)

FIRST EDITION.

To Ron

THE ADVENTURES OF DUKE LAGRANGE BOOK I
HOW TO PICK UP WOMEN WITH A DRUNK SPACE NINJA
JAY KEY

HOW TO PICK UP WOMEN WITH A DRUNK SPACE NINJA

BOOK ONE

CHAPTER ONE

A NINJA CAN BE QUITE *handy when he isn't drunk off his ass.*

The crowd slowly poured into Cyborg Joe's Grill N' Go & the Why Not Saloon—voted the loudest bar in the galaxy for the past twelve cycles and home to the MechaBurger 8000, a treat that kills twenty-three percent of the life forms that try to digest it. Duke LaGrange clicked his fingers against the uneven wooden bar top and stared into a slightly dirtier-than-it-should-be glass containing just a small remnant of golden Glyptodian ale. The bounty hunter shook his head as his mind raced to solutions for his quandary. How was he alone and all of these other life forms, if they wanted to call themselves that, were lining up their prospects for the evening? He concluded that he had just grown too damn accustomed to the tried-and-true method of luring in intoxicated females with his sidekick's conversation-starter party tricks, most of which included an element of sword play and damage to the bar. It had to be. Regardless, this evening Duke knew he would have to revise his strategy or give up and join his masked friend on the barroom floor. And Cyborg Joe's wasn't known for having the cleanest floors.

"You know, Duke, you need to move your companion. That area of the floor is reserved for tonight's musical act," said the barkeep as she wiped down some sullied glass goblets imprecisely.

"Who's the act?"

"The Trampling Death Robots." She held the glassware to the light to examine its cleanliness.

"Any good?"

"Well, that depends. Do you like loud explosions and large objects crashing to the floor?"

"I'm not into the performance arts. Can they work around him?"

"I wouldn't advise it."

"Fair enough, Queen, I'll grab him. Nothing better to do, I suppose," the bounty hunter replied in a sullen tone.

"Alright, LaGrange. Hold up. Lay it on me. What's with the pouting?"

"Huh?"

"Look, you've frequented my little watering hole more than I care to recall—but, through all of the time that you've graced us at Joe's with your presence, I've come to know Duke LaGrange quite well. In fact, it's amazing what you can learn by pouring a man's drinks for as long as I have."

"I really don't know what you're talking about. Everything's fine. Great. Grand. Hunky dory, even."

Duke lobbed a forced smile in the Queen's general direction. She countered. All things considered, a snarky glance was getting off easy with someone like the Queen. No one really knew much about the Queen outside of a few key details: she was quite possibly the most powerful sentient being in the galaxy, she was a damn good bartender, and she was the only one that could control the portals that made Cyborg Joe's one of the most frequented establishments by space travelers from every sector. Portals connecting destinations in the universe and allowing intergalactic travel were by no means unique, that's how most spacecraft got from point A to point B. But portals so small and controllable that they could transport individual beings without ripping them to shreds at the atomic level just simply didn't exist. Except at Joe's. These portals also made it a key point of interest for the government du jour. Scholars quipped that the reason that there hadn't been a universal governing body for eons was because the Queen refused to give her endorsement to any one system of rule. There was always someone or something trying to unite the planets—dictators, religious groups, military coups, you name it—but none managed to stabilize for more than a moment. The universe wasn't in anarchy, though some individual worlds subscribed to that political arrangement— everyone just did their own thing. It was a system that received general approval.

Her age was also a point of debate amongst patrons of Joe's. She joked that she was old enough to have dated the single-celled organisms that were the very genesis of life. For some reason, Duke believed it. It just made sense to him.

Outside of those well-known characteristics, she was a complete mystery. No home world. No rumors or memories or accounts of a time before Cyborg Joe's. Not so much as a single eyewitness testimony of her existence outside of the bar itself. Even her name—"Queen Joe"—was just the product of legions of guests associating her with their favorite drinking locale. No one really thought her name was Joe—but it made everyone feel good. She never fought it.

"Duke, I know your typical game—hell, I've seen your

game for going on ten cycles. The whole bounty-hunter-by-day, playboy-by-night gig isn't exactly new in these parts. It's just that you play the part with such conviction. I don't see anything resembling conviction tonight. So what's going on? Mazilda Cloax again?"

"Seriously, Queen. I really think that..."

"Duke, for the sake of all that's right in this galaxy! You haven't even hit on me tonight!"

The bounty hunter, like most beings with the gift of sight, found Queen Joe attractive—very attractive, at that—but not even he had the audacity to engage her seriously with amorous intent. His flirtations had become almost a fixed prelude for ordering a drink at the bar. The Queen even told him once that she stored a few of his best lines somewhere deep in her memory as she felt they might one day be useful to another patron of Joe's, and only in the direst of situations.

"I'm sorry, you're off on this one, Queen."

She bent down to grab a bottle of Erontian saké behind the bar. Duke's eyes migrated southward and lingered.

"At least I know that you're not entirely broken."

"Sorry. Habit."

"So, talk straight to me. What's with the 'woe is me' shtick? Maybe I can help."

The bounty hunter inhaled deeply, exhaled slowly.

"Queen, well, it's quite—" he stumbled over his words uncharacteristically. "—embarrassing."

"You know good and well, Duke, that all I ask for in my clientele is that they show tolerance; understand that beauty comes in many forms; and pay me properly if they choose to use one of my portals. That's it. In return, I promise them a place in which they can unload their grievances without fear of condemnation, meet members of a new species or two, and enjoy a well-made martini. You've definitely met a 'friend' or two under my roof—and you've imbibed your weight in martinis. Now I think it's time that you let me know what's wrong and unload those grievances."

"Fine."

Duke paused, each of his thoughts waging a war against the others. The "shoulds" had a slight upper hand on the "should nots."

"I've lost *it*," Duke cried out. His admission dissolved a tightness in the pit of his stomach that he likened to a prisoner finally succumbing to cycles of torture.

"What exactly do you mean by 'it'?" Queen Joe questioned cautiously.

"You know... 'it.'" Duke let out an audible sigh. "My talent. My power. My mojo. My 'it.'"

"You can't hit on women anymore?"

"Not successfully."

The Queen turned away from the bounty hunter.

"Are you laughing? I thought this was a place where you could unload without condemnation?"

The Queen didn't respond but reached down and unlocked a small cabinet. She pulled out a dusty, transparent vessel containing darkened liquid the color of toasted caramel. *Earth whisky.* She slung two small glasses on the bar; one slid toward the bounty hunter and stopped just short of the bar's edge. Duke plucked it off the bar top and planted it before the Queen. She topped off both glasses in the potent liquor.

"To misplaced mojo!"

They both downed their drinks. The Queen refilled them as soon as they hit the wooden bar top.

"And finding it again," she said, finishing her two-part toast.

The whisky hit the back of Duke's tongue and immediately warmed his very being.

"Duke, I'm sorry, but I don't think that I can help you with your lady troubles—"

"I figured."

"Though maybe the whisky can. In fact, there isn't much that a little whisky can't fix."

Duke pondered this for a second and didn't disagree.

"However, I do have an opportunity for you. It might be the thing you're looking for to get your mind off of your current quandry."

"An opportunity? Queen, you've never asked me to track someone down for you—I'm honored. My 'bounty hunter slash playboy' billing always lists bounty hunter first, ya' know—I'm quite good."

"This certain opportunity falls outside of your current job description. It's a bit bigger in scope, I'm afraid."

"Go on."

Queen Joe pointed across the stage to the wall on the east side of the building. It was battered and beaten as if an entire armada had released a heavy concentration of hate upon its stone-like façade. Duke was familiar with this wall —in fact, all of the patrons, first-timers and regulars alike, were familiar with this wall. He surveyed the slender door frames that spanned the entirety of the barrier. Each frame surrounded an ornate door—all of them quite distinct.

"The portal doors?"

"No, not *my* portals. Over there. Beyond them, in the far corner."

Duke noticed it for the first time; tucked behind the portals, in the center of a recessed area hidden within the few shadows that escaped the glow of Cyborg Joe's neon advertisements. The bright beams danced erratically, crackling and sizzling.

"Another doorway? When did that happen? Where did it come from? Those wild lights shooting out of the opening are quite trippy though—nice touch."

"That gateway appeared without my consent a few days ago. The others I can control, for the most part—however, when I showed up to the bar today, this mess had ripped through the wall. We did our best to board it up but it's hard to not notice."

"Any ideas?"

"I don't know. It's been some time since I left Kelt or even the bar, so I get most of my adventures secondhand through those that stumble in here. I was curious if you had seen or heard about anything like this."

"I got nothing. I'm up the proverbial creek without a paddle... or even a boat. Though if I stare at it any longer I'm going to feel like I'm messed up on some Gheo'to Morphio root. Freaky."

"My final conclusion was that it's a dimensional tear similar to my other doors—but far more unstable. After examining it, I feel it leads somewhere."

"So it *is* a portal."

"I think so. However, my intuition tells me that it's not the sort of portal that leads to a happy field of lollipops. There's a negative energy; not necessarily evil—but negative."

"So what's this opportunity about? I'm assuming it has something to do with the door."

"Yes. I'm extremely worried about this intrusion. It isn't sitting right with me—and now some of the patrons are starting to not only notice it, but ask questions too. Questions that I can't answer. Cyborg Joe's doesn't *allow* questions that I can't answer. This is very unsettling."

"So, the opportunity?"

"Here it is. If you can successfully find out why this tear

is occurring in my bar and get rid of it—I'll give you access to my portals. Free of charge. For the next cycle. No questions asked. No reservations needed. Unlimited use. Needless to say, I've never offered this type of deal before."

Duke paused. "Why me? Because I'm depressed about losing my mojo?"

"No—but if you think about it, becoming the first person ever to be granted unlimited access to the portals— free of charge—can only help your reputation. I win, you win."

"That is, if I don't get obliterated by this pissed-off dimensional door."

"True. But I have faith in you, Duke LaGrange. I won't ask any questions about what you plan on doing or how you plan on doing it. Your methods are to your own design. Just as long as that thing is gone."

"How about another shot of that Earth whisky and I'll think about it. When can I give you my answer?"

"Tonight. If I'm not serving, tell Earl to track me down. I really hope you consider it."

Duke pounded the next glassful of whisky.

"Tonight... I can do that. I think I'm gonna see if this whisky is helping with my problem, first. I would prefer to get back on track without risking my life trying to exterminate an unhinged inter-dimensional anomaly."

"Do what you need to do. However, my offer will expire at the end of the night. Try not to get into trouble, Duke. This is not an offer that you will see again."

"One last question. Can Ishiro'shea come with me?"

"Of course. And you *do* realize that he is still on the floor?"

"Thanks for the reminder, Queen. Those damn ninja sidekicks—can't live with 'em, can't keep 'em from rendering themselves unconscious on overpriced beer. Am I right?"

Joe smirked. "Overpriced beer?"

"You know what I mean," the bounty hunter stammered. "C'mon, Queen—it was just a joke."

She responded only with an enigmatic smile—equal parts playful banter and genuine offense—and effortlessly tossed her rag to an approaching armor-shelled Glyptodian barkeep named Earl.

"I'll let you know by tonight," Duke replied as the Queen locked up the Earth whisky, "even though this little venture could come at a hefty cost!"

"Anything without a cost isn't worth having."

She disappeared into the rapidly burgeoning crowd of Cyborg Joe's.

CHAPTER TWO

THREE-HEADED ICE WOMBATS

THE BOUNTY HUNTER SAT STARING at eight feet of hulking Glyptodian.

"Hey Earl."

"Greetings, Mr. LaGrange. Welcome back to Cyborg Joe's. Can I be of any assistance in relation to your alcohol consumption or culinary desires?"

Earl was very capable behind the bar and had been employed at Joe's for as long as Duke could remember. Earl's coat carried only a trace of its once brown hue; now it shone mostly silver—in fact, Duke couldn't recall a time when the large biped appeared "young." The Queen once told him that she felt Earl added much-needed sophistication and class to her operation. Duke was aligned with that statement—though, in his travels, manners were never high on the list of requirements when choosing a place to knock back a few refreshments. Duke liked Earl but found him overly formal and a substantial downgrade in appearance from the Queen, so he decided it was the perfect time to go fetch Ishiro'shea.

"I'm okay right now, Earl. Just a little ninja retrieval on the to-do list."

"Sounds exhilarating, Mr. LaGrange. If you need anything, don't hesitate to ask. And give my regards to Mr. Ishiro'shea. When he awakens from his rest, that is."

Duke spun around on the stool, which gave a shrieking whine produced by a lifetime sans upkeep. As he headed over to his passed-out sidekick his attention was diverted by the high-pitched giggles of two young female humanoids. They appeared uninterested in the advances of two heavy-set humanoids adorned in tactical gear and looking very serious. *Military attempts to take over the universe must be in season. When will they ever learn?* Almost involuntarily, Duke performed a lightning-quick scan of the two female targets to make sure that they had at least two limbs and no more than three eyes. He wasn't picky but did have some standards. The pair possessed figures that Duke found instantly appealing. He particularly appreciated, at least aesthetically, the airtight polymerized chloroprene body suits that both females wore—jet black and with no discernible markings of any kind. His imagination was aroused by the question of where certain parts of their anatomy began and ended. *How did they get those damn things on,* he thought to himself, *and how do I get them off? I have a few minutes before the Robots go on—I'm sure Ishiro will be fine. Anyways, I need to test drive this whisky before I get back to the Queen with an answer about her little opportunity.*

"Ladies. Can I buy you both a drink?"

His line was met with more giggles and the batting of electric violet eyelashes—or at least, they were close enough to eyelashes. Any new adventure—especially one involving unknown dimensional tears—could wait a bit longer. *Tonight is saved.*

"If you don't know already, I happen to be Duke LaGrange..."

He waited for a sign of recognition. When it didn't come, he continued, "Adventurer. Trailblazer. Poet. A true man of the universe."

"Is that so, handsome?" retorted one of the females, followed by even more giggles. Her voice was surprisingly confident and possessed an almost soothing quality. However, she let the last syllable of each word dangle until she started the next. And that damn giggling never stopped. "This is my best girlfriend and fourth cousin on my quasi-aunt's side, Arlut. You can call me Turla, sugar. On Hilteria, it means 'very generous.'"

The corners of Duke's mouth shot upward in a sly grin. His voice, already deeper than most upright humanoids, lowered even further to become the velvety tones of an experienced seducer. "There is nothing I love more than a charitable soul."

After the third round of especially fiery Glyptodian Summer Ale, Duke launched into his adventurous tales of capturing the scum of the cosmos with nothing more than his wits and bare hands. His overly embellished accounts of danger and heroism were interrupted only by the thunderous explosions of the Trampling Death Robots that echoed through the cavernous dimensions of the bar—its ceilings as tall as a Quibbian erecto-varmint.

"So there I was on Tardasio 7 staring down a rabid, blood-sucking, three-headed ice wombat. He had just killed the entire staff of Sol's Bail Bonds-O-Rama and was headed for a local petting zoo," Duke said.

The two magenta-skinned females oohed and aahed in tandem at every exaggerated piece of the chronicle. They never missed an opportunity to bat those purple eyelash things.

"Now remember, ladies, I had just captured an entire gang of speed cycle assassins before lunch and was quite the worse for wear—but there was no way that I was going to let this demon beast get away with eating my benefactors." A bit of honesty somehow managed to slip through his defenses.

"What'd you say, hun? Benefactors?" asked Arlut.

Luckily, the Trampling Death Robots hit the crescendo of "I Want to Smash You, My Binary Baby" and Duke's delicate game of romance was preserved.

"I'm sorry, my beautiful belles," he replied with faux annoyance. "I was saying... there was no way that I was going to let this raging, maniacal demon beast get away with eating the poor, innocent, sweet, young orphans visiting the local children's petting farm." Emphasis on *orphans*.

Flawless recovery. He was also proud of his ability to augment his description with even more adjectives that were neither necessary nor true. *The whisky must be working.*

"Duke, honey, you're simply amazing."

The bounty hunter did not shy away from the praise.

"And utterly gorgeous. Are you sure you aren't lawfully bound to something?"

Turla's flirtations overwhelmed her companion's attempts. She was the alpha flirter.

Duke's chin raised triumphantly.

"My beautiful Turla, I am now and have always been lawfully bound to my oath of protecting the innocent, defending the peace, fighting for the freedom of all that deserve it, and honoring my home—the proud colony of Nova Texas. But maybe, just maybe, I have been waiting for someone equally as amazing to stroll into my life."

Duke thought he might have overstepped the bounds

into the realm of low-budget romance films; luckily, the Hilterian ate it up, as so many had before her.

This was the all-too-familiar homestretch. Duke was a hunter and his prey was wounded. He extended his hefty and calloused—yet comforting—hand and gently covered Turla's delicate digits that dangled from a perfectly circular palm that resembled glowing porcelain. He tilted his well-worn stone-colored Stetson so that his glare could pierce her defenses. *Kill time.* The intoxicated laughter morphed abruptly into a longing gaze that immobilized Turla. Even though his brown eyes were locked into the deep smoky obsidian of his conquest's, Duke could sense that Arlut—or as Duke christened her in his head, "Option B"—was growing increasingly jealous. Being his second choice would pierce her inebriation with a jolt of sobriety and Duke knew it. *Can't have that—not when the finish line is in sight.* Duke was well aware, from combing the vast unknown of the universe as the most infamous bounty hunter playboy of the last fifteen cycles, how to guarantee that a night of spoils would not be sabotaged by a really pissed off best friend. He decided to pick up the pace.

"Babe, how about we get outta—"

"Turla, I'm tired," interjected Arlut in a pouty tenor.

"I want to hear more stories from Duke," Turla snapped back emphatically. There was an implied "go away."

The purple visors attached to her eyelids fluttered rapidly and the back of her cranium pulsated, showcasing that she was ready for some mature recreation.

"Turla!" shrieked Duke's newest archenemy.

His autopilot set in. Unfortunately.

"Have you ever seen someone cut off their own head?" he directed at Arlut.

One of the more reliable lines in the world of misdirection.

"My friend would like to show you..."

Both females looked perplexed as Duke's words seemed to fade into the dense stagnant air of the bar. His eyes peered around, hoping to land on his emerald-clad sword-wielding Irish-Japanese cohort, who had a mastery of warding away potential killjoys like Arlut. Duke recalled the hundreds of instances in which he had used that asinine phrase and how he never needed to wait for Ishiro'shea to leap into action. It was the split-second sleight of hand that had allowed Duke to leave with "Option A" on countless occasions. By the time the victim typically collected themselves enough to respond to the bounty hunter's answerless riddle and fully take in the fact that a stout martial artist decked out in a bright green *shinobi shozoku* appeared seemingly out of nowhere, Duke had escaped with the top prize. When the victim had discovered she had been hoodwinked and turned back to address Ishiro'shea, the ninja would vanish. He was a ninja, after all. However, at this moment, Duke was ninja-less.

The Trampling Death Robots cacophonous guitar solo filled every pocket of breathable air at Cyborg Joe's—and triggered Duke's cognitive functions instantaneously.

Holy hedgehogs! Ishiro'shea! Damn this whisky.

Duke shouted to himself in a fit of sudden awareness, "Trampling Death Robots!"

A vision crept into his head of a messy puddle of squashed ninja. *And for what? A night of bright pink ecstasy with the faint undertones of average beer? Ishiro'shea probably wouldn't consider that a good enough reason.*

The bounty hunter started for the stage but was quickly halted by Turla's tight grip.

"Duke, honey, your friend would like to show us what?"

"What friend?" interjected Arlut. "I don't see any friend. I told you, Turla! I knew he was a lying sack of..."

"Shut up, Arlut!"

The Beta Hilterian cowered.

"Duke, now what were you saying?"

"Sorry ladies, I must attend to something kinda important."

Duke felt Turla's grip tightening.

"More important than me, sweetie?"

He writhed his hand out of the slightly moistened clutch of the Hilterian and tried to think of a clever, if not a bit flirtatious, response. He dug deep—but came up empty.

"I'll call you."

The next sensations that Duke felt were the simultaneous four-digit slap across his right cheek and the showering of Glyptodian Summer Ale all over his face. He cleared the booze from his eyes just in time for one last glance at the polymerized chloroprene-clad package of sensuality that he was letting slip through his fingers.

Okay, focus. Find Ishiro. But damn, those bodies. Focus. Yeah, those bodies.

CHAPTER THREE

THE WRATH OF SPRINKLES

T HE BOUNTY HUNTER RACED TO the stage floor where the Trampling Death Robots were about to begin their opus—a power ballad trilogy known as "Moonlight Over the Squashed Bones of Puny Beings, Parts I–III in E Flat"—and he hurled himself onto a table of animated Jungafallowians who were each clanking their two heads together with reckless aggression. The Trampling Death Robots were huge on Jungafallow III though, oddly enough, on Jungafallow IV they topped the planet's most wanted criminals list. Either way, they were in demand.

Upon his clean landing, Duke studied the performance area, his eyes darting with the speed and accuracy of lasers. He saw the Trampling Death Robots. He saw their devotees gathered around them, attempting to make the loudest sounds that their individual anatomies would permit. He did *not* see any flattened remains of an intoxicated assassin. *Is he really that good a ninja that he could have vanished postmortem?* Duke hated to admit it, but he was actually considering that hypothesis. Moments after he had come to terms with Ishiro'shea as a zombie magician, he caught a glimpse of what appeared to be a lime green comet. As his focus steadied in on the speedy Ishiro'shea—now stationary —he noticed that his musical instrument of choice was an ancient Earth katana. In the known universe, there were many types of swords, daggers, rapiers, blades, sabers, cutlasses, scimitars, and knives— but none of them doubled as a guitar.

He seems to be having fun and no one seems to mind; no reason to interject, I guess. If anything, this should be entertaining, Duke thought.

As Duke watched his partner in crime—well, his partner in stopping crime (in most cases)—wail away alongside the Trampling Death Robots, he took a seat next to a pair of two-headed Jungafallowians and an anthropomorphic musk ox.

"Hello there," the musk ox bellowed quite formally, "my name is Lilly and I come from one of the moons of Gartosh."

Duke did not reciprocate the niceties. Lilly seemed accustomed to being ignored.

The bounty hunter didn't really care for the explosion-centric rhythms of what constituted popular music in this area of the galaxy; however, even he couldn't deny the energy that the band generated. In fact, he even caught himself tapping the soles of his boots to the melodic tones of plasma grenades being detonated. There was no debate that the band had a really, really good percussion section.

As the sentient mechanical rock stars crushed both the stage and the occasional security guard, it became apparent to Duke that they were, in fact, not aware of the sword-wielding assassin dashing feverishly amongst them. As they smashed and crushed and kaboomed, Ishiro'shea added to each pounding roar a circular whip of his arm across the invisible strings of his katana-guitar. Duke hoped that the

Trampling Death Robots would just play on without noticing his enigmatic green sidekick but, as in so many cases, the alcohol outpointed the ninja. Ishiro'shea, who had perfected not only agility and nimbleness but also the ability to remain unseen in broad daylight, stumbled like a toddler trying to navigate through a field of tripwire in a rainforest. He crashed violently into the frontman of the Robots. Duke, while not knowledgeable in the realm of music, recognized the mechanical goliath immediately— mostly from wanted posters and the best cosmic gossip rags available. It was the infamous Sprinkles. *Damn*. Ishiro'shea managed to fall sword-first into the thigh plate of the raging lead singer and detonation specialist, who was known more for his destruction of hotel properties than for his lyrical genius.

The music screeched to a sudden halt. With Ishiro'shea still gripping his katana, Sprinkles grabbed the ninja's shoulder with his well-constructed human-like left hand. Duke didn't know the true origins of the Trampling Death Robots or which assembly-line conveyor belt they had fallen off—but he did not doubt the craftsmanship of their myste-rious creators. *Neither did Ishiro'shea's right shoulder*, the bounty hunter concluded. Ishiro'shea was paralyzed in the restrictive grasp. Sprinkles' right arm possessed less of a hand and more of a blunt instrument of obliteration. Extending from a thick silver gauntlet was a 900-pound (give or take) hammer that would make Thor embarrassed for toting a mere plexor in comparison. The robot slowly lifted his right arm upwards and into kill position. Ishi-ro'shea's bloodshot eyes remained half closed. *It has to be a pretty good night on the sauce to fail to react to your impending death by an extremely heavy hammer*. None-theless, Ishiro'shea—now held immobile by Sprinkles' hand —drifted into an alcohol-induced sleep. Sprinkles didn't seem to notice his adversary's narcolepsy and was more focused on the continued extension of his right arm. Sprinkles was a showman.

Duke's right hand fell to his hip and to the handle of his laser revolver. Even after a night of flirting, Earth whisky, and Glyptodian brew, he could place a shot from his laser revolver between the eyes of a pygmy hamster, blindfolded (not that blindfolding the hamster makes the shot anymore difficult). *Sprinkles will be a dead robot before he has a chance to drop that hammer on the skull of my inebriated lil' buddy*, thought Duke. And if a blast from his trusted pulse pistol—fabricated to appear like a vintage laser revolver for that more romantic feel—wasn't enough to take down the behemoth, there was always Ol' Betsy. Betsy was an out-of-date, out-of-production Widowmaker sonic shotgun that had been used during the settlement of the colony planet of Nova Texas. It had been the first firearm to harness the power of hydroxy re-gen explosion technology, now used in the majority of handheld weaponry in the galaxy, including Duke's pulse pistol. If hydrogen and oxygen particles were within a light year from the gun, it could generate the proper combination to create exploding projectiles. There was never a need to reload or, more importantly, worry about what color ammunition strap clashes with the user's favorite warmongering ensemble. Newer models sported elegant ammo—Betsy, not so much. What she lacked in sophistication and design, she made up for in pure noise. When Betsy sang, people listened. As much as Ishiro'shea was his sidekick and most trusted confidant, it was hard to tell if Duke LaGrange ever cared for anything more than he did Ol' Betsy.

It was known by all travelers in this part of the universe, Duke included, that Cyborg Joe's had really great drink specials and a better-than-average karaoke night, but even more so, it was known for its criminally loose firearm policy. This made it a hot spot for the criminally loose of mind. It was also why Ol' Betsy was resting nicely in Duke's custom-made Ootrelian tanned leather back holster without drawing even the faintest of regard from the other patrons. The one-sided staring match between Sprinkles and Ishiro'shea seemed to last for eons as Duke awaited the next move. His fingers twitched ever so slightly across the titanium butt of his revolver. His eyes fixated on the optical visor of the angered musician—in a situation such as this he always anticipated the next move by reading eyes (or a well-crafted mechanical vision apparatus). A less experienced man would have been nervous, but this was not a new position for Duke and his Irish-Japanese companion.

The robotic musician waited for the drunken stage crasher to make the first move. Time passed slowly and nothing happened. After all, Ishiro'shea was asleep. Duke could sense that Sprinkles was losing his patience and was concerned that his street cred as a bad mutha' was slipping —it might appear as though he was going to show mercy. The silence was broken by a few inebriated calls from the back of the bar.

"Wuss!"

"Poser!"

"Hack!"

"You can't even stop a squirrel monkey!"

These insults appeared to shake the metal performer. When a loyal Jungafallowian questioned his robotic manhood, Duke saw him snap. Sprinkles' cerebral processor sparked and his visor tinged a deep red. Just as Duke assumed, the eyes told the story.

The Queen's opportunity isn't looking like such a bad deal at the moment.

A loud crash rang through Cyborg Joe's. It was the

sound that a penguin makes when you put it in a blender and then drop it on a landmine.

Sprinkles dropped the ninja and his hammer fell from attack position.

Duke was standing on the top of the table, drawing the bewildered stares of the two Jungafallowians and Lilly, the anthropomorphic musk ox from one of the moons of Gartosh. The Trampling Death Robot frontman glared directly at the Stetson-wearing humanoid with his firearm in plain sight. But it wasn't the laser revolver that he held firmly in his hand—it was Ol' Betsy, smoke still curling from the barrel. The shotgun pointed not at the musical goliath but at the ceiling of Cyborg Joe's.

Hopefully that broke the tension.

Duke figured that Sprinkles didn't really want to kill Ishiro'shea; however, not killing him would be detrimental to his reputation and, thus, his musical career—and he needed a way to divert the focus away from this powder keg. Of course, there was always the possibility of the explosion triggering the robot to drop the hammer instinctively, in the process creating the galaxy's first ninja pancake. Luckily for all involved, Duke's lightning-quick psychoanalysis was spot on. He gambled—and the early returns were favorable.

"Okay, Mr. Sprinkles, let's all calm down. I'm not here to cause any trouble," Duke said with diplomatic caution. "I'm deeply sorry for interrupting your transcendent set—as is my intoxicated friend, there. And I am sure he would be apologizing profoundly if he was, ya' know, awake. How about I just pick him up, we'll go on our merry way, and you can continue to entertain your legions of fans here at this fine establishment? Sound good?"

Sprinkles inched closer to the bounty hunter. His eyes sparkled an intense shade of contempt. *No deal, I guess.*

"We can be civil about this quite insignificant imbroglio.

24

And, with all due respect, I don't think you want to have a chat with Betsy here."

Duke aimed the wide-mouthed firearm at the oncoming musician. He continued to try to reason: "I can see you're a bit upset. I get it, believe me I do—but there's no need to cause another scene."

Sprinkles continued to approach, his metallic frame convulsing to the point that it almost appeared organic and elastic.

A second crash!

The robot halted. The bounty hunter dropped the barrel of his shotgun. They both looked around Joe's in unison. *A Jungafallowian? That big musk ox chick?*

Duke saw what constituted a sly grin on Sprinkles' mechanical mug. He looked up.

Looks like this is not going to be my night, the bounty hunter thought.

The loud crash manifested itself in the form of fragments falling from the ceiling. The rapid descent was slowed—albeit not to the point of no longer being life-threateningly dangerous—by the bounty hunter's headwear. The debris knocked Duke from his feet and he collapsed amidst a pile of ceiling rubble, splintered table shards, and sticky puddles of spilled Glyptodian brew.

CHAPTER FOUR

THE GOOEY BITS

DUKE WASN'T SURE QUITE HOW much time had elapsed; he opened his eyes and stared up at Lilly and four angry Jungafallowian faces.

That could've been a lot worse.

"He's alive," moaned the Gartoshian beast. "Everyone! The odd-looking primate with the interesting choice in evening wear is alive."

Duke awaited audible sighs of relief from the patrons of Joe's—he heard nothing, resulting in a slight bruising of his ego.

"Wait a damn minute. Who are you to be calling me odd-looking?" he muttered hazily.

"Shut up! You ruined the show, you moron," interjected one of the heads of the larger Jungafallowian.

"No one messes with the almighty Sprinkles and gets away with it," barked the other head in a slightly sinister tone.

"Damn skippy."

Duke recognized that voice. Cold. Robotic. Tone deaf. Sprinkles. *Guess the ceiling missed him.*

He sat up and tried to focus on the approaching mechanized madman. His concentration bounced around erratically from the throbbing pain in his skull to the blurred pair of Sprinkleses that wouldn't stand still long enough to merge back into one another. And Betsy wasn't within reach. He quickly grabbed the laser revolver but his disorientation from the falling ceiling debris certainly wasn't going away. *50–50 chance.*

Just as Sprinkles was mere strides from Duke, a green flash pounced up like an Erontian River Camelcat and landed firmly in a strike position with katana raised. Ishiro'shea stood resolutely between his cohort and the performer. He held his sword in his right hand parallel to his shoulders at eye level. The blade glistened with reflections of the neon that covered the walls. His stance suggested the alertness of a person that had never downed even the slightest drop of firewater—a remarkable trait in which Duke knew Ishiro'shea took pride.

Defending his partner—that's why he's the best sidekick in the business.

Ishiro'shea, without moving any other part of his body, made eye contact with his longtime friend. Duke gave him a shaky thumbs-up from within his tomb of fallen debris. The ninja glanced at Sprinkles, his eyes smoldering to the point of being able to boil water. It was quite easy to see that Ishiro'shea didn't appreciate the singer's manner—looking all guilty and up to no good. He knew that Ishiro felt confident in his gut, no matter how much of it was filled with fermented grain. *Cycles of being placed in precarious situations with me will do that to you. Hey, we have fun,* Duke reasoned.

The ninja's strike was lightning fast. Sparks and metal shrapnel exploded from Sprinkles' titanium chest and abdomen—the blow would have halved most sentient beings, but it was a mere annoyance for the multiton, multi-platinum artist. Sprinkles retaliated with a hammer strike that narrowly missed the stealthy and now very much sober martial artist. The thunderous crash of the hammer into the floor of Cyborg Joe's caused the onlookers to cover their ears (or whatever they used to hear) and left Duke wondering if Earl was already reviewing Cyborg Joe's insurance policy. Sprinkles struggled to remove the head of the hammer from the divot in the flooring; this was the opening that Ishiro'shea needed in order to thrust his katana straight into the optical visor of his adversary. As the blade pierced the lens, the sizzle of skewered circuitry resonated throughout the bar. Duke noticed a hint of sadness and regret in the giant musician's pulsating vision apparatus. Ishiro'shea plunged his sword directly through the glass-like eye. It was a sight worthy of pity—one of the most recognizable figures in robotic explosion rock flailing in agony, one hand stuck four feet into the sweat- and booze-covered stage floor while the other hand grasped at what was left of his optical visor plate as bursts of sparks and smoke escaped through his fingers. But Duke had no time for pity.

The remaining Trampling Death Robots stood momentarily frozen as this diminutive menace rendered their charismatic and controversial lead singer immobile; but they soon collected themselves in an attempt to extinguish the career wrecker. The three bandmates charged Ishiro'shea, their instruments doubling as weapons, bent on sending him to that great dojo in the sky. They encircled Ishiro'shea and took turns at trying to decapitate him. One swung his Panatynian Earblaster guitar with reckless abandon. Another swatted inelegantly with his signature 14-string Grevlon Electro-Bass. Another jabbed rapidly with his iron drumsticks, trying to skewer the dwarfed combatant. Ishiro'shea parried each oncoming strike and dashed his way around the three attackers.

"You doing okay, little buddy?"

Ishiro mirrored Duke's thumbs-up from moments earlier as he continued his masterful ballet of devastation.

"Thought so. How about we head out of here? You're sober now, and I've got a massive headache—that usually means that we've worn out our welcome."

Though he was effectively toying with his opponents, Ishiro'shea was still preoccupied fighting off the angry mechanical musicians and making sure he didn't get a Panatynian Earblaster to the skull.

Duke stood up and grabbed Betsy. *Okay, time to shut these guys up and end this mess. I have to get back to the Queen with an answer about this damn door.* He aimed the gun at the bassist of the Robots, Doug (Model 8). *I never understood the bass guitar.*

Before he could fire, there was a firm tap on his shoulder.

He spun around. Standing in front of him was one of the Jungafallowians—the larger of the two, armed with a wooden shard from the broken table and a sharp steak knife. *That might break the skin.*

"You aren't going to get away with this, human."

I can't be done in by booze, bad music, poor roof maintenance, and low quality cutlery.

Duke felt a firm tug on his biceps and realized very quickly that he was pinned up against something. He inhaled deeply and realized that the "something" was the other Jungafallowian. *Hard to mistake that smell of rotting meatloaf smothered in expired mayonnaise.*

"You're dead, human. Nobody does that to the Robots," a slithery voice hissed from behind.

Duke struggled but the Jungafallowian, even though he was the smaller of the two, had a grip that was unbreakable.

"Where should I stab him, Flakka-Grog? I can't remember where the gooey bits are on humans."

A duo of cream-colored reptilian heads on muscular neck stems slowly peered around either side of Duke. Both sets of red eyes scanned the bounty hunter meticulously. *Creepy.* Duke noticed Ol' Betsy resting on the floor, out of reach; his revolver rested firmly in his holster—but his arms weren't going anywhere if the Jungafallowian had any say.

"Flakka, do you think we stab him in here?" the head known as Grog whispered as he glared at Duke's chest.

"Oh no, Grog—I think we should have Orbo-Terg stab him here." Flakka's snout touched the bounty hunter's left ear. "Humans can't survive losing this part, I don't think."

"How about you let go of me, your friend can drop the knife, and we can talk this through?" pleaded the bounty hunter.

"Just like you wanted to talk it through with Sprinkles?" asked the scaly Flakka-Grog. "You will pay for what you did, fleshy."

"Can I stab him yet?" barked both of the larger Jungafallowian's heads in unison. "Revenge for Sprinkles! Revenge for the Robots!"

The barbaric alien pumped his oversized fist in the air. Duke noticed, for the first time, that the T-shirt Orbo-Terg wore was for the Trampling Death Robot's "Four Faces of Death Galactic Tour" and, emblazoned on the black fabric, were the faces of the four band members. Duke's life hung in the balance of four much uglier faces. Regardless, he appreciated the symbolism.

"Orbo-Terg, calm down. We want to make sure this primate suffers for what he's done to Sprinkles," hissed Flakka. It was clear to Duke that Orbo-Terg was the physically superior of the two; however, Flakka-Grog pulled the strings.

"Yes, he's committed the ultimate sin against the Holy One—we need to do more than merely kill him," continued Grog.

"Hurry up and decide!"

"Okay, we definitely think we should stick him here."

The long neck supporting the Flakka head curved around and nodded toward the human's midsection.

"There?"

"No, lower—between his legs. Under that ridiculous ornament."

"Ridiculous? My buckle? What are you talking—oh wait, where are you going to stab me?"

"There!" grunted one of the heads of Orbo-Terg as he pointed a knobby finger at an area of Duke's anatomy that the bounty hunter held in high esteem. The Jungafallowian coughed up a laugh from deep in his innards.

"C'mon guys, no need to stab me there—I mean, I have plenty of other good parts. I promise they will hurt a lot more."

"Is that right, human? No, no, I think we are going to stick to our plan."

Duke struggled, but it was futile; he was held almost inert in the powerful grip of Flakka-Grog. *I am about to get castrated by a smelly two-headed metal junkie all because I was distracted by some cheap floozies. Screw symbolism.*

Duke kicked his legs frantically in an attempt to prevent Orbo-Terg's impending charge.

"Hold still!"

"So you can stab me? Yeah, I'll get on that."

"Flakka-Grog, make him hold still!" Terg shouted in a borderline temper tantrum.

A thick stump of a leg wrapped around Duke from

behind, limiting the bounty hunter's movements even more. *This bastard is strong.*

"Stab him!"

Orbo-Terg charged knife first.

Duke closed his eyes, awaiting a pain that he was not prepared to endure. He felt a gust of wind surge across his stubbled face and heard a loud thud a few paces away.

He opened his eyes. Orbo-Terg was curled up on the barroom floor—out cold. Lilly stood over him, thin-lipped with nostrils flared and breathing heavily. Her hands remained clenched in boulder-sized fists.

Duke was thrown to the ground ferociously by the Jungafallowian; he scrambled to grab Betsy. The two-headed beast rushed toward the Gartoshian female but Lilly about-faced before the sinister reptiloid could get on top of her. She lowered her massive cranium and lunged headfirst at her attacker. Duke heard the Jungafallowian's sternum crack. From his seated position on the floor, clutching his prized shotgun, he noticed Flakka-Grog stumble backwards.

"No, no, no, no..."

He immediately found himself sandwiched between the floor and the limp and odorous body of Flakka-Grog.

"Get this—oh my god, it smells so bad!"

"Let me help," proclaimed a booming voice, twice as deep as Duke's and as full-bodied as the richest of Noctdaryan wines.

In one swift yank, the anthropomorphic musk ox easily winched up the Jungafallowian corpse with one massive three-fingered hand, then dropped it beside the recovering bounty hunter. Duke remembered scorning the fem-beast at the table, only moments ago.

"Thanks?"

"I see that you're confused, Mr. Human."

"You could say that. Don't get me wrong, lady, I'm glad you saved me—but why? I wasn't overly 'interested' earlier." Duke dusted Jungafallowian grime from his clothes.

"That's okay. I wasn't offended by your silence—I just assumed you were too ignorant to understand anything more than simple language. I mean, you don't look overly intelligent."

"Insult aside, thank you. But why risk your life to save me from those moronic rock nuts?"

"Oh, Mr. Human. No matter how discourteous your gesture might have been—what those two uncouth reprobates said to me was beyond heinous. After you caused your scene with the ceiling tiles and started your little tiff with that robotic bandleader, I decided to be the better being and exit the situation—no need to engage with those lower life forms. Then, of course, I saw them about to impale you with a steak knife—*my* steak knife, no less—and I felt obligated to punish those two and, in turn, save you."

"A moral crusader, huh? Well, thank you, Lilly. It was Lilly, right?"

"Good memory."

Duke made it to his feet and extended his hand.

"I hope that I can return the favor someday."

"I hope that won't be necessary. But your cute friend appears to need your help."

Holy hedgehogs! Ishiro'shea!

The bounty hunter turned around and saw his cohort still countering every blow from the three members of the Trampling Death Robots—at least, the ones without an appendage lodged into the floor. But he was tiring visibly. Even the most skilled martial artist has his physical limits.

"Enough of this garbage," the bounty hunter muttered to himself as he aimed.

KURGHUFFINSHOBEPOW! (BOOM! never really captured the true sound.)

The bassist of the Trampling Death Robots dropped to the floor. He had a hole in his chest the size of an exceptionally large ice wombat. Ol' Betsy was angry. The other two froze and then attended to their second fallen comrade of the night. Amidst the turmoil on the stage, Ishiro'shea stealthily made his way over to Duke.

"Ishiro, what took you so long with those guys? I would have thought..."

Ishiro'shea gave Duke an expression that the bounty hunter interpreted as *Shut up, you conceited redneck. I was fighting for my life while you managed to get pinned by a piece of ceiling tile.* At least, that's how Duke interpreted it.

"This has not been my night. Long story. Let's just say that I'm lucky that I'm only half as big of a jerk as those two idiots over there." Duke pointed to the unconscious Orbo-Terg and Flakka-Grog. "Thanks again, Lilly."

The Gartoshian gave him a blasé wave from across the bar as she pushed through a cluster of military conspirators and entered the ladies' room. Ishiro'shea looked confused as he tried to catch his breath.

"*Really* long story."

Ishiro'shea responded with a lengthy eye roll.

"Oh, but hey—I do have some news. The Queen gave us a crack at a small opportunity. Could be exciting."

The ninja halted. Duke knew what his partner was thinking.

"No, a *legitimate* opportunity. Nothing impossible. Seriously. You don't believe me?"

The masked man shook his head with undisguised incredulity.

"Fine. Follow me."

They headed to the bar, ignoring the chaos that they had—in large part—caused.

"Greetings, sirs," Earl said as they approached. "How may I help you? I see that you have had quite the eventful evening here at Joe's."

"Earl, can you fetch Queenie, please?"

"I'm right here," came a voice from behind the bar. Queen Joe rose elegantly from a crouched position near where she kept the pricier bottles of happiness.

"Startled me there, Queen. Anyways, please tell Ishiro'shea about our opportunity."

"Ah yes, what we discussed earlier, I presume?"

"Yes, ma'am," Duke said with a smirk.

"If you could've solved my problem regarding an unknown and seemingly uncontrollable astral anomaly that was creeping into my bar—I would've given you both access to my portals free of charge."

"See, Ishiro! I told you—wait—'could've'?"

"I'm sorry, Duke. The 'portal' is gone. Sometime between you hitting on those Hilterians and getting crushed by the ceiling, it left. No wild portal, no free portal card. Sorry."

"You've got to be kidding me? This is really not my night. Any chance for another shot of that whisky, at least?"

Ishiro'shea seemed reenergized at the thought.

"Guys, I'm not so sure that this is the time to be drinking. I mean, for one thing—you did a number on my bar tonight. More than usual. I'm not overly happy about that. You also seriously injured two members of one of our biggest musical draws—during their performance, no less. Oh yeah, and you shot a hole in my roof."

"So, you're telling me that we probably aren't going to get another shot of whisky?"

"Turn around."

Duke could see the Trampling Death Robots starting to collect themselves—and repair themselves. *They're gonna be pissed.* Flakka-Grog wiggled around a bit. *Damnit, he's not dead?* He could sense the crowd getting louder and bolder. *If they riot, I'm public enemy* numero uno.

"We'll just take the bill, if it's all the same to you, your Highness."

"We can settle later. I would probably just leave before things get to a point where even I can't help you."

"Thanks. Much obliged."

Duke and Ishiro'shea headed for the exit opposite the stage.

"At least you got your 'it' back, Duke!" shouted the Queen.

"Good point! I might hit up those Hilterians next time we're in town!"

The bounty hunter stumbled over what appeared to be a black polymerized chloroprene suit clinging to a magenta-skinned body. It was motionless. In its perfectly circular palm was a half-eaten MechaBurger 8000.

Okay, maybe I won't, Duke thought to himself as he and Ishiro'shea exited the bar.

CHAPTER FIVE

THE BEEPS AND BLINKS OF SPACE TRAVEL

"TONIGHT WAS KINDA CRAZY, HUH?"

Ishiro'shea did not respond to Duke. In fact, he accelerated the speed of his march towards the parking area.

"Slow down, bud. Are you mad at me? Or are you just trying to get as far away as possible from what's brewing inside the bar?"

The rumbling from inside Cyborg Joe's continued to intensify.

"Fine. I'm sorry for leaving you on the floor—and choosing to hit on those Hilterians; but you can't blame me for your ill-fated attempt to join the band. And I didn't force you to puncture Sprinkles' eye with your sword. You gotta cut me some slack there, Ishiro."

Still the ninja did not respond; he kept his hurried pace.

"Oh yeah, sorry for the whole table thing, too. I didn't mean to leave you fending off those robots—I was truly in a bit of a predicament myself."

Once again, the ninja did not respond. But Duke was not surprised by Ishiro'shea's lack of reaction—in fact, Ishiro'shea hadn't said much of anything since he took his vow of silence upon graduation from the College of Cohorts, Consorts, Co-Conspirators, and Other Assorted Sidekick Types many cycles ago. He was the Salutatorian. Duke and Ishiro'shea had a partnership solidified by more than simple words and pats on the back. They didn't need to communicate in the traditional sense; they had true bonding experiences. Real friendship-forging stuff. However, Duke was quickly realizing that he, at present, was bonding more with his own guilt than with his sword-wielding colleague.

"Can you even imagine what we could've done with unlimited access to those portals?"

Duke LaGrange and his silent sidekick stared up at the *Deus Ex Machina*, or at least the parts of her that towered over the other ships parked at the loading dock. She was an old ship, but she was *their* ship, twice the size of Cyborg Joe's and twice the alcohol consumption. She looked as if she came off of the same assembly line as Ol' Betsy. She was loud and weathered and battle-tested; she possessed nothing new, sleek, or sexy—she encompassed the phrase "they don't make 'em like that anymore" in both the positive and negative connotations. It was without a doubt that ecological regulations were ignored to produce such a spacecraft. She was a priceless relic to half of those that laid eyes on her and a worthless pile of junk to the other half—she was art. Duke and Ishiro'shea loved the *Deus Ex Machina*—no matter the pickle they were in, no matter how impossible a solution seemed, no matter if they backed themselves into a corner with no plausible manner in which to escape—she always bailed them out.

"Mr. LaGrange, your keys," exclaimed the Glyptodian valet at the loading dock.

"Thank you, my good man," Duke responded as he took the keys from his furry grasp.

The valet held out his hand for the customary tip. Duke

paused at the sight of the extended arm and upright palm. He then slammed his hand down, probably bruising the Glyptodian's metacarpus.

"Alright, son! Stay in school."

The valet appeared to be caught off guard, then seemed agitated. Duke launched himself down the loading dock until he reached the *Deus Ex Machina*.

"Come on, Ishiro'shea—we need to book it before those pissed-off patrons figure out that we vamoosed."

As Ishiro'shea patted the young Glyptodian on the shoulder and flipped him some monetary units, Duke yelled out, "My tip wasn't good enough?"

Ishiro'shea rapidly made his way to the parking spot just as Duke was opening the hydraulic hatch on the left side of the massive ship. For such a large ship, the entry hatch was quite confined. The door closed with the noisy clang of a dropped pot on a ceramic floor and the elevator shot them up towards the bridge. It was only a ten second climb but those ten seconds contained the same maddening elevator Muzak that was installed the day that Duke acquired the ship during a rousing game of No-Limit Nova Texan Strip Skeeball. It had been fifteen cycles of the same melody; fifteen cycles of that same earworm-planting monstrosity.

"I'm going to install a new song in this damned thing. I mean it this time. I've had it!" Duke barked.

Ishiro remained silent.

The door slid open with a nails-on-a-chalkboard screech to reveal the austere bridge of the *Deus Ex Machina*.

"Seriously, I mean it. I'm thinking the Nova Texas Planetary Anthem. How about that, huh?"

Ishiro'shea ignored the statement and approached the main control panel. It mirrored the appearance of the ship, in that it was oversized and underwhelming to the eye. A bit long in the tooth for a modern onboard controls system, but it still worked for the majority of the time. With speed befitting a ninja, Ishiro'shea's dexterous digits poked and prodded the luminescent buttons of the panel. Duke loved the beeps and blinks of space travel.

The bounty hunter made his way up to a raised platform in the geometric center of the bridge. There, in all of its glory, was his captain's chair. His leathery throne. The most comfortable place to rest one's tired body in the whole of the known universe. Over the cycles of use, the chair had formed around the shape of Duke's backside—he took pride in knowing that this piece of furniture was now customized for his needs. He kicked up his feet along the surrounding rail as he sank into the warmth of his favorite seat. His headache started to dissipate, his eyes closed, and he took in a deep, long breath. As he approached a moment of true bliss, he broke in and out of muddled song.

Hail Nova Texas, a beauty under the sun,
It gets hotter than Hell,
For which it ain't much fun,
But we have cacti and critters and fried meats on-the-go,
Don't tell us what to do 'cause we have our shotguns in tow...

...and we don't have sex with our livestock.

He petered out. "Yep, definitely gonna make this the new elevator tune."

Duke had almost forgotten about the damage that he had caused back at Joe's and was about to drift off into a long overdue nap, until the familiar rattling of *Deus Ex Machina*'s shell signified takeoff. The ship departed the loading dock with a clamoring "see ya' later" to Kelt, then headed into the vast playground of space.

"Where to, Ishiro? Anywhere tickle your fancy?" Duke asked with a slight yawn.

Ishiro'shea pressed a few buttons and swiped his right hand quickly over a holopad. It glimmered. Immediately, the large view screen at the front of the bridge appeared above the control panel. The split-panel view screen showed both the actual space in front of the ship, and also a more technical interface with all of the scanning data, systems status checks, and other miscellaneous bits of information needed to keep a spacecraft flying. Front-and-center on the dashboard, the long-range scanner results were materializing.

"Not a lot of traffic in this sector right now, is there? Okay, want to bounce on over to Oscavia? I think we have a few free massages from those triplets that we helped out—remember? I'm pretty sure that we need to collect on that. Two for me, one for you."

The ninja's glare was icy.

"One for me, one for you—flip for the third?"

Ishiro'shea repositioned the long-range scanners to examine the area to the right of the vessel. More blinks and beeps. He didn't acknowledge Duke's suggestion.

"Okay, no to the Oscavian Caves. Want to do some work? We can make it to Tardasio 7 in no time and see what Sol has cookin'—sound good?"

Suddenly, something appeared on the scanner. The icon on the interface was that of a spacecraft. But it was big. Really big.

"What in Nova Texas is that?"

Ishiro'shea's hands were working at a speed that Duke had never seen before. *He must be pretty curious as well.*

"It looks like... like... a school bus? At least we didn't fire on 'em. That would've been messy. On to Sol's."

Duke relaxed back into his chair and tilted his hat over his eyes. In a matter of seconds, he was startled by a slap on his shoulder. It was as firm as frozen peanut brittle. *How did he get up here without me knowing? Oh yeah, he's a ninja.*

The ninja pointed towards the screen.

"You've got to be kidding me. That's no ordinary school bus!"

The goliath ship continued on a course straight towards the *Deus Ex Machina*. It engulfed the view screen. Upon it, dead center in crudely applied stencil work, were the words:

TRAMPLING DEATH ROBOTS FAN CLUB & ATTACK SQUAD, JUNGAFALLOW III CHAPTER.

"I guess we're gonna get to finish that scuffle after all. Let's get in position, little buddy."

CHAPTER SIX

BUTTONS WHERE THERE WEREN'T NO BUTTONS

T HE SHIP DWARFED THE *DEUS Ex Machina* in the same manner that a peanut is dwarfed by a macadamia nut—if the macadamia nut is the size of a high school gymnasium.

"Ishiro, patch me in."

The ninja swiftly darted over to the far left side of the control panel and began to input digits with rapid-fire precision. After a few moments, he threw his hands up in frustration.

"Not answering our hail? See if you can override."

The ninja worked with speedy aggression.

"Hurry... hurry... they're firing up their weapons. And not to add any more pressure or anything, but they've got an Ootrelian star cannon."

Ishiro paused momentarily. The Ootrelian star cannon was one of the most deadly weapons in the known universe.

"I thought those were outlawed," said Duke, mostly to himself.

Ishiro'shea threw his thumb up.

"Excellent, little buddy."

Duke cleared his throat and began.

"My name is Duke LaGrange. Adventurer. Trailblazer. Poet. A true man of the universe. And I'm sure that this is just a big mix up."

Silence. Then a small crackle of interference.

"Mr. LaGrange. It is nice to finally meet. Your reputation precedes you."

"And who are you?"

"You have indeed put some of my closest friends away for long periods of time," the voice said, ignoring Duke's question. "You're probably the eighth or ninth most decorated and respected bounty hunter in this sector."

"Eighth or ninth? I would like to meet the other seven. I'm..."

"However," the voice interrupted, "I am afraid that you are severely overmatched and outclassed this time. Your folksy charm and overactive libido will not save you. I will take pleasure in knowing that I was the one responsible for ending your life. The Robots and my fellow brothers must be avenged. Plain and simple."

Word travels fast.

"Mister, I am afraid it is *you* that's run out of luck."

"You and your ego amuse me, LaGrange. Your systems, if they are working properly that is, have probably detected the fact that I have an Ootrelian star cannon. Your dilapidated ship won't withstand one direct hit. On top of that, my other armaments are immeasurably more advanced than anything on your floating junk heap."

"I think you underestimate us. Which is surprising for a school bus driver." Duke knew it was obvious he was bluffing. "But indulge me: to whom must I credit for finally putting me out to pasture?"

"I am Prince Korzo-Tapor of Jungafallow III."

Duke muted communication.

"Hey Ishiro, I thought there was a revolt against his government and he was hung? Double-looped noose and all."

The ninja motioned that he could not confirm the incident.

"You are probably thinking that I was killed in the Not So Great Revolt of 4392?" the voice said.

"Never crossed my mind."

"Needless to say that I was not. And I have taken back what is rightfully mine—Jungafallow III. With the help of the loyal and proud members of the Trampling Death Robots Fan Club, of course."

They really are loyal.

"But alas, I must end this autobiographical interlude," a distinctly different voice said.

Must be the other head.

"Only a fool could think that they could take out Duke LaGrange with a school bus full of fanboys."

"I am not a fool and this is no school bus. In fact, its design is what allowed us to approach without any suspicion. So, who's the fool, Mr. LaGrange?"

As the prince spoke, the interstellar school bus decloaked and a boxy Jungafallowian Fighter materialized. The only two characteristics that remained consistent were the Ootrelian star cannon and the fan club stenciling.

"So how did you survive the revolt, your highness? Or is it highnesses? What is the proper way to greet dual-craniumed royalty?"

"Mr. LaGrange, you are simply stalling now—and I am sure that your mute comrade is planning some sort of chicanery as we speak. I hear he is the brains of your outfit."

Duke noticed Ishiro'shea's smile beneath his mask.

"You're right, your Royal Scumbag, I *was* stalling. My

old floating junk heap managed to lock on its tractor beam undetected. More advanced, my ass."

"Tractor beam?" the prince laughed. "LaGrange, it really was a pleasure to meet you. But now, you must die."

"Go, Ishiro'shea!"

Ishiro'shea redirected the tractor beam onto the Ootrelian star cannon in a narrowed field of pure concentrated power. The *Deus Ex Machina* descended with a jarring jerk. An explosion engulfed the front of the larger spacecraft. The star cannon was ripped off like a dirty bandage. Clearly, the cannon had been a custom after-market addition to the ship, so there was no gaping hole left where the weapon had been—the innards were completely guarded. This was unfortunate for Duke and Ishiro'shea.

"What were you saying about a star cannon? You might be the one with the ego problem, o great exalted ones. I think it's now a bit more of an even playing field, as they say."

"Well played."

The poise and lack of emotion—traits not common among the prince's species—made Duke quite uneasy.

"Commander, I'm ready to engage with the rest of our artillery," hissed another, decidedly more Jungafallowian voice.

"Proceed, Lieutenant."

"Rest of their artillery?" asked Duke, directing his query to Ishiro.

The gigantic vessel roared with a thunderous salvo of weapons. Duke stood on the bridge as the ship unleashed a round of fury that he knew was likely the last thing that he would see in this lifetime.

"Brace for impact, little buddy."

The *Deus* was rocked.

"And now for the final blow to the mildly famous Duke LaGrange," Korzo-Tapor's voice echoed over the speakers.

"Mildly?" Duke smirked.

The sizzles of frying wires and the clangs and cracks of failing infrastructure throughout the doomed ship redirected his focus to Ishiro'shea.

"It's been a real pleasure," Duke said solemnly as he tipped the brim of his hat in the direction of his friend. "Didn't think this was how it was going to end."

Ishiro'shea continued to plug away at the control panel. He turned around and gave his longtime companion a simple wink.

The *Deus Ex Machina* was overwhelmed by the Jungafallowian artillery barrage. Explosions consumed the aging shuttle. Its crippled body fell limp as it began to float away against the infinite tapestry of space.

"Well, that wasn't fun."

Duke tried to lift himself up into the captain's chair, while ignoring some very serious bruising.

The emerald-clad swordsman slowly made his way back to the control panel. He looked around and touched different parts of the control panel tenderly, presumably checking on the welfare of the systems. Groggily, he extended his thumb, signaling that the unit was in working order, then he collapsed with a plop onto his chair stationed at the control panel.

The *Deus'* view screen was still functional. To Duke's surprise, Prince Korzo-Tapor and his mega-ship were nowhere to be seen.

"How in Nova Texas did we survive that? I'm not *that* lucky."

Ishiro'shea pointed to the far right side of the controls. A plastic dome-like hatch had been smashed, revealing a clownish red button.

"What the hell is that?"

Ishiro'shea shrugged.

"I've spent the last fifteen cycles on this ship and I've never seen that thing. Giant buttons just don't spring out of nowhere!"

A look of realization overcame Ishiro'shea's face.

"You got something?"

The ninja pointed to his right thigh. Part of his green *shinobi shozoku* was torn and shards of broken glass gracefully clung on to his hip.

"That explains *how* the glass was broken. But where'd it come from? Do we have a manual or something?"

Duke knew Ishiro was thinking something along the lines of "Are you serious?" But being a good sidekick—Salutatorian-worthy, in fact—he searched for the manual. He unlocked a drawer under some newly exposed circuitry from the attack and pulled out a dusty tome covered in filth and grime. Duke grabbed it and read aloud:

"*Owner's Manual for the* Deus Ex Machina: *You Must Be in Pretty Deep, Volume I*," Duke began. "They aren't wrong about that."

"'Foreword.' 'Chapter One: Getting to Know Your Ship.' 'Chapter Two: Taking Off amidst Intergalactic War.' Wow, they don't waste any time." He continued to scan the table of contents.

"Got it! 'Chapter Eleven: Buttons.' 'Section Three: Buttons Where There Weren't No Buttons.' Pages 283 through 284."

Duke thumbed to the pages in question.

"'You probably have noticed by now that the *Deus Ex Machina* has pulled you out of some real jams, huh? Well, that isn't the half of it,'" Duke read. "'The *Deus Ex Machina* is equipped to instantly birth survival tech when recognizing a situation in which there is no way to possibly escape. It's quite convenient when you are backed into that proverbial corner with no hope for continuing your adventure. Some discerning thinkers call it a big "cop-out" but they can kiss our collective asses. Love, the builders of the *Deus Ex Machina*.'"

The entire next page was an image of a furry creature clinging to a wire above a pit of ravenous serpents; a word bubble above the struggling fuzzball enclosed the phrase: "Persevere. It will all work out." The two companions looked at each other. "I'm guessing that's supposed to offer some encouragement. But is it encouragement for the little hairy guy clinging to the wire? Or those snakes anxiously awaiting their dinner?"

Duke then noticed the small print below and continued, "P.S. Always push the big red button."

Sound advice.

"Well, that explains it," Duke rejoiced. "I guess, at the last moment, the ol' girl became the proud mama of some new anti-Jungafallowian shielding. That explanation works for me. You good?"

Ishiro'shea nodded hesitantly.

"Remind me to thank the builders if we ever meet 'em."

It's best not to question mysterious red buttons that save your life, Duke concluded.

"Okay, since we have that sorted out, we need to go bring those bastards to justice."

Ishiro pointed to the barely functioning control panel. The maroon light signifying their tracking device was blinking rapidly.

"Ishiro'shea! You genius! You sent out a tracker as we

were being blown into oblivion? *That* is why you were Salutatorian."

The emerald-clad ninja smiled under his mask for the second time. *I guess a little recognition does go a long way.*

"There's no way that they would even think to scan for trackers—they probably just assumed we were scrambling to get our shields up. Remind me to give you a raise. We can split the bounty, 70–30."

Ishiro'shea's smile dissipated.

"Ok, fine, 51–49. The usual. We have no time to lose; let's see if we can make up ground pronto. Did the ship happen to evolve a better engine?"

Ishiro shook his head.

"Worth a try. Let's go. I can't wait to see the prince's face—or is it princes'? I'm not really sure; I mean with the two heads but one body and all. Can you imagine that day in grammar school when you have to learn plural possessives? That could get ugly, real quick."

The bounty hunter seemed to snap back into his original thought.

"I can't wait to see him *or* them when we show up—two badass ghosts with vengeance on their mind. This is going to be epic, little buddy."

Ishiro set a course out of what should have been the site of major wreckage and their untimely deaths—but with some noticeable caution.

He should be more excited. Oh wait, I guess we need a plan or something; we are still a bit of an underdog, militarily-speaking. Unplanned vengeance usually ends poorly.

"Don't worry, Ishiro, I have an idea," Duke bluffed.

The *Deus Ex Machina* halted suddenly.

"Hey, what's with the brakes?"

Before the ninja could respond, though he wouldn't have even if there was time, a light overwhelmed the bridge

—brighter than the Jungafallowian attack, but a lot quieter. The bounty hunters covered their eyes involuntarily as the illumination permeated the ship. With his forearm draped over his eyes, Duke gingerly opened one eye to a squint.

"Holy hedgehogs! Try to patch into the Queen... now."

Ishiro did as Duke requested.

"Hello, thank you for calling Cyborg Joe's Grill N' Go & the Why Not Saloon, home of the MechaBurger 8000. I'm Earl; how may I be of assistance on this fine evening?"

"Earl! This is Duke—put the Queen on the phone! Now!"

"Mr. LaGrange, it is truly a pleasure to speak to you again—"

"Earl! For the love of all that you hold dear, put the Queen on—I don't have much time. It's about her uninvited portal friend—and our recent opportunity."

"Mr. LaGrange, if I recall—the unknown astral entity disappeared earlier today and has not returned. I believe the Queen has terminated her previous offer based on these circumstances. I am truly sorry. Is there anything else that I can help you with?"

"You hairy Glyptodian bastard! Tell the Queen that I'm looking right down its bright red gullet as we speak; not too far from the Keltian atmosphere. I think she might want to know."

"You do make a valid point, Mr. LaGrange. I will seek her out with unrivaled haste. Do you mind if I place you on hold briefly?"

"Yes, I mind, Earl!"

"Thank you."

"No, I said, I do mind—"

The hold music interrupted and chimed away, a ringing annoyance that was meant to keep telemarketers at bay. The Queen's assumption was that if the blood-sucking

51

reprobates could withstand an hour or so of agonizing high-pitched musical aggravation, they earned a few minutes of her time.

"Duke, Earl tells me that you have something to share with me. Proceed, by all means."

The Queen's voice was a refreshing interlude to the hold music.

"I wanted to revisit our proposed deal, Queen. It appears that your unknown portal buddy is back—and it doesn't look happy to see us."

"Interesting."

"Interesting? So is it back on? Will you hold up your end of the bargain if we venture to the other side?"

"Duke, I'm—"

A crimson tsunami of the most intense illumination hit the bridge of the *Deus Ex Machina*. Duke and the sure-footed Ishiro'shea hit the ground unceremoniously. The beams were more than simple light—and they rattled the ship to its core.

"What was that, Queen? You broke up," Duke shouted from the floor. "Yes or no? Do we have a deal?"

The Queen responded but a barrage of noises—whizzes, whirls, and a few mini-explosions for good measure—overwhelmed her voice.

Then everything went black.

CHAPTER SEVEN

BORING OLD SPACE

THE HULL OF THE *DEUS Ex Machina* rumbled like the stomach of a ravenous yak, then mellowed to a slight murmur. Amber sparks danced about the control panel, intermingling with sporadic puffs of willowy smoke emitting from the mangled metal and pulverized plastic. The cabin's lighting system flickered as the onboard emergency systems tried to put out fires that had risen up in various locations on the ship's bridge. Alarms sounded as the craft tried to self-diagnose a catalog of ills all at the same time. Many things were happening inside the *Deus Ex Machina*, but Duke LaGrange was even more curious as to what was happening outside.

"Any chance of getting the view screen up?" Duke said solemnly as he stepped over what appeared to be a piece of the main panel. "I want to have some idea of where this son of a bitch dropped us off."

Ishiro'shea sat Zen-like amidst flashes and smoldering electronics. He clearly was more prepared to handle portal travel—especially one that had an unknown destination.

"Diagnosis?"

Ishiro'shea popped up with the same display of energy that he had showcased during his jam session with the Trampling Death Robots. With a single downward motion, he struck the impaired main panel with a forceful *shuto-uchi*. The view screen fizzled—and then resumed its bright, shiny high-definition glory.

"Thank you. That's a new one."

Ishiro bowed.

"Holy hedgehogs, there's nothing out there. Looks like our favorite portal is gone too—so I guess that's a win. I was half expecting to be dropped into an intergalactic shootout or the stomach of some moon-sized cosmic zebra. We are just in... boring old space. Seems like a lot of trouble to gobble us up and spit us out in the celestial boondocks. Something doesn't make sense. Or maybe there was a glitch in the portal. I mean, there wasn't even an in-flight film. Portal travel isn't what it used to be."

Ishiro's expression led Duke to believe that he shared the same uneasiness about how anticlimactic the whole situation had been.

"Any chance we get the auto-nav back up? Another one of your karate chops?"

The stout ninja pointed aggressively at the tattered remains of a helm. He shook his head with noticeable pessimism.

"That bad, huh?"

Ishiro then began to repeatedly jab his finger in the air— pointing to the view screen.

Duke cringed.

"You want me to fly this manually? It's been more cycles than I care to recall since I actually had to drive."

The ninja did not yield; he continued to point.

Damnit.

Ishiro sat down and started to clear away as much debris

as possible from the control station. Most of the fires were out by now. Duke knew Ishiro was more than capable at the helm of the *Deus*; however, Duke also knew that he was better. Even rusty, he was better.

"Fine. Let's see if we can figure out where we are—and if we can get back. Maybe the Queen will give us something for reporting that the portal leads to absolutely nowhere of consequence. You know, she could sell access on the black market—I'm sure someone would pay to send his enemy to an exile complete with a horrific death by boredom. And now that death by boredom has been officially outlawed in most sectors, it should fetch a pretty penny."

Duke sat down at the helm. *This has been a long time.* He wiped away a bit more of the accumulated debris and let out a long, drawn-out sigh. The ninja swiftly positioned himself in the vacant seat beside him.

"Well, crap." Duke shrugged. "Should we go left or right?"

Ishiro'shea pointed directly ahead.

"Straight it is, partner, straight it is."

The ship rattled and flexed its inflexible bits as it made its way into manual drive for the first time in many cycles. It jerked ferociously.

"Whoa, simmer down now. Easy does it."

Duke noticed his loyal companion appeared uncomfortable.

"Hey now, Ishiro. This was your idea, remember? I got it under control. Just like breakin' in a new horse," Duke said with a slightly exaggerated accent. "Easy, easy." He had never broken in a horse.

The *Deus Ex Machina* steadied and gradually accelerated into open space.

"Any chance we can get the other systems back up and running, Ishiro? I don't mind driving the girl but it would be nice to get some comm, in case we actually encounter something out here. We might want to strike up a conversation, after all."

The ninja went to work on the panel, seeming somewhat optimistic. Duke smiled.

"Seriously, there is *nothing* out here. I don't recognize the star patterns at all. They're entirely different than any that we've encountered—in any sector. Maybe the ship will think this is one of those 'backed into a corner' moments and spontaneously produce a star map for us."

Ishiro ignored Duke's far-fetched hope.

"A boy can dream, right?"

The *Deus Ex Machina* pushed on. The star patterns became no more recognizable to the displaced bounty hunter.

"Cheers!"

Ishiro'shea grabbed the beer and inhaled it. Duke cranked back his head and poured the sweet nectar of Glyptodia down his throat. He repeated this a few more times.

"Don't worry. I drive better after a few drinks."

Ishiro responded with a thumbs-up, then slugged another Erontian brew. And then another. And another. He then proceeded to the alcohol storage and dissemination unit. He reached down and pulled out a bottle of ancient Earth saké, regarded as possessing slightly higher quality than its Erontian cousin, and fetching a higher price.

"Buddy! Hey now! That's the bottle we, uh, relieved from that archeological pirate that we busted. Are you sure this is the special occasion to make you want to open it? You know what? To hell with it! From aimlessly piloting our ship in unknown and uncharted space to finding a probably dead-end planet that we'll spend our dying days on, it sounds like a special occasion to me. I've definitely never done it before. Cheers, hombre!"

The ninja removed his katana and swung it down upon the bottle with a silent precision. The glass did not shatter but the top inch of the bottle fell on the bar counter—introducing a rich aroma of fermented rice to the atmosphere of the bridge.

"Well done."

Ishiro'shea pulled his mask down to under his chin, hoisted the bottle skyward, and rotated the exposed bottleneck towards his open mouth. The liquid sparkled as it left the bottle and flowed ceaselessly into Ishiro's throat. Duke nearly choked on his beer.

"C'mon man! Don't hog the juice. Save some for me."

Duke shot out of his chair and stumbled towards his partner. The ship jolted abruptly. Duke lost his balance and hit the floor. Ishiro started to laugh, but the *Deus* kangarooed again and he fell on his posterior—without spilling a single drop of saké, however.

"Holy hedgehogs, I forgot—I'm driving this thing, right?"

Ishiro responded with a lazier thumbs-up.

"But I *really* want some of that saké. Choices, choices."

The ninja shook his head and pointed toward the helm.

"Oh, you think I should get back to driving, huh?"

The ninja repeated his headshake-and-point routine.

"Ishiro, c'mon, man, buddy, pal. I just want one shot before it's gone. We're best friends; why are you being such a bastard?"

Ishiro stood woozily and extended the bottle to his longtime companion.

"Thanks, little buddy. Cheers to us and finding our way. Our way *somewhere*."

Duke held the bottle aloft but was swiftly robbed of his balance due to the ship tipping again. The saké bottle crashed to the floor and shattered.

"No! The saké —"

Duke fell to his knees and tried to lap up the remaining liquid pooled on the ground. It was not his most shining moment. The ship violently rolled to starboard. Duke was thrown from the floor into the wall.

"Eyes *off* the prize, Duke," he said to himself. "Getting back to the controls."

Ishiro appeared a bit more focused and found his way back to the panel before Duke.

"Ok, let's wrangle this gal in."

The *Deus* rocked and rolled, herked and jerked, and did some stuff that would make a roller coaster vomit.

"I got it, I got it. Steady... steady."

The ship stabilized.

"How was the saké, jerk?"

Ishiro smirked.

"Look out the view screen! How long were we drinking?"

Duke aimed the newly-steadied ship at the planet—now much larger in the view screen—with a gradual, almost calming, acceleration.

"Get a load of that. It appears to be almost all water except for those two landmasses. They're connected. Looks like a giant upright dumbbell. I know we can't scan for life or tech or anything worthwhile—but maybe we can get a bit closer to see if we can identify a city or something."

The silent ninja nodded in agreement.

The *Deus* crept closer to the planetary body.

"I really hope it's not a planet of primitives. I can't stand primitives. Terrible conversation and nine out of ten haven't mastered brewing yet. And the women are so shaggy."

The hull rattled.

"Brace for some turbulence. Entering a stronger portion of the planet's gravitational pull."

Ishiro buckled his seat belt.

"What the—? Since when did we get seat belts? Where's mine?"

The ship rocked again. Duke and his seat parted ways.

"Damnit."

He climbed back into his chair and feverishly searched for his buckle without success.

"Fitting. Let's see if I can settle her down."

The view screen was now completely engulfed by the planet with the odd-shaped continent front and center. Ishiro pointed to the heart of the southern landmass.

"I see it, buddy. A city. Doesn't look like a megalopolis, but definitely civilization. Oh look, there's another one on the top half. And a few more sprinkled in. Maybe this isn't some deserted wasteland. Any ideas?"

Ishiro'shea shook his head.

"There seems to be a bit more cover around the first one. I think it makes the most sense. We have to chance it, right? Thoughts? Alternative ideas?"

The ninja seemed to agree.

Duke manually input a final descent and landing sequence into the tattered remains of the control panel.

"No chance the scanners will be up soon, huh? Let's hope this Podunk planetoid has an atmosphere suitable for two handsome bounty hunters with a boatload of questions."

The *Deus Ex Machina* broke through the outer atmosphere.

CHAPTER EIGHT

SOUFFLÉS

"I REALLY DO HATE THIS music."

Ishiro'shea said nothing, as per usual.

"I also hate thinking that this will be the last thing we hear before we die. The place looks habitable enough from the bridge but without working instruments on the ship, it could be toxic land, for all we know. And what a time to leave the exploration enviro-suits at the dry cleaners! Anyways, if I haven't told you before, little buddy..."

Ishiro'shea looked up at his dear companion.

"...if this is the end... it's been a hell of a ride!"

The ninja nodded.

The elevator pinged as it hit the floor of the entryway hatch; the door swung open wildly, inviting the planet in for an atmospheric tea party. Duke and Ishiro held their breaths.

The Nova Texan counted down on his fingers. Three... two... one. The duo stepped out onto the grass-covered ground and took in the atmosphere of this new world.

Duke began to choke immediately. He fell to the

ground, hacking and convulsing. Ishiro'shea stood above him, his eyes wide. And not choking.

"The air is so—clean. I hate it!"

The bounty hunter made it to his knees and eventually stood with the wobbly legs of a newborn giraffe. He clutched the supporting arm of his lifelong friend.

"Thanks, Ishiro," he hacked. "This is going to take some getting used to. I need a smoke. There has to be *some* pollution somewhere. Tell me there's some pollution somewhere."

His companion did not respond. In fact, he looked as if he enjoyed the change.

"It'll support us, at least," he continued between coughs, "despite this major headache."

Ishiro'shea inhaled even deeper and exhaled with a look of enjoyment.

Asshole, thought Duke.

"Do you think our parking job is good enough?" Duke pivoted to see the *Deus* expertly tucked away in a small patch of vegetation. He only counted four trees that had been severed in half by the hulking mass of the ship. He always strived to be eco-friendly.

"Let's hope these folks can help us out—and they don't find the *Deus*. I don't think my lungs can stand this planet longer than a few hours."

The ninja rolled his eyes.

"How can you stand this?" Duke wheezed. "Fine, maybe I won't die from it—but at least let me adjust to it. You know how long it's been since I've taken in something so damned clean?"

Ishiro'shea ignored the question—*probably doesn't know either,* concluded Duke—and started to head towards the city.

"By my best estimation, we're a few miles away. I'm hoping they can give us something useful."

They left the lush foliage that had served as their landing pad and started the trek across the grassy plain. It was a simple place, very different to the harsh deserts of Nova Texas, or the urban chaos of Kelt, or the dank labyrinths of Erontia, or the caramel sky-piercing mountains of Oscavia. And very different to the alcohol-induced bedlam of Cyborg Joe's.

The bounty hunters had been walking for less than an hour before Duke was able to see the outskirts of the city on the horizon. It was becoming much brighter and Duke was finally adjusting to the atmosphere. As they closed in, they could make out huts and other unsophisticated single-story dwellings.

"Primitives. As if this day couldn't get any worse, we've landed amongst some backwards aboriginals that probably haven't figured out basic plumbing or electricity or quantum-time manipulation. Or soufflés."

Duke knew soufflés were often perfected after a civilization had mastered quantum-time manipulation—and ninety percent of all major civilizations never made it to the "Soufflé Stage." So he didn't hold that one against them.

"I'm sure these furry cavemen are either going to charge us with bloodlust and uncontrolled aggression—or they're going to worship us as gods. Just in case, let's be ready for both."

Duke tapped the butt of his revolver, double-checking it was there. He didn't need to do the same for Betsy; he could feel her on his back. Ishiro'shea flashed his katana. Duke liked that.

"What are you thinking, Ishiro? Stroll in nonchalantly? Sneak around and try to get into the city center undetected? It does appear to be a bit more advanced than this dump and, I'm sure, more likely to provide some answers."

Ishiro'shea aimed his finger at an area about a ship's length from the outermost hut—here the grass was twice as tall with pockets of messy, dense bushes. The thicker undergrowth extended well beyond the primitive homestead and appeared to end at the foot of the walled township.

"Think that's good enough cover to circumnavigate this outpost?"

Ishiro was already in stealth position and darting towards the hedges.

"I forgot. You're a ninja," Duke chided himself. "Wait up!"

The two blended in with the flora and eased their way around the settlement. They encountered no one and no thing in the fields. The two sat, entirely concealed from any potential lookouts from the village, and peered through an opening in the foliage.

"Where is everyone? We are literally a stone's toss away from this joint and I don't see a soul anywhere. Deserted? Raided? Nah, not enough dead bodies."

Ishiro thumped Duke's shoulder. He rested his cheek on clasped hands.

"Not the worst idea, Ishiro. Maybe their species is nocturnal. Remember the nightfolk of Ruddia Gophp? Those cats were spooky. And their cats were even spookier."

Ishiro motioned a slicing movement with his hand, signaling decapitation.

"Spooky and messy."

"As much as I want to know about where all these hut dwellers are—which is absolutely not at all—I think our answers are gonna be right over there."

Duke nodded in the direction of the city center.

"Let's keep moving."

The ornate doors appeared to stretch to the sky. There was no other way to enter the walled city, at least none that were easily identifiable to Duke.

"I dig the design. Imposing but artful."

Ishiro'shea nodded.

"Maybe those village folk moved inside here and didn't bother to knock down their old homes. This *would* be an upgrade, ya' know. Although, not the most functional, if you think about it. You spend the dough building these giant walls but don't have a single sentry tower? Not real thinkers, it seems; unless this joint was designed to keep people in— not out."

The emerald-clad ninja gave a look that suggested he agreed with that assumption.

"I guess we knock, amigo?"

Ishiro ignored him and began to inspect the door meticulously, gently testing the façade for any weaknesses or clues. He crouched down and started to follow along the base of the wall for a few yards.

"No time for that, Ishiro."

Duke raised his right hand and struck the behemoth doors purposefully. A ringing thud vibrated out from the door—as loud as anything from the Trampling Death Robots' holiday album.

Ishiro quickly returned to Duke's side and slapped him on the shoulder. *Oh, he's pissed.*

"What? We didn't have time to sneak in. I want answers now—and maybe we've got a chance to get out of this godforsaken fresh air!"

Ishiro feverishly signaled in multiple directions with an angry jabbing motion.

Maybe we should have chatted first.

"Ishiro, look at this place. A fairly basic structure with a rinky-dink village in its shadows. How dangerous can it be? When we were scooting around in the bushes, I just kept thinking about how these primitives are probably going to be more scared of us than we are of them."

Duke's friend simply shook his head as the bounty hunter tried to rationalize his hasty decision.

"Seriously, buddy. Listen—we know they aren't advanced and they obviously aren't paying too close attention to us. They were too stupid to know that they should have some lookout posts along their wall. The more I think of it, my guess is that they finally discovered how to build something stronger than a wooden hut a few cycles ago—and moved the whole family in here. Nothing more, nothing less. Just another entry on the long list of primitive, backwoods, who-gives-a-damn planets."

Ishiro pointed at the intricate metalwork adorning the oversized gates.

"Okay, maybe they didn't *just* discover how to build these—apparently, they have *some* skill. But, I think you're giving them too much credit. Look, they didn't even send out a welcoming party—"

Duke's gabbling was halted by a thunderous groan. The doors began to swing inward at a deliberate pace. The noise reminded Duke of the moans of Joe's patrons after consuming a MechaBurger 8000.

"Why, hello there," chimed a high-pitched voice. The 'hello' was elongated and seemed never to end. It was an unusually cheery tone.

CHAPTER NINE

THE THING ABOUT ORBS

OUT FROM THE SHADOWS OF the doors appeared the deliverer of the jovial greeting. He was humanoid, but unusually gaunt; his drab blue skin clung to his skeletal frame. His quasi-ellipsoid face was as emaciated as his body, and hung slightly out in front of his chest; it was connected to a thin neck that jutted out from between his shoulders. His circular, murky eyes were devoid of pupils.

"I can assure you, my fine fellows, we are not stupid nor 'backwoods'—as you call it. Nor are we dangerous. It does appear, however, that I *am* your official welcoming party. I'm afraid that we don't have many visitors here; thus, we don't spend too much time on preparing formal greetings and the like."

As he came farther into the light, the cylindrical headgear balanced atop his cranium reflected the sun's rays. It stood as tall as his narrow face was long, and was studded with petite blue jewels; they matched a single stone of similar color affixed squarely to his chin.

We have an over-accessorizer, thought Duke.

"That's okay," Duke said.

"Oh, I apologize again, my handsome visitors!"

He's quite the chipper one. But it's obvious he has keen observation skills.

"As you have probably noticed, I'm a bit rusty at this hospitality thing. Let me introduce myself, my new friends. I am High Priest Vernglet Wip, a proud member of the Order of the Orb, and appointed steward of this modest municipality in which you now find yourself. The gates of Dre'en are open and we are humbled by your presence." The last phrase was uttered with an attempt at a more grandiose announcement.

Vernglet Wip knelt down with a simple bow, steadying himself against his gilded walking staff resting in his right hand. The jeweled chains dripping from his decorative breastplate rattled and jingled. Small spheres of gold hung from each chain, mirroring the larger sphere atop his staff.

"Where are we, exactly?"

"You are at the gates of the city known as Dre'en."

"I don't mean to be rude, but this joint wasn't on our itinerary. Can you tell us what... um, planet... we're on?"

Vernglet paused for a moment. An uneven smile crept across his face.

"You have found your way to Neprius—and Neprius welcomes you."

"Neprius, huh? Never heard of it."

"Oh, you don't say? I can't say that I'm shocked, my ruggedly adorable off-worlder," chirped Vernglet. "Like I said, we don't get a lot of visitors to our beautiful home. Truly a shame, I suppose."

"Yeah, it doesn't look too bad—but this air... You gotta do something about this air."

"Is it not to your liking?"

"It's borderline toxic to my kind," responded Duke.

Ishiro'shea shook his head.

"Interesting. What exactly is your kind?"

Duke began to answer but the priest cut him off.

"Please forgive me. I have been entirely rude and offensive. What is your kind—what are you thinking, Vernglet? You know better than that," he muttered to himself. His voice quivered as if he expected to be tortured for his hosting faux pas. "I should've asked you the required questions that a respectable host extends to his guests. What are your names? Where do you visit us from? Tell me all about yourselves. Please."

Once again, Duke's retort was interrupted by the slightly feminine tone of their one-man welcoming party.

"I am so rude again! We are just standing here at the gate—come in, come see the city of Dre'en—the southern jewel of Neprius. I hope you like it!"

What an odd person. Duke glanced over at Ishiro and noticed that the ninja was diligently scanning every visible nook and cranny. The bounty hunter had known him long enough to tell that he was feeling skeptical about Dre'en—and possibly about High Priest Vernglet Wip.

"As we make our way in from the gates, you will see the road directly in front of us—yes? That leads straight into the heart of Dre'en and the Altar House of the Orb. I must admit, if I'm being honest—and we are honest people here on Neprius—there isn't much to write home about for quite some time if we travel this path to the center. I hope that you can withstand our toxic air, my lovely friend. However, it will give us time to get more acquainted. Then, we can enjoy the marvels of our quaint town."

The trio started down the uneven path. The priest's prediction had been accurate—to the left and the right of the road, for as far as they could see, was nothing but dense forest. Duke noticed that Ishiro continued to examine their surroundings—never focusing on the road for more than a second at a time. Duke was impressed with the road itself—despite its wildly irregular stonework, the tops of each individual rock were polished to an almost mirror-like quality. But they weren't slippery. *I'm guessing the lady Neprians don't wear a lot of skirts.*

"So friends, as we were about to get to earlier, what are your names and where do you visit us from?"

"My name is Duke LaGrange," the bounty hunter decreed boastfully; his chest puffed out. "Adventurer. Trailblazer. Poet. A true man of the universe."

"Oh, is that so? I can see it. Definitely can see that. Very impressive."

"This is my longtime friend and trusted sidekick, Ishiro'shea."

"Hello, there Ishiro'shea, sidekick to the great Duke LaGrange."

Ishiro bowed. Vernglet mimicked the movement to reciprocate the greeting.

"Don't worry, Ishiro doesn't say much."

"And why is that? Does his species lack the ability to speak?"

"Vow of silence."

"Then, Mr. Ishiro'shea, I commend you on this solemn vow of vocal condemnation. As the High Priest of the Order of the Orb, I too know about commitment. But tell me, travelers, where did you come from—and why did you choose our world as a place to visit?"

"The universe is our home," Duke retorted. Only he knew that the line was plagiarized from a Willie's World of Galactic Winnebagos television ad. ("The universe is our home, so make it yours... Now with flushing toilets compatible with up to 85 species!")

"Interesting."

"Our work takes us to many planets, and we've been

doing it for so long that our birthplaces are almost a distant memory. Our ship back there is the closest thing we have to a home. But, if you must know, the story of yours truly started many cycles ago on a rugged, yet embracing, rock known as Nova Texas."

"I see many similarities already between you and this Nova Texas in which you speak."

Duke soaked in the unwarranted praise.

"Ishiro'shea is from a place known as Earth."

"Earth, you say? Interesting."

"Heard of it?"

"Um, no," Vernglet hesitated. "I don't think so. Yes, definitely a 'no.'"

"Well, you nailed the best way to describe Earth. 'Interesting.'"

"Do you not visit this Earth much? What do they have there that makes it so intriguing?"

"Wars, mostly."

"But do they have great crops that reach to the sky?" Vernglet asked somewhat dramatically, with his arms reaching upward.

Peculiar question.

"Um, sure there are crops—I think. There used to be, at least. Not sure if they reach to the sky—but what do I know? Ishiro? You know anything about giant crops from living on Earth?"

Ishiro shrugged.

"Why do you ask?"

"Oh, just curious. I was a farmer before I joined the priesthood and I like to know that there are places out there with bountiful harvests for all. I apologize for sidetracking the conversation. So why did you two assuredly unrivaled cosmic explorers choose to come to Neprius?"

"Ya' know, Vern—" Duke caught himself. "Can I call you Vern?"

"Whatever suits the great Duke LaGrange."

Out of the corner of his eye, Duke caught Ishiro shaking his head at the compliments being heaped upon him.

"We didn't quite *choose* to come to Neprius."

"Interesting."

I knew he was going to say that.

"It was more that we hitched a ride, you could say."

"Hitched a ride? What do you mean?"

"We actually were hoping that you could help us out with this? We essentially were gobbled up by a giant red star blob—and it conveniently dropped us off on your front doorstep."

The priest paused as if to collect his thoughts.

"Can you describe this 'star blob'?"

"Sure. It first appeared in one of our favorite bars—"

"In a bar? As in a place to consume beverages and to partake in assorted merriment?"

"Yes, a bar. And yeah, it was much smaller then but kept trying to break in through the wall, but Queen Joe— she's the proprietor of the joint—said it decided to stop bugging her about the time that Ishiro and I left."

Duke noticed the Neprian's increased concentration.

"Then Ishiro and I had some business dealings with some Jungafallowians—"

"Jungafallowians?"

"Smelly creatures. Terrible taste in music. They are of no consequence."

"Did these Jungafallowians send this 'thing' to kill you?"

"Oh no, they're way too moronic for that. But once we parted ways with these Jungafallowians—"

Ishiro snorted at Duke's choice of words to describe their encounter with Prince Korzo-Tapor.

"—our little astral friend resurfaced. And he wasn't so little."

"What did you do?"

"We didn't do much. We *couldn't* do much. We held on as tight as we could as he swallowed us whole."

"This is quite—"

"Let me guess: interesting?"

"I'm sorry, I will think of another word to use in its place," Vernglet said with an apologetic curtsy.

"Just messing with ya', Vern. But, in a blink of an eye, we were deposited, ship and all, in the friendly neighborhood we now know as Neprius."

"Wow, quite an interesting—I mean, fascinating —journey."

"So, Ishiro and I were kinda hoping that someone here might know what this is all about. Why would this unknown disturbance in space want to plop anyone or anything down in your general vicinity?"

"I am afraid that I am unaware of any such disturbances. When we get to the center of Dre'en, I can ask some of my colleagues. We have a few priests that concentrate on all things in the sky and space. They might be of better assistance."

"Can't hurt," replied Duke, though his tone was tinged with pessimism. "Anyways Vern, we've talked enough about ourselves. Tell us about Neprius. And Dre'en. And your fascination with orbs."

"My new comrade, it is not a fascination with orbs—it is a fascination with *the* Orb."

"*The* Orb?"

"Yes. The Orb That Controls Everything and Must Be Respected."

Neprius is in dire need of a good advertising agency, thought Duke.

"It is the reason for our being, our salvation, and our progression. Our leader and our savior is the almighty Orbius, the Orbmaster of the Orb That Controls Everything and Must Be Respected."

"Orbius?"

"Yes, the Orbmaster of the Orb."

"Redundancy aside, what does that actually mean? This might shock you but Orbmaster is not a common occupation in most parts of the universe."

"Orbius is the Orbmaster of The Orb, the Sultan of the Sphere, the Guardian of the Globe, He Who Controls the Orb that Controls Everything and Must Be Respected. He is our savior."

"So is that what he puts on his business card?"

High Priest Vernglet Wip did not laugh.

CHAPTER TEN

A LIBRARY WITH LESS SEX

THE VIEW FROM THE WINDOW framed the town square of Dre'en. The sun was setting; nightfall was imminent, but a few shafts of radiant orange peeked from behind the buildings. The square itself was actually almost circular, with the center plaza made of the same polished stone as the road into Dre'en. At the rear of the cul-de-sac an ornate set of steps led up to an equally ornate door of a single unornamented tower, stark and plain. The dour building and its indulgent entrance seemed an unhappy marriage. Two Neprians—clothed in the same manner as Vernglet—stood guard outside. More nondescript buildings of muddy stone and auburn timber encircled the court, punctuated only by the single road. Rising from behind the structures was the continuation of the wall where Duke LaGrange and Ishiro'shea had met Vernglet Wip.

"My friends, is this accommodation up to your standards? I know you have traveled to many exotic and, no doubt, luxurious lands with opulent lodgings; I hope that you will not be disgusted with our quaint room. The view of the heart of Dre'en is the best that we have."

"It'll do, Vern," said Duke as he peered out onto the arcade. "This is the southern jewel of Neprius, eh?"

"Why yes, Mr. LaGrange."

"Doesn't seem to be a whole lot of folks. Where's the foot traffic? The hustle and bustle? The actual Neprians? I mean, since Ishiro and I met ya', we've strolled through ninety percent of Dre'en on that road and have only seen you—and those two guards out there standing next to that interesting-lookin' door. See Vern, now you got me saying 'interesting.'"

"Ah, yes, Mr. LaGrange. That 'interesting' door is the entrance to our most beloved building—the Altar House of the Orb. And, believe me, you will meet many of our lovely residents. It happens to be a day of work for many of us, and clergymen like myself are busy preparing for our evening services."

"What about the villages that we passed before we came into the city? They looked as if they'd been recently abandoned."

"Oh, no, I assure you—they are not abandoned. The villagers are working."

"All of them?"

"Yes, all of them. And they tend to be shy."

"Do they all work together?"

"I almost forgot—you said you wanted to discuss the red 'blob' with our star scholars, yes? I will arrange an appointment first thing in the morning with our leading minds. You will be impressed with their celestial knowledge. If there is anyone on Neprius that can provide you some direction or insight that relates to your cosmic query, it will be one of our scholars here in Dre'en. We haven't quite figured out space travel as your species has, but we are very aware of the possibility thanks to the presence of our savior. Maybe one day we will earn Orbius' trust and he will teach us the ways of travel amongst the stars."

"Thanks. But what about—"

"Mr. LaGrange, I do apologize but I need to run down to check on a few things for the evening services. You and Mr. Ishiro'shea get comfortable, and I will send someone up shortly to escort you both to dinner. I think you will like our local cuisine. Until then..."

The door shut quickly. Duke could hear Vernglet scurry down the hallway at a frantic pace.

Ishiro tapped Duke on the shoulder.

"Yep, I noticed it too. He seemed a bit squirrely about those villagers and their 'jobs.'"

The ninja looked around at their surroundings without appearing to focus on anything in particular in their wholly uninteresting room. Duke knew that he was uneasy—and had been since they met Vernglet Wip and trekked through Dre'en.

"I know, little buddy. Something doesn't feel right. But then again, it might just be that it's been a bumpy ride since we decided to hit up Joe's—and we're projecting our bad luck onto this situation as well."

Ishiro shrugged his shoulders. *He's not going to buy that.*

"I knew we totally should've gone to Goddess Larry's Gin Palace for drinks instead."

His companion smirked. Duke hoped that Ishiro'shea appreciated his attempt to lighten the mood.

"I wonder how this Neprian cuisine stacks up. Can't be any worse than a MechaBurger, right?"

Duke propped Betsy up in the corner of the room and sat down on what he assumed was a bed. The cube-shaped furnishing seemed to combine the roles of mattress and frame—the bottom was plush and buoyant—the top was made of something resembling iron, if the iron had been frozen in the tundra of Garlomb for a thousand cycles and then encased within the impenetrable metal of the black-smiths of To-To Megro Minor.

"Yeah, definitely not a five-star establishment."

Duke wiggled his posterior until he got as comfortable as he was going to get, then stretched out his legs and placed his hat beside him on the bed.

"A bit better. So what do *you* think is up? Do you think he knows something about the astral anomaly that gobbled us up?"

Ishiro shook his head.

"Really?"

The ninja pointed up at the sky and then proceeded to retreat to a cowering position.

"You know, Ishiro, you're right. He did seem shocked when I mentioned the blob. It's almost as if he was startled —then realized he needed to collect as many facts as possible. But to what end? Did we stumble on—or through, I suppose—some sacred religious wormhole? Seems a bit far-fetched—even for us. All he seems to care about is that damn Orb That Does Stuff and the all-powerful Orbius."

The ninja offered only another shrug.

"Have we considered the possibility that maybe he's just a weird dude? He loves orbs and crops and seems to think that this boring-ass city is somehow the 'jewel of the planet.' Yikes. It's more like a library—but with less sex."

The ninja placed his katana on a stone shelf that protruded from the wall. He walked to the window again and studied the plaza intently.

"After a good meal—well, I guess I shouldn't get ahead of myself—after *a* meal and a good night's sleep..."

Ishiro walked over and thumped the "mattress."

"...fine, after a *horribly uncomfortable* night's sleep, then we can talk to those astronomy priests and figure out as much as we are going to. We can keep an eye out for any funny business and, by midday, we'll be back at the *Deus*. Sound good?"

Ishiro'shea agreed to the plan with a nod of his head. He turned back to the window and continued to study the plaza as the night finally swallowed the last remaining flickers of sunlight.

"So, any clue on what Neprians eat? I have a feeling we're going to be underwhelmed."

CHAPTER ELEVEN

PLOOB KALARTI

"I MUST SAY, VERN. I'M impressed. Stuffed and impressed. What do you call this again?"

Duke held up a half-eaten conical fruit covered in minute violet fibers.

"Ah, a personal favorite of mine—ploob kalarti. They can only be grown in southern Neprius. Where I come from—far north of here—we are sadly denied adequate ploob kalarti harvests."

"Bummer. What's this?" A slight gaseous belch escaped the bounty hunter at the conclusion of his question.

"That is roast leg of greattu; a local delicacy as well. It is an agile six-legged bit of fauna—about the height of Ishiro'shea but with horns. They feed off of the ploob kalarti fields—that is why their meat is slightly syrupy but with the right amount of acid to cut the rich sweetness."

"Well, I'm a fan. And it was nice to meet some of the other priests. We were starting to think that you were on this rock alone. They were some good dudes, a little high strung—but, all in all, y'all are a decent lot. What were the twins' names? They were some characters!"

"Twins? Oh, Hoblet and Delix? They are not twins, Mr. LaGrange. In fact, Delix is considered quite attractive in our race—and poor Hoblet..."

"He relies on his personality, huh?"

"You could say that."

"Well, I liked 'em, nonetheless. A pretty okay crew ya' got here, if you ask me."

"I am so pleased to hear this. Mr. Ishiro'shea, I see that you have not consumed quite the same quantity as Mr. LaGrange. Was everything to your liking?"

Ishiro'shea nodded politely and tilted his plate upward to show the priest that he had finished off the majority of his ploob salad.

"Very nice."

"Did you manage to get us on the schedule with your scholarly cats tomorrow to chat about our favorite little cosmic incursion?"

"I am very glad that you asked. Yes, I did. We will meet with them tomorrow in the late morning at their laboratory. It is merely across the plaza and directly to the right of the Altar House."

"Very good. Oh, how did your last-minute preparations for the evening's event go?"

"Oh, all is well. Thank you for asking."

The rugged playboy tipped an invisible hat.

"My friends, it is time for me to head over to the Altar House for our services in honor of the Orb. I hate to leave you, but you know your way back to your room, I believe. Try and get some sleep. Your journey would tire even the most stamina-blessed traveler."

"Cheers to that, Vern!"

"I will come and get you in the morning."

Vernglet stood up and exited the dining hall.

"Looks like we might've been wrong about ol' Wip. Usually when there is something afoot, the food sucks."

Ishiro agreed.

"Let's just hope those eggheads can help us in the morning."

The ninja nodded and swiped an untouched ploob kalarti for the walk back to their room.

The duo proceeded down the dimly-lit corridor that led to their chamber. It was slightly dank and smelled musty with a dash of concentrated cleaning solution.

"They really should redecorate this joint. The haunted castle craze is so seven cycles ago. I guess they get a pass—they probably don't get a lot of fashion trends from—"

A muffled shriek echoed around the hallway. Both Duke and Ishiro'shea paused.

"That's coming from the dining hall."

Duke lowered his shoulder and rushed the dining room door. *Now this is going to be an entrance!*

The collision was not as loud as he had hoped—and the outcome was definitely nowhere in the vicinity of what he had in mind. With a subdued thud, Duke LaGrange collapsed to the floor of the hallway like a soggy noodle losing a limbo contest. He sat up and cleared his head.

"Well," he grimaced, "what's Plan B?"

Ishiro'shea stealthily glided past the recovering Nova Texan and examined the door intently. The muffled screams that they had heard moments before had stopped as soon as Duke collided unsuccessfully with the door. Ishiro'shea continued to examine it with a surgical focus. He extended his right hand to the octagonal knob, clutched it tightly and turned.

Click. The door swung open.

"It wasn't locked? Suspicious noises and cries for help are almost always behind *locked* doors. Sloppy work from these chaps; if they turn out to be bad dudes, that is. Neprian criminals have a lot to learn about being sneaky and shady."

Duke's train of thought was interrupted as the dining room came into full view. The table at which they had feasted was mostly cleared away; only a few plates of half-eaten greattu and goblets of an overly-sludgy liquid laughably referred to as "nectar" remained. In the far-left corner, facing the wall, was a Neprian priest. Directly below him, crouched and recoiling, was another life form, much smaller than the Neprian and with a skin tone somewhere between bronze and carroty. It had a single stringy, unkempt mat of hair clinging to the top of its head; but outside of the unusual hairdo, slightly larger ears, and the absence of eyebrows, it looked human. More specifically, it looked like a human child.

The Neprian turned around slowly. His expression morphed rapidly, but Duke caught a glimpse of anger before his gaunt face produced a haunting smile.

"Hello again, Mr. LaGrange. Mr. Ishiro'shea."

"Geezer, is it?"

"Geezu, Mr. LaGrange. Geezu. But very close—you are picking up our assuredly odd-sounding names like a native son of Neprius."

"What—I mean *who* is that?"

"This troublemaker is of no consequence. I apologize for causing alarm."

Duke ignored the Neprian's response and walked toward the child-like creature. Ishiro followed closely.

"Mr. LaGrange, I assure you—"

"Geezer, I wasn't aware that there were other species on this planet. Where do they live?"

Duke knelt down a few paces from the Neprian and the child-like creature.

"Hey there, it's your 'Uncle Duke.' Are you a nice fella?"

"Mr. LaGrange," Geezu interjected, "I must ask you to leave this delinquent to me as it is official priest business."

"Official priest business?"

"Yes, Mr. LaGrange. We are very honored to have you here in Dre'en, but this situation is purely a matter for our clergy."

"Geezer, you're acting a little squirmy now."

"Squirmy?"

"What's the true story with this little guy?"

"There is no story, Mr. LaGrange. Maybe Vernglet can explain it to you at a later date. But I must ask you again to leave."

"No story? Nothing?"

"He hit me," squeaked a voice.

The bounty hunter froze. His brain tried to take in the child's comments and weigh the risks of a plethora of actions that could be taken.

"And I'm a girl, not a 'little boy.' And I'm actually taller than most my age, so I'm not little either."

"Geezer here hit you?" Duke asked.

"Yes."

"You silly mongrel, I am a man of the Orb. I would not strike an inferior life form."

"Inferior? Says who?" asked Duke.

"He makes me work in the kitchen and hits me when I'm not fast enough," the voice chirped again.

"Is this true, Geezer?" Duke drew closer to the priest.

Geezu's almost translucent skin was pulled taut against his cheekbones.

"No, Mr. LaGrange. In your short time, you must have a good grasp of us. It is a mere child's prank."

"Liar! Look at this!"

The child rotated her head to the left and exposed the back of her neck. A deep bruise came into the light.

"You little good-for-nothing!" Geezu shouted at the child. With his right hand he reached out and snatched the human-esque creature by the patch of hair on her head and yanked her to her feet. Dirt and dust flew off of her ragged clothing.

"I warned you!" shouted Geezu. "Mr. LaGrange, you have stuck your nose into a matter that does not—"

Geezu hit the floor with a thud more dramatic than Duke's shoulder-first crash into the door. The bounty hunter was pleased; Geezu's face revealed that he hardly felt the same.

"His face was harder than it looked," Duke quipped as he shook his now unclenched right hand.

Duke turned around.

"Holy hedgehogs!"

Two Neprian priests rushed toward him javelin-first. Duke turned and grabbed the closest dining chair; he reared back to swing it—but hit nothing. He looked down.

Both Neprian priests were on their backs, their eyes closed. The lethal javelins lay harmlessly on the floor beside them. Ishiro'shea stood over them in attack position.

"Ishiro! Love ya', man. But what took ya' so long? I would have knocked 'em out way faster."

The ninja pointed to the corner where the girl had been cowering.

"She's gone?"

The door to the kitchen was ajar. *She must've snuck out through there*, the bounty hunter concluded.

"We need to find Vernglet and let him know what went down here. I haven't seen a jail on Neprius, but I'm sure these guys will be thrown in something not-so-nice. Damn these bastards, pickin' on an innocent little street urchin."

Ishiro gave Duke a quizzical stare.

"I guess I don't know *for sure* that she's a street urchin. She looks like one, though. Who knows, maybe she comes from a very respectable family."

Ishiro's stare did not waver.

"Oh right! Why didn't Vernglet mention anything about folks that look pretty similar to us living on this planet? I hope he has his reasons."

One of the guards began to regain consciousness; his thin arms pressed his torso up, but his knees were still anchored to the floor. He reached for his pointy killing instrument.

Duke's boot struck the guard's face—which, in turn, struck the stone floor with a plop.

"Gettin' rusty, Ishiro?"

The ninja ignored Duke's comment, but the bounty hunter knew his friend would be miffed that the guard had recovered from his attack sooner than he would have liked. Ishiro'shea gracefully floated through the dining hall and out into the hallway.

"Okay, okay. Let's go find Vernglet. He has some explaining to do. His abusive priest buddies. This mysterious kid that claims to be an indentured servant. The fact that it appears there's another race on this planet." Duke counted on his fingers. "What else?"

Ishiro was already outside of the dining hall. He nudged his head in Duke's direction.

"Okay, I'm comin'."

Duke waded through the Neprian bodies and met his cohort in the hallway.

"I guess we finally get to see the inside of this Altar House of the Orb? Let's go chat with Vern."

Ishiro'shea started to head down the corridor leading to their rooms.

"Where ya' goin', Ishiro? The exit out to the plaza is this way."

The ninja mimed a sniper.

"Good call. Probably want to have something more than our bare hands just in case we run into any more of those un-priestly priests."

CHAPTER TWELVE

VANITY KILLED THE NEPRIAN

DUKE AND ISHIRO'SHEA STRODE BRISKLY along the corridor. It led to an unfurnished annex that marked the halfway point between the dining hall and their guest room.

"Didn't think I would have to use Ol' Betsy today. Goes to show ya'."

Ishiro'shea paused. Duke followed suit. He trusted Ishiro's senses.

"Yeah, I hear it too. I think it's down by our room."

Both men slid up against the wall with as much stealth as possible.

"Think they heard us?"

The ninja shook his head.

"Me neither," whispered Duke.

They crept around the corner, out from the annex, and into full view. Ishiro crouched down, making himself as small as possible. Duke remained upright, but his back pressed against the wall as if he hoped to cave the partition in with his weight.

The Nova Texan continued to whisper across the

hallway to his compatriot. "These Neprians will taste the explosive thunder of my trusted Betsy soon enough—and it's a taste not easily washed out of one's mouth."

Ishiro froze.

Duke tried to contain it, but a laugh escaped him. "Hey Ishiro, don't you wish you wouldn't have taken that vow of silence now, huh? You miss out on all the great and heroic lines."

The ninja, for the first time that Duke could remember without the aid of alcohol, lost his composure. He hit Duke with a hearty bellow—at least, it would have been hearty if it hadn't been silent.

The sound crackled again and Ishiro's silent chuckle evaporated instantaneously. *That's definitely coming from our room.*

Without a single spoken word, both men charged down the last leg of the hallway. A mere ten paces from reaching the door, two Neprian priests emerged from the confines. One held Ol' Betsy and Duke's laser revolver. The other carried Ishiro's cherished katana.

"Whoa now. Hold up there, boys," yelled Duke, having decided that events had already moved past the need-to-whisper stage.

The priests turned to the duo in surprise.

"Hoblet? Delix? You've got to be kidding me!" Duke howled in recognition. "I thought we were friends, man."

The Neprians looked at each other. *What are the chances that they know how to use those guns?*

"We are not your friends, Mr. LaGrange."

"I can see that now," smirked the bounty hunter.

"And now you are without your beloved armaments. You stand no chance as I see it." Hoblet raised the sword above his head and brought it down with a vicious slashing motion. *Okay, he knows how to use that.*

"What makes you so sure? We took out your spear-toting friends in the dining room without even an iota of effort."

"You will not be so lucky this time."

"Luck?" Duke laughed. "And why's that, fellas? We've beaten up twins before—and in more dire conditions than this. In fact, beating up identical twins is our specialty."

"Twins?" shouted Delix. "We are *not* twins!"

"Whatever. You guys are totally indistinguishable. Right, Delix?" Deliberately, Duke directed his question toward Hoblet.

"That's not Delix. I'm Delix, you... you... you moron of the highest order."

"Ouch. Guys, I'm sure you are unique in your own way but looks ain't one of them. I've seen many twins in my day —let me tell ya', and I've had some good times with twins— but that's a story for another time..."

"We look nothing alike. How dare you compare us like that?" Delix's face turned a nasty shade of raspberry. "I knew Vernglet Wip was a fool. Orbius knew all along that you are nothing more than marauding vagabonds sent to destroy our way of life. You aren't smart enough to possess any worthwhile knowledge. You are going to die by your own prized death toy, Mr. LaGrange. For Orbius and the Orb!"

Delix aimed Ol' Betsy at Duke and pulled the trigger. An all-too-familiar sound erupted from Betsy's inner depths, followed by smoke and the smell of fresh carnage. Blood and innards filled the corridor.

Guess he didn't know how to use a gun.

Duke firmed up his stance, his chest protruding proudly. "See, Mr. Hoblet, vanity is not a good trait. It'll get you killed. That... and holding a gun backwards."

Hoblet was petrified. He was covered in bits that, seconds ago, belonged to his good friend, Delix.

"So, you can do one of two things. You can drop the sword and run away—which I highly advise. Or you can try to fight us—and most likely end up like your friend there. And there. And over there. And I think some of him is stuck up there as well."

The Neprian placed the sword on the ground, pivoted away from Duke and Ishiro, and limped away with noticeable shakiness.

Ishiro'shea lobbied a grin at his longtime friend.

"Yeah, yeah. I, too, can take advantage of the psychological deficiencies of a weaker being. One might say I'm quite brilliant. Vanity is always a killer—when not in moderation, of course. It proves once again that I'm more than just a handsome face with a ridiculously large gun."

The ninja did not give any sign of agreement. He pointed at the ground a few feet in front of the Nova Texan.

Duke swiped at a large chunk of Delix with his boot; the gelatinous mound of flesh jiggled away to reveal Duke's laser revolver. He picked it up, examined its condition, and slid it into his holster. Then he turned and tugged violently at a musty tapestry that hung from the wall. It crashed down to the floor, landing in a deep puddle of Neprian entrails. Duke was able to keep a tiny piece dry. He knelt down and picked up his old friend, Betsy.

"She definitely needs a scrub down. I think part of Delix is lodged down the barrel. We don't have time to break her down and perform a diagnostic, do we?"

Duke answered his own question. "No. We don't."

He scrubbed Betsy down with the scrap of tapestry to the best of his abilities, and slid her into his back holster. *That feels good.* Ishiro'shea picked up his katana, but he did not conceal it.

"You wanna go to the Altar House now?"

Ishiro gave a thumbs-up.

"Look, Ishiro, I want to smash these bastards as much as the next guy—and find out about these slave children or whatever—but I don't like the odds of us versus the entire city of Dre'en. Stacked deck. I say we go back to the *Deus*. Let's see if these cats will talk when our ship is staring down at 'em. Probably a bit more persuasive."

The ninja sheathed his blade. The sound of footsteps echoed down the corridor.

"Seems like we aren't alone anymore. I bet they heard the explosion. Or Hoblet must've made it to his friends already. My vote is to get outta here *now*."

Duke and Ishiro'shea snuck away into the cool night air of Dre'en and accelerated to a brisk pace along the single road of mirror-like stone.

CHAPTER THIRTEEN

NINETEEN PACES

"I DON'T HAVE A GREAT feeling about this."

Ishiro'shea signaled his alignment with that assessment.

"I'm assuming most nights they don't just leave the front gate open like that. They either wanted us to leave to meet our impending doom—and made sure we weren't slowed down by some pesky wall—or they didn't think we would be in a position to leave this joint—because our doom had already impended upon us. Either way, we're walking into a mess that I don't care to be in."

Once again, Duke's colleague appeared to agree.

"If memory serves, we should be coming up on the *Deus* soon, right?"

Ishiro did not respond.

"Okay, must be talking to myself," Duke muttered. "Let's see then, we've already passed through the gates, we've already passed by the village—oh yeah, come to think of it, that bastard Vern never did tell us where all those cats in the village were working. He conveniently changed the subject when I asked; I did *not* pin him for being as sly as he is. Crafty little devil."

Duke scratched his chin. "But, then again, remember what Delix said? Vern thought we were here for a reason. Sounds like he might've been the only one that wanted us here—even if it was just a temporary curiosity. Vern's a bit more complex than I gave him credit for, I guess."

Duke caught up to Ishiro.

"Oh yeah, and what about the kid, Ishiro? How can those priest blokes not tell us about another intelligent—or seemingly intelligent—race on this planet, assuming there's more than one little street rat running around." Duke's stream of consciousness rant continued. "And it goes without saying, I doubt there were really any astro-scientists that could provide guidance on the red space blob that brought us here. There's just not a damn thing that's made any sense since we arrived on this rock. And another thing—"

Ishiro halted and stopped Duke with an extended right arm. Without hesitation, Ol' Betsy was out of her Ootrelian home and into Duke's hands.

"Holy hedgehogs!" Duke cried as he gazed across the expanse of terrain before them. "Those sons of bitches."

The trees and foliage around the *Deus'* hiding place had been mown down with the delicacy of a blind bonsai tree caretaker.

"Be careful, Ishiro, they could still be lurking around here."

The two bounty hunters descended a shallow hill and onto the flattened patch of grass upon which, less than a day before, their ship had rested comfortably and out of sight. However, the *Deus* was nowhere to be found. Both men had their weapons drawn.

"This cut here is fresh," Duke said as he examined a brutishly hacked sapling.

His companion pointed at a grouping of footprints beyond the scene of spacecraft abduction.

"Ah, those sure look like Neprian flippers if you ask me. And there seems to be a ton of 'em. All heading that way—over that hill east of here."

Ishiro'shea gestured beyond the hill.

"Good call. There's probably a way back to Dre'en around the wall. They could avoid running into us down the road back into the city. I guess we head that way and try to catch up with 'em, huh?"

The ninja glanced behind the bounty hunter. Duke swiveled around.

"No way, Ishiro. You're not trying to tell me that they somehow carried our ship through those woods, are you? I'm not buying it."

Ishiro shook his head. *Okay, he's frustrated. Man, of all the sidekicks in the universe, I had to pick the one that doesn't talk. Well, the one that still has his tongue and doesn't talk.* The ninja slapped Duke's shoulder to re-emphasize his observation.

"Okay, okay—what about the forest? Oh wait, I see it. Barely. I think. Okay, yes, I really do see it. Something's definitely flickering in that forest. Movement? You think it's some Neprian leftovers ready to ambush us?"

The ninja crouched down and focused intently on the edge of the forest, densely packed with alien flora.

"Probably just some bioluminescent forest critter," the bounty hunter said, kneeling beside Ishiro. "Maybe this will help. It's getting pretty dark now—not Keltian dark—but dark nonetheless."

Duke handed his compatriot a set of travel-size night vision binoculars from his belt. The ninja did a double take.

"I found them on the *Deus* right as we were about to leave. I thought that they might come in handy. You never know."

Ishiro'shea grabbed them and continued studying the wooded area.

"Anything?"

His partner did not provide any answer.

"I tell ya', Ishiro, I know you want to see what's out there—and, believe me, so do I—but the *Deus* is *that* way." Duke pointed to the crest of the butte, east of their location. "We don't have time to explore this place. We gotta catch up to those ship-stealing priests and, unless we can ride that thing in the forest and chase down Vern, we need to get going. I mean, I know we're faster than an entire legion carrying the *Deus* and all—but they do have a nice head start."

Ishiro adjusted the vision enhancers to their maximum capability.

"C'mon, buddy, we need to go. And, it's not *that* dark to go max power on those things."

Duke paused for a moment.

"In fact, it seems like it just got a bit lighter? Or am I going crazy? Seriously, it's getting lighter out here. It can't already be morning and, if it is, this is the most rapid ascension of daylight in any planet beyond the Ecclox System. I hate that system; how Eccloxians don't have countless seizures from the frequent day-night transitions, I have no idea. Remember when we went there last time? I think the days were down to about forty-five seconds each."

Ishiro'shea removed the binoculars from his eyes and adjusted them meticulously.

"Yeah, you noticing it too? I guess they have early breakfasts here. I don't remember seeing this when we landed. Makes no difference, anyways—we need to head back, bud.

We're losing precious time on the Neprian bastards. And I can't wait 'til I have a chance to bash their heads in."

"Your wait will be shorter than you think," shouted a familiar voice.

Duke and Ishiro'shea turned away from the forest to face eastward. Along the entire rim of the hill were a dozen Neprian priests, torches held high—this simulated sun illuminating the Neprian sky.

"But I don't like your chances," the voice continued.

"Oh hey, Vern! What's happening?" Duke responded, hoping to throw off the Neprian by not acknowledging the precarious situation in which they found themselves. "Thanks for turning the lights on for us. It was starting to get a bit dark. But I do have a question."

"And what is that, Mr. LaGrange?"

"I seem to have misplaced my ship. Any idea on where it might be?"

"Humorous, Mr. LaGrange. Your ship is now en route to Orbius, the new owner of your interesting spacecraft. I'm afraid this is the end of the line for you," proclaimed Vernglet Wip with the wooden oration of a community theater flunkie.

"What gives, Vern? I thought we were buds—I mean, I also thought old Hoblet and Delix were too, and now Delix is a pile of Neprian goop on a curtain somewhere. You might need to get that hallway professionally cleaned, by the way."

"I figured something did not go as planned. I warned Hoblet and Delix that their plan was foolish. Regardless, Orbius demands this. I am truly sorry, my friends."

The Neprian priests widened their formation and encircled the duo. In almost perfect synchronization, they each attached their lit torches to the business end of their javelins. Their weapons dropped into kill position.

"Vern, not to be a nitpicker, but friends don't attack each other with fire-covered spears."

"Mr. LaGrange—"

"Seriously, what's going on here? I mean—if we are going to be skewered like shish kebabs, at least tell us why. We deserve that. You give us a place to rest, break bread and ploob kalarti with us—which was simply divine by the way —and then kill us? Why not kill us at the gate and take our ship?"

"Orbius has demanded it. He has seen enough from you. I cannot go against his wishes."

"So you *don't* agree with it? You kept us around to see if we were worth saving?"

"Mr. LaGrange, Orbius' will is final. You and Ishiro'shea must be destroyed."

"You really believe that, Vern? Do we look like we need to be destroyed? We are as good of dudes as you're ever going to see in this universe. Surely, you have to recognize that? And we are super fun at parties."

"There is no process for appeal, Duke. I am truly sorry. Maybe the Orb will grant us an opportunity to meet again in an afterlife."

"Sounds like a blast."

"Advance." The Neprian motioned and his squad of priestly warriors marched down the hill toward the bounty-hunting duo. Vernglet Wip disappeared behind the apex and out of view.

"Looks like this is going to happen, Ishiro. Do you think they realize that I've got a gun? Actually, two guns."

Ishiro gave a rapid shrug that constituted a chuckle.

"Going by Delix's sharpshooting expertise, I'm guessing not. This Orbius fella must not be all-knowing after all. Who sends in ten skinny clergymen armed with over-sized toothpicks against Duke LaGrange?"

The Neprians progressed slowly towards them.

"Okay, stand back, Ishiro. Watch a master at work," Duke said confidently as he placed Betsy back in her holster and dropped his right hand to his side. His fingers twitched as he whispered to himself, "Wait for it—thirty paces out... twenty-five... twenty..."

With an unmatched fluidity, Duke rapidly pulled his laser revolver from his hip and rattled off eleven quick, powerful pulses. Eleven Neprian priests hit the ground— approximately nineteen paces from Duke LaGrange. Ishiro sheathed his katana.

"Where are you, Vern?" shouted Duke. "Come back! Is that all you got? Orbius isn't a god or a savior—he's a bona fide idiot for thinking a handful of priests could stop Duke LaGrange."

There was no response. Silence filled the air.

"I guess this means we go after him and get the *Deus* back?"

Ishiro concurred.

Now an even brighter light crept from behind the pinnacle of the mound to the east. An audible trembling was building steadily. Duke and Ishiro'shea exchanged inquisitive gazes. *This can't be good.* Flame-tipped javelins were first in view. Dozens. Hundreds. The numbers kept growing. Then the drawn and gaunt faces became visible, each set of eyes focused on the bounty-hunting duo. The group kept expanding and their numbers spilled out beyond the ridge to form a wide arc between the twosome and Dre'en. This was not Vernglet Wip and a gang of priests; this was a legion of Neprian Holy Warriors.

CHAPTER FOURTEEN

CHANGE OF PLANS

FROM THE CENTER OF THE Neprian army emerged another priest adorned in a pewter-colored robe—a very different look to High Priest Vernglet Wip. In the torchlight, his skin matched the color of his attire and his eyes were bloodshot spheres of hate. The headgear atop his cranium was also grander than Vernglet's: greattu horns extended from the sides and multicolored streamers flowed in the breeze. He took a few steps to stand in front of his troops and held aloft a sword with a hilt of bones and a winding blade, half the length of the Neprian javelin. It appeared to be a timeless relic that had dished out its fair share of pain and suffering.

"Vernglet Wip is no longer here, nor is he any concern of yours, off-worlders," boomed a voice richer than that of any Neprian the duo had spoken to so far. "The great Orbius has grown tired of your presence. Your termination will now be enforced—something Vernglet Wip was incapable of performing."

"Tired of our presence? After a day? And we didn't

even meet the guy?" shouted Duke. "Remind me not to vacation here next cycle."

"I'm glad that you find humor in your last moments of life, Duke LaGrange. May your laughter bring you comfort during your descent into the afterlife."

"Alrighty, big guy. If you say so. But if you recall, I just laid out some of your minions without as much of a thought —what makes you think that I won't do the same to you and your horde of toothpick-toters?"

The hulking Neprian priest laughed.

"I invite you to dispose of me and my legion, by all means, my off-world friend. Make the first move, Mr. LaGrange. But the subsequent move will be your immediate death."

The fingers on Duke's right hand twitched. His stare hardened. The Neprian's laughter increased in volume.

The bounty hunter pulled his laser revolver from his hip and directed a pulse at the leader of the warrior-priest gang. With an unnerving calm, the muscle-bound Neprian twisted slightly to the left. A soldier collapsed behind the colossal commander, falling face first into the soil with a gaping hole in his chest.

"Your aim seems to have failed you, Duke LaGrange," laughed the brute.

"It won't fail me again."

Duke extended his arm and pointed his gun at the commander once again.

"Attack, my legion, attack. Kill the two off-worlders!"

The seemingly infinite mob of Neprian priests surrounded their superior officer. Duke's next shot disappeared into the mass of charging warriors.

"For Orbius!" The bellow resonated from behind the enemy line. "You fail again, Duke LaGrange."

Ishiro'shea stood in attack position, bracing for the

oncoming charge. Duke rattled off pulse after pulse, taking down one Neprian after another.

"Ishiro, they're getting closer and I'm not taking out nearly enough. Any ideas?"

The ninja tapped Duke on the shoulder.

"No way, Ishiro. They *want* to drive us into that forest. You saw the movement earlier—I guarantee that they got a few more uglies in there just waiting for us."

Ishiro seemed agitated. He gestured to the oncoming swarm, now so close that Duke could see the sunken features of their emaciated faces.

"We can take 'em. We've been in worse situations. Remember that one time..."

Neprian javelins filled the air. One of the golden rods struck the ground a single pace in front of the bounty hunter.

"Ok, you win. Change of plans, Ishiro. The forest it is!"

The bounty hunters turned and sprinted toward the dense foliage. The repeated sound of the Neprian spears hitting the soil continued to follow them.

"Damnit, how many of those things do they have?"

A javelin struck just to the right of the sprinting Nova Texan.

"Looks like we got another problem, little buddy," Duke said between deep breaths. "How do we get through this brush? Doesn't look like there's a way in."

Ishiro didn't answer but picked up his pace beyond Duke's ability to match. In a few moments he was three or four body lengths ahead of his companion. The ninja leapt in the air toward the opaque barrier of intertwined branches with his katana pointed skyward. His strike was quick and effortless; the martial artist landed without a sound. The wooded barricade split open, revealing a pathway just wide enough for the two bounty hunters to continue their retreat.

"Thanks, Ishiro. But one more thing…"

Duke stopped a few paces within the forest and let off a few rounds of his laser revolver at the overhanging foliage. Debris crumbled down and sealed the katana-hewn doorway.

"That should slow 'em down a bit. Let's go, we need to put as much ground in between us and those skinny punks as we can."

They reduced their speed to a heavy jog as they navigated the unfamiliar forest. As they traveled deeper, the remaining light from overhead was swallowed up by the forest canopy.

"Listen, Ishiro," Duke said. He stopped. "Nothing. I don't hear a thing."

Ishiro'shea appeared to focus his auditory senses in order to confirm Duke's assessment.

"Did they give up? I don't hear a solitary branch cracking or a single voice. You know, I *should* be happy about this—but I keep thinking that there could be a reason they aren't following us. Maybe they drove us right into their trap?"

Ishiro unsheathed his blade. Duke pulled his laser revolver from its holster.

"Let's keep an eye out, little buddy. I have a bad feeling —again. Man, I really hate this planet."

Ishiro'shea knelt down and rummaged around a few fallen branches.

"Good idea, Ishiro. I'll cover you while you get us a torch going. I don't think we can go any farther without some light. I don't really want to hunker down now and wait until the morning; those priests might change their minds and follow us in here. But I don't think we can go down the path in the dark either—we'd be sitting ducks."

Soon a flame flickered at the ends of two sticks. Ishiro'shea handed one of the makeshift torches to Duke.

"Thanks. Okay, at least if we get ambushed, we'll see 'em. Gives us a fighting chance, right?"

A gust of wind hit both men in the face; darkness consumed them instantaneously. A heavy canvas screen knocked Duke and Ishiro'shea off their feet and flattened them against the forest floor. Their newly-created flashlights left their hands upon impact and returned to their wilderness home.

"Holy hedgehogs! Ishiro, you okay?" Duke asked in a muffled tone, pinned against the ground by the weighty net.

He didn't hear a response. *Definitely not a great time to have a partner that doesn't talk.*

Ishiro whistled. *Good.*

"Well, I'm glad we had those torches so we could prevent ourselves from walking into their trap, right?"

Duke soon realized it was a bad time for sarcasm.

CHAPTER FIFTEEN

BLINDFOLDS

"**H**OW ABOUT TAKING THESE BLINDFOLDS off? I mean, you got us... you win."

Hushed tones and jumbled speech echoed around what Duke believed was a cave of some sort.

"Actually, scratch that request. I'm tired of looking at your ugly priestly mugs. It's bad enough that you morons captured us—I don't think I'm ready to see the smug look on your bony faces."

Their conversations continued to elude Duke's understanding.

"I guess I'm talking to myself here. Well, you guys should feel pretty tough. It only took a thousand of ya' to catch Ishiro and I—not very efficient if you ask me. Pretty piss-poor, in fact."

"Seriously, do you ever shut up?"

The response was tinged with genuine frustration, and sounded nothing like the Neprian voices to which Duke had grown accustomed during his time on the planet. Not even the big ugly warrior priest's.

"Oh, hey there. What's happening, friend?"

"I'm trying to find a gag for you. Your constant gibberish is going to give our position away. No prisoner is worth that!"

"You must be related to that oversized priest dude with the flamboyant hat."

"Why on Neprius would you think that I'm related to General Tsarano Gar?"

"You're the only ones with deep voices. All of your other brothers and sisters—wait, do you have sisters? I didn't see any. Anyways, all of your brothers sounded like puberty was a long-term goal. Kudos for not being a squeaky toy."

"See, I told you!" This new exclamation was a bit more alto than bass.

"Now that's what I'm used to," replied Duke. "Hey, Mr. Priest."

"I'm not a priest, you idiot! I'm a kid. And I'm not a 'mister.' This is how I'm supposed to sound."

"Whatever. Is that you, Vernglet? Hoblet? I know it's one of you lot."

"I told you, Po'l. Both things that I said. Number one—he is not on the side of Orbius. And number two—" The voice broke off into a whisper. "He's an idiot."

"Wait a damn second! Holy hedgehogs! You're that puny street varmint. I knew I was going to regret saving you."

"You didn't save me, off-worlder," cried the kid. "I had those Northerners where I wanted."

"Right. Can you at least take off these hoods now that you know we aren't in with the killer clergy?"

"Absolutely not," replied the deeper-voiced being. Duke assumed this was Po'l. "The Northerners have pulled off sneakier ruses than this, under the guidance of Orbius. You could be part of yet another elaborate setup."

"Po'l!" squeaked the kid.

"Sorry. I'm still going to recommend that we execute them—to be safe."

"We're not going to consider that option, Po'l." The voice was soft yet with a firm confidence.

Female.

"Hello, ma'am," interjected Duke. "My name is Duke LaGrange. Adventurer. Trailblazer. Poet. A true man of the universe. You, my lovely Neprian goddess, must be the leader of this band of warriors. Your speech is that of a leader and a visionary."

The creamy voice began again. "You know what? Maybe we do keep execution on the table."

"Thank you, Ja'a. This guy and his henchman add no value to our cause," exclaimed Po'l.

Ishiro'shea began to rustle in the cage.

"Calm down, Ishiro. You aren't a henchman."

"Po'l, I'm kidding," replied Ja'a. "To be honest, I'm quite impressed. I've never been hit on through a blindfold—by someone that hasn't even seen me."

"You can tell a lot from a voice, my beautiful belle."

"Mr. LaGrange, I said I was impressed—not stupid. Remove the hoods."

"Ja'a, you're acting irrationally. Kid, keep the hoods on!"

"Po'l, I know this is hard for you, but the leaders put me in charge of the capture and maintenance of these two peculiar aliens. Let me do my job."

"No worries, Miss Ja'a! See!" The kid had already removed the hoods, obviously ignoring the barking of Po'l.

Duke scanned his cage. *Primitive.* Then, the kid. *Yep, same little urchin.* Then, who he believed was Po'l. *Athletic, probably could handle himself in a brawl.* Then, Ja'a. *My senses haven't missed a step.*

"Thanks, kid. Well, hello, there. You have to admit, I

was spot on about one thing. You're quite the sight to behold. Breathtaking."

Ja'a was slender and lean—but muscular. The exposed skin of her arms, midriff, and face were gently bronzed. Other than her ears—which were slightly too large for her head and shaped like tilted ovals—she looked exceptionally human. *Way better looking than those Hilterians at the bar.*

All three of them sported similar hairstyles; the sides of their heads were completely shaven and the hair that they did sport appeared to grow from a single circular pad on their cranium. The kid's hair was a stringy, discombobulated mess, matching her clothes. Po'l's darker hair was neatly groomed into a perfect circle, no hair longer than half a blade of grass. Ja'a's stretched beyond the back of her shoulders, wound in a tight ponytail—an attractive whip of dirty blonde sass. Of the three captors, she was the only wearing face paint—a silvery-blue pattern that stretched around each eye and continued around her head. The choice of cosmetics highlighted the steely crystal of her eyes. *Stunning.*

"We removed your blindfolds, but that's it. We still need to know who you are, where you come from, and why you're here—at this, undeniably suspicious, juncture in time."

"I'm Duke LaGrange. Adventurer—"

"Please stop. Please. If you say that again, I'll send you straight back to Gar and his men. I'm sure they'll have something a bit more *annoying* than our blindfolds."

The kid chuckled. As did Ishiro'shea.

"Ishiro? Really?"

"Ja'a, he *wants* to go back to Gar. Gar is his sworn master. I know misdirection when I see it."

Have you ever seen anyone cut their own head off? Now that's misdirection, thought Duke.

"I'm not sure they have anything more annoying than this guy!"

"Po'l, please be quiet. We need to see if Duke and his quiet friend provide any insight, or add any value for us."

"Okay, fine. My name *is* Duke LaGrange. This is my sidekick, Ishiro'shea. I'm not sure we have great answers for the rest of your questions."

"Why is that?"

"We were brought here by a giant space blob; a red astral anomaly just gobbled up our spaceship and deposited us neatly in an orbit around your gem of a planet."

"Interesting."

"The skinny priests said the same thing. I'm assuming y'all don't get along."

"For now, we'll ask the questions."

"Fair enough, all things considered."

"Yes, all things considered. So you were sent to Neprius against your will—and then what?"

"Ishiro and I parked our ship—which was stolen by those damn priests, by the way—and walked toward what we thought was civilization. We passed a few deserted villages—" Duke paused. "I'm assuming those are yours? Similar décor to this cave prison."

"Continue your story, Duke."

"Thanks for not calling me 'Mr. LaGrange.' So, we made it to the giant wall and that's where Vernglet Wip met us. He seemed like a good dude—odd, but good. He loved him some Orbius though. And crops. Never understood that. So, he invited us into the heart of Dre'en to meet with some Neprian scholars to help us find out about the weird star thingy that brought us here."

"Seems plausible."

"Ishiro and I were given a room and then we met Vern for a nice dinner. We didn't suspect any funny business."

A grunt came from behind Duke in the cell.

"Okay, I didn't suspect anything. Ishiro never felt good about the whole ordeal. We headed back to our room after dinner and heard some rumbling in the dining room, so we went to check it out. That's where we ran into your diminutive jailer over there being harassed by some Neprian thugs."

"Is that true?"

The female child nodded.

"She escaped and we bashed up some priests. When we made our way back up, our weapons were being stolen by two other pale-faces."

"Your weapons over there?" Ja'a pointed at Betsy, his laser revolver, and Ishiro's katana.

"You got it."

"How'd you survive? We noticed the destruction that these items caused on Gar and his troops."

"They're pretty rad, right? However, our buddy Delix didn't quite know how to use 'em. Betsy's pretty much a point-and-shoot firearm, but you really can't mess up the 'point' part if you're going to nail the 'shoot' half of the equation. Seeing his buddy splattered against the wall must've not sat right with Hoblet—so he vamoosed."

"Lies!" Po'l shouted. "He wants to make us seem like we can't figure out his magic weapon so we ask for his guidance —then he kills us, for Orbius."

"Her name is Betsy."

"You name this bringer of death? I knew it—they're sick, sadistic assassins."

"Po'l, let him finish."

"It was obvious that someone didn't want us here so we booked it back to the *Deus*—our ship."

"You guys sure like naming things."

"When we got there, it was gone. I'm assuming that

Vernglet and his priest friends jacked it. I don't know why, though. Or how. If they can't figure out a gun, good luck with a spaceship."

"It does seem odd. Maybe it was Orbius?"

"Whoever it was, my ship's gone. And before we know it, Vern and his buds surrounded us. I mowed some down with my other weapon."

"What's its name?"

"Actually, it doesn't have one."

"Pity."

"So Vern disappears and that ugly Gar pops up and tells us not to worry about Vern—which I wasn't because we had bigger fish to fry—and he brings out hundreds of his soldiers."

"Why didn't you just shoot Gar?" asked Po'l.

"I tried. But I missed."

"Wait, you blasted an entire group without missing— but can't hit a single target? And a huge target at that. I'm not buying it." He turned to Ja'a. "They're pulling one over on us—if he wanted to hit Gar, he would've."

"As hard as it is for me to admit this, I just flat missed."

"Mr. LaGrange—" Ja'a started.

"Oh great, we're back to 'Mr. LaGrange.' I thought we were making progress."

"I have to agree with Po'l. That part does seem far-fetched. Let's pretend you are telling the truth—continue."

"I *am* telling the truth."

"Go on."

"Gar's army rushed us with their spears and we ran into the forest. I felt we put some space between us and then BAM! We're here with you crazy cats."

"Complete garbage," raged Po'l. "I think this needs to be brought to the council. They'll side with me, I guarantee you, Ja'a."

"I think they can help us," replied Ja'a.

"Me too!" shouted the kid.

"You're both wrong. LaGrange is full of greattu dung. His friend can't even speak."

"You know we can hear you, right?"

"Yeah—and I don't really care. Please just shut up and start acting like a prisoner."

"Oh, Po'l, I think we got off on the wrong foot."

"Ja'a, let's just take their weapons and leave them to die. I can't handle this guy one second longer. I'm sure we can figure out how to use the weapons. I mean, they did—and look at them."

"You heard what he said—the priest tried and he exploded," said the kid.

"Lies."

"What if they aren't lies, Po'l? What if they are the only ones that can master them?"

"Ja'a, do you seriously believe that?"

"I don't know. But based on what we saw, they could be the tools we need to turn the tide against Orbius. It's worth the risk."

"Yeah!" screamed the kid, directly at Po'l. He sneered back.

"Hey guys," interjected Duke. "You think my guns are the secret to defeating Orbius and Gar and his armies?"

"Maybe."

"Y'all are crazy."

"*We're* crazy?" said Po'l.

"Let me rephrase that. Y'all are crazy but you, my good sir, are insane."

"And why is that?"

"Well, it's one thing to think two guns are going to win a war—even if I was operating them—but then to think that we blasted some dudes into their graves as part of some elaborate hoax to get in close with you... that's a whole new level of stupid."

"Exactly what I would expect you to say."

"Fine! Go use it. Shoot me and Ishiro. Do your best, Po'l!"

Ishiro'shea kicked Duke squarely in the back.

"No worries, Ishiro. He won't figure it out. In a few minutes, he'll be splattered against the wall like Delix—and then we won't have to listen to his dumb-ass conspiracy theories anymore."

Po'l flashed a smile at Duke. "Sounds like a plan to me—"

"Po'l, stop! Whether they're who you think they are—or who they say they are—we aren't going to try out their weapons. That is for the council to decide."

"I've had enough of this, Ja'a. I'm not sure whose team you're on—or why you'd side with this murderer and his mute lap dog."

"Po'l, be reasonable."

"You know what? You can stay here with these two, I'll head out and keep watch."

"We've got guys out there."

"Maybe they could use some company." Visibly frustrated, Po'l stormed out.

"Let 'em go, Ja'a," the kid begged. "He's wrong, I know it."

"I hope you're right. I really do."

"She is," interrupted Duke. "But tell me one thing."

"Yes?"

"What exactly are we trying to learn from you? Why are we supposedly playing this epic trick on y'all? Oh yeah, and why are you so pissed at Orbius? I mean, I know why I'm mad at 'em—they jacked my ship and tried to kill me."

"One thing?"

"Okay, maybe three."

"I'm not sure I'll tell you any of that—just in case."

"But Ja'a," the kid responded, "if they are spies working for Orbius—they know all of this."

"Good point."

"Wow, you're a wise little street varmint," commented the bounty hunter.

"Thanks."

"Do you have a name? Or just 'kid'?"

"It's Uu'k."

"Okay, 'kid' it is. So, what's the story here, Ja'a? What's the beef with Orbius?"

Ja'a sat down on a makeshift chair just outside of the pair's cage. Uu'k sat cross-legged to her left, seemingly eager for the yarn that was about to unfold.

CHAPTER SIXTEEN

RUPTURED EARDRUMS

"I GUESS WE CAN START with the droughts. I remember it quite vividly. My family and I lived outside of Dre'en and, out of nowhere, the weather changed," Ja'a paused reflectively. "Crops began to die. Our villages suffered greatly."

"What caused it? What did your scientists say?"

"Scientists? We had no scientists. We're simple folk, Duke. We farmed—and farmed well. Or so we thought. We handled bad weather in the past but weren't able to figure it out this time. Food dried up and villages began to fight with each other over whatever scraps could be collected."

"Did it affect everyone? Or just the rural villages?"

"Most of us lived the same lifestyle. Even in Dre'en— though it was the center of our land—they ate from the same crops as our village and the hundreds of villages in southern Neprius."

"So, how'd you figure it out?"

"It was so bad that our leaders traveled across the land bridge that connects the north and south to talk with the Northern tribes."

"Northern tribes?"

"Yes, your priest friends. Those possessing the pale skin; they come from the northern land mass."

"I thought they controlled Dre'en? That place seems to be crawlin' with 'em."

"That was not always the case. In fact, until the droughts no Northerner had set foot in Dre'en for countless ages."

"I'm confused," said Duke.

"As I was saying, our leaders trekked northward to meet their high priests—and ask for aid and assistance. However, it was clear that their fate was no different than ours. The extreme weather had ravaged their lands with the same blatant disregard for life. When we arrived, they were welcomed by the council of the Northern tribe to try and solve the horrible situation that had fallen upon the whole of Neprius."

"Did the two sides not speak a lot?"

"No. After generations of warfare, the two tribes settled in different halves of Neprius and swore never to cross the land bridge. Both sides lived up to their end of the bargain; cycles and cycles of life came and went and we weren't even sure if they existed anymore. I'm sure they felt the same."

"Fascinating."

"You haven't heard the fascinating part yet, Duke!" shouted Uu'k.

"Uu'k, I'm getting to it."

"Sorry, Ja'a."

"Unfortunately, 'fascinating' carries a fairly negative connotation in this case. Unknown to most of us in the south and, my assumption, to most in the north, the histories of our two tribes were connected by a powerful source that was beyond our ability to grasp. Only a few leaders on our council knew the truth. To everyone else it was just a legend that you told children."

"Yep," Uu'k added.

"There was a hidden temple near the center of the land bridge," continued Ja'a, "guarded by clergy from both lands —it remained secret for millennia. These guards' lifelong duty was the concealment of this shrine and what was inside."

"I'm guessing this is the 'fascinating' part?"

"Yes, inside the temple was an Orb. An Orb that—"

"Must be respected and controls stuff, right? I've heard about it from Vern."

"In their words, they do refer to it as something like that. In ours, the Orb is referred to simply as Peace."

"Cute. I'm not much into round rocks determining the paths civilizations take. Seems like your people and those wacky nutjobs up north are a bit simple minded. A bunch of utter hogwash."

"Duke, I don't think you understand. This Orb is an ancient relic that, whether you want to believe it or not, helped to end the war between our two tribes. Its power was uncontrollable and unimaginable; both sides stole it from one another and caused more pain and suffering on themselves than their rivals. It led them to a treaty and thousands of cycles of peace. Both tribes decided to build a secure place to house Peace and closed off the land bridge from both sides. Of course this meant that our races would never be in contact with each other from that point on—but it was worth it to maintain a truce. The sheer unharnessed power of this artifact kept everyone grounded and put into perspective how puny we really are—and how the death and destruction caused by war over petty differences of opinions was senseless."

"Seems a little harsh. If you realized that, isn't that

enough? Did you really have to separate the two tribes permanently?"

"I don't know but, for some reason, they did."

"So, what happened next regarding the dying crops and food shortage?"

"The leaders of both races were perplexed and lacked a solution. They ended up sending the High Priest of the North, his name was Jilarian Togg, and our Tribal Chief, He'j, to the temple and see if the Orb could help save Neprius."

"Did they just walk up and ask it to help? It's a flippin' rock."

"Duke, there is much that you don't know about Peace."

"Fine. Go on. But you're losing me."

"The story goes that He'j and Jilarian Togg retrieved the Orb and sat on the banks of the swamps around the temple for days. Nothing happened. And finally He'j grabbed the Orb and shook it—and shouted at the top of his lungs, 'Bring us someone or something that will make an impact on Neprius and rid us of our plight. Thousands will die of thirst and hunger if you don't help us, Peace. You did it once before—please, do it again. Bring us someone that will end this suffering.'"

"Inspiring. Did he have a speechwriter?" Duke directed this quip at Ishiro'shea, who did not return a chuckle.

"Maybe Po'l was right."

"My apologies. I promise I'll be quiet."

"I'm not sure you deserve the rest of the story, but I will continue."

"Thank you."

"Peace began to glow a bright purple, and tremble, and then hover above the two men. The swamp bubbled ferociously. The sky went completely black, with the exception of the Orb."

"Then what?" Duke asked, his interest reengaged.

"Then nothing."

"What?"

"Not for a few days at least. Just as He'j and his men were preparing to leave, reports from the north—near their capital of Sansagon—trickled in of a mysterious off-worlder. They brought him to meet with He'j and Togg. His name was Ot Vangu—of Earth."

"Ishiro, ever heard of him?"

The ninja shook his head.

"Figured. And that's why Vern was so squirrely when we mentioned Earth. What was Mr. Ot Vangu up to?"

"The Orb summoned him."

"Of course it did! You would think if a magic rock wants you to save the planet, it could've got him here a bit faster than a few days."

"Vangu couldn't explain it but it was clear that the Orb had brought him here."

"How were they so sure?"

"He was the person that He'j had asked for. His job back on his home world was to bring vegetation and crops to barren lands. He grew life from nothingness; he brought hope to Neprius. He saved us."

"So all was going so swimmingly. What happened?"

"Both tribes decided to elect Ot Vangu as supreme governor; he was wise and had no bias towards either race. He was a heaven-sent impartial leader."

"No such thing."

"I agree with you there, Duke. For Vangu learned of Peace and became obsessed with it—locking himself in a room for weeks and months and cycles. Both tribes became worried and tried to reason with Vangu. Somehow, during his time as leader of the two tribes, he discovered how to control the Orb—something thought to be impossible. He demanded that both tribes pledged their allegiance to him. High Priest Togg confronted him first—as the story goes, it was in the town square of Sansagon—and Vangu struck him down with one blast of light from Peace. Togg, a proud leader, died in the street as the other Northerners watched in awe. It was clear that the Northerners would not fight Ot Vangu. He gained his loyal followers almost immediately."

"And the Southern tribes? And He'j? Your people?"

"We fought Vangu for many cycles. We were no match for Peace—under Vangu's control, it killed many of my people. We surrendered. Vangu was not kind to us for resisting and so we were enslaved. My entire race was sent to the mines to dig for stones for his palace; stones used as decoration. We slave and die underground for a frivolous cause—and Vangu just laughs at our peril. He made sure that we would not die honorable deaths."

"What happened to He'j?"

"He died at Vangu's hands. That is all we know."

"A corrupted warlord with a magic rock that enslaves farmers to dig for some home decor—well, it's a new one for Ishiro and I. So, I'm assuming you're part of some sort of ragtag rebellion?"

"Yes. Our numbers are small but not insignificant. The sad fact is that many would rather die in the mines in ten cycles than fight for freedom in one."

"Honey, that's most sentient races. Cowardice is not unique to Neprius."

"Vangu's forces continue to grow—the Northerners worship him as a god. In fact, Vangu and the Orb have become one to them and, thus, Orbius was born."

"I was about to ask about 'Orbius.' It's nothing more than Vangu rebranding himself, huh?"

"Yes. He's successfully taken over the entire planet. Dre'en fell to his followers quite easily and now the few left that oppose Orbius are scattered across the southern land-mass. It makes it hard to organize; but we might have caught a break."

"And what's that?"

"You. More accurately, your weapons. They seem to be able to at least challenge Orbius."

"Ah. Yes. My weapons. As much as I love Ol' Betsy, I'm not sure they will be much help against a supernatural orb and its lunatic master."

"You might be right. After all, General Gar managed to elude death. However, maybe we'll be able to master your weapon at a level that you aren't able to achieve."

"You must be kidding, sister. That's as crazy as your story."

"The story isn't crazy. It's true," chimed in Uu'k. "You have to help us!"

"Uu'k, I'm not sure Mr. LaGrange and his friend have any interest in helping us. But maybe the fate that brought them here will be enough to make an impact through the usage of their armaments."

"Fate? It sounds like I got caught up in some of Orbius' manipulating-space-and-time practice sessions with his little magic ball. Not sure if that's fate or really bad luck."

"What's the difference?"

"Touché," replied Duke. "Just wonderful. I would have preferred my chances with Korzo-Tapor and the Robots. Right, Ish?"

The bounty hunter then turned his attention to the child. "Hey kid, you know all of this means that y'all are going to take our guns and leave us here to rot in this cage."

"Ja'a, no! You can't do that! They might be simple, but they did try and help me! I know they're good people that can help us."

"I wish I shared that same optimism, Uu'k."

"So, Ja'a, what if Ishiro and I agreed to help you?" Duke paused as Ishiro'shea kicked him in the back again. "We can help you take out some of the Northerners and get to Orbius. We can strike a deal. Hell, we have to get our ship back anyways to get home. I don't have time to wait around for your lot to invent space travel."

"I'm sorry, Duke. Your weapons are too powerful and we are too few in number. With what I have seen—the General Gar episode aside—if I give you the weapons, you can kill us too easily. There is nothing, outside of Uu'k's belief in you, that can make me agree to that. Our elder leaders maybe—but not me."

A loud scream permeated through the cave. A Southern tribesman stumbled backward into the room and collapsed. He had a Neprian javelin lodged in his stomach.

"Ja'a! They found us!" screamed Po'l. "One down. We're outnumbered! Ten to one!"

Po'l let loose an arrow from his bow. It whizzed through the cave and out into the unknown.

"Hurry, Ja'a!"

A crackling of rapid-fire 'dings' filled the air as the pointed tips of Neprian javelins crashed against the stone exterior of the cave.

"Hey, guys. I have an idea!"

Ja'a and Po'l both looked back at the smiling bounty hunter.

"Shut up!" Po'l shouted. "Can't you see that we're under attack? I don't have time for your plans."

Another spear entered the opening of the cave hideaway and skipped across the rocky floor before coming to a stop near to the cage that held the two bounty hunters.

"Uu'k, go hide behind the cage! Okay, Duke. What do you got?"

"Seriously, Ja'a? Are you crazy?"

Another javelin whizzed by Po'l.

"Their aim's getting better, ya' know," smirked the Nova Texan.

"What do you propose, Duke? Make it fast!"

"Well, first off—make Po'l apologize."

Ishiro, for a third time, kicked Duke squarely between his shoulder blades. Duke responded with a laugh lacking anything resembling panic.

"What?" screamed Ja'a and Po'l in unison.

"You're insane!" continued Po'l.

"Give me my guns and this will all be over," Duke responded in a calm cadence.

"You just want those guns so you can escape."

"Partly—yes. I don't want to be killed in a cage on a primitive third-rate planet by some malnourished priests with really big needles—so escapin' has crossed my mind. It's kinda funny if you think about it."

"What is?"

"You're worried about us killing you if we escape—but if you would've never caught us, maybe they would've never tracked us here. So, either way—we killed you. Sorry, bud."

"Duke, I want to help you—but this is ridiculous."

"Ja'a, wait a second. Hear me out."

"Hurry, we don't have much time to hear you out," Ja'a responded.

"They're closing in," shouted another rebel from just outside the entryway. "We've taken a few out but we're running low on arrows. We didn't pack to fight off a full squad of Northerners."

"Duke?"

"Okay, you don't trust us, right? Give us a chance. Let us out—give us our weapons. We'll get y'all out of this jam. Or try to, at least. If we survive, we promise to go with you to meet your council and see if we can help your cause. We'll give you a chance to persuade us."

"That's it?" shouted Po'l. "You need us anyways."

"And why is that?"

"You don't know how to get to Orbius' fortress up north —where your ship is."

"True, but—"

"No 'buts'. He's useless, Ja'a. I'm going to end this."

"Slow down, Po'l."

Po'l headed over to a patch of dirt and stones along the inner wall. He kicked aside some of the chunkier rocks and picked up the Widowmaker sonic shotgun.

"Hey, get your hands off Betsy!"

"Or what?"

"Ja'a, look, you better warn him. This is not advisable. If we die here, not only do we, ya' know, *die* but our weapons end up in the hands of your enemies. Even if we ran out on ya', at least our guns'll run out on Orbius' minions too."

"I'm tired of this guy. I'm going to end it." Po'l examined Betsy. "Doesn't look too hard," he muttered. "This is how I saw that moron do it before."

"I can hear you."

"Something like this."

"Is that a question? Not a lot of confidence, huh?"

"Shut up!"

Po'l marched to the cave opening and pressed his back against the rigid wall. Veins protruded from his neck all the way down to his pectorals, which were visible above the rounded neckline of his chest plate. *Dude needs to chill. Never a good idea to operate a Widowmaker sonic shotgun when you're this tense.*

"I know what I'm doing. I'm not one of those Northerners."

Po'l held the gun and pointed it in the right direction.

Okay, he's one better than Delix. Betsy's butt rested comfortably on his cheek.

"Yeah, I wouldn't hold it that way—"

The roar from Betsy filled every crack and crevice of the cave; the sound waves ricocheted like a pinball in a rubber-lined hallway. Debris fell within the dwelling; small pebbles doing their best impression of a light rain. Duke heard Uu'k's scream from behind his prison. *That had to rupture an eardrum—assuming they have eardrums in those giant head flippers they're sporting. Poor kid.*

Then silence. The athletically-built Neprian rebel lay halfway between the entryway and the makeshift jail cell —motionless.

"What happened in there?" a watchman shouted from just outside the cave. "Tell Po'l to fire again! All he hit was a tree! They're preparing another volley!"

Ja'a slid to where Po'l's body had been launched after his ill-advised handling of Betsy.

"Po'l! Are you alive? Answer me! Please!"

She shook him—no response.

"Uu'k, get me some water. Quickly, child."

Uu'k ran and grabbed a leather pouch and filled it with water. She delivered it to Ja'a, cupping her hand over one ear. *Yep, ruptured. Dumb-ass, Po'l.*

"Is he alive, Ja'a?"

"I don't know. I think so. Answer me, Po'l!"

She lifted his face. One side was completely blackened and seared by the gun; blood flowed steadily from the left side of his mouth. His eyes remained closed, already morphed into deep purple mounds of swelling.

The familiar sounds of Neprian javelin tips hitting the façade returned. The rebel fighters retreated to the confines of their bunker.

"What are you doing? We can't let them in here!"

"Ja'a, we can't hold them off out there. They're picking us off one by one. There's too many."

"What are you saying?"

"Look, Ja'a—we're beat. We have no chance. Let's have our stand and take out as many of those bastards as possible."

"Heroic," smirked Duke.

"No time for your quips! We probably have a few minutes before those priests are on top of us. How many are left?"

"We took out a good number. So, maybe twenty or thirty."

"How many do we have? Just everyone in here?"

"Afraid so."

Po'l moaned.

"He's alive! Uu'k, get some more water! Uu'k? Where are you? Uu'k!"

Two more javelins bounced into the cave.

"Help me move him!"

Ja'a and one of the watchmen helped drag Po'l to the side and propped him up alongside the walls as he continued to unleash wails of agony.

"Okay, grab your arrows—let's pick them off as they make their way in. One at a time. When we're out of arrows, we'll fight at close quarters. Just like we trained. Understand?"

"Yes, Ja'a!" the soldiers replied in harmony.

"Let's make sure Orbius and his brainwashed lackeys remember us this day."

The five Neprian rebels formed a wall a few paces from the opening. They readied their bows.

"Don't waste a shot—let's drop them all!"

"Where do you want me? Betsy doesn't like hanging out in the back, ya' know."

The bounty hunter stood behind the line with his beloved firearm resting on his shoulder, propped up by his left arm. In his right hand he held his laser revolver. Ishiro'shea stood a step behind him to the right, his sword in attack position.

"How—"

"Ja'a, no worries. We'll take care of this."

"But how—"

Ja'a turned back to face their prisoners' recent residency.

"Uu'k! How could you? How *did* you?"

"Please don't be mad, Ja'a. The keys flew off of Po'l when he tried to use Duke's weapon. I just picked 'em up and let 'em out. I know Duke and Ishiro will help us. I trust them. I just know it!"

"Smart kid."

"They're about to penetrate," shouted a rebel solider, turning the line's attention back to the battlefront.

"No worries."

"So you said," retorted Ja'a.

The first shadow crept across the cave floor—gaunt, emaciated, and possessing an elongated instrument of puncturing prowess. In a fluid dance of muscle memory, Duke sheathed his revolver, transferred Betsy to his right hand, and lined up his shot. She let off a scream of epic magnitude. As quickly as it appeared, the Neprian shadow was no more. Betsy returned to her Ootrelian home.

"Ishiro, that should be enough confusion to take these stooges out. Let's do it."

The two bounty hunters entered the cloud of smoke caused by Betsy's blast, Duke with laser revolver drawn, Ishiro'shea with katana at the ready.

"Goodbye..."

"See ya'..."

"Can't run, buddy," Duke shouted as he rattled off pulses from the laser revolver.

His laughter cut through the gunshots.

"How many is that, little buddy? Twelve? Fifteen? Oh, don't run away, guys. We're just starting to have fun!"

Duke returned to the cave; five Neprians looked at him with stares comprised of equal parts thanks and concern.

"Well, guys, like I was saying—no worries!"

"Thank you," said Ja'a in a tone of disbelief. "We are truly in your debt."

"Even Po'l?"

"Yes, I'm sure Po'l won't question what you did for us today. You saved our lives. I am sorry for doubting your intentions. Please forgive us."

"It was nothing. Okay, it was *something*." He bowed as he accepted their praise. "By the way, Ishiro, sorry that I didn't let any more of 'em make it up here. I know you wanted a piece, too. How many did I get? Twenty?"

Duke turned to face his companion. In place of his emerald-clad ninja friend stood a Neprian priest warrior, battered and bloodied. Hate and revenge filled his pupil-less eyes and a javelin filled his hand—a javelin aimed directly at Duke.

"Not if I get you first," Duke muttered to himself as he reached for his laser revolver.

He did not get the shot off.

The Neprian fell to the cave floor. Ishiro'shea stood next to the corpse, a bloody katana at his side.

"Thanks, Ishiro. I should've known that you'd get yours somehow."

Duke pivoted and faced the Neprian rebels again but his eyes skimmed past their collected gazes.

"Oh yeah, most importantly... Thank you, ya' little street urchin."

CHAPTER SEVENTEEN

MR. SHARPSHOOTER

"I DON'T SEE ANY," SHOUTED one of the rebel watchmen.

"Yeah, but some got away," replied the Nova Texan from the entrance of the cave.

"So?" yelled another rebel, checking for stragglers in the foliage outside of the rebel camp.

Duke shook his head slowly and turned to Ja'a, who was tending to the slowly recovering Po'l.

"Your team— Well, they ain't the smartest, huh?"

"They have heart."

"That organ will put you in some pretty precarious situations if you let it."

"Duke, I fully agree with you—we don't have much time before they come back with an even larger army. And possibly General Gar."

"Bring that jackass on. I'll finish him for good," Duke replied, seething.

Ishiro'shea slapped Duke on the shoulder and kept his hand clamped there in a comforting manner.

"Thanks, bud. I'm just pissed. None of this woulda'

happened had I not missed that jerk."

Ishiro repeated his gesture.

"I guess there's only one thing to do now. Pack up and head out."

"And where are you and Ishiro'shea heading?," Ja'a asked. "Though I do hope you consider joining us, I have no right to object. You've truly earned your freedom."

"Even though it took the kid over there to trust me enough to let us out, I'm still going to hold up my side of the bargain. I'll stop by and chat with your leaders; you know what we can do and you know how to get to my ship. Seems an arrangement could be in the cards."

"Thank you, Duke. I do appreciate it."

"That's very kind of you, Ja'a. I don't usually have beautiful creatures like you appreciating me—" Duke paused momentarily. "—except for... ya' know. I mean, I've been known to—"

The bounty hunter was interrupted by the faint garbled cries of Po'l.

"Oh yeah, you. I forgot about you," Duke paused. "And it was glorious," he finished.

"He does add a bit of a wrinkle into our plan of a speedy exit," started Ja'a. "I don't think we have time to build a vessel to drag him."

"Definitely not. Let's leave him."

"Duke! No!" shrieked Uu'k. Ishiro'shea had made his way over to the young Neprian and was doing his best to tend to her bloody ear. "I know Po'l can be mean sometimes, but you can't leave him!"

"Oh, alright."

"I knew it. I knew you wouldn't leave anyone behind," Uu'k said through a giant smile.

"Settle down, kid. We still don't know how we can get 'Mr. Sharpshooter' outta here."

"I'm fine," mumbled Po'l. "Let me up."

"Po'l, take it easy. We'll figure something out."

The Neprian rebel started to lift himself up with the aid of Ja'a.

"Quick, guys. Help me with him."

The other two rebel soldiers in the cave flanked the injured Po'l; he draped his arms behind each of their necks for stability.

"You two think you can get him down to the forest and then keep up with us?"

"We're going to try," said the soldier supporting Po'l's right side.

"Or die trying," whispered Duke to himself.

Ja'a stared at the bounty hunter, clearly having heard his less-than-optimistic retort.

Duke decided to change the subject. "So, how long of a trip is this to see the brains of your operation?"

"A few days, maybe more—depending on whether the planet cooperates with us. We have to travel northwest and trek through most of the southern lands until we reach the coastline just below the land bridge."

"Great. Not to be a downer but, since Ishiro and I've been here, we haven't had the best 'cooperation' from this rock. What are you expectin', Ja'a? More priesties? Scary monsters? Avalanches and cyclones? Giant fire-breathing flying panthers?"

"Oh, I didn't know that you were aware of the grundar."

"Huh?"

"Not many Neprians that grew up on the southern landmass have ever seen a grundar in the wild; they are native to the northern lands. They're quite ferocious. Most that do see them don't live to speak of their unique observation."

"What are you talking about? What's a grundar?"

"Giant fire-breathing flying panthers. Like you said."

"Did I ever tell you how much I hate this place?"

"The likelihood that we encounter a grundar is slim—there are so many other annoyances that I'm more concerned about. Most notably, Gar's henchmen."

"Speaking of those smelly punks, we better pick up the pace," Duke reminded the team.

The other two watchmen returned to the cave. Ja'a tossed them their ration bags and some additional arrows.

"Te'o and Ma'n are going to carry Po'l for the first leg of our journey back to the coast. You'll need to carry their bags. We can swap out every few hours."

"Yes, Ja'a," they spoke in concert as they each plucked a second ration bag from the air.

"I don't need their help. I'm fine. Let me walk," Po'l muttered. His words trailed off and mutated into an aching groan. "Where's my sword?"

The tall Nova Texan stepped in front of the two soldiers propping up Po'l. He hunched over slightly and placed his face as close to the injured Neprian's without it actually touching.

"I know you don't like me," Duke whispered, "or trust me. I'm not sure why especially, since I just saved your collective asses. If it was up to me, I'd leave your sorry carcass in this cave to be eaten alive by who knows what horrors live in this forest—but Ja'a and the kid, for whatever reason, want to save you. So, if you would keep the moaning and complaining down to a minimum, it would be much appreciated. If not, I can always give you another go-round with Betsy. You have a whole other side of your face to cave in with your excellent gunmanship."

"Don't lecture me, off-worlder," Po'l countered. "Even if you aren't working for Orbius, that doesn't mean I have to trust you." He pulled one arm from around the neck of the soldier and wiped away some spittle, sprinkled with droplets of blood, from his lip. "In fact, I don't. I don't know your endgame and whether Orbius is involved or not, but I get the sense that you'll screw us over without hesitation to get what you want, regardless."

"Maybe so. But what choice do you have? You need me."

"We don't need you," Po'l said between coughing episodes. "We've been doing just fine without you."

"Oh, you have? Okay, so you got Orbius under control. Let me say, Po'l, you guys do a pretty bang-up job of making it look like you're runnin' around with your heads cut off."

"How are you going to find your ship though? It's probably at Orbius' palace right now."

"Ishiro and I can head north and I feel confident that we can persuade a few folks to point us in the right direction." Duke tapped his right hand against his holster.

"Scaring innocent villagers and threatening them with a weapon? You're such a swell guy. And Orbius is just going to give the ship to you? Why? Because you're such a likable person?"

"And I *need* your band of nitwits with your bows and arrows? *That's* going to help us?" Duke's voice raised from his earlier hushed tones.

"This planet will eat you alive, Duke. And your silent friend."

"Leave Ishiro outta this. What's your real beef with me, Po'l? First, you accuse us of being really committed spies—"

"I don't like you," Pol' interjected.

"Didn't your momma teach you not to interrupt?"

Ja'a wedged her arm between the faces of the two rivals. "Po'l, you are in no position to argue. Duke saved our lives— whether you care to admit it or not. Plus, you're only slowing your healing by bickering. You need to rest. We need you in this fight."

"Yeah, Po'l—listen to your boss," Duke jabbed. "Except for that 'needing' you bit."

"Duke, in all due respect and knowing that we are in your debt for your heroics earlier, Po'l is a great warrior and has been loyal to our cause for a long time. It's important for us—to me—to get him back to our leaders safely. I don't blame his distrust, though I can't say that I ever thought you were a pawn in Orbius' game. The truth is, you *are* an off-worlder and an outsider to our cause. I would be suspicious if he *did* trust you without hesitation."

Po'l managed a wry grin.

"You believe this?" Duke aimed his question firmly at Ishiro'shea.

The ninja returned a glance that Duke knew all too well. *Dammit, he agrees with her.*

"For the last time, we must make haste before we are consumed by Gar and his troops. Those that fled are probably back now and letting Gar know where we're holed up."

Ja'a exited the cave, followed by the two soldiers carrying Ma'n and Te'o's satchels, then Uu'k and Ishiro'shea. Duke stepped to the side and allowed Ma'n and Te'o—with Po'l balanced between them—to leave next. Po'l struggled to keep his head raised; his swollen eyes never left Ja'a as she led the group into the Neprian forest. *Wait a second! He's got a thing for her,* Duke thought to himself. *How'd I miss that? In love with his commander—maybe that's why he's so surly. Can't say I blame him. Whoa, be careful now, Duke.*

Duke descended the natural ramp that led from the cave. He unsheathed Ol' Betsy as he watched the rebels and Ishiro'shea disappear into the opaque Neprian vegetation.

CHAPTER EIGHTEEN

UU'K'S DAY JOB

AS FAR AS DUKE COULD see, sloping grasslands intermingled with abandoned plots of farmland—a far cry from the dense forest that concealed their cave hideaway south of Dre'en. Beautifully translucent ponds dotted the countryside; the stillness gave them the presence of being frozen. Outside of a gentle breeze, basic movement in the southern Neprian ecosystem seemed as if it were an extinct species. Duke couldn't help but feel as if he were walking from one end of a two-dimensional painting to the other.

"This has been quite a boring stroll."

"Boring is good, Duke," replied Ja'a. "That means that we haven't run across Orbius' soldiers or anything else that this country can throw at us."

"You're probably right."

"I know I am on this one. It's been two days and nothing —that's a good two days in my book."

"It's funny if you think about it."

"What's that?"

"Two days ago, you had Ishiro and I cooped up in a cage and thinking we were Orbius' spies."

"Is that why you've been avoiding me? Still upset about that?" asked Ja'a.

Duke tilted the front of his hat up with his thumb.

"No, Ishiro and I were just getting our bearings and, ya' know, taking in this beautiful scenery," he smirked.

"Well, I never thought you two were spies," Ja'a said with a subtle smile. "That was Po'l. But, *ya' know*, you can't blame him."

Duke snorted at Ja'a's gentle mocking, then he flashed a far less subtle smile at the Neprian.

"Oh, I *can* blame him. You aren't entirely without blame, yourself. I didn't see you trying *that* hard to convince your underlings to free us. Thank goodness for Uu'k. You had us locked up—and now you need us to help you. Heck, you need us to help your entire race."

"That's a tad dramatic."

"I don't know."

"Anyways, Duke, we're actually interested in your weapons—you are just an added complexity."

"Don't you mean an added 'benefit'?"

"I know what I mean."

The bounty hunter chuckled. "You're alright, Ja'a."

"I'm not quite sure about you, Duke. You've already had a few moments that lead me to believe that you could be this planet's savior or the final nail in our coffin. I just don't know quite yet."

"So, if I'm hearing you correctly—you think I'm pretty extraordinary."

"For now, let's call it 'interesting.'"

"Fair enough. Not to change the subject—because I *do* love talking about my favorite subject—"

"You?"

"Yes, me. But look over there."

Duke pointed to Ishiro'shea. "Seems that Ishiro and Uu'k are becoming buds."

"That's nice to see. She could use a friend. You know, Uu'k has been quite a valuable asset in the rebellion."

"You're kidding, right?"

"No, not at all."

"You mean because she freed Ishiro'shea and I—and we're gonna save the day?"

"Uu'k has been one of our best sources of local intelligence from inside Dre'en—specifically around the halls of the Altar House. Isn't that where you found her?"

"Close to it. She was near the kitchen in a dining hall. Ishiro and I had just had dinner with Vernglet Wip."

"She was under their employment—or rather, she was being forced to perform menial tasks like cleaning and preparing food."

"She's only a kid, though. How does—"

"Duke, I promise you, she volunteered. Her parents did not survive Orbius' wrath and she wanted to contribute."

"She's a kid."

"No one ever wants to be in a war. No one ever wants a child to be involved in that conflict, especially. Uu'k is special, though. I believe she actually fully grasps the entire concept of what's happening to her people—and knows that she has to sacrifice to have a chance to restore happiness and prosperity to Neprius."

"Ja'a, this is hard for me to swallow. And I've had a MechaBurger 8000."

"Ask her. Talk to her. She's an amazing kid."

"Where I come from, we do our damnedest to keep children out of harm and away from violence. We leave that for the grown-ups."

"Have you ever had to save your race from a mad, murderous tyrant?"

"Nova Texas has too many of those to count."

"Seriously, Duke. Our struggle needs every bit of help that we can muster."

"Even if it means putting a good kid like Uu'k's life in danger by spying on insane priests?"

"Yes, even if it means that."

"Ja'a, your methods are unusual—even for me. I do commend the commitment. If you say that Uu'k fully comprehends the likelihood of a violent and grizzly death, I believe you. You haven't lied to me yet. But, wow, what a day job for that little runt."

"Duke, don't take my word for it. Talk to her. Or talk to Ishiro—I'm sure he knows her story by now. It's been two days and I haven't seen her stop talking to him."

"And we know Ishiro's not hogging the conversation."

"True."

"I guess, at the end of the day, looking at it from a practical and functional standpoint—no one would suspect her of being anything more than a kid. Fooled me, that's for sure."

"She was the one that alerted us about you."

"That weasel! She led us into the cage—and freed us. Door-to-door service, I guess."

"We heard about an off-worlder—it had been some time since the last one."

"Vangu."

"Yes, Vangu. And we know how that turned out. We'd heard whispers from our network of sympathizers that a large metal vessel had crashed somewhere near Dre'en. Naturally, we assumed that Orbius had found a way to bring more evildoers from his home world to help him control the rebellion."

"Naturally. Lots of evildoers on Earth."

"We sent out a message to our local spies in and around Dre'en—but no one could get close. I knew Uu'k and her location at the Altar House. I guessed that if Vernglet Wip came out to meet you, he would probably get you to his compound as quickly as possible. I relayed the message through our runner network from where I was stationed south of the city and, luckily, it made it to Uu'k uninterrupted."

"I only saw her for a second—her information couldn't have been that in-depth."

"She has a knack for hearing things that shouldn't be heard. In fact, she let us know that the priests were planning to trick you and abduct your weapons."

"How did the priests recognize my guns? There's nothing on this rock remotely similar."

"Their communication network runs as fast as ours. Probably faster. The Northerners use winged flurn to carry messages over great distances."

"Orbius?"

"That was our thought. We can only assume that they used winged flurn to transport the message all the way to Sansagon—a method we ourselves are trying to master. If he was interested in these items, they must be important."

"And I bet that once we stepped off the *Deus*, accounts of our appearances made it all the way to Orbius and back before we made it to the gates of Dre'en. Vangu must've recognized the descriptions of the guns."

"That's our assumption as well."

"Sneaky troll."

"Uu'k gathered intelligence that day and uncovered a plan to steal what the priests called 'tools of monstrous calamity.' She quickly relayed the message down the network but, by the time it made it to me, you and Ishiro'shea were already heading southbound. A band of us, stationed near your crash site—"

"Landing site. I didn't crash the *Deus*. Duke LaGrange doesn't crash ships."

"—near your landing site, then, moved to the forest where we met you."

"Met? Not the word that I would've used."

"We scouted you and waited to assess the situation."

"We saw you moving about in the forest. Or rather, Ishiro saw you."

"Good eyes. Then before we were able to press on and introduce ourselves—and offer sanctuary, Vernglet and his troops moved in." She paused. "And then we saw them fall with a thunderous clap. Dead. Immediately, we knew what Orbius was referring to as 'tools of monstrous calamity.' Po'l wanted to charge—but I held us back since I didn't know if you would think that we were friend or foe."

"Smart move."

"When we collected ourselves enough to create a sensible plan, General Gar had appeared with his legion. The rest was a bit of luck."

"For who?"

"Both of us, really. When you and Ishiro'shea started to head toward the forest, our team quickly relocated our snare trap—and, once again by luck, you ran right into it. Lucky for us that we now have the services of someone who could provide a serious advantage over Orbius; lucky for you and Ishiro that you weren't hunted down and murdered by Gar's troops."

"This is assuming that we actually get back to the *Deus*, get rid of Orbius, and get off of this planet."

"I hope those aren't doubts, Duke LaGrange."

"Let's call them 'concerns' for now." Duke grinned and removed Betsy from his holster. He stroked the barrel and patted it gently. "Forget I said anything. I can win a war with this old girl."

"That's what we're banking on."

CHAPTER NINETEEN

IF A PERSON HAS A SWORD, DON'T
CALL HIM STUPID

"THIS SEEMS LIKE A GOOD place to set up camp," Ja'a said.

The land had hardly changed over the course of the day's march. As the evening approached, an unnerving calm continued to reign over the Neprian landscape. Aside from a gentle hill—the lone grassy mound alongside the level prairie path—it appeared no different than the previous dozens of miles.

"I agree," said Po'l. "Don't anticipate much danger lurking around these parts."

"No offense," Duke replied, "but the most dangerous part of this trip has been the stench coming from 'Mr. Sharpshooter' over there." He nodded in Po'l's general direction.

"What does that even mean?"

"Never mind. But seriously, can we give our friend Po'l a bath tonight? I think I saw a pond a few clicks back."

"Duke—"

"Fine. If you don't mind though, I think I'm going to camp up ahead at the edge of the hill. Your watchmen over there can take a turn being downwind from our fragrantly-challenged friend."

Duke walked up to Ma'n and Te'o, who were still propping up the banged-up Po'l.

"Guys, I feel for ya'—I really do. I've been in the drunk tank at Cyborg Joe's when the toilet broke—for two days—and it wasn't this bad."

"You're lucky that I'm not at my best right now, off-worlder," Po'l snapped back.

"What, so you can hurt yourself again? I don't even have to lift a finger with you, Po'l—you knock yourself out."

"Both of you, cool it." Ja'a interjected before Po'l dared a comeback. "Actually, here's an idea—it's about time to rotate positions. Fresh eyes up front and on the flanks; weary legs in the middle. We're probably halfway to the coast. Halfway to meeting with the leaders."

"And to figure out how Ishiro and I get the *Deus* back," added Duke.

"Of course." Ja'a walked a few paces away from the convoy. "Everyone! Let's call it a day and get some rest."

The entire group save the watchmen came to a stop.

"We're going to shuffle it around now before our final stretch," she shouted. "Everyone's doing great."

Ja'a motioned to Ma'n and Te'o, indicating Po'l. "Guys, can you help him down?"

"Bet you're pretty happy about that, huh?" Duke directed his snippy query at Ma'n and Te'o.

They did not respond.

"Enough, Duke."

"I'm fine, Te'o!" huffed Po'l as he pushed away his fellow rebel. "I don't need your help anymore."

"Don't be ridiculous. You need to rest up. We've got a long way to go before we get to Orbius. We need you—not a shell of you."

"Ja'a, I'm fine. I might be a bit slow when we start again —but I don't need anyone else holding me up. Ma'n, Te'o— thanks, but I can't ask you to do any more than you already have. I'll heal in due time, being carried or not."

"I don't know how I feel about this, Po'l."

"I'm fine."

"Okay, so you can hang in the middle tomorrow with Ishiro'shea. If you need assistance, I feel better having Ishiro'shea near you."

"I don't need anything from that masked goon who's too ignorant to even speak. He's like an untrained pet."

"Looks like you *do* need him, actually," Duke said.

"What?" Po'l responded.

"Turn around, genius."

Po'l about-faced and his nose nicked the edge of Ishiro's katana—drawn in utter silence and ready to decapitate the Neprian rebel.

"You can't hear on account of having taken a sonic boom from Betsy right in the kisser, you can't walk, you definitely can't defend yourself—I think you *need* all the help you can get," Duke said. "Starting with the fact that you *need* Ishiro to *not* cut your head off."

"Lower your sword," Po'l commanded.

Ishiro'shea did not budge.

"He doesn't like you," Duke sneered.

"Lower your sword."

"Po'l, not sure if you're hazy or what—but we aren't exactly your prisoners anymore. No rinky-dink cage separating us from you. You need to apologize."

"That's not going to happen, off-worlder."

"So proud. But so dumb."

"He's sorry," chimed Ja'a, but Ishiro'shea remained steady.

"Not good enough, I'm afraid. When you insult an

Irish-Japanese ninja of the cachet and standing of Ishiro'shea—he was Salutatorian, you know—you can't expect him just to lower his blade because some pretty girl asks him to. Po'l's slanderous jab insulted Ishiro's honor—he's sliced folks in twenty neatly cut ribbons for far less than what your colleague did."

Po'l and Ishiro continued to lock eyes. Pol's brash self-assurance slowly became something resembling panic—or at the least, anxiety. *He knows Ishiro means business.*

"Fine, I'm sorry."

"You're sorry—about what?"

"I'm sorry that I called you ignorant."

"Because you know—what?"

"I know—I know." Po'l searched for the words.

"C'mon, Po'l. You can do it, buddy."

"I know that you are actually quite intelligent."

"Not bad," commended Duke. "So, Ishiro—is it enough? Or should we make him grovel a bit more?"

"Duke, please," Ja'a begged. "Enough. Stop this. You made your point."

The ninja lowered his katana. Ishiro and Duke exchanged glances and then cackles.

"Not funny at all," Ja'a steamed.

"Sorry. 'Mr. Sharpshooter' needed to be taught a valuable lesson."

"And what's that?" Po'l inquired with a tone of annoyance.

"If a person has a sword, don't call him stupid."

The bruises on Po'l's face turned from dark violet to a shining red, signaling his embarrassment. *It's amazing that embarrassment looks the same on so many worlds and with so many species,* Duke pondered.

"Let's change positions before it gets too dark," Ja'a said. "Like I was saying before, Po'l, you stay in the middle until you get your strength—Ishiro'shea will move from the right flank and join you. Ma'n, you take the right flank—where Ishiro'shea was. Te'o, you grab the left flank, where I was. Duke, you can replace Ty'n and Bu'r and be our scout. They'll replace you in the rear."

"Aye, aye captain!" Duke quipped as he performed a half-hearted salute.

"Let's hope they do a better job than you."

"Hey now, you enjoyed my company. Admit it."

"What about me?" squeaked Uu'k.

"Uu'k, you stay by Ishiro'shea, please. In the center. With Po'l too."

"Not a problem, Ja'a. I like Ishiro. He's a good listener."

"Hey, what am I? Erontian Camelcat liver?" Duke whined.

"Duke, no offense, but you're more my 'small doses' friend."

Po'l erupted into laughter.

"Okay, I guess I can't argue with that," replied Duke.

The tension seemed to ease a bit.

"Ma'n, Te'o," Ja'a continued, "take your bows and be on alert. I want you to extend our flank a bit. I know it's been smooth sailing thus far but I want to make sure nothing slows us down before the coast."

"Yes. We'll camp out in our new positions tonight."

"Told you that they wanted away from Po'l and his cloud o' funk."

Ignoring Duke, Ja'a shouted, "Bu'r! Ty'n!" She turned. "That's odd, I only see Ty'n. Duke, I might need you to go up ahead and relay the message to them that we're going to rotate."

"Aye, aye captain... again."

Ishiro'shea slapped Duke on the back. *Fine, I'll stop.*

The skinnier of the two watchmen on scout duty came

sprinting back. "Ja'a! I came running as soon as I heard your voice."

"Where's Bu'r?"

"He's up ahead. We're close to his old village; he wanted to see if it was still standing."

"He doesn't know if it was taken over by Orbius?"

"No, he left to join up before they made it out this way. It could've avoided their control—it's a good ways away from any other village."

"It *would* be a nice place to rest—a true rest," Ja'a said, thinking aloud.

"And real food!" shouted Ma'n.

"Yes, that would be quite nice."

"Maybe some ploob kalarti," Duke said hopefully.

"He should be back anytime," Ty'n continued. "He said he was only going to check out a few miles ahead. Then again, that was a good while ago. Regardless, once he sees that I'm not at the post, he'll come back here."

"So not every village is under Orbius' control?" asked the bounty hunter.

"We don't know, Duke. There could be some that survived but they would likely be quite remote. We've been trying to find holdouts to help our recruiting efforts and strengthen our numbers. We just don't have the manpower and resources to engage in battles for every town to land a few able-bodied soldiers."

"But if one was entirely free of Orbius, you'd get supporters without any bloodshed."

"Exactly."

A few moments passed.

"There's Bu'r!" exclaimed Ty'n, pointing beyond the grassy hill.

"He looks excited," Uu'k noticed.

"Or scared," commented Duke.

Bu'r was muscular and broad shouldered—bigger than Po'l but not as athletic in appearance. He was barrel-chested but his bulbous stomach extended beyond his belt. He was the only rebel that Duke had seen that did not sport any hair atop his head—it was completely shaven. He did make up for this lack, though: he sported a well-trimmed beard that extended from each ear to just before his chin. His chin was bare save for a thin patch of hair that extended from the direct center of his bottom lip to the midway point of his throat. *Maybe it's a regional look.*

"He can run for a big boy, huh?"

The hearty-statured rebel decelerated as he approached. "I saw it!" he huffed, out of breath.

"Your village?"

"Yes, Ja'a. Only a few miles away. I know we can help them."

"So, they've been controlled?" asked Ty'n.

"The village was dead but I saw movement around the entrance to the mines. They have to be digging for Orbius' precious mustangsen."

"Mustangsen?"

"The decorative stones that Orbius hoards at his palace in the north. He has our entire village performing these vanity tasks to prove how powerful he is—it's how he controls us."

"Bu'r, I'm sorry. We need to get to the coast. The village is a detour we can't afford right now."

"Ja'a—"

"I'm sorry, as much as I want to help your village—it could derail us from freeing our entire race."

"I'm sorry, Ja'a, but I must go. I simply have to."

"Bu'r, you can't defeat an entire group of village guards by yourself—none of us can."

"Duke and Ishiro can!" exclaimed Uu'k.

"That's right, kid," Bu'r concurred, "the off-worlders can save my village."

"You know, Ja'a," Po'l added, "we could use some fresh soldiers helping our cause. As much as I hate to admit it, the off-worlders do give us the ability to strike quickly and effectively."

"Hold on. Saving villages wasn't in the deal. I was going to go to your secret hideout, talk to your old timers, agree on a plan to get back my ship, and if I save your entire race as part of that plan—so be it. There was nothing on there about freeing villages."

"He's right," Ja'a stated. "We cannot expect Ishiro and Duke to help us."

"Borrowing a phrase from an old robot friend of mine, 'damn skippy.'"

"And I don't think that it's wise. It's too risky and takes us off course. In good conscience, I just can't agree to this. I'm sorry, Bu'r."

"Ja'a, there are people that are being tortured and forced to mine for wall art as their lives slowly slip away."

"Bu'r, I get that. More than anyone, I get that. The horrors that Orbius has enacted on my family would rival anyone's—but, bigger picture, we have to go at Orbius, not his lackeys that oversee rural villages on his behalf."

"It's quite an intelligent move on Orbius' part," Duke interposed.

"Excuse me?" Bu'r grunted.

"What better way to keep the focus off of him by enticing freedom fighters to charge after each and every enslaved village; he's manipulating you emotionally. It's a trap. Even if you succeed and free the villagers—it'd be a Pyrrhic victory at best. He doesn't mind losing meaningless battles because it will help him win the war."

"But what about the recruits? We could triple our numbers."

"Possibly. But my guess is that those that are devoted enough to fight for the greater cause have already joined. Orbius' gamble is a smart one."

"Shut up already, off-worlder. I'm with Bu'r. I will help you save your village," said Po'l.

"Thank you, Po'l. You are a true Neprian patriot."

"Me too!" Ty'n joined in.

"Us, as well," shouted Ma'n and Te'o.

"I'm sorry, Ja'a," started Po'l. "We respect your leadership but we aren't going to let Duke scare us away from helping our people. He just wants to get his ship back—and what he thinks of as an inconvenience, we think of as our duty to the cause."

"Is this really how you all feel?" asked Ja'a.

"Yes," the rebels concluded in unison.

"Ja'a, you're making a mistake," warned the Nova Texan.

"Maybe so, Duke. I'll admit, I don't agree with this plan—"

"Aren't you the commander? Command!"

"Duke, I don't lead that way. That might be the way of your people or others that you've encountered—but I accept the fact that I can be wrong or that I can change my mind. We all have a say and I can see the emotion and desire of my team. That trumps my opinion in this case."

"This is a mistake. Oh yeah, Ishiro and I are sitting this one out."

"Duke, your help would be greatly appreciated."

"Off-worlder, you're in this with us now—you might as well do your part and help us. It will only help you," said Po'l.

"And think of the recruits! We'll have dozens of my fellow villagers—and I know we have some fighters—that will accompany us on our final push to the coast. Maybe even join up on your quest to get your ship back from Orbius!"

"You're sure of that?"

"Yes, without a doubt."

"Sorry if I'm not quite so optimistic. But I guess it does beat hanging out here in what could possibly be the most boring place in the known universe."

Ja'a's eyes caught Duke's. She mouthed silently, "Thank you."

"I do want us to camp here tonight," she said to the team. "We can make our way to the village tomorrow and assess the situation. It can wait a night."

"Yes!" shouted the Neprians.

"Great. Tomorrow the life of Duke LaGrange could end on a world of no importance during a half-baked raid of a farming village controlled by anorexic killer clergy. How's that for an epitaph? Whatever. I'm heading up front to keep a look out tonight—I need to get away from you crazies just in case it's contagious."

"Wait up, Duke. I'll join you," Ja'a stated.

"Ja'a, you aren't going to stay back with Uu'k and I?" asked Po'l.

"You'll be fine. Ishiro'shea will guard you."

"I don't need guarding. It's just—"

Ja'a and Duke headed out toward the scout locations previously occupied by Ty'n and Bu'r.

CHAPTER TWENTY

A GOOD NIGHT'S SLEEP

THE FLAME OF JA'A'S TORCH hissed as she sat at the apex of the knoll. To her left, Duke sprawled out against the downward slope with his arms behind his head.

"Do you really think I should've pushed back harder on the team?"

"Honest answer?"

"Yes."

"Then, yes, I do. I'm a big proponent of leaders leading —and not this democratic, 'it makes us feel good inside' hogwash. If you really feel we should press on to the coast, we should."

"They'll go on to the village whether we're with them or not."

"Let them go."

"I can't, Duke. They're my people. Each one has a role to play and can help us take down Orbius."

"Not if we all end up dead and buried in the mines."

"True—"

Duke interrupted. "Are you scared of 'em?"

"Scared? No. Not at all."

"Are you sure? Po'l seems to carry some weight in your decisions."

"Po'l and I have known each other for a long time."

"He likes you."

"I hope so, we've been friends since childhood."

"No, Ja'a. He *likes you* likes you."

"I don't understand."

"He *likes you* likes you means that he is interested in some amorous recreation. Some physical repartee. Some carnal deviance. Some—"

"I get it. I don't agree—but I get it. We've known each other for so long; he's a brother to me. I just don't see him in that way."

"You probably should tell him, then. Because he sees *you* in that way."

"I think you're mistaken, Duke. Our customs and interactions could be something new to you."

"I doubt that," Duke chuckled. "If there's one thing that I know and have a keen intuition for—regardless of the planet or species—it's lustful intent. Okay, also tracking down fugitives and all-around bad dudes. And I'm pretty handy knocking down any sort of booze. But, lustful intent —I can spot it a mile away."

"That's an interesting skill."

"It's an extremely rewarding skill in many cases."

"Not something that I care to hear about."

"It's got me out of some tight pickles." Duke tried to not make the obvious joke.

"So, you're quite the seduction specialist, huh?"

"I don't like to brag but I've been known to woo a pretty lady or two. Or three. This one time, in the Oscavian Caves —I lost count at seventeen."

"Just because you've had some luck on that front doesn't mean that you have any idea what Po'l's thinking."

"You've had to have noticed, right? He was about to piss his pants after you told him that you were joining me up at the lookout position."

"No, he wasn't."

"Yes, he was. Most definitely. And when we were leaving the cave, he couldn't take his eyes off of you. I don't blame him, after all."

"Duke," she said shaking her head.

"Seriously, he digs you. The question is—do you dig him?"

"No, absolutely not."

"Why? He's a strapping young buck. He's a bit of a meathead, but he'd help you breed out some little rebels to fight orbs, emaciated clergy, and crap."

"Maybe so, but my love and devotion lies elsewhere."

"And who's the lucky guy?" Duke's voice inflected upward.

"My cause. Destroying Orbius and saving my planet."

"Oh," the bounty hunter responded in a dejected tone. "Well, I guess that's good. Won't get you hot and sweaty and satisfy those pesky carnal needs—but I guess it's a good thing to 'love.'"

"It does the trick."

"You know, this entire you-and-Po'l dynamic also explains why he doesn't like *me*."

"How do you mean?"

"You might not understand since you aren't a guy."

"Try me, Duke," said Ja'a, rolling her eyes.

"He's there playing his game to win you over, right? He might be playing a long game or he might just be a natural meanderer. Doesn't matter. Regardless, out of nowhere, in comes this good-lookin', ruggedly handsome galactic man of mystery."

"Who's that? I must've missed him."

The bounty hunter ignored the playful jab. "It's obvious, if you think about it."

"Oh, it is?"

"Yes, Po'l feels challenged by me—as it relates to winning you over. He's scared that your heart will not be able to withstand someone as 'interesting' as me."

Ja'a remained stone-faced. *She's not buying this?*

"I think you might be stretching to reach that conclusion."

"Is that so?"

"Po'l really thinks—or thought—that you were part of Orbius' plan. I really don't think it's anything more than that."

"See, I knew you wouldn't fully grasp this idea. You've got to be a dude."

"Actually, he thinks you are an egotistical, reckless, self-absorbed bastard," Ja'a started, "that—in his opinion—still could be a mindless pawn in a twisted game of power and death initiated by the most heinous murderer that has ever graced our entire planet. How's that for grasping?"

"Ouch, sister. I guess we'll agree to disagree."

"So, is there a Mrs. Duke LaGrange?"

Thank goodness, she changed the subject, Duke thought to himself. *Though it doesn't sound like a real winner either.*

"No. Not really a 'settle down' sort of guy."

"Doesn't that get old?"

"Not if you don't let it. Always keep it moving."

After a brief pause, Ja'a stabbed the bottom of the torch into the soft earth and slid down to relax in the same manner as Duke.

"What about Ishiro'shea?"

"What about Ishiro? I mean, he's my best friend, but he's not my bag if you know what I mean."

"No, not that—what about Ishiro'shea, as in, what's his story? Why doesn't he talk?"

Changing the subject again. Thank you.

"Ishiro and I have been doing our thing for quite some time. He was Salutatorian, you know."

"I'm not sure I know what that means."

"It means that he's a damn good partner. And has the paperwork to prove it."

"That's good. How did you meet?"

"On Earth, actually. A city called New Tokyo in an area referred to as Ireland."

"Was it like Dre'en?"

"Way worse. Way bigger but mostly way worse. It was the center of the largest and most intense turf war in a hundred cycles."

"Why were you both there? It's not your planet, right?"

"See, Ishiro is half-Japanese and half-Irish—meaning his family was divided along the battle lines. His mother was Japanese royalty—or rather a descendent of the most famed samurai warrior in history. So, the one side wanted her as a rallying symbol of the conflict. And Ish's dad was an Irish spiritual leader in New Tokyo—and a famed military strategist. So, it was obvious why they wanted him."

"How did they choose a side?"

"They didn't. They hated war. So, they made it very clear that they were going to remain neutral. Which, as you can probably guess, pissed *everyone* off. Being neutral on Earth is another way to say that you have no friends."

"What did they do?"

"How I understand it is that a young Ish was dropped off at the edge of the city and picked up by a family friend that enrolled him in the local school—the College of Cohorts, Consorts, Co-Conspirators, and Other Assorted Sidekick Types. That's all I know."

"And the not talking bit?"

"He swore a vow of silence upon his graduation; it will be his burden until he finds his parents. They went missing in the conflict—some believe they died, some think they fled and are living it up on an island paradise on some uncharted world."

"I can't imagine."

"In fact, I think it's what bonded us together."

"Are your parents missing as well?"

"Not missing so much. More like dead."

"I'm sorry, I didn't—"

"No need to be sorry. I never knew them. I was orphaned. Dropped off on the doorstep of a brothel and raised by a rogue outlaw and his favorite lady of the evening."

Ja'a appeared visibly flustered.

"At least, she was the madam."

Once again, Ja'a struggled to respond. After a while she managed, "That had to make for an interesting upbringing?"

"I learned a lot. But after Mistress Trixie died, my father—if you want to call him that—left."

"I'm sorry."

"And I think that our unique parental situations made Ishiro and I the perfect team. Every corner that we turn in every new city on every new planet that we visit—there's a bit of us that's hoping that we run into our parents or, in my case, the man that raised me. We both know the odds of that happening but it's still with us. What would we even say, anyways? Especially Ishiro—I mean, does he even remember how to talk? But we get each other. Same wavelength, you know."

"I hope you find the man that raised you. And I hope that Ishiro'shea finds his parents."

"Enough of that. Let's talk about something more upbeat."

"You never did tell me how you met on Earth," reminded Ja'a.

"That's for another day."

"Then what should we talk about?"

"How about how we're going to kill these slave drivers and save an innocent village."

"Right. We need to come up with some sort of plan if we're going to do this successfully."

"Kinda hard without seeing the lay of the land, having an estimate on 'bad guy' count, or really knowing *anything*."

"True. We can survey the village tomorrow from a safe distance, then figure out our strategy. Bu'r should be able to help us. I guess for tonight we can focus on making sure no one finds us out here relaxing and resting up."

"Hey, I'm a mighty fine lookout. Even when it's pitch black and we only have that wimpy torch." The bounty hunter rustled around in a small compartment affixed to his belt. "Oh yeah, I've got these."

He handed Ja'a his travel-size night vision goggles. "Check 'em out! They help you see at night."

The Neprian examined them and placed them over her eyes. *That was natural.*

"These look like our bifocal telescopic sight enhancers— but ours don't work in the dark. These are fascinating. I mean, I'm sure they would be fascinating if there was anything to see."

"True, not the best subject to view, but we can take turns as lookout—just in case we see an oncoming group of nocturnal marauders."

Ja'a reclined onto the yielding grass of the hill with the binoculars still pressed to her eyes.

"I've got another question for you, Ja'a."

"What's that?"

"How close has this rebellion come to overthrowing Orbius? Have there been any wins or progress? Or are we shooting in the dark?"

Ja'a hesitated and sighed. "Do you remember that I spoke of a leader called He'j?"

"Yes, with Jilarian Togg."

"Great memory."

"Thanks. I try."

"He'j was very much the face of our rebellion, as you know. You could say that he was like Ishiro'shea's mother and father—the symbol of our cause and the one leading. He was very close to destroying Orbius."

"How close?"

"He told us that he had a theory about the Orb—but it was just that, a theory. He couldn't bring himself to have troops go into battle over his hunch so he and a select group of soldiers traveled to Orbius' palace in a stealth manner."

"What was his theory?"

"That's just it, he didn't tell a soul. Not even his companions on the mission."

"Why? Seems like an odd thing to do."

"He said that if he was right or wrong, he couldn't tell anyone. If he was right and failed to kill Orbius, the simple fact that Orbius would know that we are aware of his great weakness would bring greater harm to Neprius."

"Interesting."

"We learned not too long ago that He'j's mission had failed. Orbius killed He'j. Word spread fast. He wanted all of us to know that he'd *personally* ended our great leader's life."

"To weaken the resolve of the cause."

"Yes. He's good at that."

The night continued to curtail visibility but Duke

noticed, in the faint glow of the flame, a narrow rivulet of tears on Ja'a's cheek.

The rebel leader's eyes caught his stare. "I'm sorry. It's just that—He'j was my father."

Duke attempted to digest this news. "Why didn't you tell me that before?"

"It shouldn't matter—it doesn't matter. My devotion to the cause is independent of my relationship to my father. Whether he was a significant leader or an enslaved peasant, I would still be where I am now—fighting Orbius with every ounce of energy in my bones."

"I don't doubt that, Ja'a. Not at all."

"Thank you, Duke. That means a lot."

Ja'a rolled onto her side, facing Duke. Her face was illuminated by the torch flame; highlighting her striking features against a backdrop of celestial darkness like a spotlight focused on a single actor standing before a murky theater curtain.

"Good night, my friend."

Duke didn't like the term 'friend.' But he also didn't feel right about what he typically would have done in a moment such as this. Restraint was never his forte when it came to lying next to vulnerable females—but he found a way to dig deep and not act like a total asshole.

He took the binoculars from Ja'a and started the first shift of lookout duty.

The morning light eased its way under Duke's eyelids, ending his peaceful slumber. Along with the light, the dawn brought intermittent clouds of fog that hovered over the expanse of fields. It was slightly cooler than the previous mornings. Duke always enjoyed a breeze, having grown up in the living furnace that was Nova Texas.

The bounty hunter stretched his arms and embraced the day—and the inevitability of having to deal with a village under siege; another roadblock between him and the *Deus*. However, his pessimistic outlook was quickly diverted to one of a more pleasurable connotation.

"Good morning."

Ja'a had been on the last shift of lookout duty. She was already packed and ready to return to the rest of the group. Her long pearwood hair was pulled back neatly and arranged in the style that Duke was accustomed to seeing during their trek. The cosmetic stylings that adorned her face had already been reapplied, albeit with a slightly ashier palette, though they showcased her steely eyes no less than before.

"Good morning to you," Ja'a said softly as she knelt down, adjusting elements on her bow and examining the remaining arrows. "Ready to go save a village?"

CHAPTER TWENTY-ONE

UNIVERSE'S BEST RULER

"**Y**OU DON'T THINK I'M EVIL, do you?"

The servant immediately halted his feathering of a trophy proclaiming that the owner was the "Universe's Best Ruler" and stared back at the questioner.

"Of course I'm not evil," Orbius said to himself before the servant could respond.

The Neprian priest exhaled and continued to clean the ruler's assorted awards that accumulated on his shelf.

"I just don't get why these rebels keep trying to resist. Do you?"

The servant froze again. His trembling was more noticeable: he knocked over a framed photo of two orcas trapping a poor sea lion on a floating shard of ice with the caption, "Teamwork."

"Of course you don't. You get it. You see it. You know that I'm the only one that can harness the power of the Orb and prevent it from corrupting the entire planet. Right?"

The priest simply nodded and bowed slightly.

Orbius stood up and walked towards an enormous window that looked out over the whole of Sansagon. The priests—*his* priests—were running drills and distributing weapons. Preparations for battle were underway. Orbius smiled.

He raised his hand and stretched his fingers skyward; his bulky rings scratched one another. Whoosh. An electric purple filled the area and the Orb skimmed across the room at eye level and came to rest in Orbius' palm. He examined it. His gaze lingered.

"What do you think?"

The priest cleared his throat. He looked around the room as if to make sure that the Orbmaster was actually addressing him.

"Yes, *you*. What do *you* think?"

"Almighty Orbius, my lord, what do I think about what?"

"About the current events on our happy little world. Your pesky cousins to the south not seeing the error of their ways and realizing that I'm their savior too. And now rumblings about some flying monsters coming out of the west."

"I do not understand their actions."

"I know, right? Ridiculous."

"Yes, my lord, ridiculous."

"And another thing—"

Orbius' thought was interrupted by the sound of two more servants entering his chamber, pushing a wheeled tray containing plates and glassware.

"Excellent! There better be some greattu under that lid."

The priests stopped and looked at each other. They performed a complete turn and shuffled back through the door. A shrill "We need greattu—fast" was audible from the hallway.

"I love greattu. Maybe the best thing about this planet. What was I saying before?"

"I believe you were questioning the actions of those opposing you."

"And not just me, my good friend. They are opposing *you*. And your families. And—if you think about it—the entire planet of Neprius." Orbius paused. "They are waging a war against the long-term health and safety of the planet."

"That is very true, my lord."

"You could say that on top of everything, we are eco-warriors."

"You could say that," stammered the servant.

"I know. And I am *going* to say it. Oh, and you missed a spot over there."

The priest doubled down on his dusting.

"But why don't they see it? You see it. Your race sees it. I mean, outside of that Togg character. Why is it so difficult?"

"I think—never mind."

"No, go on—*please* go on." Orbius' demeanor turned to grim concentration.

"From what I hear—you know, the word from around town, if you will—"

"Yes?" Orbius asked impatiently.

"The rebels think that you are the evil that the planet should fear. They think that you are trying to make them slaves."

Orbius' eyes widened and his pupils dilated. He gripped the Orb even tighter and its glow pulsed with the increased tension. The veins in his necked stiffened. The servant cowered.

"Which is, of course, crazy. And why they must be punished," babbled the servant. "Who could honestly think that? Especially after you saved us once from the droughts with your advanced knowledge of harvests."

Orbius relaxed. "That's right. They are crazy. What if I relinquished the Orb and someone who couldn't control it ended up with it? What then?"

"Disaster," responded the servant hesitantly.

"Disaster, indeed. You could end up like Earth. Wars, feuds, conflict. Every good thing that we created or discovered was overshadowed by greed, corruption, and baseless violence. If it wasn't a gang war driven by races with different values about who knows what, it was two governments fighting over a few extra bits of currency or a few scraps of insignificant land. Did I ever tell you that my lab was fire-bombed by a group of people that felt I was violating the right of plants by testing chemicals on them? Tests that potentially might end hunger throughout our entire planet?"

"No, my lord."

"And then I was stoned by another group of wackos as I was fleeing the burning building. They felt I was infringing on God's will by trying to eradicate hunger."

"I'm sorry, oh great Orbius."

"If that wasn't bad enough, I also avoided a corporate assassination because I switched the brand of chemical compounds that I was using, costing some high-level executive a big payday after he promised his mistress a new beach house."

"Truly a planet with many issues."

"There wasn't a singular power to unite the planet. There wasn't a singular point of reason that could govern everyone correctly. Hell, that's the problem with the whole of the universe, if you ask me. I won't let *that* happen to Neprius. The Orb called me to save this planet—save you and your people—and I will stop at nothing to make sure that I do. If I had the Orb on Earth, I could save that planet too."

"They would all be very grateful, I'm sure."

"You better believe it. I will get enough power in due time—and then I *will* save Earth in the same way that I'm saving Neprius. And then on to another poor planet. And on and on."

"A glorious plan, my excellency."

"It is, isn't it?"

Another knock at the door.

"Yes, it's open. Come in."

"Almighty Orbius. Orbmaster. Savior. The one true—"

"I get it, I get it. What do you want?"

"Vernglet Wip of Dre'en is here to see you."

"Send him in."

"Yes, my lord."

"Oh, and will you check on my greattu?"

CHAPTER TWENTY-TWO

WELCOME TO SHUD'NUT

DESPITE THE PIVOT SOUTHWARD TOWARDS the village, the scenery remained consistent. For the short excursion, Duke, Ishiro'shea, and the Neprians traveled together—foregoing their previous positions and adopting a 'safety in numbers' approach. Duke figured that if the climate of the mission changed to one of an unfriendly ilk, Ja'a probably didn't want the look-outs to be on an island without immediate backup. *Sensible,* thought Duke.

"We're close. Can you see the smoke?" asked the barrel-chested Neprian, Bu'r.

"The mines?"

"Yes. See that patch of trees just north of town over there? It'll provide us with some cover as we map out an attack plan."

"Slow down, Bu'r. I don't like the aggressive under-tones," snapped Ja'a. "Our goal is to free this village of Northern guards and recruit. We will focus on efficiency and safety—you can't do that with vengeance driving your actions."

Bu'r looked dejected.

"I understand. Freeing my village is enough reward."

"I would hope so."

"Hey Bu'r, what do ya' call this home of yours?"

"Shud'nut."

"Shud'nut' we be focusing on getting my ship back?" Duke deadpanned.

The rebels all glanced at the bounty hunter—obviously, not in the mood for a morning jest. Duke had had a feeling that his quip wouldn't land but the rebels' scowls displayed more anger than he had imagined. Even Uu'k seemed disappointed. *Even Ishiro!?!*

"Sorry, that was in poor taste," the bounty hunter acknowledged.

"And it wasn't funny," added Uu'k.

"Not surprising coming from you, off-worlder," snapped Po'l with a nasty bite.

"It's too early to fight you on this one, Po'l."

"Why are you in such an agreeable mood?"

Duke didn't respond to Po'l's query. However, Ishiro'shea snuck up and slapped Duke in the small of the back.

"What?"

Ishiro'shea's eyes asked a tricky question: *Did you do what I think you did?*

Duke motioned back something resembling a *No, nothing happened* gesture. Ishiro'shea seemed to understand.

"You alive, Duke?" Po'l interrupted. "Are you just going to ignore me?"

"It's a great day to be alive. And with you lot. We're about to save a village—hard to beat that! Right?"

"Right. Okay," said Po'l in a confused tone.

"How about over there?" interjected Ma'n. He pointed towards an open patch of soil blocked from the view of the town by some midsized trees. "This looks like the only cover before we're in plain sight."

"Aren't we a bit worried that—since this *is* the only cover—that the Neprian guards are probably watching it like a hawk?" asked the bounty hunter.

"I think you give them too much credit," said Po'l.

"I don't know. They did manage to take over your whole planet. How's your face feeling, by the way?"

"Yeah, I'd like to see how long you would last against the Orb."

"I've handled a lot worse than a rock filled with magic and mumbo jumbo."

"Calm down. Both of you," Ja'a said soothingly. "We're on the same team."

"Are we?" Are you sure, Ja'a?" asked Po'l.

"You know that we are. Our motivations might differ from Duke's—but our goal is the same. We need you both to defeat Orbius."

Ishiro'shea hopped down into a crouch and slid in front of everyone—he pointed toward the outside wall of Shud'nut.

"Down," Duke shouted at the group. "I see them too, Ishiro. Only three. No wait, four."

The ninja confirmed the latter count and stared back at Duke inquisitively.

"Yep, I agree."

"You agree with what?" asked Po'l in a slightly annoyed tone.

"I agree with Ishiro. He's not a 'what'; haven't you learned your lesson about insulting my friend?"

"Duke," Ja'a interjected, "what does Ishiro'shea have in mind? Do you have a plan?"

"Sort of."

"Sort of?"

"Yeah, sort of. We see four guards—and we're going to dispose of them."

"Yes, but how? What's the plan?" pleaded Ja'a.

"That *is* the plan."

"Ja'a, I told you these two weren't going to help. I have an idea."

"Okay, Po'l," said Ja'a. "Gather round, everyone. What are you thinking?"

"First, if we can distract the guards long enough for Ty'n and Bu'r to flank them—that will set us up for minimal casualties. Ma'n and Te'o can provide—" Po'l stopped mid-thought. "Where are y'all going?"

Duke and Ishiro'shea were already out from their camouflaged hiding spot and in the open field that led right to the perimeter walls of Shud'nut. In a few hundred yards, they would be easily spotted by the guards.

"You know, Ishiro. What if there are more *inside* the walls?"

The ninja hesitated momentarily—then continued toward the village.

"Yeah, best not think about it, right? We got this. Yeah, most likely, we got this."

Duke drew his laser revolver. Ishiro'shea unsheathed his katana.

"So, you think they'll just let us in?"

Ishiro did not blink.

"Probably not."

They continued their brisk saunter towards Shud'nut.

"Duke! What are you doing? You're going to get killed!"

The two men ignored the shouts from behind them; Duke wanted to reply with a snarky comment about Po'l being happy about that potential outcome but he decided against it. *Best be remembered as a brave, albeit stupid, hero than a smart-ass if this thing goes sideways.*

"Well, they seemed concerned for us but they don't seem to want to join us, huh? Better this way. They would just get in the way."

The bounty hunters were within an arrow's shot from the wall when they were finally noticed by one of the Neprian priests.

"Halt, strangers. Who are you?"

"We're here to clean your jacuzzi," Duke fired back.

"I'm not certain I understand your request," shouted the confused Neprian.

"Ja-cuz-zi," Duke yelled back, enunciating each syllable.

"Hey, have you ever heard of a jack-yoozi?" the priest screamed back to his colleague.

"A what?" the other one began, a jo-kawzi? What's that? Hey, is this some kinda Southern trick? Who are those guys?"

"We aren't Southern Neprian trash, if that's what you're asking each other," Duke called up. He imagined how offended Po'l would be at that comment. He smiled.

"You don't look like a piece of Southern Neprian trash, that's true."

"Why thank you, kind sir."

The priest was still confused. He motioned for his fellow priest to come over and discuss their predicament in more detail. They deliberated, out of Duke's earshot, for a few minutes.

"What are y'all talking about up there?" asked Duke. "That jacuzzi won't clean itself."

"I'm sorry, I'm not certain what you mean by jow-cooli, stranger," shouted back the priest.

"Let us in and I'll show you."

"I think not," returned the second priest.

"But Orbius sent us."

The priests paused.

"You know—Orbius. Orby. The head honcho. Boss man. The Dude of Dudes."

"We know who Orbius is. We need to discuss further."

A third priest joined the brainstorming session.

"Hey there, friend," Duke shouted to the newcomer. He didn't receive a response. "Also, not only did Orbius send us to clean your hot tub but he also told us a super important, highly confidential secret that we must relay to you. It's about the defense of this village. We've received updates from General Gar about the positions of the Southern rebels."

All three priests looked even more confused.

"We will need to consult with one more of our colleagues. He is a direct report to the General."

"Great! Why don't you invite all of the guards in the city? You can all weigh in on how you want your pool cleaned—and on how to handle this top secret intel."

"Strangers, we still don't understand this term, 'jaw-kwayze,' and our colleague is the last of us guards here in this rotting cesspool of a village."

"We could ask Gander Vorv. He's on mine duty."

"Oh yeah, Gander is pretty well-versed in protocol," the other agreed.

Duke and Ishiro'shea exchanged glances and smiled.

The fourth priest was slightly larger than the other three and appeared agitated by this impromptu debate.

"What do you want? What's worth waking me up for? It's bad enough they moved me to this dirty outpost babysitting slaves and away from killing Neprian rebels."

"Sir, we wanted your opinion on a situation."

"What situation?"

"Do you know what a 'ja-zuki' is?"

"What? No. Is this some game that you lot made up? I'm not interested."

"I said that you wouldn't know," said the first priest.

"Maybe I do? Say it again."

"Jow-cootie."

"Use it in a sentence."

"I don't know how."

The fourth priest grew even more annoyed.

"It's just these strangers down there said Orbius sent them to clean ours," the first priest said, and pointed to Ishiro'shea and Duke.

"Hi." Duke smirked and gave a sly wink.

"You morons," exclaimed the bulky priest. "These are the off-worlders that I mentioned."

"Oh."

Four pulses beamed in rapid succession. All four Neprian priests collapsed. Dead.

"Well, they made it easy for us, huh? It was nice of them to let us know that there weren't any more inside—and then huddle up all nice and close."

Duke placed the revolver back in his holster and took out Betsy.

"And now about this door."

He aimed at the wooden door that stood between them and the innards of the city of Shud'nut.

"I hope no one is standing behind it."

Betsy screamed and let off a thunderous emission. The door was obliterated instantaneously. It did not appear to have hurt anyone—in fact, Duke couldn't see a single villager through the gaping hole that now served as their entryway.

"Hey, hold there!"

Duke turned and faced the mines. A Neprian priest was running towards him. He had a whip and was flailing and popping it with ruthless animosity as he charged the bounty hunters.

"Ishiro, this is all you."

The ninja nimbly accelerated towards the oncoming priest with his katana drawn. *Poor Gander Vorv.*

The priest hurled the whip in the ninja's direction, but Ishiro'shea leapt into the air and avoided its impact. He landed soundlessly and, with a simple slash, struck down the slave master. It was quick, silent, and clean. It was ninja.

CHAPTER TWENTY-THREE

A SKILLED POLITICIAN

BETWEEN BETSY'S EXPLOSIVE GREETING AND the shattering of a giant wooden door, the villagers of Shud'nut started to appear, presumably in order to see what was going on. Many made their way out from the mines. Others scurried deep within in the village, emerging from dimly-lit storefronts and huts.

"What did you do, Duke?" Ja'a asked as she and the other rebels rushed up from behind.

"We freed the village. You're officially welcome." Duke removed his hat and bowed.

"We didn't say 'thank you,'" Po'l reminded him.

"Oh yeah. Well, you can say it now. No more priests. Everyone is free. And no one got hurt."

"Thank you!" shouted Bu'r. "Ja'a, this is great! Shud'nut is free!"

"Excellent, Bu'r. We need to direct the villagers to the town square and start inquiring about potential recruits."

"Of course," responded Bu'r. "Let's go—they're going to be so happy!"

Bu'r, Ty'n, Ma'n, and Te'o rushed off in four different directions to direct the villagers to the center of the town.

"So—" Duke began.

"Yes?" said Ja'a.

"Do I get a big thank you?"

"You were reckless. And dangerous."

"And successful."

"I suppose," Ja'a muttered as she walked towards a gathering of confused villagers.

"No appreciation from this lot, Ishiro. No appreciation whatsoever."

The two off-worlders migrated to what they thought was the town square, where the inhabitants of Shud'nut had begun to gather around a raised platform, presumably designed for such keynote addresses. Roughly three hundred Southern Neprians filled the clearing with little room to spare. They all appeared to be in a state of shock and bewilderment. Most took a keen interest in the two odd-looking guests that had disposed of five guards and a door without as much as breaking a sweat.

Ja'a ascended to the top of the platform; her feet stood eye level to an adult Neprian.

"Fellow Neprians," she began, "please be calm. I am Ja'a, daughter of He'j."

At this, the crowd immediately ceased all conversation. A hush fell over the audience.

"Thank you. People of Shud'nut, as you know we have been enslaved by an evil in the North—an evil known as Orbius. We continue to fight against him and his followers—and we will defeat him."

Duke was bracing himself for an uncontrollable roar of support, but the villagers said nothing. *Very odd.*

"Thanks to our new friends from a land far from

Neprius," Ja'a continued, "you are no longer condemned to this tyrannical slavery. People of Shud'nut—you are free!"

Nothing. *Very odd, indeed.*

"Who are these strangers?" shouted a villager. "Maybe they want to enslave us too." The other villagers seemed to agree with this notion.

"These strangers just saved you from your captors. Isn't that enough to make you trust them?"

"Yes, so they could enslave us for themselves!" erupted another villager.

"Friends! They have saved the lives of our company already on this journey—would they do that if they only wanted to enslave you? They are the allies that we so desperately need in the fight against Orbius!"

"What's in it for them?" shouted another townsman.

"Tough crowd, Ishiro," Duke said to Ishiro'shea as the rumbling sounds of dissent seemed to escalate amongst the villagers.

Ja'a attempted to salvage the discussion. "Our friends have a mutual benefit in the destruction of Orbius. It is their only way to get home. So, please, I'm asking you to join us in our fight. For our people!"

"Why? So we can die with you?"

"You will certainly die as slaves under Orbius. Be part of the solution and free our people!"

Many in the crowd erupted into laughter. Ja'a was visibly shaken by the response.

"*You* are going to defeat Orbius? You and these castaways—*and a kid?*" exclaimed an older male Neprian that stood directly under Ja'a. "You have a kid fighting with you, for the sake of Neprius! The only thing that you bring us is pain."

"Orbius is going to punish us for sure, now," another villager shouted. The crowd seemed to agree.

"Your father couldn't defeat Orbius," the older man continued, "so what makes you think his naive daughter can? This is hopeless. Your interference will cause us greater pain and suffering."

Bu'r climbed to the platform to accompany Ja'a.

"Everyone, I am a son of Shud'nut. Ja'a speaks the truth. We can defeat Orbius."

"A son of Shud'nut brings this calamity upon us. A sad day for us all," the old man said.

"What are we to do, Ye'f?" a villager asked the old man.

"We must ask for forgiveness from Orbius so that we can return to how life was before this intrusion."

"And live as slaves?"

"Better slaves with breath in our lungs than free and rotting in the ground," Ye'f replied.

Duke, still at the outskirts of the town square, found a stone wall and stood upon it. He was not as elevated as Ja'a and Bu'r, but he was high enough to be seen by the entire gathering. He grabbed his revolver and fired it in the air. Silence descended upon the group.

"Hi there. My name is Duke LaGrange. Trailblazer. Adventurer. Poet. A true man of the universe. And I'm here to free you. And I'm here to kill that nasty bastard, Orbius. Don't believe me? Watch this."

Duke rattled off another round of energy pulses that removed parts of the wall with ease.

"Y'all should be thanking Ja'a and her crew."

"Off-worlder, we don't need to hear from you. You helped bring this upon us. There is only one clear thing for us to do." Ye'f turned to face the crowd, as any skilled politician would, and proclaimed, "We must appease Orbius by capturing these rebels and turning them over to him. Maybe he will be lenient in his punishment and, eventually, let us get back to mining with only the lash of a whip to worry about."

There was a short pause. Then the village cheered in unison.

"No, please don't listen. We are giving you freedom," pleaded Bu'r from atop the pulpit. Ja'a looked as if she had been hit in the midsection with a blunt ax.

The crowd closed in on the platform. Duke aimed his revolver at the mass of villagers.

"No, Duke! Stop!" shouted Ja'a. "Don't kill them; they don't know any better. We can't turn on our own people!"

"It appears that it might be you or them."

"Please don't," Bu'r pleaded.

Ishiro'shea hopped up onto the stone wall next to Duke and tapped him on the shoulder. He pointed to the apex of the pole that supported the platform—which was much higher than the actual platform itself.

"Good plan, little buddy!"

"Ja'a! Get everyone on the platform and be ready to make a break for it!"

Duke wasn't sure if the Neprian rebels understood. He fired off a pulse from his revolver—and another.

"Stop!" screamed Ja'a involuntarily.

She looked around and saw not a dead villager, but the large vertical beam behind the platform beginning to shake and sway—and then fall directly into the mosh pit of angry villagers. The townsfolk scattered to avoid being mashed into Neprian goop. The seven rebels, now understanding Duke's intentions, sprang on top of the fallen pole and sprinted to the now-permanently-open doorway out from the town. Duke and Ishiro followed, with weapons drawn. As they cleared the threshold, Duke fired a few more rounds at the top of the entryway. Stone and wood fragments fell, making a temporary seal that kept the mob inside the walls.

"That was close," exclaimed Po'l, collapsing to the ground. It was obvious that he was far from one hundred percent.

"Listen," Duke said.

"I don't hear anything," replied Ty'n.

"That's the problem. Why aren't they following us? I mean, that debris blocking the door won't hold them too long—do they give up that easy?"

Ishiro'shea pushed aside Po'l and Ma'n and darted back toward the village. He disappeared within the dust cloud made by the impact of the door fragments on the soil.

"Ishiro? What are you doing?" Duke shouted.

"Duke. Oh no," Ja'a moaned.

They all looked at each other.

"Where's Uu'k?" Duke asked, without wanting to hear the answer. "Ishiro!"

Duke and Po'l rushed to follow Ishiro'shea.

"Stay back," Po'l demanded. Ja'a and the rebels didn't argue.

"Okay, you ready? This could get messy." Duke said to Po'l as they reached the pile of fallen stone and wood.

He noticed that Po'l had not recovered completely. "Need help?" Before Po'l could respond, Duke extended a hand. They locked hands and Duke helped the rebel warrior scale the mound.

As they both touched the ground on the inside of the wall, Ishiro'shea appeared with sword drawn and Uu'k on his shoulder.

"Is she okay?" asked Duke.

Ishiro'shea merely winked. With surprising ease, he glided over the rubble with Uu'k.

Po'l and Duke surveyed what was in front of them.

They looked at each other. Duke placed his hand on Po'l's shoulder.

"Best we keep this to ourselves."

"For once, I agree."

"Let's get out of here before they see us."

The two left the entrance to Shud'nut and joined their band—now complete again.

"What happened in there?" asked Bu'r.

"Uu'k is safe," Duke replied.

"Did he kill my people?" Bu'r asked in an agitated tone. "Did he?"

Duke was silent as he tried to think of the proper words.

"Uu'k is safe. That's all that matters. Ishiro'shea did what all of us would've done—and he did not go in with violence on his mind."

"But—" started Bu'r.

"That's enough, Bu'r. Let us move on," Po'l said, ending the conversation.

Duke nodded at Po'l. Po'l did not return a reply.

Ja'a approached both men. "Thank you both. And especially you, Ishiro."

Ishiro bowed.

Duke began, "Are you sure this cause of yours is worth it? We just had an entire village try to kill us because they would rather be slaves of Orbius than join your rebellion. That's typically not a good sign."

"I don't know what happened in there, Duke. Truly I don't."

"All you care about is getting your ship back anyways, LaGrange."

Ah, there's the Po'l that I know and love.

"Yes, I'm doing this to get my ship and get off this horrible rock—but are you certain that *you* are on the right side? They seemed pretty content working the mines for

Orbius. Maybe he's a steady employer? I'm just a little worried."

"I promise, Orbius is the tyrant that we claim him to be. I'm as shocked by the response of the Shud'nut villagers as you."

"My people. My neighbors. I don't know what happened." Bu'r sat looking into his open palms, his face wet. "I don't why they responded like that. We aren't a big village but we are a proud village." The broad-shouldered rebel paused. "We *were* a proud village. I'm sorry that I made you all risk everything for that."

He looked at Uu'k. Ishiro'shea was still holding her upright; her face was pale and her eyes frozen.

"Most of all to you, Uu'k. I'm sorry," Bu'r sobbed.

The child spy did not return as much as a blink.

"Maybe we can clear things up with our leaders once we get to the coast," offered Ja'a.

"I guess."

Duke was not as optimistic as Ja'a.

CHAPTER TWENTY-FOUR

UNCLE LO'N

"THIS IS IT?"

"This is where the senior leaders of the cause reside. Yes."

"It's kind of a—" Duke cleared his throat and continued, "—let's just say it leaves a bit to be desired."

"Judging by your tone, I'm assuming that's not a complimentary term," returned Ja'a.

"Doesn't seem like a place from which one would launch a planet-saving rebellion, if you ask me."

"I didn't," Ja'a replied. She picked up the pace and headed under a natural archway created by two trees—one cracked into a right angle, the other with a posture crippled by age.

The archway led to a clearing surrounded by a grove of tropical trees and brush. It was dense, but not like the forests south of Dre'en where Duke and Ishiro'shea had first met their Neprian allies. Grass was in sparse clumps on the light tan soil which merged into grainy sand extending beyond the outer rim of trees west of the compound. Duke couldn't see the ocean, but he could hear the waves just beyond their forest wall.

"Can you smell it?" Po'l asked boastfully.

"Is that a rhetorical question?" Duke smirked.

"That's the smell of our beloved aquatic goddess; she who has both nurtured us from the bounty of her watery bosom and has buried men in her darkest depths for them never to return," Po'l proclaimed triumphantly.

Duke and Ishiro'shea exchanged glances.

"He has a way with words," whispered the Nova Texan to his mute friend.

"This perfume means that we are home, we are with our true friends, and we are in her tender care," Po'l continued.

The other rebels stood around him, overcome with pride and admiration. All except Ja'a. Duke locked eyes with her and felt that he could read her mind—and it was telling him not to say what he was about to say.

"You know, Po'l," Duke began. Ishiro immediately covered Uu'k's ears. "Maybe it's different here on Neprius, but if a woman's parts smell like rotten fish and saltwater—maybe she needs to scrub her darkest depths a bit more."

For a split second, Duke was hopeful that Po'l wouldn't quite understand his meaning. He did.

"How dare you insult our land!"

"Technically, I insulted your water."

Po'l, still a bit worse for wear, charged at Duke. The bounty hunter assumed a martial stance—but Te'o and Ma'n caught the lunging Neprian.

"It was just a joke, Po'l. Lighten up," said Duke.

"A poor joke at that," Ja'a interjected as she turned and headed towards the largest of the buildings.

"Ja'a, wait. I didn't mean it like that. It was just a joke."

Duke took a step towards her but Ishiro extended his arm and halted his progress.

"Why's Ja'a so mad?" asked Uu'k.

"Your Uncle Duke said something really dumb," he said softly as he knelt down to her eye level.

"Figures," Uu'k retorted.

"Hey!"

"And you aren't my Uncle Duke."

Ishiro was clearly pleased by his small companion's attitude. However, she was soon interrupted by a very angry Po'l.

"LaGrange, I've had it. You may think this is a joke still and you can poke fun at me—I'm man enough to take it—but don't insult the very place that we are fighting and dying to preserve."

"Lighten up, Po'l. I get it."

"I don't think you do. But one day you will get it, oh, you will."

"Is that a threat?"

"Greetings! Welcome, great warriors!" boomed an abrupt interruption. "Old friends, little friends—hello there, Uu'k—and these new friends that Ja'a has delivered to us."

Seemingly out of nowhere, an elderly gentleman appeared before them, accompanied by Ja'a. He had wide shoulders and a stocky build, much like Bu'r but without the bulbous midsection. Duke could tell that he was once a warrior. Or a bouncer. His hair, cut short, was a sparkling white and he sported a neatly trimmed beard. The man's skin was of a darker hue than any of the other Neprians—it had the look of worn leather.

"There is no need to fight amongst ourselves when there are so many out there that deserve to feel the wrath of our fists and the sting of our arrows," he bellowed. His voice was that of a leader that commanded respect. It was clear that

Po'l was trying to mimic his swagger. *And without much luck*, thought Duke.

"This is the leader of our cause and a great hero, General Mo'a," proclaimed Ja'a. "He heads our council."

Mo'a nodded slightly. "Just Mo'a, please. A council leader without a council is no leader."

The entire group remained silent as they absorbed Mo'a's comment.

He continued, "Sure, there are council members scattered about—but what do we council? We have no government to oversee. No positions to appoint. We plan raids and sneak attacks against Orbius; that's it. I feel that the only title that I'm worthy of is 'old man that can't accomplish anything.'"

"Pleasure, regardless." Duke tipped his cap. Ishiro'shea bowed in respect.

"Ja'a, tell me about your friends here," Mo'a requested, regaining his jovial tone.

"Po'l, obviously. And I believe you've met Ma'n and Te'o—they served my father."

"Oh yes. It is good to see you again, old friends."

"Yes, great Mo'a," Po'l replied humbly.

"Stop groveling," said Mo'a. "I'm not anyone's king. I'm just the old man that's trying to keep our operation afloat. Nothing more, nothing less. We all have our roles to play and our input to provide. Right, Uu'k?"

Uu'k smiled.

Ja'a continued, "Let me introduce Bu'r of Shud'nut and Ty'n of the Southern Forests."

"Greetings, my good men. Your service is beyond appreciated."

Both men nodded at the Neprian leader.

"And who are these two curious-looking souls standing next to Uu'k?" Mo'a asked.

"These are the off-worlders, Duke LaGrange of Nova Texas and Ishiro'shea of Earth."

"Hey."

The entire crew of rebels cast piercing stares at Duke—or rather, hurled, like an octopus practicing dagger throwing.

"What?" Duke asked, knowing full well that his informal greeting had not been well-received.

But Mo'a only returned a great laugh.

"Duke—oh, it's nice to have someone that's not so stuffy around me!"

The Nova Texan winked at Ja'a. She returned a slight grin.

"My beautiful Ja'a, you know that I have viewed you as one of my own; your father was a brother to me. I miss him every single day—but not as much as our cause does. I fear I lack his leadership—rather, I *know* I lack his leadership."

"Mo'a—" interjected Ja'a.

"Hush, girl. I know my shortcomings. I also know that he would be very proud of you."

Ja'a blushed. It was the first time Duke had seen her so vulnerable.

"And he would be proud of you, great Mo'a. He often spoke of your fighting prowess."

Mo'a laughed. "Something I haven't had in many cycles. And it takes more than swords and arrows to defeat an evil like Orbius."

"He also spoke to me—many times, in fact—about your spirit and conviction. And if I believe in something as strongly and passionately as his friend Mo'a, I would live a richly fulfilled life."

It was Mo'a's turn to blush. His eyes glazed over and he stared at nothing in particular. *He must be caught in a good —no, a great—memory*, thought Duke.

Mo'a jolted from his momentary trance. "That is very kind, Ja'a. Very kind. You've made an old man very happy."

Ja'a bowed her head gently.

"But, sweet daughter of He'j, I have someone else that you might remember even more fondly than my ancient bones."

He pointed to the entrance that led into the base. Leaning up against the frame was an older Neprian male— not as old as Mo'a, but definitely old enough to be Ja'a's father. He was extraordinarily fit for his age; he appeared to be sculpted from hardened mud. His ink-colored mustache curved downward and extended well beyond his chin. Atop his shaven head was a neatly groomed row of thick black hair that stretched from the midpoint of his cranium to the start of his neck, transitioning into a braided mane which fell to the middle of his back. He stepped out of the shadow of the doorway and approached the group.

A smile flashed over Ja'a's face with such power that her cheeks almost exploded. She dropped her bow and sprinted towards the mysterious Neprian. She leapt into his arms and he swung her around with great enthusiasm. His smile mirrored that of Ja'a's.

Duke looked at Po'l. *Surely* he had to be upset at this. But Po'l also sported a grin.

"Hey, who is this character?" Duke bent down to ask Uu'k.

"That's Lo'n," she whispered back.

"Boyfriend? Grandpa? Massage therapist? Who is he?"

Uu'k looked at him, "that's Lo'n."

Unprompted, Bu'r tapped Duke on the shoulder.

"Duke, that's Lo'n. Can you believe it?"

Duke looked around and Ma'n was mouthing to him silently, clearly saying, "That's Lo'n."

The bounty hunter clenched his teeth.

Ja'a turned to everyone—her hand still around Lo'n's waist—and proclaimed, "Everyone, this is Lo'n—"

"I know it's Lo'n! Everyone knows frickin' Lo'n!"

They all turned to face Duke. Ishiro'shea looked at the ground.

"I mean—" Duke cleared his throat. "Nice to meet you, Lo'n. I've heard so much about you."

Duke awkwardly knelt down in an exaggerated curtsy. Mo'a laughed.

"Is that right, off-worlder?"

"But of course. The great and all powerful Lo'n. Your exploits are known throughout the universe. Entire races are sacrificed in your honor every cycle. The mere mention of your name can impregnate certain species. Both male and female. You are a god, my friend, a true god."

Lo'n's eyes locked on to Duke's. Silence fell upon the group. Not even Mo'a chuckled.

"Off-worlder, I like you!"

The Neprians exhaled audibly and some broke into a light giggle.

"Where did you find this one, Ja'a? And his masked companion?" asked Lo'n.

"It's a long story, Uncle Lo'n."

"So you were He'j's brother?"

"Not by blood, off-worlder. But we were very close. Ja'a was always like a niece to me."

"So you're a fake uncle?"

"I guess. You could say that," Lo'n replied, confused.

Duke turned to Uu'k and smirked. "See, I *can* be your uncle."

Uu'k stuck her tongue out. Ishiro'shea patted her on her head and smiled through his mask.

"Uncle Lo'n, this is Duke LaGrange and Ishiro'shea. They came to us when their ship was swallowed by a giant star portal, as they call it, and then had a run-in with the Northern priests. They escaped and joined us."

"Aren't you forgetting how you captured us and treated us like spies? And how we saved everyone? And then you drug us to some ragtag village and they turned on us? And we saved Uu'k from being kidnapped and sent to Orbius?"

Ja'a looked cross.

"Duke, that is very interesting," said Mo'a. "Sounds like you already have some tales to tell."

"Very interesting, indeed," Lo'n said. "How did you survive these trials?"

"Cunning. Brute strength."

"He has special weapons," Po'l interjected. "His weapons are quite powerful—in fact, Orbius likely wants them to help squash our cause."

"Hey Lo'n, ask Po'l what happened when he tried to operate my 'special weapons.'"

Po'l grumbled.

"I take it that their power is only fully realized in the hands of an expert?" asked Lo'n.

"Yes, you got it, Uncle Lo'n!" said Duke with a large smile. "I like this guy. Where've you been keeping *him*? We could use some enlightened thinking in this crew."

Po'l grumbled even louder.

"Duke, unfortunately, the last stretch of time has not been kind to me. I've just now found my way back to the coast and Mo'a's protection."

"Where were you?"

"Out there taking care of Northerners, huh?" shouted Bu'r. Ty'n and Te'o echoed with their own shouts of approval.

"A few, my proud friends," Lo'n answered, "a few."

"He's being modest," Mo'a chimed in. "Lo'n was on the mission to Orbius' fortress with He'j."

"A mission that failed," Lo'n said in a low tone.

"A mission that was doomed for failure; rushed and ill-planned from the onset," Mo'a retorted.

"Maybe so, Mo'a, but He'j was lost to us. It's our greatest loss since we started battling Orbius and his minions."

"You were with my father?"

"Yes, Ja'a. A very small group of us joined him. We felt it was the only way to penetrate his base and take him out. Even if we mustered a massive army, which you know would be impossible, it would be dwarfed by Gar and his priest warriors. Not to mention the numbers we would lose on the march north."

"Our next attempt will have to be of a similar approach," said Mo'a.

"But this time, we will have their weapons, right?" inquired Ty'n.

"It seems that our new friends have been a great help to us," Mo'a continued, "but what we ask is more than simply fighting off low-level priests. This is not their fight. It is our cause. I don't feel comfortable about potentially leading these two visitors to their deaths."

"Mo'a, I understand your concerns, but these visitors bring us an advantage that we have so desperately been missing. I think they should join us."

"Hey guys, over here. Stop acting like we aren't standing right next to you."

"Apologies, Duke," said Lo'n.

"We make our own decisions. Not to be an ass, but you can't make us do anything."

"Understood," began Mo'a, "and to echo what Lo'n said —apologies."

"Just because you have those weapons," Po'l growled. "You wouldn't be so tough if—"

"Enough, Po'l," demanded Mo'a.

"What about your ship?" chimed Ty'n. "Surely it will be an easier journey with us."

"Holy hedgehogs, can you all just shut up? You're arguing over nothing. Mo'a—appreciate that you're lookin' out for us, but Ishiro and I are planning to come along. Not because of your cause or how cool 'Uncle Lo'n' is—solely because we need to get to the *Deus* to get off this damn planet."

"This makes me very happy," Lo'n announced. "We will drink the finest Neprian wine that the coast has to offer in celebration of our newest ally and the impending trek northward."

"Hear, hear," responded Mo'a.

Ishiro'shea looked at Duke and extended a thumb.

"Finest Neprian wine? You keep getting better and better, ol' Lo'n-y boy," started Duke. "Maybe over a few glasses, you can share with us any weaknesses that you noticed."

"And what else we might encounter," added Ja'a.

"Ah, yes. Both excellent questions. I can tell you are both great leaders. And an unbeatable team."

Po'l groaned. Mo'a slapped him on the back.

CHAPTER TWENTY-FIVE

NEPRIAN WINE

"WHAT IS THIS STUFF—" DUKE began, "and why did you wait until now to share?"

"I'm glad you like it, Duke," responded Lo'n.

"Easily the best thing we've come across on this rock. There isn't even a close second."

"You surely can't mean that," replied Lo'n. "What about our lovely Ja'a? Surely, this wine falls short when compared to her beauty."

"Shut up, Uncle Lo'n," said Duke, blushing.

"I agree, shut up," Po'l blurted out in an aggressive tone.

Never mind. If it's making Po'l uncomfortable, sign me up.

"I stand—err, sit—corrected, oh wise Lo'n. I've never seen anything as beautiful as Ja'a in the whole of the universe," Duke began rather theatrically. He stood and struck a pose of an actor preparing to deliver the climactic speech of a staged drama. "I've traversed the cosmos and nothing—from the twinkling crystals when the light of the twin moons shine against the caves of Oscavia to the seemingly never-ending skies over Nova Texas, which are the bluest of blues that your baby blues could ever see—would even come close to the radiance of this beloved daughter of Neprius."

"Now *you* shut up," said Ja'a.

"I cannot be silenced! As I look up into the celestial cloak that descends upon us this evening—with only the flickering flames bestowing luminescence upon our merry crew—I can't help but think, why are we so lucky? Why are we so fortunate to have stood in the presence of a beauty that would start wars and topple kingdoms—and the millions of worlds floating above our heads will never be so blessed."

Duke bowed.

After a momentary pause, Lo'n stood up and applauded. Mo'a let loose a laugh that shook the ground. Bu'r and Ty'n whooped and cackled. Ma'n and Te'o applauded. Ishiro'shea rolled his eyes and shrugged his shoulders. Uu'k was already asleep, curled in a ball beside the ninja.

"Seriously, shut up," repeated Ja'a. She took a long sip of her Neprian wine.

"This is ridiculous," Po'l huffed.

"Oh, Po'l, lighten up," said Mo'a.

"No offense, General—"

"I'm not a general anymore."

"Whatever. No offense, Mo'a, but we are on the verge of risking our lives. No, that's not true—we are on the verge of most likely dying for this cause, and we are sitting around getting drunk and listening to this off-worlder spew nonsense."

"Calm down, Po'l. We're just having fun," said Lo'n. "It's good to laugh. There's more to life than war and heartache. In fact, if life was solely pain then why are we fighting to restore it?"

"Hear, hear," said Duke, offering a toast.

"What are you toasting, off-worlder? You have no business here. This planet doesn't need you. This cause doesn't need you or your weapons. I don't need you. Ja'a doesn't need you."

Duke made a mocking pout towards Ja'a.

"I know that you saved us in the cave with your little weapon—"

"My weapon happens to be quite large."

Ishiro'shea slapped Duke on the leg. Po'l ignored the bounty hunter's interruption.

"—and you saved Uu'k from the villagers but we don't need you anymore. You are nothing but a self-centered, egotistical pain in the ass. You are *more* likely to get us killed. It gets a lot more dangerous than peasants and priest soldiers."

"First off, Ishiro saved Uu'k," Duke said under his breath.

"What if we defeat Orbius with these weapons? With *their* help."

"What do you mean, Po'l?" asked Ja'a.

"Do you think that someone that loves himself so much will just walk away without our entire race having to kiss his feet? He will become a tyrant more dangerous than even Orbius."

"Po'l, that's enough!" screamed Ja'a.

"I agree, Ja'a. This is not the attitude and composure of a future leader of Neprius," added Mo'a.

"Neprius has no future if we need his kind to save it. We are defeating a villain with an even greater threat."

Silence fell upon the group.

Duke stiffened his stance, which no longer bore any resemblance to an actor's. He gently placed his wine on the sand as his smile dissipated.

"Po'l, I was just kidding around about Ja'a—well, I mean she is beautiful, but—"

"See off-worlder, you aren't capable of being serious."

"Look, I get it. I'm not part of your cause and, quite frankly, I don't want to be part of your cause. However, circumstances have made it apparent that my cause and your cause are symbiotically linked. I'm not saying you have to like me—in fact, it's been obvious that you don't, ever since you were convinced I was a spy and you almost killed yourself trying to work Ol' Betsy. Guess what? I don't care for you either. You're reckless. All of that's okay with me. But I do need my ship back. And if me getting my ship back helps Ja'a and Uu'k and the guys over there have a better life, that's just gravy. But we stand a helluva lot better chance working together."

"It's obvious that Ja'a and Duke are working together," Lo'n added. "So are you saying that she has poor judgement?"

"No. Well, yes. Maybe. I don't know. I'm sorry all, but I can't continue. Not with him."

"Po'l! You can't leave. We need you," cried Ja'a. "Why are you behaving this way?"

"This cause is my life. I will defeat Orbius alone."

Po'l threw his full glass of Neprian wine towards the sea. The rebel stormed into the central building of the compound, muttering under his breath.

"Well, that happened," said the bounty hunter.

"Duke, I'm sorry, I don't know what got into him," said Mo'a.

"I do, but that's for another day."

"What?"

"It doesn't matter," Ja'a interjected. "We are all tired and have been through many perils already—and we haven't even started the final journey. And the wine might be getting the best of us."

"Yeah, he didn't even have any—"

"Duke," Ja'a continued sternly, "the wine is probably getting the best of us. Right, Duke?"

"Fine."

"I'm going to go talk to him."

"I'll go with you, Ja'a," Mo'a said. "He is my nephew, after all."

"No, Mo'a. I think it would be best if I handled this alone."

Ja'a followed Po'l's path into the compound.

"So wait," Duke began, "we actually have a real 'uncle' here?"

Mo'a, his head hanging, sauntered away from the gathering.

"It's hard to see your kin behave in such a manner," said Lo'n. "Can't help but feel like you have something to do with it."

"He doesn't," retorted the Nova Texan.

"Why do you say that?"

"It has nothing to do with Mo'a—it's Ja'a."

"I'm not following you, Duke."

"Po'l has the hots for her."

Lo'n's face was overrun by an empty stare.

"It means that he's got feelings for her. You know, googly eyes, sweaty palms, heart beating fast. He loves her."

"Oh, that *is* interesting."

"Yeah, and I think that's why he hates me."

"I don't follow."

"Ja'a and I have, you know, gotten along real well and all. He probably feels threatened. I mean, before me, she was surrounded by some real B-teamers." Duke swiveled on the spot to make sure Ma'n, Te'o, Ty'n, or Bu'r weren't looking. "They're good guys and all, but Po'l was the only alpha in the lot, so he never feared them stealing his woman."

"This makes more sense. You might have been the straw that broke the greattu's back. I wasn't aware of this situation and with all of the other pressure that he's under—what transpired doesn't shock me."

"Other pressure?"

"See, Duke, Po'l is Mo'a's nephew—"

"Yep, got that."

"—and is in line, or rather expected, to be the next great warrior-general of the Southern tribes. It has not gone according to plan thus far. He's not even the leader of this band of rebel guerrillas."

"That accounts for his awkwardly dramatic speech when we arrived here. I think its aim was to be inspiring."

"Probably so. Mo'a is a great orator—and has given speeches to troops and townsfolk alike that roused their spirits to the point that they would do anything for him."

"And now the woman he loves is preventing him from achieving his destiny. That's not that uncommon, if you think about it. Women be ruining everything, right?"

Duke playfully punched Lo'n in the shoulder. The meaning of the gesture seemed to be lost on the veteran Neprian warrior.

"Po'l is reminded every day that he will likely never be the great leader that he was groomed to be by seeing someone else control his squadron. And now that I realize that the person that represents his failure as a commander also represents his failure in personal happiness—I see why he acted the way he did."

Duke took another swig of his drink.

"I can sympathize."

"Really?"

"Yes, I once had a 'Ja'a' back many moons ago. She also

was better than me at my job. And she also got away. Now she's simply a ghost."

"To lost loves and moving on," Lo'n said, raising his glass. "Now let's rejoin the group before they drink all the wine."

"Cheers to that."

The duo made their way back to the torchlit semicircle. Mo'a seemed to be leading the storytelling.

"Duke, my friend, they were just telling me about your adventures thus far. And the magic that those weapons of yours possess. They say that Betty is quite the eradicator of priest warriors."

"Betsy."

"Oh, yes, Betsy. Can we see this Betsy in action?"

"And the little one," added Ty'n.

"Sure, why not?"

"Ishiro, toss a rock up in the air—and I'll blast it."

The ninja shook his head and pointed down at the sleeping Neprian on his lap.

"Oh, sorry. Anyone? Pick up a stone and throw it as far as you can towards the sea."

"This sounds like fun!" boomed Mo'a.

"I'll take a stab at it," said Lo'n.

He reached down and grabbed a rock roughly the size of his hand. He reared back and chucked the object towards the seashore. As it began its descent back to the soil, Duke relieved his laser revolver from his holster and fired a single shot in the direction of the stone. Direct hit!

"Impressive. What if I did this, however?"

Lo'n grabbed three rocks in one hand and quickly tossed them away from the camp. They sailed in different directions and at different trajectories. Duke, with his gun already in his hand, rallied off three pulses in rapid succession. The courses of all three stones were altered—all direct hits.

"Duke, I see why everyone thinks that you can turn the tide for us," belted Mo'a. "I've never seen anything like it."

"Indeed," confirmed Lo'n. "Now what about this Betsy you speak of?"

"Wait until you see this!" shouted Bu'r.

Duke removed Betsy from his back and presented her as if she were a prized jewel from the royal family of Oscavia.

"See that gathering of trees over there?" asked Duke to Mo'a and Lo'n.

"Yes."

"See how dense it is—almost like a wooden wall separating this area from the water? Be prepared to be amazed and awed by Betsy's singing voice."

He aimed the Sonic Widowmaker shotgun at a dense area of foliage where five or six large trunks appeared to intertwine into a single tree.

"Sing for us, ol' girl," Duke whispered as he pulled the trigger.

The bellow of the firearm knocked Mo'a to his knees. Lo'n seemed shaken by a bad case of secondhand recoil. Both gazed in wonderment at what remained of the trees.

"Duke, I don't know what to say."

"I do!"

Ja'a sprinted toward them.

Not good, thought Duke.

"Are you kidding me? This is a hidden base. Keyword—hidden. If Orbius or Gar or one of their henchmen find this place, our cause is over with, done. Duke, I'm not surprised—"

"They made me do it—" interjected the bounty hunter.

"—But Mo'a? Lo'n? Guys? I'm sure someone heard

that... that... sound—someone that's not supposed to hear it. And, on top of that, you woke up Uu'k."

Even Ishiro'shea seemed to side with the enraged rebel.

"The noise reminds me of when," Lo'n started, as if he were in a trance, ignoring Ja'a completely, "a—err—I can't put a finger on it. It's impressive, I must say."

"You're probably thinking about a penguin in a blender —" Duke began.

Ja'a cut the bounty hunter off. "Enough! Of course, when I heard the weapon go off, I immediately assumed that we were being attacked. Then I come out and witness this? A bunch of fools and their wine."

A crowd of Neprians had started to trickle out of the base.

"Nothing to see here," shouted Duke. "Go back in and do your rebelling. Or whatever it is that you're doing in the base."

"This is why I will be joining you, after all," came a voice from behind the irate female. It was Po'l. "Someone needs to make sure this mission doesn't implode."

"And that's you, is it? We don't need you, Po'l. We have Lo'n. He's survived Orbius' fortress once and he will again."

"Thank you, Duke, my friend," began Lo'n, "but we could use everyone to help us overcome the perils of a journey to Sansagon. It *is* quite dangerous."

"Did you not see his weapon, Lo'n?" asked Bu'r. "It can't be stopped."

"I wish it were so. But there are many things that pose great dangers even when you have this Betsy," replied Lo'n. He turned his attention to Ja'a. "I'm sorry, I will take full blame for this distraction. You are right, it was foolish."

"Very."

"Yes, very foolish. Don't blame Duke. I take full responsibility."

"Yes, but it was that moron that fired it," said Po'l, pointing at Duke.

"You changed your mind awfully quick about the mission. What was it? Worried about Lo'n and I becoming best friends and kicking total ass? Or that I might be an evil spy sent by Orbius in what would be the most elaborate and well-orchestrated double cross in history? Or is that I might be getting a bit too close to—"

"Shut up!" shouted Ja'a. "Everyone sit down—and shut up."

The group, including Mo'a, followed her command. Ja'a herself sat down and grabbed someone's wine that was sitting on the ground. She took a big swig.

"Mo'a, I'm sorry. I feel I'm letting you and my father down. And the cause."

"I won't even entertain a thought like that. Your father would be proud of you and what you've become—regardless of if you are the one to drive the stake through Orbius' heart or not. That reminds me—I have something for you." Mo'a headed back into the main building.

Ishiro'shea patted Ja'a on the back. She appeared to find it comforting.

"So, Lo'n, what are we to expect on this journey?" Duke asked in a focused, sober tone. Ja'a's eyes lit up. The rest of the Neprians and Ishiro'shea leaned in and awaited the old rebel's response.

Lo'n took a hefty drink of his wine. "It was not an easy road. That's for sure."

"So what are we talking about? More priests?"

"Yes, we have no idea of knowing how many of Gar's troops we will encounter. Maybe none. Maybe hundreds. My guess is that he has his eyes and ears out, awaiting our approach."

"How would he know?" inquired Duke.

"He knows that you and your unique armaments aren't in his control—so rest assured, he's on high alert. I'm sure he has squads out in every nook of Neprius."

"Okay, aside from an unknown number of skirmishes with those javelin-tossin' bastards, what else?"

"Up first..." Lo'n paused. "The land bridge."

The Neprians groaned collectively.

"I'm guessing that means the land bridge isn't a viable vacation spot," asked Duke.

"Remember when I told you about our warring tribes and how Peace was buried and sealed off in a temple?" said Ja'a.

"Yes, until He'j and Togg recovered it and brought Vangu here," replied Duke.

"Right. The hidden temple is on the land bridge," began Ja'a. "Some guards were sent in to watch the temple. Every decade or so, others would enter the land bridge to assume the same position. However, no one knew if they ever made it to the temple to actually guard it. There was nothing allowed out—no news whatsoever. Not until He'j and Togg led the mission to recover Peace."

"And?"

"There were no guards. The temple could have been unguarded for hundreds of cycles," she replied.

"At least the Orb was still there."

"Yes, that's because they decided to seal off the land bridge. No one in, no one out for generations—except for the guards."

"Sacrificial lambs, it seems," replied Duke.

"But I didn't mention that the bridge was sealed off rather... well, hastily."

"What do you mean?" asked Duke.

"Entire communities were living within the swamps of the land bridge."

"Why weren't they evacuated?"

"I don't know," replied Ja'a.

"So, I'm guessing that these villagers just didn't die out," commented Duke.

"According to He'j and Togg—," began Ja'a.

"They are monsters," interrupted Lo'n.

"Monsters?" asked Ty'n.

"Yes. They've become one with the swamp. They're wild animals—inbred to the point where they are barely recognizable as Neprians, just a grotesque mix of the two races."

"That sounds fun," replied Duke.

"And, what we learned was that they're tired of eating the bounty of the swamp," said Lo'n.

"Cannibals? I hate cannibals," Duke quipped.

"Does anyone *like* cannibals?" asked Po'l in a sarcastic tone.

"We were caught off guard. We lost some of our best men. Those that escaped the swamps alive were lucky."

"Any weaknesses?" asked Ja'a.

"Vegetables?"

Lo'n ignored Duke's comments. "Actually, we did notice that they're nocturnal. We never encountered them during the day. I would suggest swift travel during the day—and being as quiet as possible when the darkness descends."

"Not to be an ass, but why don't we just build a boat and sail around this strip o' death? Seems like the logical thing to do."

"It is logical," responded Lo'n. He paused. "But—"

"Here it comes."

"Orbius has already thought of that. He has guards along the coast in boats. And he's sunk the few that we maintained in the South anyways."

"Right. That officially sucks."

"It's not ideal, no. He's forcing us to go directly through the swamp."

"Smart. And they can get down here much quicker with control of the sea."

"Yes."

"Damn. So with these swampfolk running the land bridge, did they take over the temple?"

"Oddly enough, no. Something about the temple spooked them."

"Not sure what would spook an undead swamp monster," said Duke.

"I think He'j knew. He never told us why, but he said that re-entry into the temple would be certain death. Neither he nor Togg ever mentioned the reason. He'j was not prone to exaggeration and, coupled with the fact that the cannibals didn't take it over, that was good enough for us. We all assumed that traps were in place to protect the Orb and that they remain still. Traps that only He'j and Togg knew or that they placed on their exit."

"Or maybe something worse," added Po'l.

"I hate to agree with Po'l," Duke began, "but, in my experience, it's *always* something worse."

Po'l looked shocked.

"What else, Lo'n? Let's say we get past the flesh-craving inbreds... What's next? I'm assuming they'll have a welcoming party in charge of guarding the northern entrance to the wall and making sure no one gets in. Or, in our case, gets out."

"It is heavily guarded."

"Great."

"But, I'm not too worried about that."

"Why? Because of Ol' Betsy?" Duke said with a grinning confidence.

"No. Because I know where the gaps are. It's a bit rougher terrain but they leave it open because—"

"Let me guess," interjected Duke, "because they don't think anyone could make it through whatever is on the other side."

"Yes. We would have to go through the heart of the swamp."

The Neprians exchanged glances without saying a word.

"So instead of just having to avoid these cannibals, we're going to break into their house, urinate on the living room floor, and try and leave without being caught?"

"I'm not sure I follow but, yes, it will be a trickier proposition."

"Is that how you and my father got through?" Ja'a asked.

"No, not exactly. He'j remembered a passage from his trip with Togg that was clear—however, it was blocked up after we got through. But to our knowledge, they never added support to the area that marks the end of the swampland. Togg said it was pointless and Orbius—once again, to our knowledge, hasn't any reason to go against that thinking."

The bounty hunter stood up and paced around the group. He tipped the brim of his hat. "Let's say we get through the cannibal-infested swamp and beyond the wall—without having to fight through the priests. Then what?"

"It's a long trek to Sansagon. The direct route is mostly grasslands. Not a lot of hiding; we'll be exposed. On the positive side, there aren't many towns or outposts that could spot us. We will probably have to deal with a few scouting parties, but I don't think that will be our biggest concern."

"And that would be?"

"Grundar."

"Oh, right. I forgot about the damn grundar."

"You don't think we'll actually come in contact with them, right?" asked Ja'a.

"Probably not. You never know."

"Have you seen them?" she asked.

"No."

"No one here has seen one? And yet we are freaking out over a potential attack?"

"Yes."

"I think someone might be pulling one over on ya'. I mean, invisible beings forcing you to do and not do certain things based on extreme consequences—pretty sure that's a relatively common annoyance in most every developing civilization."

"Grundar are very real, Duke."

"Believe what you want to believe. If we're lucky enough to avoid these mysterious, magical flying kitty cats, is it a straight shot to the fortress?"

"Yes."

"And can we get in?"

"I believe so. Our theory—that a small unit can penetrate Orbius' base—is sound. We could never win all all-out attack, even if we had greater numbers."

"Did you actually make it in last time?" asked Po'l.

Lo'n looked around at the group. "No."

There was some mild grumbling amongst the team. Even from Ja'a.

"Hey, he's been closer than any of us," Duke started, "and he witnessed He'j make it through. Tell 'em, Lo'n."

"You're right."

"So what happened on that mission?" inquired Po'l.

Lo'n looked at Ja'a.

"Ja'a—"

"Go ahead, Uncle. I can handle it. I know my father was killed at the hands of Orbius—it's something that has petrified my heart—so the details of your attempt won't change anything. We need to know what you know, if we are to have any chance at success."

"Very well." Lo'n cleared his throat. "Our party was about the size of this one. As we descended upon the fortress, we decided to split up and search for weaknesses around the entire perimeter. Unfortunately, most of us discovered guard units. We fought valiantly. He'j found a way in—through an underground tunnel—and came back to tell us. He discovered me engaged in a brutal fight with three priests."

"What happened?" asked Bu'r.

"He'j helped me defeat them. We quickly went to the defense of our other comrades... but were too late. We lost everyone. Then He'j told me to do something that I regret to this day."

Lo'n bowed his head.

"It's okay, Uncle. Go on. Please."

"He told me to go back to the coast. I needed to tell everyone that there was a way in—a natural tunnel system that originated from a cave north of the base. If we both attempted entry and failed, the cause would have to start over from the beginning. He said the knowledge was greater than both he and I."

Lo'n hung his head. A tear ran down Ja'a's cheek.

"And so I left him," Lo'n continued. "I left him there to die. I can't help but think that I could have saved him; that we could have defeated Orbius... together."

"But Uncle, if my father's fear came true, and you both were killed, we wouldn't know that there's a way in."

"However," Duke began, "since He'j made it through—"

"They probably have sealed off that passage. Doubled down on any weakness," Po'l said, finishing Duke's thought.

The rebels looked around at one another. No one said a word. Their gazes focused on Lo'n as they awaited his response.

"My gut tells me that it's still open."

"And why is that?" asked Po'l.

"He'j didn't go in that way. He discovered it, yes, but he didn't use it."

"What?"

"He felt that if I could bring back a party—armed with the knowledge that I had gained about the fortress—it would be better than this one single shot. We could send a troop or two through the tunnels and then a few to do exactly what he did."

"And that was?"

"Walk right up to the front door and knock."

"But why?" Ja'a cried. "That would've been suicide. My father didn't have a death wish."

"No, but he cared about this cause more than anything and he knew that he wasn't destined to be the savior. That honor—that destiny—would fall to someone else."

Ja'a began to weep softly. Ishiro'shea put his arm around her.

"I made my way back to the coast—but, as you know, that took me much longer than I had hoped."

"What caused the delays?"

"Traveling alone with no food and in enemy territory is not easy. I had to scavenge and—I hate to admit this—steal from villages along the way."

"Did you have any run-ins with Gar's men?"

"Yes, I evaded capture once, just east of the Valley of the Grundar."

"And the cannibals?"

"I was lucky. I traveled by day, and at night they paid me no interest—or did not pick up my scent."

"I'm glad you made it back, for one," started the bounty hunter, "and I feel you give us the edge we need to take down Orby, Gar, and whatever else is up in that fortress."

"For the *Deus*, right?" added Po'l.

"Yes, for the *Deus*, of course," Duke replied. "What else would it be for?"

Ja'a began to laugh. Ishiro slapped him on the leg.

"Now Duke, if I didn't know any better, it seems that you might be coming around on this idea of helping out the cause," added Lo'n.

"I'm here for one reason and one reason alone—"

"Yourself," Po'l said, again finishing Duke's thought—this time using a word selection he personally wouldn't have chosen.

"Well..."

"Ja'a, I'm so glad that I found this," interrupted Mo'a.

Saved by the Mo'a.

"What, Mo'a?"

Mo'a extended his arm and in his hand dangled a long chain necklace. The interlocking rings were thick and clunky and appeared quite heavy. They were an odd mix of silver and black; almost like matted pewter. On the chain hung a pendant, lighter in color but chunkier in design. It was a half circle with a jagged edge down the center. It seemed to be part of a two-piece emblem, missing its complementary half.

"What is this?" asked Ja'a.

"This is something that your father wanted me to give you. He gave it to me before he left for Sansagon. I have no idea what it is, what it means, or anything. It's nothing of value—it's made from regular mustangsen. And I have no idea what the emblem means. I've never seen it before."

"Did you ask him when he gave it to you?" inquired Duke.

"No, Duke, I did not. He was so very adamant about making sure she has it, I thought it might have some special meaning, like a family heirloom."

He handed it over to Ja'a. She examined it.

"I have never seen this before."

"I have," began Lo'n. "Your father wore the other half. He said it was good luck because he knew you would eventually wear the other half. The pendants formed a perfect circle—and, even though they were broken, they would be whole again. He believed it symbolized the Neprian struggle. The planet would be whole again. The mustangsen also served as a constant reminder of Orbius' greed and evil—for it's the very material that our brothers and sisters are dying in the mines to recover for his own vanity."

Ja'a placed it around her neck. Her tears evaporated and resolve hardened her expression.

"Thank you, Mo'a. This means a lot. More than you will ever know. And thank you, Lo'n, for that story. When we defeat Orbius, I will find my father's half and restore it—just as we will restore this planet."

The Neprians cheered. Duke and Ishiro'shea raised a glass next to their new comrades.

"Let us enjoy these drinks. Tomorrow, we head north!"

CHAPTER TWENTY-SIX

MISSED MEETING

"MAYBE WE SHOULD'VE TAPPED THE brakes on that ninth bottle of wine, huh?"

Ishiro'shea raised his arm groggily and signaled a thumbs-up in the slowest of slow motion. His hammock rocked a bit... then some more... then the ninja was deposited face-first onto the hard stone floor.

"Not very ninja-like, little buddy."

Duke splashed some water on his face, sat back down on the slab of weathered padding that constituted a bed, and covered his face with his hands.

"Seriously, I think we might've hit it too hard—especially the day before an extremely long walk."

Ishiro repeated his earlier gesture—this time from a position face down on the ground.

"At least the room's an upgrade over our last Neprian accommodations."

"Off-worlders, you ready? We're all meeting in the main hall." The voice passed by the doorway and faded. *Shut up, Po'l.*

"We'll be there," Duke shouted, but he knew it was hopeless that Po'l actually heard his response. He then turned to Ishiro. "Are you kidding me? They want us now? Do Neprians not get hangovers?"

Duke closed his eyes.

The pattering of feet continued to fill the hallway outside their room; a symphony of voices followed. Duke picked up his sidekick by the arm and propped him up against the door frame.

"Look alive, Ishiro. Let's just hope this is a quick strategy session. I mean it's not like we won't have days of walking... and walking... and walking to discuss how we're going to hide from cannibals and hide from flying panthers and hide in tunnels. Damn, our entire game plan is to walk and hide. Anyways, let's not keep 'em waiting anymore. They probably can't even start the meeting without us."

The duo left their room and made their way down a narrow stone corridor. A torch protruded from the wall every few paces so that the hall was adequately lit despite having no windows. The two exchanged stares with rebel soldiers and other assorted followers of the cause as they passed; it was obvious that these people knew more about Duke and Ishiro'shea than vice versa.

The bounty hunters followed the sounds of commotion and turned right halfway along the corridor. They entered a vast circular public space; hundreds of Southerners navigated the room in rapid crisscross patterns without colliding with one another. Chatter, laughter, and animated discussion filled the room. Both men had to cover their eyes—the intense light was a drastic change from the torchlit halls. Duke looked up to see that the entire ceiling was a glass dome.

"Hey you!" Duke shouted at a group of what appeared to be soldiers. They ignored him. "I said, hey you!"

All four turned around in unison.

"Yes, Duke LaGrange of Nova Texas," one replied.

"How do you know who I am? Never mind, don't have time for it. Where's the great hall?"

The quartet laughed. "This is the great hall."

"That lying ass, Po'l. He said to meet him in the great hall. He thinks he's so funny."

"I saw Po'l moments ago," began another one of the soldiers, "but he was heading into the main hall."

"Are you serious? It's way too early for this. Can you at least show me how to get to the *main* hall?"

The soldier pointed to an oversized wooden door at the side of the room.

"It's just on the other side of that door. When you enter, there's a hall—on the right is the hatchery for the winged flurn; keep following the hall and take a left immediately following the mail room. After a few paces you will see two spiral staircases—take the one of the left. The one on the right goes to the arts and crafts center."

"Where does the one on the left go? The opera house?"

"No," replied the solider, "that's on the other side of the base."

"Of course it is."

The rebel continued, "But follow the right staircase down and you will see the door to the main hall."

"Thanks."

"Good luck."

"We might need it."

They followed the instructions to a tee, Duke only stopping to ask the hatchery attendant if he could order a bucket of fried flurn. The attendant did not find it humorous.

Duke looked up at what had to be the door to the main hall, on the basis of the humongous placard that read: *Main Hall*.

"Sorry we're late!"

The room was empty, with the exception of Lo'n and Ja'a.

"Hey guys, you missed our chat."

"I see that."

"We leave after we all have a bite to eat. Sound good?"

"Not really. What's the plan?

"I can fill you in on the way."

"Hopefully we won't have to use these too often," Lo'n said, hoisting a curved saber that was almost as tall as Ishiro'shea. *Impressive.*

"Hey, buddy," Duke said, nudging Ishiro. "Sword envy?"

The ninja ignored him.

"Okay, well then—where's the grub?"

"Ishiro'shea! Duke!" screamed a juvenile voice. It was Uu'k. "You can't leave without saying goodbye."

Duke glanced at Ja'a and mouthed, "Not going?"

"Uu'k is going to stay here with Mo'a," Ja'a replied. "She has earned some time away from Dre'en and from adventure. Also, she expressed interest in learning how to handle a sword."

Ishiro'shea knelt down beside Uu'k and they embraced.

Duke patted her on the head. "See you soon, Uu'k."

"You better. I want Ishiro to teach me some of his sword tricks."

"I'll do everything I can to make that happen, kid."

"Thanks."

"Now can I get an 'Uncle Duke' before we leave?"

"No."

Lo'n laughed and handed Uu'k the hilt of his saber. The blade clinked against the ground with an excruciating sound. It was obvious that the Neprian child did not quite yet possess the physical strength to hold the sword aloft.

"It will come with time, Uu'k. If we hurry—and if Ja'a says it's fine—maybe we can do a quick beginner's lesson before we have to leave."

Uu'k rushed out in her excitement to learn from the Neprian swordsman.

CHAPTER TWENTY-SEVEN

A COUNTER-ORB?

THE TREK FROM THE REBEL hideout to the entrance of the land bridge was a day and a half—at a brisk walk. Of the nine travelers, only Bu'r seemed to struggle with the pace. Lo'n, despite being the oldest, appeared to be affected the least. Duke's earlier challenges to acclimate to the fresh air were behind him. *Maybe I could get used to this whole non-pollution thing*, he thought. It reminded him of his youth on Nova Texas. The good parts, at least.

The wall itself was an ominous structure that could be seen miles away, rising above the forest. It was nothing like the divider that ran outside of Dre'en—it was more archaic, more primitive. Boulders made up its base—they decreased in size as they moved skyward. The top of the wall curved out and was laced with sharpened wooden pikes, presumably to annoy would-be breachers.

From the coast, they had mostly traveled through uninhabited areas of forest and field, but the last few miles had been on a cleared path from one of the villages to the land bridge. The road led directly into a narrow archway in the wall—the only potential entryway visible from their location.

"I was kinda expecting some guards," remarked Duke. "Wouldn't the Northerners want to prevent y'all from gaining access to their home?"

"They don't feel it's necessary," replied Lo'n.

"That bad, huh?"

"Unfortunately. They don't think we would risk trying to make it through the swamps and whatever else might be there."

"What about those guys gettin' out? Maybe they could go terrorize some priests and help us out."

"That would not be a good thing, Duke. You don't want these guys out of the swamps. But, luckily, they won't."

"What do you mean?"

"They are part of the swamp. It's their home and they won't venture far from it."

"How can you be certain?" asked Duke.

"Yeah, how can you be sure?" echoed Ty'n.

"Once we get inside the wall, you will see. There are hundreds of these beings—maybe thousands—and they only live in the swamp. They haven't even moved out to other areas around it. Their homes—if you want to call them that —blend into the muck; they are truly one with their ecosystem."

"I hope we don't have to see—but I get your point," Duke replied. "And the swamp runs all the way to the northern wall?"

"It's concentrated near the wall. In fact, we probably won't even smell the swamp until the end of our first day."

"How far is the walk?"

"Walk? Duke, we will be going a bit faster than a walk."

"How far is the jog?"

"We should cover the majority of the land bridge in a

full day. I think we should camp near the temple—which, I hope, will spook the swampfolk. When daylight hits, we will go as fast as we can until we hit the exit. Even though the cannibals won't be out during the day, the terrain is tough. Other creatures lurk there—and the path won't be as easy as what we've experienced thus far."

"Kinda figured that," smirked Duke.

"Any more questions?" Lo'n asked the group.

"Are you sure you'll know the way to the hidden temple?" inquired Ma'n.

"Yes. When He'j and I crossed, we marked a path—I'm hoping the markers remain. If not, as long as we get to the swamp, we can follow it to the wall."

"My man, Lo'n! We're lucky to have run into you!" Duke extended his arm to give Lo'n a high five; Lo'n did not reciprocate the gesture. Duke assumed the Neprian didn't know what a high five was.

"Wish we could say the same about you, off-worlder," grumbled Po'l.

"Guys, let's get focused," said Ja'a. "This is going to be a perilous journey. Let's do everything in our power to avoid these creatures and get through the swampland intact."

"So, how do we get... in?" asked the Nova Texan.

"Open the door, moron," heckled Po'l.

Duke walked over to the archway and gave the door a firm push. It slowly creaked open.

"Don't even bother locking it, huh?"

"It was sealed from the outside—on both ends—until He'j and Togg excavated and discovered these doors," explained Lo'n. "And since securing the walls isn't high on Orbius' to-do list, they just remain unlocked."

What's with this planet and not locking doors?

The road that led to the archway stopped abruptly on the other side. For as far as the eye could see, a maze of branches dominated the landscape. Twisted, tangled, intertwined—the work of a hundred cycles worth of unimpeded growth. *This is an old forest*, thought Duke. No intuitive paths could be identified—it was just wooden chaos.

"How do we, um, get through this mess, Lo'n?"

"By enduring a lot of scrapes and scratches, my off-world friend."

"Great. What about—"

Ishiro'shea jumped to the front of the line and hacked away with his katana. Branches fell with far less noise than one would expect. He slashed and cut as he marched forward.

"One step ahead of me, little buddy."

"Not a bad idea," added Lo'n. He removed his saber and joined Ishiro'shea. They hacked through the forest in unison, clearing enough space for the party members to pass through with ease.

"Once we get out of this—which shouldn't be much longer—we should see our first marker. From there, it's a relatively treeless run until we get to the temple and set up camp."

"I'm all for that."

Amidst the foliage was a solitary scrap of orange cloth flickering gently in the breeze, fixed to a lonely branch jutting out from a thorny bush. *Marker number one*. The bounty hunter squinted and focused his sight up ahead—another dot of orange.

"What do you think is so bad about that place?" Duke asked Ja'a, pointing at the parts of the temple that peeked out from the mangled trees.

"I'm not sure—probably some traps so that no one else would successfully enter again. Like Lo'n said."

"That doesn't make sense to me."

"What do you mean?"

"If he took the Orb out, why would he waste his time placing traps until after he returned it? Why would he add obstacles for himself when he came back to seal it away again?"

"Maybe—"

"Maybe," Duke interrupted, "there's something else down in that temple."

"Don't be foolish," interjected Lo'n, who had overheard their conversation.

"Think about it, Lo'n. There has to be something in there that He'j wanted to keep a secret."

"Probably, for good reason," added Ja'a.

"Yes, Ja'a is right. He'j only had the best interests of his people. If there is something down there, we don't want to, nor can we afford to, encounter it."

"I don't doubt that *at all*—but what if it's something that can help us? Maybe He'j was being overly cautious."

"Like what?"

"What if there's another Orb?"

The group engaged in a collective gasp. A drawn-out hush permeated the camp.

"I don't think that's the case," said Lo'n, breaking the silence.

"But why?"

Ja'a began, "If my father felt there was any way that a person, creature, artifact, or other thing could help the cause —he would have explored it. He certainly wouldn't have told his most trusted friend to stay clear of it at all costs."

Lo'n smiled and nodded in Ja'a's direction.

"I think it's worth a visit," proclaimed the bounty hunter.

"No!" shouted Lo'n. "Duke, when daylight hits we are going to make it through the swamp and into enemy territory. We are so close—why would you risk everything on something that can be avoided?"

"Curiosity."

"Haven't you heard that curiosity killed the humpback tyorf-gella?"

"I can honestly say that I have not—but I get where you're going with it, Lo'n. But what if there is something useful in there? What if—"

"Enough. This cause isn't going to be dictated by 'what ifs' and 'maybes.' We have a mission," Ja'a said with conviction. "We need you and Ishiro'shea to help us—and I know you need us to get your ship back—but as mission leader, I forbid you to go into that temple."

Duke's mouth hung open. *She has guts, that's for sure.*

"Isn't it enough that this temple is providing us a shield —for whatever reason—from the beasts that lurk mere paces away?"

"I get it—don't look a gift horse in the mouth, right?"

Ja'a offered only a blank stare. *Probably didn't get that one.* "I don't know, but you shouldn't question it."

"If your father hadn't been the one to issue the order, would your judgment be as ironclad?"

"What does that mean?"

Ishiro slapped Duke.

"Answer me, what does that mean?"

"Ja'a, you would do anything for this cause—so why refuse to open a door that could help us?"

"Because my father told us that door shouldn't be opened—and I would trust him until the end of our planet."

Duke could sense her blood beginning to boil. *I should back off,* he thought. But Duke liked to ignore his thoughts.

"What if your father was... mistaken? What if the end of your planet will only be prevented by what's in that temple?"

Ja'a stormed towards Duke, her eyes burning.

"I'm in charge and the final command is to stay away from the temple. Got it?"

"What if I don't—"

"What if you don't follow my orders? Is that what you were going to say? You don't have to. You're right. We don't control you. But good luck getting to the wall at night through the swamp. Without a team. You'd be good as dead. Or you could go back south—away from your precious ship. Have at it! Good luck!"

Silence fell over the group again—this time even more suffocating.

"You're right. I'll stop. You're in charge. I will follow you to my death, oh fearless leader of mine," Duke said in a snarky tone. He removed his hat and bowed.

Ja'a turned away without responding to the bounty hunter's demeaning gesture; she grabbed a large branch and drove it into the ground at a low angle. She started to shape a pointed tip near the end with an arrowhead.

"Get back to work, everyone. Those that aren't shaping pikes to give us a barrier, start working on fire pits. We only have a few more moments until the night is upon us. Our meaningless discussion ate up precious time—"

"And if we don't get these fires lit and pikes sharpened, we could be the ones that are 'ate up.'"

"Nice one, Lo'n," Duke said as he bunched dry pieces of tree debris into a pile.

"Duke," Lo'n whispered, "I get it. Don't tell Ja'a but I've also wondered what lies in that temple—and why he was so adamant about it. But this is not the time. If we can get off the land bridge without losing anyone—that would be amazing. He'j and I weren't that lucky last time."

"What do you think is in there—honestly?"

Lo'n paused. "Ja'a doesn't know this about her father but he didn't trust many. He trusted Mo'a, me, his late wife —but that's about it. There could be something in there that's really powerful but which he felt could complicate the situation if it fell into the wrong hands."

"So maybe another Orb? Or a counter-Orb?"

"Possibly. I think if it was an indestructible creature that was to be left undisturbed—he would have told us. I think if it was a set of traps—"

"Which is what you originally said," interrupted Duke.

"Yes, if it was a set of traps, He'j probably would have told us. So, the fact that he wasn't open about it—even with his trust issues—leads me to believe it could be something more complex."

"Something that if not discussed in the proper context could be misconstrued or manipulated."

"Exactly."

"Like another Orb!"

"Well—"

"Well, I guess it doesn't matter. I'm not going to betray Ja'a."

"You must really like her, Duke."

"She's not too shabby. For a Neprian," said Duke. "And I do respect her. Anyways, I appreciated the chat, Lo'n."

"Who has first watch?" shouted Ja'a as she drove another pike into the ground. Duke and Lo'n exchanged looks, ending their clandestine conversation.

"We do!" Duke replied, raising his hand.

"I'm not so sure that's the best idea."

"You don't trust Ishiro'shea and I? When have we ever broken your trust?"

"True," Ja'a answered. "But—"

"I'll take the first watch with them," interjected Po'l. "They won't do anything stupid on my watch. Nothing more than usual, at least."

"I can live with that," replied the rebel leader.

"I'm a bit offended," returned Duke directly to Ja'a. "After all we've been through."

The commanding Neprian paid no attention to the bounty hunter's comment.

"Now let's finish our camp and hope we have an easy night ahead of us."

The dozen or so mounds of crackling fire provided ample illumination; Duke would be able to spot an encroaching swamp cannibal from a decent range. *They won't get to fifty paces from the camp before I could pick 'em off*, he thought to himself.

The night was silent—as was the swamp. No moans. No groans. No growls. Nothing resembling grotesque man-eating swamp creatures seemed to be lurking about, waiting to pounce on the sleeping Neprians. He shifted his legs and backside upon his rock seat and tipped up the brim of his hat. He twirled his sidearm by the trigger guard.

"So, looks like we might make it outta here without running into those flesh-gobblers."

"It's still early, off-worlder," replied Po'l. "I think you should probably be more on guard, like your talkative friend."

Ishiro'shea had his katana unsheathed as he crouched behind a row of pikes.

"He's somewhat of a worry wart."

"You aren't worried at all?"

"Nah, I think we'll be alright. With me, Ishiro, Ol' Betsy, Lo'n, and this guy here," Duke said, twirling his laser revolver with even more pizzazz, "we can take care of anything."

"You know there are a few more of us here, too."

"Yeah, we'll be fine despite that."

To Duke's surprise, Po'l chuckled. *Has he finally snapped?*

"You know what—that was a solid joke. I'll give the devil his due."

Po'l extended his hand and Duke reluctantly shook it.

"How much longer do we have in this shift, you think?" asked the Nova Texan, not expecting an answer. He stood up and walked around the perimeter.

"Everything okay?"

"Outside of losing the battle to boredom, I'm just peachy. It's been a weird day."

"Because Ja'a got pretty annoyed at you? That was quite amusing. She made you look like a scolded child. Actually, Uu'k would've put up more of a fight than you," Po'l said with a grin.

"Hey, watch it. That's big talk coming from a guy that got beat up by an inanimate object."

"Not my brightest moment."

"I hope not."

"But back to today," Po'l said in a more serious tone, and at a lower decibel level. "Do you really think there's something in the temple?"

"No need to start it up again. I'm done talking about that. I said my piece and Ja'a—"

"Shut you up."

"Kinda. She was furious."

"Seriously, do you think there's something in there?"

"No... yeah... yes, probably... maybe... I don't know."

"Was that a yes or a no?"

"Honestly?"

"Yes, honestly."

"I can't believe I'm telling you, of all people, this—but I do think it's a little strange about how cryptic Ja'a's dad was about the whole 'Don't go in there no matter what' mumbo jumbo. If it was that bad, wouldn't you tell someone so they would definitely know to avoid it? I would. So yeah, if you twisted my arm, I think there's something in there."

"I see."

"But no matter what it is, it's not worth angering Ja'a again."

"I agree with you."

Duke sat back down and leaned over until his nose was almost touching Po'l's.

"Say what?"

"I agree with you. I think there's something powerful and dangerous and potentially useful in that temple. I bet it's the same reason the cannibals don't go near it."

"You agree with me?"

"I don't know if there's another Orb as you suspect—but a system of booby traps doesn't seem like something that would keep away flesh-craving sub-Neprians for ages."

"Exactly, right?" exclaimed Duke. "The story doesn't jive."

It was as if Duke's past quarrels with Po'l were distant memories; he spoke in a voice befitting a lifelong friendship.

"Not at all," Po'l concurred.

A moment later, the bounty hunter spasmed as he caught himself in his own excitement—his body unconsciously rejecting Po'l's agreeable tones.

"Nope. Never mind. Not going to do it."

"What if—"

"Stop, don't want to hear it. Not gonna do it. No way."

Ishiro'shea must have overheard, which was hardly surprising given the quietness of their watch. He walked over and glared at his longtime friend. *He must know when I'm about to do something stupid*, thought Duke.

"Hear me out, Duke," Po'l pleaded. "Everyone here is asleep. We can all make a quick dash in and take a look around. If there's something in there, we can take it—or leave it—"

"Or kill it."

The bounty hunter started to squirm; he *wanted* to side with Po'l. *Why is this so difficult?*

"We do have to chance the fact that there aren't any traps—at least traps that we can't overcome," Po'l continued. "But I'm willing to risk it. If there's something that can help us out against Orbius, I'm willing to die for it. I know it's against Ja'a's wishes, but it's worth the sacrifice. Lo'n is in agreement as well. He told me."

Ishiro'shea was shaking his head and pointing at the sleeping rebels.

"Oh yeah, good call, Ishiro. Who's gonna stand guard in case we get attacked by the children of the oozy lagoon?"

"I didn't think of that," Po'l said. "I'm definitely going in —how about Ishiro'shea?"

"Not exactly the best alarm system if something did happen. Also, if we go missing, it might be more difficult for him to explain where we went than one of us."

"Good point. Do you want to stay?"

"I can't. If there is something in there, Betsy will want to greet 'em. And you aren't... well... qualified to handle her."

"Fair point. Never mind then. There's no way I'm not going. I have to find out what's down there."

"Listen here, Po'l, I love this new attitude—we'll need it for when we cross Orbius' path—but the only way that makes sense is for Ishiro and I to head in and you stand guard."

"I hate that. Are you sure?" asked Po'l in a pleading tone.

"Yes. Right, Ish?"

The emerald-clad ninja threw his hands in the air in what could only be construed as more than mild disagreement.

"So you're out too?" Duke asked Ishiro'shea.

The ninja silently sighed in response. *He's in.*

"Great, let's make this quick," said Duke. He turned towards Po'l. "Thanks. I appreciate this. We'll be as discreet as we are fast. In and out and we'll report back if our suspicions are correct. For the cause!"

"And your ship, right?"

"Yes, and our ship."

CHAPTER TWENTY-EIGHT

A GARDEN FERTILIZED WITH COTTON CANDY

"THIS SHOULD JUST ABOUT DO it."

Duke rammed Betsy's butt end into the temple door. The giant slab moaned and opened inward. It was completely black inside.

"Voila, little buddy. Yeah, He'j set an intricate system of traps but yet forgot to lock the front door? My ass."

Duke pushed aside the vegetation that had grown to the point of almost covering the temple entrance. He struggled with a particularly stout branch that had fallen as the door swung open.

"He could've at least cleaned up the front porch. Some help?"

Ishiro'shea removed his sword and sliced the stubborn branch into three neat pieces that dropped to the ground.

"You ready to do this?"

Ishiro'shea nodded.

"Ja'a is going to be so pissed," Duke began, "unless we bring back something of value. And she'll still probably be pretty pissed. So let's be fast, quiet, and productive."

Ishiro ignored his friend. Duke remembered that he was, after all, talking to a ninja.

Duke continued to talk, now more to himself than Ishiro'shea. "I guess if there isn't anything of value to get, we're just going to have to take it from Ja'a."

In response, Ishiro'shea grumbled.

"Fine, *I'm* going to take it from Ja'a. I'll take the heat. I'm already kinda in the doghouse."

Duke lit his makeshift torch. Ishiro'shea followed suit as the bounty hunters stepped inside the ancient dwelling.

The flames illuminated what could be best described as nothing. *Kinda anticlimactic*, thought Duke. The room was cavernous; the walls, floor, and ceiling were all constructed from goliath stone rectangles, all equal in size. There were no ornaments hanging from the walls, no furniture, no dead bodies, and no tasteful rug to pull it all together. It was empty. It was nothing. Well, basically nothing. The lone exception was on the wall opposite of the entry. One of the bricks was marked with sloppily-applied white paint streaks.

"You think that means something? Of course it does. Lift me up."

Ishiro'shea didn't budge.

"Okay, fine. I'll lift you up."

Duke knelt down and Ishiro'shea placed his thighs on the Nova Texan's shoulders, straddling his neck. Duke struggled but made it to his feet with his companion on his shoulders, as if they were about to play a game of especially demented chicken fighting.

"Make this quick!"

Ishiro'shea pressed his hands down on the top of Duke's hat to restore balance.

"Holy hedgehogs! Watch the hat!"

Duke was barely done speaking when Ishiro nimbly

vaulted up so that his feet replaced his straddled legs on the bounty hunter's shoulders. He stood completely erect; Duke grabbed his ankles for additional support, though it was likely unnecessary.

"Can you get it?"

Ishiro'shea reached out and pushed the brick. Nothing. He slapped it with a bit more force. Nothing.

"Hit it harder!" yelled Duke.

Ishiro'shea wiggled his ankles, signaling Duke to let go.

"Maybe I can shoot it?"

But Ishiro'shea sprung from Duke's shoulders and, in midair, connected with a swift kick to the direct center of the stone. He landed on the ground without the slightest of noises. The stone rattled momentarily. The wall began to slowly suck the brick inward. Sparks danced as the slab scraped against its neighbors.

"A heads-up would've been nice, Ish. You coulda dislocated a shoulder."

The rattling increased at a rapid rate—the entire wall vibrated. It sounded as if an entire truckload of chains had been dropped from a two-story building. The vibration escalated.

"This can't be good."

Clouds of dust bellowed from the ground at the base of the wall. The shaking became more intense and the wall began to ascend.

"Or it can be—amazing!" exclaimed Duke.

An entrance to a cave had been exposed. It was pretty standard as far as cave entrances went—not as ostentatious as those in Oscavia, but not as menacing as the Great Tunnels of Zyrma Chuk'nik. But it did feel ancient. And it was dark—as all good caves are. Duke stepped beyond the threshold and extended his torch.

"Nothing. I can't see a damn thing in here."

The light provided almost no help in distinguishing the depth or height of the tunnel; if his feet hadn't been firmly on the ground, Duke would have believed he was floating in the abyss of deep space. He knelt down, holding the light as close to the ground as possible.

"If He'j did set any ambushes here, we'd be goners. I haven't been in something this dark since—"

Duke broke off suddenly. He gripped Ishiro'shea's forearm.

"Hey, wait a second. You smell that? Tell me you smell that?"

There was no response from the ninja—as per the norm.

"It smells—" Duke struggled for the right word. "Pleasant?"

He released his grasp on his friend's arm.

"Like—" Duke again had difficulty coming to terms with his thoughts. "—fresh cut flowers."

Caves, on the whole, usually lived up to the stereotypes —dark, dank, musty, spooky. This one was dark, yes. Spooky, a bit. But dank and musty, it was not. Duke tilted his chin upward and expanded his nostrils as wide as possible to soak in the enjoyable fragrance. Ishiro'shea did the same, after pulling down the portion of his mask that covered his nose and mouth.

"It's like a garden that's been fertilized by cotton candy."

Duke waved the torch in front of his face, aiding his navigation from one wall of the cave to the other as he searched frantically for the source of the odor. Ishiro'shea followed suit.

Something's not right, the bounty hunter thought to himself. *It doesn't feel right. It smells right—in fact, it smells wonderful. But too wonderful.*

The two men continued to search in the darkness,

pressing their hands against the rocky corridor walls. The blaze of the torch flame barely provided enough visibility to see an arm's length in front of their noses. The darkness seemed to suppress the flame, winning the eternal battle of shadow and light. As they moved down the path, the glow from the torch became even fainter and their visibility was reduced to mere inches. Still the pair trekked on. Even though he couldn't see Ishiro'shea nor would the ninja break his vow of silence to say it, Duke knew what was going through his companion's mind: *We probably shouldn't have done this*. But Duke pressed on stubbornly. And Ishiro'shea accompanied him faithfully.

"I think we're gonna find something big like an Orb. A real game-changer. You know the story—rain and rainbows, darkness and dawns, Erontian saké and freshwater mermaids. We're gonna turn a corner and see the light at the end of tunnel."

Duke wasn't wrong. But the bounty hunters did less of turning a corner and more of falling down a steep, jagged incline—landing with a thump as they hit an equally jagged rock pit. But, on the bright side, they did see a light in the distance.

"Told you."

Duke stood up and brushed off the dust and debris from his clothes using his hat.

"We should probably check it out, right? I can feel something. Something big. I can't wait to see Ja'a and Lo'n when we come back with the saving grace of their cause. Hell, even Po'l."

The ruddy glow was only the length of a standard spacecraft from where they had fallen. It was flickering irregularly. As the two approached the source of the light, they could see it was emanating from an extremely tall archway, reaching a height equal to the entrance into Dre'en but much less welcoming. There was no door or gate. The two off-worlders entered.

"Halt!" boomed a monstrous roar. "You are trespassing on private property and holy ground."

Duke drew his laser revolver. Ishiro'shea readied his katana. The massive beast that sat before them, its legs crossed within a brightly lit chamber, didn't even pay attention to the flashing of armaments.

"Getting pretty brave, aren't you, swamp maggots? Take this—"

The gargantuan creature—as tall as four Jungafallowians and as stout as the entire Trampling Death Robots welded together into one humongous musical nightmare—thrust a glass bottle in their direction with his right hand. His other hand was firmly placed on a bulbous pump. Duke fired. The shot hit the monster's left bicep. It was as if the giant didn't even notice it. Before Duke could rattle off another pulse, the monster squeezed the pump. A cloud of pink translucence filled the room, caking Duke and Ishiro'shea in a chalky dust that smelled like... fresh-cut flowers fertilized with cotton candy.

"Did you—" Duke said between coughs, "—did you just douse us with perfume?"

"What?" bellowed the beast in a thunderous voice.

"I said, did you just spray us with perfume? I shot you—and then you make us smell better?"

"You can speak—intelligibly?" asked the monster.

Duke caught eyes with Ishiro'shea and began, "Well, I can."

"The other one, is he your pet?"

"Well—" Duke began. Ishiro'shea threw a glance as sharp as his katana back at the bounty hunter. "No, he just doesn't speak."

"But how is that you can stand this?"

The beast held up his glass holster containing an electric pink fluid.

"It's quite nice, actually."

"Oh no. I will now have to kill you and think of a new way to keep you pests out. This worked for so long," he muttered dejectedly.

"Wait, what? No. Hey, we aren't pests. Who do you think we are?"

"You come from the swamps, right?" the brute said. He finally seemed to notice his wounded arm. He placed some pressure with his hand and it seemed to stop bleeding almost immediately.

"You think we come from the swamps? No, I'm from Nova Texas. Outer space. Far, far away from this rock. Ishiro'shea here is from Earth."

"Outer space? You swamp creatures are gaining a sense of humor, I like that. Maybe next—who knows? Soufflés?"

"We are *not* from the swamp!"

"You seem pretty annoying—which is a trait of the people in the swamp."

"Yes, but we don't have the most important trait."

"And what is that, swampy?"

"I don't know—how about living in a swamp?"

The giant laughed and the vibrations shook the walls. He placed the perfume canister down gently and then stood up. His muscular frame filled the entire space of the room. His skin was a muted orange and he wore no clothes outside of a strategically placed loincloth made of a furry substance. Duke did not want to find out how he came across this piece of clothing—nor how long he had been wearing it. Bulky gauntlets adorned his wrists and ankles.

"Before I kill you, can you at least tell me what compelled you to explore my home? Call it basic curiosity. To be honest, I haven't seen one of your types in a while."

In the full light, Duke could see that the monster had two large lower canines that extended beyond his lip so that when he spoke, Duke thought he was going to put his own eyes out.

"Okay, first off, we aren't from the swamp. We came here to look for something."

"What exactly is it that you are seeking?"

"I'm not entirely sure."

"Not very convincing, swamp man."

"See, there's a war going on. We're trying to help the southern Neprians take out this guy named Ot Vangu."

"A war going on? Outside my home? I haven't heard any troops or battles or anything of the sort. I think you're making this up, pond dweller."

"Enough with the names, alright? I'm telling you the truth. We are camping out here, next to the swamp—"

"Swamp! I knew it," the giant roared and reached for a wooden club to his right. He raised it.

Duke grabbed Betsy from his back and uncorked a frustration-filled load. The club splintered and fell limply to the floor. The echo from the explosion drove a stake directly into Duke's eardrum.

"Hey, that's a neat gadget. What do you call it?"

"Her name is Betsy," Duke screamed, still trying to regain his hearing.

"I like Betsy. And I don't think a swamp man would have a toy like that."

"You finally believe me?"

"Trial period. But tell me again—why are you in my lair?"

"Look, Mr. Giant—wait, what's your name?"

"Let me think about that. No one has asked me in so many cycles—I'm not exactly sure." The behemoth looked a bit embarrassed. He then snapped back and said in a proud belt, "They used to call me the Keeper."

"The Keeper of what?"

"Of the Sphere of Power."

Duke and the ninja exchanged glances.

"A sphere?"

"Yes."

"Of power?"

"Yes, that's what I said, you odd little thing."

"So, it's an orb?"

"Sure, if you want to call it that. It's around here somewhere."

The Keeper turned and began to rummage around the floor of his lair. Bottles of his potent perfume, bulky canisters, and odds and ends—all of an ancient patina—were tossed and hurled in the air. Clinks and clanks echoed throughout the chamber.

"Nothing of value, it seems. A bunch of junk. Most of it's that mustangsen garbage," Duke said to Ishiro'shea.

Ishiro'shea narrowly avoided being impaled by what could only be described as a hat stand for someone with a cranium the size of a galactic Winnebago and a deeply-rooted affinity for headwear.

"Ish, are you hearing what I'm hearing?" the bounty hunter asked, dodging a gravy boat hurled at a hazardous velocity. "I knew there was another Orb! Oh man, the looks on their faces. I can't wait. Can't believe they doubted our hunch."

"Where could it be now?" the Keeper mumbled to himself.

"Let us help," the bounty hunter said. "How about we look over here?"

"No, it's not over there."

"Are you sure?"

"Yes."

"How about over here?"

Duke and Ishiro'shea ascended a dozen steps that led to a platform full of another hodgepodge of useless objects. They began to dig through the heap of artifacts.

"Be careful. Some of those are pretty important."

"To who?"

"I can't remember, to be honest, but I know they're pretty darn important."

Duke and Ishiro'shea continued to discard the items at a rapid pace and with a blatant disregard for the preservation of the artifacts.

"Okay, no spheres, orbs, or balls—or anything that could be misconstrued as roundish in nature—up here. Just a bunch of knickknacks."

Duke kicked the mound. Items spilled over and hit the floor with ringing clanks.

"When's the last time you saw it?" he asked.

"I don't know. It's hard to keep track of time in this place."

"All of this junk and not a single clock to be found," Duke muttered to himself.

"Was it before or after you gave the other sphere to He'j and Jilarian Togg?"

The Keeper halted mid-toss. He looked perplexed.

"What other sphere? And who's Hodge and Jilarpian Targ?"

"Seriously, big guy? The two dudes that borrowed the first sphere. You know, to save the planet and all that."

The Keeper began to laugh. "Oh, I get it, a joke to lighten the mood! Very funny. Next you're going to tell me that they make a toilet compatible for over eighty species. I haven't laughed like this in a good while."

Duke and Ishiro'shea did not laugh. It was a few

moments before the Keeper realized. His hooting ceased abruptly.

"You're aren't serious—are you?"

"Dead, unfortunately. They came here not too long ago —maybe a few cycles back—and borrowed the Orb. I mean the Sphere of Power."

"Not to my knowledge, they didn't."

"That's what I was afraid of," Duke said in a dejected tone.

"What?"

"I think you might have been robbed."

The Keeper let out an audible sigh and plopped down, legs crossed, causing a slight tremor in the room.

"Not again," he said.

Duke and Ishiro'shea slapped their foreheads with the palms of their hands in unison.

"I'm slightly afraid to ask—but what do you mean, 'not again'?"

"Sit down, my diminutive pals."

"It's that bad?"

"Afraid so," huffed the monster. "I am the Keeper of the Sphere of Power—a job that I take very seriously."

"Uh-huh." Duke expected the worst.

"But it's a job that I might not have been the best choice for. I'm a mover and shaker, deep down. I want to be out there—you know, doing stuff."

Ishiro'shea proceeded to sit down and prepared himself for a lengthy yarn. Duke followed suit, albeit less gracefully.

"Did you know that I was once an artist?"

"Considering we literally stumbled upon you a few minutes ago... No, we weren't aware of that amazing piece of trivia."

"I was. I dabbled in a lot of media—I liked mixed media; some found objects here, some painting there, maybe even a touch of sculpting. I was quite good. Had a few retrospectives at the local museum, way back when."

The bounty hunters had no response to the rambling biography, but Duke tried. "Not to interrupt what I'm sure is a fascinating trip down memory lane, but we have to get back to our friends soon—so we would appreciate getting back on track."

"Right, of course," apologized the beast. "So, I wasn't the best for the job. But, as the only remaining member of my race—really, of any race from the time of my people—I felt it was my duty to prevent the same calamity that ended our reign on this planet. Then, there were these two creatures that came in—two distinct races, it seemed—"

"Whoa, stop! What two races?"

"See, my new friends, my time on this planet goes back to when the mountains were but pebbles and the seas mere puddles of rain. When the—"

"We get it," Duke said cutting him off, "you're old and have been here a long time. Continue."

"Right. But even before that, my race cultivated this planet and built a society of caring and prosperity and progress—and, eventually, exquisite art. Did I mention my retrospective?"

"Yes."

"One day—and I'm not sure where or who or when—but one day, our people discovered the Sphere of Power. It allowed us to do things that we never could before. It helped us clear mountains for roads and save villages riddled with disease and grow the best ploob kalarti for our festivals. It was all-powerful."

"And then what?"

"Like all things that grant you power without having to earn it, it corrupted the minds of my people. Cycles turned into hundreds of cycles and into millennia. Control of the

Sphere bounced from one tribe to another. Death and madness permeated the land. Eventually, we assembled into two tribes and the war raged on. Near the end, the two factions didn't even resemble each other—the sphere had manipulated our minds and altered our physical appearances. Even I have been affected—my current state does not reflect how we once were. But we battled our former brothers, now heinous and ghastly and terrorizing the skies on the backs of demons. We were shorter but stronger and hurled boulders at them as they swooped down to skewer us with fire-covered spears."

"Near the end, you say? What happened?"

"The races destroyed each other. Death prevailed. Unharnessed power rendered the powerful powerless." The Keeper took a deep breath and a solemn expression erased his earlier scowl. "And left in this wasteland was myself, my house, and the Sphere."

"How did you survive?"

"Not really sure, to be honest. When the weather started to change and chaos seemed to replace normalcy, I retreated here and remained for cycles. Eventually, I returned to the surface and there was nothing. As I started to explore... there, in an open field, was the Sphere. Needless to say, I decided to take it—it's not like *more* harm could be done. I think part of me thought I could control it."

"And I guess the story ends with the fact that you couldn't?"

"Actually, no. I took it home and it responded to me. Right away. I sat right here, where we are now, for ages, trying to better control it. Become one with this power that eradicated my entire family, my entire race. It didn't seem inherently evil—and I didn't feel evil as I bonded with it. I definitely didn't feel like going out and starting a war even if there had been someone to start a war with.

"Ages passed as the arrow of time points in but one direction—memories of my people, the festivals, and even my art retrospective became very distant."

"Obviously, not too distant," Duke chimed in.

"Not *too* distant, no, but they started to feel like a dream. I must have been with the Sphere for a thousand cycles—or two or ten—when I was startled by a simple knock on the outside of my house. It was a duo of odd-looking creatures—about your size—the first living creatures that I had seen in many cycles. Needless to say, they assumed that I was a monster and lobbed pointy objects at me. I finally settled them down and invited them in. We talked for hours. They explained that their people had been the original race on the planet—of course, I chuckled and politely corrected them. I didn't want to say it, but I think they evolved from the parasites that survived the wars. I told them about the Sphere and the history of the planet—they seemed particularly interested in the Sphere, almost mesmerized."

"Let me guess what happens next—they stole the Sphere?"

"That predictable, huh?"

"I had a feeling."

"I'm not sure what exactly happened after that, but sometime later two different people from these two races came to me. This time they had the Sphere with them and asked me to keep it with me forever. They said it was the only way to prevent their races from killing each other—I could sympathize with that, and wished my people would have thought of it. They offered to guard my home, even send soldiers to protect it. I appreciated the gesture but, as you can see, I could've defended it myself in battle. I let them 'guard' me."

"They also blocked off the entire land bridge that

242

connects the northern land mass from the south," added Duke. "You've been isolated here for another thousand cycles. Just you and this swamp—and the swamp people that have evolved from whatever was left here when they blocked off the bridge."

"And now someone stole it out from under my nose—again. I wonder who—and why?"

"It was the same race that gave it back to you for safe keeping. They are called Neprians."

"Why would they do that?"

"To save the planet. They were experiencing a great drought and famine—and entire villages were being wiped out."

"That's rich," smirked the Keeper. "It took me countless ages to be able to control it—as much as it would let me—and they think they're just going to summon it to do their bidding? It's just going to start to glow and then prepare a fancy dinner for everyone?"

The Keeper was visibly upset. "I wonder why they didn't just ask me? Probably knew I would just say no."

"Probably. And it's probably a bit difficult to explain to the masses that a giant monster has been watching their precious Orb for countless ages. Even a bunch as gullible as these Neprians."

"True," the Keeper continued, "but I wish I could have told them about its true power. It has a mind of its own. If it winds up in the hands of someone evil, it will be an instrument of death and annihilation."

"Yep, already there, big guy. They asked it to help with their crops and it brought a being from across the universe that could make the crops grow again. He fulfilled his job—but, instead of leaving, he became consumed with learning how to control it. The people of the North became his army and he enslaved those in the South that resisted."

"What is his name?"

"He goes by Orbius."

"Not very original."

"Agreed."

"Sounds like he probably could've taken over this lot without the Sphere."

"Agreed, again."

"So, can he control it?"

"From what we hear—yes."

"And how do you fit into this story, my new friends? Since you are not from this planet of Neprius, as you call it."

"A bit of bad luck. Orbius' tinkering led to the Sphere sending an astral portal near our neck of the woods—and we happened to get consumed by it. Because of his unchecked insanity with this magic rock, I'm stuck here instead of enjoying some Glyptodian Summer Ale at Cyborg Joe's."

Ishiro'shea perked up at the mention of Glyptodian Summer Ale.

"I see. And you aim to help these Neprians defeat Orbius."

"And get our ship back."

"Ah yes, I assumed there was something else too. Needless to say, it is imperative that you bring it back soon. Otherwise, this Orbius will destroy Neprius—whether he means to or not."

"No offense, Keeper, but you've lost it twice now. Not sure if bringing it back makes a ton of sense. Is there a way to destroy it?"

"Destroy the Sphere of Power? It is without a doubt indestructible, my spacefaring comrades." The Keeper seemed a bit miffed at the question, and their lack of faith in his "keeping" abilities.

"Okay, so we'll get it and bring it back to you."

Duke glanced over at Ishiro'shea. *Unless we figure out something better.*

"I promise I won't lose it this time."

"Great."

"Let me see if there's anything that can help you in your attempt," the Keeper said as he picked through his mound of decorative homeware and miscellaneous décor. "You probably don't need a spatula, do you?"

"I doubt it. How about a bottle of your perfume? A smaller bottle, of course. We have a trick that we want to play on a friend of ours that doesn't bathe as often as he should."

"Not a problem, take two."

Duke snatched a pair of ornate glass containers and affixed them to his belt.

"Many thanks, Keeper. I hope we see you again soon."

"If not," the Keeper replied, "I fear the planet will be no more."

CHAPTER TWENTY-NINE

FIGHTING THE SWAMP

"GUYS, YOU WON'T BELIEVE WHAT we just—" the bounty hunter shouted. Then, immediately, he froze. Ishiro'shea followed suit.

Their campground was unrecognizable, turned into a warzone infested by proto-humans covered in leaves and mud and moss; sluggish and lumbering. Their gaseous body odor was so putrid and thick that it appeared as an opaque cloud of green above their heads. Their ghastly faces were reminiscent of the Melted Skin art movement made popular by Treglor of Phleg-Mem—especially the early cycles. It was clear that the swamp people of the land bridge were not scared of the temple or, at least, anyone camped in its shadows—and they appeared to be pissed off.

Duke and Ishiro'shea hustled down an incline towards the scuffle. Duke immediately rattled off a few pulses, striking three creatures squarely in their heads. All fell to the muddy bank with a squish.

Duke pivoted sharply at the feeling of a moist, cold weight on his left shoulder. His eyes locked with the swamp being—but only one eye returned the gaze. The beast's other eye socket was not where it should have been—it sat squarely in the middle of his left cheek as if it had slowly migrated southward. The grotesque appearance immobilized Duke.

"Gross."

The cannibal opened his mouth to reveal mangled, mud-colored teeth sharpened to fine points. The stench was unbearable. He lunged at Duke as he clamped down his jaws; his ferocious bite snapped mere inches from Duke's right ear. The bounty hunter shook himself out of his trance and threw a right jab to the monster's face. It pushed the cannibal back a few paces but didn't seem to do any harm. Duke swung again and connected to the stomach region. This had even less effect. The cannibal reached out with both arms and grasped Duke by the neck. He proceeded to lift the Nova Texan in the air; Duke hung on to the creature's wrists to slow down the choking process. A swift gust of wind passed Duke's face and he fell to the ground. Landing right next to him was a rotted, pock-marked appendage. He looked up. The monster was without his right arm.

"Thanks, buddy."

Ishiro gave a quick nod toward the cannibal, who was seemingly unaware that he lost his arm but very aware that he lost his prey.

"Tough bastard," Duke muttered as he lifted himself onto one knee. He spun his laser revolver out of his holster and let loose two shots into the belly of the beast, who dropped to the ground with a groan.

Ishiro'shea was slicing and dicing his way to the center of the camp; Duke was blasting and punching a parallel path to the same destination. A few short moments of carnage led them to the pikes that they had placed as a temporary fence.

"Can you let us in, Ja'a?"

"And take down our last line of defense?" interjected Po'l. "Are you serious?"

"You're going to leave us out here to die?"

"If that's what's necessary."

Ja'a barked orders at Ma'n and Te'o; they dropped their bows and ran to the perimeter of the fence where Duke and Ishiro stood fighting off encroaching mutants. Ma'n hoisted his ax above his head and crashed it down upon the base of a pike. It crumpled to the ground. He repeated this two more times, creating a space large enough for the two off-worlders to enter the safety of the camp. However, it was also big enough for swamp cannibals to follow them in.

"Thanks, Ja'a," yelled Duke. "I knew you wouldn't—"

"No more talking. Simply, no more. You left us out in a bad place, Duke. Your fun adventure left us without a lookout and much needed support."

"Wait, Po'l said he would look—"

"Don't blame this on Po'l. He's been asleep in the camp ever since you went on lookout," Ja'a said. She sent off two arrows into the mass of swampfolk in rapid succession. "You and Ishiro'shea were on duty... and now—this!"

Po'l, you little rat.

"Can you believe that, Ishiro?" Duke asked as he dropped five more raiders. "I thought these guys were scared of the temple?"

"It appears that I was wrong," replied Lo'n.

"No kidding," retorted Duke.

"I promise you, Duke, the last time that I was here—with He'j—we figured that the temple held some sort of power over them. We used it as a shield."

"Maybe they saw you in the temple and realized that it couldn't be that bad if *you* would go in," interjected Po'l.

"Thanks for screwing us over, Po'l. And I thought we turned a corner. We need to have a chat one of these days."

The moans of the approaching monstrosities continued to escalate. Their numbers appeared to be multiplying, with more emerging from the murky river all the time.

"We're running short on arrows," shouted Ty'n from the far end of the camp. He dropped his bow and pulled out his duo of daggers. He began to jab and poke at any body part, or anything that resembled a body part, that made it through the openings between the sharpened fence posts.

"Same here," shouted Te'o. "Need some help now!"

A section of three pikes parted and a steady stream of cannibals were poised to enter the inner confines of the camp.

"No you don't!" shouted Lo'n. He sprang from another part of the perimeter and swung his saber down on the torsos of the first monsters to penetrate the fence. He swung his oversized blade at the mutant force with elegant aggression.

"Impressive," Duke said in between shots. "You starting to feel a bit jealous *now*, Ish?"

The ninja ignored his companion and continued to keep the horde at bay with his own nifty swordsmanship.

"Duke, I could use you right now," Lo'n shouted. The numbers appeared to be getting the best of him.

"We need help over here now," cried Po'l.

"Breach! Breach!" bellowed Bu'r.

"Over here, too!" screamed Ma'n.

"Not to be a backseat general, Ja'a, but I'm not sure how much longer we can hold out. Two of these bastards are coming in for each one I send to his maker."

"Duke's right," Lo'n confirmed. "What's the plan?"

More portions of the fence were rendered useless as the

cannibals swarmed the campsite. Ja'a did not offer a response.

"I can't hold them much longer," groaned Lo'n as he cleaved off two of the creatures' heads in one swing. "Ja'a?"

"We need to leave the swamp," Ja'a exclaimed.

"I think we're aware of that," Duke countered.

"Everyone, fall back. Over here, near the fire. Duke—give us as much cover as you can."

"Yes, ma'am," he shouted. He unleashed a rapid-fire salvo from his laser revolver as he walked backward toward the group.

"What's the plan, Ja'a?" asked Po'l urgently.

"Grab your weapons—as many as you can carry but won't slow you down," Ja'a shouted, calmly and with confidence. *Much different than Shud'nut,* thought Duke.

"Everyone good?"

After a smattering of affirmations, Ja'a continued. "We're going to break through their ranks and head north through the swamp, along the bank. We're going to run until we hit the wall. I know it's going to be challenging—but it's our best bet to get out of here."

"Is this even possible?" asked Bu'r.

"It's possible," confirmed Lo'n. "That's the path that we were going to take anyways, the same one He'j and I followed—now we will just do it a bit faster. And at night."

"Great. Not to be a downer but how are we going to break—"

"When I say 'now,' stop firing," Ja'a said, interrupting the bounty hunter as if he'd never started speaking, "I will cover you as you get Betsy ready. Fire her into the north part of their lines. It should give us an opening—then we fight our way through until we get behind them. Then run."

Never going to work.

"Let's go!" shouted Ma'n.

"Alright!" screamed Po'l.

"Great plan, Ja'a. Your father would be proud," Lo'n added.

Idiots.

"Stop, Duke."

He holstered his laser revolver and removed Betsy from his back. The encroaching mass continued to advance. Ja'a released two arrows that struck the two closest cannibals in the middle of their faces, dropping them instantly. She grabbed a handful of arrows and reloaded her quiver.

Betsy roared.

An entire section of swamp cannibals collapsed.

Betsy roared again.

More toppled over each other.

"Fight until you're out the other side. Then run north to the first clearing."

The Neprian rebels charged in, Lo'n leading the group.

"Stay between us, Ja'a," shouted Ma'n and Te'o as they surrounded her with their axes. "Your bow won't be much use in this scrum."

Duke stored away Betsy and retrieved his revolver. He followed Ishiro'shea into the smoke-filled clearing. Rapidly, he volleyed off pulses at anything with a feculent odor. The sounds of his comrades' voices were drowned out by the sounds of limbs being severed or blown off and splashing into the gloomy waters. He hoped the limbs didn't belong to any of those comrades. The cannibals screamed and moaned but Duke wasn't sure if that was from dismemberment or just their general disposition. He didn't want to wait around and find out.

"Duke, you're the last through," Ja'a screamed from a clearing ahead, alongside the bank of the swamp. "You, Ishiro'shea, and Ty'n need to make a break for it!"

"Don't need to tell us twice!" Duke pivoted and ran, a

few paces behind his much speedier ninja companion. He turned to his left, "Hey Ty'n, don't run so close to the swamp—that's where—"

Out of the corner of his eyes, Duke saw the cannibal leap from the water and grab Ty'n's ankles. The Neprian rebel hit the ground and rolled onto his back. The monster dived on top of Ty'n in an attempt to smother him—but he received a dagger in the throat.

"Get up!" shouted Po'l from up ahead. "They're heading towards us."

Duke stopped and dropped two more of the cannibals that were closing in on Ty'n. He made his way out from under the deceased creature and started to head to rejoin the team.

He increased his pace to a full sprint—partly to get away from hundreds of flesh-craving aberrations, partly to beat Ishiro'shea.

"Okay, made it. What are we waiting on?" Duke huffed.

Bu'r pushed Duke aside and charged back into the oncoming horde.

Ty'n was back on the ground again. Two more cannibals halfway submerged in the swamp held his legs down. One had a dagger in the forehead but still appeared to be keeping the rebel at bay. Before Duke could blink, one dove on top of Ty'n. Then another. And another.

Ty'n was no longer visible.

Duke went to fire his gun, but halted.

"Bu'r, come back here," screamed Lo'n. "It's too late. You're going to get killed!"

Bu'r swung his mace at the pile of swampfolk covering Ty'n's body. He knocked down two at a time—but he made no gains. His face was red but his eyes were focused. He killed more cannibals in that burst than he had the entire day. But they kept coming.

"Die! Die! Ty'n, can you hear me? Die!" Bu'r cried, still swinging.

"We don't have long before we're back in the same situation that we were in a few moments ago," Lo'n reminded Ja'a.

"Somebody has to get Bu'r, right?" asked Te'o.

Duke began to fire his revolver at the massive blob of mutants. He picked his march up to a jog.

He looked back at the rebels and screamed, "Holy hedgehogs, are you morons? Run!"

"But Duke?" shouted Po'l.

"Run! Damnit, run!"

Duke heard the splashing of puddles and the squishing of mud against boot soles. It became distant and faint very quickly.

Duke was now behind Bu'r.

"It's time to go back," Duke said calmly in between shots from his revolver. "Nothing you can do here, nothing you could've done."

The barrel-chested Neprian did not respond. He just kept bashing and clubbing. Cannibals fell to the left and right of him. But they kept coming.

"Ty'n wanted to free his people. You can't help him when you're dead."

"Ty'n's not dead!" shouted Bu'r, his eyes red and wet.

"Bu'r, he's dead!" Duke countered as he pushed back cannibals with more pulses.

"Leave me alone! Go! Let me fight!"

"You're letting down Ty'n. You're letting down Shud'nut. You're letting down everyone. Don't be selfish."

Bu'r let out a deep roar and swung his club in an elongated looping motion, crushing four skulls in the process.

He turned to look at Duke. Pain riddled his gaze. Tears

253

covered his upper cheeks. His stare said it all. He knew it was time to go.

"For Ty'n." Bu'r started to sprint north.

"About damn time," Duke said to himself as he followed Bu'r into the deeper part of the swamp.

After a lengthy sprint, Duke could finally see the rest of the party up ahead. They were all sitting around a twisted tree, breathing heavily.

"I'm sorry, Bu'r," began Ja'a in a soothing tone before the distraught Neprian had any time to catch his breath. She placed her hand on his shoulder. They stared into each other's eyes for a moment, then the husky Neprian sank to his knees. He wept loudly.

"Ty'n fought valiantly. Your friend will be remembered with great reverence. Be proud of that, Bu'r."

"That skinny bastard wasn't supposed to die like that," Bu'r cried. "He deserved better. It's my fault."

"Enough. You've seen great men and women die for the cause—and innocent people, too. Ty'n knew the risks and he wanted to make a difference. We need you alive to make sure that we *do* make a difference. Do you understand me?" Ja'a's tone grew more unapologetic, more direct. "We will honor him by ridding Neprius of Orbius and his rule. We can't do that without your help."

"Yeah, I've never seen an ass-whuppin' like you put on those guys back there," Duke added. "Quite impressive, if you ask me."

Bu'r looked up at the off-worlder. He wiped the tears from his cheeks.

"Thank you, Duke."

Lo'n stepped in front of the bounty hunter and nodded at Ja'a.

"I know we've been through a lot, but I must urge us to press on. And fast. They won't stop following us. What they lack in foot speed, they make up for in perseverance."

"We don't have to make it through the swamp—just until daylight. They won't chase us in daylight. And that's fast approaching," Ja'a clarified.

"Exactly. We need to put as much distance between us and them—and when the sun comes out, they'll return to the swamp."

"Let's hope we don't have another 'They won't come near the temple' moment again."

"I couldn't agree with you more, Duke."

The morning light began to peek through the clouds above the land bridge—and, thankfully for Duke, it was only a short run. Traversing an entire alien continent—no matter how small—by foot was pushing his limits to begin with; having to run a marathon at the midway point was not his idea of a good time. *Still, the swampy atmosphere of the land bridge was preferable to the cleanliness of Dre'en,* he thought.

"Much better," Ja'a said as she stared up at the rays of light. "We should take some much-needed rest before night falls again."

Cheers erupted from the group—especially Duke. The northward march continued along the tributary; all members made sure to keep their distance from the water to ensure that Ty'n's fate wouldn't be replicated.

"How are we doing, Lo'n? We should be close, right? Does this look familiar?"

He did not respond.

"Lo'n?" asked Po'l again.

"I'm not sure. We followed the swamp until it hit the wall—that's what I remember. But this vegetation—"

"Yes?"

"I don't recall seeing it."

"Great!" shouted Po'l as he threw his hands in the air.

"Everyone stop for a second," Ja'a commanded, "and let's give Lo'n a chance to collect his thoughts. You followed the river to the wall, right? And we've been doing that."

"I'm sorry, but this doesn't seem right. In our haste fleeing from the cannibals—I think we might have gone down a different path than the one He'j and I took."

"But we *are* heading north, right?" asked Ma'n, looking up at the sky.

"Yes."

"That's good at least," said Po'l. "I say we just push on north. Right, Ja'a?"

"I'm sure there's more than one way to get to the wall," added Te'o.

"Yes, but I don't know what lies in front of us down *that* path."

"How close are we?" asked Duke. "Approximately."

"I really don't know."

"We couldn't have steered off course too much. I mean, it wasn't that long of a jog."

"I tend to agree with Duke," said Ja'a. "Chin up, Uncle Lo'n. Whatever is ahead of us, we can handle."

"I'm more worried about what's behind us," chimed Duke.

"So, does that mean we are on the march again?" asked Po'l. "Or can we rest?"

"I think we should push on—just in case we are farther away than I remember."

"I agree," said Ja'a.

Her statement was met with grousing from the group.

"Are you sure?" asked Po'l in a pleading tone. "It's been a pretty taxing trip. Between the sneak attack and Ty'n—"

"Ja'a's right," interjected Bu'r, surprising everyone.

"Are you sure you can continue?" asked Po'l. "You've had a worse day than any of us."

"I think we should go. While it's light outside. I don't want anything else to happen to us."

Ja'a smiled back at Bu'r. He blushed and returned a nod. On that exchange, the entire group picked up their weapons and started to jog northward—but stopped as they approached the gargantuan patch of foliage that first alerted Lo'n that they weren't on the same path as he had previously trekked.

"Left or right?"

"I guess I should make that call, huh?" answered Lo'n. He pointed his saber to the left.

"Sounds good to me," added Duke.

And the group was on the move again.

"So far, so good, huh?"

"Seems that way," replied Lo'n.

"I would consider getting out of the swamp to be good," smirked Po'l.

"I don't disagree with Po'l," added Ja'a. "Lo'n, any feeling on how much longer?"

"I'm sorry. I don't know. But it can't be much farther to the wall. At least I don't think so."

"We do have daylight on our side," said Ma'n, clearly searching for a silver lining.

"I'm afraid that might not be the case."

At Ja'a's statement, the group halted immediately. She pointed ahead of them. To their left remained the ever-present swamp; to the right, the thick dense forest. The light pierced through the sparse canopy overhead, illuminating their path. However, the road seemed to end. The forest and swamp merged together with only humps of solid ground peeking up from the fetid muck as if they were tiny islands amidst a great sea. Even worse, the canopy's coverage became much less sparse—in fact, it became a shield against the sun's rays. They would have to enter a realm of pure darkness during the middle of the day.

"Weapons out. Let's light some torches. Only enough to see," Ja'a barked. The team followed her commands promptly—even Duke.

"Surely there's another way," muttered Te'o.

"We don't have time to turn around and try another path. We push on."

They picked up the pace as they entered the swampy forest. The last few shafts of light petered out as the water began to cover more and more of the muddy terrain. Even the trees seemed to become more twisted and sinister. The concentration of the odor increased—the smell of death and rot was so potent, Duke felt it might crush his lungs. His eyes stung.

The rebels hopscotched from dry patch to dry patch, trying to avoid watery missteps. They didn't want to find out what the noise from an echoing splash might waken. They had already lost one valuable team member to this swamp. Losing another was not part of the plan.

"This isn't getting any less spooky."

"Scared, Duke?"

"No, Po'l, but—"

Ja'a silenced them with a simple shush.

"Stop," she whispered. "Be alert."

"Holy hedgehogs," Duke said, mimicking Ja'a"s whisper.

Eyes appeared within the foliage along their right flank. Then subtle gurgles. The limbs of the dying trees rattled.

Heads started to bob out of the swamp in front of them, behind them, all around them.

"We're surrounded."

The swampfolk started to mobilize on their right—the others held steady.

"This isn't some primitive brawl. They're coordinated," noted Duke.

"Hold still, keep your weapons drawn," commanded Ja'a. "If we move, we go in one direction—straight ahead and try and outpace them."

"The water is going to slow us down—it won't be a simple footrace like before," corrected Lo'n.

"It's our best bet."

Lo'n concurred with a look of defeat.

"Look, they're moving. Over there," said Ja'a.

The swamp creatures on the right flank parted to allow other creatures to advance towards the rebels. These two mutants carried torches and what appeared to be clubs rendered from the sturdy swamp trees. However, these fire-bearing swamp men stopped well before the group.

"Guards," said Duke.

"Of what?" asked Po'l.

"Him."

Emerging from behind the line of cannibals was a creature nearly two heads taller than the largest mutant that they had fought off. He was draped in a cloak of mud and leaves and barbed branches. Moss seemed to cover his entire cranium, dripping down from his forehead and over his eyes. Glimmers of mustard-colored eyes peeked through. It was if he was a living extension of the swamp itself. It was clear that he was the Alpha King of the Swamp.

He stared directly at Duke. It was as if he knew that Duke was not like the others. He then raised his hand above his head and closed it, clenching his fist.

The arrow that Ja'a loosed was swift and struck the Alpha King squarely in his wrist. It did not exit the mutant; he looked at the arrow resting lifelessly in his flesh. He then pulled it through his body slowly. The King roared with laughter.

"He means business," said Duke.

The King dropped his arm and the legions of quasi-humans screamed and grunted in unison. They charged. Duke's first pulses didn't make it to the King, clipping the guards instead.

"Run, everyone!"

Ja'a made it only a few paces before she encountered an impenetrable roadblock of mutant cannibals.

"Looks like another dogfight. You ready, Ish?"

The ninja nodded back at his companion.

The mutants closed in.

"Or maybe not," said Duke slyly. He pushed Ma'n and Te'o aside and proceeded to the front of the line. He put away his revolver.

"Little buddy, if this doesn't work and you get out of here—tell the Queen that she owes you a few drinks."

The Nova Texan strutted to the barrier of swampfolk nonchalantly, sporting a nervous grin.

"So," he started. "Someone told me that you might want to try a free sample of our latest fragrance."

The monsters returned blank stares.

"He's lost it," chimed in Po'l.

Duke grabbed the perfume bottle and sprayed a few puffs in the general vicinity of the beasts. They paused—then let out glass-breaking shrieks of agony. Many fell immediately to the ground and contorted in pain. Others dove back in the swamp. However, this clearly angered the other mutants surrounding them but out of the radius of the perfume spray. They pushed on.

"Okay, you can go now," Duke said to the group. He sprayed more perfume, clearing a way for the rest of the party.

Almost out.

"They're still coming," shouted Lo'n.

"You'll need to run faster, then."

The King himself was now approaching the group, keeping pace—it was clear that he knew how to traverse the shallow waters better than the rebels.

"Glad I grabbed another one," Duke said to himself. He threw the bottle up in the air—high above the head of the King and the most aggressive pursuers. One blast from his pulse pistol shattered the bottle—creating a dense perfume mist that fell on their heads. Some of the cannibals dropped like flies; others turned and ran in the opposite direction of the escaping Neprians.

Duke and Ishiro'shea headed toward the group. The sprint seemed like a blur, but the two covered more ground than they thought.

"The wall's just up here," shouted Lo'n. "It might be a tough climb."

"No time for that," returned Duke, now caught up. "I'm done with this swamp."

Betsy 1, Wall 0.

One by one, the members of the group climbed through a gaping hole in the wall and landed on the drier surface of the northern land mass.

"So, Duke, where did you get that—spray?"

"Long story. Remember the temple? Yeah, we met this guy."

CHAPTER THIRTY

NICE TO SEE YOU AGAIN

"THAT'S QUITE A TALE," LO'N said. "Don't you think?"

He looked towards J'a.

"Yes, quite." She spoke softly, as if she was still contemplating what Duke had told her.

"I don't believe it," Po'l said forcefully. "Not for a solitary moment do I believe that. He'j wouldn't steal anything."

"He might," Ja'a began, stunning Po'l, "if he thought it was in our best interest."

"And who *wouldn't* be freaked out by a giant monster guard? Introducing himself probably wasn't high on He'j's ol' 'What should I do now?' list," Duke reminded them.

"True." Ja'a paused. "But to the more pressing issue. There's no excuse for abandoning your post and leaving us in a very precarious situation."

Duke had no retort.

"I think he's making it up," Po'l started again, "so we'll think his nighttime escapade that left us vulnerable to those cannibals wasn't for nothing."

"How do you explain the perfume?" asked Duke.

"Po'l, we don't have time for this now," Ja'a said. "It's a lot to digest. We've put a good distance between us and the swamp so I don't see us having to deal with this 'Keeper.' But it's all very interesting."

Ja'a picked up her pace and moved to the front of the group, lock step with Ma'n and Te'o, before anyone could blink. She motioned the pair away and proceeded to take on the scout position independently.

"You believe me, right?"

"Most definitely," said Lo'n. "There are many things in Neprius that I don't understand—that *we* don't understand —especially when it comes to that Orb. And *that* swamp. I'm just glad he gave you that fragrance. Dumb luck or not, we owe you yet again."

Po'l grew red in the face. Duke shot a smile in his direction.

"I'm sure it won't be the last time either. We're making good time now that it's open land ahead of us, but we still have a few more days trek to get to Sansagon."

Now Po'l's face was the shade of the astral anomaly that brought the bounty hunters to Neprius in the first place.

The group journeyed for the better part of the day. The landscape of the northern land mass resembled that of the south, with its long sweeping grasslands and low sloping hills. *Equally as boring*, thought Duke. The only difference was that the terrain was dotted with unique rock formations, the likes of which Duke had never seen. Massive boulders jutted out of the ground at odd angles—some as gargantuan as the *Deus Ex Machina*, others not much bigger than Duke himself. Their jagged edges made it appear like lodged spear tips from a race of ancient titans that would have made the Keeper seem pocket-sized.

Regardless, they were everywhere. Some standing alone, others in clusters.

Ja'a must have trekked a great deal farther than Ma'n and Te'o's previous scout position: when she approached the group she was sweating and trying to catch her breath. She inhaled deeply.

"Up ahead—" She hunched over, hands on her knees. "—priests. They're tailing someone."

"Who?"

"Not sure. They weren't on lookout, they were definitely following someone."

"Any guesses?"

"My guess would be a runaway."

"As in someone that escaped the mines?" asked Duke.

"Yep."

"How many did you see?"

"Just two. I'm assuming they're tracking a lone runaway."

"I don't think there are any mines around here, so they must've made it pretty far," said Lo'n. "And to send two armed guards... Seems like overkill for a single runaway."

"Maybe it's someone of importance," Po'l said. "Or at least someone that would join our cause. Surely, if they made it this far, they are a force to be reckoned with."

"Let's go," said Duke. The rest of the group turned to him, appearing shocked. Even Ishiro'shea did a double take.

"So, you didn't want to help out the villagers at Shud'nut—but *this* is fine? Blindly going off course to track down a mysterious escapee?" asked Po'l.

"Or maybe they are just tracking down lunch?" added Bu'r.

"Sure, I mean, you said it yourself—they could be important," Duke replied. "If they can help us, let's do it."

"Because you want your ship back?"

"Whatever the reason, I'm saying I'm in."

Duke looked at Ja'a. She didn't acknowledge him, her eyes fixed on the ground.

"I don't like this," said Po'l.

"Oh, the ever-trusting soul," Duke said with a groan. "I always took you for a 'shoot first, ask questions later' type of guy. Maybe I misread you. I mean, if they need two guards to take down this runaway, they might be too dangerous for you anyways. I *did* see you struggle with those cannibals back there."

"Enough!" Ja'a barked, cutting Po'l off before he could lash out. "Thoughts, anyone? Productive thoughts."

Duke smiled at Po'l.

"How off course?" inquired Lo'n.

"Probably an hour or so. Without knowing how far behind they were from their prey, it's hard to tell," replied Ja'a.

"Doesn't seem too bad," Duke said. "I'm still for it."

"Me too," Bu'r chimed in.

"What do you think, Lo'n?" asked Po'l.

"I think we should press on. The risk isn't worth the addition of one member of the group. And what if it's a child or someone injured? Are we prepared to leave them and push on?"

"Wouldn't a child or an injured person only need a single tracker?"

Lo'n continued, "I say that we maintain our course and focus our efforts and energies on Orbius."

"Lo'n, my good buddy, I'm going to have to disagree with you. I say we take the chance—it's only a few hours, after all. If they can't help us, then we free them and let them travel with us until we can safely drop them off. Or if they want, they can continue on their merry way—they're obviously heading somewhere. It's worth the risk, to me."

"We are wasting precious time arguing!" screamed Po'l.

"He's right," said Ja'a, prompting a smirk from Po'l. "Let's vote. There are eight of us, so I'll abstain to allow a majority."

The group circled around their leader. Softly, she said, "Those that want to track these priests and see who—or what—they are pursuing, raise your hands."

Duke shot his hand up first. Bu'r followed. Ishiro'shea was next. Ma'n and Te'o stared at the ground.

"I'm sorry, friend, but it looks like you lose this round," said Lo'n.

"Actually—" started Po'l.

Po'l stood with his hand raised. Duke felt as if his intestines had just exploded. It was obvious that Po'l seemed to enjoy shocking the bounty hunter—even if it meant siding with him.

"Very well," the elder Neprian sighed. "I don't agree with this. But if we can make it quick, there's no harm, I guess."

"Okay, this way," ordered Ja'a.

"If we double-time it, maybe we can get there before they catch him," added Duke.

"Or her," said Ja'a.

"Or it," countered Duke. "But let's hope it's not an *it*. I hate *its*."

"Exactly what I feared," said Lo'n. He remained hunched behind one of the jagged rocks protruding from the Neprian landscape. "A waste of our time. If we pick it up, we can make up a ton of the ground that we lost before night hits."

"Are you kidding me?" Duke shouted, only to be met

with an aggressive "shhh" from the group. "You know who that is, right?"

"Yes," Lo'n replied, less than enthusiastically. The others seemed to come to the same conclusion.

"That's Vernglet Wip. He knows stuff. Important stuff. And, if he doesn't tell us this important stuff, I want to make sure his skull is properly smashed in for setting us up and getting us into this mess."

"We came here to free someone being enslaved for no reason and who could potentially help us in our quest," Ja'a said. "I'm sure this Wip character deserves everything that he gets—and those two guards seem like they can do an adequate job. Now let's go."

Duke looked at Ja'a. Her glance in return offered no insight into what she was thinking. The others tried not to make eye contact.

"Guys, he knows *stuff*. We can get information out of him and, if he doesn't, then Ishiro can slice him into neat little pieces. Win-win."

"He knows stuff? What stuff?" Lo'n chirped back, in a tone of frustration.

"He knows where his ship is," Po'l added. "He only cares about that, remember?"

"You're right. He probably does know where the *Deus* is. And the Orb. And weaknesses at Orbius' place. And the easiest route in and out. He made it this far before getting caught. Well, I guess he isn't caught *yet*."

Duke peeked out from behind a particularly odd-shaped rock formation. The rebels remained hidden from the scene that was unfolding below; safely behind a cluster of the unusual rocks at the ridge of a slight incline nearly a hundred paces away from the trackers. Duke assumed that they were out of earshot—as long as they spoke with their "inside voices."

"Okay, he's caught now," Duke corrected himself with a huff.

The two Neprian priests had Wip backed up against a boulder. Their spears were mere inches from his face.

"C'mon guys! We came this far, let's at least see if we can get something from him. What do we have to lose?"

"Lives," Ja'a replied calmly.

"Fine, I'll go alone. If I die, no big whup. You guys can run away and keep pursuing Orbius. I'll even leave Ishiro'shea for you as a parting gift."

Ishiro'shea shook his head.

"I knew this was a bad idea," Lo'n began, "even if rules are rules and the majority won. Bad outcomes—even when following the rules—are still bad. I simply cannot stand for us risking anything to help a runaway priest. Nothing he can do is worth this. It's a total waste. I say we leave now. No, I *demand* it."

"But then we can't pick his brain—no matter how warped it is. *That* would be a total waste. There's no point to any of this if we don't at least try to see if we can get something useful from him," professed Duke.

"The point is that this is *pointless*," Lo'n hissed.

"Calm down for a second. Let's think about this," Ja'a said.

"No," Lo'n roared. "This is ridiculous."

"Hey," Duke started, "no need to—"

"I demand that we leave," Lo'n repeated.

"Friend, let's take a deep breath—" Duke replied.

"Ja'a, tell them to go," Lo'n continued, without acknowledging the bounty hunter.

"Duke brings up a good point. He might know something," said Ja'a.

"Unbelievable. 'Something.' 'Stuff.' That's all you got." Lo'n stood up and headed back towards their original path.

Based on their expressions, this is a Lo'n that no one has ever seen before, surmised Duke. *Especially Ja'a.*

"Lo'n!" screamed Ja'a.

The subtle, indistinguishable murmurs of the priests' voices suddenly stopped. Ja'a immediately realized what she had done.

That was not an inside voice.

"Who goes there?" shouted one of the trackers.

"Help!" screamed Vernglet Wip. "Help me!"

"Shut up, Wip. Who's behind those rocks?"

"Me," shouted Duke gruffly. But it was Ishiro'shea that slowly stepped from behind the rock and into plain sight. The ninja moved his mouth under his mask, giving the impression that the words were his own.

"Stay there! Hands up. You are now the property of Orbius, Orbmaster of the Orb."

"Okay, I give up. Please don't hurt me. I'll lie on the ground and be a good little boy," Duke bellowed from his unseen location. Ishiro'shea gave him a venomous stare and then proceeded to lie down on the ground—behind the first row of boulders.

One of the trackers made his way to Ishiro'shea, face down in the dirt.

"Who is he?" shouted the guard that remained with their prisoner. "A rebel?"

When the guard was a few paces from him, Ishiro'shea sprang up and darted back behind the rocks.

"Stop or—"

The guard never saw the club coming. Bu'r's swing had the force of ten Neprians and dropped the priest with ease.

"Hey, what's going on? Did you let him escape? I know I should've gone," shouted the other tracker. "Stay there, Vern."

"Idiots. Lather. Rinse. Repeat," whispered Duke. "Okay, get ready. He'll be here in five... four... three... two..."

BLAMPH! The second tracker was out.

"Good job, Bu'r," congratulated Duke.

Ja'a chased towards Lo'n.

"Ja'a, let him blow off some steam. We have a chance to get some... answers, maybe," Po'l said optimistically.

She didn't hear him. Moments later, they were interrupted by a familiar voice.

"Thank you! Thank you! You saved me!" came Vern's high-pitched voice from his place of would-be capture. "I can't thank you enough. What can I do to repay you? Whomever you are?"

"Not sure you want me to answer that," Duke said as he stepped out from his hiding spot and positioned himself in Vernglet's line of sight.

The Neprian priest's face sunk within itself before it sank into his hands. Duke interpreted the next sounds as some sort of Neprian curse words.

CHAPTER THIRTY-ONE

A THUD IN THE NIGHT

"YOU'RE GOING THE WRONG WAY," squeaked Vernglet Wip. He squirmed, trying to find a comfortable position amidst his roped bonds. "Right into Orbius' central army."

"Shut up, priest," barked Po'l. "You're lucky we kept you alive."

"A massive mistake in my estimation," said Lo'n gruffly. It was clear that he was still angry about the decision, but he was now calming visibly.

"He might come in handy, still," pleaded Duke. "We just don't know yet."

"You said he would have information—and did he?" asked Lo'n.

"Not as such," started Duke, "but—"

"No, he's now a liability. I went along with saving him, but he's of no value. And he's evil. Orbius' stooge," said Po'l. It was clear the tide of his opinions was shifting in Lo'n's direction.

"I don't think he would have sent two trackers to bring him back if he was totally loyal to Orbius," added Bu'r.

"Yes," chimed in the prisoner. "Like I told you, I was being sent back to Sansagon to my death for being a traitor."

"Convenient story. Maybe Orbius knew we would take you in—and you are supposed to sabotage our mission," said Lo'n.

"That does make some sense," murmured Po'l.

"You love your conspiracy theories," jabbed Duke.

"I don't believe his story about going against Orbius' wishes for the greater good of the planet," Po'l said defiantly. "I don't think he has the spine for it."

"You all know what Orbius has done to your people. But look what he's done to mine. We are no less slaves than you. Maybe we lack actual chains—but we also lack free will. Is it that hard to believe that one of my kind has come to realize this?"

"Yeah."

"Yep."

"Totally."

"You set yourself up for that, Vern," said the bounty hunter, "but I see where you're coming from. Don't get me wrong, I'm still royally pissed—but I get it."

"It's true. Gar knew it. He saw it in me. He ordered my imprisonment. He claimed that I gave you an out—that day in the field where your ship was—set you up to kill our troops and flee. I didn't know that he brought an entire legion with him."

"Utter nonsense. Surely you can't believe this drivel," groaned Lo'n. "Ja'a, let's cut our losses and leave his carcass to rot in the sun."

He held up his saber mere inches in front of Vernglet's face.

"Lo'n, no. I don't know if I believe him but he doesn't have any weapons and doesn't pose a threat. I think we should continue on, and an answer will present itself."

"He's slowing us down."

"I don't think that's the case."

"As long as we don't listen to him, I'm fine. He would love for us to follow his directions and bring us right to Orbius' warm embrace."

"That's where you're heading now," Vernglet pointed out.

"For now," Ja'a began, "we will listen to you, Lo'n. You know these lands and how you made it to Orbius last time."

"That's a mistake—"

"It might be wise to keep your mouth shut," said Lo'n, raising his sword again.

"Hey now, chill. He can hang back here with Ish and I. We'll watch him. I still have some questions for him."

"Fine."

Lo'n stormed to the front of the group. Ja'a looked back at Duke and locked eyes. He couldn't figure out if she was confused or angry—or simply disappointed in how her "uncle" was behaving.

Vernglet seems to bring out the worst in people.

Duke whispered to the priest, "You gotta help me out here, Vern."

"What do you mean?"

"They really want to kill you."

"But isn't the enemy of your enemy your friend?"

"Not if that person is a slimy Neprian priest with a long history of enslaving their people."

"Fair point."

"Is everything that you said true?"

"Yes."

"We are walking directly into the jaws of Orbius' army?"

"Directly. I've been running from his clutches for some time now. I know."

"I don't know why I'm trusting you, after you sold us up the river back in Dre'en. I mean, not cool, dude."

"I had no choice."

"I'm willing to entertain that notion. Thoughts, Ish?"

The ninja looked Vern up and down, from toe to head. He glanced back at Duke and shrugged.

"Helpful."

The fabric on Ishiro's mask tilted upward. He was smiling.

"How long do we have until we meet them head on?"

"A day. Maybe a bit more."

"Not much time. It's getting dark, so maybe we can sleep on it and come up with a plan to at least consider the fact that you might not be part of some complex orchestration by Vangu. Oh man, can you imagine Po'l if there *is* a conspiracy? He would be unbearable. And we would likely be dead."

"I will continue to think of ideas, Duke."

"So, are you sure you don't know anything else about the *Deus*?"

"Just what I told you. Orbius was very interested in it. I'm guessing he is going to use it as a weapon—another means of controlling us."

"Maybe. Not sure he could fly it—it's a bit finicky. And I definitely know he couldn't teach your lot to drive it." Duke paused momentarily. "No offense."

"None taken."

"And it's just at his fortress?"

"I wasn't with the group that delivered it to him."

"One last thing, Vern. This has been bugging me."

"Yes?"

"Don't take this the wrong way, but why does Orbius care so much about you? It doesn't seem like you know the inner workings that could help bring him down. One traitor doesn't win a war."

"But it can lose a war."

The bounty hunters looked at each other. *What the hell does that mean?*

"He fears that my resistance—and his inability to publicly punish me—"

"You mean kill you."

"Most likely, yes. His inability to dispose of me will spark rebellious thoughts that are buried deep in our people. I know Ja'a and her people don't view us as capable of standing up for something—but it's there. Somewhere. Our servitude to Orbius without even a hint of defiance has been our lowest point. Some of us recognize this and refuse to let it happen again."

The bounty hunter scratched his chin.

The troop marched on as night fell over the Neprian landscape. Ja'a directed them to a dense collection of rock formations surrounded by a few rogue trees.

"See those formations ahead?" asked Ja'a. "Forward lookouts can post up there. We can camp under these with a single scout on the other side. Any volunteers?"

"I'll take the forward lookout," said Te'o.

"I'll join him," huffed Lo'n.

"Okay, and I'll watch the back first. Vern can come with me, too."

"I think he should be up front with us, Ja'a. I know you're a great warrior but two trumps one if he does decide to get feisty," remarked Lo'n.

"I can handle it."

"I know you *can*. But it's not wise."

"I agree with Lo'n," interjected Po'l. "It's logical."

"You and logic have met?" snapped Duke.

"Enough," said Ja'a. "Unnecessary, but I will yield to the group. And to logic."

Lo'n turned to Vernglet. "Don't even think about trying any of your priestly trickery. I'll behead you before you can say Orbmaster of the Orb."

He grabbed Vern roughly by his rope cuffs and led him to the lookout position. Te'o followed.

"Good night."

"What is it, Ishiro?"

The ninja was kneeling over the Nova Texan, peering out into the dead of the night.

"It's nothing. Go back to bed."

The mute martial artist tugged at Duke's shoulder again and pointed. Off in the distance a faint flicker of light was losing a battle against the ominous darkness.

"That's just Lo'n and Te'o. You're losing your touch. You're better than that. Now go to bed."

Ishiro'shea tapped Duke again—this time with more force.

"Hey!"

The ninja pointed to his ear.

"Listen to what?"

Ishiro pressed his palms down, signaling for Duke to shut his trap.

"Fine," Duke said, and waited. "Nothing. You're hearing things."

A subtle thud. Duke stood to attention.

"Okay, I heard it that time. You don't think—" He paused. "No. Vern *did* set us up? It's a trap? That means— holy hedgehogs, that means Lo'n and Te'o are in trouble."

Ishiro'shea started to sprint nimbly in that direction.

"Wait! Should we tell—nope, answered my own question. We need to ambush this bastard and any friends that he might have brought along to help. They'd smell Po'l a mile away."

Ishiro'shea pointed to the large rock barrier behind their campsite.

"No, I think we need to leave Ja'a out of this, too."

The duo ran towards the lookout position with as much stealth as they could muster. *Ishiro'shea's much better at this*, thought Duke. The terrain was flat, so their path weaved from rock to rock to whatever piece of the Neprian topography would provide cover.

"There it is again," whispered Duke as he slunk behind an oversized boulder angled into the Neprian soil. "There might be an entire band of priesties waiting on us."

They continued on.

"One more hiding spot before their camp—and it's pretty well covered. If we need to snipe them from there, we should be fine. Let's go."

The collection of stones was to the east of the scouting location. It had a slight incline that reached a pinnacle at a point almost as high as the hill where Lo'n and Te'o were camped with Vernglet Wip. It was the perfect spot for reconnaissance—*super secretive* reconnaissance at that. The pair crawled silently to the apex of the formation and laid belly down. They could hear the crackling fire from a torch stuck in the ground.

"I don't see 'em. Too late?"

Ishiro'shea pointed.

"That's... that's Lo'n. Hey—" Duke started to scream for Lo'n's attention but Ishiro'shea quickly covered his mouth and shoved him down. Duke mumbled unintelligibly through Ishiro's hand. It wasn't a particularly nice comment.

After a few moments, the ninja and the bounty hunter rose again to survey the area. Ishiro'shea pointed at another person. On the ground.

"Is that one of Vern's henchmen?" Duke said softly. "Did Lo'n take him out? That would make this much easier."

He examined the figure more closely. "No," he whispered to himself.

Lo'n scanned the area, standing over the prone body. Ishiro'shea threw Duke's head down to the surface of the rock again.

More mumbles.

"That can't be," Duke said as they hid on the downward slope of the rock. "That can't be," he gulped, "Te'o?"

Ishiro'shea nodded in affirmation.

"Lo'n was too late. They got to Te'o. We should definitely go give him backup."

Duke leapt to his feet at the summit of the hill. Ishiro'shea tried to stop him, but the bounty hunter was undeterred.

"What the—Look, Ishiro."

Duke drew his laser revolver and rushed down the rock face. His companion followed suit, katana drawn.

"Duke, Ishiro'shea," Lo'n huffed as they approached. "I'm glad you're here. As I had feared, Vernglet Wip was leading us on the entire time. This was all a ruse. His fellow priests tracked us down and attacked. They killed Te'o. I was able to fight them off and they fled. I knocked him out and was about to finish him off."

He pointed at Vernglet Wip's motionless body.

Lo'n's saber was hoisted high in the air with his right hand. Te'o's ax hung at his side, gripped in his left hand. The priest was slowly coming to.

"Drop the sword."

"What?" the aging rebel asked, staring in confusion. "This cancerous wretch killed Te'o. Who knows how many are on their way now."

"None," Duke said emphatically.

"Excuse me?"

"None. There aren't any that are coming for us. At least, none directly caused by our friend Vern here."

"What are you talking about, Duke?"

"Don't play dumb. I watched you drag Vern's body and drop it next to Te'o."

"Your eyes mistake you, off-worlder."

Ishiro'shea took a step toward Lo'n with his katana at the ready.

"Hold, Ish. We saw you drag the body. I get it. You didn't want to slice him into two Vernglets and have to drag the blood and entrails over here—we woulda seen through that. Po'l probably woulda seen through that."

"You're wrong."

"Why'd you do it?"

"Do what?" he pleaded.

"You know what. And drop the sword."

Duke aimed his gun directly at the rebel's chest. Lo'n paused, breathing deeply.

"I can't do that," Lo'n said, his voice changing from confusion—or a poor performance of it—to one of cold calculation. "This guy here has to die. And then you and your friend have to die. You shouldn't have come here, Duke. Orbius might have only imprisoned you, but now you'll have to be silenced."

"Orbius?"

"You know so little of this land, off-worlder. Orbius is our only hope. Our savior. The only one that can control the Orb. He'j was foolish—and he paid for it. I had to make sure that he wouldn't be in the way anymore. And now, you. You are in the way. This fruitless rebellion is in the way."

"Haven't you heard the old saying about absolute power?"

"The Orb *is* the absolute power—and Orbius is our buffer from its evil magic. He is our guardian."

"Why does a savior need to enslave people to mine for jewels and rocks?"

"Non-believers must be punished. If they stop Orbius, our planet is doomed."

"He's not very all-powerful if he's worried about a few disorganized farmers. You honestly believe what he's saying?"

"I do. It's the truth."

"And you know this how?"

Slight movement came from under Lo'n's foot. A groggy Vernglet Wip moaned and tried to roll onto his back.

The Neprian turncoat did not answer Duke's question.

Lo'n lobbed his saber at Duke. Duke fired.

CLINK!

The sword fell to the ground; next to it, Ishiro's katana. Lo'n crumpled to the ground on top of the wounded priest.

"I did *not* see that coming," Duke said to no one in particular. He walked over and helped Ishiro'shea move Lo'n's body off of Vern. "Man, could really use an anthropomorphic musk ox from one of the moons of Gartosh at a time like this."

"What... what happened?" asked Vernglet.

"Not really sure. But let's just say that I'm going to be making the case that we seriously consider your navigational recommendations."

Vernglet stared at Te'o's dead body. He glanced to Lo'n's.

"Orbius has many spies. He plays many angles."

"This one was a strong hand," Duke began, "I have a feeling that this is going to be harder than I thought."

Ishiro'shea picked up his sword.

"Thanks, Ishiro. I *really* owe you this time."

All three turned as a slowly accumulating rumble crept up behind them. *Everyone's awake.* Duke turned to his compatriot.

"How are we going to explain this to Ja'a?"

Ishiro'shea's expression offered no helpful suggestions.

The group stampeded towards them. Ma'n led the way, presumably due to the worry that if something went wrong, his lifelong friend Te'o was likely affected—and this was, of course, precisely the case. Po'l was next—his enthusiasm likely relating to blaming Duke for the entire mess. Bu'r followed. Ja'a came up last, since she had been stationed furthest away. Duke could see the dread on her face—she was probably in the process of calculating the worst possible outcomes.

"Whoa! Same team! Same team!" shouted Duke as Po'l aimed an arrow at his nose.

"Are we?" Po'l countered with equal force. "What happened?"

"No, no, no," cried Ma'n as he finally noticed Te'o's body a few feet from where they stood. He rushed over and slid to the ground. He felt his pulse. It was very clear that Te'o had not survived the massive slash wound across his chest.

"Ma'n," Duke started, "it was—"

"Shut up, off-worlder!" Po'l said, cutting him off. He stepped a few paces closer to the bounty hunter. Duke and Ishiro'shea had put away their weapons to prevent the situation from looking any worse. Bu'r scrambled over to Te'o's body and consoled the clearly heartbroken Ma'n. Duke overheard him mentioning "Ty'n" and "honor" and "courage."

"What happened?" barked Po'l. "Tell me. Now."

"What do *you* think happened? Lo'n wasn't who we thought he was."

"You expect us to believe that? You're partners with him, right?" Po'l said, nodding in Vernglet's direction. "It was an elaborate setup. This entire time."

"Not this again. Really?"

"We're to believe that Lo'n, one of our greatest warriors and comrade of He'j, is a traitor? And that he killed one of his own? You've lost your mind, LaGrange. Or you think we are just that stupid."

Duke gritted his teeth. *Not going to say it.*

"Look—"

"No, you look. You killed Lo'n. You killed Te'o."

Ja'a had finally arrived and stepped in front of Po'l. She signaled for him to drop his weapon. She knelt down and examined Lo'n's body. She traced her finger to the wound. She wasn't crying, hysterical, or even sad. She wasn't emotional. *Odd.*

She rose and locked eyes on Duke's, cold and steely. She gave him nothing. She then walked to Te'o's slain body and put her hand on Ma'n's shoulder. She repeated the action with Bu'r. Her eyes fixated on the slash mark that had clearly been the death blow to her former ally. There was a sense of eeriness about the entire situation. No one moved or spoke. Ja'a walked back to stand directly between the two off-worlders and Po'l.

"Tell me. From the beginning. Leave nothing out."

Po'l began to speak, but she halted his response with a simple glance. During her mediation, Ja'a was not going to suffer emotion.

"Not now, Po'l. I want to know what happened. Or at

least what Duke is going to *tell* us the story is. Let's start with why you are here."

The bounty hunter cleared his throat and started.

"Ishiro'shea heard something. A noise. I thought he was crazy—especially when he pointed in this direction. But then I heard it too."

"How did that not wake us up?" Po'l blurted out, to Ja'a's visible dismay.

"Let him finish. Do not interrupt again."

Scolded, Po'l's face sunk in on itself. Duke enjoyed it.

"I don't know. It wasn't a loud noise by any means. Just a soft thud. No screams or shouts."

"Go on," said Ja'a.

"Right. Then we both snuck over here as quietly as possible. We hid on the top of that rock over there." Duke pointed at their recent stakeout locale. "Then we witnessed everything. Most everything."

"And that is?"

"Lo'n standing over Te'o's body. Blood dripping off his saber."

"That doesn't prove anything." It was Bu'r, still consoling Ma'n, who interjected this time. His tone was more curious than angry.

"Like I was saying," Duke continued, "Lo'n stood over Te'o. Then he started to walk over to Vern who was passed out—or rather, knocked out—a few paces away. Right over there. Then, what put this whole thing together was that Lo'n started dragging Vern over to Te'o's body. Ish and I showed up just as he was about to deal the death blow—making it look like Vern did the deed."

"And that deed was?"

"Vernglet's conspirators came in and killed Ma'n before Lo'n fought them off and they fled."

"But why knock the priest out first?" asked Bu'r.

"It would have been easy to tell that he killed him first and drug the body. Especially if it was a messy death."

"Even if this was all possible, why? Why would Lo'n risk this to kill the priest and Te'o?"

"It was just Vern that he wanted to kill."

"But why?"

Duke and Ishiro'shea looked at Vernglet and signaled for him to tell the story.

"Because I knew Lo'n was working for Orbius."

"That's it, Ja'a," snapped Po'l. "I've had enough of this. I mean it this time. Lo'n going crazy and killing people, I'll buy that. A cunning trap from this sleaze—I'm very likely to buy that. I could even give you the craziness of this weak little bastard breaking free and killing Te'o under Lo'n's watch. But I'm not going to sit here and let you believe that Lo'n was a traitor."

Po'l stormed off to the rock that Duke and Ishiro'shea had recently used to spy on Lo'n.

"Why didn't you say anything?"

Vern took a deep, chesty breath and retorted, "Would you have believed me?"

"No," Ja'a answered honestly.

"And that's why Lo'n wanted to leave you or kill you initially," chimed in Bu'r. "He knew that there was a chance —albeit a slim one—that you could convince us."

"Right," answered Duke.

"This is a lot," Ja'a began. "I don't know what to think. No, I do know one thing. Our friend Te'o deserves a proper burial. That is not to be questioned. Let's dig and honor him. He gave his life for the cause. Maybe in this darkest hour some clarity will present itself."

The entire group—*sans* Po'l—started to dig. Even Vernglet Wip.

"Po'l," shouted Ja'a. "Please come help us honor Te'o."

"I'm not going to dig a grave for one of our own alongside his murderers. A priest that sent countless droves of our people to their enslavement and two off-worlders that likely helped him—that's not what Te'o would have wanted. You all taint his honor."

"Be reasonable."

"I am, Ja'a. I very much am. My time with this group is done. I'm going to follow Lo'n's path and kill Orbius myself. I can't stand being part of this embarrassment—this disgrace—any longer."

"Po'l—" Ja'a pleaded.

"I should've left when we met with Mo'a, back at the base. I let you talk me into this—but not anymore. Not now."

He turned and walked away.

Ja'a began to go after him but Bu'r grabbed her arm. "He made his decision."

"And it's a decision that proves that I've failed as a leader."

CHAPTER THIRTY-TWO

VALLEY OF THE GRUNDAR

"DO YOU HAVE TO KEEP him tied up?" Duke asked Ja'a. "I mean, we are following *his* directions—so you have to trust him to some degree."

"I'm not sure that I can ever fully trust a priest. You're new to Neprius and haven't witnessed all that they've done to our people."

"But it was under the threat of death by Orbius."

"That makes no difference. They could've resisted. They blindly followed evil. Even if Vernglet is an outlier, it doesn't excuse him from the monstrosities that he allowed for cycles. I will have a hard time trusting everything that he tells us."

"Baby steps?"

"Yes, baby steps. In time, I hope that I will conclude that he is honest and true and there aren't any sinister motives. Until then, he remains tied up."

"But we follow his directions?"

"Yes."

"Sorry, Vern. I tried." Duke shouted back at the Northerner.

"Her points are valid and understandable," responded Vernglet. "In time, I hope that they see my true colors."

"That's what I'm afraid of," chimed in Ma'n. "We haven't had the best of luck regarding people's true colors as of late."

The group pressed on. Now down to only six—including the quasi-prisoner, Vernglet Wip—they did not have a scout or flanks, and traveled in a single huddled mass. As they pressed northwest, following the priest's guidance, the landscape began to slowly change. Increasingly, the sprawling grasslands were dotted with giant angled stones. On the horizon, bluffs sprouted up in the shadows of a mountain range that seemed to touch the sky.

"The Valley of the Grundar," Vern said, pointing at the first set of rocky cliffs. "There is a passage that leads through to the valley. From there, we can approach Orbius without detection—or, at least, reduced chances of detection. It's only a two-day march."

"The valley is safe?"

"Safe from Orbius' men—yes. Other than that, I cannot guarantee anything."

"That's reassuring," said Bu'r.

"It's the best that we have," responded Ja'a. "If we push, we can make it to the passage and into the valley long before nightfall."

"I'm not camping out there, Ja'a," shouted Ma'n. "What if the legends are true? What if there are actual grundar?"

"Not this again," interjected Duke.

"Then we need to push harder and make it through the valley and en route to Orbius."

"I'm okay with that!"

The rebels picked up their pace. Ma'n and Bu'r moved ahead of the others, clearly spooked by the thought of the flying fire-breathing felines. Ishiro'shea remained at the back with Vernglet, who was having trouble moving faster due to his arms being bound behind his back.

Duke turned to Ja'a. "How do you think Po'l's doing?"

"I'd rather not talk about it. I hope he finds his way to Orbius safely. That's all that I can say."

"Understood. Can we at least talk about Lo'n?"

"What about him?"

"Ja'a, I didn't see a speck of emotion from you when everything went down. Surely—"

"I'm fine. A leader does not let emotions dictate their decisions. It was obvious what happened."

"It was?"

"Yes, it doesn't make sense as to *why* he would do it—but I know he did it."

"Don't you feel betrayed?"

"He was the closest thing that I had to a father outside of my own. Of course. However, I feel worse for my father. His best friend not only betrayed him, but tried to send his daughter into the clutches of the very thing that he fought against. I don't want to know what he would think now."

She clutched her necklace. Duke could see that sadness was trying to break through her defenses.

"I've been around this universe too many times to count, but I've yet to find a leader so dedicated to their cause as you. I mean it. No joke. I know we haven't seen eye-to-eye on everything, but—"

His rare and heartfelt plea was interrupted by a shout from Ma'n. "Is that the passage?"

"Vernglet?" asked Ja'a.

"Yes. We go through that opening and within moments the sky will open up and we will be standing in the Valley of the Grundar."

Ja'a turned to Duke. "Thank you."

She then picked up her pace and took the command position as they approached the cave.

As Vernglet had predicted, the walk through the passage was short and uneventful. And it did open up to a valley—and quite dramatically. Duke estimated the valley was the size of the whole of Dre'en. The mountainous cliffs surrounded the lush landscape. Greens, yellows, and whites adorned the beautiful palette; the valley seemed untouched by even the primitive level of civilization elsewhere on Neprius. It was picturesque and, more importantly, quiet. The lack of life was almost unsettling.

"It's a direct route to the other end of the valley," said Vernglet. "There is another passage—not too dissimilar than the one we just left. That will put us out due west of the base. When we near the village of Horteyaya, we can take a northern route to avoid Orbius' many eyes and soon we will see the fortress."

"Thank you. And I do believe that I owe you this." Ja'a walked to him and drew out a single arrow from her quiver. The priest winced involuntarily, but Ja'a grabbed his rope bonds and sliced them off in one single motion with the edge of the arrowhead. The priest exhaled.

"You haven't led us astray and I want to show you trust. Our people have battled for so long that trust will be the hardest gift to bestow, but I want to start that process now. Here. With you. We are both children of Neprius and we can never heal unless we both see that."

Vernglet Wip bowed in appreciation.

"Enough of this—let's go kill us an Orbmaster!" Duke said, twirling his laser revolver on a finger. "How about it, guys? Let's do this!"

His attempts at rallying the troops fell flat. "Hey Ja'a, tell me about the grundar again? Winged fire-breathing panthers, right?"

"Yes, that's the legend. Though I've never seen—"

"I think you're wrong."

"Wrong about what?"

"They're *big-ass* winged fire-breathing panthers that look *really* pissed off—oh yeah, and you're about to see one."

The entire group turned to see what Duke had witnessed. Landing without a sound was a massive flying cat. The saber-like teeth that protruded from the upper jaw were each about the length of Duke's arm.

As one, the group drew their weapons.

"It's a grundar. A real one," uttered Bu'r in amazement. "I can't believe it."

The beast let out a deafening growl. *Perfect murder machines*, thought Duke. *Almost beautiful, if you take out the whole "likely to kill us" part.*

"Hold fire," said Ja'a. "It could be scared of us. It probably hasn't seen a Neprian before."

"It doesn't look too scared," replied Duke. "And it looks like we're about to meet its friends."

A dozen more grundar were flying from the cliffs on a direct path to them. They landed, encircling the rebels and providing no exit.

"Back to back, everyone!" shouted Ja'a. "Hold steady."

"If they really can breathe fire, we're about to be toast. Literally," Duke added. "Great, another one. And it's really, really big."

A final grundar descended from the sky. It was a grundar a head taller than the next largest. But the major difference was that it carried a passenger. A not-friendly-looking passenger.

Duke had wondered if he appeared gargantuan only because he was sitting atop the majestic beast—but he was quickly proven wrong. When the grundar rider dismounted he stood twice the height of the tallest human. His face was almost skeletal in appearance, gray skin pulled tight against his bones, but his frame was muscular. His eyes were pupil-less; as if someone had stuffed a pair of polished onyx stones into his eye sockets. Somehow, though, they contained life and emotion. The weathered shroud that he wore matched the color of his eyes and its tatters and rips flowed in the air upon his descent. He carried a staff of warped wood, almost the size of a young tree, and marked with wounds inflicted by combat and time.

The rebels kept their weapons drawn. The grundar rider snarled in his displeasure, showing jagged teeth that could cut iron.

Two of the grundar parted as he approached the encir-cled band of warriors. Duke fired his laser revolver impul-sively. The giant raised his left hand and deflected the energy pulse. Not even a scratch.

"You guys are getting more and more daring."

There was a slight hiss to his voice.

"Wait... what?" Duke blurted out. "What are you talking about?"

"I didn't think that your leader would send you into *my* valley."

"This seems familiar," Duke whispered to Ishiro, recalling the Keeper's confused insistence that they were swamp cannibals.

"Our leader?" asked Ja'a.

"The one that stole the Orb and is trying to bring the end to life."

"Wait... what?" Duke said again.

"Enough of your stalling. Girls, ready to pounce..."

"We are not the warriors of which you speak," Ja'a proclaimed. "We are trying to *stop* him. We are trying to destroy the Orb."

The grundar were growing restless.

"Nice try," the grundar rider said dismissively. "I've seen your types. And I know that *he* is your leader." He pointed.

Vernglet looked genuinely shocked.

"What? Vern?" Duke blurted out. "He's actually our prisoner. Well, sort of. He *was* our prisoner."

"A prisoner that sports no bonds or chains?"

"Good eye. I can explain that," replied Duke, with a touch of embarrassment.

"Your people must have a very liberal interpretation of 'prisoner.' He looks like all of the others—digging and mining and destroying. I knew it was only a matter of time before you made it to my valley."

"I assure you, Master of the Grundar, I am no leader. And these people speak the truth," began Vernglet. "My people—my former people—follow the orb-stealer. I'm afraid he is unstoppable with the power that it brings him."

The rider seemed to consider Vernglet's claim.

"Nice try, again. You are but six. Am I to believe that you are going to take down this Orbmaster? And his army?"

"His name is Orbius."

"Cute."

"We are going to try," proclaimed Ja'a.

"You are a feisty one. Are *you* the leader?"

"Yes, and, kind sir, if we were part of this horde, do you think that the Orbmaster would have sent only us six to capture the Valley of the Grundar?"

"Very good point." He scratched his cheek with a spindly finger which ended in a hooked nail.

"But how did you learn that this Orbmaster knows of my existence? I've been in this valley for ages without a single interaction from your kind. Or yours." He pointed at the priest.

"It's clear that you've been in battle."

She motioned towards a grundar with a gash on its right front leg, then at another with a cut between its eyes.

"You are quite observant and correct, leader."

"My name is Ja'a. From the Southern landmass. A long way from here. My people were enslaved by Orbius. We are fighting back against him and his army. We want to be free again. We want Neprius—this planet—to be free again."

"And us two, we're from outer space," Duke said, trying to imbue the term "outer space" with mystic spookiness.

It was apparent that the grundar rider was not shocked or impressed by the concept of cosmic life.

"I'm Duke LaGrange," Duke concluded weakly. "This is my compatriot, Ishiro'shea."

"Is that so?"

"And sorry about shooting you earlier. Habit."

"Wait, was that thing that you hurled at me supposed to be a weapon?"

Duke opened his mouth but at first nothing came out. He cleared his throat. "Sorry, anyways."

"Why are you fighting Orbius?" asked Ja'a.

"He has the Orb—and therefore he has the ability to levy uncontrolled carnage to my valley. The Orb only brings destruction. My friends and I are not ready to see our home destroyed again. We will eventually have to face this Orbmaster. I was in battle with a garrison southeast of here, until I heard that someone had entered the valley."

"You were battling an entire garrison by yourself?" Ma'n blurted out.

The rider gazed at Ma'n and then nodded.

"How did this Orbius get hold of the Orb? I thought it was lost to time; its stories and legends all but evaporated with the ancient races. With *my* race."

"It was stolen," Duke jumped in, "from the Keeper."

"The Keeper?"

"Yes, the only other thing on this planet that's as big as you. He was guarding it in his temple."

"Oh, wait—do you mean Toby?"

The rebels looked shocked.

"Toby?" asked Ma'n.

"Now that makes so much sense," said the grundar rider, appearing more relaxed. He repositioned his staff to support his weight. "I can't believe he's still around. I'd like to give him a piece of this!" He raised a fist. "Calling himself the Keeper, huh? If there's one thing that he's not good at, it's keeping things. You know he's lost it before, right? And he's not much good at finding things either, I guess."

"Yep, he told us. He also told us that he was the only thing to survive the destruction caused by the Sphere of Power. So how do you know him?"

"That's not entirely true," the grundar rider said, ignoring the question. "Maybe near his home, he was the only thing to survive. The sphere sunk much of the land to the bottom depths of the sea."

"That explains the narrow land bridge," added Ja'a.

"But a few pockets of survivors remained—mostly in secluded areas. Not sure if they are still around, to be honest. I doubt it—that was a long time ago. Even we have expiration dates. I stayed in the mountains and started to breed grundar. It seemed like the best thing to do. I mean what else was I to do? An art retrospective? This is my seven thousand, three hundred and forty-eighth litter here."

He turned to his cats. "And my favorite!" he added in a playful tone.

The grundar purred joyously. The rebels collectively relaxed.

"You know about the people that gave it back to him after he lost it, then?"

"I do. Peculiar race that came out of nowhere. I blinked —couldn't have been but an age or two—and we had civilization again. Primitive, albeit, but civilization. Hadn't made it to the soufflé stage yet."

"You knew they had the Orb—and that's what was causing the war?"

"I did not—not until I saw them give it back to Toby and block off the land bridge. Their skirmishes didn't make it to my lands. I would occasionally scare an ambitious explorer in the valley but, other than that, I ignored them entirely. Had I known sooner, I would have tried to destroy it then. But Toby seemed to do a better job that time around. Until this latest fiasco. So this Orbius character stole it from good ol' Toby?"

"Actually, my father stole it from him," Ja'a replied.

The rider seemed taken aback by this tidbit of information. "This is getting really juicy now. Do tell," he said eagerly.

"Don't you have a battle to go back to?" asked Bu'r.

"They'll wait. Go on," the rider said, waving away Bu'r's comment.

Ja'a proceeded to fill the grundar rider in on the droughts, He'j and Jilarian Togg, the arrival of Duke and Ishiro'shea, and Lo'n's betrayal. Vernglet explained his role in the tale. Duke talked about his conversation with Toby.

"That's quite a yarn. I'm actually inclined to believe it. It's too ridiculous to make up. And Looloo over there seems to like you. I trust her."

The winged grundar nudged her nose into Bu'r's back, knocking him down. She licked the top of his head.

"So what should we call you?"

"I am Fazeek, Shepherd of the Grundar. But you can call me 'Shepherd of the Grundar.'"

"Not where I thought he was going with that... but okay," whispered Duke to Ishiro'shea.

"Shepherd of the Grundar," began Ja'a in a formal, almost regal, voice, "do we have your permission to leave your valley and try and stop Orbius?"

It was obvious that Fazeek loved the formality—and the fact that it was referred to as *his* valley.

"By all means," he responded. "But to truly be part of this, we need to get you to this Orbius a bit faster than your tiny legs can carry you."

He whistled and six of the winged beasts approached and submitted for mounting. Looloo leapt eagerly to Bu'r's feet and knelt down.

"I guess we go bareback," remarked Duke. "Anyone else feel a bit uneasy about this?"

The bounty hunter looked around. All of the others were already on their grundar and hovering above the ground. Duke hopped on, then was jolted back as the cat leapt to the sky to join the others.

"My new friends—we have two goals. Destroy this Orbius. And find a way to destroy the Orb. It will not be easy. I will rejoin my loyal menagerie south of Orbius' hideout and try and eliminate his main force. My lovelies will take you to the location of your desire—and then they will return to me and our battle."

"How do we tell them?" asked Ma'n.

Fazeek looked perplexed.

"With words."

"They understand us?" questioned Bu'r.

"Of course," Fazeek replied.

The rebels all looked at each other. Duke didn't know if he believed Fazeek.

"And what about saddles?" asked Bu'r. "You don't expect us to ride—"

"Bareback, yes," said Fazeek.

"So, you're telling me that these monsters are just going to let us hop on their backs and fly away; all the while, we are supposed to be skilled enough to balance without any saddles right out of the chutes?" questioned Bu'r again.

"Not if you refer to them as 'monsters' again," replied Fazeek.

"This seems like a tall task," added Ma'n.

"Oh, I'm sure you'll figure it out," said Fazeek. "You seem like an intelligent lot." He sharply pivoted his over-sized grundar and darted into the wide sky.

The group of rebels stared at each other again, this time with downward turning lips and scrunched brows.

What just happened?

"Well, you heard the man," Duke began, breaking the silence. "Vern, where are we going again?"

"The outskirts of the village of Horteyaya."

"Okay, Mister Grundar—"

The cat bucked.

"Miss Grundar?"

It meowed, affirming Duke's correction.

"Take us to Horteyaya."

Nothing. The feline turned to Duke with a look of confusion on her face.

"She doesn't know what we've named these places," Ja'a reminded the bounty hunter. "Try this."

She cleared her throat.

"There is a village west of Orbius' fortress. You know the fortress that I speak of?"

The grundar loosed a throaty growl.

"Can you take us to the westernmost rim of that town— and make sure no one sees us?"

The grundar exchanged roars of varying decibel levels, relaying Ja'a's message. They flapped their wings in unison; the squalls generated from the motion almost knocked the riders from their steeds. They leapt into the Neprian clouds as they headed towards Horteyaya—or wherever it was that the grundar thought Ja'a had commanded them to go.

CHAPTER THIRTY-THREE

CAMPS

THE FLIGHT OF THE GRUNDAR was actually pretty smooth, all things considered. It wasn't executive platinum on a galactic cruiser—but it wasn't coach on an Oscavian Cavehopper, either. For his first foray into feline flying, Duke scored it a solid B+. The team waved goodbye as the majestic creatures vaulted into the night air soundlessly. With a single flap of their silvery wings, they were propelled beyond the bounty hunter's range of visibility to become one with the starry backdrop.

"We don't have much time," urged Ja'a. "If we are to go around Horteyaya and into the shadow of Orbius' fortress, we need to move swiftly. And silently."

No one countered her order. *Why would they? She's right.* The grundar had travelled speedily—and had certainly been superior to the alternative of walking—but the evening was already reaching a mature stage and they had ground still yet to cover. The team crested the hill that had hidden their descent. They lit no torches for fear of being seen. The light from the nearby village would have to suffice. For now.

The slinking and slouching reminded Duke of too many recent events—from the grasslands outside of Dre'en, to the hallways of their hotel imprisonment by the Neprian priests, to the witnessing of Lo'n's ultimate betrayal. He wasn't a fan. He was almost looking forward to a straightforward confrontation with Orbius. Even if his Orb controlled everything and must be respected.

The village of Horteyaya wasn't walled like Shud'nut. *Maybe walls are a Southern thing,* pondered Duke. The individual dwellings seemed to be larger and more rugged than the tiny huts outside the city walls of Dre'en; they were boxier with clean lines and smooth edges. Cubes with a slender rectangular door. All were the same color, height, and shape. Not the elegant kind of simple; the boring kind of simple. It was as if they were mass-produced. Duke wondered if anything from Toby's art retrospective could have brightened these places up.

"A typical Northern settlement," whispered Vernglet over Duke's shoulder. "It reminds me of home."

"A bit on the—" Duke searched for the word. "—simple side, don't you think?" It was difficult for him not to call them "drab." Or worse.

"Why would we want our quarters to be exciting? Isn't the point to provide a place to sleep in and keep the elements out?"

"I guess. In many cultures, beings put their own individuality into their houses. Different colors they like. Big paintings on the walls. Swimming pools. You name it. It's been done. I heard that Sprinkles has a taxidermied three-headed ice wombat in his bathroom."

"I don't know this Sprinkles but it sounds interesting. However, I like these abodes. Call me old-fashioned."

"Have it your way."

Ja'a halted the company as they approached a clearing.

It looked similar to the area outside of Shud'nut, with one major exception. Wooden pens taller than two Neprian priests were scattered outside the entrance of a cave.

"The mine," said Vernglet as he pointed into the mouth of the cave.

Duke ignored him. He couldn't help but fixate on the goings-on *in* the pens. In the wooden coops were Neprians. Dirty, unwashed, hygienically-unsound Neprians. Each one covered in mud and indistinguishable muck; their hair matted to the point it looked like it was carved from stone. On their faces were downtrodden, vapid expressions, vacant eyes barely ever looking up from the equally filthy pen floor as if eye contact was a capital offense. Sadness didn't do it justice. Down-on-their-luck was way too nice. They were simply beaten.

"Ishiro, are you seeing this?"

"What did you think we meant when we said we were slaves to Orbius?" asked Ma'n, noticing Duke's shock.

"I thought they took a few of you down in the mines for manual labor. A few guards here and there. Not ideal, but not *this*."

"Maybe in Shud'nut," said Bu'r. "It's a Southern town out of the immediate sight of Orbius. They're going to be much more *by the book* here in Horteyaya."

"They don't want Orbius to stop by for a quality control check and see anything that could be misconstrued as leniency," Vernglet chimed in. "That would be very bad for all."

Duke sat crouching behind a bush, his mouth agape. Sure, he had heard of this type of treatment. But a few paces away, he could see it. Hear it. Smell it. It made him sick.

He reached for his pulse pistol. Vernglet stopped his hand. "This is not the way."

"What are you talking about? Look at 'em."

"I know. If you shoot now, you will spoil the plan. You will take a few lives and save a few. But Orbius will know that we are here. The element of surprise is our greatest ally."

"How can you let this happen?" Duke's emotions caused his voice to increase in volume. Ishiro'shea tapped him on the shoulder; Duke returned his voice to an acceptable level. "How can you let your people do this to other living things?"

"I am guilty, Duke. I cannot run from what I've done or —or, more accurately but no less damning, what I let happen. Orbius has corrupted us all and the servitude to his rule has clouded any chance at rational thoughts from my people. I cannot defend this, nor can I expunge my past—I hope my small part in this cause will at least show that some of us are capable of changing. I wish for a time when that will be important, because it will have meant the demise of Orbius." Vernglet's face twitched and his eyes flickered.

His voice waned. "I don't deserve a second chance for everything that occurred under my watch in Dre'en. It shouldn't have taken a trip to Sansagon for me to realize the full extent of what was happening. But it did. And if I can help you stop this, then maybe I did something right in this life. And the next generation of Neprians—both races—will have a chance to live in peace."

Overhearing the conversation, Bu'r interjected. "I wish my friends back home could see this. They wouldn't have treated us the way they did."

Ishiro'shea put his arm around the beefy rebel to comfort him. Duke could tell that Bu'r carried the weight of his people's rejection, and that it was slowly crushing him.

Three priest guards emerged from the cave carrying wooden rods longer than the javelins that Duke was accustomed to seeing in the hands of the Northern folk. The last third of each pole was dotted with sharp tacks and barbs. Not enough to kill, but more than enough to produce the desired outcome of the prodder.

"No," Duke said to himself.

The priests inserted the rods into the pens and began shouting. The slaves squirmed and tried to move but they were packed in so tightly that they ended up falling over each other and being subjected to more pokes and slices. The priests increased the frequency and the force of the strikes and, with each violent episode, they increased the width of their smiles. Despite their confinement, the prisoners still lunged for an unattainable freedom, scratching and clawing their fellow detainees to flee the reach of the pointed tip of tyranny.

It was impossible for Duke to separate the pain-riddled screams of those being caught with the javelin's point from the agonizing groans from the slaves being crushed by their fellow prisoners. It was a single amorphous bloodcurdling wail that burrowed deep into Duke's mind.

Vernglet's expression mirrored those of the prisoners. He looked at the ground.

"I hope you see now why my decision was to leave and separate myself from Orbius' influence. I was in Dre'en for far too long. Setting up altars and having kids clean pots and pans was much different than what I experienced here."

Duke wanted to understand. Vernglet wasn't *that* good of an actor. He also knew the timing was suspicious and made for textbook spy work. However, he gave the priest the benefit of the doubt. He just hoped it was more than simply proving Po'l wrong that was driving his faith.

They trekked until the sun began to turn the northern sky a radiant orange. The sounds from the mines were but a faint memory, but Duke knew it would take much longer to erase the images of what he had seen in Horteyaya. As they continued, their surroundings provided less and less cover.

"There. Do you see it?" said Vernglet, pointing to a ridge on the horizon. "That's directly outside of Orbius' palace. Beyond the hills is a steep decline into a ravine. In that ravine is the fortress—and farther out is the heart of Sansagon."

Ja'a turned to her team. "We made it. Now we must finish this."

The team cheered—but not too loudly.

"Let us all rest before our final push. Vernglet, you have led us honestly and without deceit. We are grateful. Now, we must ask you for one last favor."

"Yes, noble Ja'a of the Southern landmass."

Duke rolled his eyes at Vernglet's incessant formality.

"Help us strategize a way to enter Orbius' fortress and dispose of him before he can use the Orb to wreak havoc upon us."

"I would be honored. And I happen to have an idea."

Before Vernglet could continue, a black speck appeared in the sky to the south. It was growing and growing—or rather, it was getting closer. It wasn't long before it was easy to see what it was—a grundar.

"Surely they didn't change their mind and are coming back to eat us?" asked Duke.

"There's only one, so I doubt that," replied Ja'a. "And, it looks like it's carrying something. Or someone."

"It appears much too small to be Fazeek," chimed in Vernglet.

"And Fazeek doesn't ride his cat like he's taking a nap," said Duke. "Whatever is on that flying feline, it's unconscious."

"Fazeek could be unconscious. Or what if he's dead?" retorted Vernglet.

Before Duke could answer, the huge cat hit the ground with a plodding gallop and came to a halt a few paces before the group. It lowered its body to the ground. From its back rolled a beaten, bloody body. The thud sounded painful. The living corpse looked up.

"The bastard was right," the injured passenger said through bruised and swollen lips.

Po'l.

"Quick, get him some water," shouted Ja'a.

Ma'n and Bu'r rushed to the injured Neprian's aid.

Duke walked over to the grundar and placed his hand on its nose. It purred softly.

"Thanks, girl. You did good. You don't know how happy I'm going to be to hear Po'l admit he was wrong."

The purr rose to a muted roar and then the grundar was off the ground and heading back towards the battle.

Po'l was sitting upright, downing liquid from Bu'r's canteen. "I just flew on a grundar. And there was some giant skeleton that said he knew you. And Orbius' army... it's... heading south. Lo'n was leading us right to them."

"Wait a second," interrupted Duke.

"Yes?" moaned Po'l.

"So you *were* wrong about Vernglet?"

"No time for this, Duke," hissed Ja'a.

The Nova Texan extended a hand and helped Po'l to his feet.

It can wait.

"Good to have you back, old friend."

CHAPTER THIRTY-FOUR

SMUGGLER'S DOOR

"VERN, WE TRULY COULDN'T HAVE done this without you."

"I'm glad to help, Ja'a. This passage through the ridge and around the ravine isn't even known to most. It was a smugglers' tunnel long before Orbius rose to power."

"It must be the tunnel that He'j mentioned," remarked Bu'r.

"It is not," countered Vernglet.

The rebels' faces contorted with confusion.

"He'j did not find this tunnel. Nor any tunnel."

"I don't understand," said Ja'a.

"Lo'n was deceiving you. In the off chance that you didn't fall for or survived him leading you into the teeth of Orbius' invasion force, you would have been sent into a side entrance that was already laid with a trap and a dozen-plus soldiers."

"So He'j—"

"Yes. He'j *did* try to go in through the front door."

"Suicide," whispered Duke to Ishiro'shea.

"He was a fierce warrior," said Vernglet.

The group fell silent, absorbing the priest's words.

"So this smuggler's tunnel," said Duke, attempting to refocus the conversation, "it drops us right into the fortress?"

"For the most part. It opens up into an attic chamber of a supply closet, just off one of the halls leading into the throne room."

"Great. I'm guessing that Orbius will be there, in the throne room?" asked Duke.

"That is the most likely scenario," replied Vernglet.

"And soldiers? Will this supply closet be guarded?" asked Duke.

"I don't remember it being attended."

"But you don't know for sure," noted Po'l.

"No."

"I think it's a risk that we have to take," replied Ja'a.

Everyone nodded in agreement, including Po'l.

The voyage through the cave system was unexciting. Its lack of use was apparent. Pools of stagnant water dotted the uneven path. A few holsters for torches jutted out intermittently from the passageway; Duke lit each one as they moved farther along. Surprisingly, they encountered no smugglers' traps. Duke thought this was odd—but then again, it was odd that Vernglet knew of a secret passage into Orbius' fortress that the almighty Orbmaster wasn't aware of. The bounty hunter began to talk himself out of believing Vern, but then thought better of it. His internal struggle grew fierce. *I've been on Team Vern from the get-go—best not abandon him now.*

Time was hard to determine in the darkness of the tunnel, but Duke thought it was likely still in the early part of the morning when they approached a cylindrical room that marked the end of the passage.

"Wrong turn?" asked Duke.

"If you want to get into Orbius' house uninvited and without him knowing, Mr. LaGrange, then this is definitely not a wrong turn."

Duke puzzled over the convoluted response for a moment, then replied, "Good."

Vernglet Wip approached the wall and then began to caress it.

"It's here somewhere," he said to himself. "I think it's right—"

A loud click echoed through the chamber. A panel, until now hidden in the stone, swung open.

"—here," concluded Vernglet.

He grabbed a ladder from within the opening, placed it on the cave floor, and started to unfold it. It appeared to Duke that it was the perfect height to reach the top of the room. *But then what? There isn't a door, or at least a noticeable one.*

The priest struggled to bring the ladder upright.

Po'l limped over, still suffering from his wounds sustained during the battle with Orbius' army, and helped Vernglet lift the ladder and lean it against the cave wall.

"Thank you. It's heavier than I remember."

"Wait, Vern," began Duke. "Were you a smuggler? I thought you were a farmer before becoming a priest."

"I had many jobs before I served Orbius. Bringing in goods that were misguidedly outlawed by Togg's government to Sansagon for purchase was one of them."

"So... a smuggler?"

"I preferred 'merchant of exotic and hard-to-come-by goods.'"

"You continue to surprise me."

"I also sold crop insurance for a time."

"Not as surprising."

"Okay, now what?" interjected Ja'a, cutting off Duke's conversation with the former smuggler.

"My apologies," said Vernglet. "Memory lane can be quite the detour."

"Is there an opening beyond our sight?" asked Ma'n.

"It's beyond everyone's sight. You have to activate it with a special code."

"I'm not following," said Po'l.

Duke was about to offer a retort that would have assuredly been ill-received, but Ishiro'shea tapped his shoulder forcefully. *He's probably right*, thought Duke.

"At the top of the room, where the wall meets the ceiling, there is a small inset. It won't be visible until you're up there—it's well-hidden from anyone that might have accidentally stumbled into the caves. You have to know *where* to look. I positioned the ladder so that when you ascend, you will be led right to it."

"Then what?"

"Inside are five circular holes and a pile of brightly-colored pebbles and stones. You must place the stones in a certain pattern. The door will unlock. Then you have to remove them in another particular order and the door will open. It will remain open for exactly the time it takes to sing 'Sansagon the Beautiful.'"

"How long is that?" asked Duke.

Vernglet broke into a rendition of the patriotic tune. It wasn't the Nova Texan planetary anthem, but it was catchy.

"Okay, so we have about a minute and a half," Duke said to Ishiro'shea.

"What's the pattern?"

"It's pretty easy to remember, Ja'a. It's a red stone, two blue, another red, and a yellow. If you are reading it from left to right."

"Red, blue, blue, red, yellow. Got it," said Duke. The

bounty hunter started to climb the ladder. He looked back at the group. "Come on now."

"Once we're in the attic of the supply room, we're in. There isn't a way to open the door from that side. That's one of the reasons it has remained hidden from Orbius."

"Got it. Once we're in, we're in," Duke shouted back as he continued his ascent. "Let's go, everyone. We have a tyrannical maniac to squash."

Bu'r and Ma'n followed the bounty hunter, then Ja'a and Ishiro'shea. Vernglet brought up the rear.

Duke made it to the top and felt around the surface of the wall. Sure enough, there was a small inset panel about the size of his laser revolver. He readjusted his position so that he could see inside the cubbyhole. As Vernglet had described, there was a pile of colorful rocks—some even looked like jewels. *Typical smugglers*, thought Duke. There were also five tiny craters, each the size of one of the rocks.

"I see it, Vern," Duke shouted. "Wouldn't a button have been easier?"

"Buttons can be accidentally pushed. This requires previous knowledge that had to be acquired."

Vernglet's voice lowered as he uttered the word "acquired"—likely harkening back to his days as a smuggler.

"Makes sense, but my hand barely fits in here. Okay, red, blue, blue... uh..." Duke stopped to think.

"What happens if you place the stone incorrectly?" Ja'a said to Vernglet.

"The ceiling opens up and boiling oil is dropped down over the ladder. Instantly transforming those on the ladder into a gruesome, mangled, gnarled—"

"We got it," Duke screamed. "Red, blue, blue, red, and YELLOW."

"Yes."

A loud click resonated throughout the cavern.

"Great, it's unlocked," said Vern. "Now remove them in this order—yellow."

"Okay, yellow removed."

"The first red that you placed," continued Vernglet.

"Done."

"Both blues at the same time. Then the last red."

"Here goes nothing," said Duke with a quaver in his voice.

A squeaking shriek and a whoosh of air followed. A soft light filled the room. It was a light from *another* room—on the other side of the now-open door.

"We're in, my friends," exclaimed Duke.

"Careful," Ja'a reminded the group. "We have no idea what's in there."

Duke crawled through. The room was empty and quite cramped.

"No way we're all fitting in here," relayed Duke. "What next?"

Vernglet responded from inside the cave. "There is a door at the far end of the attic floor. Open it and you should be able to fall right into the supply room. It shouldn't be exposed to the hallway; we should be hidden."

Duke followed the orders, traversing the restricted attic crawlspace until he discovered a hatch. He opened it and dropped directly into the supply closet, as Vernglet had described. *That was easy.*

The others followed suit. Ishiro'shea and Vernglet were the final two to make it to the attic door. As the ninja hit the supply closet floor without a sound, the door suddenly opened, exposing the group to the hallway—and to a dozen priests with javelins pointed at them.

"General, we have intruders!" screamed a guard in a high-pitched, nasal tone.

"Vern!" shouted Duke.

There was not a response. Then a whoosh and click. *The smugglers' door.*

Duke could sense Po'l's smug "I told you so" from the back of the supply room. He thought that was the worst feeling in the world—but then was reminded that the dangerously sharp spears being thrust in his general direction might hurt a bit more.

CHAPTER THIRTY-FIVE

FOR THE GOOD PART OF NEPRIUS!

THE ARROW FLEW MERE INCHES from Duke's ear and struck one of the guards in the chest. Duke's reflexes kicked in and he rattled off a few pulses. Most landed effectively. The guards retreated a few paces, providing the rebels with a little more separation from their assailants.

"Quick," Ja'a commanded. "Let's get out of this damn deathtrap of a room!"

The group sprinted down the ornate hallway until they reached a grand foyer sporting equally grand doors at its terminal point.

"Maybe that's the throne room," said Ja'a.

Bu'r and Ishiro'shea tried to open the door, but it wouldn't budge.

"Move," shouted Duke. He drew Betsy. She shook the entire hallway. The doors splintered and collapsed inward. *Orbius knows we're here now.*

"Even better than a throne room," said Ma'n. "The armory."

The sound of the footsteps of Orbius' troops were growing louder. Their approach was rapid.

"Let's prop these doors up. They should provide some cover," Duke said to Ishiro'shea.

The bounty hunters began to form a rudimentary barricade. Bu'r noticed their efforts and quickly joined in. Po'l, Ma'n, and Ja'a started to grab as many projectile weapons as they could—javelins, arrows, spiked stones, skins filled with flammable oil—and stockpiled them behind the makeshift barrier.

"This should make for one hell of a final stand," Duke said to Ishiro'shea.

"Who said this was our final stand?" Po'l interjected. "Our business is unfinished. A trap by that wormy priest won't stop us."

"*They* might have something to say about it being our final stand," Duke said. He pointed Betsy's barrel towards a horde of javelin-toting priest soldiers.

"A mere delay."

"I appreciate the optimism, Po'l. And, just so we can get it out of the way—I'm man enough to say it—"

"Say what?"

Duke knew that Po'l was aware of exactly what the bounty hunter was about to say. He wanted to milk it. *That bastard.*

"About Vernglet and—"

"Yes?"

"I never thought this would be the last word uttered in the life of Duke LaGrange, adventurer, trailblazer—"

The footsteps came to an abrupt end.

"Rebel trash and off-world scum." The voice was booming. It sounded like fresh death. Tsarano Gar. "I'm surprised that you decided to drop in on us like this. More courage than I thought."

"I'll give it to you, Gar," Ja'a responded, "your spy fooled us. But there's a massive chasm between placing us in this trap and actually stopping us."

Gar did not respond immediately. He looked around, almost confused at Ja'a's retort.

"Fine. Whatever you say, rebel. Prepare to die as your father did, begging for forgiveness."

The general released a throaty baritone laugh.

Duke could hear Ja'a gritting her teeth.

"But before you put up this annoyance of a resistance, remember that whatever you do now will affect what I do to this ingrate."

The general reached behind two of his soldiers and yanked out a ratty-haired Neprian child—gagged and tied.

"Uu'k!" shouted Duke.

Ishiro'shea's teeth were now grinding even louder than Ja'a's.

"How?" asked the bounty hunter.

"Lo'n," replied Po'l, his voice full of defeat.

Duke drew his gun and aimed it at Gar's head.

"Kill me and this puny accident of a life will be skewered."

Before Duke could respond, he felt a body leap past him.

"Come back, Ma'n!" shouted Ja'a.

The rebel hurdled the barricade and charged the entire Neprian line, his bow drawn. He sent arrows into flight toward the mass of soldiers without breaking stride.

Gar held the soldiers from advancing. He shoved Uu'k back and she disappeared behind the ranks.

Ma'n threw the bow down as he approached Gar. He drew his ax. Two soldiers stepped in front of their commander and were chopped down in a single motion from the irate rebel. His momentum carried him to Gar and he came down with a powerful stroke. However, his ax was halted in midair by Gar's twisted sword.

"Weakling," shouted Gar passively.

Ma'n countered with another swing, but again it was blocked by Gar's blade. Gar reached out with his free hand and clamped down on Ma'n's throat. The rebel struggled and dropped his ax as he gasped for air. Gar's death blow was quick but he held the blade firm so that the other rebels could see and digest what had just happened. With a slight shrug, Ma'n's corpse slid off the sword and fell limp to the floor.

"Attack!" screamed the general as he sank to the back of the line.

The soldiers stormed the rebels.

Between Duke's marksmanship and the constant barrage of deadly projectiles lobbied from behind the barrier, the priests weren't immediately successful in breaching—but their numbers never dwindled. It was a constant flow. And though Duke could keep shooting forever, the rebels' other ammunition was running low.

"We can't hold them off much longer," said Po'l. "And Gar is getting away with Uu'k."

"And pretty soon Orbius will turn up—with the Orb," added Bu'r.

"At least I could get a shot at him," said Duke.

"Orbius is not that careless," reminded Ja'a. "He won't put himself in harm's way—especially since we aren't posing much of a threat at the present."

"So, basically, this *is* our last stand?" questioned Duke.

"If Uu'k has been kidnapped, then Mo'a must have pieced together Lo'n's betrayal," Ja'a said, changing the subject. "They will be working on another mission as we speak."

"Or those that abducted her with Lo'n's help already

destroyed the base and everyone in it," Duke replied grimly, "and we *are* the last hope."

"I refuse to believe that."

"They've been pretty successful thus far in one-upping us," countered Duke. "They stole Uu'k from right under our noses; a betrayal from one of the trusted rebel brass."

"And your priest friend," added Po'l.

"Yes, and Vern. I'm not making myself immune from anything. I was fooled, the same as you."

Po'l seemed surprised by Duke's honesty. And then he lobbed a javelin into the chest cavity of a charging priest.

"I refuse to believe it. I have faith in Mo'a."

"We don't have much left," screamed Bu'r.

"Here, Ishiro, catch." Duke tossed his pulse pistol to the ninja. Ishiro'shea dropped the bow and arrow that he was using. Duke took Betsy from her holster. "At least we'll have two things rockin' when they run out of arrows."

Betsy cleared the hallway. Duke let loose another shot, pushing back the line even more. He smiled. Ishiro'shea discharged pulses into the cloud of smoke.

"As long as this door provides cover, we can do this all day. They have to run out of soldiers at some point. Right?"

Before Duke could receive an answer, a booming crack rang out. Duke and Ishiro'shea, being the closest to the door, were thrown to the ground about halfway into the room.

Duke looked up. The door that had served as their barricade was shattered. The culprit was a javelin nearly quadruple the size of the ones carried by the priests. Emerging from the cloud of dust and debris was a gargantuan mounted crossbow, pushed by four priests. The rebels were now fully exposed, and the priests accelerated in their advance.

Ishiro'shea leapt to his feet and threw Duke the pulse pistol in the same motion. He drew his sword. The meaning of the gesture was clear: if he was going to die, it would be with his sword in his hand. Duke spun the revolver on his finger and slid it into his holster. He drew Betsy. If this was going to be his last day, he would spend it with his true love. The Neprians followed suit. Bu'r, Po'l, and Ja'a drew their weapons and readied for the horde that was sure to overwhelm them.

"This should take a few out!"

Betsy sang. Smoke and the smell of burnt death filled the hallway. But the pattering of feet didn't wane. The mounted crossbow continued to roll towards them.

This is how it's going to end. On a two-bit planet in an unknown sector of the universe. Definitely not going to have a parade in my honor, Duke concluded. This was *not* how the bounty hunter drew it up.

During the course of his career as one of the best-known bounty hunter–playboys in the universe, Duke had been charged by many violent entities, so he knew the anxious feeling right before he engaged in mortal combat. When his enemy was a few paces away, he would tense up and visualize the first few moves that he planned. Maybe an offensive attack, or a counter to what the assailant was likely to do. Against a massive blob of assailants, it would be all firepower until the lights went out. He aimed Betsy at the direct center—at the group toting the rolling crossbow.

"For Neprius!" shouted Ja'a.

"But only the good part!" added Duke.

The rebels began to scream—an organic and primal sound. Worthy of a last stand.

Oblong faces, gaunt and bony, emerged from the cloud. Duke tensed.

And then they were gone.

An entire side wall collapsed on top of the soldiers. The roar of the charging mass was silenced in a mere flash. A chunk of rock lay on top of dozens of soldiers. The others that stood behind the disaster area looked shocked, then readied themselves for another charge.

"What just happened?" asked Duke, wiping dust from his eyes. There was no response.

Stepping from outside and onto the makeshift stage created by the fallen wall fragment was Fazeek. And his grundar. And the grundar's grundar friends.

"I thought I would come lend a helping hand," Fazeek shouted. "And paw. Attack, my lovelies!"

Looloo roared.

The grundar pounced and growled. The priests mostly screamed. And ran.

Fazeek turned to the rebels. "Well, don't just stand there. We've got this handled. Go get that Orb!"

"Thank you, Shepherd of the Grundar," proclaimed Ja'a, rather regally considering the circumstances.

Fazeek turned his back to them and entered battle, waving his staff and striking down the much smaller soldiers effortlessly.

"Thoughts on how to get to the throne room that Vern spoke of?" asked Duke. "I bet Orbius is tucked away in there... unless Vern was lying to us about that as well."

"With Uu'k, too," added Po'l.

Ja'a hesitated. It was clear that she didn't know.

"We can't follow Gar's route since that will lead us right through the skirmish," said Duke. "And Fazeek doesn't seem like someone that would enjoy us meddling in his business. Maybe. No..." He caught himself. "Well, maybe..."

"What?"

"This."

Duke took aim at the side wall of the ammunition room. He fired Betsy.

Once again the bounty hunter was making his own

doorway. Betsy fired again. And again. The gaping hole connected to another hallway. It was empty. No guards; nothing.

"I say we go that way," Duke said, pointing into the vacant hall.

There wasn't another option. They all sprinted into the open area, then stopped to assess their position.

"The hall looks like it wraps around to the right up ahead," said Ja'a. "Maybe it circles back to the direction that Gar was heading with Uu'k."

"Makes sense," chimed in Duke.

"In agreement?"

"Yes!" called Po'l and Bu'r. Ishiro'shea nodded.

They all made their way down the passageway, following it as it wound to the right. Before long Duke could see that they were heading in the correct direction. At the end of a long, narrow corridor was another decorative entrance—not as big as the ammunition keep, but more detailed. It appeared to be made of mustangsen and dotted with a jeweled design befitting a crazed dictator. Only two guards stood outside, both holding golden javelins.

"I'm thinking that's our destination."

Duke unleashed his pulse pistol and dropped both guards.

"Let's go meet this Orbius and his pet rock."

CHAPTER THIRTY-SIX

JUST A VILLAIN

THERE WASN'T EVEN A LOCK on the door. *How very Neprian.* The doors swung open and hit the wall with a ringing clang.

The capacious dwelling was so large that Duke had trouble finding the perimeter walls. The entire village of Horteyaya could have crammed into it with room to spare. From what Duke could see, the walls were gray, with a metallic tint. In the center of the room was a maroon and yellow rug that stretched from the entrance to a set of four steps that led upwards to an immense and gaudy throne. Sure, there were a few stones here and there—but mostly it was roughly sculpted mustangsen, matching the walls.

Standing at the bottom of the steps was General Tsarano Gar. His monstrous claw was gripping the back of Uu'k's neck. Her wiggling and writhing did not appear to faze the Neprian general. His other hand held his drawn, twisted sword, its business end facing the visitors. Extending from the throne, like wings on either side, was a contingent of priest warriors. They looked like the foot soldiers that the rebels had encountered in their march towards Sansagon, save that they wore additional armor around their chests and bulky helmets that covered the majority of their faces. Their javelins were drawn and they each held a circular shield in their left hand that seemed to reflect the remnants of light that emanated from the lanterns that hung from the ceiling.

Standing in front of the throne was a human who sported a cloaked robe of deep red accented with bright yellow. Around his waist was a rope that served as a belt. His hood was down, revealing a very ordinary face. No scars. No facial hair. No demonic eyes or fangs. His skin was a milky-cream color, with noticeable creases and age lines. *He's a bit on the ordinary side*, thought Duke, *especially for a ruthless tyrant and murderer*. The more Duke contemplated it, the more Orbius' nondescript nature started to freak him out. *So ordinary that he is terrifying.*

Orbius raised his hand, seeming about to speak.

"I see why you have so many mines," began Duke. He could tell that the Orbmaster was irritated. Duke thought that he probably had an opening line planned for such an occasion. The bounty hunter loved ruining plans. "I mean, this entire place is mustangsen. Not the most decorative material out there."

"What about it?" Orbius spoke.

"Nothing, just that a good interior design firm could make a killing on this planet," added Duke.

"I see."

Orbius' voice matched his appearance—bland. It wasn't overly masculine or feminine; it didn't fill the room, nor was it meek or inaudible. He raised his hand again, pointing into the far corner of the chamber. Duke squinted but saw nothing outside of a towering curtain, approximately the length of a spaceship.

"Guards, a little help," said Orbius in an agitated tone.

Three ran over and started to tug on a cord that also hung down from the ceiling. It matched the cord on Orbius' waist but with much more girth.

"Sorry, my friends," started Orbius. "They were supposed to be over there for the grand reveal."

"The grand reveal of what?" asked Po'l.

The spaceship-length curtain was a perfect size for what it covered—a spaceship. The *Deus Ex Machina*, to be exact.

"Your ship!" shouted Bu'r. Oddly enough, Duke didn't say anything. He tightened his grip on his gun.

"You don't look shocked, bounty hunter. And why is that?"

Before Duke could answer, Po'l blurted out, "Why do you have this ship in your throne room? I thought the point was to use it to terrorize our people and escape to other worlds."

Orbius did not answer. It was as if he knew that the gears were turning inside the Nova Texan's head.

"He doesn't want the *Deus* to go anywhere. Terrorize your people, yes, but not by flying it over settlements and blasting his way to obedience."

"I don't need your ship to terrorize these primitives."

"I don't understand," said Bu'r.

"It's what the *Deus* is made of, huh?" said Duke. "You want to harvest it as you would any mine. It's made of your precious mustangsen."

"How many more pieces of decor does he need?" chimed in Po'l.

"I thought it was quite a coincidence. I mean, think about it—the most monumental slab of mustangsen in the known universe happens to end up on my planet in the middle of my final conquest of these rebellious twerps.

Sure, you probably don't call it 'mustangsen'—but it is, you know."

"Hard to believe, indeed," Duke said, barely managing to squeeze the words through his clenched teeth. He turned to Ishiro'shea and whispered, "I guess it can get us *into* trouble as well as out? We should totally write a review if we make it outta here."

"I still don't get it," said Bu'r.

"He's not mining the mustangsen for decorative purposes," began Duke.

"No," Ja'a interjected, "he's using it to control the Orb."

"What?" asked Po'l, as confused as Bu'r.

"Yep," said Duke. "The rings on his fingers, this room, the *Deus*—heck, even the mounds of junk in the Keeper's cave—all of it was mustangsen. It somehow controls the Orb."

Ja'a looked down at her chest.

"My necklace."

"Very good. You aren't as stupid as you look," said Orbius in a congratulatory manner. He bowed sarcastically.

Duke thought for a moment. "Your father had a necklace like that as well, right?"

Before Ja'a could answer, Orbius cut in.

"Yes, your father," he rolled his eyes. "What a nuisance! He thought he could challenge me, overtake me. He started all of this, you know? He asked for help and the Orb summoned *me*. He thought he could alter it all by barging in and trying to summon a worthy adversary for me. And guess what? He failed. Miserably. The Orb brought you two."

Orbius pointed at Duke and Ishiro'shea and giggled. Duke tried to wrap his head around the fact that the Orb selected him and Ishiro'shea to save the planet. And it was He'j that had requested it, wearing the other half of the necklace that Ja'a wore at this very moment. *Heavy stuff*. He decided that he liked it better when he thought that it had been merely random chance and an insane maniac's practice sessions at dimensional portal manipulation that had sucked them into the astral anomaly and deposited them on this cursed rock.

"Yes, girl, your father failed. And then I killed him. Struck him down like I have so many of your friends. And like I will do to your annoying rebellion. Kind of sad, if you think about. I mean... sad for you. It's actually pretty great for me."

"It's not over," Ja'a insisted.

"Oh, but it is, my flower. It is."

Po'l broke through the line and charged at the throne. Orbius waved his hand and motioned the guards to halt the angered rebel. Po'l slashed down the guards with his sword. Gar released Uu'k and started to head towards Po'l.

"Halt, General. No need," said Orbius, without any trace of fear.

He held his hand high. An object floated upward at a leisurely pace from behind Orbius; when it was an arm's length above his head, it stopped and hovered. The sphere glowed a radiant violet, and tiny fragments of electricity pulsed around its outer shell. Sporadically, the pulses would halt, revealing the sphere's cloudy interior. It was The Orb That Controlled Everything and Must Be Respected.

Orbius manipulated his fingers in a calculated manner; the mustangsen rings danced. A beam shot out and crashed in front of Po'l. The explosion sent Po'l into the air with a velocity that defied the laws of normal physics. He was thrown across the room and crashed into the side of the *Deus*, then met the floor with the sound of shattering bones. A muffled scream escaped Uu'k's gag. *No one could have survived that,* thought Duke.

Orbius laughed. "Just a sampling of what I can do."

He's pleased with himself.

"You mean what the Orb can do," corrected Duke.

"It's all the same to you, bounty hunter," said Orbius. "Now put down your weapons and kick them over to me, or you will end up like your friend with the broken spine over there."

"Why should we?" exclaimed Ja'a. "You're just going to kill us anyway."

"I will squash your rebellion, yes. I will throw you into the mines—especially you, bounty hunter—but I won't kill you. I'm not a tyrant."

Orbius looked disappointed that no one appeared to agree with this sentiment.

"And, you my radiant daughter of He'j, I do need a queen. Or at least someone that is somewhat attractive. I mean, I can't even tell the male Northerners from the female Northerners. Am I right? My hometown wasn't exactly known for beautiful women—but this is another level. Then again, Newark had its other benefits."

He trailed off into self-reflection before regaining his train of thought. "I'm being serious. I had one servant pegged as a guy—a cycle later, she's pregnant."

No one shared his joviality, but it did make Duke curious about Vernglet's gender. He hoped that he hadn't insulted him/her by defaulting to masculine pronouns.

"I would rather die than have any part of this," Ja'a said boldly.

"No you wouldn't," replied Orbius. "Dying looks quite painful, if you ask me."

"You will have to kill me. I won't go to the mines and I definitely won't stand by your side."

"Such vigor. I like it."

Duke looked over at Ja'a. In a low voice, he said, "Drop

your weapons. As long as you're alive, there's hope. It will give Mo'a additional purpose. As bleak as the prospects of the rebellion look, Mo'a will always try to rescue his best friend's daughter from enslavement."

"What's that?" asked Orbius, trying to make out what Duke and Ja'a were saying. "Oh yeah, I almost forgot. If you don't, I'll have Gar slit this puny wretch's throat right in front of you."

Uu'k squirmed, but not as much as Duke would have expected. *She's tough. She's a spy, after all.*

"Fine," Ja'a huffed. She dropped her bow.

Duke knelt down and put both of his guns on the floor. Ishiro'shea followed suit with his katana and Bu'r with his mace. They kicked them all to the Neprian guards. They were officially weaponless.

"I totally should have led with the kid," said Orbius to himself.

"Hey, Ot!" yelled Duke. For a brief moment Orbius seemed taken aback at the use of his real name. It was doubtful that his priestly servants referred to him as anything other than Orbius, if they were even that informal.

"Why yes, Duke LaGrange, bounty hunter and failed rebel. Go on."

"So," began Duke, ignoring Orbius' insult, "what's the plan?"

"Why should I tell you 'the plan', bounty hunter? I mean, that's like Villain Mistakes 101."

"True. But you aren't *just* a villain. You're a villain with a magical Orb. That has to give you some leeway, right?"

"I suppose."

Gar looked back and snarled at Orbius.

"Simmer down, General," Orbius said. "We have this under control. You have the girl under control, right? That's our ticket. Their weapons are on the ground. We're good."

"So, the plan. What do you get out of running this one-horse primitive planet? Is it just ego?"

"Ego?"

"Yeah, or is this payback from being pushed down on the jungle gym at recess?"

"Compelling. But no. You're going to be disappointed by my answer."

"Try me."

"I'm actually the good guy. The one that is on the side of right. The light side. The hero. The protagonist."

Duke didn't think the joke was funny. Then he realized that Orbius wasn't joking.

"The Orb could be in far worse hands than mine."

"You're enslaving an entire race. You are aware of that, right?"

"A race that wants to free the Orb from my possession—and, in turn, it would end up in worse hands. Probably. Therefore, the Southern Neprians are necessary casualties for the greater good. You see, I'm the only one that can control the Orb—and if I control it, it's not doing any damage."

"No damage!" screamed Ja'a. "Have you seen what you are doing to my people?"

"Refer to my last comment, sweetie," replied Orbius. "Stop resisting and the pain will stop. I never understood why you challenged me in the first place. These guys didn't."

It looked like Gar was trying to muster a smile.

"You know," Orbius continued, "I'm not trying to control you or your people. Just protect them."

"From what?" asked Duke.

"I told you, bounty hunter—worse things than I."

"Any names?"

"No one has stepped out from the shadows yet, but

that's how the universe works. A great power is discovered or built or acquired—and eventually the most evil and sinister entity ends up with it. Maybe that's you, Duke LaGrange. Have your rebel friends thought about that? As it goes, tragedy ensues until balance is restored. Look at Earth. He knows what I'm talking about." Orbius pointed to Ishiro'shea. "You're from New Tokyo, right?"

Ishiro'shea did not move a muscle.

"The Orb is power that can't be harnessed by anyone other than myself."

"Or someone else with access to a ton of mustangsen," challenged Duke.

"I'll admit, it helps control the Orb. It's my remote control, so to speak. But, I am *one* with the Orb now. It's part of me and I am part of it. It called me here to bond with me. I'm the one it chose as the savior of this planet."

"It also chose us," Duke said with a smirk.

"Ah yes, it did. I thought about that when I heard that you had landed outside of Dre'en. I thought about it a lot. But, it was quite obvious to me."

"It was?"

"Yes, Duke LaGrange, it was. The Orb wasn't going to send someone to actually challenge me or overtake me, definitely not that—it was going to send someone that would prove so useless that they would actually crush the rebellion for me. The rebels view you as their best shot at taking me down. Coupled with all of the traitors that I already have—like your old friend, Lo'n—your demise will destroy all hope that's left."

"Pretty self-centered view, wouldn't you say?" asked Duke.

"I would not say. See, old He'j just asked the Orb to send help. He didn't say help for what. I killed him before he could elaborate any further. So the Orb did send help—

help for me. Help to stop this futile cause that's killing more people than necessary."

Ja'a, Duke, Ishiro'shea, and Bu'r all exchanged glances. *It isn't totally insane to consider Orbius' rationale*, thought Duke. *Could the Orb have known what He'j meant? Does it really want to quash the rebellion so it can spend more quality time with this nutjob?*

"So, if we stop the war and surrender," began Ja'a, "and acknowledge that you are the one true master of the Orb and should reign over Neprius—"

"Yes," Orbius said eagerly.

"—you will free my people from the mines."

Orbius thought about this and started to speak, but caught himself. He pondered a bit more. Gar peered back to make sure that his boss had heard the question.

"No."

"What?"

"No. I still need mustangsen mined. Duke's ship should help for a bit but it won't last forever. And, if you think about it, you kind of deserve some punishment for this annoying resistance."

"Then—" started Ja'a.

"Yes?"

"Then we won't surrender. You will have to kill us now."

"This is growing very tiresome. Fine, if you really want to die, I can make that happen. This will be as painful as it was for your father."

The Orb ascended even higher above Orbius' throne and pulsated with even brighter colors. It spun faster and faster as it prepared to strike the rebels.

The blast was blinding and deafening.

But Duke was in one piece. He looked around. So were

his companions. The blast didn't look or sound like the one that had hit Po'l.

Duke scanned the room looking for the source of the burst. His eyes panned to Orbius' throne. The Orb was no longer hovering in the air—it wasn't anywhere to be seen. General Gar and his guards had been displaced by the explosion but appeared to be alive. Orbius, though, wasn't visible.

Duke swivelled his head again, towards the *Deus Ex Machina*. In the cockpit was a barely visible silhouette. The figure was thin and boney, with a head too big for its body. *Vern.*

"Nice shot, Vern!" shouted Duke.

How did he do that? He doesn't know how to work a spacecraft—he's a primitive, thought Duke.

The Neprian priest poked his head out from a side window.

"Did I hit it?"

"You did good, Vern. Impressive shot," yelled Duke.

"It just told me what to do—it's like it knew that I needed to save you. And there was no other way. As in, no other reasonable way to survive. None whatsoever. You were goners."

"We get it, Vern," said Duke. He turned to Ishiro'shea. "Saved us again. Maybe we leave a slightly better review now."

Just as Duke finished his thought, another noise filled the throne room. The *Deus* fizzled and shook and the light in the cockpit dimmed. It was powering down.

"So it *is* still broken. Its timing is impeccable," said Duke to his ninja companion.

Emerging from behind his throne, Orbius was regaining his composure and shaking off the proverbial cobwebs. The blast had knocked him off of the altar and down to the floor but he didn't appear injured.

"What just happened?" he screamed. "And where's the Orb?"

No one responded.

The bounty hunter continued to scan the room. There was no sign of the Orb, nor was there any sign of Orb shards, fragments, or shrapnel; there was nothing that said that the Orb was destroyed.

"Is that Vernglet Wip?" Orbius asked General Gar. The general was struggling to his feet with Uu'k still in his clutches. "I thought you disposed of him. Who cares? Guards! Kill him."

The guards charged the *Deus*. The remaining guards surrounded Orbius. One of them grabbed Uu'k and passed her to the Orbmaster. Unfortunately, the rebels' weapons were still very much out of reach.

CHAPTER THIRTY-SEVEN

GIVE ME BACK MY SPHERE

F OUR JAVELIN-TOTING GUARDS STORMED the doors of the *Deus*. Duke could see the panic in Vernglet's eyes. The lifeless ship had no other option than to accept the inevitable breach. Duke, Ishiro'shea, Bu'r, and Ja'a stood next to each other—too far from their weapons to retrieve them without having to deal with Gar and the rest of the armed soldiers. However, Orbius seemed preoccupied with the attack on the *Deus*.

"You will pay for that, Wip. Not smart, man, not smart." Orbius paused and regathered himself. "Where is my Orb?"

"Destroyed," shouted Duke, diverting Orbius' attention from the *Deus*.

"Destroyed, you say? If it is, then this has no chance of working."

Orbius twinkled his fingers, rubbing the mustangsen rings against each other. Nothing. He did it again, nothing. For the third attempt, he completed the motion with a clenched jaw and progressively reddening face.

"No chance of doing what, Ot?" Duke smirked.

The Orb sped from an unseen location in the corner of

the room and into the tyrant's clutches. Orbius turned his attention back to the quartet of rebels.

Shit.

"Now, while my minions take care of that traitorous rat in the ship, I get to finally dispose of you. Despite the brief delay, this should be fun. For me, that is."

Orbius laughed maniacally.

First thing that he's done that's worthy of a true supervillain, thought Duke.

The soldiers began prying Vernglet from the cockpit of the ship. He was grabbing anything that he could, to no avail.

"I'm going to fry you after I deal with your friends here, Wip," said Orbius, though his eyes remained squarely focused on the four rebels.

The soldiers released Vernglet, unnoticed by Orbius. They also released their footing from the platform that they had scaled to capture him. They crashed to the floor.

Standing beside a confused Vernglet Wip was a bruised and battered Po'l. The metal pipe—clearly a piece of the *Deus'* exterior that had dislodged itself when it ceased operations—was covered in Northern blood. Orbius *did* notice this.

"Seriously, how many lives does this guy have?" asked Duke to his cohorts.

"How cute. You aren't dead. Whoop-de-doo. I just get to kill you *again*. Yay for me." Orbius sounded a bit annoyed, like a child receiving an extra chore just as they are almost finished with their original list. He pivoted towards the ship and raised his hands. The Orb began to spin even faster. *Po'l won't be able to survive this,* Duke concluded. *No one would survive this.*

The wall to the left of the throne exploded. Stone fragments consumed the entire room.

Despite the echoing boom, Orbius' voice could be heard above the noise. "What now? Seriously, what now?"

In the frame of the newly-created door was the outline of something big. Huge, in fact.

"You have my sphere."

Out stepped Toby, hulking and ticked off. Orbius had not expected to see a mountainous creature asking for his Orb once the dust settled, that much was clear, but to his credit he didn't panic. He appeared calm, if not a bit frustrated by the continued interruptions. Duke was impressed again with his villaining. *Not bad for a glorified gardener*, he thought.

"I think you are mistaken, my ogre friend," replied Orbius, wiping the dust from his face and hood. "This is *my* Orb!"

He motioned towards the Keeper. The Orb emitted a beautiful beam of light in the direction of Toby, who raised his forearms to shield the impact. The ray deflected off of his gauntlet and was redirected to the ceiling, greeting the surface with a crash. Parts of the ceiling fell to the floor.

"Impressive. I see your gauntlets are made of mustangsen."

"I guess," bellowed Toby, obviously not understanding the significance of the construction material. "Now, give me back the Sphere."

"I don't think—"

Orbius wasn't able to finish his sentence. He dove back to avoid the swing of Toby's gargantuan club, which sent three guards into the air and deposited them on the other side of the room. Toby swung again, cracking the throne in half. The soldiers surrounded him and heaved their javelins. He didn't seem to like that very much and demonstrated his irritation by crushing them with blunt force aggression.

During the chaos, Uu'k broke free of Gar's hold and sprinted towards the rebels. Gar followed suit with his sword drawn. Ishiro'shea made a course to intercept the grizzled Neprian general.

"Bu'r, get Uu'k to safety," screamed Ja'a.

Bu'r obliged, snatching her up and heading towards the *Deus*. Po'l and Vernglet were already down from the platform and hiding in its shadows, searching for usable weapons.

Tsarano Gar swung at Ishiro'shea with his sword but the ninja eluded it with a swift forward roll. The general turned and swung again—another miss. Ishiro'shea countered with a powerful kick to the chest. Gar was stunned but didn't lose his footing. He stabbed at Ishiro, but again came up empty. His frustration took the form of a vitriolic growl. Ishiro'shea took the offensive and leapt at Gar, but Gar blocked the strike and countered with a clubbing fist to the ninja's jaw. Ishiro'shea tumbled a few steps behind Gar. He still clutched his katana.

"Behind you!" shouted Duke. "Behind you!"

A Neprian soldier approached the ninja from behind with his javelin aimed to kill. Gar charged from the front. Ishiro'shea turned and ran towards the guard. Then, mere moments before the Neprian performed his death blow, Ishiro'shea dove to the ground feet first in a slide. He tripped the guard, who crashed face first, dropping the javelin. The rampaging Gar halted to avoid colliding with the fallen guard, who was now rolling with increased velocity. Gar returned his attention to Ishiro'shea. He swung—but the ninja, having grabbed the free javelin, blocked the swipe with the midsection of the shaft. It snapped in two under the power of Gar's swing. Ishiro'shea fell on his backside.

"So much for that, off-worlder!" roared Gar. He raised

his sword and sent it crashing down upon Ishiro'shea with all of his power. Ishiro'shea moved.

The sword was stuck. Gar tried to remove it, his muscles flexing and tensing as he struggled to dislodge it from the floor.

Ishiro'shea was quick. He leapt from the floor and appeared almost to hang in the air. In one motion, the point of the shattered javelin struck Tsarano Gar across the bridge of the nose. He shrieked in pain.

Sprinkles didn't even have it that bad, thought Duke.

Gar released his sword and stumbled backwards. Another javelin tip ripped through the general's backside and exploded through his chest. Then it was pulled back through his chest cavity. He collapsed to the floor, lifeless.

Vernglet stood above the body, holding a bloody javelin taken from one of the would-be captors that had yanked him out of the *Deus*.

"I never liked that guy," he proclaimed.

"Quick," Ja'a shouted to Duke. "Betsy! While the guards are distracted!"

Distracted, was of course, an understatement. Pummeled would be a more appropriate term, considering the power of Toby's club.

The bounty hunter hustled and dove at Betsy. He quickly checked to see if she had survived all of the falling debris. *Looks good enough.*

"Not so fast, Duke LaGrange," proclaimed Orbius. The Orb was floating above him—though not as high as it had been previously—and once again it was spinning and glowing. "Your fun is finally at an end. I'll deal with that brute in a second. You, I kill now."

"Don't I even get an overblown sinister dialogue before I go? That would be fitting, considering I'm Duke

LaGrange, after all." He paused. "You know, adventurer, trailblazer—"

The blast was quick and exact. It burst from below Orbius' neck and into the wall behind Duke.

Ja'a sat with the laser revolver in her hand.

"At least someone on this planet can shoot!" said Duke.

He could hear Po'l groan from across the room.

As Orbius' flaccid body fell, the Orb crashed to the floor. It stopped momentarily and then slowly rolled towards the bounty hunter as if it had a mind of its own and high-end rear-wheel steering. No fizzling. No sizzling. No lights or clouds. Only what appeared to be an ordinary round glass ball with the power of sophisticated and seemingly spontaneous locomotion. Duke picked it up and examined it.

All fighting had ceased. The Keeper stopped his bashing of skulls and looked at Duke inquisitively. Ja'a kept her gun drawn. The remaining soldiers stared at the bounty hunter, still gripping their weapons. Bu'r positioned Uu'k behind him. Po'l moved to provide additional cover. Only Ishiro'shea seemed to react what Duke would refer to as "normally."

Duke stood up and held the Orb above his head.

"Behold, puny peasants! I am now one with the Orb! I am Orbius... Junior!"

Nothing.

Then a laugh permeated through Ishiro'shea's mask. Uu'k joined in. The rebels all gave a deep collective sigh. Toby and the Neprian priest soldiers seemed confused.

"Here you go!" Duke nonchalantly tossed the Orb to the Keeper. Toby caught it and placed it in a satchel that hung from his hip.

"Thank you," he said. "And, I've decided that I'm

almost certain that you and your friends aren't swamp people."

"Thank you," replied Duke. "I guess."

He turned his attention to the priests. "Oh yeah, you lot. Drop your weapons."

The guards all dropped their weapons. They didn't seem too unhappy. One even smiled.

"What'd I miss?"

Fazeek entered through the Toby-created opening on the back of his favorite grundar.

"Oh hey, Toby. Long time," Fazeek said, not successfully hiding his true feelings regarding the Keeper. He glanced at Toby's satchel, his eyes squinted. His gaze shifted to Duke, then to Ja'a, and finally back to the Keeper. "You think you can keep it this time?"

Toby didn't sneer back as Duke had anticipated. "I think so. But I could use some help, old friend."

Fazeek's expression changed to one of genuine surprise. It then morphed into a wry smile.

"Sure. Not many old-timers like us around."

Duke walked over to Ja'a and extended his hand. She shook it gently.

"Your dad would be proud."

Ja'a hugged him tightly.

CHAPTER THIRTY-EIGHT

FORTY-EIGHT MINUTES

"I WAS COMING TO THE realization that this day would live only in my dreams," bellowed Mo'a. "However, here we are. Orbius is gone. And it's the daughter of He'j, my best friend, that accomplished this." He drew in a deep breath as his eyes moistened. "I am very proud of you, Ja'a. And your father would be as well."

"I already told her that," Duke whispered to Ishiro'shea.

"Great Mo'a," Ja'a began as she rose from her seat at the circular table. "My hope is to focus on the future of our planet. Yes, Orbius is gone. The mines are empty. But cycles of battle and death leave us with two strained peoples and much work to do."

She looked at Vernglet Wip; he nodded in her direction.

"Yes, Ja'a. We are aware," said Mo'a. "Once we heard the news, we started to discuss the next steps to rebuild a Neprius that represents peace and coexistence. The first question is what to do with the Orb."

"Hey there, big Mo'a," Duke interrupted. "That's been taken care of."

"What do you mean, Duke?"

"No offense to you and the council, but we went ahead and made those preparations back in Sansagon."

Mo'a looked irked. Duke could tell that decisions of this magnitude weren't typically made unilaterally.

"Ja'a, is this true?"

"Yes," she responded without hesitation. "There was only one logical decision. Even transporting the Orb back here to our base would have been too risky."

"I see," Mo'a said unconvinced. "What has happened to the Orb, to Peace?"

"It's back in the hands of the ancient Keeper."

"The beast that you spoke of? The one that lives in the old temple in the swamp?"

"Yeah, his name is Toby," added Duke.

"Didn't he lose it? Twice?"

"He did, Mo'a," said Ja'a. "But he has help this time around."

"Help?"

"Yes, the Shepherd of the Grundar has promised to monitor the skies above the Keeper's lair."

"Interesting. I'm not sure what I think about this arrangement."

"They've put aside their differences to forge a powerful symbiotic union."

"We hope to do the same," said Vernglet Wip. Duke noticed that it lacked its usual nasal whine.

"I see."

Mo'a contemplated the news. He placed both hands upon the table and leaned forward. He slowly peered up and made eye contact with all of the attendees. Bu'r. Ishiro'shea. Po'l. Ja'a. Duke.

"A wise move."

A collective gasp of relief came from around the table.

"A wise move befitting of an empress."

Ja'a's smile dissipated and shock consumed her elegant profile.

"Mo'a?" she queried.

"Yes, Ja'a. You may have made the decision of how to protect the Orb from harming us without our input—but this, we are adamant about, and will not accept counterarguments."

The room was silent. Duke stood. Ishiro'shea followed suit. They raised their glasses of Neprian wine.

"To Empress Ja'a!"

Everyone in the room cheered. Vernglet Wip walked over and hugged the newly-appointed monarch.

"Not a lot of paperwork required to be an empress here," Duke muttered to Ishiro'shea.

The ninja nodded.

"Once I heard the news of Orbius' downfall," shouted Mo'a above the congratulatory cheers, "I went ahead and planned a bit of a celebration. I hope that's okay, Ja'a. It won't have the scale of our past ceremonies naming dignitaries and rulers, as we were short on time to plan. And, to be honest, we've never had an empress before."

"That explains the lack of paperwork," added Duke to Ishiro'shea.

"So, I'm afraid it will just be a big party."

"Cheers to that!" Duke added.

"I'm honored, Mo'a. That is, if I accept this position."

"If?" questioned Mo'a. "Ja'a, the people of Neprius *demand* it."

Ja'a continued, "As part of this celebration, I do have one order of business that must be addressed."

"Go on."

"I will only take this responsibility if Vernglet Wip—the *honorable* Vernglet Wip—is named the Ambassador of the North."

"Vern, you hear that?" Duke said, slapping the gaunt Neprian on the back. "They called you honorable. Who would have thought that?"

"Are you sure, Ja'a?"

"That's *Empress* Ja'a," Duke reminded Mo'a.

"We're going to work on that title also," added Ja'a. "Empresses are only in fairy tales."

"Title aside, are you sure that you trust this priest to help in the rebuilding?" asked Mo'a.

"Mo'a, had Vernglet not risked his life and shot the Orb down from Duke's ship, we would have been destroyed."

"Yeah, you pulled a fast one on us, Vern!" Duke said to the priest. "We thought you sold us up the river."

"I knew I was no help in combat, so I fled—if I had said something, you wouldn't have believed it anyway. My only hope was to sneak into the throne room. Luckily, the ship knew what I needed to do."

"Well played, ol' Vern."

"And Mo'a, it will take both races to rebuild our planet. No one understands that more than Vernglet Wip."

Mo'a thought hard about Ja'a's request. His temples contracted and his brow wrinkled.

"You are right, daughter of He'j. It is a great idea."

"I would be honored," Vernglet Wip said, bowing to the elder Neprian rebel. He then turned to Ja'a and repeated the gesture. "Empress Ja'a—or whatever designation that you choose for yourself—may we begin healing the unnecessary wounds of conflict."

"How about president?" said Duke. "President Ja'a—has a nice ring to it."

Ishiro'shea kicked him.

"Oh yeah, bad track record with those."

The Neprians were stone-faced.

Duke attempted to get the conversation back on track. "Now, about this party..."

The coastal compound came alive as the moon shimmered across the crashing sea. Brilliant colors and exotic smells permeated through the base. Southern Neprians danced and hugged and drank. Many came up to Vernglet and embraced him with the same emotion that they did Bu'r or Po'l. Vernglet seemed genuinely happy. He told them all that the real hard work lay ahead but that they would undo the evil of Orbius' reign. He eventually found a handful of partygoers intoxicated enough to want to engage in this deeper sort of dialogue. Most just hugged him.

A thick meathook of a hand landed on Duke's shoulder. The bounty hunter turned around to see Bu'r.

"How's the wine tonight?" asked the broad-chested rebel.

"Not bad, not bad at all."

"Thank you, Duke LaGrange of Nova Texas. We couldn't have done this without you and Ishiro'shea. I believe the Orb did summon the right people."

Duke blushed and quickly gave Bu'r a big "Nah." He proceeded to change the subject. "What's next for you, my friend?"

"I'm going to return to Shud'nut. It's my home and they need my help. It won't be easy. I'm sure they are embarrassed about how they acted."

Duke couldn't help but think of how the citizens of Shud'nut would react after seeing what Ishiro'shea had to do to get Uu'k back. *Bu'r's job will definitely not be easy.*

"That's very noble of you. I'm sure that if you decide to

stay here, the brass will shower you with honorary titles and all of that stuff."

"Maybe. But with Ja'a in charge, I think they have it under control."

"You're probably right."

"I just wanted to thank you. I probably won't see you again, off-worlder." Duke noticed Bu'r's sly grin as he used the term. "And I wish you the best in your return home to the stars."

The bounty hunter raised his glass of wine, then clinked it against Bu'r's.

"To Ty'n. His sacrifice was a worthy one."

"And to you," Bu'r said, fighting back a tear. "Thank you for helping us make it a worthy one."

Ja'a ascended to a platform constructed in the middle of the open plaza. Vernglet and Mo'a flanked her. Fire-tipped pikes surrounded the stage. The Neprians began to coalesce around the platform, raising glasses and cheering. Mo'a stepped to the forefront and calmed them down.

"Everyone, I present you, Ja'a, the first empress—" He looked at a scowling Ja'a, "—or similar designation as yet to be ironed out—of Neprius."

The cheers turned into roars, then halted as Ja'a began to speak.

"My father loved our planet. He died trying to do what we did—end the reign of an evil ruler. A ruler that sent us to the mines to be whipped and beaten as slaves, killing us if we resisted. But let's not forget, he enslaved our neighbors to the North as well. He corrupted their minds with fear and forced them to harm us—or die. I beg you all to not hold grudges against our fellow beings. It will be hard, I know that. Death and suffering are not easily forgotten. But we must try. We will not have a single, harmonious Neprius unless we can all forgive and move on."

The crowd applauded. Vernglet smiled.

"This gives me much hope. But as my good friend, Vernglet Wip, has reminded me—the hard work still lies ahead."

Her tone turned from hopeful to reflective. "I could never even attempt to thank and honor those that sacrificed their lives and health for our cause. However, I do want to mention the names of those that accompanied us and did not make it back to enjoy this moment. I want to be very clear—we would not have survived without their efforts. The noble Ty'n of the Southern Forests held off voracious swamp cannibals so that we could make it through to the North. The honorable Te'o fell victim to an unexpected traitor, whilst doing his job, providing us a lookout as we traversed the hostile lands leading to Sansagon. And the courageous Ma'n. He challenged an entire squad of soldiers, as well as Gar himself, to save a child. Please honor them and all others by doing your best to make Neprius a better place. A place that they died for."

Organically the crowd raised their glasses as silence overcame the entire plaza.

"Thank you," Ja'a continued. "And to those that did make it back. The great warrior, Bu'r of Shud'nut!"

Cheers erupted.

"His mace and passions carried us through many perils. You all know Po'l—his bravery is unrivaled."

More cheers.

"He escaped death's grasp on countless occasions."

Duke rolled his eyes.

"He provided our band with a warrior's spirit. I hope that he will accept my offer to continue the legacy of his uncle Mo'a and lead our army—though I hope that we never need to use it."

Po'l received pats on the back and handshakes from all of the attendees around him.

"And, lastly, to our new friends from the stars. The silent Ishiro'shea—I've never seen a fiercer soldier. His lack of words is made up for by his actions, which speak volumes of his character."

Duke put his arm around the neck of his ninja companion, "Attaboy! I never knew I worked with a real life hero."

Ishiro'shea returned the snarky comment with an elbow to the bounty hunter's ribcage.

"And to Duke LaGrange. Adventurer. Trailblazer. Poet. A true man of the universe."

Duke tipped his hat. Ja'a, the new leader of Neprius, returned a smile.

"Enjoy tonight," she concluded. "Tomorrow, we welcome a new Neprius."

The loudest cheers of the evening filled the seaside air as Ja'a left the platform and returned to the party.

"Ishiro, we did good. I think."

Ishiro'shea responded with a thumbs-up. Like a flash of light, reminiscent of the ninja himself, a smallish figure affixed to Ishiro's left leg.

"Ishiro!" shouted Uu'k, not releasing the hug. "Before you leave, can you teach me some more sword fighting? Today was fun!"

Ishiro'shea knelt down and examined the wooden training sword he had given her earlier in the day. He gave her a thumbs-up.

"Thanks! See you in a bit! And thanks to you too, Uncle Duke."

The child spy sprinted off into the crowd and disappeared.

"Uncle Duke. Finally."

Ishiro'shea took his turn and extended his arm around Duke's neck.

"Okay, okay! But don't teach her *all* of your tricks—she's pretty salty. For a filthy street urchin."

Uu'k scrunched her nose at Duke, then smiled. Ishiro'shea nodded and followed the child spy's path to the perimeter of the party.

Duke examined the wine in his glass against the moonlight. He slurped down the last remnant.

"Need a refill?"

The voice was beautiful. It sounded the same as when he heard it blindfolded in a cave south of Dre'en.

"Your highness."

"No need for that, Duke."

"Thanks for the mention in the speech."

"You know, I didn't always know where you stood."

"Join the club."

"But I always knew where I wanted you to stand."

"I don't follow."

"I could tell—even during those early attempts at flattery—that you had a heart."

"It's what keeps me alive."

"No, our cause. Our group. Me. We—*I* needed someone with passion to fuel our cause. We needed a heart."

"I wasn't so sure after Shud'nut."

"I wasn't either, if I'm honest. And you challenging that was a good thing."

"You sure didn't act like it."

"You can be an ass. I'm still not entirely over you leaving us in the swamp solely to scratch the itch of curiosity."

"Fair point. But, you have to admit, Toby did prove to be a useful ally."

"But don't miss my meaning, Duke LaGrange, I'm very

appreciative of everything that you have done. Whether it was for the cause, or to get back your ship. It doesn't matter. We couldn't have accomplished what we did without you."

"Thank you."

"One more thing before you leave our 'primitive, two-bit world' as I believe you called it."

"Something like that," Duke said, blushing.

"Do you remember that night on the hill?"

"I do."

"You told me about—how did you put it? Pesky carnal needs?"

"I did? I mean , yes, I did."

Ja'a grabbed Duke's hand and led him to the *Deus Ex Machina*.

For the next forty-eight minutes, the Nova Texan experienced a different side of Neprian culture and, specifically, a different side of this gorgeous and giving Neprian female.

It was a side that he very much liked.

He was pretty confident that he had the best time at the party of anyone there.

The rat-a-tat-tat knock on the exterior of the *Deus* woke up both Ja'a and Duke. They looked at each other and exchanged smiles.

"About last night—" started Duke.

"Duke, you don't have to say anything or expect anything. It was what it—"

"I was just going to ask how I did?" he interrupted.

Ja'a grinned as she turned her head away. He heard a discreet laugh from the attractive Neprian.

"I'll take your silence to indicate a job well done."

"Duke," Ja'a began, "I have to admit—it was like nothing else that I've experienced."

"That's what I like to hear."

"I won't challenge you on your prowess in that department, but I'm truly sorry if I led you on or took advantage of you. The long journey, you being thrown into my life and my cause, the emotions, and everything else just bubbled up and it seemed like the right thing to do. And it was everything that I needed—passion, escape, connection, pleasure. I hope it was enjoyable for you as well."

"Wait a second. You used me?"

"Duke! No, no. That's not what I meant."

"Sure sounds like it," Duke retorted.

Ja'a struggled to find her words.

"I'm yankin' your chain."

Ja'a responded with a blank stare.

"Oh, right. It means I'm just messing with you. In fact, I appreciate anyone that can take advantage of Duke LaGrange. If anything, I'm impressed."

"That's not what I did. I acted on impulse—but I find you very—"

"Ja'a," Duke said, cutting her off. "You don't need to explain yourself. I'm a big boy. And it was enjoyable for me. A moment that I won't forget."

His tenderness seemed to catch Ja'a off guard.

"You know my place is here," she said.

"I do. I've never doubted that. And you know my place is—"

"Out there," Ja'a said, finishing his thought. "But I do want to give you something."

She removed her necklace and handed it to Duke.

"No way. That's a gift from your father. I couldn't."

"You helped me realize my father's dream. And this could help you get home."

"I'm sure there's enough mustangsen here on the *Deus*. I mean it's *made of* mustangsen."

"It would make me feel better. I want to give you every opportunity to get back to your part of the universe."

"It's an honor." He draped the necklace around his neck —it was a little snug but it didn't choke him.

The pounding noise increased in volume and frequency.

"Okay, Ishiro! We're coming."

Duke and Ja'a descended to the entrance closest to the incessant knocking. The door opened.

"Oh, it's you Po'l," said Duke, somewhat surprised and unsure of the impending reaction.

"Duke," he began. "Good morning."

"Good morning to you," Duke responded tepidly.

"Ja'a, I had a feeling that I would find you here. I need to tell you something."

"Do we need to go somewhere private?"

"No need. I wanted to tell you that I'm not going to take you up on your offer."

"What?" Ja'a asked. "But this is your chance to become our general. It's been your dream."

"It was. I've learned a lot. My eyes have been opened to all that I *don't* know. I've been a fool." He faced Duke. "Not everything that I've done was foolish—but more than I care to admit. I still have my doubts about you, LaGrange—but not about you being a traitor or a liar. Just about you being anything other than a giant ass."

Duke grinned.

"Not the first time that I've been called that in—well, since last night."

Po'l looked confused but continued. "Ja'a, I'm honored to have received your trust but my path is much different than yours. You have been my greatest friend and I know that you will bring peace to our planet."

Ja'a stepped towards Po'l and kissed him on the lips. His eyes widened. She pulled him close and embraced him as a brother. "I love you, Po'l. I hope you find what you're looking for."

"I will."

Duke heard a child's voice in the distance. Ishiro'shea and Uu'k approached. Ishiro'shea had his katana drawn; Uu'k did not have her wooden training sword—instead, she had a simple but very much real dagger. They parried back and forth as they shuffled towards Duke, Ja'a, and Po'l.

"It looks like you're taking to this naturally," Ja'a said to Uu'k in a maternal tone. "Maybe you will be a general one day."

"Ishiro'shea's the best teacher ever!"

"Already migrated to an actual blade?" asked Duke.

Ishiro'shea gave a thumbs-up to Duke as he continued to fend off Uu'k's swipes and swings. She stopped and withdrew her dagger. She gave Ishiro'shea an elongated embrace.

"Thank you, Ishiro'shea. Good luck getting back home. And come visit again."

Ishiro'shea returned the embrace.

"I guess it's that time," Duke said, regretting the cloud of sadness his statement cast over the gathering. "Time for us to hit the road and for you to rebuild your planet."

"I almost forgot," Ja'a said. She rummaged inside a beat-up leather satchel. She removed a bright purple glass Orb.

"Ja'a! Why? How? What?" Po'l stammered and struggled to pick which question to ask first.

"Po'l, it's okay," she said reassuringly. "The Keeper, Fazeek, Duke, and I made the decision. The Orb needs to leave our planet for us to have a chance to rebuild without the worry of its corruption—but we don't want people thinking that it has escaped. Both of the ancients have decided to go along with the ruse. In fact, it was Fazeek's idea."

"Yeah, I don't think he trusts Toby," Duke added. "Can't blame him."

"Also, it will give Duke and Ishiro'shea a better chance to get home. If it deposits them somewhere other than their home, then they can always try again until it gets it right."

"And we have a place in mind that it will be safe."

CHAPTER THIRTY-NINE

CYBORG JOE'S, REVISITED

"MR. LAGRANGE, CAN I GET you another Glyptodian Summer Ale?"

"No thanks, Earl. I'm more in the mood for—"

"Whisky?" asked Queen Joe.

"How'd you know?"

"Lucky guess. That was quite the tale. Who would have thought that damn red blob would have led you to such an adventure?"

"I have a feeling that *you* did."

Queen Joe sunk below the bar and appeared with a dusty bottle of Earth whisky. She did not respond to Duke's comment. She placed five glasses on the bar top and slid them along, the first four stopping in front of the desired patron at even intervals. The fifth remained in her hand.

"To adventures," said the Queen, "and restored mojo."

"Definitely to restored mojo," added the bounty hunter.

Duke clinked his glass with Ishiro'shea's. The ninja sucked up the shot in a flash. Duke swivelled in his chair, facing the patron to his right.

"And to Po'l," proclaimed Duke.

The Neprian nodded and drank the whisky.

"So what's mojo? And what's this drink?" asked the Neprian.

"Your new friend has a lot to learn," added Joe.

"What better place than at Cyborg Joe's?" exclaimed Duke.

"Very true. And I think Lilly is eager to help. She seems to like him."

Duke looked along the bar. The anthropomorphic musk ox from one of the moons of Gartosh was batting her eyelashes at the rebel. The Neprian responded with an expression of fear and horror.

"Hey Lilly," said Duke, "Good to see you again."

"Thanks for the whisky," she replied.

Duke raised his glass and downed the brown liquid. He turned back to Queen Joe. "What's been going on since we left? How'd everything shake out with Sprinkles?"

"I haven't heard from the Robots in a while," she replied. "I think they were arrested on Jungafallow IV. But we just repaired the ceiling last week. So—let's keep Betsy quiet, please."

"Sounds good."

"Oh—someone was asking about you the other day."

"Who?"

"Prince Korzo-Tapor."

"That guy? He tried to kill me, you know. All because of the Robots."

"Are you sure?"

"What else could he have been pissed at?"

"You are Duke LaGrange, remember."

"True."

"But he was asking a lot of questions. Earl was pretty coy, but the prince *did* press."

"What did he do?"

"He ended up using a portal. Probably to gamble."

"Ah."

"But—"

"But what, Queen?"

"Soon after, someone that you know *very well* also used the same portal. Mazilda Cloax."

Duke was silent. His face lost emotion. He extended his glass to Queen Joe and she refilled it without hesitation. He sucked the whisky down aggressively.

"I'm done with portals."

"Probably a wise move," said Queen Joe. She returned the now much lighter bottle of whisky to a cabinet below the bar top. A faint purple glow rose from behind the bar. Her eyes met Duke's. "Don't worry, it will be safe."

"Who's Mazilda Cloax?" asked Po'l.

"You know how I'm the renowned bounty hunter?"

"So you say."

"She's better."

"She? Is she the one—"

"Another time, another place, my friend," Duke said, cutting off Po'l. "Now we have to teach you how to survive Cyborg Joe's Grill N' Go & the Why Not Saloon. If you can make it here a night without being killed, you'll be just fine out in the universe."

Duke pointed at the MechaBurger 8000 sitting before the Neprian. "Lesson one. Don't eat that."

"Why not?"

"Trust me. Earl, are you trying to kill him?"

"I'm sorry, but he ordered it."

The Glyptodian barkeep removed the plate as Po'l took another sip of his Erontian saké.

Duke picked up the menu and ordered two soufflés.

A booming thud rattled Po'l, causing the Neprian to spring to his feet.

Duke laughed. He looked down.

Ishiro'shea was out cold on the barroom floor.

"Lesson two. How to pick up women with a drunk space ninja."

HOW TO WIN AT PIT FIGHTING WITH A DRUNK SPACE NINJA

BOOK TWO

CHAPTER ONE

REAL HERO STUFF

THE CATAPULT RELEASED WITH A swoosh and hurled a glowing rock at breakneck speed towards the enemy lines. Mid-flight, the boulder caught fire, an iridescent flame that formed a tail. It was a man-made comet—or, in this case, a Psitakki-made comet—and it was usually pretty effective. The projectile landed in a huddled mass of the attackers, which was, after all, the specific aim of the catapult operator. Unfortunately, the rock found a way to miss them all and collided with the ground instead. Grozzel couldn't help but think of all of the other places on Psitakki that he'd rather be than watching the loyal battalions of his home world hurl giant flame-covered rocks with the accuracy of a blind furgosi bird. The thunderous thump of projectile-meeting-earth reverberated all the way back to the Psitakki camp. The flames fizzled and the enemy marched forward, undeterred.

"Are they ghosts?" Grozzel asked his commander. "Who can avoid something like that? I don't think they even blinked. I don't think they even have eyes."

Commander Churzzel grunted back at the infantryman. It was hard to tell if his annoyance stemmed from the fact that he was being addressed informally by an inferior, or if he just didn't have a good answer. The commander about-faced and marched behind the front lines.

Typical, thought Grozzel.

"Infantry, prepare for the push," shouted Grozzel's battalion leader, an overly zealous, hardwired Psitakki named Serjarzzel. He stomped on the dirt with his bare feet, his posture remaining authoritative and almost statuesque.

The Psitakki were one of the few cephalopodan species in the known universe that had not only developed the ability to walk on land, but had became extremely adroit at it. They had evolved into a rather athletic bipedal race, equally at ease climbing trees as being submerged in their murky aquatic abodes.

"A bit enthusiastic to start your own death march, oh fearless leader of mine," whispered Grozzel to himself.

"What was that?" yelled Serjarzzel, looking around to identify a culprit. "Who said that? If you have a problem with my orders, you have a problem with Commander Churzzel. And if you've got a problem with him—you have a problem with High Command."

Grozzel mouthed the last of these comments silently in sync with Serjarzzel. It was a statement that he had heard numerous times.

"Got it?" Serjarzzel roared.

The battalion grumbled half-hearted affirmatives.

"What was that?"

The collective "Yes, sir" had a bit more volume and body, but it still lacked complete conviction.

Serjarzzel stroked the tentacles that extended from above his upper lip. He appeared satisfied enough with the level of pep amongst his troops.

"Prepare to march!"

The foot soldiers began to mobilize. A large homogenous chunk of Psitakki warriors slowly began a path toward the mysterious invaders. Grozzel estimated that there were at least a few hundred in his battalion—and probably a few hundred battalions on the front line. The indestructible enemy force was only a fraction of their size—but they were *indestructible*, so the size of their army wasn't relevant.

"This is idiotic," Grozzel said to a soldier next to him as they paraded towards the enemy.

"Shut up, Grozzel. What are we supposed to do? Tell High Command to go suck a finback jorquoia egg?" responded Zorzzel. Zorzzel had been Grozzel's best friend since primary school, when they merged the district lines so that some of the residents of the swampland would comingle, scholastically speaking, with the residents of a few of the towns in the much dryer plains. Due to the places of their rearing, they were of slightly differing skin tones—Grozzel being a muted grayish-green, Zorzzel somewhere between heavy cream and sunburned grass.

"I mean, it would probably be the most productive thing they've done in a few cycles."

"You can't honestly blame them for this invasion? These creatures, these things came out of nowhere. It's not like High Command provoked them."

"I don't blame them for the invasion, of course not. I *do* blame them for having every able-bodied Psitakki march blindly into the teeth of a monster that we don't understand. And can't seem to hurt. Not even a 'boo-boo on the knee' hurt."

"What would you do then, General Grozzel?" Zorzzel said sarcastically.

"Run away," Grozzel replied assuredly.

Zorzzel's eye ridges raised. "Run away?"

"Yes."

"Dare I ask—where to?"

"Yes, you may dare," Grozzel snickered. "To the swamps."

"To the swamps?"

"Yes. Any of them. All of them. And hide."

Zorzzel rolled his eyes as another rock, destined to fail, whizzed over their heads. "You're made of real 'hero' stuff, you know."

"When they first came to our planet a few days back, they didn't hurt anyone. They crept around. Floated here and there. Sure, they spooked a few kids. I mean, who wouldn't be scared by a creepy floating demon thing that's taller than three male Psitakki and doesn't have a face or feet?"

"And can't be hurt in any way," reminded Zorzzel.

"Yes, and can't be hurt in any way that we've discovered," continued Grozzel. "Then High Command, in their infinite wisdom, said, 'Hey, let's lob some rocks at 'em.' I'm not even sure they're made of solid matter. They look like a cloud of smoke with arms. So, even if we ever managed to hit one with our catapults, it'll probably just go straight through 'em. And that's how we ended up where we're at now."

"But what good would hiding do?"

"First off, we won't die. Or we're less likely to die. I give you and I a—I don't know—two percent chance to survive this direct attack on these guys."

Zorzzel nodded several times, perhaps processing the odds himself.

"If we hide, let them do their thing, whatever that thing might be, then they might leave. We live. The race goes on."

"You're missing the obvious 'what if,' Grozzel. What if

they just stay? Or what if they're looking to drain our resources and leave us to die on a dried-up planet?"

"I still like the odds."

"It's not too late to go present your well-crafted plan to High Command. If you run back now and Serjarzzel doesn't execute you as a deserter, I'm sure Churzzel will be an eager audience."

"I think I've quickly come to grips with my destiny— complaining about High Command while I get ripped to shreds by one of these shadow demons."

"I'll be ripped to shreds right by your side, old friend."

"Thanks."

Another comet flew overhead and deposited itself onto the ground harmlessly. The gaseous ghouls barely seemed to notice.

"Hey now, that was too close for comfort!" shouted Zorzzel. He gestured wildly. "The bad guys are *that* way."

"Do you think it would hurt more to be friendly-fire catapult fodder, or lunch for those bodiless monstrosities?"

"You're insane, Grozzel. Can we just march ahead and try and not die?"

"We can try."

The sky above the shadow demons' encampment began to rumble. The clouds turned from their usual deep green to a smoky metallic gray. Moments later, they were charcoal black. The sky seemed to pulse like the heart of a celestial deity that was going into cardiac arrest. Rain came crashing down irregularly; Grozzel even thought he saw it flow into the clouds from the ground. But he just chalked that up to exhaustion and his state of rapidly coming to terms with his mortality.

The Psitakkian infantry instinctually halted.

We're sitting furgosi birds, thought Grozzel.

The shadowy invaders began to emit bolts of obsidian

lightning from their faceless, feetless floating bodies. It struck the Psitakki ranks and killed instantly any soldier within a radius the size of a small farm. The bolts came from every angle and at erratic intervals. The armor that the Psitakki wore provided no defense to the salvo. The line broke and they began to flee.

"Okay, you got your wish, Grozzel," screamed Zorzzel as he sprinted away from the chaos. "We can run *and* hide."

"Hiding from curious terror-beasts was what I had in mind, not hiding from lightning bolts conjured out of nowhere."

"Beggars can't be choosers," Zorzzel replied.

The pair leapt over their deceased comrades and plunged into a grove of ancient tarzantia, brawny and impenetrable trees that will only grow near the edge of a swamp.

"This way," barked Grozzel. "This isn't far from my home. I know a good place to hide."

"I'm right behind you."

A piercing crack echoed through the grove of tarzantia trees. Grozzel stopped and turned back. Zorzzel was on the ground, face down. Smoke rose from his back. Grozzel could smell the charred skin. Zorzzel looked up—his eyes glassed over—blood dripped from the corners of his mouth, along his tentacles.

"Hide," he mouthed as his head hit the ground, his life force extinguished.

Floating above his lifeless body was one of the invaders.

They're bigger than I thought, concluded Grozzel. *Maybe he didn't see me?*

The shadow demon whipped its substanceless arm towards the Psitakki. A stream of black electricity zipped by him and struck down an entire tree.

Grozzel fled deeper into the swamp. He wasn't as fleet

of foot as Zorzzel—or any land-born Psitakki, for that matter —but once they entered the thick liquid of the swamp he was as adept as any in his race. But he wasn't really sure how fast these shadow creatures could float, or if they would even want to chase a single soldier deep into an unfamiliar landscape. Then again, Psitakki with titles far more prestigious than his had been wrong about everything to do with these beasts. Grozzel assumed that his pursuer was hardwired to massacre him at all costs.

He finally approached the edge of the swamp. He leapt in. The lukewarm water hit his skin and his body instantly relaxed. He was at home. A grimy home, but home nonetheless. His feet kicked, propelling his streamlined body deeper into the water. The sediment and debris floating about made the water too opaque for most life forms, but the Psitakki's vision was specially adapted to navigate these depths. It was an evolutionary trait that helped his race become the alpha species. Even though other animals evolved keen smell or the means to echolocate, being able to see trumped everything. Grozzel pivoted underwater, turning his body to face the faint glow penetrating the surface of the swamp.

Damnit, he's following me, concluded Grozzel.

The Psitakki stayed submerged for as long as he could withstand. Though their ancestors could breathe underwater indefinitely, the Psitakki lost that benefit eons ago. Grozzel couldn't help but think that his ancestors would point and laugh at him for needing boring old air to survive.

Grozzel hoped that the shadow monster would eventually give up and leave. No such luck. Hours passed. The greater battle on the surface was probably over, with the peculiar intruders likely claiming another easy victory. More would likely join his pursuer in his chase, and soon.

However, Grozzel had to resurface. Knowing he only

had a few more moments before he would pass out underwater, he shot himself as far as possible from the beast's location. His propulsion landed him near the opposite bank of the swamp and, he hoped, out of sight of the enemy. But Grozzel couldn't help but think that his guesswork about the monster's range of sight wasn't likely to yield useful results since he had never known another life form that had no face. *Nothing really to compare it to; no point of reference. He might be able to see into outer space for all I know,* he thought to himself.

He gulped air as he emerged from the murky water. He scanned the area. Sure enough, the shadow demon remained hovering over the swamp. Its faceless torso angled downward until it was nearly touching the surface. *How could something with no eyes see?* Regardless, Grozzel came to the conclusion that it was definitely contemplating what it was going to do next. It then raised an arm and sent another bolt into the water. It pierced the surface and cut through the water as if it was air. Grozzel could see and hear the crash as the bolt struck the swamp floor. Fish and swamp worms and water womblers scurried in every direction. *That's not good.*

The shadow beast loosed another strike, with the same result. It seemed pleased with the outcome; it was shrugging what could be best described as shoulders up and down rapidly as if it were in a state of uncontrollable hysteria. Grozzel, on the other hand, was frozen at the realization of this physics-defying weapon. He now knew his cover would provide no safety from the beast. Unfortunately, his catatonic state lasted a few moments too long. The shadow demon ceased its movement. Its body shifted; it didn't need a face for Grozzel to realize that it was facing him. It darted to intercept the Psitakki soldier.

Grozzel didn't know which gave him a better chance at

survival: diving to the bottom and hoping that the beast's aim was predicated on having a clear view of its target; or making a break for it on land and hoping to locate a hiding place before he was fried with one of those lightning beams.

If I'm going to meet the Colossal Calamari in the sky, I'm going to do it on my own terms... in my swamp, decided Grozzel. He quickly dunked his head, turned effortlessly in the water, and darted to the other side of the swamp.

The electric bolts entered the water at a frantic pace. Grozzel bobbed and weaved to avoid a fatal strike. They came with such rapidity that they appeared to form a sort of underwater latticework. Grozzel didn't stop to admire them; he swam as far away as possible from the onslaught.

The demon paused, presumably waiting to see a limp corpse float to the top. After a brief moment, he moved on to another area. And Grozzel did as well. This game continued for what seemed like hours. Outside of brief moments of surfacing for air, the Psitakki stayed one step ahead of the tenebrous predator.

Regrettably for Grozzel, the invader had friends. They showed up in droves and surrounded the body of water. Grozzel surfaced near the far bank under the exposed roots of a tarzantia; the shadows and mud made him invisible to the naked eye of most biological entities. He wasn't so sure with these guys.

Grozzel noticed that the beast was communicating with his comrades. He must have been telling them that the ammunition that they flung from their bodies penetrated the water, because they all started to test it out. In short order, the real estate within which Grozzel could hide shrunk dramatically. The demons unleashed a coordinated pelting; the strikes stirring the swamp into an ocean of sludgy waves. If Grozzel re-entered the swamp, it would only be a matter of time before he was struck down by the same kind of bolt that had killed his best friend.

This is it, he thought to himself. *At least I get to die in the place that birthed me.* He liked the symmetry of it.

He took one last deep breath and submerged himself in the comfort of his swampy home, waiting for the bolts to appear. He wasn't sure how long he could dart about and avoid their sting, but he would try until he took his last breath.

As soon as a charge snaked past his head, he pushed off from the submerged bank and headed in the opposite direction to a portion of the swamp that he hadn't yet used as a hiding spot. He dove deeper and deeper. *This is new*, he realized. He continued his descent towards a nook that was easily four times deeper than most of the swamps in the area. He hoped that the added depth would provide added cover. The frequency of the bolts decreased. *Maybe this will work*, he hoped. *Until I have to resurface for air, that is.* The latter thought deflated his newfound optimism rather quickly.

The velocity of the bolt that zipped by was so great, even underwater, that it spun Grozzel around completely. It struck something solid; the crash sent him into another aquatic tumble. He felt more crashes in rapid succession but saw no additional bolts. It was as if the strikes had triggered the eruption of an underwater volcano. But Grozzel knew that swamps typically didn't have volcanoes. The shaking stopped.

Maybe it scared away the shadow beasts?

The Psitakki swam through the newly-created debris, searching for cover from any subsequent attacks. As he navigated through the murky water, he noted that the swamp kept going and going. *I should've hit the bank by now*, he thought to himself. It was clear that the strike had opened up the mouth of a hidden cave. Some of the larger swamps in this area had submerged caves, but Grozzel was familiar with this particular body of water and had been relatively sure it didn't possess one. He was very happy to be proven wrong.

Maybe this is my lucky break... or my future tomb.

The passage narrowed. A tunnel. He pursued the trail and swam for some time until he surfaced in a cavern. He had never seen or heard about this place, though Psitakki had traversed all of the swamps and waterways on their home world.

He took in a deep breath of stagnant cave air, enough to fuel him for another prolonged retreat. He treaded water as he tried to collect his thoughts. His meditation was interrupted by an unusual glow coming from behind a cluster of stalagmites. It was bright white—blindingly bright. Even though a large portion appeared to be blocked by the rocky formations, Grozzel didn't look at it directly as he feared it might burn out his pupils.

Oddly, as he approached it, the intensity of the glow lessened. He wasn't even sure why he approached it. As a young squidling he had been taught to avoid bright and shiny objects stashed away in hidden caves. But investigating just felt right.

He peeked around the stalagmites. The glow was now faint and subtle. It was coming from a mound of circular disks. The pile extended farther than Grozzel had realized.

Shields? Why is there a heap of glowing shields in a secret cave on Psitakki? His mind began to race. *Clearly not made by the Psitakki smiths. Alien? Could this be what those demons are looking for?*

He knelt down and picked one up. It wasn't heavy at all; in fact, it was extremely light—too light. The material was foreign to Grozzel and he concluded that it wasn't likely to be able to withstand much impact. That wasn't a good trait in a shield. He slid his arm into the strap and the shield rested on his forearm. *Kinda useless*, he concluded.

A dozen or so explosions rocked the cavern and pushed Grozzel onto his posterior. The strikes ripped off the ceiling of the cavern, exposing Grozzel and his mound of alien shields to the night air. Five shadow beasts peered down at the trapped Psitakki soldier. But they didn't pursue.

All five slowly entered the dwelling. Grozzel hadn't previously seen them act in any manner that would be described as cautious. After the initial five beasts entered, one after the other, more flowed in. The sky was obscured by the mass of shadow demons. It was impossible to tell where one stopped and the other started. Grozzel's game of hide-and-seek was finally at an end. He cowered and covered his face with a forearm, though he knew it would provide little defense against one of the demons' obsidian death bolts.

The shield on his arm pulsated and vibrated, then shrieked and whined, then swished and whooshed. It let out a reverberating bellow and shot out fiery flares from its perimeter. The bellow turned into a wheezing sound as if the shield was inhaling. Then out shot a ray of light that permeated every crevice of the roofless cave. The explosion of light from the shield caused a massive recoil. However, the force didn't knock Grozzel off his feet. It pushed against his forearm but the pressure was manageable. The light continued to blast through the cave into the night sky for what seemed like hours. The banshees wailed and screamed in pain. The blast stopped and then the beam seemed to be sucked back into the middle of the round shield.

Grozzel opened his eyes and looked upward. Nothing. Not a single shadow beast remained. The shield had obliterated them all. Every one of them.

This is exactly what they came for, he concluded.

The Psitakki was too shocked to move the shield—or to move at all. He stood petrified near the stalagmites, the shield still strapped to his forearm. He lost all track of time.

"Is that you, Grozzel?"

The gruff voice belonged to Commander Churzzel. He unfastened himself from his rappelling harness and approached Grozzel. Other Psitakki soldiers were also careening down the cave wall from the newly formed roof entrance.

"Yes," Grozzel replied meekly.

"We saw a light shoot out from the trees and hurried over here. What's left of us, that is. What happened?"

Grozzel did not respond right away. He collected himself and glanced at the mound of shields. Churzzel also seemed to notice the pile. Grozzel straightened his posture.

"Commander, tell High Command that I have a much better plan."

CHAPTER TWO

SOL'S BAIL BONDS-O-RAMA

S OL WAS NOT THE MOST hygienically sound being in the universe. In fact, he flat-out stunk. But he ran one of the most lucrative bail bond outfits in his sector of the galaxy. So a bounty hunter looking for a payday could turn a blind eye—or nose—to Sol's unsavory fragrance. That was exactly why Duke LaGrange and Ishiro'shea were on Tardasio 7 in the waiting room of Sol's Bail Bonds-O-Rama. It had been a month or so since the bounty-hunting duo had returned from their adventure on Neprius. They had been canvassing the sector but hadn't picked up a single gig in that time span. It was a record low. It was even crazier that they hadn't heard of any sub-space chatter from any other bounty hunters. The only thing bounty hunters love more than bounty hunting is bragging about how good they are at bounty hunting. Maybe Duke wasn't the only one suffering from a dry spell.

The lobby of Sol's was as unkempt as the owner. If the furniture wasn't broken, it was dirty. If it wasn't broken or dirty, it was uncomfortable. Pictures of Sol shaking hands with the who's who of bounty hunters adorned the walls.

Some of the frames had pieces of glass missing or noticeable cracks. All of them hung crookedly. It annoyed Duke to no end, especially the ornate frame made of faux jewels hung above the receptionist's desk that housed a warped photo of Sol raising the hands of Duke and Ishiro'shea as if to announce that they had both won a prize fight. Duke was one of Sol's top clients.

What was unusual, however, was that Sol's waiting room was empty.

"Sol will see you now, gentlemen," whined the over-weight receptionist. Women on Tardasio 7 were typically bigger boned than most humanoids in the sector, so they tended to carry a bit more girth, but she was especially flabby. And sweaty. *She might be related to Sol*, thought Duke.

The Nova Texan tipped his hat and smiled. The receptionist swooned and giggled. As one of the most recogniz-able bounty hunter-playboys over the last fifteen cycles, Duke LaGrange knew that behind every unattractive lady could be a more attractive best friend. His Irish-Japanese ninja sidekick bowed slightly.

Other than his sloped forehead and narrow cylindrical nose that came to a sharp point—both typical traits of Tardasian males—Sol could have blended in with the humans on Earth or Nova Texas. At least, the grotesquely obese ones. Even though he was a disgusting man in a disgusting office, he was good at his job. From its outward appearance you couldn't tell it, but Sol's Bail Bonds-O-Rama was a well-oiled machine. Duke and Ishiro'shea had brought in bounties for Sol on hundreds of occasions. He was a fair businessman and easy to work with, if you could stand the stench.

He waddled towards Duke frantically.

"Close the door, LaGrange. Close it now," he said in

between grunts. He had to hike up the waist of his pants with every step to prevent them from falling to his ankles. *Probably don't make belts in his size*, thought Duke.

"Sol, my good buddy," Duke began. "How goes it? Any more sightings of three-headed ice wombats?"

"No time for chitchat, LaGrange," growled the bondsman. "We gotta hurry."

"What are you talking about? Why do we have to hurry? What's going on, Sol?"

"Those damn toughs from that government thingy, they're trying to shut me down."

"What toughs? What government thingy?"

"You know, those hard military bastards. With the guns and the warships and whatnot."

Duke looked blankly at the overweight Tardasian.

"Come on, LaGrange! The organization that's trying to take over the frickin' universe, man!" Sol yelled, throwing his hands in the air in frustration.

"I got nothing."

"Where have you been lately?"

"Actually—"

"Never mind, I don't care. Anyways, out of nowhere, this organization starts claiming to be the one true government in the known universe. All I know is that they're big. Real big. They sent squads to every corner, every planet of any consequence, and started to... well... govern."

"Come on, Sol," Duke protested. "And all of the planets and races just went along with it?"

"Of course not, meathead. Some resisted and were shut down—but not as many resisted as you'd think."

"Did they come over from some alternate reality? Have they seen how successful governments are in *this* universe?"

"This one seems different, LaGrange. In one month, they've done more than any of the previous outfits. More than the Cosmic Council, or the Planetary Senate, or that one weird tyrant guy with the eyepatch, or..."

"I get it, I get it," Duke interrupted. "So why are you freaked out? You said they've only gone to planets of consequence. Seems like Tardasio 7 is pretty safe, then."

"Funny, LaGrange. They're on their way."

"Why are you so worried? It's just some government pencil pushers with submachine guns. You've seen worse. It'll probably be just a few more minutes of paperwork a cycle—maybe a tax hike or two. Nothing you can't survive."

"You don't know, do you?"

"Know what?"

Sol paused for the first time since Duke and Ishiro'shea had entered. He took in a deep breath.

"They're outlawing bounty hunting."

Duke and Ishiro'shea looked at each other.

"They're outlawing bounty hunting?"

"Yes, what are you, deaf? No offense, Ishiro'shea."

"He's mute, not deaf," Duke said. "And it's by choice. But why?"

"I don't know, ask him. He's your friend."

The bounty hunter pinched the bridge of his nose with his fingers and sighed. "No, Sol, why are they outlawing bounty hunting? It's not exactly a bad thing. I mean, we bring bad guys in. For the most part."

"Yeah, LaGrange, but you see... it's not regulated."

"So?"

"So, these guys don't like what they can't control."

"Tough," scoffed Duke. "Not my problem."

"Oh yeah," Sol snickered. "How's business? The last month in particular?"

Duke looked at Ishiro'shea again. Then he pulled up a chair and sat down. "That's why no one has been returning my calls, huh?"

"Yep. They shut down Big Rudy yesterday. Warthog Phil went down last week. Mama Fong fought back—no one has heard from her since."

"Mama Fong, the three-eyed Zylantian? The one that used to be a bounty hunter?"

"Yes, *that* Mama Fong," smirked Sol.

"It doesn't make sense. In the whole scheme of taking over the universe—"

"Not taking over the universe, LaGrange. Controlling it. They don't seem to care for power like a mad dictator would, they just want to control it. Have everything be neat and tidy. A single set of laws. In my opinion, it's worse. At least a crazed power-hungry megalomaniac is relatable to most of us. Order, structure—who needs that nonsense?"

Sol mimed spitting on the floor.

"But outlawing bounty hunting and upstanding bondsmen like yourself seems pretty petty and insignificant at the onset of a universal takeover," said Duke. "Right? Even if what you've said is correct and they've accomplished a ton in the last month, more than others that have sought to organize the infinite number of planets and races, are they that efficient that they can also enact bylaws to eliminate harmless little sub-industries like bounty hunting?"

"Honest answer?"

"Yes."

"Yes," said Sol. "They are. And they're coming for me next."

He rushed behind his desk and started organizing items and miscellaneous decor. He tossed them into a duffel bag.

"Why are you running?" asked Duke. "Can't you just say, 'Fine, I'll shut down'?"

"I've heard that they've been burning the places down

to the ground and taking every valuable on the premises. Right down to the clothes you're wearing."

"I don't think they have any interest in seeing you without clothes," joked the bounty hunter.

"Laugh now, LaGrange, but what are you going to do without any benefactors, huh? Not sure the playboy racket pays enough. I know and you know that bounty hunting pays the bills. Keeps your freaky ship in the air. Keeps your bar tab at Joe's paid off."

Duke couldn't disagree. The playboy part of his title—bounty-hunter-slash-playboy—was the part that typically got him in trouble. Bounty hunting was the steady gig and he knew he couldn't let it slip away.

After watching Sol load up his getaway bag, Duke asked, "So what about the other bounty hunters in this sector? Surely they're trying to fight this?"

"Bounty hunters trying to unite against this?" Sol snorted. "Are you mad, LaGrange, or just stupid? Once the word went out and a few bondsmen disappeared or were kicked to the curb, the hunters scattered. They hid. Did you see my lobby? Not a damn soul. I was shocked when I saw the *Deus* arrive. I thought you'd skedaddled with the rest of 'em."

"You know there's a Bounty Hunters Union, right? It's on Brenatto in the Gordget system. Or maybe it's Torlanus in the Protitroxx Limpor system. I'm not sure, but I get the mailers."

"You're kidding, right?"

"What?"

"It's a myth, LaGrange. There's no union for bounty hunters. It's a scam to swipe a few coins from your purses."

"Shut up, Sol."

"Seriously. I think they busted the guys that made it up.

They made a fortune before they were caught. Don't tell me that you paid dues to that thing."

Duke looked at Ishiro'shea. The ninja provided no help.

"Oh man, Duke."

"It's real, Sol," pleaded Duke.

"Gotta give 'em credit. Always best to exploit folks that are rich and dumb. If they kept their mouths shut, they probably would be in some Oscavian cave right now, living the life."

The Tardasian zipped his bag shut and hurried past the bounty hunters. He opened the door and motioned for them to follow him. "You guys leaving? Or are you gonna wait around for these feds to show up? I don't think they are the talkative type."

Duke and Ishiro'shea entered the lobby.

"Come on, Wanda!" shouted Sol. The pudgy receptionist left her post to stand next to the bondsman. She carried a duffel bag equally as robust as Sol's.

"Duke, Ishiro'shea—this is Wanda. Wanda, these are—"

"I know who they are, silly," she interjected in a wheezy tone. She batted her eyelashes and blushed. Sol looked a bit peeved at her reaction.

"Well, these two morons didn't even know that these new government types outlawed bounty hunting. They came looking for work," Sol said with a bitter laugh.

"You didn't know about the decree making bounty hunting illegal?"

"Nope."

"What about the one on brothels?" she asked.

Duke threw up his hands up. "My day just got a little worse."

"And portals," she said.

Duke and Ishiro'shea turned as one to stare at Sol. He cowered.

"Wanda, we gotta get out of here," Sol said. "Let's go. See ya', guys."

He trudged to the door, pulling Wanda with him. A few items fell out of his duffel bag.

Duke fired his laser revolver above their heads. The pulse hit the wall above the entrance, knocking down a photo of Sol hugging the noted bounty hunter, Maxx Gemstarr. Duke hated Maxx Gemstarr; the placement of the blast wasn't entirely unintentional.

"Sol," he said. "Why didn't you tell us about the portals?"

"Whoa, whoa, whoa," the rotund Tardasian said, his arms in the air. "It slipped my mind, it slipped my mind. Okay? Yes, they've announced that unregulated portal manipulation is illegal." He gulped in air and continued, "Extreme force will be used to prevent the breaking of this law."

"There's only one place with portal manipulation, regulated or otherwise. And that place doesn't respond nicely to extreme force."

"Yep," Sol groaned.

He tugged Wanda's arm firmly. She winced but didn't say anything. The two plump Tardasians fled through the door.

Duke and Ishiro'shea were left standing in the deserted reception room of Sol's Bail Bonds-O-Rama on Tardasio 7, a shattered photo of Maxx Gemstarr and a stray pair of Sol's socks on the floor next to them, and instead of a new gig, all they had been able to secure was a basketful of confusion and unanswered questions.

"Let's go see the Queen," said Duke after a moment's thought. "She might be having a worse month than us."

CHAPTER THREE

ASSISTANT DEPUTY ASSOCIATE
DIRECTOR

THE *DEUS EX MACHINA* WASN'T a quiet ship, nor did it have a smooth ride—not like certain newer, sleeker, sexier craft. But it was reliable when it needed to be reliable and, more importantly, unpredictable when it needed to be unpredictable. It always managed to pull Duke and Ishiro'shea out of jams when there was no hope. Surviving massive offensive attacks from disgruntled Jungafallowian princes even when its shields weren't operational—done. Teaching primitive alien races to access and fire its weapons system accurately, ignoring a good thousand generations of evolution in the process—sure, why not. And this was only in the last few months. There was no doubt that the two bounty hunters that called this ship home would have been cosmic roadkill countless times over had it not been for the *Deus*.

Currently, the *Deus* was on a trajectory to the planet Kelt and, more specifically, Cyborg Joe's Grill N' Go & The Why Not Saloon, having left Tardasio 7 a few hours prior. Duke and Ishiro'shea had some questions that needed to be answered, and they wanted to warn Queen Joe about the new sanctions that were being levied against her by this new bureaucratic upstart.

"How many times have we made this trip, Ish? Sol's to Joe's. Sol pays us. We give that hard-earned cash to Joe. We need more money. We go to Sol. Lather. Rinse. Repeat. An unhealthy cycle, if you ask me."

The ninja nodded in agreement.

"But a fun one."

Ishiro'shea concurred again.

"I still don't get why Sol was so squirmy. I mean, I get it. He doesn't want to be the next 'missing' bondsman or have his stuff taken away, but why didn't he tell us about the portals? Joe has to be pissed, if she knows. Or at least a bit annoyed."

The ship trembled.

"Inertial stabilizers operational?"

Ishiro'shea gave Duke a thumbs-up, then quickly tapped a few buttons on the control panel. The ship ceased its convulsions and steadied.

"Thanks, little—"

Duke was interrupted by a more violent jerk. And another. The ninja threw up his hands in confusion.

"Screens up."

Nothing appeared on the front view screen.

"That's odd. No visible culprits," Duke observed.

The *Deus* began to slow, but the rocking continued.

"Did you check the back scanners?"

Ishiro'shea projected the rear view to the main screen.

"What's going on? This doesn't make any sense. And it's nothing with our equipment? Is she malfunctioning?"

The ninja shook his head and flashed up the diagnostics report to the main viewer.

"She should be purring like a kitten," Duke concluded.

The ship dipped precipitously and Duke fell out of his captain's chair.

"Hey, wait a minute," he said from the floor, squinting intently at the screen. "Look there. On the back of the *Deus*, connected to us. Zoom in."

The projection focused in on the back of the *Deus Ex Machina*. Four metal suction cups were affixed to the outer shell. They were massive but barely visible due to their being camouflaged.

"Those aren't part of our ship. At least not normally. Do you think it's another one of the *Deus'* 'improvements'?"

The ninja did not respond.

"Me neither. I have a feeling that we might have company, little buddy. I don't like uninvited guests."

Duke stood up, vaulted over the rail that separated his captain's chair from the rest of the bridge, and landed gracefully next to his companion.

"Let's try this," Duke said, punching sequences into the panel.

A symphony of lasers lashed out from the posterior of the *Deus* in all directions. The beams rotated and fanned out to cover as large a footprint as possible. Tiny explosions appeared in what seemed to be open space.

"Extend the phasers out. I know they won't be as strong, but this is more exploratory in nature."

Ishiro'shea followed the order and increased the range of the lasers.

The tiny explosions remained but, farther out, they grew in size. The lasers were hitting something. Something invisible.

"Let's ratchet up the intensity. Let's make 'em feel it!"

The *Deus* roared and unleashed a more persuasive wave of firepower.

Four long towing cables appeared where the explosions

were sprouting up. Three snapped immediately due to the intense fire. At the ends of the cables, four towing ships uncloaked.

"Recognize these guys? They obviously have some cool tech. Not even the *Deus* can cloak. But what do they want with us?"

The ninja shrugged his shoulders.

"Can you hail 'em?"

Ishiro'shea opened up a communication line. Within seconds, an image appeared on the screen. It was a humanoid male dressed in tactical gear. He looked like he could be from Earth or Nova Texas, on the whole, generic and unremarkable. Duke did, however, remember seeing a similar uniform during one of his recent visits to Cyborg Joe's.

"Greetings, my sneaky little friends," began Duke. "I'm Duke LaGrange. Adventurer. Poet—"

"Mr. LaGrange, I'm the Assistant Deputy Associate Director of this ship."

"Wow, they really threw the big guns at us, huh?" Duke snickered to Ishiro'shea.

"And you have been deemed a criminal by the new galactic government," the deputy continued. "You are to halt and be boarded by our team. You will await trial at the star system of our choosing. Please do not resist. Intergalactic Infrastructure—"

Duke cut off communication.

"He was boring me, little buddy. So since we are so close to Joe's, I think we head that way. See if we can outrun 'em. I don't really want to fight off four of these guys, especially since we don't know what type of firepower they're packing. If they can cloak, they probably have some pretty good gear."

Even as Duke was finishing his thought, Ishiro'shea had

initiated a course to Joe's at top speed. The immediate acceleration jarred the bounty hunter enough to send him backwards into the railing around his chair.

"Holy hedgehogs, one's still attached to us," shouted Duke. "Hey, I have an idea. Try this."

Duke hopped in front of Ishiro'shea to sit at the manual controls. The *Deus Ex Machina* dove and wiggled, spasmed and spun, all at max power. The tow ship chose not to release the cable. Bad decision.

"Watch this!"

The fourth tow ship, still clinging to the cable, struck the neighboring vessel. The explosion was much larger than Duke had imagined. The cable fell limp as it released from the demolished tow ship. The two operable ships swiftly exited the immediate space as the other two continued to disintegrate into a pile of space junk. But they didn't flee.

"Now, wasn't that easy? Two down, two to go. Poor Deputy Assistant... whatever he was. Anyways, let's step on it and outrun these bastards to Joe's."

The bounty hunters sped towards Kelt with two government tow ships on their tail. Duke was once again a wanted man—but he wasn't exactly sure why they were so keen on flushing him out.

Duke looked at Ishiro'shea.

"You don't think that Sol set us up, do you?"

"Sol totally set us up. That fat son of a bitch."

The federal blockade surrounded the entirety of the planet Kelt. There were at least a dozen battle cruisers, a ton of single-seat fighter scouts, and one behemoth Armada Titan, one of the largest makes of warship in the known universe. Duke had never seen a force of this size so close to Kelt. Joe had to be really pissed now.

"That bulbous bastard. He told us that portal crap because he knew we would beeline it directly to Cyborg Joe's to talk to the Queen. Those four ships were waiting on us. Even if we escaped, they'd drive us directly into an entire flippin' fleet. They even have an Armada Titan, for crying out loud. Who has a godforsaken Armada Titan?"

A pulsing light flashed on the screen.

"They want to talk again," Duke sighed. "Might as well hear what they have to say, right? Maybe it will buy us some time to figure out how to get outta this jam, because right now I'm out of ideas. Barren. Empty. I got nothin'."

Ishiro'shea pressed the button to open the hail.

"What do you want now?" barked Duke.

"Mr. LaGrange, it is now time for you to surrender. There is no hope for you as you are now facing our entire 42nd legion. Did you see the Armada Titan? If you attempt to escape again, we will render your ship inoperable."

"You think I'm scared of that oversized tin can?" Duke asked. "The *Deus* has taken out badder ships than that more times than I can count."

"Please stop your advance," responded the officer, ignoring Duke's question. "We will board you. It will be painless and swift. You will be taken to the Armada Titan to await—"

Duke cut the communication off again. "Nope. He's still boring me." He stood, arms crossed, and tapped his foot. "What to do, what to do? Any ideas?"

Ishiro'shea was also deep in thought. A moment later, his eyes expanded, bugging out of his head.

"What?"

The ninja pointed to the captain's chair.

"Not again."

In the middle of the left armrest was a plastic dome the size of a big-boned hamster. Inside it was a clownish red button. Duke remembered what the manual said: *Always push the red button.*

He looked up at the ceiling of the *Deus.* "Hey girl, you know I love you, right? I'm sure I'm going to really appreciate whatever that button does—but I also know it probably means that any second we're going to be in a pretty dire situation. I'm not overly thrilled with that part. But thank you. I think."

He sauntered to the chair and opened the dome. He gave Ishiro'shea a timid thumbs-up. He pushed the button.

A buzzing sound consumed the *Deus.* Duke closed his eyes and clenched his teeth, bracing for something dramatic... and painful.

Nothing.

The buzzing stopped and all was as it was before.

"You're losing your touch, old girl," he said to the *Deus.*

The communication light pulsed again.

"I really hate this guy," he sighed. "Let's see what he has to say this time. I'm sure it's exhilarating."

The enemy ship's representative reappeared. His face was bright red.

Why's he so mad? thought Duke.

"Mr. LaGrange, whatever you're trying to do, whatever your game is, it's futile. You can't just disappear and escape our entire fleet. We will find you in due time."

Duke didn't respond. He cut the communication immediately. He turned to his masked co-conspirator.

"You don't think..." He paused. "No way. Do something for me, Ish. Let's head directly toward that ship—the battle cruiser directly in front of us."

Ishiro'shea shot back a confused look.

"Trust me. Do it. I have a hunch."

The ninja hit the thrusters and the *Deus* darted directly towards a well-armed battle cruiser.

"Check the back scanners."

Ishiro'shea pulled the rear view on the screen. The tow ships hadn't moved. They weren't chasing them. Ahead of them, the battle cruiser remained equally motionless. Their weapons systems were very much idle.

"Holy hedgehogs," Duke proclaimed as he hugged the rail around his captain's chair. "Thank you, old girl. Thank you."

Ishiro'shea still looked perplexed.

"Ish, we're cloaked. They can't see us. That damn button gave us cloaking tech. It probably saw that those puny tow ships had cloaks and decided it wanted the same. She was probably a tad jealous. This ship, man." He shook his head in disbelief.

"So, if we know anything about the *Deus*, it's that these upgrades don't last forever. I say we try and navigate this minefield and get to Joe's before it wears off and we become sitting ducks again."

Ishiro'shea jabbed his finger in the opposite direction.

"You're right, we *could* run and get out of this mess. However, if they got to Sol, who's to say that they haven't gotten to our other friends? I'd feel better talking to the Queen. You know they didn't get to her. They're trying to make her illegal. There's no place safer than Joe's. From an invasion, at least."

Duke could make out a smile through Ishiro'shea's mask.

Yep, he agrees, thought Duke.

"But let's stay as far away as possible from that Titan."

CHAPTER FOUR

FOUR I'S

"THANKS, EARL," SAID DUKE. "DRIVING through an entire armada can really make a man thirsty."

Duke downed his purple liquid. His face puckered.

"Is it not to your liking, Mr. LaGrange?" asked the mannerly Glyptodian barkeep.

"Is Ootrelian oyster juice to anyone's liking? I can't believe y'all are out of Erontian saké. And Glyptodian ale."

"And most of our whisky selection," chimed in the enigmatic Queen Joe. She was an attractive female and most believed she was one of the most powerful beings in the universe. Duke tended to align himself with that hypothesis. She also controlled the portals that made Cyborg Joe's Grill N' Go & The Why Not Saloon one of the most popular destinations in the universe.

"Hey, Queen. Yeah, I guess if I was a supplier, I probably wouldn't want to try and traverse that blockade, either."

"It's unfortunate. Earl said that you wanted to see me."

"Well, yes. There's an entire fleet of battle cruisers in orbit around Kelt. And you're violating their new mandate."

"The one about my portals?"

"Yeah."

Queen Joe rolled her eyes and helped Earl clean some glassware.

"Aren't you worried?" asked Duke.

"Not at all. How many times have we seen these pop-up governments?"

"Queen, no offense, but they always ignored you before now. These guys are on your front doorstep."

"You should be more worried about their ban on bounty hunting."

"And brothels," slurred a familiar voice from the table behind them.

"Oh hey, Po'l. How ya' doing?"

"Amazing," said the intoxicated Neprian. "I love this place. Best thing that I ever did was leave that boring rock that I was on. Right, Queenie?"

She turned to Duke and leaned in.

"He's been portaling more than any other patron that we've ever had. Hits up a pleasure planet one day, goes on some 'epic quest'—as he calls them—the next. I'm worried about him."

"How does he afford it?"

"He's been working here. Earl hired him."

"Hey, how 'bout some more of this purple stuff? It's my new favorite drink, Queenie!"

She ignored him. Earl picked up on the clues and brought another round of Ootrelian oyster juice to Po'l.

"Last round, Mr. Po'l," bellowed the Glyptodian. "Your shift starts in a few hours."

"Alright, you big hairy..." Po'l trailed off, but then perked up and refocused his attention. "Good seein' you,

Duke. Ishiro'shea," he said between belches. He pounded his drink and headed to the back of the bar.

Duke flashed a bewildered look at Queen Joe.

"We threw a hammock up in one of the back closets. He likes it."

"He's always been an odd one," replied Duke. "But back to the question at hand, what are you going to do about these guys?"

"Duke, I told you. Nothing. They'll go away."

"I don't think they will, Queen. These guys seem different. They got to Sol. He set us up. They've already taken over a few not-so-insignificant planets in a few weeks. No one has ever done that before, not this quickly. This just seems *different*."

"We're fine, Duke."

"They said they're going to use 'extreme force' on you."

"They haven't yet. I can take care of myself and this bar. I'm not concerned."

The bounty hunter knew that he was fighting a losing battle. He had to trust the Queen—because why wouldn't he? She was the Queen.

"Earl, get Duke and Ishiro'shea a drink. On me. See if we have a shot of whisky left. Guys, it might be Erontian. I know it's not the best. But, hey, free is free."

"Sounds good to me."

"You know, Duke, I'm more worried about what I'm hearing from some of my customers about the goings-on at the other side of the sector."

"What's that?" asked the bounty hunter, puzzled.

"I've been hearing some whispers that Admiral LePaco is back and causing trouble."

"LePaco?"

"Didn't you try and track him down before?"

"I'd rather not talk about it," snapped Duke.

"I'm just telling you that his name's been popping up here and there. Seems like he's out of hiding again. He's insane enough to actually do something dangerous. These uptight middle-management types with battleships, they don't worry me; a sociopathic murderer that's escaped *your* clutches—that makes me nervous."

"Not interested. At all. He's probably just trying to scheme on folks while everyone else is so focused on this new group of misfits. Not worth my time."

"Okay, what *is* worth your time?"

"This," said Duke as he plucked a glass full of whisky from a tray balanced on Earl's oversized, furry paw. "This is worth my time. At no point in my existence, no matter how gruelling the situation or how tranquil and beautiful the moment, would *this* not be worth my time."

He stared longingly into the glass before he downed the booze in one fluid motion.

"What about Mazilda Cloax?"

Immediately, Duke choked on the remaining splashes of whisky still working its way down his throat. A cough slipped out. And another.

"Thought so," Queen Joe smirked. "You know that she came through here not too long ago."

"You mentioned that a month ago. If I recall, you dropped that on me right when we returned from Neprius after dealing with a maniac and his magic rock. Thanks for that, by the way."

"You're welcome."

"How is my favorite magic rock?" asked Duke.

"It's safe," replied the Queen soberly. "I promise you, it's safe."

"That's good to hear. The only thing so far that has been. I mean, since I've showed up, it's been LePaco,

Mazilda, and a giant Armada Titan floating above Kelt. Are you trying to get me to leave?"

"And Prince Korzo-Tapor."

"I almost forgot about that two-headed whackjob."

"He came through a bit before Mazilda. They both went through the same portal to the same destination. I forget which one. Not even sure of the planet. Something about getting ready for a tournament of some sort. Maybe a combat tournament? I think I recall something along those lines."

"I doubt Mazilda would enter into a combat tournament," replied Duke smugly.

"No, she never struck me as someone that would get dressed up and fight for the amusement of others."

She paused and a smile crept onto her face.

"But her new boyfriend did."

"What new boy—" Duke began, but caught himself. "Don't care. None of my business. Don't care one bit."

He tried to stop his teeth from gritting but failed. He tightened his grip on his empty glass.

"Okay," the Queen said, shooting a glance towards Ishiro'shea. Duke interpreted it as a not-so-subtle 'yeah right.'

"You don't care about Mazilda and her new boyfriend?" began Queen Joe.

"Nope."

"Or Prince Korzo-Tapor?"

"Couldn't care less."

"Or that Admiral LePaco's name is popping up again?"

"Who?" Duke feigned.

"Okay then," responded Queen Joe.

"But I do care about that armada outside of your bar."

"Like I said before, I'm not," the Queen replied. "They're harmless. If we ignore them, they'll go away."

"You can't ignore a flippin' Armada Titan!" Duke shouted.

The Queen appeared to be caught a bit off guard. It wasn't every day that someone raised their voice to Queen Joe. *I hope she doesn't kill me*, thought Duke.

After a brief pause, she went back to cleaning more glasses. She looked up momentarily, locking eyes with Duke. "If you're so worried about them, why don't you ask them to leave?"

"What?"

"One's coming over, right now."

Duke pivoted on the barstool.

Standing in the entryway of Cyborg Joe's was a humanoid wearing the same attire as the two tow-ship officers that they had engaged with on the *Deus*; he was clearly a representative of the enterprise that was currently surrounding the planet Kelt. He looked important, or at least he appeared to possess a high rank, as he wasn't in traditional tactical gear. The officer wore glasses and medals adorned his left breast. He looked as if he was after something—and Duke didn't like that.

"Prepare to be bored to death by this Four I's paper-pusher," said Queen Joe.

"That's a bit beneath you, Queen," gasped Duke. "Heck, that's beneath most primary schoolers. I thought you were all about tolerance, blah, blah."

The proprietor looked genuinely confused, which, for a nearly all-powerful being, wasn't a common look. Then she appeared to come to some sort of realization. "No, Duke. Not 'four eyes.' Four I's. Acronym. The organization that's surrounding us—the one that you are so freaked out by. They are Intergalactic Infrastructure Improvement, Incorporated. Their mission is to improve the order of the universe with a sound infrastructure—or something like that. I. I. I. I. Four I's."

Duke looked embarrassed.

"They have a jingle, I think, if it helps you remember," the Queen added.

The bespectacled man was still standing at the entrance of Joe's. He stood perfectly erect with his arms folded behind his back and his chest puffed out.

He cleared his throat. "Patrons of this establishment," he boomed.

The amplification of the man's address reminded Duke of a behemoth monster named Toby he had once encountered on Neprius. The bounty hunter was impressed by the volume that this average-sized humanoid was able to unleash.

The officer continued, "I'm looking for a criminal that is likely seeking refuge amongst you."

"What did I tell you guys? I'm not going to go peacefully. If you bug me again, I'm going to get really angry," shouted the Queen from the bar. "There's really no point in you trying. You're just going to waste time, resources—all the things that you guys preach about maximizing with your —what do you call them?—'pillars of efficiency.'"

The Four I representative remained stone-faced.

"Queen Joe, we've received your warnings and are taking them into consideration. Our decision on how to move forward with you and your alleged crimes of portal manipulation are still under discussion. As are our plans to turn this lackluster, low-output planet into an effective member of the universal community. This visit, however, is about something else. *Someone* else, to be precise. The outlaw bounty hunter Duke LaGrange and his accomplice, Ishiro'shea of Earth, are to report to Four I's Disciplinary Committee immediately."

Duke stood up and faced the representative.

"Hey, we haven't bounty hunted since the law was enacted. Ask anyone. Look at my bank account."

"Bounty hunting is the least of your offenses, Mr. LaGrange. The destruction of two Four I tow ships is the reason I am here to collect you both this evening."

"Oh yeah, that. We *did* do that. You are one hundred percent right."

"Please come with me."

"I don't think that's going to happen."

Duke unholstered his laser revolver and spun it on his right index finger.

The representative did not fail to notice the firearm. "It might be worth noting, Mr. LaGrange, that we've confiscated your ship."

Duke immediately pointed the gun at the representative. "Not a smart move, man. Not at all."

As if on cue, a squad of armed Four I soldiers burst through the door and surrounded the representative. They were heavily armed and armored.

The Queen whispered in Duke's ear. "You and Ishiro'shea go. Now. I'll handle this."

"To the portals?"

"Yes."

"Just any? Where do they go?"

"Not sure where I had them programmed to. Probably a pleasure planet—thanks to Po'l."

"Not a bad hiding place," responded Duke. "What about the Bounty Hunters Union headquarters? We could rally some support there and come back and fight."

"Duke, I don't think that's a real place."

"It's a real place! Why doesn't anyone believe me?"

"Just go."

Queen Joe stepped from behind the bar and parted

with Duke and Ishiro'shea. She headed towards the Four I squadron.

"I said go," she yelled without turning around.

The bounty hunters vaulted over the bar and headed towards the portals.

"You better not harm my ship!" Duke shouted as they stepped through one of the ornate portal doors. He heard what sounded like a firefight breaking out behind him. It became fainter and fainter as his body deconstructed and was sent through the portal.

CHAPTER FIVE

CEPHALO-GOD

S HAMAN OF THE HIGH COMMAND Klorzzel IV ordered Grozzel to the edge of the overlook. Commander Churzzel flanked him and Serjarzeel followed a few paces behind. Grozzel looked down on the thousands of Psitakki that filled in the grasslands below the cliffs. They roared and cheered as he stepped to the ledge. Shaman Klorzzel and Churzzel both raised Grozzel's hands. The gathering erupted with even greater fervor.

The Shaman hushed the crowd. He leaned into his voice amplifier and spoke. "Psitakki, you've come from all corners of our home to celebrate our continued freedom. We, as a people, together and undeterred, have driven the shadowy interlopers from our world."

The Psitakki whooped and shouted. Flags waved and trumpets made celebratory honks.

"But, as you may have heard, and I can confirm it this very moment as gospel, we would not have made it to this day without a great discovery by the fearless Grozzel."

The Shaman motioned to Grozzel, who waved timidly. Churzzel draped his arm around Grozzel, sharing in the boisterous applause from the spectators. *Of course he is,* thought Grozzel.

The Shaman repositioned himself at the vanguard and the crowd silenced immediately.

"It has been determined, following much debate and counsel, that the trove of magic shields that were discovered on the final day of battle by our dear Grozzel here were, in fact, sent to us by the Colossal Calamari in the sky."

Murmurs of discussion rippled through the droves of Psitakki in attendance. *Not sure they're buying the Cephalo-god angle,* thought Grozzel. *Typical High Command brainwashing.*

The Shaman slammed his staff on the ground and the muddled debate halted.

"I repeat, my Psitakki brethren, it has been decided that the almighty and all-knowing Colossal Calamari sent us these tools to defeat our demonic foes. If anyone thinks differently, please speak up. Don't be shy. The elders of this world and I would love to discuss this with you."

The catapults rumbled to the edge of the cliff, in plain view of the audience.

Chants of "Ca-la-mar-i" broke out. The Shaman smiled. *Figures.*

"Excellent," began the Shaman, the leader of High Command, still grinning wryly. "Now that we know where they came from, it's time to decree how we will celebrate our great fortune that they were given to us and, of course, discovered by our beloved Grozzel."

The Psitakki cheered at the idea of a celebration.

"We will hold a tournament. The Tournament of the Shield..."

They erupted. The Shaman motioned for silence.

"...of the Colossal Calamari!"

They clapped less enthusiastically. A chuckle escaped Grozzel. Churzzel sneered at him.

"It will be a tournament of combat. Being versus being. Sixteen of the bravest, strongest, and most honorable combatants will battle. The winner will be awarded one of the very shields that saved our species!"

The valley below the cliff was jolted into excitement.

"All one hundred shields will be awarded over time, in order to honor our triumph and signify our perseverance."

Shaman Klorzzel IV held aloft his staff in dramatic fashion as the Psitakki below fell silent.

"And the first tournament begins in a fortnight!"

He slammed the staff down. A thunderous roar filled the Psitakki countryside.

Grozzel sighed dejectedly.

After surviving his first three opponents by outsmarting them—more or less—Grozzel found himself in the finals of the first Tournament of the Shield of the Colossal Calamari. He thought that since he was the symbolic hero of the war, the tournament planners may have given him some easier competition to avoid upsetting the adoring masses. Grozzel wasn't even sure how they chose the tournament entrants, since thousands had applied. He wasn't complaining.

Staring at him from across the arena floor, however, was a different opponent to the ones he had faced so far. This one was bigger. Meaner. There was a good chance that he represented Grozzel's imminent death. Even though death wasn't required to win your tournament bout—the rules specified submission to your opponent or the physical inability to continue as the official outcomes—no one was going to get too upset if someone was mortally wounded, especially to honor the Colossal Calamari. For some reason, the Shaman and High Command thought death and mortal sacrifice were the best ways to become buds with the celestial cephalopod. Most of the regular folks on Psitakki didn't have time to worry about what a squid in the sky was thinking.

Of all the possible opponents, it had to be Churzzel.

Grozzel could hear the grizzled commander's growl from across the arena. Churzzel pounded his chest; his eyes filled with primal rage.

Grozzel looked up at the sea of spectators. The arena was packed. A temporary third deck had been built in the last week to accommodate the anticipated crowds. He turned to look at the decorated seats in the center of the primary grandstands. The Shaman sat there, his staff in one hand, a drink in the other. He tapped his staff and the crowd cheered.

This is going to hurt, thought Grozzel.

Since no projectile weapons were allowed, Grozzel didn't have his sling with him. It was his favorite toy. He used to practice on the tarzantia trees near his house. He could knock a rogue twig off a branch from the other side of the swamp. For this fight, he had opted for a wooden club. It wasn't particularly ominous, but Grozzel felt that he could swing it with some authority. Churzzel toted around an iron mace the size of a Psitakki female, making Grozzel feel wholly inadequate. The commander twirled it around to the crowd's delight. Even across the arena floor, Grozzel could feel the breeze that the humongous weapon generated.

This is going to hurt a lot.

The first part of the bout didn't go so well for Grozzel. It mostly involved Churzzel picking him up over his head and tossing him to the ground, to the accompanying sound of admiration from the crowd. Churzzel would then turn and soak in their praise. With each toss, they cheered louder. Grozzel had lost his club after just one swing—Churzzel had blocked it with his mace and then pushed Grozzel to the ground, forcing him to release it. He had tossed it away from the action.

Grozzel was bleeding from the mouth. The urge to submit began to overtake him. For some reason, however, he pressed on. *So many of these folks here think I'm a hero,* he thought. *I must continue.* But he wasn't a hero—just some guy who had found some shields in a cave when he was running away. He decided he would give it one more go before admitting defeat. One more last-ditch effort. He owed himself that much.

He charged Churzzel. The commander turned around as Grozzel was leaping for an attack, and swatted him down in midair.

That was anticlimactic.

The attendees clapped. Churzzel picked up Grozzel and flung him to the other side of the arena. Grozzel skidded to a stop, his face resting a few paces from his club.

He gathered himself and gripped the baton.

What to do? What to do?

His hand hovered over a stone. It wasn't an insignificant rock—but it wasn't large by any stretch of the imagination. It could be categorized as being between pebble and mountain range.

Grozzel didn't know what came over him or why he thought of it—he tossed the rock in the air and struck it with the club. It arched across the arena floor and hit the commander square in the back. Churzzel stumbled forward a few steps, then turned around slowly to see Grozzel standing with his club in hand.

Churzzel charged. Dust kicked up behind him and

formed an arch of spray as he raced towards Grozzel. He waved his iron mace erratically.

Grozzel picked up another rock and struck it. Wide right. Churzzel was closing in. Another rock. It hit the commander in the knee. Churzzel stumbled momentarily, then collected himself and continued his approach. Grozzel had one rock left.

"This is for Zorzzel."

He threw the rock in the air. It connected with his club with a loud crack.

The rock struck the commander with such force that it burrowed into the area between his eyes upon impact.

Churzzel collapsed. He was unconscious.

The Shaman smashed his staff against the stone floor. The sound echoed throughout the arena. The fight was over.

What just happened? Grozzel thought to himself in disbelief.

"The winner of the first Tournament of the Shield of the Colossal Calamari—our own war hero, Grozzel!"

Grozzel fell to his knees in exhaustion. All went black.

He was suddenly awakened by a splash of cold water. The Psitakki opened his eyes to see the Shaman looking down at him. Two guards lifted him to his feet. Grozzel wasn't sure if the crowd was cheering or if the sound was the ringing in his ears. Either way, it was loud.

"Friends, I present to you our champion, Grozzel," boomed Shaman Klorzzel IV's voice through the amplifier.

He handed one of the shields to Grozzel. It radiated with a glow that seemed to fill the arena. The crowd seemed mesmerized by its beauty. Grozzel couldn't tell if it was the actual shield that he used to obliterate the shadow demons in the hidden cave, but he wanted to believe it was.

The dazed victor tapped the Shaman on the shoulder. Klorzzel looked back with an expression of disgust.

"You're really going to give away all of these shields? Is that smart? I mean, you know best and all, but it seems—"

Klorzzel's sneer stopped him in mid-sentence. The Shaman leaned in and whispered, "Don't question what I do, peasant. Shut up, take your shield, and did I mention shut up?"

The guards released Grozzel and he fell to the arena floor still clutching his shield.

"And friends," the Shaman began, "to honor the ten thousand Psitakki that lost their life forces at the hands of these ruthless marauders, we will hold the tournament again in ten thousand cycles. And every ten thousand cycles after that."

The entire arena went silent. The Shaman looked back at Grozzel and rolled his eyes.

Of course it's every ten thousand cycles. The Shaman would never let something so powerful out of his sight until he has milked it for all its worth.

"I really hate High Command," Grozzel said under his breath.

Grozzel didn't feel like a champion anymore. It had been many cycles since he had won the Tournament of the Shield of the Colossal Calamari. The shield sat on his table, serving no purpose other than acting as a window into his past. A window covered in the fingerprints of time, rendered opaque with the smudges of irrelevance. There were no more promotional appearances, no more autograph signings or store openings. He shook no more hands and kissed no more babies. He was a relic, just like his magical shield.

The aged Psitakki sat down with a bowl of hashed jiarfu as a late breakfast. His body ached. The shield pulsed softly as he ate. It had seen better days as well.

One more daily entry in the boring book of my life, he thought.

The jiarfu slid down his throat. He was delighted that it was so mushy. Chewing hurt.

Only those clinging to the last cycles of life would find happiness in soggy breakfast food.

The shield started to pulse at an increased rate.

"What's wrong with you?" Grozzel asked the shield. "You haven't blinked like that in ages, old friend."

The speed of the shield's pulsing picked up exponentially. The light grew brighter. It illuminated Grozzel's entire home.

"Hey now, stop that," he screamed at the inanimate object.

Why am I talking to a shield? I've really gone crazy.

The shield started to buzz and whirl.

Then it exploded.

Grozzel, his house, and the tarzantia trees that lined his swamp were wiped from the face of Psitakki in the blink of an eye.

CHAPTER SIX

CRASHING THE PARTY

"I THINK I HAVE A fork in my armpit," grimaced Duke. "No wait a minute, that's a... is that a spork?"

They had successfully materialized upon exiting their hastily-chosen portal; it just so happened to be about five feet above a banquet table. Covered in plates. And silverware. And a spork. The impact of the two bounty hunters hadn't even dented the monolithic slab; the only tabletop casualties were a fruit platter and some congealed pudding substance. Duke and Ishiro'shea were the clear losers in the collision.

They both sat up, sending a few more plates crashing to the floor. The hall was jam-packed with beings from all corners of the universe. Duke didn't even recognize some of the species. The room was elaborately decorated; it was a full-on gala.

Within moments the bounty hunters were surrounded by Psitakki from all angles. Those seated at the table they had crashed into quickly made room for the armed cephalopodan guards. The barrels of their rifles were mere inches from Duke's and Ishiro'shea's faces.

"Who interrupts this celebratory evening?" boomed an artificially projected voice, coming from the direction of a stage at one end of the hall. The speaker was an elderly Psitakki cloaked in a dazzling lavender robe. His upper lip tentacles hung down to his chest.

He has to be really old, thought Duke.

"My apologies," began Duke, finding and donning his Stetson. "I'm Duke LaGrange. Adventurer. Poet. True man of the universe. And this is my faithful partner, Ishiro'shea. Salutatorian of the College of Cohorts—"

"Why have you chosen to crash our party?" the Psitakki interjected. "And when I say 'crash our party,' I quite literally mean crash our party."

"Again, apologies. It seems our portal did not calibrate properly. This was not our intended destination."

"What was your intended destination, Duke LaGrange?"

"I don't know, man. A pleasure planet, probably. That was what I was hoping for."

"I'm not surprised by that," chimed a familiar voice from somewhere behind the guards.

A curvaceous female stepped out in the light. Her skin was a subtle yellow hue whereas her eyes, hair, and lips were electric purple, the color of Ootrelian oyster juice.

"Oh hey, Mazilda," Duke said nonchalantly, without making eye contact.

Duke turned to Ishiro'shea and mouthed, "Of all the portals..."

The ninja shrugged.

"State your business," shouted the Psitakki elder.

Duke looked at Mazilda. She gave him nothing. He looked at Ishiro'shea for some guidance but the ninja provided no aid either.

"We just want to get outta here."

"I think that could be arranged."

"Great. Wonderful. Apologies again," said the bounty hunter. He brushed some unknown culinary substance from his pants.

"However, before we let you leave our planet," said the Psitakki, "we do want to take you in for some questioning. It's standard procedure."

"Smart thinking, Grand Shaman," shouted a muscular human adorned in bright spandex.

Not him, Duke pleaded internally. *Please don't let that be him.*

"It's what I would do," the beefy partygoer continued. His hands were on his hips, his elbows fanned out. His chest jutted out and his chin pointed to the ceiling. His striking pose was positively camera-ready. "That's exactly what Maxx Gemstarr would do."

"I'm glad you agree, contestant Gemstarr," replied the luxuriously-clothed Shaman.

"You're a tool, you know that?" Duke said to Maxx.

Gemstarr did not respond. Instead, he pulled Mazilda Cloax closer to his side. He planted a kiss on her cheek, then winked at the Nova Texan.

Duke's intestines constricted as if he had just been kicked by a Quibbian erecto-varmint.

"Take them away," said the Grand Shaman.

The guards yanked Duke and Ishiro'shea off the table and led them to the back of the hall.

"Easy, tiger," Duke snickered at one of the guards, "I thought this was just some standard questioning."

The guard ignored him. Four rifles were trained upon the two party crashers at all times.

They were ushered to the back of the hall and forced to sit against the wall. The guards did not take their weapons, but Duke did not consider fighting back. A little interrogation never hurt anyone—nor were he and Ishiro'shea likely to take out an entire dining hall worth of guests. With any luck, they would be off of Psitakki by the morning.

One of the guards returned to the main stage and whispered something in the Grand Shaman's ear. He nodded and sent the guard back.

"Friends, as we wait for our Chief Interrogator General to arrive and take away our uninvited guests, I feel we should continue."

The crowd clapped politely.

"I am Grand Shaman Klorzzel XVMMMDCCXXIII, the direct descendant of Klorzzel IV, the first Shaman of the Tournament of the Shield of the Colossal Calamari."

More applause.

"I wonder how you get promoted from Shaman to Grand Shaman?" Duke whispered to Ishiro'shea. The ninja did not respond. His eyes remained focused on Klorzzel.

"It is my honor to announce the one hundredth and final tournament honoring the unique magic shields sent by our always-present deity, which saved our people from invasion so many eons ago, when time was young and our planet was a mere infant. The winner of this tournament will not only win the final shield, the last link between the present day and that fateful event that saved our race, but they will also bookend the million-cycle history of this contest with the inaugural champion, our legendary hero and finder of the shields, Grozzel the Great."

The applause picked up a notch. It was still classy and dignified applause, only much louder.

"Your participation honors the Colossal Calamari in the sky. I know that you have all been busy for the last month training, meeting locals, conducting interviews and other assorted pre-event tasks. We appreciate the focus. It honors our planet and our ancestors. It shows that you respect our customs and our history. Truly, it honors us all. I wish you all luck and a good battle."

The Shaman bowed and exited the stage.

Another Psitakki took the stage. He sported no robe and generally looked less prestigious.

"Honorable combatants and guests, as by ancient law, I shall read the rules of the tournament. Many originate from the first tournament; others have been modified over the course of time."

"I thought this tournament was a joke," Duke said to Ishiro'shea. "It doesn't seem up Maxx's alley, though. Unless he plans to blow so much smoke up their asses that they all explode. It's a pretty good superpower if you ask me."

The Psitakki on the stage unrolled a scroll and began to read aloud.

"As you know, the Tournament of the Shield of the Colossal Calamari will pit sixteen of the most honorable beings against each other in fair and regulated combat. Fifteen, from as far as the mystic Silver Mountains of Mrelock to the turbulent tides of Zylantia, have been selected by the Grand Shaman and awarded invitations. All fifteen have accepted and no alternates were required."

"Ladies and gentlemen," Duke muttered to Ishiro'shea, "I have discovered the fifteen dumbest individuals in the universe and they're all in the same room."

The Shaman continued, "The sixteenth spot will be determined tomorrow, on the eve of the tournament, by means of a voluntary melee battle in the arena."

"Okay, *they* might be the dumbest individuals in the universe," Duke said, correcting himself. "A melee battle to get into a tournament of death? So dumb."

"The rules of combat," the Psitakki continued, "are simple but final. No contestant can be robotic, mechanized, cybertronic, or artificially manufactured. If you have some upgrades here or there, we're cool with that."

A few hoots and hollers came from pockets of the great hall. Duke and Ishiro'shea looked at each other quizzically.

"I hope one of those cyborgs beats Maxx's face in."

"There will be no projectile weapons allowed. No guns or lasers or arrows—unless it's part of your natural biology. If you spew a toxic muck from your belly button, we'll allow it."

Duke could hear some hissing from the front.

"Weapons are fine but need to be preapproved. We have all of the submissions from the combatants. All are approved!"

Boisterous applause filled the room.

"Magic is strictly prohibited."

"Hear, hear!" shouted Maxx Gemstarr.

Duke rolled his eyes. *What an ass. He probably still believes in magic.*

Duke had always believed that magic was just undiscovered science—but then he remembered the mysterious Orb on Neprius, which was now under the Queen's watchful surveillance. On reflection, he decided that he was firmly *undecided* on the topic. Anyway, Maxx had other quirks to mock and snicker at; no need to waste time on such a gray-area issue.

"In order to advance in the tournament, you will need to defeat your opponent," said the orator.

That's the usual requirement in a tournament, Duke smirked to himself.

"This can occur by your opponent giving up and submitting to your dominance. Or if the Shaman considers them unable to continue. Or if they die. We will do our best to prevent victory by death but, hey, stuff happens."

"It would take a *complete* idiot to fight in this thing," said Duke. Ishiro'shea nodded in agreement.

"Good luck and good battle. For the Colossal Calamari!"

"For the Colossal Calamari," the crowd responded in unison.

"What a bunch of—"

"Morons?"

The speaker of the voice that interrupted Duke appeared from the shadows. He had a reptilian head on top of a long, cylindrical stalk of a neck. It was next to an exact duplicate neck and head.

Jungafallowian.

"Nice to meet you in person, Duke LaGrange," the newcomer said in a slithery voice.

"And you are?"

"Surprised to see that you survived my attack."

"Prince Korzo-Tapor, I presume?" Duke said despondently.

"Yes, the pleasure is mine." Both of his heads bowed to the bounty hunters.

"Come to finish the job, with us handily tied up and surrounded by gun-toting squids? You are extremely brave, Princey."

"Oh, not in the least. I have no need. I've lost interest in avenging your misdeeds against the Trampling Death Robots. Water under the bridge, my friends."

"Right."

"In fact, I agree with you. It would take an idiot to fight in this tournament."

"Why are *you* here then? Seems like a perfect weekend activity for a Jungafallowian."

"It is. But not for *this* Jungafallowian. I have more, let's say, refined interests. However, I am here supporting my own entrant. He's not here at this particular moment. In fact, I don't take him out in public that much. He tends to —" The prince paused. "—cause a scene."

"Not a black-tie sort of hombre?" quipped Duke.

"That's an understatement, I'm afraid."

"Well, good luck with all of this. I hope he bashes in Gemstarr's head."

"As do I. He's quite annoying," Korzo-Tapor remarked.

"Not that we don't love your company and all," Duke said sarcastically, "but why are you over here talking to us? Don't you need to go strategize, or something, for this dumb tournament?"

"You know that Psitakki interrogation is actually a euphemism for torture, right?" said the prince, changing tack.

"What?"

"Yes, you two are scheduled to be tortured for ruining— or almost ruining—the Shaman's gala."

"Shut up."

"I'm being serious," the other head hissed. "This Shaman really likes burning people alive. Or is it flaying them in public? I can't remember. He's a being of many unorthodox desires."

"If you're telling the truth, why? Why would you, of all people—peoples? Is it peoples? Anyways, why should we believe you?"

"I think it would be interesting to see you in this tournament. This tournament of morons."

"No chance, Princey."

"It might behoove you to know that if you put your name in the proverbial hat for that final spot in the melee bout tomorrow, you will be spared the inquisition. The toasty inquisition. Or the skinless inquisition. You get the point. It will be bad."

"I'll take my chances. I have two guns and a ninja. It could be worse."

"True. That disappoints me, it truly does. But good luck to you, Duke LaGrange. It was nice meeting you before you die a ridiculously agonizing and stomach-turning death."

Duke grimaced. *Why do I believe this guy? I shouldn't believe him, I really shouldn't. He tried to kill us, after all. But I kinda believe him. I hate myself a bit more now.*

"And the author of your grizzly demise approaches," said Korzo-Tapor. "I present to you the Chief Interrogator General. I hear he's a lovely man."

Korzo-Tapor slid away, back into the shadows from whence he came.

A hulking Psitakki lumbered towards Duke and Ishiro'shea. He walked with a limp and had a crude hooklike instrument in place of his right hand.

Wonderful. Just wonderful.

CHAPTER SEVEN

CHIEF INTERROGATOR GENERAL

"THIS JAIL ISN'T THAT BAD, is it little buddy?"

Ishiro'shea did not respond. Duke knew what his answer would have been.

"Okay, fine, it's not the *best* jail we've ever been in," Duke admitted, "but it's not the worst."

The ninja turned his back to the Nova Texan and walked to the bars that separated the duo from freedom. He gripped them and examined them intently. He rattled them. And then some more. The usually stoic martial artist allowed an inkling of frustration to creep through; his shaking grew more violent.

"Hey, Ish. Calm down. We'll figure it out. That interrogator guy didn't seem too bad, ya' know."

Ishiro'shea's eyes shot lasers at Duke. At that moment, Duke would have preferred actual lasers.

"Fine, the hook hand wasn't super inviting. But we've had it worse. Remember—"

Duke was cut off by loud shouting from another room. The muddled grumbling of the Chief Interrogator General was apparent—but the other voice was distinctly female.

Mazilda?

"Are you going to tell me that just because two morons are dropped onto a table by some obviously unhinged portal, you have to tear their eyes out and burn them alive?" Mazilda said.

"Miss Cloax," began the interrogator, "I assure you that I won't be tearing anyone's eyes out. Not today."

"Or burning alive?"

"Well, I do like that part. But, sadly, no. It's not on the schedule."

"That's better, I guess," Mazilda's tone became slightly more relaxed.

"For their crime against the Shaman, I'm going to slice off their feet," the Psitakki added.

Even though Duke couldn't see him, he had a feeling that the interrogator flashed a creepy smile at the thought of them writhing in footless agony. Shivers racked Duke's body.

"You've got to be kidding, Interrogator," Mazilda said, her voice back to a scream. "These two buffoons aren't to be blamed. If anyone, it's whomever is operating the portal. They sabotaged the Shaman's gathering. Not these two."

"Do you consider a gun without any ammunition a weapon?" asked the interrogator calmly.

"What? What are you talking about?"

"Do you, Miss Cloax?"

"Yeah, sure. I guess."

"And the ammunition?"

"Yeah, of course. The ammunition is what does the damage to the target."

"And it only works with a gun."

"Uh, yep. That's the usual arrangement."

"So, both are guilty of causing the damage?"

"I guess. What does this have to do with anything?"

Mazilda was clearly angered at the interrogator's byzantine questioning; her voice doubled in volume. "What are you talking about?"

Duke and Ishiro'shea could hear footsteps as the interrogator and Mazilda approached the cell. The thick-bodied Psitakki stepped from around the corner, followed by Mazilda, her pewter robes flowing behind her. The interrogator pointed at the bounty hunters with his hooked appendage.

"Miss Cloax," he bellowed, "these two are the ammo. The portal is the gun—or rather, the portal operator. And we know who that is. Both are to blame—but, unfortunately, at the moment I can only interrogate these two. And I don't think I would try and interrogate the Queen of Cyborg Joe's."

"You know, Mazilda," Duke began calmly, "this one here has more layers than I gave him credit for. You aren't as dumb as you look, are you, Chief?"

The Chief Interrogator General didn't pay any attention to Duke's remark. He produced a rectangular metal box seemingly from out of nowhere and placed it on a knee-high table in the corner of the room. Under the table were an old Sonic Widowmaker shotgun, a laser revolver, and a katana. The latches of the box opened with a dull clank and the top of the box swung back to reveal a plethora of metallic instruments. Duke had a good idea as to the purpose of these instruments. He did not like it.

He also didn't like the expression on Mazilda's face, a ferocious glare aimed directly at him. She could be quite scary. This was one of those moments.

The majority of the time, Duke just thought of Mazilda as cunning. Really, really cunning. The most painful part was that she was a whole lot better at bounty hunting than he was. She was also extremely beautiful.

Even now, with a look of pure disgust upon her face. Duke always thought of her attractiveness as singular and distinct—in a universe filled with infinite complexities, she was unique. Her skin had a yellowy tint; a healthy sort of jaundice that gave her a splendid luminosity. Typically, one could only achieve this unique tan with increased levels of bilirubin in one's extracellular fluid, or a really painful tattoo—but Mazilda Cloax had no time for liver disease or body art. All of her visible hair—which sprouted in the same places as an Earth or Nova Texan woman— was a deep blue violet. She possessed penetrating pupils and full lips that perfectly matched the radiant color of her locks, painted by the same biological paintbrush. Her build was athletic yet voluptuous. She always knocked Duke's socks off—when she wasn't knocking other people's heads off.

"You're going to make jokes now? I'm here trying to plead your case and you think it's a good time to be funny? I knew you were an idiot—"

"I believe you called them 'morons,' Miss Cloax," chimed in the interrogator as he sharpened a nasty-looking utensil that sported four razor-sharp prongs.

"Shut up!" she screamed back at the Psitakki.

He paid the retort no attention and went back to preparing his equipment.

Mazilda approached the cell. Duke wasn't sure what material the bars were fashioned out of, but the visible pulse marks led him to believe that his laser revolver wouldn't have done much damage even if he still had it. Ol' Betsy would, no doubt, have turned the bars into a smoldering pile of ash, but, at the moment, she wasn't in her leathery home across Duke's back. Mazilda glanced at the bars. She seemed impressed at their construction.

"Nice to see you, Ishiro," she said in a voice barely

above a whisper. "I'm working on getting you both out of here."

"And how's that going?" quipped Duke.

Mazilda's gaze did not leave Ishiro'shea. "I'm not talking to you. I'm talking to Ishiro."

"And you know how much of a conversationalist he is. Why are you helping us, Mazilda? I mean, it's been a long time since we..." Duke searched for the proper terminology.

"Were friends?" Mazilda said, finishing his thought. "Since we were friends."

"Sure, since we were friends. Why are you helping us?"

"You know, Duke, most people would be content having someone trying to free them from a round of torture with that psycho." She pointed at the interrogator.

"Thanks," the Psitakki added, genuinely appreciative of Mazilda's acknowledgement.

"But I'm not 'most people.' That's why I—" Duke paused again. "—intrigued you so much. That was our thing, Mazilda. There was no one like you, no one like me. It worked."

"Did it? If I recall, it did lots of things... Working wasn't one of them."

"So, why are you helping us then? If I was such a pain in your ass."

Mazilda went silent for a second. She glanced at Ishiro'shea, then back at Duke. She looked back at the interrogator. He was polishing a blunt pipe covered in tiny metallic teeth. It looked painful. She refocused her attention on Duke.

A voice broke the silence. "There you are! That Jungafallowian goon told me that you were in here. I thought he was joking; I'm glad that I am such a thorough investigator."

"Hey Maxx," said Mazilda with a half-smile.

"Hello, my fair love," Maxx replied in his naturally booming voice.

Maxx sported his trademark polished yellow helmet with its color-changing fins and placed it in the crook of his arm. Duke thought the helmet made him look like a radioactive dolphin.

"And hello, friends. It is an honor to be here tonight. I know that you must be saying—what in the cosmos is Maxx Gemstarr doing here in a prison?"

Is this guy for real?

"Nope. No one's saying that," said Duke.

Maxx ignored the bounty hunter and turned his attention to the Chief Interrogator General.

"My good man, I'm honored to be here in your quaint prison. As a public servant, I am sure that you are well aware of the Shaman's upcoming Tournament of the Shield of the Crispy Calamari."

"*Colossal* Calamari," Mazilda whispered to Maxx, but his self-centered theatrical trance rendered him oblivious to Mazilda's attempt at correcting his faux pas.

"I, Maxx Gemstarr, the universe's most beloved crime fighter and bounty hunter, a man that has saved countless lives, civilizations, and planets, has embarked on yet another grave and perilous challenge. One that, you know, I will meet head on and overcome in the name of all that is good and right in the universe."

Maxx's pectorals were puffed out so far that Duke expected his internal organs to burst through his chest cavity.

"Let me guess, you're in the tournament," the interrogator said blandly. "Good luck with that. Try not to die."

"Ha, my good man! Maxx Gemstarr needs no luck. For I have honor on my side. And a good woman."

He squeezed Mazilda. She smiled.

I think I'm going to be sick, thought Duke.

The Chief Interrogator General rolled his eyes.

At least the guy that's going to gut me with extremely sharp tools also thinks Maxx is a fool. There's that.

Maxx turned his attention to his girlfriend. "My sweet love, why are you here talking to these criminals?"

Duke sneered. "We asked her the same thing. I guess she needed a real man again."

Gemstarr's face turned an intense shade of red. His muscles—which were plentiful and covered the entirety of his body—flexed and almost tore his baby-blue spandex jumpsuit. He snarled and took a step towards the cell.

Mazilda grabbed him by the arm and spun him around. She pulled his face down to hers and planted an aggressive yet sensual kiss on his lips.

"I have a real man, Duke," she said when she re-emerged. "Maybe I was wrong to try and help out an old friend."

"I still can't believe that you used to date this guy," Gemstarr said. His face had returned to its amber hue.

"We all make mistakes."

"You're lucky that I am so forgiving. Duke LaGrange is a pretty big blunder to look past," said Maxx.

He slapped Mazilda on the backside. She leapt up in the air a few inches.

Duke clenched his teeth. He felt like he was going to be sick.

The interrogator butted in. "It's time for a few questions," he said with a smile. In his good hand he held a cartoonishly oversized needle. Duke recognized the pink slime oozing from its tip as an immobility solution. One prick and they would wake up strapped into the interrogator's favorite chair.

"Let's go, Mazilda," said Maxx. "I need to rest before the tournament. I fight in two days, remember?"

"Yes, I remember," Mazilda said. She turned her attention back to Duke. "Why do you have to be such an ass?"

Duke knew that she wasn't picking a fight—she was truly curious. Maybe she was right. Maybe this was the one step too far that would send Ishiro'shea and him over the cliff and into the torture chair of a sadistic squid man with a hook hand. Events were certainly trending in that direction.

"Wait a second," he screamed as the interrogator reached the cell. Mazilda and Maxx paused and turned to face Duke. "In this tournament, Maxx, will I get to fight you?"

Maxx looked Duke up and down. He smiled.

How are his teeth that perfect?

"If you survive the melee tomorrow and earn a spot—which is highly unlikely knowing your..." Maxx coughed. "...skills, then yes, you could potentially meet me in the arena. However, the chances are—"

"I'm in."

"Duke," Mazilda began, "this tournament isn't—"

"I'm in. You hear that, you gross bastard? Put the needle away. I'm in."

The interrogator appeared genuinely sad. Upon his droopy face was an even droopier frown. Then he turned to Ishiro'shea and smiled.

"Nope," said Duke. "He's my trainer. He's free, too. You can go away now. Tell the Shaman guy that Duke LaGrange—adventurer, trailblazer, poet, true man of the universe—will take part in that melee fight tomorrow."

Mazilda stormed out. Maxx followed suit.

"Bye Maxxy," Duke called. "See you soon."

"Good luck, Mr. LaGrange," said the Chief Interrogator General, "I think that you will find that a day or two in my company would have proven to be a lot less painful than what you are about to endure."

He inserted a key into the lock, turned it, and the door opened.

"But don't expect me to say 'adventurer, trailblazer, and whatever' to the Shaman. That's below me. And I stick objects into folks for a living."

Duke and Ishiro'shea grabbed their weapons from under the table and left the jail.

"What does Mazilda see in Maxx, Ish?"

CHAPTER EIGHT

THE PONDSCUM TAVERN

T HE PONDSCUM TAVERN WASN'T CYBORG Joe's and Duke wasn't sure if that was a compliment or not. It was what one might call "traditional" in its styling.

"So this is the only bar on Psitakki?" Duke asked the young Psitakki bartender.

"Yes sir. It's a sacred place."

"Most bars are, my young friend, most bars are," replied the bounty hunter philosophically.

"No, sir, it's *actually* a sacred place."

It just seems like an old dingy cavern with a sunroof, thought Duke. *Not exactly awe-inspiring.*

"And what, pray tell, makes it so sacred? If you don't mind me asking, that is," he queried.

"Not at all. The legend is that the Pondscum Tavern was built in the very place that Grozzel found the magic shields—the very ones that repelled the shadow demons and saved Psitakki. Are you familiar with that story?"

"Increasingly so."

"This is the very place where that seminal moment in our history occurred."

"And you built a bar over it?"

The Psitakki froze, his eyes unblinking. It was clear that he did not know how to respond to his patron's inquisition.

Duke sipped his drink and smiled. "Maybe Psitakki is my kinda place after all."

He downed the rest of the liquid and asked for another.

The Psitakki barkeep, seemingly oblivious to the most recent exchange, launched back into his train of thought. "Over the course of a millennia, bars would come and go, except for this one. After a while, we just gave up trying and the Pondscum Tavern became the only bar. It didn't seem right to have other bars take away potential patrons from this holiest of holy places."

"Well, it's a lively little dive, that's for sure," commented Duke.

The bartender nodded and handed Duke and Ishiro'shea another drink.

"It's not typically this crowded, but it's been ten thousand cycles since the last Tournament of the Shield of the Colossal Calamari—so folks are making sure they pregame appropriately. And I think the locals are hoping to see a fighter or two before they... you know?"

"Before they what?" asked Duke cautiously.

"Before they fight."

"Ah yes, before they fight." Duke exhaled.

"And, most likely, die," the bartender added.

"Wait a second, I thought that fighters died only on the rarest of occasions."

"Yes, but our Shaman is a bit—well, a bit of a sadistic blood-hungry maniac."

"Great," Duke replied. "Just great."

"Just be glad you aren't fighting in it, sir."

Duke nodded and tossed the bartender a tip.

"I think we're going to go grab a seat over there. Thanks for the history lesson, kid. Maybe I can score an autograph from one of the combatants tonight."

"Good luck, sir. If they're in the melee..."

"Yes?" Duke eagerly asked.

"You better hurry up. It's likely your last chance."

"Dumb kid," said Duke under his breath.

He and Ishiro'shea sat at a long wooden table against the back wall of the bar. The Pondscum Tavern was buzzing; combatants, locals, and media personalities from all over the sector were mulling about, imbibing alcohol, conducting interviews, and generally having a pretty okay time.

Duke was drinking, but he definitely wasn't having a good time. His entry in the tournament had been made official, much to the chagrin of the Shaman and Maxx Gemstarr; now he just needed to find out what in the cosmos this melee match was all about.

"We meet again, Duke LaGrange and Ishiro'shea," said Prince Korzo-Tapor quite formally.

"You know, Prince, you tried to kill us not too long ago. I'm not sure I'm over that," Duke replied, drawing his laser revolver and spinning it around his finger. "I'm not really looking to become best buds and strike up a lively conversation with you. Bygones aren't quite bygones yet."

The prince did not flinch. "Fair point. In fact, when I left you, I thought you *were* dead. The ship was wrecked."

"Duke LaGrange always has a few tricks up his sleeve," the Nova Texan proclaimed.

He didn't look back, but he knew Ishiro'shea was either rolling his eyes or shaking his head.

"That was the case then. However, Duke, this is now. And I hear that you've entered the tournament. How exciting. I for one am interested to see how you fare in this unique event."

"Yeah, thanks again for that bit of information. It actually was quite helpful." *Why am I thanking this guy?* Duke asked himself.

"I guess we're even now?"

"You tried to blow me up! We aren't even. Not even close."

"Fair point again," replied the prince. Up to this point, only one of the heads had been talking. The other head had been constantly surveying the room, either trying to find someone or make sure someone didn't find him. "Now I must say, I do wish you the best but if you do happen to fight my entrant, you will meet a quick yet painful defeat."

"Oh yes, I forgot about your mysterious, invisible 'sure thing.' Where is he? Or she?"

"He is preparing for the battle in two days. We aren't sure of his first opponent, but we were told it won't be the sixteenth participant."

"The melee winner?"

"Yes."

"He's just going to have to wait for me to kick his ass."

"The melee winner has never won the tournament before—not in the previous ninety-nine attempts. Not good odds, I'm afraid, Duke."

"I'm not one for odds. I just hope it's paired with Gemstarr. I owe that punk a few."

"Yes, he is quite—" the talkative head began, but it was the other that finished the thought, "—annoying. Full of himself. Impossible. Awful."

"I like this head much better," smirked Duke.

"Yes, Gemstarr is not our particular cup of tea," the alpha-head began again. "But he has one thing going for him."

"And what's that?"

"He doesn't have to fight in the melee tomorrow. And you do."

"So what's this melee all about?"

The prince cleared his throats. Once again, it was the more formal head that addressed the bounty hunter's question.

Why did both of them have to clear their throats?

"The night before the tournament begins, the sixteenth entrant is determined by a battle royale in the arena. The same rules apply, but instead of one-on-one, it's every man for himself. You could be in the process of knocking someone out and then get a club to the back of the head. It's less about skill and more about survival."

"Like a barroom brawl?"

"On an epic scale, yes."

"So like a barroom brawl at Cyborg Joe's," Duke added.

"I've heard that there are thirty fighters registered for it —that's the most ever. It's just not the sort of thing that someone volunteers for. Mortal combat has its romantic element, no doubt, but this is so—primitive."

"And no one who's qualified via the melee has ever won the entire tournament?"

"I'm not sure if anyone has ever made it past the opening round. It does take quite a toll."

The bounty hunter was quiet, deep in thought. Beside him Ishiro'shea continued drinking his Psitakki booze.

"And Prince, do you know anyone else in the melee tomorrow?"

"Let me think," the prince said rubbing both of his

chins. "I know a few Psitakki toughs joined up. They have a champion in the main tournament—apparently a descendant of Grozzel the Great—but these other guys are just some local loudmouths, likely out to impress a mate."

"Idiots," Duke murmured. Ishiro kicked him under the table. He turned to his masked sidekick.

"What? You think I joined up to impress—" Duke didn't finish his sentence. "I saved us from getting prodded by the old kook with a trunk of very sharp toys. That's it. Drop it."

The ninja turned away and finished off his drink, then rose to his feet and headed back to the bar.

"I'm surprised that your companion didn't enter his name. I hear that he's quite the master. His attack on our great Sprinkles has been frequently referenced throughout the Jungafallowian system."

"He probably would fight in my place had I asked him. Probably has a better shot at winning, too."

"Then why don't you?"

"I caused this mess. I cause most of our messes. Don't tell him I said that. It just wouldn't be fair. I don't know, call me honorable."

"Not a word that I have typically heard associated with your name."

Duke grinned, tipped his hat at the prince, and walked over to join his companion at the bar.

———

"Are you friends with that Jungafallowian?"

The Psitakki asking the question was muscular and had a youthful exuberance to him.

"That guy?"

432

"Yes, the one that you were talking with at the table. And the other night at the gala. Are you friends?"

"Kid," Duke sneered, "that guy tried to blow us up a month ago. No, we aren't friends. In fact, there are few things that I hate more than Jungafallowians."

The Psitakki glared intensely at the bounty hunter. *Some sort of Psitakki lie detector test,* thought Duke. The Psitakki did not break his eye contact.

"I believe you," he said, relaxing and shifting his eyes off of the bounty hunter.

"Thanks?" replied a confused Duke.

"My name is Gjrazzel. I'm a descendent of Grozzel."

"Who?"

"Grozzel. The one that made this tournament possible. It's first champion. Our species' savior."

"Right. Grozzel. Of course. He's the reason why we're here, good ol' Grozzel."

The Psitakki male seemed perplexed.

"Would you like a drink?" asked the bounty hunter charitably. "My treat. And you can tell me why you care if I'm buds with the prince."

"I will pass on the offer of a drink, stranger. I am actually a participant in the tournament—the grand champion of Psitakki—and my training does not allow me to consume alcohol."

"You don't say? I'm in the tournament as well."

Now the Psitakki looked totally perplexed. "*You* are in the tournament? I know all of the contestants; I've seen many of them fight. Except for one."

"You haven't seen me fight."

"Are you the Jungafallowian's secret entrant?"

Duke took a deep gulp of his strange beer. He could sense that Ishiro'shea was giggling inside. "No, I'm in this melee tomorrow."

"I see," Gjrazzel said after a slight hesitation. "Good luck."

"Thanks."

"Should you prevail, stranger, it appears that I will be your first opponent."

"You don't say. Well, cheers to that!"

Duke hoisted his drink in the air. Gjrazzel's expression remained unchanged. Never one to leave a toast unclinked, Ishiro'shea stealthily sneaked to their side and pounded his mug against Duke's.

"Thanks, little buddy. Meet Gjrazzel. I'm going to fight him, apparently."

Ishiro'shea bowed.

"Pleasure to meet you," said Gjrazzel.

"Don't worry, kid. Ish here doesn't talk. He's not being rude."

"I see."

"So what's your beef with the prince? Not a fan of the Trampling Death Robots? Ish almost single-handedly ended their music careers, ya' know."

"I'm not familiar with the Trampling Death Robots but I am familiar with the prince. At least, I'm familiar with what he represents."

"Bad musical preferences?"

"Have you seen his arm?" asked Gjrazzel. "Right below his elbow?"

"No, I hadn't looked."

"He has a tattoo."

"So do a bazillion other folks. Probably half the people here at this bar sport some sort of ink."

"The tattoo is that of a fish."

Duke paused and placed his drink on the bar. Ishiro'shea did the same.

"Let me guess," began the bounty hunter, "a fish with a mustache."

"Yes. You are familiar with what that insignia means, then?"

"Unfortunately, yes. Admiral Lothario LePaco."

"I'm afraid that Prince Korzo-Tapor has something planned on behalf of the admiral. I don't know what or why, but I have a hunch that his mysterious combatant might have some role in this."

"How did an unknown fighter get an invite?"

"The Jungafallowians are known for their fighting prowess. Their government was awarded the right to send their system's champion—this was their selection."

"No name?"

"He's listed as 'Combatant 2.' No one has seen him."

"You know, Gjrazzel, I think I'm on your side on this one. Something isn't right. But I'm sorry, I don't have any insight."

The Psitakki looked dejected. "Thanks for your time, and I hope to meet you in the arena."

"Sure thing, kid."

"Good luck tomorrow."

"Cheers to my luck."

CHAPTER NINE

BLOPS, DURPHS, AND SABROMMS, OH MY!

THE VENUE ITSELF WAS NOTHING more than an underground cavern with a circular pit within which the combatants could wage martial war. The seating consisted of simple benches carved from the cave wall, but from the arena floor it was impossible to see where the seating stopped. Duke assumed there were at least two hundred rows encircling the pit. Maybe more. Even from the holding cell under the floor, the bounty hunter could hear and feel the rumble of the crowd that had gathered to view the spectacle of the melee fight.

When he stepped out, the roar generated a sound wave that almost knocked him over. Upon the announcement of "Duke LaGrange, human from Nova Texas," from the loud-speaker, he tipped his hat to the crowd. He quickly realized that all of the contestants received similar greetings. This bruised his ego slightly.

As he waited for the other participants to be introduced, he surveyed the landscape. In the middle of the circular pit was a mound of assorted weapons—mostly clubs and other bludgeoning instruments. Each contestant emerged from a tunnel at the perimeter of the pit, all equidistant from the pile of weapons. Since Duke didn't own a tournament-approved weapon, he grabbed a standard-issue spear from a tournament official. It was sturdy enough to do some damage, but its metallic makeup made it far too heavy to be a potent projectile.

I thought I was done with spears in Neprius, Duke thought to himself.

As he looked around, he noticed that many of the combatants were Psitakki—the "local toughs" that Prince Korzo-Tapor warned him about. He also noticed a particularly menacing-looking Jungafallowian opposite him. The sight of the two-headed reptilian behemoth instantly reminded Duke of a really bad day he had had at Cyborg Joe's recently. In addition to the Jungafallowian, Duke also made note of two Sabromms. If he avoided their massive skulls that they slung around violently on elasticized necks like powerful hammer whips, he felt confident that they wouldn't knock him out of the competition.

There was also a Durph. Duke hadn't dealt with Durphs too frequently, but he knew they had a reputation for being really ill-tempered. This particular Durph stood as tall as Duke, which was impressive for a quadruped. Its four red eyes were barely visible in a sea of thick matted fur that covered every part of its body. Though it was powerful —probably the strongest in the arena—it wasn't likely to sneak up on anyone; and Duke knew a club to the face could render its power moot.

The bounty hunter was shocked to see a warrior from Hausen-Ra. Their race lived in a remote system protected by an asteroid belt; their space travel was rudimentary and their piloting skills novice, so they rarely left. The Hausen-Ra were enigmatic from an evolutionary standpoint; they appeared like basic humanoids, but with no skin, no eyes, and no hair.

Except for the fact that they could walk, talk, and fight, they could have been sold to any middle school science class learning human anatomy. In one of the universe's many quirks, the organs and overall life-supporting functions of the Hausen-Ra developed *inside* their skeletal frames. Despite their inside-out evolution, they were renowned fighters as they had no soft spots to attack—but a broken bone could be fatal.

The rest of the field was made up of some species not particularly known for their combat prowess, like the bird-like Dysortimom, and the sickle-armed Sicythian, and some species that Duke had never seen before.

He wasn't particularly concerned with any of them—however, he was intrigued by the smallest combatant. The top of his head wouldn't have reached Duke's waist and his hunched posture was so pronounced that he required a cane to stand upright. The diminutive being was almost formless, as if a naked mole rat infant had mated with a glob of used chewing gum. He was announced as Blop, a Blop from Blop.

He didn't have a very inspired mom, thought Duke.

As the introductions concluded, five Psitakki entered through a tunnel and surrounded the pile of weapons in the center of the arena. They each wore full bodysuits that glowed bright red. Duke surmised that these were the referees, the beings that would make the ultimate call about whether the participant could continue or if he was eliminated. They all faced the combatants, standing like statues with their backs to the mound of armaments.

The voice over the loudspeaker echoed throughout the arena. "Combatants, ready. Those in attendance, ready. Referees, ready. You've been waiting ten thousand cycles—well, *you* specifically haven't been waiting that long. Unless you're ten thousand cycles old—and if you are—kudos to you, because that's pretty sweet. I've never met anyone that's ten thousand—"

The voice suddenly stopped. A moment passed. The crowd seemed confused. Duke looked up and saw Ishiro'shea in the first row. They exchanged thumbs-up.

"Fight!" screamed a new voice over the PA system.

The crowd erupted, as did Duke's sweat glands.

The bounty hunter hung back along the perimeter wall, hoping to prevent sneak attacks. Some of these entrants were so amped up that he hoped they would take each other out and leave him with a clearer path to victory. For the most part, that was the case. The Psitakki attacked each other. They attacked the Dysortimom and Sicythian. The more ambitious locals tried to take out the Jungafallowian and the Durph, but proved little more than an annoyance. Many were racing to the pile of weapons to see if they could upgrade their own gear. It proved to be an unsuccessful strategy—typically, they were struck down from behind as they dug for better arms. The two Sabromms were fighting each other. Each cranium smash was louder than the previous one. Within a few moments, the referees had already carted out a handful of combatants. Duke looked over and saw that Blop, the Blop from Blop, was standing alone by himself.

I guess they don't consider him much of a threat. Duke felt a bit sorry for him.

An ax struck just to the right of Duke's head, taking out a piece of the wall behind him. It was one of the local Psitakki fighters. He reared back again but Duke struck his face with the shaft of his spear. The Psitakki staggered back but regained his composure and charged again. Duke sidestepped and swept the Psitakki's legs out from under him with the spear. As the Psitakki's body hit the arena floor, the ax flew from his hand and landed out of his reach. The Psitakki slowly sat up. His eyes narrowed.

"Come on, squid face," shouted Duke.

The Psitakki snarled.

The rock came from a few rows into the audience, and landed squarely on the head of the Psitakki.

He was out cold. Duke looked up and the crowd cheered.

The referee ran over and signaled that the Psitakki was eliminated.

"Hey," Duke said, grabbing the referee's arm, "the fans can throw stuff?"

"Yes, the Shaman encourages crowd participation. Especially when fighters aren't entertaining them."

"Great."

Then Duke noticed the Blop, who was still standing motionless. The fans near to him were starting to grow restless.

Out of the corner of his eye, Duke saw that the Jungafallowian, the Durph, and the Hausen-Ra combatants were each disposing of lesser fighters. The Hausen-Ra warrior engaged with the Jungafallowian and had the upper hand. The Jungafallowian was bigger and stronger but the skeletal soldier's trident kept the two-headed behemoth at bay. However, the Hausen-Ra likely didn't count on the Jungafallowian's alliance with the beastly Durph. The monster leapt and landed on the skeleton's back. If he had skin and squishy parts, there would have been a splat. Instead, there was the sound of cracking bones. The referee checked and there was no response. The Hausen-Ra was out.

Duke did not want to think about the two nastiest combatants joining forces to set up a mutually agreed one-on-one battle. He didn't like his odds of surviving that situation. But before his worry transitioned to unmitigated despair, he noticed that a group of Psitakki were surrounding poor Blop. Duke hustled over and stood next to the mushy alien.

"What are you doing?" said Blop in a plodding and melancholy voice.

"I know this is an 'every thing for himself' ordeal," Duke replied, "but five-on-one hardly seems fair."

Blop did not immediately respond. He appeared deep in thought, even as the Psitakki prepared to charge. "That is very kind of you, human."

"You can thank me later. Let's fight off these meatheads."

"Agreed."

"What's your skill? What do you do?" asked Duke frantically.

"What do you mean?" answered Blop, seemingly in no hurry.

"Can you punch? Kick? Breathe fire?"

"You are funny, my new friend."

"Okay. Get ready to do whatever it is that you do."

The Blop remained silent. He lifted his cane in front of Duke, signaling for him to stay put. He walked forward a few steps, now within striking distance of the bloodthirsty Psitakki. The Durph and Jungafallowian also approached a few paces behind the Psitakki. Duke wasn't sure if they were going to ambush the Psitakki or join in the beatdown that was likely to ensue. He was hoping for the former.

The Psitakki raised their weapons and charged.

This isn't going to be pretty.

Blop dropped his cane and extended his arms as if he was going to give the entire group a great big, affectionate hug.

The flames momentarily blinded Duke and knocked

him back against the arena wall. Through squinted eyes he saw a wall of fire emerge from where Blop was standing. It rose above the arena floor and crashed down like a wave of lava. Blop turned to Duke and smiled.

"Thank you for your help, human."

"*My* help? You're doing everything."

"My pleasure," said the Blop, still grinning.

"Why are you helping me?" asked the bounty hunter.

"Why were *you* helping *me*?"

Duke thought about it. "It seemed like the right thing to do," he said, unsure if that was the "right" response.

"*This* seems like the right thing to do," Blop replied.

"What do you mean?"

"I don't mean anything. Have fun, human. Good luck."

As the flames continued to set everything ablaze and the screams of the other combatants rang throughout the arena, Blop vanished in a puff of smoke. The fiery rain ceased and self-extinguished. The victims of Blop's attack were sprawled out, but all remnants of the fire were gone, as if nothing happened.

The referees ran over and counted the Durph, the Jungafallowian, and the Psitakki out. The crowd roared in approval. They had seen amazing martial theater this evening.

Despite the attack, Duke wasn't alone. On the far side of the arena and out of reach of Blop's spontaneous combustion, the Sabromms continued to fight each other, ignoring the goings-on that had consumed the rest of the arena floor.

They must really hate each other, thought Duke.

Duke slowly stepped over the unconscious bodies and made his way to the Sabromms. They didn't acknowledge his presence.

Their heads were cracked and caving in due to the

constant attacks on each other. They were formidable combatants.

Duke was only a few paces away when they both stopped their battle and looked at him, their chests heaving at an alarming pace.

Oh great. I have to fight both of 'em.

They pivoted to face the bounty hunter. Then both Sabromms crumpled to the floor.

Huh. Well, I'll be damned.

The referee sprinted over to Duke and raised his hand.

The loudspeaker voice shouted, "Your winner and final participant in the Tournament of the Shield of the Colossal Calamari—Duke LaGrange, human from Nova Texas."

Duke looked up and Ishiro'shea exchanged thumbs-ups. Just above the ninja sat Mazilda Cloax. She locked eyes with the Nova Texan, the corners of her mouth turned up. Duke blinked and she was gone.

CHAPTER TEN

LIGHT OF GOD

"I HOPE THIS PLACE IS still open," Duke said to Ishiro'shea as he opened the back door of the Pondscum Tavern.

Inside he could hear a lively round of congratulations. "I guess they don't really have many options, do they? One bar, remember."

The ninja nodded.

Roars and chants rang throughout the bar. Duke wanted to believe that they were chanting his name but the sheer number of voices and the varying tonalities, decibel levels, and accents made it sound more or less like the groans of a chipmunk giving birth to a full-grown panda. It goes without saying that it wasn't very melodious.

Duke tipped his hat and gave the customers a wave. They continued to chant as he sat down at the bar.

"The drinks are on the house, Mr. LaGrange," said the young bartender. "And, about earlier..."

"No worries. Why would you have thought that I was competing in the tournament? Not your fault."

"Regardless, drinks for you and your friend are on us. Enjoy."

"That's mighty kind, and I do believe that we'll take you up on that offer. Two of your best... whatever you got."

"Coming right up."

The Psitakki barkeep made his way to the far end of the bar, unlocked a small cabinet, and poured a clear liquid into two cylindrical tubes. The liquid was transparent but glowed brightly; Duke wasn't able to tell if it was the actual drink or the container that caused the effect.

"Sirs, here's our finest imported alcohol. It's from the neighboring planet, Psitakki Minor. They call it the Light of God."

"So, the Colossal Calamari?"

"Oh, no. The Minors don't believe in the Colossal Calamari. They have their own god. It's some wandering commoner that ascended into the night sky with a special magic that he found in a mountain or something. I think there's something about snakes or maybe it's lightning. Not sure. Some real off-the-wall stuff, if you ask me."

"Not as logical as a massive mollusk watching over all of us and tossing shields down to save his people," smirked Duke.

"Exactly."

The bounty hunter's sarcasm was totally lost on the bartender. Duke turned his attention to the glass and cautiously sipped the illuminated liquor.

Divine.

"Holy hedgehogs, kid! This is spectacular."

He gulped the remainder of his drink; Ishiro'shea followed suit.

"I'm glad you like it, Mr. LaGrange. Needless to say, it's truly an honor to serve someone that has actually won a match in the tournament. It's a dream that I never thought would be a reality. Thank you."

"I'll have another, please," Duke said, ignoring the Psitakki's praise.

"I'm sorry but I have to limit you both to a single glass."

"Wait, what? You're cutting us off after one drink?"

"I'm sorry, Mr. LaGrange. It's—"

"I just fought in a brawl with thirty other nutjobs and you're cutting me off after one glass?" Duke asked, with bite.

"I'm not cutting you off because I think you're intoxicated. It's just that it's really bad luck to drink more than one glass in a lifetime." The bartender slunk backwards in fear.

"One in a lifetime? So you're pretty confident that I'm not going to be around to partake in the drink after today, huh?"

"That's not what I meant," said the barkeep in a pleading tone.

"What did you mean? Please enlighten me."

The cowering Psitakki shrank even further, almost into a fetal position behind the bar. He said something inaudibly.

"What's that?"

The Psitakki once again whispered something that even a four-eared trondylpip would have difficulty deciphering.

"Come again?" The agitated bounty hunter's voice grew louder.

"I'm sorry, Mr. LaGrange. I was just trying to do something nice. I want you to have a seamless ascension to the Colossal Calamari in the Sky—and the Light of God, despite its heathen origins, is said to provide its drinkers a beacon to follow in the afterlife."

Duke sat back down on his barstool and looked at Ishiro'shea. The ninja was still sipping on his drink and appeared amused by the goings-on. Duke folded his arms and sighed. "This place," he huffed.

The bartender made his way back onto his feet but leaned against the back cabinets, maximizing his distance from the enraged Nova Texan.

"So, what you're telling me, kid, is that I'm as good as dead tomorrow. I just won this melee, I'm pretty much unscathed outside of a few singe marks from Blop's fireworks, yet you think this is my last night alive."

"It's just that," the Psitakki stuttered, "no one has ever—"

"I know, I know," said Duke, cutting him off, "no one who has won the melee match has ever won the tournament."

"No. No one has ever—"

Duke cut him off again. "I know, no one has ever won their first-round bout."

"No one has ever *survived* their first-round bout," the Psitakki corrected him, speaking more quickly so that Duke wouldn't cut him off a third time.

Duke stared at the bartender. "Is that right? Wonderful. I guess that just means that I'm gonna have to win the whole damn thing."

He placed his foot on the barstool and vaulted himself to the bar top itself.

"Attention, attention," Duke shouted. "It seems that no one in my esteemed position has ever won—has ever survived—their first round fight after winning the melee. In fact, this guy here gave me a free glass of magical potion that is supposed to ease my transition into the great beyond because he's so sure that I'm as good as dead. Well, people, quasi-people, media, and local tramps and degenerates here in attendance, Duke LaGrange—adventurer, trailblazer, poet, true man of the universe—doesn't plan on continuing that trend. In fact, I plan on not only not dying, I plan on winning the entire tournament."

Some of the crowd cheered but it was obvious to Duke that most sided with the bartender's prognostication. He felt he did have the support of the local drunkards.

"And if I win tomorrow night, everyone in this bar will drink entirely on the house!"

The Pondscum Tavern erupted in raucous admiration. The chant that Duke wanted to believe was his name filled every crevice of the cavern. He leapt to the floor and was immediately embraced by the patrons nearest to him. He felt hands and tentacles and talons pat him on the back. He looked back at the bartender, whose jaw hung open.

"You better hope that I lose tomorrow."

"But I didn't promise that—"

"Kid, I'll let *you* tell them that."

"But I can't, they'll—"

"That stuff wasn't that good anyway."

CHAPTER ELEVEN

POTATO LIPS

EVEN IN THE BACK CORNER of the Pondscum Tavern, Duke was being hounded by locals and journalists. He enjoyed the praise and attention—and the free alcohol—but it was getting a bit repetitive.

"How do you plan on beating Gjrazzel?" one reporter asked. She was a Dysortimom.

"That's *my* secret. But I'm not scared of a squid-face. Bring 'em on."

Duke knew that most journalists, regardless of species, just wanted digestible soundbites with a hint of controversy. It helped them sell whatever they were hawking and Duke could give them what they needed. And the tastiness of the soundbites only improved as the drinks continued to flow.

He turned to face another gaggle of media types. "This punk has no chance!"

He turned to another group. "The Shield is mine! Gjrazzel won't know what hit him!"

And again. "Better get that squid a shot of Light of God because he's got a date with the Colossal Calamari!"

And again. "Maxx Gemstarr is a pansy and has really poor hygiene!"

The reporters frantically wrote down, recorded, or telepathically communicated Duke's many quotations back to their respective publications and forums.

Duke felt confident that his rapid-fire commentary would give them what they needed, but they continued to try and extract even more nuggets from the bounty hunter.

Suddenly, the sea of reporters parted and then scattered.

"Go away, Mr. LaGrange is done for the evening." The voice was booming but had feminine undertones.

Emerging from the mass of reporters was a hulking frame of fur topped by a set of boney horns that covered the skull like a cap and curved out just in front of the ears. She resembled the Gartoshian musk ox that Duke and Ishiro'shea had met a month back at Cyborg Joe's Grill N' Go & The Why Not Saloon, but she was even broader in stature and her fur was a sandier shade of brown.

The Gartoshian about-faced and snorted at the few reporters that had ignored her demand. They scattered immediately. She sat down at the table.

"Mr. LaGrange. Nice to meet you. Your speech earlier was interesting."

Duke tipped his cap and Ishiro'shea bowed.

"Thanks, and a real big thanks for pushing out those reporters. I know I probably deserved it for giving them some red meat to sink their teeth into, but it was getting annoying. Can we buy you a drink?"

"Thank you for the offer," the musk ox snorted, "but, like you, I have a match tomorrow. Unlike you, I'm choosing to stay away from the drink until I have finished the competition."

"No way! Well good luck to you. You know, I'm not

surprised. We know a Gartoshian and we've seen her duke it out. She almost killed two Jungafallowians without even breaking a sweat. If you're half as tough as Lilly, you'll be a tough in this odd little dance, that's for sure."

"Lilly, you say? Lilly Arnaq of Moon Colony #3?"

Duke looked at Ishiro'shea for an answer. The ninja returned a blank stare and then shrugged his shoulders.

"Maybe," Duke replied. "She looks like you—maybe a bit darker—and can throw down like nobody's business. We met her at Cyborg Joe's on Kelt."

"Ah yes," the Gartoshian began, "that's Lilly. She's a great fighter. She was my toughest opponent back home on Gartosh."

"You fought her?"

"I have."

"And?"

"We only fought once, when she was just getting back into the game. I think that was the only reason that I prevailed. She demonstrated true grit. But, alas, with my victory, I became the Gartoshian champion and received an invite to this tournament. You see, we are known to excel at the combat arts and the annual winner of the Miss Bovine Boxing contest is held in high esteem throughout our system."

"You beat Lilly to win Miss Bovine Boxer of Gartosh? That's impressive," Duke said. "You have to be the odds-on favorite to win this whole shebang. I'm sorry, I didn't get your name."

"Yvonne. Yvonne Angerdlarnek. I'm from Gartosh Moon Colony #1. And no, Mr. LaGrange, I'm not considered a favorite to win this tournament. The other fighters here are much more accomplished. It's a pretty remarkable field."

"Oh."

"Do you know anything about the other fighters, Mr. LaGrange?"

She knows the answer to that.

"Please call me Duke. And no, not really. I mean, I know *you* now. And I know I'm fighting Gjrazzel. I met him yesterday and he seemed like an alright guy. Not too worried. And I know that there's some mystery fighter from Jungafallow III."

"Yes, we are all curious as to what the Jungafallowians are doing. They are not my favorite race."

"Join the club. Oh, and speaking of the universe's worst slime, I know Maxx Gemstarr."

"He's quite handsome though," said Yvonne.

"If you like pompous, arrogant, no-talent hacks. Anyways, this isn't a beauty contest."

"I've heard he's quite a skilled warrior too," added the musk ox.

"Not even in the top twenty toughest bounty hunters, if you ask me," Duke answered.

From the corner of his eyes, Duke noticed Ishiro'shea trying to convey to Yvonne that Maxx might not be as worthless as his compatriot was making him out to be. It was clear that she was having trouble understanding the ninja's non-verbal communication.

"What? You think he's a tough guy? So *you* like Gemstarr too. First Mazilda and now my best friend," Duke said gruffly. "Maxx is really pushing the limits of my hatred."

Ishiro'shea simply rolled his eyes and went back to his beer.

"There are others in the tournament besides the contestants that you mentioned," said Yvonne, redirecting the conversation.

"I guess some advanced scouting can't hurt, right?" said

Duke, while still sneering at Ishiro'shea.

"Most people are concerned about the Jungafallowian entry because it's an unknown. No records. No name. Just listed as Combatant 2."

"So I've heard. His handler tried to blow us up once. I would expect the worst."

"And the Psitakki champion that you mentioned is a skilled fighter. He will have a decided home field advantage; not only is he a Psitakki but he's the descendent of Grozzel himself. It's going to be loud."

"Anything that I should be aware of?"

"He will try and finish you off with a Psitakki staff made from a tarzantia tree. I've seen him practice; he strikes quickly and effectively."

"Great."

"The field is quite diverse. There is a Hiritai warrior. She is considered a favorite by many."

"I'm intimately familiar with Hiritai. And I mean intimately. Know what I mean?"

"I think I do," replied Yvonne.

"Aggressive in every way that you can imagine," added Duke.

"Right," Yvonne replied, "and a Gurlfian Goother Rat."

"A Goother? Those critters are insane."

"And tenacious fighters," Yvonne added. "Their size is their greatest strength because most underestimate them because of it."

"I've seen one tear up a Zylantian pirate in a bar once. It was pretty ugly."

"There's a Zylantian here as well."

"They let one of those four-armed sleazebuckets in this thing?"

"Have you ever been to Planet F?" asked Yvonne.

"No but I'm aware of it. A bunch of flying bugs, right?"

"Yes. One of the Queen's Royal Guard has been entered in and, well, he can fly. That's makes him a tricky opponent."

"Great."

Yvonne looked as if she was about to launch into more detailed biographies of each combatant when the trio was interrupted. The visitor slid into her seat without a sound and removed her hood. Duke saw deep blue-violet hair and matching eyes.

"I'm sorry to interrupt," said Mazilda, bowing slightly to Yvonne. She extended a hand. "It's a pleasure to meet you, Yvonne. I've heard many tales of your pugilistic prowess and renowned fighting spirit."

Yvonne countered with a bow of her own and gripped Mazilda's hand. Duke noticed that Mazilda was trying to hide a wince. *That musk ox is strong.*

"I see why they call you the Furry Mountain of Moon Colony #1," complimented Mazilda.

"Cool nickname," added Duke. "Do I get one for this tournament?"

"You are officially registered as Duke LaGrange—" began Mazilda.

"Adventurer. Trailblazer. Poet."

Mazilda cut him off. "No. You're officially registered as Duke LaGrange—a bounty hunter."

"Are you serious?" Duke sighed dejectedly.

Mazilda turned her attention back to the anthropomorphic musk ox from Gartosh.

"Good luck tomorrow with Reginald. I hear he's a bit of a scrapper."

"Thank you..." the musk ox paused.

"Mazilda. Mazilda Cloax. I'm an old friend of these two."

"And a *friend* of Maxx Gemstarr," Duke announced with disgust.

Mazilda scrunched her face and glared at Duke.

"It seems that you have some catching up to do," began Yvonne. "It was nice to meet you, Duke LaGrange. And your friend. I will tell Lilly that I ran into you if I see her again."

"We'll do the same," replied Duke. "And thanks for the insight about the other fighters. Much appreciated."

"See you tomorrow at the Grand Entrance. And, Mazilda, it was nice meeting you. You must be quite the woman to catch the eye of Maxx Gemstarr."

Duke mimed being sick.

Yvonne "The Furry Mountain of Moon Colony #1" Angerdlarnek stood up and exited the Pondscum Tavern. The reporters that had hounded Duke earlier avoided the musk ox as she made her way out. Duke chuckled at the dread and fear on their faces.

"I saw you tonight," Duke said with a smirk.

"So?"

"Just saying."

"I wanted to make sure you didn't get yourself killed. I had two daggers at the ready just in case one of those Psitakki bastards got a bit too aggressive."

"That's sweet," Duke said, batting his eyelashes. "You still care about me."

"I don't know why that's such a shock to you. Yes, we were awful together. But I still care about you. And Ishiro'shea."

Ishiro'shea was on his twelfth or thirteenth beer. He acknowledged Mazilda with a groggy thumbs-up.

"I haven't seen you in a long time," said Duke.

"I know. I've been busy. You've been busy. In fact,

where *have* you been? My sources said something about you getting eaten by one of Joe's portals."

"Something like that. I'll fill you in later. It's a long, long story."

"Let me guess, it includes some blue-skinned, big-breasted beauties—"

"Hey, don't go making fun of my choices in that arena. Do I need to remind you that you're here with Maxx Gemstarr? The galaxy's biggest ass. What do you see in that guy?"

"I will fill *you* in later on that."

"No thank you. The less I have to hear about Gemstarr, the better. I'm just surprised. I know we were a disaster but I thought I knew you better than that. I guess I don't."

"We weren't always a disaster," Mazilda said with a smile. "Some parts were great."

Duke pondered that thought for a moment. He wasn't sure if Mazilda was flirting, but he didn't want to chance it and get one of her daggers in his eye.

"Some were great. Key word being 'were,' unfortunately," replied Duke. "So why are you here *now*? What's so important?"

"Potato Lips."

Duke lifted his glass in the air and examined the liquid. Confusion consumed his expression.

"How much have I had? I could have sworn you said 'potato lips.'"

"You never were a good listener," Mazilda jabbed. "Yes, Seamus 'Potato Lips' O'Hoolihan. Ring a bell?"

"Nope. Should it?"

"He's from Earth."

"So are twenty billion other life forms."

"He's from New Tokyo. Ireland."

Duke slapped Ishiro'shea on the back of the head. The ninja sprang up and drew his katana.

"Simmer down, Ish. Mazilda has something that we need to hear."

Ishiro'shea returned to his seat sluggishly and stared cross-eyed at Mazilda.

"I've seen you in better shape," she said.

The ninja tried to focus his eyes but the booze was making an impact.

"You know that it takes Ish a night for his body to acclimate to new types of booze. He'll be drinking everyone under the table by the time we leave this rock."

"I have no doubt about that," said Mazilda.

"So who is this Potato Lips?"

"O'Hoolihan is a decorated soldier who worked for the Irish gangs back in New Tokyo. But he's no ordinary soldier, he's a mutant. His mutation gives him unmatched strength and skin as thick as a brick wall; he's so valuable that they've sent him on the most important mission of all."

"To win the Tournament of the Shield of the Colossal Calamari?" asked Duke quizzically.

"No, Duke. To track down Ishiro'shea's parents."

Instantly, every bit of intoxication drained from Ishiro's face, like a popped water balloon. He was sober. He inched closer to Mazilda.

"So why is he *here*?" asked Duke.

"I don't know. But someone here must know something. Why else would O'Hoolihan join the tournament while the wars rage on?"

"I have no idea."

"And you two haven't made any headway on finding Ishiro's parents?"

"None, unfortunately. We've been a bit busy of late."

"Oh yes, the portal thing."

457

"Yes, the portal thing," Duke replied with no shortage of sass.

"I want to do whatever I can to help."

"Why now?"

"What do you mean 'why now'? How many missions have I gone on with you two searching for Ishiro's parents? More than I can count. I was happy to do it."

"Yes, but we haven't seen you in a long time, Mazilda. Why help us now? You weren't seeking us out or anything. We kinda dropped in on the festivities, if you don't remember."

"Yes, I remember. And when it happened, it..." She paused. "...it reminded me of some good memories. I'm not one to get nostalgic, but I feel that this is something that I left unfinished. It's always haunted me. I was given a second chance to help you guys out. You two falling onto that table during the Shaman's gala was the universe's way of telling me something. I won't mess this up. And one more thing."

She reached into her robe and removed a communication device. It was an older model, mostly used for short range, which made it very difficult to intercept or decode. It was a popular design for thieves and other positions of ill repute. Mazilda pressed a few buttons and turned the screen towards Ishiro'shea and Duke.

It was a grainy image of two humans. The male was gray-haired and mature in cycles but broad-shouldered, and looked to be in prime physical condition. The woman looked around the same age but she was petite. She also had grayed but her beauty wasn't tarnished by her advanced age; if anything, it was enhanced.

The ninja's eyes widened. Duke noticed a twitch in his partner's upper cheek. It was as if joy and disbelief were dueling to see what emotion would win out on the ninja's face.

Ishiro'shea's parents.

"I was able to acquire this image from Potato Lips without him knowing," Mazilda said in a hushed tone. "I'm not sure where it was taken. I don't recognize the buildings in the background or any of the reference points. But—"

"They're alive," Duke said finishing Mazilda's sentence.

"Maxx is here," she said with a sense of urgency. "I have to go. Here you go."

She pressed a few more buttons on the device and a printout of the image was produced. She handed it to Ishiro'shea.

"Do you have to go?"

"Yes, but we can talk again. Good luck tomorrow against Gjrazzel. I have faith in you."

Mazilda placed her hand on Ishiro'shea's shoulder and smiled at Duke. Then, in a blink of an eye, she was gone. Duke turned around to see her arm in arm with Maxx Gemstarr, exiting the Pondscum Tavern.

Man, I hate Maxx Gemstarr.

The bounty hunter turned to Ishiro'shea, who was still motionless from the shock.

"Little buddy, regardless of how this tournament turns out, it's been a worthwhile detour if you ask me. We finally have a lead on your folks."

Ishiro'shea did not budge.

"Let's go get some sleep. Tomorrow, we can try and find Mr. Potato Lips and ask him a few questions." Duke twirled his laser revolver. "Okay, maybe one more round."

CHAPTER TWELVE

RATINGS KILLER

DUKE WAS HUNGOVER, WHICH WAS surprising considering it was midday. In fact, he and Ishiro'shea both would have still been asleep had it not been for a tournament official beating incessantly on their hotel door. Since most of the local accommodation had been booked up cycles in advance in anticipation for the Tournament of the Shield of the Colossal Calamari, and Duke and Ishiro'shea just happened to drop in at the last minute, their room wasn't exactly topflight. It wasn't even bottom flight. It was next-to-the-ice-machine bad. But it was near the bar, so it had that going for it. The official's rapid-fire hammering caved the door in. It swung open on a single hinge and hung limp.

"I'm not paying for that," Duke mumbled.

"Mr. LaGrange, you need to hurry up. You can't be late to the tournament's Grand Entrance."

"I'll catch the next one," said the bounty hunter. He repositioned his pillow to block the light.

The Psitakki official stepped over a sleeping Ishiro'shea

and hoisted Duke up by his arm. "Mr. LaGrange, we have to go. Now."

"I thought the fight wasn't until tonight," Duke moaned.

"The Grand Entrance starts in..." The Psitakki looked at a communication device. "...it starts very soon. If you aren't there, the Shaman is going to be irate. He'll probably blame me."

"Who are you anyways?"

"I was assigned to make sure that you don't escape before the tournament."

"The Shaman thinks I'm going to run away, does he?"

The Psitakki sighed, clearly not wanting to begin a debate with the half-drunk Nova Texan. "Let's just say that we were concerned with the amount of alcohol that you had last night at the Pondscum. We just wanted to make sure that you actually made it to the arena. By the looks of it, our concerns were justified."

Duke reached for his hat and placed in on his head. It slid down over his eyes. "Can I rest for a few more minutes? I promise I'll meet you at the arena."

The Psitakki official jerked Duke harder, but lost his balance. He stepped on the snoozing martial artist. Ishiro'shea leapt to his feet and connected with a *shotei* strike to the official's chest. His eyes were still closed. *He's on autopilot*, thought Duke.

Ishiro'shea shook his head and came to his senses. He glanced at the door, then at the unconscious Psitakki at his feet, then at Duke.

"You just knocked out our ride to the arena, Ish."

The ninja knelt down to make sure that the Psitakki was still breathing.

"He's fine, he's fine," said Duke. "Apparently we have to go to some big ceremony at the arena. You know how to get there?"

Ishiro'shea shook his head.

"Do they have taxis on Psitakki?"

Ishiro'shea responded with a glance that seemed to convey his lack of hope for a suitable Psitakki public transportation system.

"If we get to the arena, maybe we have time to chat with Potato Lips before the show."

The ninja seemed to perk up at this suggestion.

"Mr. LaGrange! Mr. LaGrange, we are about to start. Get in your place. Hurry! Hurry!"

The Psitakki yelling at Duke was easy to identify as a member of the production team responsible for broadcasting the event across the universe. His headset was oversized to the point of being comical; it screamed, 'Hey, look at me! I'm important!'"

"Not there; *here*," he said, pointing to a compact metallic room.

Glad I'm not claustrophobic.

Duke recognized that they were near the holding area that led to the arena floor. His memory was a bit hazy, but the thunderous booms of thousands of spectators cheering, mere paces away, made it quite obvious as to where they were.

"Who are you, peanut?" asked the production supervisor in a pugnacious tone.

Ishiro is not going to like that.

"Only the combatants and their corner men are allowed here. Get out. Get out. Get out."

Ishiro'shea's eyes focused on the Psitakki and he grabbed the hilt of his sword. Duke gently took the ninja's wrist to make him halt.

"*He's* my corner man," said Duke.

"I was told that you didn't have one," snapped the producer. "He wasn't at the melee."

"I didn't know that I could have someone in my corner. Now I do. And he's it. Deal with it."

The producer flashed a scowl that could have bent steel. He screamed into his headset and stormed off.

"I guess this means that you're my corner man," said Duke. "Now sober up and look alive."

Ishiro'shea shot him a glance almost as menacing as the producer's.

"Fine, I'll try and sober up too. Apparently, I'm going to die today."

The roars of the crowd were accompanied by equally deafening trumpets. And then by ear-smashing drums. It was like being serenaded by the Trampling Death Robots while locked in a midsized sports utility vehicle. Duke grimaced; his headache had spread all the way down to his spleen.

"Maybe that room has a door," Duke said, his hands clamped over his ears.

He and Ishiro'shea entered the chamber. It wasn't as cramped as it appeared and, most importantly, it had a door. Ishiro'shea slid the door shut and the noise abated.

"Holy hedgehogs, that was loud," Duke proclaimed. He sat down on a smooth white bench that jutted out from the wall.

"Are you in your places?"

Duke and Ishiro'shea looked around confused.

"Who said that?" asked Duke.

"Look up, Mr. LaGrange," the voice said, sounding annoyed at the question. "See that tiny black box? That's called a speaker. I'm not some scary invisible god that is talking to you, right? I'm just a production manager that wants this event to be broadcast without any major screwups. Got that?"

Duke contemplated leaving the room and tracking down the producer. He wondered how the Psitakki would react to looking down the barrel of Ol' Betsy.

But, uncharacteristically, the Nova Texan took the high road. "We didn't see the speaker. We see it now."

"Good. First, remove your guns and give them to your corner man. It is strictly forbidden to have them on your person when you walk out for the Grand Entrance."

"Done," replied Duke, handing his revolver and Betsy to Ishiro'shea.

"When the door in front of you opens—not the one that you just closed—"

"Let's tone down the condescension a notch, huh?"

"Fine," the producer barked. "When the door opens, follow the path to the empty pedestal. Stand on it. Wave. Bow. Do whatever you want. When everyone is done, you will exit in reverse order and return to this room. Stay on the path."

"Sounds easy enough."

"It does, doesn't it?" replied the producer in a snarky tone. "In the meantime, you can watch the live broadcast from this screen."

The wall next to Ishiro'shea opened up and a monitor extended on a metallic arm. It turned on to reveal a still shot of the arena overlaid with text in a grandiose and gaudy font. It read: *The 100th Annual Tournament of the Shield of the Colossal Calamari—The Grand Entrance. Sponsored by Uncle Tofu's Adventure Land, home of the Screamin' Vegan, the universe's first roller coaster made exclusively from a fungal-derived meat alternative. Fun with less fat.*

"Wow, looks like the Cosmic Superstation is picking this up."

"Yes, and the Universal Superstation," chimed in the producer's voice from the speaker. "And the Galactic Superstation. Everyone is carrying this. It's the biggest event in the last ten thousand cycles."

"When do I go on?"

"You're second to last. Gjrazzel is last, for obvious reasons."

"Hometown boy?"

"Yes. A Psitakki hasn't won this tournament since his ancestor, Grozzel. That was ninety-nine tournaments ago. The world—no, the universe—wants him to win."

"So, I guess that you aren't rooting for me?"

"You, Mr. LaGrange, would be a ratings killer."

"Thanks. If it's all the same to you, I think my buddy and I would like to watch some of the broadcast and relax. You know, before I kill the ratings and all."

"I'm not worried about you killing the ratings."

"Because you don't think I can win."

There was a long pause. "Don't screw this up. When the door opens, follow the path..."

"I got it."

The broadcast cut to two announcers sitting in a booth suspended above the arena floor. One of the announcers was a well-dressed Trevlon. The Trevlon were about as nondescript a bipedal race as you could find, but they had deep and soothing voices. Most Trevlons left their home planet to seek employment as voice actors, lounge singers, and, if they were lucky, broadcasters. Next to the Trevlon was a brightly-colored robot wearing a top hat.

"Hey, Ish, we're famous. Look who's calling the action. I love these guys."

CHAPTER THIRTEEN

RANDY AND ZEL

[INTRODUCTION MUSIC ENDS AND TITLE SCREEN DISSOLVES. BROADCAST OPENS WITH SHOT OF THE ANNOUNCERS.]

ZELARIOUS ZAN ALON: Hello, everyone in the universe! And welcome to the one hundredth annual Tournament of the Shield of the Colossal Calamari, live here on Psitakki. I'm Zelarious Zan Alon and, man, I tell you, I am honored to be here calling this exciting tournament. You are in for a treat, my friends. You won't see anything like it again, I can promise that. And to help me call the action is the best color commentator in the business. He's a veteran of over forty-two thousand broadcasts that span everything from the Slinky Racing Nationals to the Extreme Armadillo Juggling Grand Prix to Paint Drying Watching Battles on Gorma Gorma Zed. Yes, you know him, you love him—it's everyone's favorite spunky little android, Randy!

RANDY: Thank you for that kind introduction, Zel.

Beep. I'm ready to see some pain and suffering. And I don't just mean from your play-by-play call. *Boop. Beep.*

Zelarious Zan Alon: Oh wow, starting out strong, Randy.

Randy: That's what Mrs. Zan Alon said last night. *Beep.*

Zelarious Zan Alon: Let's leave that monster out of this, because we have sixteen other monsters that we need to talk about today. In a few moments, the final Grand Entrance will happen and we—along with the thousands in attendance—will lay eyes on the combatants that are fighting for that unbelievable prize, a shield of Grozzel. It's a million cycles old and is the last of the artifacts that helped Grozzel save the people of Psitakki from those mysterious shadow demon invaders. The previous ninety-nine have been lost to time, along with their owners, but we get to see the final one handed out. Pretty special, huh, Randy?

Randy: Sure. *Beep.*

Zelarious Zan Alon: Before the introductions start, here's a word from our sponsor. Uncle Tofu's Adventure Land—It Won't "Meat" Your Expectations, It Will "Meat Substitute" Them!

Randy: Speaking of meat, Zel... *Beep.* Your wife called me, asking about a pork. *Boop.*

Zelarious Zan Alon: Now that word from our sponsors.

[UNCLE TOFU'S ADVENTURE LAND COMMERCIAL PLAYS.]

Zelarious Zan Alon: Welcome back, fans, to the Tournament of the Shield of the Colossal Calamari. You can hear the music and the crowd cheering and that means it's time for the entrances. Sixteen of the fiercest, most distinguished warriors in the entire galaxy will do battle in a single elimination, no-holds-barred tournament. There can be only one winner. It's not for the faint of heart or the weak of stomach. It's going to be brutal, nasty, painful, and destructive, but oh so glorious. And all to honor that big squid in the sky. Do you have any favorites in the field, Randy?

RANDY: *Beep. Boop.* Yes, I do, Zel. The Grand Champion of Psitakki, Gjrazzel, is quite a specimen, especially with that weapon of his.

ZELARIOUS ZAN ALON: Yes, his tarzantia tree staff is deadly.

Randy: Oh, yeah, that too. *Beep.*

ZELARIOUS ZAN ALON: What are you talking about, Randy?

RANDY: Ask your wife. *Boop.*

ZELARIOUS ZAN ALON: Anyone else catch your eye?

RANDY: I really like the combatant from Hiritai. *Beep.* What's her name?

ZELARIOUS ZAN ALON: Sulaw. What makes you think she will go far in the tournament?

RANDY: I don't know if she'll go far in the tournament. But she catches my eye. *Beep.* She's smoking hot. Isn't that what you asked me? Zel, you really need to step it up. You're embarrassing yourself tonight. *Beep. Boop.*

ZELARIOUS ZAN ALON: She *is* a fierce combatant, no doubt about it. But don't forget about the entrant from that messed-up sphere we call Earth—Seamus "Potato Lips" O'Hoolihan.

RANDY: He's nasty, for sure. *Beep.* And ugly. *Boop.* And probably drunk.

ZELARIOUS ZAN ALON: Quite possibly, Randy, quite possibly. We have some intriguing first round matchups. How about Yvonne "The Furry Mountain of Moon Colony

#1" Angerdlarnek going one-on-one with Reginald the Mega-Troll? That should be explosive.

RANDY: And what about Maxx Gemstarr? *Beep.* He's hunky enough to cause my gears to spin the other way. *Boop.*

ZELARIOUS ZAN ALON: He sure is a handsome man. And a favorite to win the entire tournament. Watch out for the Universe's Favorite Bounty Hunter. But don't forget about the two big mysteries.

RANDY: Ooooooh. *Boop.*

ZELARIOUS ZAN ALON: First, and to be honest, what I'm most excited about, is to see this unknown Combatant 2 from Jungafallow III. All we know is that he was awarded their government's invitation to the tournament and he's seconded by the esteemed Prince Korzo-Tapor. I know the prince personally and he wouldn't endorse anything less than a sure-fire winner. And, lastly, the wild card entrant and winner of the melee, Duke LaGrange—a bounty hunter.

RANDY: Who? *Beep.*

ZELARIOUS ZAN ALON: Exactly, another mystery indeed. When we return, the entrances will begin. Now a word from Willie's World of Galactic Winnebagos—Where the Universe is Our Home, So Make it Yours... Now with Flushing Toilets Compatible with up to Eighty-Five Species!

[WILLIE'S WORLD OF GALACTIC WINNEBAGOS COMMERCIAL PLAYS.]

ZELARIOUS ZAN ALON: Welcome back, fight fans from across the universe. It's about time to see our combatants! I'm really excited, Randy.

RANDY: *Beep.* Me too, Zel. *Beep.*

Zelarious Zan Alon: The lights are down and the trumpets are blasting. The crowd is in a frenzy. I haven't heard anything this loud and indistinguishable since the Trampling Death Robots' holiday album. This is quite a sight to behold. Wait a second, Randy. The first door is opening, and we have our first entrant into the Tournament of the Shield of the Colossal Calamari. It's Not Very Good at Math.

Randy: But is it good at fighting? *Boop. Beep.*

Zelarious Zan Alon: No, Randy, that's his name. Not Very Good at Math. He's the representative of Zylantia and a renowned pirate lord back on his home planet.

Randy: *Beep.* What a dumb name, Zel. *Boop.* Who are these Zylantian pirates anyways? Beep. I've never heard of them. *Boop.*

Zelarious Zan Alon: I can tell, Randy. Zylantia is a harsh cloud-covered world filled with villainy and treachery, with overtones of male chauvinism. Amongst this collection of vile scum, those that successfully earn a spot on a pirate vessel are considered royalty. Due to their affinity for theft and general terror, Zylantian pirates always have substantial disposable income. These blood-soaked nest eggs allow them to travel off-world to engage with other races and, if they're lucky, learn new ways to lie, cheat, steal, and torture.

Randy: And they have four arms. *Beep.*

Zelarious Zan Alon: Great observation, Randy. They can utilize all four hands to slice, stab, and claw at their opponents. They are a devious race, no doubt. Just look at Not Very Good at Math. He's taunting the crowd with two arms, stroking his icy-white mustache with another, and... What's that other hand doing?

Randy: That's even too gross for me to comment on, Zel. *Beep. Boop.* And what about that funny name?

ZELARIOUS ZAN ALON: It's customary on Zylantia that a child does not receive a proper name given to them by their biological parents. In fact, parenting is a bit of a lost art on Zylantia. Names just sort of evolve based on characteristics, traits, behaviors, or really stupid things that you do. Famous Zylantians include Pointy Elbows, Dried Spit on Mouth, Really Small Eyes, Trips More than Average Zylantian, and the universally-acclaimed chef that invented "never-ending mayonnaise," Mother Looks Like Dirt Bug.

RANDY: *Beep.* Looks like our second contestant is coming out now. *Boop.* It's my personal favorite! Wives, hide your husbands, because Sulaw is here. *Beep.*

ZELARIOUS ZAN ALON: That's right, Sulaw is the next competitor in the Grand Entrance. And wow, she's a fan favorite. Listen to these fans! Listen to those cheers!

RANDY: *Beep.* That's the sound of drool hitting the ground, Zel. *Boop.*

ZELARIOUS ZAN ALON: She's not just a pretty face, Randy. She's an accomplished warrior from Hiritai. Her tribe is the current ruling group, which makes her one important woman. Look at her now, paying respect to the Psitakki as she walks to her pedestal. What a class act. She knows honor. And how beautiful is that *chunki*?

RANDY: *Boop.* She looks pretty damn fit to me. *Beep.*

ZELARIOUS ZAN ALON: No, you crazy robot. *Chunki* is the golden material fashioned to form her breastplate and twirled around her waist like a skirt. The interconnected rings covering the midriff and fastened to the shiny brassiere and kilt are also made from the impenetrable *chunki*. But, as is common with the Hiritai warriors, her legs—muscular legs, at that—and feet are exposed. If you grow up in the harsh terrain of Hiritai, your feet become as tough as any cobbler's creation.

RANDY: *Beep.* You know a lot about these Hiritai women, Zel. *Boop.* Think you can introduce me to Sulaw?

ZELARIOUS ZAN ALON: You wouldn't want that, Randy. The Hiritai hate men. They *loathe* men. They view them as tiny-brained, sex-driven nuisances. They put up with them for procreation until they can figure out a solution to eliminate them entirely. I've heard nearly a third of the gross national product goes towards male eradication technology. But as much as they hate men, they love parties. And being the center of attention—a trait that anthropologists believe they inherited from their ancient Earth ancestors. A Hiritai may take a husband for the sake of having a bitchin' bachelorette party and wedding and, before the honeymoon is over, the husband will either be subjected to a life of slavery in the Hiritai mines, or killed simply for being in the way. Once again, anthropologists see numerous similarities to their Earth-bound relatives.

RANDY: *Boop.* Well, I'm a robot, Zel.

ZELARIOUS ZAN ALON: You might have a chance, then.

RANDY: *Boop.* And I'm not really into gross generalizations of gender tendencies and furthering outdated stereotypes that demean entire populations. *Beep.*

ZELARIOUS ZAN ALON: You are quite the progressive, Randy. Oh wow, Randy, look at that. Did you see that? Not Very Good at Math and Sulaw are having a bit of a stare down. The crowd is eating this up. They meet in the first round, you know. Going to be quite the battle.

RANDY: *Beep.* Who's that coming out now? *Boop.* Or rather, slithering out. *Beep.*

ZELARIOUS ZAN ALON: That's the infamous Tor-torta of Krawn. The serpent people of Krawn are widely known for their advancements in two major industries: the torture industry and soybean harvesting. They lack hind legs, but they are quite agile slithering around. The arms on their upper torsos are ridiculously strong, as they are their primary means of locomotion. And they're covered in nasty spikes.

RANDY: *Beep.* He's pretty gross, Zel. Does he have any special skills? *Beep.*

ZELARIOUS ZAN ALON: Just wait a second... watch this.

RANDY: Oh wow! *Beep.* He can breathe fire! That's got to help his chances! *Beep.*

ZELARIOUS ZAN ALON: But he has a tough challenge in front of him. The representative from Earth is a bad dude.

RANDY: *Beep.* Aren't most people from Earth 'bad dudes'? *Beep.*

ZELARIOUS ZAN ALON: I think that might be a bit of an exaggeration, but this guy here comes from the heart of the gang wars in Ireland—New Tokyo, to be exact. Seamus "Potato Lips" O'Hoolihan.

RANDY: Beep. Why do they call him—never mind. I see. *Beep.*

ZELARIOUS ZAN ALON: Yes, he's not your average Earther. His mutation has given him abnormal strength and mass. Including on his face. I've heard of O'Hoolihan's exploits as a street tough before he became the chief enforcer for the Irish. You don't want to mess with this guy.

RANDY: *Beep.* Was he born this way? *Boop.*

ZELARIOUS ZAN ALON: He was, Randy.

RANDY: *Beep.* That had to be a painful birth. I feel sorry for his mother. Hopefully, she had good birthing hips. *Beep.* But the crowd seems to love him. I guess when you bring out two mugs of beer and toast the crowd, what's not to like? *Boop.*

ZELARIOUS ZAN ALON: No doubt! His legendary

473

drinking adventures rival that of his fighting prowess. He and Tor-torta should be an interesting bout. Look who's out next. The biggest competitor in the field, it's Reginald!

RANDY: *Beep.* You aren't kidding, Zel. This Mega-troll is massive. How can anyone beat this guy? *Boop.*

ZELARIOUS ZAN ALON: He will be a tough out, that's for sure. Look at him saunter to the pedestal. Four steps and he's there. You know what, I don't think the pedestal will support him. He's a true goliath. But, Randy, they grow them big in the Silver Mountains of Mrelock.

RANDY: *Beep.* And stupid. *Beep.*

ZELARIOUS ZAN ALON: You're right, Randy. The Mega-Trolls aren't known for their mental dexterity and intelligence—but when you're that size and that strong, it makes up for areas where you're lacking. Look at Reginald playing to the crowd! His pounding of the chest signifies that he's very appreciative of the fans, and those primal screams are his way of saying that he's going to give it his all in this tournament.

RANDY: You're fluent in Mega-Troll? *Boop.*

ZELARIOUS ZAN ALON: His opponent is one of the crowd favorites. Wait for this cheer.

RANDY: *Beep.* They do love this lady! *Beep.*

ZELARIOUS ZAN ALON: I wouldn't be surprised if this is the second or third loudest ovation today. There she is, ladies and gentlemen, Yvonne "The Furry Mountain of Moon Colony #1" Angerdlarnek! She's quite impressive.

RANDY: *Beep.* Even I know not to mess with an anthropomorphic musk ox from any of the moons around Gartosh. Their fighting skill is known throughout the cosmos. *Beep.*

ZELARIOUS ZAN ALON: And Yvonne is the best. She won Miss Bovine Boxer over Lilly Arnaq last cycle in a hard-fought contest. She's a no-frills competitor and I'm curious to see how that plays out in the Tournament of the

Shield of the Colossal Calamari. She's going with no weapon and will rely on her mastery of the pugilistic arts.

RANDY: *Beep.* And her boxing. *Beep.*

ZELARIOUS ZAN ALON: Yvonne versus Reginald the Mega-Troll should be a fascinating and hard-hitting matchup. I can't wait for that one. And the next two fighters will round out the first bracket. A lot of us are anxious for this one as well.

RANDY: *Beep.* Look at this guy! He's rolling out from the holding area. I haven't seen anything like that before. *Beep.*

ZELARIOUS ZAN ALON: Randy, that's Kitar! He's showing off his patented rolling spike attack. His race, from the Olamandrian System, represents one of the few successful porcupinoid races in the entire universe.

RANDY: *Beep.* Why do you think that they have such a problem sustaining a civilization?

ZELARIOUS ZAN ALON: There's been a lot of debate about that, Randy. Most scholars seem to think it has to do with their inability to reproduce without sustaining major puncture wounds.

RANDY: *Boop. Beep.* I seem to do fine reproducing with my massive spike. *Beep.*

ZELARIOUS ZAN ALON: As much as Kitar is a legitimate contender for the Shield, I think most in attendance are more curious about this next entrant—Jungafallow III's mysterious Combatant 2.

RANDY: *Beep.* He sure is taking his time. *Beep.*

ZELARIOUS ZAN ALON: I know. Where are you, Combatant 2? The universe is waiting.

RANDY: *Beep. Boop.* I don't see anyone or any thing. I'm sure the backstage staff isn't happy about him missing his cue. *Beep.*

ZELARIOUS ZAN ALON: Hold up, Randy. I'm getting

an update from backstage. One of the producers is telling me that Combatant 2 is delayed. It looks like we'll have to come back to him. Let's not hold up the broadcast any longer. Who's next? Hey, I recognize that guy.

RANDY: *Beep.* How do you know it's a guy? It looks like a big pile of mush.

ZELARIOUS ZAN ALON: That's because it's Jin-Jin-Jin; he's a Globuloid from Hobunk Alpha. And man, is he going to be a tricky one to beat!

RANDY: *Beep.* Seems a bit soft. *Beep.*

ZELARIOUS ZAN ALON: By design, Randy. It's hard to knock out a Globuloid due to their nebulous form. But they pack a mighty powerful wallop. They've been known to squeeze the life out of prey—and rival mates. It's still a bit of a primitive world on Hobunk Alpha. But it's cycles ahead of Hobunk Beta.

RANDY: *Beep.* I don't think the crowd knows what to think about this guy. *Beep.*

ZELARIOUS ZAN ALON: They'll get a treat watching him duke it out. He trained under the legendary Nin-Jin-Nin, the Grand Victor of Slimo. Slimo, of course, being the primary martial arts discipline of those species lacking a tangible bone structure. The celluloid classes really love them some Slimo.

RANDY: *Beep.* And who does the hunk of gelatin get in round one? *Beep.*

ZELARIOUS ZAN ALON: Have you ever met a Goother Rat?

RANDY: *Beep.* I have not, Zel. *Beep.*

ZELARIOUS ZAN ALON: Consider yourself a lucky little android, because they are diabolical critters from the swamps of Gurlf. And this guy is no different. This is Gha. And that's his stone-tipped flail, the weapon of choice down home in the swamps. I believe he hails from Swamp Blorg in Gurlf, an especially tough marsh. He should feel quite at home with the Psitakki.

RANDY: He has to be our smallest competitor, Zel. *Beep. Boop. Beep.*

ZELARIOUS ZAN ALON: Yes, Randy, but don't let his size fool you. It will be interesting to see if the Goother Rat and the Jungafallowian entry meet at some point in the tournament. You know, there's bad blood there.

RANDY: Why? *Beep.*

ZELARIOUS ZAN ALON: I'm glad you asked. Goother Rats aren't only native to Gurlf. In fact, their lesser-evolved brethren are all over the universe, including Jungafallow III. But the fascinating part is that most astrozoologists believe they originated on Jungafallow III.

RANDY: How did they get to Gurlf? *Boop.*

ZELARIOUS ZAN ALON: The Jungafallowians tried to colonize the insignificant swamp planet we now know as Gurlf, but gave up after they deemed it just too damn disgusting.

RANDY: *Beep.* It has to be nasty for a Jungafallowian to say that. *Beep.*

ZELARIOUS ZAN ALON: Take my word, it's a bubbling ball of gaseous sludge. But a family of Goothers, who were being kept as pets by the landing party, escaped. A few millennia later, they developed speech, written language, quasi-complex social structures, and moderate levels of technology, including space travel up to one hundred light years. Back on Jungafallow III, they're still kept as pets or raised for their pelts.

RANDY: *Beep.* No love lost between these two then, huh, Zel? *Boop.*

ZELARIOUS ZAN ALON: It gets better. About two thousand cycles ago, a Gurlfian priest was blown off course and landed in the Jungafallowian system. When he voyaged back to Gurlf, he shared what he had witnessed to his people. He even brought back one of the lesser-evolved Goother Rats.

RANDY: *Beep.* What happened?

ZELARIOUS ZAN ALON: Immediately, five of the planet's religions toppled. The ruling parties demanded an invasion of Jungafallow to rescue their proto-cousins. But cooler heads eventually prevailed.

RANDY: *Beep.* Sounds like a Gurlfian probably won't be inviting a Jungafallowian to his birthday party anytime soon. *Beep.*

ZELARIOUS ZAN ALON: I think you're right, Randy. But let's not lose sight of Gha. He's a particularly angry and violent Goother. He medaled in four straight Gurlfian marsh-hopping events, but shunned the endorsements and a lifetime of celebrity in order to see the universe. Well, the nearest one hundred light years, at least. But, as it is with many space travelers, he grew bored and decided to enter the glamorous world of underground cage fighting. His success earned him a spot in this tournament.

RANDY: *Beep.* That's an impressive rat. *Boop.* And he seems pretty skilled with that twirly thing. *Beep.*

ZELARIOUS ZAN ALON: Yes, the rock-tipped flail or, as the Gurlfians call it, rock-on-the-end-of-a-rope-attached-to-a-pole.

RANDY: *Beep.* A creative bunch, no doubt. *Boop.*

ZELARIOUS ZAN ALON: We've spent so much time on Gha, we have two more coming out now. These two will be battling in round one, and I for one can't wait. Almost at his pedestal is Jorb of Karr.

RANDY: He looks like a giant sludge monster. *Beep. Beep.*

ZELARIOUS ZAN ALON: ...that spits acid, Randy. A giant sludge monster that spits acid. Not much is known about these creatures. No gender. Just that they are made of sludge and spit acid. He has a bit more structure than Jin-Jin-Jin, the Globuloid, but he's also a lot more sedentary. If he can connect with that green saliva, it's game over.

RANDY: *Beep. Boop.* What about his opponent? He seems to have the fans jazzed up! *Beep.*

ZELARIOUS ZAN ALON: Oh yes, our only contestant that flies. It's a real treat to have him here. That's Glux Xyphormog II—a royal guardsmen of the Queen Mother of Planet F.

RANDY: The Mother F'er? *Beep.*

ZELARIOUS ZAN ALON: As you can see, Planet F is home to a dominant insectoid species. We have millions of those in the galaxy, but the F'ers are regarded as the most honorable and chivalrous in their sector. Glux splits his time between training in combat, protecting the royal Queen Mother, and helping sire her legions of offspring.

RANDY: *Beep.* My kind of gig, Zel. *Beep.*

ZELARIOUS ZAN ALON: Not only can Glux whizz past you with his aerial attacks, he's also an elite-level master with the signature weapon of the royal guard, the two-sided halberd. It's a deadly tool. But in round one, he will have to find a way to avoid that toxic drool of Jorb.

RANDY: Oh, Zel. *Beep.* I forgot about this guy! I know him. *Beep.* That's the Grand Blademaster of Gyork! *Beep.*

ZELARIOUS ZAN ALON: You've done your homework, Randy. You are absolutely correct. The Grand Blademaster of Gyork is a swordsman like no other.

RANDY: *Beep.* Yeah, it looks like he's made of sword parts. *Beep.*

ZELARIOUS ZAN ALON: When a Gyorkian wins the title of Grand Blademaster, not only does he have to forego his given name to become referred to as the Grand Blademaster of Gyork, but he also has to embed bits and pieces of swords into his skin surgically. He's a walking armory.

RANDY: *Beep.* How does he... you know? *Beep.*

ZELARIOUS ZAN ALON: Let's just say that when you earn the designation of Grand Blademaster of Gyork, you take an involuntary vow of celibacy.

RANDY: Ouch. *Boop.*

ZELARIOUS ZAN ALON: Exactly the point.

RANDY: *Beep.* Good one, Zel. *Boop.*

ZELARIOUS ZAN ALON: What? Oh, Randy. Get your head out of the gutter. But, unlike the porcupinoids of the Olamandrian System, only a chosen few have this issue—not the entire race. So, the race has a chance to make it.

RANDY: *Beep.* I think he's my new pick to win this entire tournament. *Beep.* Give me the Grand Blademaster of Gyork. Who does he fight in round one?

ZELARIOUS ZAN ALON: Get ready for the answer to that very question, Randy. This place is about to go crazy!

RANDY: Who? Who is it? *Beep. Boop.*

ZELARIOUS ZAN ALON: Listen to that music. He's the only one with custom entrance theme music. And look at those lasers. This is quite a show.

RANDY: Is it... *Beep* ...is it?

ZELARIOUS ZAN ALON: Yes, here he is, ladies and gentlemen! But mostly ladies. The Universe's Favorite Bounty Hunter, Maxx Gemstarr!

RANDY: *Beep.* I change my mind, Zel! I change my mind! *Boop.* Maxx is my pick. Not the Gyorkian. Maxx is my guy! *Beep.*

ZELARIOUS ZAN ALON: Calm down, Randy. Calm down. Maxx is quite the specimen. Not only does he have super strength, but he's as cunning a competitor as you'll see. One strike from Maxx's power gauntlets and you're going to be down for the count.

RANDY: *Beep.* I haven't heard this many females swoon since I posed in the Mister Nuts and Bolts Calendar last cycle. *Beep.*

ZELARIOUS ZAN ALON: They do love him. And he loves them. He knows how to put on a show. And look at this! He's walking down the aisle and shaking the other competitors' hands—or whatever they have resembling hands. This guy here is classy, Randy. We all could learn a few things from him.

RANDY: *Beep.* If I was running from the law and he was after me, I would just give up. *Beep.*

ZELARIOUS ZAN ALON: Many do! Oh, hold the phone, we have an update. We have the final pairing about to come out—one of them is the hometown favorite, Gjrazzel. And afterwards, Combatant 2 will come out and greet the crowd. Seems that he was running a bit late.

RANDY: This next guy intrigues me, Zel. *Beep.*

ZELARIOUS ZAN ALON: And why is that?

RANDY: He won the melee match, right? *Boop. Beep.*

ZELARIOUS ZAN ALON: That's correct.

RANDY: It was a pretty lucky win if you ask me. *Beep.*

ZELARIOUS ZAN ALON: He did have some good fortune on his side, thanks to an explosively suicidal Blop.

RANDY: Can he have the same type of luck against Gjrazzel? *Beep.*

ZELARIOUS ZAN ALON: We will have to wait and see—but I know one thing: he will not have the crowd support. Listen to these boos and hisses greeting Duke LaGreen, a bounty hunter. Hold up, something from backstage. Yes. Yes. Sorry, ladies and gentlemen, it's Duke La*Grange*, a bounty hunter.

RANDY: *Beep.* Where's he from, Zel? He looks like another Earther. *Beep. Beep.*

ZELARIOUS ZAN ALON: Actually, he's from Nova

Texas. It was once an Earth colony but gained independence many cycles ago.

RANDY: I know it, Zel. *Beep*. They have a great planetary anthem. *Boop*. What are Duke's chances?

ZELARIOUS ZAN ALON: He's definitely the underdog in the field. Apparently, he's well known in bounty hunter circles, but I can't say that I know much about him.

RANDY: He's no Maxx Gemstarr, that's for sure. *Boop*.

ZELARIOUS ZAN ALON: No one is, Randy. I'm not sure what this Duke LaGrange is good at, but maybe that can be an advantage up against the hometown hero, Gjrazzel.

RANDY: *Beep*. Duke's having a little trouble getting up on the pedestal, Zel. *Beep*. He looks hungover. *Beep*.

ZELARIOUS ZAN ALON: I doubt he would drink before a battle with the likes of Gjrazzel. But if anyone can recognize a drunk shaking off the cobwebs after a particularly rowdy night of the drink, it's you, Randy.

RANDY: *Beep*. You're too nice, Zel. *Beep*.

ZELARIOUS ZAN ALON: Speaking of Gjrazzel, it looks like he's about to enter the arena. To our viewers at home, Randy and I are going to stop talking for a moment for you to be able to soak in the spectacle that we are about to witness. Thousands upon thousands of fans—mostly Psitakki—are going to go absolutely crazy for this fighter. He's a descendent of the first champion and savior of his planet, Grozzel, and one of the most feared combatants in this part of the universe. I give you... Gjrazzel!

[BROADCAST FIZZLES. BLACK SCREEN. DEAD AIR. BROADCAST RETURNS.]

ZELARIOUS ZAN ALON: Oh my gods! What is going on? We need help now!

RANDY: *Beep*. I think Gjrazzel may be dead! *Beep*.

ZELARIOUS ZAN ALON: He was just thrown out of the waiting room as though he was a tenth of his size. He's not moving! He's not moving!

RANDY: Zel, look! *Beep. Beep.*

ZELARIOUS ZAN ALON: That has to be... No... It can't be...

RANDY: *Beep. Boop.* Is that— *Beep.*

ZELARIOUS ZAN ALON: That has to be Combatant 2. Yes, it is! Look who's next to him—Prince Korzo-Tapor. I've never seen anything like him.

RANDY: He's bigger than the Mega-Troll! *Boop.*

ZELARIOUS ZAN ALON: He's exactly that. A Mega-Troll-sized Jungafallowian. He has to be an experiment gone wrong. The crowd is throwing objects into the arena. I wouldn't advise that. Some of the other competitors are surrounding him. Keeping him at bay. The medical staff are tending to Gjrazzel. It doesn't look good, friends. I'm speechless.

RANDY: How can anyone stop this monster? *Beep.* Will Gjrazzel be able to compete? *Boop.*

ZELARIOUS ZAN ALON: All great questions, Randy. And you'll have to tune in tonight to find out. The one hundredth and final Tournament of the Shield of the Colossal Calamari begins in a few hours! Don't miss it. The madness! The carnage! We need reinforcements!

[BROADCAST FADES TO BLACK.]

CHAPTER FOURTEEN

A FEISTY CORNER MAN

"THIS ISN'T FAIR! DISQUALIFY THAT overgrown bastard," shouted a short Psitakki built like a brick house as he charged through a door in the backstage area. Duke assumed this was Gjrazzel's corner man.

"What just happened?" screamed the broadcast's producer as he steamrolled his way into the gathering. "That brute ruined my show. Exalted Grand Shaman, I expect you to do what needs to be done."

"Yeah," began the stout corner man, "disqualify him! Execute him if you have to. He deserves a date with the Chief Interrogator General at the very least."

"And what of Gjrazzel?" asked Grand Shaman Klorzzel calmly.

"He advances, of course," replied the corner man as if there were no other correct answer.

"I meant how is he doing?" explained the Grand Shaman.

"Oh, he'll live," responded the irate corner man. "I think so, at least. But he should advance, regardless."

"Hey, wait a minute, guys," interjected Duke. "Why am

I being punished for what this two-headed oaf did to the kid?"

"I don't have any time for you," snorted Gjrazzel's trainer. "Consider yourself lucky that you don't have to fight Gjrazzel. You should gladly do the right thing and let him advance. It's the only way you would survive this thing anyways."

"Maybe. Or maybe I might just win the entire thing," Duke boasted.

All eyes rested on the Nova Texan. *They don't think I'm serious*, he thought.

The corner man started to laugh. It was a deep, visceral laugh that almost took him off his feet.

"Now now," the Shaman stepped in, "I appreciate confidence in a fighter. This one here—"

"Duke LaGrange."

"Yes, Duke LaGrange has confidence. I will give him that."

"But he obviously lacks smarts," added the diminutive cephalopodan. "Do the right thing, human."

"Or what, short stack? What are you doing to do?"

The corner man's face lit up with rage. His fists clenched and his teeth ground together audibly. He lunged at the bounty hunter but his progress was quickly impeded by the Shaman's staff. The corner man halted his attack immediately.

"Lower your weapons," the Shaman said, pointing his staff at Duke and Ishiro'shea. "No need for that now."

"Can we get back to what's actually important?" yelled the producer. "I'm broadcasting this garbage to half the universe and I don't even know what's going or *when* it's going on. I don't like surprises in my programming schedule. This tournament is our big bet ratings-wise, and now I don't even know if we have a full slate. If I get fired over this, Shaman—"

"Calm down," said Prince Korzo-Tapor, emerging from behind the Shaman. "You should be thanking us."

"I'm glad you came, Prince," said the Shaman.

Korzo-Tapor bowed.

"What do you mean I should be thanking you?" the producer protested. "You ruined my show. Maybe my career."

"Check the early ratings."

The producer pulled out a device from his belt. He input a few codes and a holographic image materialized over the instrument. He turned his back and walked a few paces away from the group. After a few moments, he turned back to the gathering, his eyes wide and the corners of his mouth turned up.

"You see," began the prince. "Controversy creates cash. Or in this case, ratings. And ratings create cash. You're welcome."

"We have a show to shoot. I'll get everyone ready. We're on in a few."

The producer ran out of the room, shouting, "Places, places, places!" to anyone in earshot.

"You're lucky the Shaman's here," said the corner man, "otherwise I would tear you apart, Jungafallowian."

"There will be time for that later," said the prince, "but, I will admit, you might have to get through my friend first. He's resting after his difficult scuffle with your man, Gjrazzel." He chuckled. "Who am I kidding? He didn't even break a sweat with your pathetic excuse of a champion."

The enraged Psitakki's muscles twitched and pulsated. He charged again. The Shaman once again prevented him from carrying through with his attack—however, this time, the Shaman's staff landed across the corner man's face. He hit the ground with a muted thud. As he scuttled to his feet, two of the Shaman's personal guards appeared and apprehended the feisty corner man. Korzo-Tapor's smirk only seemed to anger him more as he struggled to free himself from the grip of the two guards.

"I will not tolerate this," proclaimed the Shaman. "The final Tournament of the Shield of the Colossal Calamari will not be defamed by this behavior. Nor will it be derailed by the actions of Combatant 2."

"But honorable Grand Shaman—" the prince began, but he was silenced by the tip of the Shaman's staff.

"I'm disgusted by what I'm about to say," he began, "but I will not alter the rules or bylaws of this sacred competition, despite some of its participants doing their best to do so. What occurs outside of the tournament's bracket—be it in a bar or in the Grand Entrance—will not affect the competition itself. It is my final decision to allow Combatant 2 to compete as scheduled. As for Gjrazzel, if he can continue, he will face Duke LaGrange tonight at their scheduled time. If he cannot compete—and based on these injuries, I assume that to be the case—the Nova Texan will advance in the tournament."

"Unbelievable," barked the corner man. "You should be ashamed. How can you call yourself a Psitakki? Grozzel is turning over in his grave." He spit at the feet of the Grand Shaman.

Without even a gesture from the Shaman, the guards hauled the corner man away.

The prince bowed towards the Grand Shaman and began to walk away.

"Jungafallowian," shouted the Grand Shaman, "I won't be as lenient on you and your fighter if you push the limits again. This is your final warning."

"To a fair and entertaining event," said Prince Korzo-Tapor, bowing repeatedly.

As the Jungafallowian walked past Duke and Ishi-ro'shea, he paused. Both of his heads were so close to the bounty hunters that Duke could make out the markings on each individual scale of the royal reptiloid.

"Look at you, Duke. Seems like we did you a favor as well. You can thank me later."

"I don't want your help."

"Maybe not. But you *need* it. I'm sure we will run into each other again. Good luck."

CHAPTER FIFTEEN

THE SNAKE AND THE MUTANT
IRISHMAN

STILL HUNGOVER FROM HIS NIGHT out at the Pondscum Tavern, Duke stretched out on the floor of the pre-fight holding room to try and sleep off the lingering headache. He couldn't help but dwell on his predicament. He wasn't unhappy about the possibility of advancing without a fight, but he also knew that the crowd wasn't going to be kind to whomever was on the receiving end of such good fortune. It was especially worrisome that his good fortune was the direct result of the bad fortune suffered by their home world's favorite son. And what if Gjrazzel tried to fight? The bouts had been moved around so that they were now last on the schedule; maybe they thought the extra time would be enough for Gjrazzel to heal.

He couldn't get comfortable enough to rest. His mind was racing with an eclectic menagerie of memories. The moment he closed his eyes, images of Mazilda and Maxx crept in, followed by the prince and the behemoth Jungafallowian, and snippets of the other combatants in the tournament. *How many different ways could I die at the hands of these crazies?* He kept going back to Mazilda and trying to figure out what she saw in Maxx. The Chief Interrogator General. The Grand Shaman. The annoying producer and the hotheaded corner man. The bartender who was confident that Duke wouldn't make it out of the tournament alive. The Four I's surrounding Joe's. They all peeked into Duke's mind as he tried to relax.

"Hey Ish, turn on the view screen when you can. I think the fights are starting. If I can't sleep, I might as well scout my competition."

The ninja turned on the monitor. The broadcast was just getting underway.

"That Randy guy is great," laughed Duke.

Ishiro'shea nodded in agreement.

The opening bout of the tournament pitted the Earth representative, Seamus "Potato Lips" O'Hoolihan of New Tokyo, Ireland, against Tor-torta of Krawn.

"Man, we really need to talk to O'Hoolihan," Duke said to Ishiro'shea. "Let's hope this snake guy doesn't burn him to a crisp."

The two beings made their way to the center of the arena as they were introduced to rousing ovations. The Psitakki referee appeared to be giving them the rules and then backed away. The bellowing howl of a ceremonial horn signaled the start of the altercation and the official start to the tournament.

Tor-torta slithered back on his tail and pressed his chest down to the arena floor. He tried to get as much distance between him and O'Hoolihan's dreaded shillelagh. The Irish mutant twirled the club around but didn't charge. Tor-torta encircled O'Hoolihan and then lunged with a fang-first strike. The serpent's bite narrowly missed O'Hoolihan and forced him to stumble backwards awkwardly. As the Irishman fell, the Krawn native rose high on his tail and came down hard, leading with his spike-covered forearm.

Seamus moved and countered with a glancing shillelagh strike to the back of the head. Tor-torta rolled a few paces but seemed uninjured.

The two danced and bobbed and weaved for some time. O'Hoolihan consistently tried to stay clear of Tor-torta's head—not only could he tear large chunks of flesh out with a single chomp, he had the ability to breath fire. One direct hit and Seamus would be done. *Well* done.

The slowly developing chess match between the two fighters suddenly turned into a slight advantage for Tor-torta when he tripped O'Hoolihan with his tail. He let loose a fireball that narrowly missed the Irishman but managed to dislodge his shillelagh, which fell to the arena floor engulfed in flames. The Krawnee wasted no time and pounced on his fallen opponent. His muscular tail wrapped around the waist and legs of the Irish gang thug and pinned him to the ground. He punched and clawed but Tor-torta showed no signs of stress. O'Hoolihan reached into his vest pocket and pulled out a knife. He stabbed Tor-torta—which got the serpent warrior's attention—but the action wasn't damaging enough for Tor-torta to release his grasp. He tightened his grip and Seamus flailed to the ground. Tor-torta removed the knife and tossed it aside. He gestured to the crowd; they responded with cheers, signaling their approval of the impending death blow.

The injured Earth mutant reached into his vest again. He threw out a chain, some brass knuckles, a pair of dice, and some other items that weren't distinguishable on the broadcast. They all piled up next to the shillelagh, now almost entirely covered in Tor-torta's flame. A tiny flask also spilled to the floor. Duke recognized that immediately. Seamus grabbed the vessel and downed the contents.

To make this less painful, thought Duke.

O'Hoolihan smashed the empty flask into a collection of

sharp shards. He started to stab his captor's tail over and over. Tor-torta noticed this and prepared for his final death strike. The frill from his shoulders to the top of his head expanded, showcasing an imposing display. His mouth widened and he thrust his torso towards the Irishman still pinned against the arena floor.

As Tor-torta attacked, O'Hoolihan grabbed the fiery shillelagh and blew a mouthful of whisky onto the club. The fireball that emerged from the stick engulfed Tor-torta's face and upper body instantaneously. He released his vice grip on O'Hoolihan and squirmed around the arena floor, screaming in a high-pitched shrill. His pain was reflected on the faces of all in attendance. He was blinded and burning alive. In his chaotic scramble, he inched close to O'Hoolihan. The Irishman struck hard with the shillelagh, smacking Tor-torta's face. The serpent collapsed to the floor. Medics ran to the Krawnee and doused him with water to extinguish the flames. After a few moments, it was apparent that Tor-torta was closer to death than he was to continuing in the tournament.

The referee raised the hand of Potato Lips. The riotous crowd shook the arena with their passionate screams and chaotic gyrations. It was clear that the fans loved the extreme violence. The bar for such violence had been set high following the quick-thinking carnage of the Irish gang member.

Duke turned and locked eyes with his partner.

"What did I get myself into, Ish?"

CHAPTER SIXTEEN

RECORDS ARE MADE TO BE BROKEN

D UKE AND ISHIRO'SHEA WATCHED THE other first round battles from the confines of their holding room. Each was more savage and unbridled as the one before. In the opposite side of the bracket, they witnessed the femme fatale, Sulaw, overpower and outsmart the devious four-armed Zylantian pirate, Not Very Good at Math. True to his chauvinistic nature, the Zylantian would not acknowledge that the Hiritai was the more powerful and skilled competitor and in the end he paid for it. However, Not Very Good at Math escaped with only two broken arms; had Sulaw given in to her hate-fueled desire, he would have been crushed unmercifully.

The third contest pitted Yvonne "The Furry Mountain of Moon Colony #1" Angerdlarnek against Reginald, the Mega-Troll from the Silver Mountains of Mrelock. Duke and Ishiro'shea were worried for their Gartoshian friend; Reginald stood taller than any combatant in the field, save for the Jungafallowian entry. On numerous occasions at the Pondscum Tavern they had heard, or rather overheard, about Yvonne's fighting aptitude. She was a definite favorite, but it was hard to overlook the behemoth brute that stood opposite her in the arena, swinging a massive steel mace.

Size does matter occasionally, thought Duke.

When the ceremonial horn sounded, Reginald tossed aside his mace and rampaged weaponless towards the musk ox.

Yvonne has the brains advantage, concluded the bounty hunter.

The Gartoshian hadn't brought a weapon into the arena, relying solely on her boxing abilities. But how would fisticuffs fare against an ogre four times her size—no matter how skilled the puncher? As Reginald rumbled toward her, Yvonne sidestepped the Mrelockian. Due to his massive size, his momentum drove him into the arena wall with a crash. He turned and sat up, resting his back against the barricade. It was obvious that he was dazed. Yvonne pounced, leaping to his midsection and unleashing a furious barrage of rights, lefts, and uppercuts. Blood flew from the Mega-Troll's lips and nose, splattering plasma across a section of spectators. They loved it. Reginald swiped his left arm, lifting Yvonne into the air, then planted her a quarter of the way across the arena floor. That single blow would have killed most sentient species, but Yvonne regained her composure and prepared for another attack. Reginald and Yvonne locked eyes and the Mega-Troll charged again. This time Yvonne didn't wait around. She picked up speed and headed on a direct collision course with the beast.

What is she thinking? She'd have a better chance surviving a headlong crash into a dwarf planet.

Reginald let out a primal yell as he closed the gap between himself and Yvonne. At the last moment before contact, Yvonne leapt into the air, leading with her horns. Just as Duke had seen—or rather, heard—Lilly crack the sternum of a Jungafallowian back at Cyborg Joe's a few months back, he witnessed the awesome power of a Gartoshian musk ox. Yvonne blasted Reginald square in the nose with her cranium-first attack. She fell back to the ground. Reginald collapsed with an elongated moan. He was knocked out. Yvonne showed no signs of movement either.

Slowly, she lifted her hand. The crowd, noticing her efforts, began to cheer and scream for her to get to her feet. The Psitakki referee had already ruled Reginald out of the contest, it was now just a matter of whether Yvonne would advance—or no one would. The referee surveyed the injured boxer intently. Some members of the crowd chanted "Y-vonne," some chanted "Fur-ry-Mount-ain," others screamed "Go Musk Ox, Go"—it came out a garbled mess, but it seemed as though Yvonne appreciated the support. She raised herself onto all fours and tried to stand. She wavered and fell back down. She tried again. She winced as she strained to muster the strength to stand. Her balance wavered but, finally, she made it upright. The referee signaled for the horn and raised Yvonne's hand in victory.

"Ish, I think she deserves a drink after that one," said Duke. "Who goes head-to-head with a Mega-Troll... and wins? I do hope she heals quickly."

Ishiro'shea nodded in agreement.

The next two quarterfinal matches were no less intense in their dangerous dance of devastation. Glux Xyphormog II, a Royal Guardsman of the queen of Planet F, used his ability to fly to give him an advantage over Jorb, the sludge monster of Karr. Though Jorb had the edge in strength and a noteworthy special ability—spitting deadly acid at his opponent—it was Glux's quick thinking and aerial acrobatics that allowed him to prevail over the bipedal mound of waste. Jorb managed to dissolve the midsection of the insectoid's double-sided halberd, but he couldn't quite connect with his projectile saliva when the guardsman took to the air. In fact, Jorb's poor aim forced many spectators to evacuate; syrupy lumps of corrosive phlegm went astray and landed in the seats. It was an attempt to bring down Glux as he flew directly overhead that led to Jorb's demise. His acidic spew missed the insectoid and came splashing down on his own face. Jorb, writhing in agony at the pain caused by his own venom, screamed his submission and was escorted from the tournament immediately.

In the longest bout of the opening round, Gha, the Gurlfian Goother Rat, met up with Jin-Jin-Jin, the Globuloid from Hobunk Alpha. Gha's flail did little damage to the surprisingly quick-moving mound of shapeless goo. Conversely, Jin-Jin-Jin's attempts to capture and squeeze the fleet-footed rodent into a premature death were futile. The match was so heated and hotly contested that it spilled out of the arena and into the locker room. The brawlers knocked down lockers and reporters and anything else that got in their way. The producer's legion of cameras caught every moment of the heart-stopping contest. It raged on, leaving the back room and heading out into the streets and exhibition area. The pair battled through concessions stands, kiosks selling memorabilia commemorating the event, and sponsors' booths hyping the latest and greatest in their respective industries. It was in one of the sponsors' stalls that the duel reached its dramatic conclusion. Jin-Jin-Jin managed to catch Gha in his nebulous clutches after the Gurlfian slipped on a puddle of nacho cheese sauce. He hurled Gha over a Psitakki military recruitment table, passed a stand stocked with souvenir shields, and into the side of one of the Willie's World of Galactic Winnebagos showroom floor models. The collision rocked the massive vehicle and almost tipped it over. Gha retreated into the Winnebago, seemingly to collect his thoughts and reevaluate his strategy against the fighter from Hobunk Alpha. Jin-Jin-Jin followed. The exact details of what happened next were known only to the two competitors. Inside a Winnebago in the exhibit hall adjacent to the arena had not been on the producer's list of areas to station a camera. After some shaking within the automobile, Gha emerged, raising his hand in victory. The Psitakki referee entered the vehicle and, after some moments surveying, returned and declared the Goother Rat the victor. The violent thuds and thumps coming from the vehicle's septic receptacle laid to rest any concerns that the claims of the flushing prowess of Willie's World of Galactic Winnebagos were anything less than one hundred percent accurate.

It had to be the tournament's first ever victory by flushing, thought Duke.

Duke turned from the screen to catch a glimpse of the producer hurrying by his room. The bounty hunter shot his head out of the door. "Hey!" he screamed.

The producer stopped in his tracks, turned around, and sent a menacing gaze towards Duke.

"What, Mr. LaGrange?" he barked.

"It's almost time for my match. Any updates on my opponent?"

The Psitakki didn't answer. He threw his hands in the air and scurried off, presumably to do something more important. Duke heard a faint mumbling about Winnebagos as the producer stormed away.

"Looks like we still don't know if I have to actually fight anyone tonight," complained Duke. "Ish, who's up next?"

Ishiro'shea made a face that could only mean one thing. *Maxx Gemstarr*.

The crowd was still restless after the last match had ended up leaving the actual arena. Given the prices that tickets fetched, the vibe in the arena was trending towards disappointment. Then the festering malaise simply stopped. Dead in its tracks, it stopped. Wonder, excitement, and unadulterated joy regained control over the collective in mere seconds.

That damn music. I hate that damn music. And those lasers.

There was no denying that Gemstarr knew how to make an entrance. He was a showman. Duke would argue that he wasn't much of an actual bounty hunter in practice, but he was great at marketing himself.

The crowd was rocking. The entire building felt as if it was moving off its foundation and rolling along the Psitakki countryside. Maxx ate it up. He motioned to each part of the arena, elevating the volume of their cheers to a fever pitch. He made victorious gestures, flexed his impressive muscles, and pointed to his power gauntlets. Each carefully planned movement received a bigger ovation than the one before. Duke was disgusted.

The Grand Blademaster of Gyork was shocked when he stepped out in front of the audience and was pelted with a loud chorus of boos and derogatory chants. He seemed visibly rattled by the reception. The swordsman flashed the two steel blades surgically implanted to the top of his hand, and started to taunt the crowd. They screamed louder and louder. He then drew his two shining broadswords from each thigh and raised them above his head. The two sets of blades, one set in his hands and the other *in* his hands, formed an "L" at the end of each arm. In response to this impressive display, trash and bottles rained down on the Gyorkian. Most ricocheted off without any damage, but a tub of piping hot nachos landed square on his face. Duke wondered if it was from the same batch that almost cost the Goother Rat his bout against Jin-Jin-Jin. The crowd broke into laughter as the Blademaster dropped his swords and stumbled about in panic.

The horns sounded and the match officially began. Maxx Gemstarr leapt in front of the Gyorkian and connected squarely with his power gauntlet to the swordsman's chest. He flew back across the arena and crashed into the retaining wall. Even before the referee could call the match in favor of Maxx, he was celebrating in the first row celebrity boxes, shaking hands and posing for photographs.

The loudspeaker rang out: "Maxx Gemstarr has just set a new tournament record for the quickest victory—ten seconds."

Maxx's iconic theme music filled the arena as what seemed like the entire planet cheered uncontrollably.

I really hate that guy.

Maxx's music halted suddenly. A familiar voice echoed throughout.

"Who gave that guy a mic?" Duke asked his ninja friend.

"Congratulations, Maxx Gemstarr," Prince Korzo-Tapor shouted to all those in the arena. "Impressive indeed. A new record, I hear. However, my friend, records are made to be broken, even brand new ones. And I guarantee that we will break this record. Now."

The audience was trying to digest both the interruption by the Jungafallowian prince and his bold claim.

"Ten seconds," he began, "is quite jaw-dropping. But eight seconds is even more magnificent. Am I right? My Combatant 2 will accomplish this feat against our opponent, or..."

"Or what?" shouted Maxx Gemstarr from the front row.

"Ah, Mr. Gemstarr, if we fail, we will forfeit."

The buzz in the stands was deafening. No one knew what to make of the enigmatic royal.

Combatant 2 stomped in to thunderous boos. His position as the most hated entity on Psitakki had been all but settled when he had taken out Gjrazzel during the Grand Entrance. Now, it appeared he was trying to become the most hated entity in the entire universe by upstaging Maxx Gemstarr.

"Of course, the bet is off if our opponent doesn't show," the devious prince stated. "I haven't seen the Olamandrian weakling since my friend here laid waste to that worthless squid."

An avalanche of refuse spilled down on the massive Jungafallowian. He didn't even notice it.

"You simpletons are putting up a better fight than our original opponent would have anyways," the prince continued. "Is that the best you got? Trash? Garbage? I guess it's befitting of Psitakki. Nothing but a bunch of swamp-dwelling pieces of trash."

The crowd erupted as Kitar busted through a holding cell door and charged directly at Combatant 2. He was coiled, with his spikes exposed, and rolling at breakneck speed towards the two-headed brute. The horn sounded as he approached the Jungafallowian and catapulted his spinning body—a living saw blade. Combatant 2 threw out his right hand and connected with the Olamandrian's body. Kitar collapsed and fell limp, sprawled out on the arena floor at the gargantuan creature's feet. The referee signaled the end of the round.

"Ladies and gentlemen, we have a new tournament record. Combatant 2 has defeated Kitar in six seconds."

The crowd was stunned. Not a single murmur could be heard amidst the thousands in attendance.

"Like I said, records are made to be broken," Korzo-

Tapor began. "Except this new one, maybe." He walked over to Kitar and kicked his paralyzed body. "Get this off of our arena floor."

Three referees ran over to drag the Olamandrian away.

"Your new champion. Fear him. Marvel at him. Worship him. He will not be stopped!" Korzo-Tapor's maniacal laugh permeated throughout the stadium. When it stopped there was an eerie silence. Nobody in the audience could argue with what they had just witnessed.

Duke looked at Ishiro'shea.

"How are we going to beat that thing? How's *anyone* going to beat that thing?"

The ninja shrugged.

Well, shit.

CHAPTER SEVENTEEN

FIGHT OR FUNERAL

"Y OU'RE UP NEXT, LAGRANGE," SHOUTED
the producer.

"So, wait. I'm fighting? Gjrazzel's recovered?"

"Sure, I guess. Probably. I'm just shooting whatever happens out there, so if it's a fight or a funeral, it's going to be broadcast across the universe," the Psitakki snarked. "A funeral would be sure to mix it up a bit."

"How respectful."

"Just be ready. When your name is called, follow this lighted pathway to the stadium entrance. When the big door opens..."

"Let me guess. Walk through it."

"I forgot that I'm dealing with a certified genius," jabbed the producer. "And you over there?"

Ishiro'shea did not acknowledge the Psitakki's finger pointed in his direction.

"What about Ishiro?"

"He's your corner man, right?"

"Yep."

"Right outside the door, there are a few steps that lead

to a platform. He can watch the fight from there and throw in the towel if needed."

"That won't be necessary."

"You're right, you'll probably just die."

Duke wanted to respond with a witty line, but his mind was entirely blank.

The producer huffed. "Lights. Path. Door. Fight."

"Got it," Duke replied.

"And, for the love of the Colossal Calamari, try and do something that's interesting. You won't have a flammable Blop to save you this time around."

The producer stormed off, barking orders at any being he passed until he disappeared into the depths of the stadium catacombs.

The bounty hunter turned to Ishiro'shea. "Gotta give credit to Gjrazzel. He's a tough bastard to try and fight after what that Jungafallowian did to him." Duke paused. "So, any plans spring to mind? I probably should have a strategy going into this thing. To be honest, Ish, I sorta didn't think Gjrazzel would bounce back so quickly."

Ishiro'shea pondered.

"If I win, who do we fight next?"

Ishiro'shea flapped his arms, simulating wings.

"Ah, the bug. Great. A stick-twirling squid, then a giant bee-man with a double-sided halberd. Did I mention how much I hate this tournament?"

The crowd had been silent following the massacre caused by Prince Korzo-Tapor's Combatant 2. Now they began to collect themselves and isolated cheers began to swell from the arena. In short order, it was clear that they were ready for the next and final fight of the evening. Most importantly, they were ready to see if their local hero had recovered enough to wage mortal war against the long-shot melee winner for the honor of Psitakki.

The cries of "Gjrazzel" rang out. The speaker crackled and a booming voice proclaimed, "First combatant in our final fight, from Nova Texas, Duke LaGrog, a bounty hunter."

"It's LaGrange!" Duke screamed as he walked out to the loudest jeers of the tournament. "How hard is that to remember? LaGrange! You get Glux Xyphormog's name right every time. C'mon!"

Debris fell from the rafters to line the arena floor. Duke ducked and swerved to avoid being struck by stray bottles or bricks.

The announcer began again. "And now, from right here on Psitakki, our grand champion and a direct descendant of Grozzel the Great, the master of the tarzantia tree staff, our hero, our hope, the greatest being in the universe, Gjrazzel!"

The collective adulation was almost sonic; Duke had to focus to keep his balance as the decibel level reached a point that would burst many an eardrum. Gjrazzel did not make his way out.

The crowd grew louder. And louder. Then it started to subside, turning to a hopeless clamor that verged on becoming entirely pitiful. Emerging from the dark, limping noticeably, was the brave Psitakki champion. His tarzantia staff was being used as a crutch. His head and left eye were bandaged. A brace covered his back and waist; he was barely able to move. But he approached Duke with an unwavering determination. *He's going to try and fight*, realized the Nova Texan. *He's actually going to try and fight. Holy hedgehogs.*

The referee met the two combatants in the center of the arena. He looked over Gjrazzel. Then Duke.

He's going to let us fight. This officiating bastard is going to let this half-dead guy fight.

"You probably know the rules," the referee began,

"but, just in case, there aren't really any rules outside of no guns or projectiles. Or magic." He locked eyes with Duke. "No guns, okay? No matter how bad it's going. Just give up if you are getting beat to a pulp. Do not use a gun."

"I got it," snapped Duke.

"I know how you Earthers like to use guns," the referee continued.

"I'm not from Earth. I'm from Nova Texas. Do you not listen to the damn introductions?"

"I want a clean fight. No, I just want an exciting fight. So go crazy."

Duke turned his attention to Gjrazzel. He had to be heavily medicated; his eyes were glassy and vacant, a sliver of drool dripped from the right corner of his mouth and off one of his upper lip tentacles.

"Man, you don't have to do this," Duke pleaded. "You're in no condition to fight."

Gjrazzel just grumbled a particularly gurgly grumble.

"Seriously, it's not your fault. You're going to get yourself killed."

"Am I?" Gjrazzel replied softly. "Or is it you, Duke LaGrand, that's going to get killed?"

Why is this so confusing?

"It's LaGrange," he said in a defeated tone. As the last syllable passed Duke's lips, Gjrazzel hoisted himself into the air, supported by his tarzantia tree staff, and struck the bounty hunter with a left thrust kick to the upper chest. Duke stumbled back and fell to one knee.

The horn sounded.

Gjrazzel hopped towards him and repeated the same maneuver. The second kick knocked Duke to the arena floor. A third sent him crashing into the perimeter wall, where he crumpled to his backside.

"Whoa, there, Gjrazzel," Duke yelled. "I'm not going to fight you. You can barely walk."

"Then this makes your current predicament even more embarrassing."

Duke didn't disagree. Nor did the fans. Their hurrahs turned into laughter.

As Duke got to his feet, Gjrazzel approached and, for a fourth time, catapulted himself in the air. However, instead of kicking the bounty hunter, he wrapped his legs around Duke's neck. He tightened his grip. Duke struggled. Gasps of air were becoming increasingly difficult to obtain. His vision grew blurry.

Duke heard a voice. A female voice. It was telling him to hold on. It was then yelling Ishiro'shea's name. And Ol' Betsy's name. This struck Duke as odd. He always envisioned that the last words that he heard would be female but they wouldn't be screaming at Ishiro'shea and his gun. He opened his eyes and he saw Mazilda shouting something at Ishiro'shea.

She wants him to shoot Gjrazzel, Duke thought.

"No," the bounty hunter screamed in a muffled and indistinguishable bellow.

Ishiro'shea locked eyes with the bounty hunter and threw Ol' Betsy at him. It was a perfect toss. Duke caught it by the barrel and swung it at the tarzantia tree staff. It fell to the ground, along with its owner. Gjrazzel released his legs from Duke's throat. Duke choked as he tried to regain normal breathing.

Gjrazzel slowly made his way to his feet and picked up the staff. He swung it wildly, but Duke ducked and it crashed into the perimeter wall. By reflex alone, Duke stabbed the butt end of Ol' Betsy at Gjrazzel, connecting flush with his jaw. The cracking sound echoed through the arena.

Gjrazzel staggered and collapsed. The arena fell silent.

A noiseless hysteria was building within the arena. Duke could feel it. He didn't like it.

From the other side of the stadium, a diminutive figure stormed at Duke. As he drew nearer, his identity became clear. It was Gjrazzel's trainer.

Not this guy again.

His screaming became more intelligible as he approached. "Disqualify him! He used a gun! Guns are outlawed!"

The crowd recognized the possible loophole and many started fervently supporting the claims with boisterous chants. It was clear that Duke knocking out the courageous local hero was not the desired outcome of the masses. And the masses started to jump the barricade and spill onto the arena floor.

Not good.

The huddled mass moved towards the bounty hunter with hate and murder in their eyes. Duke was frozen.

He felt both of his arms tightly pinned and his body pulled backwards. He was hurled into the entryway, back first. Ishiro'shea grabbed Ol' Betsy and aimed it at the horde of attackers. He didn't shoot, but it slowed them enough for Mazilda to hit a button on the side wall, closing the door.

"Did I win?"

"I think so. But you aren't going to be a crowd favorite anytime soon," replied Mazilda.

CHAPTER EIGHTEEN

GOOD CONVERSATION

"MR. LAGRANGE, I CAN'T LET you in. I'm
sorry."

"And why is that?"

"Because these folks will want to kill you after what
happened at the arena," answered the barkeep at the Pondscum Tavern. "I just can't let you in."

"So, kid, you want to be known as the guy that refused
service to the first ever being to not only survive, but win a
match in this holiest of holy tournaments after escaping
from the melee?"

The Psitakki pondered this for a minute.

"Yes, but..."

"Never mind. I'll find somewhere else," replied Duke.

"There aren't any other bars, Mr. LaGrange. This
is it."

"I will find someone willing to give me a drink. And I'll
be sure to mention how you slandered the good name of
Grozzel the Great by turning away someone who risks his
life in the name of that great Psitakki warrior. I wouldn't be
surprised if you get a few reporters in here asking some

tough, hard-hitting questions before the night's done. Good luck."

Duke and Ishiro'shea turned around and slowly walked away from the tavern's entrance.

"Wait! Hold up!"

Duke paused, then pivoted to face the young bartender.

"Yes?" he asked, barely able to conceal a mischievous smirk.

"I have an idea."

"And that would be?"

"We have a back room. I'll bring you drinks personally. Just don't tell any reporters, okay? I won't tell the patrons that you're here, there won't be a ruckus, and you will get your drinks."

"I'm assuming they're on the house for this trouble that you've put us through and how I'm basically a celebrity now."

The bartender was visibly flustered. It was obvious that he wasn't used to beings like Duke LaGrange.

"I will see what I can do."

"And one more thing."

"Yes?"

"If Seamus O'Hoolihan comes in... You know him, right?"

"Yes, Mr. LaGrange. Potato Lips."

"Yes, Potato Lips. If he comes in, tell him to meet us in the back room. I want to talk to him. And the drinks will be on me. Well, I guess they will be on you. But you get the idea."

"What if he says no?"

"He's Irish. He won't turn down a free round."

"Yes, Mr. LaGrange, I will let him know. And let's get you to the private room before the crowd really starts to pour in. Follow me."

After traversing winding back hallways, dimly lit and smelling of exotic booze, Duke and Ishiro'shea entered a compact, square room. It was lit by torches and a single gas light fixture that hung from the center of the ceiling. The room was cool and draughty, but comfortable. There were a few barrels along the edge of the wall and a wooden bar in one corner.

"Please have a seat," said the bartender.

He bounced to the corner and opened up a barrel. He snatched two glasses from the counter of the wooden bar and scooped them into the barrel. They emerged with a glorious golden liquid.

Glyptodian Summer Ale.

"Why have you been hiding this from us? Who needs Light of God when you have the refreshing, full-bodied delight that is Glyptodian Summer Ale?"

Duke could see Ishiro'shea's smile from behind his mask.

"I thought that you might like it," said the bartender. "I hear it's quite popular in other parts of the universe. It's not a big seller here."

"Are all of these barrels full of it?"

"Yes."

"Looks like we won't be needing your services tonight. Just leave us to the beer and our own company."

The Psitakki exited the private drinking cellar.

"Things are starting to look up, Ish. Glyptodian Summer Ale, avoiding unnecessary skirmishes with locals, and—if we're lucky—a chance to ask Seamus a few questions about your parents and that photo."

Ishiro'shea raised his mug and the two clinked glasses.

The ale slid down Duke's throat, seeming to touch every part of his insides. He couldn't help but think about Cyborg Joe's.

"Reminds me of home."

"Get out of my way, boy," Prince Korzo-Tapor sneered as he pushed the Psitakki bartender away from the doorway.

"I'm sorry, Mr. LaGrange," the barkeeper stammered. "I told him that he couldn't come back here, but he—"

"It's fine," said Duke. "At least I know that the prince here isn't mad at me for beating Gjrazzel."

"Very true, Duke. It was quite an impressive win. I mean, it was impressive if you look beyond the fact that Gjrazzel was partially blind, couldn't stand on his own accord, and he was significantly concussed. But, hey, a win is a win."

"Thanks."

The Jungafallowian bowed.

"What do you want?"

"It seems that, like you, I'm not the most revered being on this rock. I just wanted to have a few drinks without being harassed. I had a feeling that you were in the same boat."

Duke huffed.

"Fine, what can it hurt?"

"That's the spirit, old boy. Oh, is that Glyptodian Summer Ale?"

Duke grimaced. "No, it's some local sludge. I would just order something from the bar."

The prince leapt over and grabbed Duke's mug in one seamless motion. Both reptiloid heads converged on the glass and took a whiff of its distinct aroma.

"I'm disappointed, Duke. I thought you would have recognized that this is Glyptodian. It's pretty apparent."

"I guess I'm a bit rusty," Duke said dejectedly.

"I love this vintage. Bartender, go fetch me two glasses. I think I will stick to the same stuff as Duke and Ishiro'shea here."

The Psitakki bartender left the room and returned moments later with two empty glasses for the prince. He walked over to the barrel and scooped ale until both mugs were overflowing with the golden liquid.

"Now run along, boy," the prince said condescendingly.

"What do you want? Really," asked Duke.

"Why do I have to *want* anything? Outside of good drink and good conversation with good company, of course."

Duke rolled his eyes. Then he grinned.

"Fine then, Prince. I have a question for you. You know, just regular ol' conversation between friends."

"Go ahead."

"What was the attack on Gjrazzel all about?"

"I thought you would appreciate that unfortunate event."

"It was a pretty underhanded move, if you ask me."

"I don't remember needing to ask you, Duke. But I had my reasons. It was not unprovoked."

"Really?" Duke asked. "Gjrazzel didn't strike me as someone that would get involved with any extracurricular activities, especially before the biggest day of his life."

The prince didn't answer right away. He seemed to be planning how he was going to respond to Duke's question. "He was being somewhat..."

"Yes?" interjected Duke impatiently.

"...snoopy."

"About what?"

"I think that falls outside of the realm of good conversation."

Duke opened his mouth to respond, but the memory of Gjrazzel asking about the whereabouts of Korzo-Tapor and if he was somehow involved with him crept into his mind.

Is the prince telling the truth? There's definitely a connection.

"Fair point, Prince. So, answer me this."

"Yes?"

"Why are you here? Why are you, well, why is your pet project, fighting in this tournament?"

The prince chuckled. "Surely you are aware of our fighting reputation on Jungafallow III, Duke? If I recall, didn't you pick a fight with two overly eager Death Robots fans back at Joe's about a month or so ago? I believe it was the prelude to our first encounter."

"Okay, so you like to fight. Once again, not you, but your friend."

"Naturally. I find physical altercations to be somewhat primitive and undignified. And illogical. That doesn't mean that I don't like to watch them, however. We all have our guilty pleasures."

"So this whole ordeal is just in the name of Jungafallowian pride and your weird fetish?"

"Yes. And don't forget ego. I like to be a winner."

"Sorry, K. T., I'm not buying it. Not one bit."

The Korzo head took a big sip. The Tapor head followed suit. They both turned inward and eyeballed each other, as if discussing telepathically what to say next. To Duke's knowledge, Jungafallowians had no such ability, but when you share the same body for dozens of cycles, it's likely some silent language develops naturally between heads.

"Let's say you're correct, LaGrange, and I'm here for some alternative and sinister reasons."

"Fine, I'm correct."

"Cute. Why would I ever tell you? You, after all, are a

sworn enemy to the Trampling Death Robots—a band, nay, a cultural phenomenon that I hold in high esteem. You are a bounty hunter and, despite the recent legal hurdles around that particular trade, it's still a profession with which someone like myself tends not to get too close and snuggly. Lastly, you are a participant in this noble tournament and, no matter how improbable, it's not impossible that you will face my precious Combatant 2 in the finals. Should I go on?"

It was Duke's turn to take an elongated sip of Summer ale. He turned to Ishiro'shea. He could sense that the prince knew they were mocking him. "Yes, please go on."

The prince appeared shocked by Duke's response.

"Let me think," he began.

"What about your boss?" interrupted the bounty hunter.

"My boss?"

"The good Admiral. Lothario LePaco. The scourge of the cosmos."

The snarky and pretentious expression that Korzo-Tapor wore on both of his faces became nondescript blankness. His right arm lowered from the table and out of view of the bounty hunting duo.

"I'm not sure I know what you mean," said the prince unconvincingly.

"Princey, c'mon. We've seen the tattoo. We know you are working for LePaco. And it's my keen assumption that he has more to do with you being here with this overgrown monstrosity than the spirit of competition."

Duke leaned back in his chair and folded his arms behind his head. He smiled a victorious "caught you red-handed" type of grin.

"I give it to you, Duke LaGrange," Korzo-Tapor began submissively, "you have seen through my ruse."

"You probably should have covered up the ink, man."

"I wasn't expecting anyone here to know the mark."

"Really? It's LePaco. He's probably the most known super criminal in the universe."

"Yes, but only those 'in the know' would have any clue about what this tattoo means—law enforcement at the senior levels only, other criminals, and..."

"Bounty hunters," Duke said, finishing the sentence.

"Yes. Most of them, at least. I'm not sure Gemstarr knows. He is, after all, a bounty hunter in name only."

"And an asshole in practice."

"Are you not a fan of his work?"

"Stop changing the subject, Prince. You're working for LePaco, fine. So are a billion other degenerates. But why did he send you here? Why does he care about this tournament? It has to be important for you to publicly humiliate Gjrazzel. That's a message if I ever saw one."

Prince Korzo-Tapor stood up and headed over to the barrels containing the Summer ale. He pushed them aside and peered behind the makeshift bar in the corner.

"I'm looking for something a bit stronger."

Got him right where I want him, thought Duke.

"Nothing," the prince said sullenly. "This will have to do."

He dropped both mugs into the barrel and pulled out another round of beer. He sat back down.

"I don't know why I'm telling you this."

"Because you know that if you don't, Ishiro'shea and I will make it our primary mission to find out what LePaco's up to, and likely cause more harm to you than if you flat-out told us."

"There's some logic in that statement. Somewhere."

"And I know LePaco, so this plan is probably so far in

motion that telling me won't even make a bit of difference," Duke said in a bit of blatant ego-stroking.

"I wasn't expecting you to give my boss so much credit."

"Look, I hate the guy. I would introduce him to the business end of Ol' Betsy if given a chance—but he's the greatest criminal that I've ever seen. I'm not going to bring him to justice by figuring out some side job scheme on Psitakki. No offense."

"None taken," replied the prince.

"So call me intrigued. I'll get my shot at the admiral one of these days. I don't think this is it. You satisfying my curiosity about your mission for the admiral, in exchange for Ishiro and I staying out of your business regarding said mission."

The Jungafallowian royal seemed to relax. He downed both mugs of beer in single gulps. The Korzo head's eyes shrank as he leaned in.

"LePaco's been out of commission for some time, right?"

"Yes, he was running the risk of being a ghost in our trade. He was a few steps away from being nothing but a legend," replied Duke.

"Let's just say that he felt that he was having some trust issues within his inner circle," said the Korzo head.

"Paranoia?"

"I don't know. I wouldn't classify myself as inner circle. But maybe a little. So he decided to take a break to revamp his network. Rebuild, or refortify in this case, his empire. And he needed to start with the muscle."

"Believable, so far."

"We did some experiments on... let's call them the 'fringe' of Jungafallowian III society."

"There's a joke to be had, but for the sake of the story, I'll refrain," Duke quipped.

"Much obliged," the prince acknowledged. "The results

were a mixed bag but then we found our star pupil, Combatant 2. He was bigger, stronger, and more obedient than all of the others. We sent him in the middle of a Trampling Death Robots fan convention with a shirt that read 'I've Heard Better Music in Elevators than at a Trampling Death Robots Concert.'"

"Don't get me started on elevator music," Duke replied, thinking of his long overdue project on the *Deus*.

"As you can guess, the thousands of die-hard TDR fanatics rushed Combatant 2 without thinking twice."

"What happened?"

"He single-handedly disposed of them all. The first ten or fifteen went down in a flash and the rest ran away. It was a roaring success."

"And so why bring him here? He passed your test. LePaco should have been happy with that."

"I'm not the admiral, so this next part is conjecture."

"Sure."

"The admiral wants everyone to know what he has under his employ. If Combatant 2 wins the Tournament of the Whatever It Is—and we have thousands of these enforcers across the universe—people will tend not to be as quick to double-cross or try and pull one over on the admiral."

"He's advertising his newfound power."

"In the most delicate and subtle way, of course," the prince added. "The Gjrazzel episode just added to our reputation."

"And if Combatant 2 loses?"

The Tapor head belted out a laugh that echoed throughout the secret drinking den. The Korzo head simply smiled.

"We don't think that will be an issue. We are quite confident..."

"Hey, there you are," chimed in a female voice from the doorway.

"Mazilda, what are you doing here?" asked Duke.

She paused and sneered at the Jungafallowian.

"What is *he* doing here?" she asked aggressively. "The company you're keeping has really gone downhill."

"An upgrade from you, my dear, there is no doubt," said the prince with a sneer. "And how is your new boyfriend, Gemstarr? Any new poses that he's practicing and planning to break out in the tournament? Or is he at his intellectual limit for flexing routines? I'm shocked he has time to take another girlfriend. I hope his mirror isn't jealous."

A laugh slipped through Duke's defenses. Mazilda treated him to a glance as piercing as any of her throwing daggers.

"Come sit down, Mazilda," offered Duke. "The prince has been sharing some interesting tidbits."

"I would rather—" began Mazilda.

"No need to finish that sentence, Miss Cloax. I was just finishing up my chat with Duke and Ishiro'shea and then I need to check in on Combatant 2. We need to strategize for our next big matchup with that Earth mutant."

The prince stood up and bowed disingenuously to Mazilda. She did not reciprocate the gesture.

"Thank you for the good drinks and good conversation, Duke. I hope to do this again soon," the prince said as he exited the room.

Mazilda sat down in the chair recently occupied by the Jungafallowian. She pounded her fists on the table, knocking over one of the empty glass mugs. "What was that about?"

"The prince was feeding us some garbage about why LePaco sent him here."

"Admiral LePaco?"

CHAPTER NINETEEN

PO-TAY-TO, PO-TAH-TO

"HE DOES APPEAR TO BE holding something back," Mazilda began, "and it's no surprise. He's a murderous reprobate that would sell out his own mother for a few extra seconds of power and a boost to his bank account."

"No arguments there," replied Duke.

"But what do you think he's hiding?"

"No idea. I have a feeling Gjrazzel knew something."

"The Psitakki?"

"Yes, the prince said he was being 'snoopy.' For some reason, I think he regretted telling us that part. I think Gjrazzel was on to his game, whatever that game is."

"What are you going to do now?"

"Nothing," Duke replied matter-of-factly.

"What?"

"I'm not here to deal with anything LePaco has cooking. I'm sure I'll have a chance at him real soon but, for now, based on what you shared with us, this tournament is about two things. Number one... staying alive."

"Number two?"

"Finding out about Ishiro's parents."

At this, the ninja perked up from his alcohol-induced trance. He raised his empty glass.

"Cheers, Ish. We'll find them. I made Seamus an offer he can't refuse."

"And what was that?" asked Mazilda.

"A free round."

"What makes you think he's going to even come into the Pondscum Tavern on the eve of his fight with Combatant 2?"

Duke smiled and kicked back once again in his chair.

"Oh, Mazilda. He's Irish."

"That's playing to stereotypes a bit."

Duke nodded his head in Ishiro'shea's general direction.

"It's still insensitive," Mazilda added.

"But most importantly, he's about to have to face that Jungafallowian science experiment. What else would one do with that looming in front of 'em?"

Mazilda pondered this for a moment, then seemed to submit to Duke's logic.

"Oh, by the way," started Duke, "to what do we owe the pleasure of your company this evening? And without the galaxy's favorite bounty hunter, nonetheless."

"The *universe's* favorite bounty hunter," Mazilda jabbed back.

"Right."

"Honestly, I thought you could use a little help. Do you know anything about your next opponent?"

"Yes, I do actually. Quite a lot, in fact."

"I'm all ears," Mazilda replied.

"He can fly."

"Great."

A booming voice redirected their attention to the door. The Psitakki bartender was already a few paces into the room; the voice didn't belong to him. No, it was a hulking brute of a man. More accurately, a hulking brute of a mutant man.

"Howya. What's the story here? I'm trying to get fluthered off this purple stuff and this eejit fella tells me someone's offering to buy me a few rounds. He takes me down to this kip of a room and now I sees you lot. What ya' playing at? Not codding me, eh?"

Duke looked at Mazilda in confusion.

"You understand that, Ishiro?" asked Duke.

The ninja shrugged.

"I mean you *are* half Irish, right?" questioned Duke.

Seamus "Potato Lips" O'Hoolihan wasn't the easiest person to understand. Duke surmised that much of this was due to the unusual mutation that caused his lips to balloon to the size of, well, potatoes. But giant lips or no giant lips, Duke didn't have the faintest clue what O'Hoolihan was saying.

"Come again, Mr. Lips?" asked the bounty hunter.

"I said..." Seamus started.

"He asked what do you want," said the Psitakki barkeep.

"Yeah, wut he said," Seamus agreed.

Duke looked to his half-Irish sidekick. Ishiro'shea concurred with the Psitakki's interpretation.

"Have a seat, please. I promised you some booze and I shall deliver."

"Got any of the black stuff?"

"Black stuff?"

"I take it that he means a local stout from his native land," chimed in the Psitakki. "Do you want me to stay and translate?"

"We got this, I'm sure you have customers that need that purple junk," snapped Duke.

"That purple drink is right manky. It will get you locked, no doubt, but it sent me to the jacks for two whole days. Know wut I mean?"

"I..." Duke stuttered, "...do not. But I'm sure I'll figure it out with some context clues in due time."

The Psitakki rolled his eyes and exited.

"It's not your black stuff but this ain't half bad," Duke said pointing to the barrels of Glyptodian Summer Ale. "Ever been to Cyborg Joe's?"

"No, but I knows of it. Everyone does. Best place in the Andromeda to get totally landers when you're out on the tear, I hear. Up to your neck in floozies, from what I've been told."

Duke stood up and grabbed an empty mug from the corner bar. He inspected it to make sure it wasn't covered in too much grime.

Clean enough, Duke concluded. He dipped it in the barrel of Glyptodian Summer Ale.

"Well, this stuff is a best seller."

Duke slid the glass along the table and it halted in front of the Irish mutant. He downed the entire beer in one gulp, then wiped his mouth with his forearm.

"Not bad. A female's drink but it'll do for now, as long as it's free."

"What is that supposed to mean?" Mazilda snapped.

"It lacks a man's strength."

The female bounty hunter stood up rapidly, knocking her chair to the ground.

"Come again, you drunk..."

"Sit down, Mazilda. We don't invite people in and then insult them," Duke said, trying to extinguish the potentially flammable situation.

"I didn't invite this buffoon in. You did."

Seamus remained sitting in his chair, unfazed by Mazilda's show of aggression. Ishiro'shea slid the refilled mug back in front of O'Hoolihan, who smiled and nodded to the ninja.

"The reason we asked you here has nothing to do with the tournament at hand," said Duke. "I know you have a big fight tomorrow with the Jungafallowian, so we won't keep you long."

Seamus' eyes widened as if he had totally forgotten about his opponent in the next round.

"See, my dear friend here," Duke began, "is Ishiro'shea."

The Irish mutant did not react. After a few moments of awkward silence, he simply shrugged.

"Ishiro'shea. *The* Ishiro'shea."

Seamus's expression of ignorance didn't change.

"The two people that you are looking for, those are his parents."

"I don't have any idea what you're talking about. You are codding me, aren't ya?"

"We know you're looking for them. *Why* are you looking for them? And where are they?"

Seamus stood up and slammed his mug down on the table. "Look, I don't know what you're talking about. Alright? I'm here to win this tournament. Not find anyone's parents."

As he turned to exit the room, Mazilda was already at the door and slammed it shut.

"Does this look familiar?"

Seamus seemed to recognize the photo immediately.

"How'd you get that?"

"It doesn't matter," said Mazilda. "What do you know about these two?"

"You're telling me that this little guy over there is their son? You must think that I'm not the full shilling."

"He is," added Duke. "He is a descendant of the

Nobunaga clan on his mother's side. His father is, well, 'The Father.'"

"No way."

When Mazilda turned around, her face was mere inches from Seamus'. One of her trusty blades was close enough to shave his amber beard clean off.

"Put that away!" Duke screamed. "Sorry, Seamus."

"You heard what he said, lass. Best not be pissin' me off."

"Is that so?"

Without so much as a sound, Ishiro'shea placed himself between Mazilda and the Irish mutant, defusing the situation.

"Seamus, I swear to Nova Texas that he is," said Duke. "He's taken a vow of silence until he finds them again. They shipped him off when he was a young boy, to avoid the conflict."

"If this was true, which I don't believe, but say it were true, why do you think I'm tracking them down?"

"Really?" asked Mazilda, shaking her head. "We have your damn photos, you drunk bastard."

"That doesn't prove anything," Seamus argued, his arms folded in defiance. He sat down and finished off the rest of his beer.

At least he's not trying to leave, thought Duke. *Maybe we can get something out of this conversation yet.*

"Seamus, can we move past this? We know you're looking for them. Why?"

"Let's pretend that I am looking for these two people."

"Okay, we'll pretend."

"Great. I'm not looking for them both."

"You aren't?" asked Mazilda.

"No, not as such. I'm looking for—" Seamus caught himself. "—assuming we're still pretending and all, that is?"

"Yes."

"I'm looking for the man."

"The Father?"

"Yes, the Father. His bird is just trash that's in our way. The Father—we know this to be true, mind you—was corrupted by this demon witch here and brainwashed. I'm going to save him."

Duke looked over at Ishiro'shea. He could tell that the ninja was boiling internally at the thought of a mutant calling his mother a 'demon witch.' Duke motioned to him to calm down. He acquiesced.

They were all sitting at the table now, and a calmness permeated through the gathering for the first time.

"So, your aim is to bring back the Father to Earth and try and un-brainwash him?" asked Duke.

"Yes. He was our greatest leader. A man of God but also a man of war. Brilliant he was. He is. I hope he is still, that is."

"But why this tournament?" asked Mazilda eagerly. "If they're out there in the cosmos and you have this photo, why are you here instead of there?"

O'Hoolihan stewed on this question for a while. He looked around as if his interrogators had the answer hidden on their faces. His face became as red as his hair. "That's for my own knowin'. I think I'm done here."

"What?" cried Duke.

"I'm done. I'm not even sure why I told you as much as I did." He glanced at Mazilda. "Oh yeah, 'cause that floozie held a knife to my throat."

Mazilda reached for her dagger again, but Ishiro'shea grabbed her arm in mid-motion to halt the action. Seamus nodded at Ishiro'shea in a sign of thanks.

"It's about leavin' time for me. Thanks for the woman's brew."

"But we can help you," Duke shouted in a last-ditch effort.

The monstrous mutant slowly turned his misshapen face around and glared at the bounty hunter. "And how are you going to help me? You, obviously, don't have nothin' that I don't... Just my photograph that you stole. You aren't any closer to understandin' where it was taken than I am. Besides, your reasons for trackin' them don't line up with mine. Those aren't ideal partnerin' conditions, if you ask me."

"True. But we have something that you don't."

"And what's that?"

"Bait."

Seamus' eyes swelled. He opened his mouth to speak, then promptly closed it.

Is he... thinking? Duke wondered.

"Bait, you say?"

"Their long-lost child. Instead of you tracking them down, this could potentially help them come to you. Assuming the word gets to them. I'm sure that you have some channels to help spread this enticing nugget of information. If they've been so good at hiding, they've got to be tapping into some back alley, seedy underbelly types. Those folks tend to pick up all of the information and sift through it until they find something profitable. This has profitability written all over it."

"If it works and they get wind of their son and, let's say, they find me..."

"Us," corrected Duke.

"They find us," Seamus said with a grimace. "What then? How do I get what I want and you get what you want?"

"All that we want is for Ishiro'shea to be reunited with his parents. I don't see how that conflicts with your goals."

"What if he wants to defend his banshee of a mother?"

"If she's as awful as you say she is, Ishiro'shea will see it too. Maybe she was the reason that he was cast aside and removed from his home. His presence might just strengthen the Father's conviction and help you."

Duke knew his argument was flimsy. He was banking on Seamus' lack of critical thinking to push this partnership through.

The Irishman folded his arms and grumbled gibberish to himself. Then he concluded, "I'll think about it. It does make sense."

Duke smiled. Mazilda rolled her eyes at the mutant's stupidity.

"After my next fight, let's chat again," said O'Hoolihan. "I might have some more information by then anyways."

"What information?"

"We have some folks working on that photo and identifying the whereabouts."

"Cross-referencing some of the background images, I'd suspect," said Mazilda. "Angles of the light, barely visible serial numbers on items, type of soil or pavement. They can be used to trim the possibilities down to a few systems and maybe a hundred or so planets."

"Sure, I guess," responded Seamus, with much less enthusiasm. "All I know is that I should have some more information tomorrow."

"And why are you in the tournament?" Mazilda asked pointedly.

"Like I said, I have my reasons."

"Seamus, if we are going to work together for both of our benefits, we need to be open and honest," pleaded Duke.

Potato Lips sighed again.

"Fine. We heard some chatter that someone else here was hot on the heels of the Father and his witch queen."

"Do you think that was us?"

"Nope. I was entered in this tournament long before you crashed into the Shaman's table. Someone else."

"Who?" asked Mazilda.

"No idea. I thought it was that Jungafallowian but I haven't found anything on him. If he knows something, he's good at being discrete."

"There are a lot of unsavory types here," concluded Duke. "We will keep our eyes out, Seamus. You will be the first person we alert if we catch on to something."

Duke stood up and walked over to O'Hoolihan. He extended his hand. The mutant brute squeezed it so hard that Duke swore he heard a bone crack.

"Quite a grip there, Seamus."

The mutant conjured up a misshapen smile.

"Let's go find us Ishiro'shea's father."

"*The* Father," Seamus replied.

"Right, a father, the Father. Po-tay-to, po-tah-to."

Seamus snarled. He had clearly never heard that expression.

CHAPTER TWENTY

RANDY AND ZEL... AGAIN

[BROADCAST OPENS ON THE ANNOUNCERS' BOOTH.]

ZELARIOUS ZAN ALON: Fight fans, welcome back to the Tournament of the Shield of the Colossal Calamari! It's day two—well, day three if you count the melee night—and this is shaping up to be the greatest event in the tournament's rich history. We've had upsets. We've had death-defying feats of strength. We've had surprise attacks. And we've seen a record broken—and then broken again moments later. It has been nothing short of amazing!

RANDY: *Beep.* Yep. *Boop.*

ZELARIOUS ZAN ALON: You are truly the most dynamic color man in the business, Randy. And what a day we have planned. In the opening round, we witnessed Sulaw, the beautiful Hiritai warrior advance over Not Very Good at Math from Zylantia, and she will now take on Yvonne "The Furry Mountain of Moon Colony #1" Angerdlarnek. The Furry Mountain was able to overcome a very game Reginald the Mega-Troll.

RANDY: *Beep.* Finally, some girl-on-girl action. *Beep.*

Zelarious Zan Alon: I predict it will be the hardest-hitting bout of the evening. They are both fierce combatants and have a real shot to win the entire tournament. The winner of that slugfest will meet the winner of the match between Seamus "Potato Lips" O'Hoolihan of Earth and Combatant 2, the Jungafallowian, in the next round.

Randy: *Beep.* Yikes. Not exactly an easy path for any of them in that bracket, Zel. *Beep.*

Zelarious Zan Alon: Agreed. Potato Lips disposed of Tor-torta of Krawn with his own flames, in one of the most dramatic finishes in the first round. Combatant 2 made waves across the universe by attacking Gjrazzel, the home-town hero, during the Grand Entrance. He then proceeded to shatter Maxx Gemstarr's record for quickest victory mere moments after Gemstarr set it. He leveled the poor Kitar in a mere six seconds.

Randy: *Boop. Boop.* I'm not sure that he can be stopped, Zel. Not even by that mutant Irish thug. *Beep.*

Zelarious Zan Alon: But you know who probably benefitted most from Combatant 2's unprecedented attack on Gjrazzel?

Randy: The unknown bum, Duke LaGrout. *Beep.*

Zelarious Zan Alon: You are absolutely right. The lightly-thought-of bounty hunter, Duke LaGrange of Nova Texas. He was able to take advantage of a hobbled and blinded Gjrazzel to win. Despite Gjrazzel's physical limitations and injuries, LaGrange still had to push the rules and regulations to sneak out a victory.

Randy: *Beep.* I think he should be disqualified. The rules clearly say no firearms. *Beep. Boop.*

Zelarious Zan Alon: Most are on your side, Randy, especially those in attendance. But the Shaman did clear his use of the butt of the gun, so LaGrange does advance. But we can't underscore enough the valiant and noble effort made by Gjrazzel in this tournament. What a true champion.

RANDY: *Beep.* And damn LaGregg. *Boop. Boop.*

ZELARIOUS ZAN ALON: He doesn't get a free pass, however. He now has to square off against the winged warrior from Planet F, Glux Xyphormog II, who was able to get a win over Jorb, the sludge monster from Karr, by using his own acidic spit against him.

RANDY: That was some nifty flying, Zel. *Beep. Beep.*

ZELARIOUS ZAN ALON: Indeed. He did lose his prized two-sided halberd in the battle, but I'm sure that he will be ready for the Nova Texan. And the crowd will be solidly behind the Royal Guardsman from Planet F.

RANDY: *Beep.* I know I will be. *Beep.*

ZELARIOUS ZAN ALON: I think we're supposed to be impartial, Randy.

RANDY: *Beep.* Screw that. Duke can go "Glux" off. *Beep.* See what I did there? *Boop.*

ZELARIOUS ZAN ALON: I did, Randy, yes I did. Finally, the round will end with Maxx Gemstarr, fresh off of a sub-ten-second victory over a Gyorkian Blademaster—impressive stuff—and the feisty Gurlfian Goother Rat, Gha. Gha had one of the more unconventional wins in the tournament —and no one is happier than one of our key sponsors, Willie's World of Galactic Winnebagos. It's a real testament to the flushing power of a Willie's brand Winnebago.

RANDY: *Beep.* I wonder if Jin-Jin-Jin ever escaped? *Boop.*

ZELARIOUS ZAN ALON: I'm not sure. And I don't want to be there when he does, that's for sure.

RANDY: I'm really excited, Zel. *Beep.* This is going to be a crazy day. Who's up first? *Beep.*

ZELARIOUS ZAN ALON: It looks like we are going to see your guy, Glux Xyphormog II, try and end the upset streak caused by Duke LaGrange, the bounty hunter from Nova Texas.

RANDY: *Beep.* I hate that guy. *Beep.*

ZELARIOUS ZAN ALON: But first a word from our sponsors.

[UNCLE TOFU'S ADVENTURE LAND COMMERCIAL PLAYS.]

[WILLIE'S WORLD OF GALACTIC WINNEBAGOS COMMERCIAL PLAYS.]

[THE BROADCAST OPENS TO A WIDE SHOT OF THE ARENA.]

ZELARIOUS ZAN ALON: We have the best sponsors, don't we, Randy?

RANDY: *Beep.* Yes, edible roller coasters and toilets with the suck force of a black hole. Hard to beat it, Zel. *Beep.*

ZELARIOUS ZAN ALON: Despite the early exit of their favorite son, Gjrazzel, the crowd is packed and buzzing with excitement today.

RANDY: *Boop. Boop.* The *unfair* exit of Gjrazzel, Zel. *Beep.*

ZELARIOUS ZAN ALON: The lights are dimming and the trumpets are sounding. Here's our first competitor. It's Glux Xyphormog II! They love him and... Whoa! Look at that! Those are some impressive aerial moves!

RANDY: *Beep.* No doubt. It's hard not to root for this crazy insect. *Beep.*

ZELARIOUS ZAN ALON: They sure are behind him in this fight. However, I'm not sure if it has to do with their love for this insectoid warrior or their hatred for our next fighter. Here he is, ladies and gentlemen—and greeted by a rousing chorus of hate-filled heckles. I'm not sure what those hand gestures mean on his home world, but I have a feeling that the crowd isn't appreciating it.

RANDY: *Beep.* I'll give it right back to him. *Beep.*

ZELARIOUS ZAN ALON: Get your hand back in here, Randy. Don't stoop to his level. Let's send it down and get an official introduction for these two.

ARENA PA ANNOUNCER: Ladies and gentlemen and beings from all corners of the universe, welcome to the quarterfinal round of the Tournament of the Shield of the Colossal Calamari! This match is the opening contest of the day and will be a fight to the finish. Introducing first, from the majestic world of Planet F, a member of the most prestigious military unit on the planet—the Queen's Royal Guard —he's the master of the double-sided halberd and has sired over three hundred and forty thousand royal larvae for the Mother of the Empire, the queen herself. It's my honor to introduce the being that defeated Jorb, the sludge beast of Karr—this is Glux Xyphormog II!

[THE CROWD GOES CRAZY.]

ARENA PA ANNOUNCER: And his opponent, from the harsh and barren world of Nova Texas, a two-bit offshoot of everyone's least-favorite planet, Earth. He's an unheralded bounty hunter that takes advantage of other's misfortune and uses illegal weapons to knock out injured competitors. He also claims to be a playboy—whatever that is. He's the melee victor—which he also won by pure luck. It's my job to have to introduce Duke LaGrunge.

[THE CROWD DOES NOT GO CRAZY.]

ARENA PA ANNOUNCER: Correction. Duke LaGrange.

ZELARIOUS ZAN ALON: The Nova Texan seems to have irked the arena's PA announcer, even.

RANDY: *Beep.* Now that's impressive. *Beep.*

ZELARIOUS ZAN ALON: Now on to the match itself. I really don't see how LaGrange can pull this one off. It's an uphill battle for sure. First off, Glux is healthy. He doesn't have his two-sided halberd, but he has a standard-issue variety and he's still lethal with it. Second, Glux can fly. Third, he trains every day of his life and is constantly in danger's bullseye as one of the most revered soldiers of the imperial force. Fourth...

RANDY: *Beep.* We get it. This is going to be a blood bath. We can finally be done with this LaGoop character. *Beep.*

ZELARIOUS ZAN ALON: The referee is reminding these two contestants of the rules, or lack thereof.

RANDY: *Boop.* There are barely any rules, but LaGrotch still managed to break them. *Beep.*

ZELARIOUS ZAN ALON: To be fair to Duke, Randy, the decision was made that his use of the gun was legal. We have to move on, no matter how despicable this guy is. But, he doesn't have the gun with him now. It looks like he was given one of the house clubs, a pretty basic bludgeoning instrument; I don't see a talent like Glux Xyphormog falling victim to something as basic as a wooden stick.

RANDY: *Beep.* Let's go, Glux! *Beep.*

ZELARIOUS ZAN ALON: They both have retreated back to their sides of the arena and we are about to get this on.

RANDY: *Beep.* I think this will be a quick one, Zel. *Beep.* *Boop. Beep.*

ZELARIOUS ZAN ALON: And Glux is on the attack! He

534

just ran across the arena and now he's laying into Duke with the halberd. Or trying to. LaGrange seems to be blocking it pretty successfully with his club. Oh, wait! He's down on his backside. Glux is not letting up! He just missed LaGrange on that jab. Duke gets to the barrier and gets to his feet. Another halberd strike just misses. Oh, this does not look good for the Nova Texan.

RANDY: I can't believe he's dodging these! *Beep. Boop.* Get him, Glux! *Beep.*

ZELARIOUS ZAN ALON: What a kick by the Royal Guardsman! Duke is on his back again. Here we go! Glux is up in the air, hovering, there he goes... Duke moves! The halberd is stuck in the ground. It's not moving at all. LaGrange swings the club and connects. He then uses it to smash the halberd in two.

RANDY: *Beep.* Glux is not having much luck with halberds in this tournament, Zel. But I think he's fine. That love tap by LaGrout didn't do any damage. *Beep.*

ZELARIOUS ZAN ALON: You're right. It did appear to be a glancing blow. Glux recollects himself and charges again, Duke swats at him. No avail. Again. Nothing. It's obvious that the bounty hunter won't be able to slow down Xyphormog that way. Another sweep by Glux, and Duke swings. Glux grasps LaGrange's forearm in mid-swing with his foot. I have never seen that before in my life. He snatches the club and flies above the reach of the bounty hunter. Glux throws the club into the audience!

RANDY: *Beep.* He wants to make this a one-on-one battle. No weapons. Just the epic struggle between humanoid and insectoid. And I don't like LaDork's chances. *Beep.*

ZELARIOUS ZAN ALON: Okay, Randy, now you aren't even trying anymore.

RANDY: *Beep.* What? *Boop.*

Zelarious Zan Alon: Another diving attack by Glux, and he tackles the bounty hunter. They roll for a few paces and disengage. Another swift thrust kick by Glux and Duke hits the ground. He takes flight and charges the downed bounty hunter. He connects again! This is not looking good for Duke LaGrange. Glux hovers, Duke is up... and back down again. This time a kick to the back of the head. This could be the beginning of the end for the Nova Texan.

Randy: *Beep*. Finish him. *Beep*.

Zelarious Zan Alon: Glux swoops in and grabs the bounty hunter between his legs. Oh, I think I know what's happening now. Glux is lifting the woozy LaGrange in the air. He's going to dangle him high above the arena. Duke will have to either embarrass himself by giving up, watched on by a viewing audience of billions and effectively ruining what little reputation he may have in the outside world. Or plummet to his death.

Randy: *Beep*. A squishy death, Zel. *Boop*.

Zelarious Zan Alon: Right you are, my tiny metal compadre. Very squishy indeed. Glux is gaining elevation. LaGrange isn't moving. He might be out cold.

Randy: *Beep*. So if he's out cold, that means he likely won't answer, huh? *Beep*. *Boop*. So, that means Glux will have to...

Zelarious Zan Alon: Send him to splat city.

Randy: *Beep*. Alright! *Boop*. *Boop*. *Beep*.

Zelarious Zan Alon: They're high in the rafters now. The crowd is loving this. As impressive as Glux's fighting ability is, the fact that he can carry a full-sized humanoid to these heights using only his legs is a testament to his strength and conditioning.

Randy: *Boop*. No wonder the queen loves this guy so much. *Beep*.

ZELARIOUS ZAN ALON: Here we go. Glux appears to be asking the motionless bounty hunter to tap out. Give up. Submit. I don't see any signs of life from LaGrange.

RANDY: *Beep.* Is that eye opening? *Beep.*

ZELARIOUS ZAN ALON: Oh wow, fight fans! Shocking. LaGrange was playing dead. He just swung his body upwards and kicked Glux square in the jaw. That's a pretty sneaky move and shows that Duke may have some fight in him. He's now firmly grabbing Glux by his ankles but he's still dangling from the height of the upper deck. He's playing with fire. Glux is trying to shake him, but Duke is holding on. He's moved up and now has a firm grip on Glux's left thigh. He's trying to mount the insectoid. Glux starts a speedy dive to try and shake the rogue from his body, but the Nova Texan is hanging on. I've definitely never seen this before.

RANDY: *Beep.* They're going to hit some spectators! Watch out! *Boop.*

ZELARIOUS ZAN ALON: You're right. Glux is accelerating down to the arena floor at an uncontrollable speed. Duke has a full mount now. He's riding Glux like some sort of Mrelockian skybeast. It's affecting Glux, too. He can't seem to steady his flight, he's all out of sorts. LaGrange is holding on for dear life. They just swooped mere inches above the heads of the patrons in the lower sections.

RANDY: *Beep.* If they crash into the stands, advantage Glux. *Beep.*

ZELARIOUS ZAN ALON: No doubt. I bet that a large portion of those in attendance would love a crack at Duke LaGrange. They just flew over the head of Duke's corner man.

RANDY: *Beep.* That tiny masked fella is his corner man? *Boop.*

Zelarious Zan Alon: Yes. Ishiro'shea, from Earth. Apparently, he's a skilled martial artist.

Randy: *Beep.* Maybe he should have joined up instead of LaGrease. *Beep.*

Zelarious Zan Alon: That's what most insiders have told me, Randy. Another swoop over the crowd, narrowly missing Ishiro'shea again. Duke reached down and appeared to slap a fan in that section!

Randy: *Beep.* Figures! Just when I thought that I couldn't hate someone more, he does that! *Beep. Boop.*

Zelarious Zan Alon: What's this? Does Duke have a knife? It looks like a tiny dagger. Where did that come from?

Randy: *Beep.* Did he steal it from that fan? *Beep.*

Zelarious Zan Alon: Oh no—he's shredding Xyphormog's wings. They're going down! LaGrange is on top. This is going to be loud!

Randy: *Boop.* Damn. *Beep.* [Randy's commentary censored on the broadcast.] *Beep.*

Zelarious Zan Alon: You can't say that on air, Randy. It's a mess down against the barrier. The two crashed headlong into the wall at full speed. The referees are checking on it. I can't believe this. I'm speechless.

Randy: *Boop.* [More censored commentary.] *Beep.*

Zelarious Zan Alon: Glux Xyphormog is not responding. He's out cold. I can't believe that I'm about to say this—

Randy: *Beep.* Then don't. *Beep.*

Zelarious Zan Alon: Duke LaGrange wins.

Randy: *Beep.* [More censored commentary.] *Beep.*

Zelarious Zan Alon: Duke LaGrange advances to the semifinals of the Tournament of the Shield of the Colossal Calamari. Fight fans, do you believe in miracles?

CHAPTER TWENTY-ONE

MAXX AND THE RAT

DUKE DIDN'T CARE TOO MUCH for the taste of his own blood. Nor did he particularly like the taste of anyone's blood. The one possible exception being the blood of the Awlravian Jumping Cow, whose plasma is a common drink amongst Awlrav's inhabitants and whose milk is a toxic poison. The Awlravian Jumping Cow's blood is a prominent ingredient in the mixed drink Coagulation Celebration, a festive signature cocktail at Cyborg Joe's Grill N' Go & The Why Not Saloon on Planet Kelt. Unfortunately for Duke, his blood didn't come with a free party hat and edible confetti.

"That was a close one," said Mazilda.

"Thanks. And thanks for the assist," said Duke, wiping blood from his mouth with his forearm.

"Those morons on the broadcast thought I was some random fan that you were taunting. Can you believe that?"

Is she mad that they thought I was cheating—or that they didn't recognize her? Duke wondered.

"Hey now, I like those guys. Randy is awesome. Easily my favorite broadcaster."

"You probably shouldn't listen to the replays then," smirked Mazilda.

"Oh," Duke responded with a frown.

Ishiro'shea patched up some of the bounty hunter's cuts.

"Ouch. That stings. You know what you're doing?"

"Toughen up, pansy," said Mazilda. "You don't want one of those cuts to open up in the next round."

"Who are my options again?"

"Shut up, Duke, you know damn well that it's Maxx."

"Or the Goother Rat. He's pretty squirrelly. The rat might get lucky and have Maxx flush himself down a toilet," Duke laughed. "Where is ol' Maxxy-poo anyways? Shouldn't you be with him?"

"We're on after Yvonne and Sulaw. He likes his alone time before a fight."

"I'm surprised he doesn't need your help to wriggle into that getup of his," said the Nova Texan, rolling his eyes.

"I do like how he looks in that," Mazilda whispered to herself. Her focus drifted noticeably.

"Whatever," replied Duke. "He's still a big dumb animal."

"A *sexy* big dumb animal."

"If you're into that sort of thing."

"Most women with eyes are, Duke."

"Only if they also lack taste," he jabbed. "But seriously Mazilda, thanks for the help. It was like..."

"Old times," she said, finishing his thought.

"Yes, old times. Good times. I don't exactly know *why* you're helping me. Helping us, really. But Ishiro'shea and I are thankful."

Mazilda seemed to blush, at least as much as could be discerned from her pale yellow skin. She grabbed Duke by the shoulders and planted a kiss on his cheek. She hugged Ishiro'shea and kissed him on the top of his head.

"I'm glad that we reconnected."

The loudspeakers started to boom, shaking the back rooms of the arena.

"The next match is up already, I should probably get back to Maxx. I'll see you tonight. Hopefully, Seamus can give us some more info."

"See you tonight."

Following a quick patch job on some of Duke's more noticeable scrapes, he and Ishiro'shea lounged in their personal holding room to watch the other bouts unfold. Duke flipped on the monitor to the broadcast; a fight was already in progress.

Yvonne "The Furry Mountain of Moon Colony #1" Angerdlarnek was panting, her thick fur matted and a single stream of blood dripping down from the corner of her mouth. Her opponent, Sulaw of the Hiritai, was breathing heavily as well, and a bulbous purple knot swelled under her left eye. The dirt from the arena floor caked her back and thighs. The two combatants were circling each other, waiting for an opening for another series of attacks. Sulaw snarled at the Gartoshian musk ox.

Somehow, she makes bloodied, dirty, and beaten-up look damn good, thought Duke.

Sulaw darted at Yvonne's sturdy legs, trying to take her down and grab a mounted position. However, Yvonne fended off the athletic Hiritai with a swift knee strike to the shoulder. Sulaw tumbled down and rolled out of striking distance. Neither woman had a weapon. This was not shocking in Yvonne's case, as she tended to rely on her boxing prowess. Duke hypothesized that Yvonne had been able to dislodge Sulaw's weapon earlier in the match. *Advantage Yvonne*, concluded the bounty hunter.

The match became a series of chess-like moves. Neither fighter gained much of an advantage until Sulaw aggressively charged Yvonne nearly an hour into the encounter. She sprinted at full speed toward the musk ox, which prompted Yvonne to start her deadly head butt charge, the move that had leveled the behemoth Mega-Troll in the opening round. Sulaw miraculously avoided the collision in midair; as she flew over the Yvonne by a good arm's length, she snagged her right horn and forced the Gartoshian to lose control and fall into a mid-flight spin. Yvonne crashed to the ground with a massive thud, then rolled near to the barrier wall.

"She totally duped her, Ish. I don't know if this is making me concerned or aroused," said Duke.

Sulaw walked over to the injured Yvonne, now on her hands and knees. Sulaw looked at the crowd and made gestures, inviting a choice: should she finish her off respectfully or in a blaze of unfiltered violence? They chose the latter.

The Hiritai took a few paces back, then began a stroll towards Yvonne; as she came closer, she picked up speed.

"She's going to punt her in the head," shouted Duke to Ishiro'shea.

As Sulaw's right leg began to swing, Yvonne jumped in the air and came down with a powerful right cross across Sulaw's jaw. The cracking of the jawbone echoed throughout the arena. The Hiritai warrior collapsed immediately. There was no chance of her getting up.

The referee made the easy call to end it. Yvonne fell to a knee, her fatigue visible. She managed a wave to the appreciative, bloodthirsty crowd but then she needed help from Psitakki officials to make it to the back.

"Now that Sulaw's out of the tournament, do you think I should ask her to drinks?" asked Duke.

Ishiro'shea did not respond.

As was customary on the broadcast, after a fight concluded, the programming jumped to some pre-taped fluff pieces hyping up each fighter's background, resume, their unique path to the tournament, and any general badassery that could be attached to their name. Not surprisingly, Maxx Gemstarr had the longest and most elaborate video montage of any of the competitors. Even less surprising, it was during Maxx's vignette that Duke decided to take a much-needed nap.

When the bounty hunter awoke, the next contest had already begun— Maxx "The Universe's Favorite Bounty Hunter" Gemstarr versus Gha, the Goother Rat from Gurlf.

"What'd I miss?" asked Duke.

Ishiro'shea pointed to Gha on the monitor and then made a motion that signified the Goother Rat was nearing his end. At a second glance, Duke realized what Ishiro meant. Gha was beaten badly. Instead of his customary frantic movement, he was sluggishly moping around, trying—unsuccessfully—to dodge Gemstarr's strikes. Maxx eventually caught Gha, hoisted him over his head and tossed him across the arena. He posed for the crowd; they cheered at his superiority over his opponent. However, this gave Gha enough time to retrieve his flail which had, presumably, been cast aside by Gemstarr at some point in the fight. The flail sat right under the designated corner man station, where Mazilda stood cheering on her man. As Maxx continued to delight the crowd, Gha hit him from behind with the flail. The muscular bounty hunter tumbled over as the crowd collectively gasped. Gha swung again, narrowly missing Maxx as he rolled away rather clumsily. Gha landed a vicious swing on Maxx's backside, causing a mild chuckle in the audience. Gha connected again.

Is the Goother Rat going to pull this off?

Another powerful flail whip crashed down across the chest of Gemstarr and sent him to the ground. Gha pounced on top of the prey. As Gha mounted him, Maxx tried to block the Gurlfian's punches, scratches, and bites. However, some of Gha's offense was getting through; Maxx was in trouble.

In his whirlwind assault, Gha must have forgot about Maxx's power gauntlets—surgically implanted forearm guards that packed enough wallop to level an especially bulky tanker that's been submerged in cement and placed behind a heavily fortified lead-lined wall. When you get hit flush with a Maxx Gemstarr forearm strike, it's like being punched in the face with an iron fist powered by a jet engine.

Maxx's forearm radiated an electric neon blue.

Move away, Gha! Get off him, shouted Duke internally. *His arm thingy...*

The bounty hunter smashed both power gauntlets against the torso of the Goother Rat. Gha flew up into the air, then crashed into the top of the barrier wall, narrowly missing the VIP suites. Smoke puffed from his wiry fur, and his eyes rolled back into his head. He was toast.

Damn.

As Maxx celebrated, thanking his fans with yet another flexing routine, Duke saw Mazilda applauding from the corner man station. He didn't like it.

After more packages and some expert analysis by well-known fighters attending the event, the last quarterfinal began. Seamus "Potato Lips" O'Hoolihan entered first, to a rousing ovation. The audience roared even louder as he downed two mugs of beer at the same time. Just as loudly as they had cheered Seamus, they hissed and jeered the Jungafallowian responsible for injuring Gjrazzel. Combatant 2 didn't even seem to notice. His corner man, Prince Korzo-Tapor, did—however, he seemed to relish it. He taunted the crowd with as much vigor as his gigantic minion physically abused his opponents.

"Hey, Ish. I think there's someone they hate more than me," Duke observed. "Let's hope that it's not both of us in the finale—we might have an empty house."

Ishiro'shea was squarely focused on the monitor.

"Don't worry, he just has to live. He doesn't have to win. Even if he's in a hospital bed, we will make sure to get the information that we need. We just have to wait until the fight is over and then we will..."

Ishiro'shea's planted his face firmly into his open palm.

Seamus "Potato Lips" O'Hoolihan was sprawled out in the middle of the arena, his shillelagh broken in half next to him, with a Psitakki referee standing over him. He had been knocked unconscious in only a matter of seconds. Combatant 2 raised his arms in victory and trash filled the arena floor just as quickly.

"At least he's alive. They're bringing out a stretcher; better than a gravedigger."

Ishiro'shea reluctantly nodded his head in agreement.

"Did you see Maxx tonight?" a voice said. "Wasn't he spectacular?"

"Oh hey, Mazilda. No, he's just a lucky bastard. I thought that little rodent had him beat."

"No chance," she countered. "He's—"

"What are you doing back here?" Duke said, cutting her off, which appeared to surprise Mazilda. "I have to fight your boyfriend tomorrow, remember."

"I thought you'd be happy about that?"

"Happy about getting a chance to embarrass that fake? Yes. I can't think of anything better. In fact, it makes this entire ordeal worthwhile."

"Then why are getting so snippy with me?"

"I'm not super jazzed about fighting Maxx with *you* in his corner."

"How sweet..."

"No, not 'how sweet.' As long as we've known each other, as much as we've cared for each other, I know you'll do anything needed to win. So, until after the fight, maybe we take a break from our side project related to Ishiro's parents."

"Duke? C'mon," Mazilda pleaded.

"Look, you're here with that..." Duke began, but he was stopped by Ishiro'shea, who pointed to the exit as a crowd of people made their way from the arena to the backstage area.

"Sorry, Mazilda, stay right there."

"I thought you wanted me to leave?"

"Okay, leave. Do whatever. We have to go see something."

She pivoted and saw the passing stretcher, upon which lay a beaten Seamus O'Hoolihan. She stepped aside and let Ishiro'shea pass. Then she stepped in front of Duke.

"I get that you don't want me here before the match. It's a bit paranoid, but whatever. But don't keep me away from talking to Seamus with you. I'm as invested in tracking down Ish's parents as you."

"Fine," Duke said reluctantly.

As they approached the stretcher, Duke could see that Seamus was fastened down but his eyes were wide open.

"Seamus," Duke began, trying to keep pace with the medical team carrying the downed Irishman.

"Hey, mate. I got my arse kicked by that guy."

"A lucky shot," chimed in Mazilda.

"Funny one, lass," Seamus said. "Good luck if you have to scrap with 'im, Duke."

"How are you feeling?"

"I've been better. Not sure why they have me strapped down like this, it's like they've never seen someone get knocked out before. I'm sure they'll give me some headache meds and send me on my way."

"That's good. It looked pretty brutal. Glad to see that you're not badly damaged."

"No more than normal."

"I know this isn't the perfect time—" Duke began.

He was cut off by Mazilda. "Any new news on the Father?"

"Actually, yes. Let's meet up at the Pondscum after I get done with these morons. I have some news that you might find quite interesting."

"Like what?" Mazilda asked assertively.

Seamus smiled back at her. He turned to face Duke. "Talk to you in a bit, mate."

CHAPTER TWENTY-TWO

A BIT OF BAD NEWS

DUKE, ISHIRO'SHEA, AND MAZILDA SAT around the table in the back room of the Pondscum Tavern. They had instructed the bartender to usher Potato Lips discreetly to them when he arrived. They had no timetable but, with a few unopened barrels of Glyptodian Summer Ale lining the back wall of the room, they weren't in any rush.

"I'm still not sure about you being here," Duke said to Mazilda. "I mean, at least not tonight, on the eve of the epic battle of bounty hunting legends. Well, one bounty hunting legend and one jerk that couldn't bounty hunt his way out of a paper bag."

"You're a legend now?" Mazilda quipped, rolling her eyes.

"Well, we aren't going to let any of our strategy slip out."

"Strategy? *You* have a strategy? I thought you were allergic to strategy, to planning, and to anything that requires you to do something that can't be classified as wingin' it."

"Why does that surprise you? We've won three matches here. If I recall, I'm the first one ever to do that after being stuck in that damn melee. First one ever. In a million cycles. *One million cycles.*"

"So, if *I* recall, your strategy has actually been: one, hide behind an explosive Blop with a death wish; two, hope that the grand champion of Psitakki gets maliciously attacked outside the tournament so he will be half-blind, concussed, and crippled; and three, ride around on the back of a flying insect and get a dagger handed to you by your ex-girlfriend so you can clip his wings and crash him into a wall?"

Duke pondered this for a moment. He smiled. "Pretty much, more or less."

"You're such an ass."

"Speaking of asses," Duke responded as he nodded towards the door.

"Maxx, baby, what are you doing here?"

Gemstarr wasn't smiling, which concerned Duke because he assumed that Maxx's face was permanently fixed into an affable expression, ready for publicity shots and whatnot. Maxx pushed away the Psitakki bartender, who apologized from the hallway. He eventually gave up and ran back to the front of the house.

"What am *I* doing here?" Maxx said. "Shouldn't I be asking you the same thing, Mazilda?"

"We talked about this, Maxx," she said softly through gritted teeth.

"Fraternizing with my next opponent? We talked about no such thing. You're already on thin ice after your debacle earlier."

"Do tell?" Duke interjected with a sly grin.

Mazilda's face grew red. She glared at the Nova Texan.

"Did you see my last fight, LaGrange?" Maxx said.

"I did. You better not try to start a career as an exterminator given how you struggled with that rat, Maxxy."

"Yeah, the match would've been over if I had a corner man with half a brain."

"Hey," Mazilda's voice rose above the others. "I said I was sorry for not picking up that flail when it was beside my seat."

"Any corner man worth their weight would've known to do that. Because of you, I had to repair a suit and get five stitches."

Wait, five stitches in his suit? Duke asked himself.

"Mazilda, you're lucky that I'm Maxx Gemstarr."

"So lucky," Duke whispered to Mazilda, out of Maxx's earshot.

It was clear that she wasn't happy with either of them.

"Do you know who I am, Mazilda?" Maxx said. "You're lucky to be the woman standing next to me. No more of those sneaky, bush league assassin gigs for you anymore. And why is that? Because of me. So, leave these two morons to themselves and let's go."

Mazilda took a deep breath.

Oh, she's going to kill him, thought Duke. *Hey, maybe I'll get a free pass to the finals.*

Mazilda reached down to her thigh.

Dagger to the face, coming up!

However, Mazilda didn't pull out one of her deadly throwing knives. She scooted the chair out gently and stood up. "Yes, Maxx. Sorry."

Duke and Ishiro'shea exchanged confused looks.

That's not the Mazilda that I knew.

"Wait a damn second, here. She might be scared of you, but I'm not," Duke proclaimed.

"Stop, Duke. Not worth it," Mazilda whispered so that only Duke would hear.

Duke ignored her.

"If she wants to stay with us, she can stay with us," Duke said. He removed his laser revolver from its holster and twirled it on his finger.

Maxx didn't seem too impressed. "And you're going to make me leave, are you? With that puny pea shooter?"

Duke then removed Ol' Betsy from his back. "How about *this* pea shooter?"

Maxx's eyes widened and he took a step back. "Hey now, Duke. No need to do anything stupid."

"If Mazilda wants to stay here with us until Seamus arrives, she's more than welcome to. She's not sharing any of your tricks or secrets because, quite frankly, I don't need them. Tomorrow I'm going to expose you as the fraud you are."

"Did you say Seamus? As in Seamus O'Hoolihan?" asked Maxx.

"Yes."

"Potato Lips?"

"Yes, Potato Lips."

"You haven't heard, have you?"

"Heard what?"

"He's dead."

"What are you talking about?"

"It's all over the news, man. How long have you been in here drinking?"

Duke didn't answer.

"What happened?" Mazilda chimed in.

"They don't know—only that when he was in the medical tent awaiting his final clearance so that he could leave, he fell on something sharp."

"Something sharp," asked Mazilda.

"Yeah, maybe a surgical tool. Or a knife. Or something. But it went right through his neck. Dead."

Ishiro'shea banged his fist on the table and sat down heavily.

"So you're probably going to be waiting around for some time," Maxx laughed.

No one joined in.

Duke slumped down in a chair despondently.

"I guess that you can come with me now, Mazilda. See you tomorrow, LaGrange," Maxx said with a subtle cackle in his voice.

"This doesn't make any sense," Duke said to his companion. "What are we missing?" He looked around the room. "Hey, where'd Mazilda go? Did she leave with Maxx?"

Ishiro'shea shrugged.

Duke strolled over to the door and peered into the hallway. He saw Maxx grasping Mazilda's arm as she struggled to keep up with his long strides.

"I don't need you, Mazilda," Maxx muttered. "You need me. Remember that. Okay? You're making me regret this relationship. Stop hanging out with those losers."

They turned the corner and were gone.

Ishiro'shea still sat at the table, gazing at its surface dolefully.

"We'll get to the bottom of this. Don't worry. This is just an inopportune setback. We're already better off than when we got dumped here. We just gotta get out of this tournament alive."

CHAPTER TWENTY-THREE

I CAN'T LOSE

"Y OU'RE UP FIRST TODAY, LAGRANGE," barked the producer.

"Are you ever in a good mood?" asked the bounty hunter.

"Not when I have to deal with the likes of you," replied the Psitakki.

"Hey! What did I do?"

"Nothing personal, LaGrange. I already told you that you're a ratings killer. In fact, the only way the ratings would improve is if you got killed."

"That can't be right. People love me."

"No, they *hate* you," corrected the producer. "Not love... hate. But it's not a 'We all want to see him beaten to a pulp' hate like the hate for Combatant 2. Yours is more of an 'Ugh, can someone just remove this guy from my screen?' hate. One gets me ratings. The other one gets me fired."

Duke didn't reply. He couldn't. He felt emasculated.

"But," the producer continued, "things are looking up."

"Fans are finally starting to get me now? Taking down that royal bug must've won me some fans."

"Nope, you're fighting Maxx Gemstarr. He's a ratings magnet. So, for once, I'm not dreading you gracing the airwaves. You know, I don't exactly get a do-over with this tournament."

"I hate Maxx Gemstarr," Duke shouted.

"You're the only who does. Any time he's on, most galaxies tune in."

"I hate him even more now."

"Regardless, try to last more than a few seconds. We need some drama."

Duke tipped his hat without answering and moved down the hallway to his holding room.

"Don't worry, Ish," Duke began as he hung his hat and holsters on the wall pegs. "I promise that we'll start investigating what happened to Seamus after the fight tonight. Win, lose, or draw, I promise."

The ninja shook his head and sat cross-legged on the floor. Duke flopped on the couch.

"You know, Seamus' mutation made his skin almost impenetrable. How could a tiny surgical instrument kill him? Even if he had areas that weren't as calloused, how impossible is it that he accidentally fell down and landed on something sharp enough to penetrate his skin in the exact location that would kill him? I'll answer it. It's *very* impossible."

Duke reclined on the couch and closed his eyes. He started to hum the Nova Texan planetary anthem. Within moments he was asleep.

"Wake up, LaGrange. You're on in a few."

"Man, that guy is annoying," Duke said to Ishiro'shea in between yawns.

Ishiro'shea stared at Duke.

"What? You don't think I'm taking this fight with Maxx seriously?"

The ninja nodded.

"I am, give me some credit. I just happen to know that I'm smarter, faster, and craftier than him. He's just a pile of muscles. One carefully placed punch and he's done. The Goother and the sword guy didn't even get a clean shot at him—his face, at least. I just have to avoid his magic wrist-band thingies. Easy enough."

Ishiro'shea looked disappointed.

"You don't think I can win? My own corner man? What do you think I should do?"

The ninja shrugged.

"Thanks, that's helpful," Duke replied sarcastically.

Duke splashed water on his face and partook in some mild calisthenics as his pre-fight preparations. He threw some punches into Ishiro's open hands. He felt good. He felt ready.

Finally, I get to kick that bastard's ass, once and for all, he thought.

As he made his way through the arena doors towards his designated area along the barrier, he was overwhelmed by the usual negative reception. He just ignored it this time. He didn't taunt. He was focused on his opponent, or at least the outcome that he desperately wanted.

The lights dimmed and the music and laser show that was Maxx Gemstarr's entrance filled the hall. It seemed more over-the-top from the floor of the arena. It engulfed the entire space; you would have had to hide in a lavatory deep in the bowels of the stadium to escape the reach of

Maxx's introductory spectacle. Duke looked up at Ishiro'shea; the ninja was bobbing his head to the beat.

"Hey," Duke shouted. "You're on my team, remember."

Duke could see Ishiro's smirk under his mask.

Unlike the first two rounds, in which Maxx had sauntered out to the crowd's praise, only stopping to flex and pose, this time the Universe's Favorite Bounty Hunter rode in on a small decorative hovercraft. Lasers and lights pulsed from every nook and cranny of the ship. Smoke billowed from below until it almost covered the entire arena floor. By the time the hovercraft slowed to a stop, Duke estimated that only his hat would be visible to the crowd. Trailing behind Maxx were two lines of scantily-clad females from a dozen different systems. They all danced in a choreographed routine and, at its conclusion, hoisted up a banner that read: *You're our hero, Maxx! Beat Duke LaGreen. Love, the Gemstarrlets.*

"It's LaGrange," shouted Duke. "It's LaGrange! How hard is it?"

Not a single spectator acknowledged his plea. Their eyes were all fixated on the pomp and circumstance around the entrance of Maxx Gemstarr.

This is pointless, realized Duke.

As the public address announcer screamed Maxx's name, the roar from those in attendance nearly shattered the roof. It was truly deafening. It would have even made Gjrazzel's ovation seem pedestrian.

It's going to be so great to shut these people up and expose Maxx for the fraud that he is, Duke thought. But just as he finished that thought, another crept into his mind. *Holy hedgehogs, what if I actually lose? What if I lose to Maxx Gemstarr? I'll be banned from every reputable establishment in the whole of the universe. The Queen might even disown me as a patron.*

As the vents in the bottom of the arena floor sucked up the excess smoke produced by Maxx's hovercraft, Duke gulped nervously. Beads of sweat rolled down his forehead.

I can't lose. I can't lose. I can't lose.

His thoughts became more and more distracting as he approached the referee at the center.

"I can't lose. I can't lose. I can't lose," he mumbled aloud.

"Oh yes you can. You can. You can," Maxx replied in a velvety baritone. "And you will. And probably rather quickly and in a humiliating fashion."

The referee tried—unsuccessfully—to stifle a chuckle.

"What?" Duke said distractedly. "Shut up, Maxx."

"Ouch. Duke, you are on fire today."

The official laughed again, this time not even trying to hold it in. Duke glared at him and he clamped his mouth shut.

"You two know the rules," the referee began, "so I want..."

"We know what you want," Maxx interjected, "and I promise to give you and the universe what they want— Duke LaGrange out of this tournament."

"Works for me," the referee concluded and walked away.

The two combatants did not budge. Duke wiped the sweat from his brow but never broke eye contact.

"You know you're a loser, LaGrange."

"Loser can mean so many things. It's a big universe, lots of interpretations."

"Your jokes aren't going to save you today. Neither will a Blop or a Jungafallowian sneak attack or an insect that can't land. You are going to get really hurt. I'm going to make sure every bounty hunter, former bounty hunters, bounty hunters with expired licenses, wives of bounty hunters, and children contemplating an exciting career in the field of bounty hunting know that I was the one that broke you down and beat you to a pulp."

"What if I beat you?"

"What? Don't be ridiculous."

"Okay, let's say that you are the favorite."

"I am."

"Fine. And you should win. But you don't. Have you worked out how you're going to explain that to your fans? It's not like you lost to a Mega-Troll or a Jungafallowian giant or the greatest boxer on Gartosh. You would lose to another bounty hunter. And one that didn't even get a proper invitation. You won't be the Galaxy's Favorite Bounty Hunter anymore."

"It's the Universe's Favorite Bounty Hunter," replied Maxx.

"Whatever. You will just go back to being a muscled-up moron in spandex. You will go back to being the fraud that you are."

Maxx seemed to ponder this notion for a minute.

Go ahead, you big dumb animal. Get your mind thinking about something else. You only have so many brain cells, thought Duke.

Maxx came to attention. "Nope, don't think it can happen. There's no way that you can beat me, LaGrange. And it will be extra special knowing that Mazilda will be in my corner watching me decimate you."

Duke peeked around his rival's massive frame. "Where is Mazilda?"

Maxx turned around and realized that his girlfriend and corner man was not in her customary position.

"Trouble in paradise?"

"Shut up, LaGrange."

"Oh, and when I beat you, I'll make sure to add in an extra shot for how you've been treating her."

"I'm real scared," Gemstarr replied, expressing faux terror.

The Psitakki referee approached them at a full sprint. He stopped mere inches from the two combatants. "Guys, get back to your spots so we can start this thing," he ordered in between breaths.

The trumpets sounded. Duke LaGrange, one of the Andromeda Galaxy's most renowned bounty hunter playboys, would finally get his crack at Maxx Gemstarr, the celebrity known to all as the Universe's Favorite Bounty Hunter.

CHAPTER TWENTY-FOUR

SEMIFINALS

A FEW MOMENTS INTO HIS bout, Duke realized that Maxx Gemstarr might be a fraud when it came to bounty hunting, but he was a more than capable scrapper. In fact, he could teach master classes in the art of asskicking. Duke was slowly becoming his worst pupil. Though he had managed to avoid a disastrous death blow from Maxx's power gauntlets, he was proving less successful at avoiding his fists, knees, and feet, all of which were introduced to Duke's body with unyielding force.

"Have you ever actually fought anyone before, LaGrange?"

"Shut up, Maxx," replied Duke. "You can't be all that tough if I'm still talking, huh?"

Maxx connected with a swift boot to Duke's chest, sending the Nova Texan to the dirt. Duke's vision was getting hazy and his hearing a bit muffled. But he was lucid enough to look up and see Gemstarr's expansive grin and hear the chorus of cheers from those in attendance. He struggled more and more for each breath. He was not only about to lose to Maxx Gemstarr, he was about to lose without landing a single punch. He was going to lose without even getting a fleck of dirt on Maxx's ridiculous spandex jumpsuit. He was about to be the laughing stock of the bounty hunting world.

"Don't you wish Mazilda was watching this?" Duke said, clutching his chest.

"Your distractions aren't going to work. I wish I could say that I've been wanting to do this for a while but to be honest, LaGrange, I kinda forgot about you."

The hulking Gemstarr stood over the reeling Nova Texan. Duke wasn't sure what was going to happen, but he knew it was going to hurt.

Then he had an idea, something that he hadn't thought of in quite some time.

"My dad taught me this one," Duke muttered.

As Maxx raised his foot to stomp on his face, Duke dug his fingers deep into the arena floor, shoveling up as much dirt as he could. He hurled it directly into Gemstarr's eyes. Maxx staggered back, wiping the soil from his eyes. His blindness was only temporary, so Duke leapt on his first opening in the contest.

Duke struck Maxx in the face with his right hand, followed by a knee to the midsection, and another right to his jaw. Gemstarr winced and dropped to a knee. He held up his muscular frame with his right arm. Duke had him wobbling and he needed to finish him off. He drove another fist into his kneeling opponent's jaw. Maxx absorbed the shot and didn't fall to the ground as Duke had hoped. Duke went in for another but Maxx rose up before the strike could land, swinging his elbow back and catching Duke flush. The Nova Texan was once again on his backside with the Universe's Favorite Bounty Hunter standing over him.

"I thought you were an orphan," said Gemstarr. "What dad teaches someone that dirty of a trick?"

Duke couldn't think of a witty comeback. He could only think about his impending demise at the hands of someone that bastardized and profited off of the noble profession of bounty hunting. This was not going to be pretty.

"You've had your fun, now you say good night," Maxx declared softly. It was the first time that Duke LaGrange actually feared Maxx. *Maybe he isn't such a joke after all.*

Maxx raised his right hand in the air. The power gauntlet embedded in his forearm pulsed neon blue. Duke could hear a buzzing sound.

"Your time in this tournament is over!" screamed Maxx. Then, "What the—"

His arm began to spark and started to spasm in every direction.

"What's going on?" he shouted frantically.

His arm, driven by the gauntlet, whipped around his body in jerky motions. The motor in the out-of-control forearm guard was quite powerful; it twisted Maxx's entire body in a series of wild convulsions. It slammed him into the ground. Again. And again. The audience sat in total silence as the cries and pleas from the muscular bounty hunter rang throughout the arena.

Duke scooted to the barrier wall to avoid the flailing Gemstarr. He looked up at Ishiro'shea. Beside the ninja, in the area designated for the corner man, was Mazilda Cloax.

"What are you—" he began.

"Finish this clown," Mazilda hissed.

She handed Duke his favorite weapon, Ol' Betsy. The crowd started to complain—they obviously weren't quite over the controversial ending to the match against their home world hero, Gjrazzel.

Duke walked up to the clearly suffering Gemstarr. He

was standing but struggling to keep his arm at bay; he was battered and bruised.

"This one is for Mazilda."

The butt of Ol' Betsy cracked Maxx in the face. He dropped to the arena floor like a felled tarzantia tree.

Duke looked back at a smiling Mazilda.

This was a good day.

The referee raised Duke's hand in victory. Then the bounty hunter collapsed, equal parts exhausted and overjoyed.

Duke was on the couch in his holding room, wet towels on his forehead.

"How long have I been out?"

"Not long, Mr. LaGrange," answered a Psitakki medic. "We're just here to make sure that you can continue. It seems you are just a bit dehydrated. We've stuck a few tubes here and here to get your fluids back up. Your species loses your fluids at such a rapid pace, very odd. I'm surprised that you can do *anything* athletic in nature."

"Thanks, doc."

"I'm done here, you've cleared my tests. Get some rest, Mr. LaGrange. You've got a big fight tomorrow. I hope your luck doesn't run out."

"Luck? That's talent."

The doctor did not respond. He closed up his medical kit and exited the room. A team of four other Psitakki trailed after him.

"Ish, where's Mazilda?"

The ninja shrugged.

"She helped us. She helped me. Not Maxx," Duke said,

his eyes wide and his smile stretching across his face, nearly touching his jawline. "What do you think it means?"

Ishiro'shea repeated his shrug.

"Oh, wait a second, is Yvonne's fight on? I want her to waste that Jungafallowian monster. If she took out a Mega-Troll, she can take out this guy, right?"

Ishiro'shea turned on the monitor just as the fight was about to begin.

"This is going to be good."

The crowd was solidly behind the Gartoshian musk ox; Duke enjoyed the hate that Combatant 2 received from the fans. He was surprised how much he enjoyed not being the most hated competitor in the field. Prince Korzo-Tapor continued his taunting of the crowd both during the entrance and while standing in the corner man's box at the barrier wall.

Combatant 2 came out as the aggressor but Yvonne was able to avoid his clutches. She ducked under his lunges and frustrated the overgrown brute. After a missed attempt at a stomp, Yvonne landed a few hard body blows to the Jungafallowian's right side, just under his armpit. Due to his extreme height advantage, she had to reach a bit and it was clear her strikes didn't have their normal power—but they were enough to annoy Combatant 2. He lunged again and missed. Yvonne peppered him again on one side. He tried to counter with a big left hand but his swipe missed the musk ox. Yvonne connected a right cross to one of Combatant 2's heads. It appeared stunned but Combatant 2 didn't lose his balance. The fact that he didn't show much damage after the blow froze Yvonne—it appeared that she was trying to process the fact that he was still upright. It was enough of an opportunity for the Jungafallowian to grab her and hurl her across the arena.

Yvonne got to her feet having suffered only a few

scrapes. Combatant 2 ran towards her. She did the same, lowering her head as she sped towards the gargantuan beast.

"This is what she knocked Reginald out with," screamed Duke in excitement. "Get 'em, Yvonne. Get—"

His words ceased but his mouth hung open.

The musk ox had leapt in the air, horns first, as she had during the earlier action. It was a tactic that appeared impossible to survive. Her cranium struck Combatant 2 squarely in the chest. Duke estimated that the collision could be heard in neighboring star systems. The crowd was silenced.

Not only did Combatant 2 survive, he stood firm. Yvonne was face-first in the arena dirt. She was out. The referee approached, but the Jungafallowian caught him and tossed him away. The referee hit the dirt with considerable force and rolled into the barrier wall.

He's not done with her, thought Duke.

The Jungafallowian hoisted up Yvonne by her throat. She dangled unconsciously from his grasp. He paraded her around the arena to rousing jeers. He motioned that he was going to crack her skull with his fist. The crowd grew even more restless.

"They can't let this happen," shouted Duke. He ripped off the tubes providing fluid to his body and stumbled to the door. Ishiro'shea followed close by, katana drawn. Duke exited through the tunnel and into the arena. The prince and Combatant 2 noticed the bounty hunters immediately. Korzo-Tapor already had the microphone in hand to address the arena.

"How sweet! Duke LaGrange, our next victim, is coming to watch the last few moments of life of the Furry Mountain of Moon Colony #1. He must be curious to see what is going to happen to him tomorrow."

"Let her go!" Duke screamed from the other side of the arena.

"What? What was that? I can't hear you, LaGrange," the prince said over the loudspeaker. "I guess we have to kill her now."

Ol' Betsy sang. The arena floor in front of Combatant 2 burst up. Only a gaping hole remained. At the edge of the crater, Combatant 2 remained as still as a statue, still clutching Yvonne by the neck.

"Drop her," Duke yelled at the prince.

"Even you aren't dumb enough to..."

In one motion, Duke had holstered Betsy and drew his laser revolver. He loosed one pulse. It cleaved the top of the microphone off.

Duke and the prince locked eyes. The stare down lasted for what seemed like ages. Korzo-Tapor broke off first and signaled to Combatant 2. He dropped Yvonne unceremoniously into the pit that Betsy had created. He marched to the prince's location.

"We will see you tomorrow, LaGrange," the prince snarled. "You're a dead man. Big mistake. Really big mistake."

Ishiro'shea ran to Yvonne's aid, signaling for the Psitakki medical teams.

Duke was caught off guard. The crowd was cheering him.

The Grand Shaman came over the public address speaker, attempting to calm the situation. He sent in his personal guards to separate Duke from the exiting prince and Combatant 2. The situation was diffused quickly. Duke couldn't help but think that this was the producer's idea.

The medical team carried off Yvonne. Ishiro'shea looked back at Duke with concern in his eyes.

"Go ahead and make sure she's fine. Meet you back at the Pondscum tonight."

Ishiro'shea gave him a thumbs-up.

It'll probably keep his mind off of the Seamus stuff, thought Duke.

The bounty hunter was ushered back to his holding room by the Shaman's guards.

"I'm fine, I'm fine. You can go," Duke protested.

They threw him forcefully into his room. His momentum caused him to fall ungraciously onto the couch.

"Thanks, appreciate the help, guys."

The guards did not acknowledge Duke. One of them slammed the door and Duke heard their footsteps as they marched away.

A knock followed shortly after.

"I'm in here. Not causing any trouble. You can go away. Thanks."

The door opened slowly. It wasn't a Psitakki guard.

"I'm fine with a little trouble."

Mazilda has never looked so beautiful.

CHAPTER TWENTY-FIVE

ONE MORE ADVENTURE

DUKE SWUNG THE DOOR OPEN to the backroom of the Pondscum Tavern. It crashed against the wall. His life-long companion, Ishiro'shea, looked up at him. Duke smiled. Ishiro'shea then glanced down at what Duke clutched in his hand: the hand of Mazilda Cloax. The ninja stood up and held a glass high in the air.

"How about you do a little less toasting and a bit more pouring," said Mazilda with a smile.

Ishiro's eyes brightened. He vaulted to the beer barrels that lined the back wall. Before Duke and Mazilda sat down, he had placed two full mugs of Glyptodian Summer Ale before them.

"It seems that, for the time being, the band is back together," proclaimed Duke.

"Let's just get you through tomorrow alive," Mazilda said.

"Sounds like a plan to me," Duke replied, hoisting up his glass for another round of celebratory cheers.

The three reminisced about past adventures and misadventures, from Mazilda single-handedly sinking a Zylantian pirate ship to Ishiro'shea's sword battles with the Shark-women of Freylonia to Duke's trials dealing with the Hiritai tribes. Mazilda didn't appear to care too much for those stories. They shared laughs and tears as they recalled the time that they'd spent together.

Duke was in the midst of recounting a particularly crazy adventure involving him and Ishiro'shea on a primitive world, a madman, and a magic orb, when their session was interrupted by an irate Prince Korzo-Tapor.

"Don't bother getting up," the prince shouted as he approached the table. All four of his eyes were enraged. One head spoke as the other cycled through a progression of snarls and scowls. "Nice to see you, Mazilda Cloax. Ditching yesterday's news for your new toy?"

"I'm actually her used toy," Duke said with a smirk. "I pre-date that goon I beat down."

"Regardless," the prince said, "you will *die* tomorrow. No bones about it. It's over, LaGrange. No one insults me in public like that. You'll wish that your shot had actually hit me."

"Where's your friend?" asked Duke.

"Combatant 2 is resting. Trying to invent new ways to destroy you."

"Neat."

"He's unstoppable. You saw him today. Not even your cow friend could faze him. He took her best shot and shrugged it off like a gust of wind."

"I'll admit, Prince, it was impressive. But I have a few tricks up my sleeve."

"We shall see, LaGrange. Tomorrow you die."

"You've said that already. If it's my last night, can you do me a favor and let me enjoy it with the best friend a man could have and the prettiest lady in the galaxy?"

Prince Korzo-Tapor looked around at the table and laughed. He stormed to the doorway just as the Psitakki bartender was entering.

"Mr. LaGrange, the prince..." the bartender began, but then stopped at the sight of the Jungafallowian.

"A bit late there, barkeep, but no worries," said Duke. "The good prince was just leaving."

Korzo-Tapor left the room as the bartender apologized profusely.

"Stop," Duke said. "Go back and serve some drinks."

"So Duke, what are these tricks up your sleeve?" asked Mazilda.

"I got nothing."

Mazilda pulled out a pair of keys and dangled them in front of Duke.

"Lucky for you, I got something," she said smugly.

"What's that?" asked Duke. He snatched the keys and examined them. "Did you swipe these off the prince?"

Mazilda nodded.

"The emblem says Psitakki General Storage for Big Stuff and Really Big Stuff," read Duke.

"Hey, bartender, get back in here!" shouted Duke.

A few moments later, the bartender arrived.

"Do you know where this is? This General Storage place?" asked Duke.

The Psitakki glanced at the key and seemed to recognize the emblem immediately. "Yes, sir. It's just around the corner. It's a huge warehouse-type facility, heavily guarded. It's actually where we keep our surplus alcohol."

"Interesting," Duke began. "Why would a prince with unlimited funds, along with his prizefighter, be staying in a shady storage unit?"

"Interesting indeed," Mazilda agreed. "Maybe we pay him a visit?"

"I don't think you'll be able to get in," interjected the barkeep.

"We will if they think we're picking up some barrels of Glyptodian Summer Ale for you," said Duke slyly.

"I don't know."

"You don't want to be known as the bartender that prevented a finalist in the Tournament of the Shield of the Colossal Calamari from investigating a potential cheat..."

"Fine, fine. Just do it," the bartender said huffily. "I'll be happy when this damn tournament is over with."

That change of heart came on fairly quickly, Duke noticed.

The Psitakki tossed the key back to Duke and relayed a passcode for entrance into the bar's storage unit.

"If you get caught, I'm going to tell them that you robbed me at gunpoint."

"Fair enough," agreed Duke as the bartender exited the room. He turned to face his companions. "Ready for one more adventure?"

"But, promise me, after we see what's up with the prince and his brainwashed monster, we refocus our efforts on Ish's parents," Mazilda said.

"And Seamus," Duke added. "Yes. Of course we will. That's the most important mission, no doubt."

"What are we waiting for, then?"

This warehouse looks like a... well, a warehouse.

"I was expecting, I don't know, more," said Duke. "If the prince is brewing up something questionable, seems like he would've picked a place with a bit more, I don't know, pizazz."

"I think he wants to hide in plain sight," countered

Mazilda. "Nothing about this place really makes you think 'Oh, hey, there might be a crazed sociopath with an unhinged monster under his control in here'. It's actually what I would've done."

Duke clicked his fingers against his chin. "Whatever. So do we knock?"

"Or should we try to get in with a bit less..." Mazilda started.

"Permission?"

"That's one way to put it."

"I think Ish has already made that decision for us."

They looked up to see the emerald-clad martial artist scaling the drab stone perimeter wall. He gave a thumbs-up, then turned around at the apex. Not a sound could be heard as he, presumably, landed safely on the other side.

"Odd. No alarms," noted Duke.

"I don't think burglary is a common practice on Psitakki. Probably don't see the need."

"Or it means that the real security is on the inside."

The rusted door that marked the side entrance opened slowly with a whine and a creak. Duke drew his laser revolver, Mazilda pulled out both of her throwing daggers. The moonlight caught the blade and twinkled.

"I really hope this is Ishiro," said Duke.

From the shadows emerged the stout ninja.

Thank you.

He waved them in cautiously; Mazilda closed the door softly behind them.

The trio came upon a second door that led into an interior building and, fortunately, it was unlocked. They proceeded down a stairwell. It was musty, with sporadic puddles of standing water, but it wasn't gross. It wasn't a cave. Duke wasn't a fan of caves, unless they were on

Oscavia. This dilapidated warehouse was an upgrade from the majority of caves.

"I woulda thought that there'd be at least one person here. It's a huge storage facility and no one is tending to their stuff? No picking up or loading up or piling in? We can't be the only ones here."

"That *is* odd, Duke. What's the prince's unit number again?"

"1314, right, Ish?"

Ishiro'shea nodded.

"That has to be around the corner to the right."

As the three approached the unit, it was clear that unit 1314 was one of the largest in the facility. It was the size of most of the single-family dwellings on Earth or Nova Texas.

"I don't get the property choice, but at least the prince has some space. Maybe he got a screamin' deal?"

"Or maybe he's hiding something that can help you win tomorrow? There has to be something that will shine some light on his dealings or weaknesses in that brute of his," Mazilda added.

"That's the plan. Let me see the key, little buddy."

The gunfire came out of nowhere. More accurately, it came from the two units on either side of 1314.

A trap.

Four Jungafallowians emerged from the depths of the storage boxes and opened fire on the trio. Ishiro'shea bolted behind a pile of metallic crates. Duke shoved Mazilda out of the way and they both rolled to an area covered by a stone barricade.

Duke rattled off a bevy of pulses.

"I got one," Duke yelled. "Three more. They're toting pretty heavy guns for Jungafallowian thugs."

"Maybe the prince loaded them up with the best from his armory. He seemed to have this planned out."

Duke did not respond. He peered up over the barricade. An errant shot crashed into the stone mere paces from his face, and sent a chunk hurtling into the air.

"That was close."

The bounty hunter let loose another salvo of pulses.

"Got another one. I think. He's at least wounded."

"How did he know we were here? And why don't you seem to care?"

"I have it under control," replied Duke nonchalantly.

"What are you talking about?"

Duke lobbied a smile in Mazilda's direction.

"I don't like that look, Duke."

"Watch this."

The bounty hunter stood up and aimed Betsy at one of the storage facilities. She sang a melodious tune of chaos.

"Let's go!" he shouted.

Mazilda didn't flinch. Duke grabbed her by her arm and lifted her into the air. A less nimble being would have landed irregularly, tripped, and smashed their face on the ground. But Mazilda was one of the deadliest assassins in the galaxy; definitely one of the deadliest that had come from the ranks of bounty hunting.

Duke slid Betsy back into her holster and grabbed his laser revolver. He fired into the ceiling.

"You aren't hitting anything!" Mazilda shouted as he dragged her through the smoke-filled corridor, dodging enemy fire.

"I just want them to chase me. Well, us."

"What?"

Duke pushed open the door that led to the exterior courtyard. He slammed it.

"Hurry, let's head to the Pondscum. They won't follow us there."

"What about Ishiro'shea?" Mazilda asked.

"All part of the plan, Mazilda."

"What plan?" she questioned the bounty hunter.

"*The* plan. The plan to lure these guys out after us and leave Ishiro there to figure out the real scoop."

"You honestly planned for an ambush?"

"Of course. The possibility of an ambush, at least. The prince is a smart guy. He'll have noticed his keys were gone. Once he didn't come back for them—like anyone that didn't have anything to hide would have done—I knew that he knew we would be heading that way."

"That's a bit of a convoluted plan. Even for you."

"What are you talking about? My plans are usually on the simple side. Shoot and run. And talk to a pretty alien if there's time."

The duo heard the interior door crashing into the stone wall.

"Let's go, Mazilda. Ishiro is going to do some digging and meet us back at the Pondscum in a few."

"If he's still alive."

CHAPTER TWENTY-SIX

THE MAIN EVENT

DUKE LEANED UP AGAINST THE wall in his holding room. He twirled his pulse pistol on a finger, his gaze fixed on the floor.

"Hey, I'm worried about him too," Mazilda said softly. "But we're moments away from you having to fight that monster. He's crushed everyone that's he faced. Yvonne. That Olamandrian. Seamus. We need to come up with some sort of plan."

"I'm good," Duke muttered as he holstered his gun. "Ish will be here."

"I sure hope so. But whether he's here or not, it won't affect what happens in that arena. You need a plan, Duke. And what if..."

"What?"

"What if the worst happened?"

"That's easy. When I see the monster, I shoot the monster."

"The Psitakkis will be on you in no time. You'll spend the rest of your life with the Chief Interrogator General."

"You wouldn't rescue me?"

"Be serious."

"You wouldn't?"

The producer entered the room and broke the silence. "I can't believe you're still in this thing, LaGrange. But hey, ratings weren't too bad yesterday. Thanks to Gemstarr, of course. We're about ready for you. Where's your corner man?"

Duke pondered this question for a second. "I don't really know."

"I'm going to step in and handle the duties today," blurted Mazilda.

"Aren't you Maxx Gemstarr's girlfriend?" snapped the producer. "Well, this week, at least."

"I'm jumping ship for a winner," she replied.

"Oh. This is highly irregular," the Psitakki said.

"Think of it," Mazilda began, "even if the fight doesn't deliver..."

"It probably won't," the Psitakki interjected.

"Even if it doesn't, you can always spin a story about why Maxx's girlfriend is now with his hated rival, Duke LaGrange. Can you see it?"

The producer thought about this for a moment. A sly smile crept over his cephalopodan face. "Not sure that they'll believe LaGroin is Maxx's rival, but I do like the scandal, the intrigue. Gossip-rag angles do work. Everyone loves infidelity and scheming partners."

Duke stepped into the hallway. He looked around. No Ishiro'shea.

"Let's go do this," Duke said to the producer, without acknowledging the Psitakki's conversation with Mazilda.

The producer didn't respond. He turned his back to both Duke and Mazilda and tapped his headset. "What? What's going on? He's not what? I'm heading that way."

The Psitakki was clearly panicked. He glared at Duke.

"You know the way. Try and be somewhat entertaining. Or just die in a really exciting way."

"Isn't that what you told me last time?"

The producer scurried away frantically, screaming into his headset.

The Nova Texan looked up at the ceiling. It was pulsing with the vibrations coming from the arena. They wanted a finale worthy of the million-cycle history of the tournament. A finish worthy of the title "Tournament of the Shield of the Colossal Calamari."

The door slid open. The entire arena was pitch black. Suddenly lights and lasers beamed across the entire width of the stadium. Music boomed. It wasn't as elaborate an entrance as Maxx Gemstarr's—there were no Gemstarrlets or hovercrafts—but it was an upgrade over Duke's usual stroll into the arena amidst boos and debris slung by the fans.

The crowd gave Duke a healthy round of applause. Once again, it wasn't Maxx Gemstarr level, or even Sulaw or Yvonne or Glux. But it was probably on the same level as Jorb, or Tor-torta. Duke, for the first time since the Grand Entrance, tipped his hat to the fans.

"Introducing first, from the Earth colony of Nova Texas," the public address announcer began. "He's the greatest underdog story in the million-cycle history of the Tournament of the Shield of the Colossal Calamari; he's the first being to survive the melee match and win his first round contest; he's defeated the Royal Guardsman Glux Xyphormog II, he's defeated the Universe's Favorite Bounty Hunter, Maxx Gemstarr. He's the unexplainable and incomparable Duke LaGrange. A bounty hunter."

That's much better. Still no mention of Gjrazzel.

The announcer boomed, "And his opponent—"

He didn't continue. The microphone was simply cut off. Duke could sense the crowd growing curious.

From the entrance tunnel designated for Combatant 2 came another Jungafallowian. A much smaller Jungafallowian. A Jungafallowian that Duke LaGrange did not care for. And he had a hot microphone, wired into the public address system.

How does he keep getting hold of these microphones? Duke thought.

"What happened? Where is he? Where's Combatant 2? You know where he's at, don't you, LaGrange?"

Prince Korzo-Tapor was clearly not happy.

"That's funny, Prince. I had a question for you about a missing person, too," Duke shouted across the arena.

"What are you talking about, bounty hunter?"

This isn't going to go anywhere, concluded Duke.

The Jungafallowian prince turned to the Grand Shaman's box, halfway up a far section of seats.

"Shaman, disqualify this man! He kidnapped Combatant 2! I have it on good authority that he and his lackeys sabotaged my hotel last night and kidnapped Combatant 2."

"Hotel? Are you referring to that storage facility? The one with the armed thugs waiting to shoot us?"

The prince did not acknowledge Duke's dig. He continued to plead with the Grand Shaman. "This fraud has disgraced the name of this tournament, he's disgraced the Colossal Calamari, and he's disgraced the memory of Grozzel the Great. He's a black eye on the entire planet of Psitakki. You must deal with him. He must pay."

The Grand Shaman rose to his feet. His handlers and attendants followed suit. His robes flowed gently as he slid to the podium at the edge of his suite. From this pulpit, he could overlook the entire arena floor and address his people.

"Now, Prince Korzo-Tapor, I understand your complaint," he began, speaking into the microphone. "This is highly irregular, indeed. If what you say is true, that is."

"What do you mean?" hissed the prince.

"I have no proof that these accusations are true. It seems a bit far-fetched to think that anyone or anything could kidnap your impressive entrant. If anything, it takes some of the shine off of what was an unblemished reputation."

"He did. I don't know how, but he did."

"And," the Grand Shaman continued, "wasn't it you, mere days ago, that claimed that what happens outside of the tournament does not dictate the actions *in* the tournament? It was *your* Combatant 2 that injured Gjrazzel during the Grand Entrance. I allowed him to continue without penalty."

The recollection of this event caused a stir in the crowd. They began to cheer and applaud the Grand Shaman's train of thought.

He's a good politician, I'll give him that, thought Duke.

"Now why should I be so lenient towards you and Combatant 2, but not to Duke LaGrange?"

"Because Gjrazzel had that coming to him," Korzo-Tapor shouted.

The crowd's hatred reached a fever pitch. The Grand Shaman had to ask for them to calm down. It was apparent that even he sensed a riot about to unfold.

It was Korzo-Tapor that spoke next. "And we didn't try to make a mockery of the tournament. Did our personal dealings with Gjrazzel get a bit out of hand? Yes. But we didn't meticulously plan a kidnapping to disrupt the finals. This stain on evolution here... he did."

"A bit out of hand? My ass," shouted Duke from across the arena.

One of the prince's heads twisted back and flashed an intense glare at the bounty hunter.

"You do bring up some good points, my Jungafallowian friend," the Shaman began. The crowd started to rustle at this indication that he had had a change of heart. "But I do pride myself on being a fair leader."

The crowd veered back to cheering the Shaman.

He knows what he's doing.

"What to do?" the Shaman said with the voice of a true games master. "What should we do about this quandary? Do I send this bounty hunter to the Chief Interrogator General for a lifetime of torture and pain unparalleled in this sector of the galaxy, all on the word of my good friend, Prince Korzo-Tapor?"

The crowd moaned, groaned, and hissed.

"Or do I award the victory to Duke LaGrange? His ingenuity has allowed him to advance—in some cases, controversially—but he, to my knowledge, has broken no rules."

The audience applauded in favor of this course of action.

"Ah yes," the Shaman said, raising an index finger, "but, if Duke wins, then you are deprived of a final battle and a public beating at the hands of the Chief Interrogator. We do strive to give you your money's worth here on Psitakki."

The applause downgraded to only slightly positive murmurs, then into complete silence, then into gabbled conversation. A chant crept from the cheap seats in the upper regions of the stadium and into the areas of premium suites. It was gaining steam.

"Torture. Torture. Torture."

Both of the prince's heads turned back to the bounty hunter and smiled.

That turned fast.

"Calm down, my friends in attendance. No need to make a decision," the Shaman shouted in the voice of a great orator. "I've just received word from the back. It appears that Combatant 2 has arrived!"

"What?" shouted Korzo-Tapor. "Where?"

"It's obvious that Duke LaGrange did not kidnap his opponent," the Shaman continued, "and so, we have our main event!"

The crowd exploded.

Combatant 2 emerged from Duke's entrance tunnel slowly. Duke saw no signs of blood or bruises. He clearly hadn't been in combat.

Could he have killed Ishiro without even a scratch to show?

Combatant 2 trudged out slowly, to lukewarm applause. His plodding was so deliberate that Duke wasn't sure if he was actually moving. The fans clearly still hated him for what he had done to Gjrazzel, but he had shown up in time to provide them with a final fight, so had redeemed himself somewhat.

The prince stepped to the center of the arena floor and assumed the role of ringmaster. "Everyone in attendance, I present to you the greatest competitor in the history of this tournament. He's already set records that will outlast the universe itself. He's the destroyer of Kitar. He's the crusher of Seamus O'Hoolihan. He dominated and decimated Yvonne "The Furry Mountain of Moon Colony #1" Angerdlarnek. Now witness him obliterate Duke LaGrange in a matter of seconds and win a holy shield of Grozzel. He's the pride of Jungafallow III, he's Combatant 2!"

The ground rumbled and quaked as Combatant 2 crashed to the floor.

Duke was lifted into the air by the shock waves from the fallen monster. Korzo-Tapor, the closest to his collapsed entrant, fell awkwardly, dropping the microphone.

"No!" cried Korzo-Tapor. "This can't be. This can't be. Get up. Get up. Please."

The behemoth didn't move. But he did smoke. And he sizzled a bit. His back leg twitched irregularly. A single row of tiny explosions raced down his back. Slightly larger explosions followed all over the Jungafallowian's body. There was no blood, no exposed muscle tissue, no bones popping through the gaping gashes on his skin.

Metal.

"An android!" shouted the Grand Shaman.

"Duke, turn around, Duke!" screamed Mazilda.

"Holy hedgehogs!"

Stumbling towards Mazilda was Ishiro'shea. He was drunk. He toppled over the wall and hit the arena floor in the most un-ninja-like manner.

Duke ran over to his lifelong companion and knelt down. "You stupid bastard. You stupid drunk bastard. I thought I'd lost ya'."

Ishiro'shea gave him a groggy thumbs-up.

"You know Prince's guy is a frickin' robot?"

Ishiro'shea nodded.

"Wait. No? You didn't? Did you get the robot drunk?"

Another thumbs-up.

"And that's how you win at pit fighting with a drunk space ninja."

CHAPTER TWENTY-SEVEN

FAIR AND SQUARE... FOR THE MOST PART

"I'M IMPRESSED, LITTLE BUDDY. I mean, I knew you could drink, like *really* drink, but to outdrink an android... That's next level, right there."

Ishiro'shea allowed a chesty belch to exit his body.

The Psitakki guards surrounded the buzzing carcass of Combatant 2 and the fuming Prince Korzo-Tapor.

"Get him!" bellowed the Grand Shaman from his perch. The guards tightened their circle around the Jungafallowian.

"If I were you, Shaman, I would tell them to back off," said Korzo-Tapor, still gripping the microphone.

"And why is that?"

"If you don't, you'll die."

"Is that right, Prince?"

"It is," said Korzo-Tapor, regaining an aura of calm. He flicked his finger at the Shaman, signaling for the Psitakki leader to turn around.

The guards stationed in the Shaman's suite had disappeared. In their place were two Jungafallowian thugs. Both pointed powerful blasters at his face.

"Now do you believe me?" asked the prince maniacally. He jerked around to address Duke, Ishiro'shea, and Mazilda. "Put the gun down, LaGrange. If you as much as tickle me, my guys up there will splatter the Grand Shaman all over his adoring constituents."

"Why would I care about him?" asked Duke.

"C'mon, LaGrange, we both know that you won't cause political upheaval on another planet for the sake of escaping unharmed."

"I wouldn't?" Duke replied. "You think much higher of me than most, Prince. But you're wrong. I'm a survivalist, and an egotistical, self-centered one at that. I will most definitely do whatever is needed to save my skin, especially if it means the universe contains one less psychotic Jungafallowian."

"Fine, then, Duke. I'll give you some points for self-awareness. Fooled me. Go ahead and do it."

Prince Korzo-Tapor opened his arms as wide as possible, giving Duke a clear kill shot. "Kill me, bounty hunter."

The Grand Shaman screamed out from his stage, "Don't do it. We can work this out peacefully. Diplomatically."

"Go ahead, I'm waiting," the prince continued.

Duke begrudgingly placed his laser revolver back in its holster.

"That's what I thought," chuckled Korzo-Tapor. He turned his attention back to the Grand Shaman. "Here's what's going to happen. You're going to order everyone to drop their weapons. In fact, go ahead and do that now."

The Shaman signaled to the guards on the arena floor and stationed throughout the arena. They all complied.

"Then, I'm going to walk up to you, and you are—with a big smile on your face—going to award me the holy shield of Grozzel. Combatant 2 will be forever known as the last champion of this tournament. If I hear of you or anyone else saying otherwise, I will come back and personally disembowel you."

"Fine," the Shaman grumbled into his podium's microphone.

"Then you, me, and my two guards are going to proceed to my ship. If anyone tries anything funny, you get blown to a billion tiny Psitakki bits. Got it?"

Reluctantly, the Shaman shook his head in agreement.

"When we're safely in our ship, we'll throw you out of the cargo doors before takeoff, and we'll be out of your hair forever."

Solid plan, Duke concluded. *Probably what I would've done were I inclined to be a tyrannical villain.*

"What's the plan?" asked Mazilda in a hushed tone. "You are 'Mr. Plan' now, remember."

"No plan. I think we just let him get away. I mean, it's just a decorative shield. Frankly, I'm kinda impressed with the lengths he went to for an antique. I know some collectors get pretty intense over certain rare pieces; did you ever see *Attack of the Hobbyists*?"

"There's the Duke I know," Mazilda quipped.

"What's that supposed to mean?"

"Do you really think that the prince built a massive robot warrior that was undetectable to anyone as an actual android, traveled to one of the most deadly tournaments in the universe, and is staging what amounts to an assassination plot, all for a shield that's just really pretty to look at?"

Duke began to speak but was cut off.

"Don't answer that," Mazilda said. "You did, didn't you? Anyways, I'm inclined to believe that the shield probably means something. Something big. Maybe it has something to do with Ishiro's parents."

The ninja jolted out of his alcoholic daze at the mention of his parents.

"You went and woke him up, Mazilda, for a bunch of nonsense."

"Think about it. Seamus was looking for someone or something here that knew about Ishiro's parents."

"Yeah."

"The prince must've discovered something linking the shield and Ishiro's parent. So, he killed Seamus to get him out of the picture. He just assumed Combatant 2 would win without any mess and without attracting suspicion to the shield."

"But he didn't count on Duke LaGrange, trailblazer—"

"Stop it. But, yes, he didn't think there was anyone that could beat Combatant 2."

"Do you think that's why he attacked Gjrazzel, too? He did tell me that Gjrazzel was getting involved in business that wasn't his to get into."

"It's quite possible," Mazilda agreed.

"I guess that means that we *do* need a plan now," grumbled Duke. "Did I ever tell you that I'm not a huge fan of Psitakki?"

The trio peered up to watch Korzo-Tapor making his way up the stands to the Grand Shaman's box. None of the audience members tried to harm the prince, presumably for fear of being responsible for the Shaman's death. However, they did make some really nasty faces at him.

Duke pinched his temples with his thumb and middle finger. "I got nothing. Think, Duke, think."

"I'm not doing much better," added Mazilda.

"I wish the *Deus* was here," concluded Duke.

The prince had reached the Shaman's suite. "Open the case, oh great Shaman of Psitakki."

The Grand Shaman followed his orders. The glass

casing atop its marble pedestal tilted open, revealing an ancient circular shield.

Not as glamorous as I would've thought.

Korzo-Tapor jerked the shield out of the case and placed it on his arm. Both heads grinned as they surveyed the priceless relic attached to his forearm.

"Grab the Shaman and bring him with us," the prince ordered his two stooges.

A wooden projectile whizzed through the air from behind the Shaman's chair in his box. The tarzantia staff struck Prince Korzo-Tapor directly in the chest. Duke could hear the Jungafallowian's bones crack on impact. It reminded him of a recent episode at Cyborg Joe's when he had been saved from another ruthless Jungafallowian by a stampeding anthropomorphic musk ox named Lilly Arnaq.

The botanical missile not only crushed the sternum of the two-headed royal, the force actually lifted him off the ground and tipped him over the edge of the Grand Shaman's suite. Prince Korzo-Tapor plummeted with extreme velocity towards the arena floor. His body lay sprawled out, lifeless, his outstretched arm still sporting its super-expensive piece of armor.

The two gun-toting henchmen whirled around, but didn't know who to shoot at. The Shaman, noticing the opening, dove under one of his chairs. Duke sent two pulses out. Each struck one of the Jungafallowian thugs, who both collapsed to the floor. Duke wasn't sure if he had killed them, as his vision was blocked by the railing, but he was confident that they were incapacitated.

Duke looked up to the box. Out of the shadows stepped a Psitakki covered in bandages, limping, and generally looking like he was in a whole lot of pain. He kicked away the guns from the immobile Jungafallowians.

"That's one tough bastard."

Gjrazzel exited the Shaman's box to a raucous ovation. As he descended the steps towards the arena floor he was mobbed by fans offering pats on the backs, pleas for handshakes and hugs, even the odd unsolicited kiss.

Mazilda grabbed Duke and Ishiro'shea by the hands and dragged them towards the corpse of Prince Korzo-Tapor. "That's your shield, Duke. Don't let Gjrazzel take it," she snapped.

"Surely he won't. He seems like a good guy. But he *is* making a beeline for it."

"Remember, he thinks you cheated," she argued. "These fans think you cheated. He will try and take it. Trust me."

Gjrazzel reached the prince's body at the same time as Duke, Mazilda, and Ishiro'shea. Neither side moved. Not a single muscle twitched amongst the two parties. The crowd, for the first time in many days, was totally silent, without a single murmur coming from the thousands in attendance.

It was Gjrazzel that moved first. He reached down and grabbed the shield. Duke unholstered his revolver. Mazilda readied a throwing dagger. Ishiro'shea drew his katana.

The Psitakki looked up at them. Duke noticed the confusion in his eyes. His body was beaten badly, after all, and he had no weapon, at least that the bounty hunter could see. The four remained in this position for some time, each assessing the situation and running the odds in their heads about what action-reaction combination would give them the best probability of survival.

Duke then put his gun away.

"What are you doing?" barked Mazilda.

He placed his hand on Ishiro'shea's katana, lowering it without any resistance.

"Mazilda, put away your knives."

"What? No."

"Please," Duke begged, never taking his eyes off of the Psitakki and the holy shield of Grozzel.

"I don't like this," she huffed as she placed her knives into her belt.

"Thank you," Gjrazzel said. "Thank you, Duke LaGrange, and his friends, for not letting this abomination ruin the legacy of our planet and its greatest hero."

Duke tipped his hat.

"I believe this is yours," Gjrazzel stated. He extended the shield to Duke. "You won, fair and square... for the most part."

Duke smiled at the Psitakki's addendum to his statement.

"Congratulations," Gjrazzel continued. "You honor the memory of my great-great-great-great-great-great..."

"I got it," Duke interrupted. "Your ancient ancestor."

The Nova Texan grabbed the shield and slid it onto his forearm. Gjrazzel put forth his hand. Duke took it and the pair shook hands to an eruption of hoots, applause, and other bodily sounds of a positive connotation. Gjrazzel raised the bounty hunter's hands in victory.

The Shaman stepped up to his podium.

"Duke LaGrange," he proclaimed, "the last champion of the Tournament of the Shield of the Colossal Calamari."

"See, I told you that I got this," Duke said to Mazilda with a wink.

She responded with a subtle shake of the head and a not-so-subtle roll of the eyes.

"I don't know about you," Duke began, "but I'm ready to celebrate."

Ishiro'shea extended two thumbs-up.

CHAPTER TWENTY-EIGHT

A CRUEL REUNION

"SO HOW WAS I?"

MAZILDA slid closer to the bounty hunter and kissed him gently on the cheek.

"I've had better," she said with a laugh. She sprang out from the bed and walked over to a hutch in the corner of the room. She started to get dressed. "It's much nicer than the holding room, that's for sure."

"You're lucky you didn't see where Ish and I had to stay during the tournament."

"A dump?"

"That's putting it nicely. I don't even think *you* would be caught dead there with your clothes off."

Mazilda grabbed one of Duke's boots from beside the hutch and hurled it at him playfully. "Not funny, not at all."

"It's kinda amazing how much better your accommodations get when you win an ancient, quasi-religious combat tournament. I could get used to this," he said as he folded his arms behind his head. "Not a bad life. What's this joint called again?"

"The Palace Royale Hotel of..."

"Let me guess," Duke interjected. "...of the Colossal Calamari."

"Yep."

"And Ishiro got his own room! He never gets his own room."

"I'm glad you're happy."

"Are you sure you have to get dressed? Do you really have somewhere to be?"

"Are you sad, Mr. Champion of the Calamari?" Mazilda said, pouting. "Are you going to miss me?"

"Yes, of course," Duke said matter-of-factly. "Who, in their right mind, wouldn't miss a naked assassin of your skill set in their bed?"

Mazilda got back into the bed, only partially dressed. She crawled on top of Duke until her thighs were straddling his stomach.

"I think we have a bit more time," she whispered seductively. She bent down and kissed him. "How about we try this?"

"I'm game. Whatever it is, doesn't matter, I'm in. One hundred percent in!" Duke said eagerly.

"I sure missed your enthusiasm," Mazilda replied. "Let me grab something."

She hopped off of the Nova Texan and glided over to the hutch. She opened up a satchel and pulled out some shiny metallic objects. Within a blink, she was back in the bed and on top of Duke. She dangled the items in front of the bounty hunter.

"Handcuffs? You tart."

"I borrowed them from the Chief Interrogator General. I had an odd feeling that they'd come in handy, one way or another," she said.

"Not the most original idea, Mazilda, but on such short notice, it'll do."

She bent down and kissed him again.

"I promise you that this will be anything but unoriginal. You'll never have experienced anything like this before," she said assertively.

"Like I said, one hundred percent in."

She snapped his left wrist into a pair of the handcuffs, then cuffed it to the bedpost. She did the same to his right wrist using the second pair. She bent down again but didn't kiss him. Her lips were touching Duke's ear.

"I'm sorry, Duke," she whispered.

She vaulted off of the bed and headed back to the hutch.

"Very funny. Come back over here, you vixen."

"I'm sorry," Mazilda repeated.

"Not funny. You got me. This is original. Faking that you set me up in a not-so-innocent position. You win. Now come back over here!"

"I'm sorry," Mazilda repeated again as she finished getting dressed.

"No, don't put the clothes *on*. Mazilda, what's going on?"

She looked at him with a stern expression. As they locked eyes, her expression transformed into one of doubt, and then sadness.

She picked up the shield from the dresser and covered it in her cloak. She placed the bundle under her arm.

"This is what's going on," she said, signaling to the shield under her arm. "I really wished that you wouldn't have come here. It was a cruel reunion for both of us."

"Decidedly more cruel for one of us, obviously," Duke remarked.

"You have no idea what this is, do you? This is a power like you've never seen."

"You'd be surprised what I've seen recently when it

comes to powerful objects," Duke said, his thoughts drifting to his adventures on Neprius. "Why do you want it?"

"I don't. But my employer does."

"Your employer? What's going on, really? I thought you were going to help Ishiro and I find his parents."

Mazilda looked at the ground.

"This was all a lie," Duke shouted. "Us getting back together was a lie. Just a ruse."

She looked up. A tear fell from her eye.

"I'm sorry."

Before Duke could respond, Mazilda Cloax and the shield were out of the room.

I guess I should start screaming for help now.

"Don't judge me."

The green ninja remained silent as he worked on the handcuffs. Duke knew what he was thinking, though.

"You didn't sense it either. She fooled us both."

Ishiro'shea stopped working and glared at his bounty-hunting friend.

"Fine, she fooled me *more*."

The ninja went back to work on the handcuffs. They weren't releasing. Duke could sense Ishiro's frustration.

"Just cut 'em off. I'll worry about the pieces on my wrists later. If we're going to try and track her down, we better hurry."

Duke pulled his arms in as far as possible, creating a taut chain for Ishiro'shea to aim at. The bounty hunter closed his eyes. A gush of wind, a loud crack, and his left arm was free, then his right.

"Thanks, little buddy. We need to go now if we're ever to find her."

Ishiro'shea paused and tilted his head at Duke's half-clothed body.

"Yes, after I get dressed, of course."

The former Salutatorian from the College of Cohorts, Consorts, Co-Conspirators, and Other Assorted Sidekick Types darted to the door.

"You got an idea?"

Ishiro'shea returned a thumbs-up and then waved his hand for Duke to hurry up.

"Give me a second. I don't want to put Mazilda and her mysterious boss away forever in just my birthday suit."

Ishiro'shea and the now fully-clothed Duke sprinted down the hall and out of the Palace Royale Hotel of the Colossal Calamari, dodging reporters and children asking for autographs.

Ishiro'shea directed them down the road to the nearby auditorium that had hosted the Grand Shaman's pre-tournament gala. Behind the auditorium was the royal space dock for the use of the Shaman's guests. It was a lovely, albeit a tad gaudy, parking garage.

"Makes sense," Duke began. "She knew that you would rescue me and, likely, in short order. She wouldn't have let that happen if she was going to be lurking around here for a while, hiding out. She was heading directly for a pick-up and exit from Psitakki. And this *is* the closest place to park a ship. Let's just hope we aren't too late."

The sky above the spacecraft parking lot was a tranquil lavender color, without even a single cloud, open and clear—other than a titanic ship that was approaching rapidly.

"Wait a second—is that one of the Four I's ships?"

The bounty hunters looked at each other in terror.

"This is not an ideal situation, little buddy."

The spacecraft was of substantial girth. Upon its landing, the vessel took up a dozen spots allocated for an entire row of standard-sized commercial ships. It sported sleek lines and appeared to be made from a single slab of material, with no sign of rivets or junctions. It was beautiful. The only things that broke up the ship's clean facade were the multitude of guns, missile launchers, plasma cannons, and the like that covered nearly a fifth of the ship's surface. On the side, painted in white letters, perfectly sized and spaced so as to not detract from the awe of the armaments, yet not go unnoticed entirely, were the words: *Intergalactic Infrastructure Improvement, Incorporated.*

As Duke and Ishiro'shea approached, a rampway emerged from the underbelly of the Four I's battle cruiser.

A robed figure made her way out of the shadows of one of the Shaman's leisure ships and headed towards the ramp of the Four I's cruiser.

Ol' Betsy fired into the air. Mazilda stopped immediately. She turned around, still grasping the shield under her arm, though it was now unwrapped. Duke and Ishiro'shea marched towards her; she did not try to flee, nor grab her throwing daggers. From this distance, she could probably still kill them.

"You can't get away that easily," said Duke, still aiming Betsy at Mazilda.

"You shouldn't have come, Duke," Mazilda said. "Really."

"From your vantage point, agreed. If I didn't come, you'd have gotten away. And these bureaucratic nutjobs would get the shield. And that would be bad, I'm guessing."

"No. You shouldn't have come because there's absolutely no way that you can escape."

"You do realize that I'm the one with the sonic shotgun in this exchange, right?"

"It doesn't matter."

A crunching noise came from behind Mazilda. A dozen

Four I's soldiers marched out from the battle cruiser in perfectly straight lines. They were dressed in black tactical gear and each individual was indistinguishable from the next. When they reached the bottom of the ramp they fanned out behind Mazilda and pointed twelve automatic rifles at the bounty-hunting duo.

"See, Duke, it doesn't matter."

"Don't get too trigger-happy, guys. In fact, put your guns down or I blow up Mazilda and the shield."

There was no movement from either side.

"Hold," Mazilda commanded the group, motioning for them to lower their weapons. "So what do we do now, Duke? You know more of them will come and you'll either have to kill me or be killed. If you leave now, you can live to fight another day, in another battle."

"It seems that you forced me into *this* battle," Duke replied.

"And I'm giving you a way out. Go. Please. You weren't even supposed to be here. Maxx was my target."

"Gemstarr?"

"Yes, he was thought to be a favorite in the tournament and I just had to get close to him. Which, as you know, wasn't hard, considering he's a moron."

"Can't argue with that," Duke agreed.

"And the prince," Mazilda continued, "had the other side covered with his mechanized monster. Our employer felt pretty confident that one of those two would win the tournament and get the shield without any additional violence or notoriety. With no one expecting a thing, he would have a much longer runway to set things in motion."

"Wait? The prince was in this too? I knew he was lying about why he was here."

"I told him that his dumb machine wouldn't work. He was going to get caught."

"But you had us go after him. Remember the warehouse?"

Mazilda simply nodded.

"No... that was a setup," Duke said slowly. "You didn't steal any keys. You led us there to get ambushed and killed. How could you?"

"That wasn't my idea," said Mazilda, a note of pleading now in her voice. "But our employer thought it would be the easiest way to get the shield."

"That's why you didn't like the fact that Ish and I had a plan that you didn't know about."

"Yes, and it worked gloriously. I'll give you both credit. Leaving Ishiro there to investigate while the prince's goon chased us. But I still can't believe that he talked that android into having a beer with him."

"He's a good listener," Duke smirked. "And so I guess I was just your insurance policy once I beat Maxx."

Once again, Mazilda's silence gave Duke his answer.

"But you helped me beat Maxx in the tournament? Never mind, don't answer that. You thought I was an easier mark."

"With our past and all, it was..." Mazilda seemed to struggle to find the words, "...more natural."

"What if that bug would've beaten Maxx? Or the slime monsters? Would you've cozied up to them too?"

"I was going to make sure that wouldn't happen but, had it happened, possibly."

"I always thought I would be the one that sunk to these depths in my career—not you."

"You don't understand how persuasive my employer is and what he's promised me. If I get him this shield, I'll never have to work again. No more assassinations. No more hunting down or running from really nasty people. It will be over."

"This shield is that important to this cat, huh? Why?"

"I don't know. I really don't know."

"It's not like you to go into a mission and not know all of the details."

"I know it's not, but the pay and the promise made up for going without a few bits of information," she argued.

"A few bits? If they're offering as much as you say they are, you know it can't be good. Are you that selfish to put beings in jeopardy? An entire planet? An entire system? Just for a little rest and relaxation?"

"Wouldn't you?"

Duke pondered. He didn't like the accusatory tone, but he understood how his past actions might lead her to believe that was the case. However, Duke LaGrange was not a bad guy.

"No, I wouldn't."

"Then I'm sorry to disappoint such a noble warrior."

"Noble warriors," Duke corrected her. "Don't forget, Mazilda, you also lied to Ishiro'shea."

She has a soft spot for Ish, thought the bounty hunter. *Maybe she'll tell us some more.*

"I guess that's true," she replied.

"You even brought a phony photograph of Ishiro's parents to get us excited. That was possibly the cruellest thing that you did, ya' know."

"That wasn't a fake," Mazilda insisted. "It's real. And I really stole it from Potato Lips. He was after your parents, Ishiro, but not for the reasons he was telling you."

"How do you know this?" asked Duke.

"Because I'm after them too."

"Aren't you the busy girl," jabbed Duke.

"I thought you might have made some progress so I risked asking you. But you hadn't made any. Then I found out that Seamus *did* discover something."

599

"And he was going to tell us," Duke added.

"Maybe. And I couldn't have that happen."

"It was you. You killed him. Not Korzo-Tapor. You."

"It had to be done," Mazilda said drily. "Seamus was probably playing you both too. Don't you see?"

Duke shook his head in frustration and re-aimed Betsy at Mazilda. She tensed up.

"Please go, Duke."

"I can't go until I know why these Four I's guys want this shield. Guys, don't be shy. You tell me and Ish and we'll go."

"We don't know," Mazilda pleaded. "These guys don't know either."

"Aren't they your employers? And they don't know?"

"No, Mr. LaGrange, *I'm* her employer."

The soldiers parted to reveal a tall, slender humanoid wearing an outlandish uniform. Medals covered his pink jacket adorned with elaborate epaulettes. His tight trousers matched the color of his shoulder pads; they disappeared into knee-high boots that likely cost more than the space-craft parked beside the battle cruiser. He sported an equally garish mustache that extended far beyond the width of his face, yet was still pencil thin.

He pointed an antiquated pulse pistol at Duke. The bounty hunter hadn't seen that model in many cycles but he knew that it packed a wallop. A sometimes inaccurate wallop, but a wallop nonetheless, compensating for its lack of precision with power. On the back of the hand that gripped the gun, Duke noticed a tattoo.

A fish with a mustache.

"Nice pink jacket," said Duke.

"It's salmon, actually."

CHAPTER TWENTY-NINE

POOR, POOR DUKE LAGRANGE

"CAN I SAY 'WE MEET again'? I've always wanted to say that," Admiral Lothario LePaco said, plucking his thin mustache. It extended beyond his cheek and curled up into a tight spiral.

"I never pegged you for someone that asks permission for anything," replied Duke.

"How have you been, my old friend? It's been some time. We were quite the bounty-hunting royalty back in the day," LePaco said in a tone of reminiscence.

"You haven't been a bounty hunter in a long time, LePaco," Duke snapped.

"Once a bounty hunter, always a bounty hunter. Or something like that," LePaco countered.

"Have you even paid your dues to the Bounty Hunters Union?"

"Yeah... that's not a thing," LePaco said dismissively. "Please tell me you haven't been sending money to that scam? I wouldn't even stoop that low and I've done about every sinister deed in the book. Oh no, wait, you *have* been sending money to them. Poor Duke LaGrange. Poor, poor Duke LaGrange."

"Enough with the talk of the good ol' days, Lothario. What's going on? I have to admit, I'm a wee bit shocked that you're the leader of the Intergalactic Infrastructure—"

"No, no, no," the admiral interjected. "These guys? You think these guys are my grand plan? My opus of power? My—"

"Then what are you doing here?" Duke said, relishing the chance to interrupt LePaco in return. "With them."

"Oh, I've bought 'em. They do work *for* me."

Duke was perplexed.

"I'm sorry for maxing out the engine in that head of yours," said the admiral, "but the Four I's are just a company that helps me organize stuff."

"Stuff? As in planets and peoples and civilizations?"

"Yeah, stuff. They are a well-run organization that offers a service that I needed—so I bought them. They've been excellent. Outside of letting you escape from Tardasio 7. Mind you, those involved were severely punished."

"Why do you need to organize governments and planets?"

"When you plan to rule over the entire universe, you need a good infrastructure. And the word 'infrastructure' is right in their name. Look at the ship."

"I see it. How are you, pray tell, going to take over the entire universe?" Duke said with a laugh. "You're a slippery crook, I'll give you that. You've built up a nice seedy empire of crime and extortion, no doubt."

"Why thank you, Duke. That means a lot," LePaco said with a subtle bow.

"But running the universe? Taking over every system and galaxy that's been charted?"

"And those that we don't have charted," LePaco added. "Don't forget them."

"C'mon, that's crazy. Even for you. How would you even start?"

Duke glanced over at Mazilda. She was nudging her face at the object in her hands—the shield.

What's wrong with her? Duke thought as he watched Mazilda spasm, seemingly in his general direction.

"I'm glad you asked," LePaco said, "because I know a few things that you probably don't. I doubt many people in the whole of the universe know these things. Myself. A few trusted advisors. That booze-peddling wench, Queen Joe."

The inclusion of the Queen's name really vexed the Nova Texan. *How is she involved in this?*

"Shut up," Duke moaned.

Mazilda repeated her gesture but this time with a bit more vigor.

LePaco must have caught the action out of the corner of his eye. "What my associate is trying to tell you is that the Shield here is part of my plan. It looks ordinary to you, maybe a bit mystic and ancient, yeah, but on the whole, ordinary. However, it is, in fact, a crucial part in what could become the most powerful weapon in the universe."

"That shield?"

"Yes, this Shield. I'm not talking, 'Oh, look, he has a big laser' powerful; I'm talking 'This will rip down the very dimensional fabric of known time and space' powerful."

"Not buying it," Duke responded. "It's a shield."

"So, Duke, have you never seen an ordinary object—like a shield—prove to be more powerful than it appears? Could it have, I don't know, let's say magical powers? Have you seen anything recently that could be a boring old object one second, then a magical killing machine the next? Maybe something round?"

"Shut up, LePaco. I know what you're referencing. I'm to believe that the Orb that Controls Everything and Must Be Respected is somehow related to this Holy Shield of Grozzel?"

"Intrinsically linked."

"You're insane."

"My mental well-being has nothing to do with the relationship between that Orb and this Shield," LePaco remarked. "It's very, very true, my old bounty hunting friend. Deep in your gut, you know it. You can feel it."

"I honestly cannot. But even if you were telling the truth..."

"I am."

"Even if you were telling the truth," Duke began again, "I've seen what the Orb can do. It's not pretty."

"No, but it's powerful," the admiral proclaimed with a twinkle in his eye and a smile on his face.

"Yes, and it corrupts those that are close to it. The bastard that controlled it on Neprius was turned from a halfway decent scientist into a ruthless, maniacal ass in no time. It turned a relatively good guy into a mini-you. He was so brainwashed and decimated by it, there was no way that he was going to do anything other than destroy that planet and himself along the way."

"So, you stole it from him. Good job, Duke the Savior."

"No, we killed him."

"You killed Ot Vangu?"

"How do you know Ot Vangu?"

The admiral's attitude became more serious. He held the aged pulse pistol a bit firmer, a bit straighter. "Then, Duke LaGrange, it seems that you killed my half-brother."

"Come again?" Duke responded.

"Ot was my half-brother. He moved to Earth when he

was a child. We kept in touch but he never knew about my history, my career. And you killed him, in cold blood."

"Wait a damn second, you crazy bastard. I helped kill Orbius—the person that the Orb turned Ot Vangu into. Your brother was dead long before I ever showed up. He didn't even recognize the name 'Ot Vangu.'"

LePaco stared off in the distance but the barrel of his gun never left its position.

Is he crying?

"His mysterious disappearance was the first domino to fall," the admiral began in a markedly more somber and reflective tone. "The residual energy left behind from that Orb was nothing that I had ever seen. No one had any idea, but I had a hunch. I searched and searched, researched and researched. A few rabbit holes later, I made a few key discoveries that led to a revolutionary hypothesis. It led me to my destiny. A way for me to rule the universe."

"You are one crazy bastard."

"The energy signals surfaced again. First at Cyborg Joe's, which was interesting considering Joe was there."

"She's always there. She owns it."

LePaco disregarded Duke's comment and continued.

"So I sent Prince Korzo-Tapor to investigate."

"He told me he was defending the honor of the Trampling Death Robots."

"What we he supposed to tell you, LaGrange? That he was there investigating the remnants of a super weapon on the dime of Lothario LePaco?" the admiral replied angrily.

"No, but..."

"Then it popped up again, not long after he said he destroyed you and your freaky ship. We analyzed it for quite some time. Of course, we had no idea that you had been sucked up into the damn thing. And now we know that it took you to my half-brother. And you killed him." The final statement was punctuated with a menacing growl.

"Slow down, LePaco. If you do anything stupid, I'll blast Mazilda and the Shield. And your dream will be over."

"Go ahead, shoot it," replied LePaco.

"What?" both Duke and Mazilda said in unison.

"That's a powerful gun, I know. Widowmaker? They don't make 'em like that anymore, ya' know. But it's not going to even dent this Shield."

"But I'll be splattered across the side of the ship," chimed in Mazilda.

"I told you it would be a dangerous mission," LePaco replied.

Mazilda dropped the Shield and sunk behind the wall of Four I's infantrymen.

"Ready... aim," LePaco began.

He didn't make it to the final command.

A swirling light appeared behind Duke. The light transitioned into a portal that was large enough to fly the *Deus Ex Machina* through. Which was good, because that's exactly what was coming through.

CHAPTER THIRTY

THE THIRD PIECE

"OF COURSE YOUR SHIP SHOWS up. No way to escape and it shows up. You're gettin' kinda predictable, LaGrange," grumbled Admiral LePaco.

"Predictable just evened the odds, Admiral."

"Who's even driving that thing?" asked LePaco.

"It has a damn good autopilot setting."

"So, the stories of your legendary piloting, I see, are greatly exaggerated. The credit should be to the *Deus* herself?"

Duke chose not to take the admiral's bait. He kept Betsy firmly pointed at him.

Even when the *Deus Ex Machina* was fully out of the portal, it didn't close. The ship kept its exposed weaponry pointed directly at the admiral and his Four I's guards. The *Deus* hovered for a moment, then landed gently behind Duke and Ishiro'shea.

Who's that waving from the bridge? thought Duke. *Earl? How did he... Never mind, best to not ask questions.*

The side hatch opened. A faint melody emanated from the elevator bank. Ishiro'shea eyeballed Duke.

"I know, Ish, I'm going to change that music eventually."

Three individuals emerged from the *Deus*. The first was an athletically-built bipedal male carrying a glimmering broad sword. Po'l. The second was a wide-shouldered anthropomorphic musk ox from one of the moons of Gartosh, pounding her fist into her open palm as she approached. Lilly. The figure in the center of the trio sported no visible weapons. She was beautiful. He had known her for a long time and really enjoyed her martinis. Queen Joe.

"Well, today must be a special day," remarked the admiral. "On top of my favorite bounty-hunting odd couple, I get to meet a Miss Bovine runner-up and the always delightful proprietor of Cyborg Joe's."

The trio did not return the admiral's niceties.

"But *you* I don't know," LePaco said, pointing his gun at Po'l.

"Name's Po'l. From Neprius," the warrior said bluntly.

"I've heard the old expression 'bringing a knife to a gun fight,' but you're literally bringing a sword to an intergalactic battle cruiser fight," LePaco jested.

"I like my odds," Po'l responded, his focus on the admiral unwavering.

"Wait," LePaco began, "where did you say you're from?"

"Neprius."

"Ah yes, that's where the magic Orb was located, am I correct?"

"So what?" Po'l growled.

"You must've known my half-brother then?"

"I doubt it."

"I don't know. Does the name Ot Vangu ring a bell?"

"Orbius?" Po'l cried. "You were related to Orbius?"

"Well, Ot Vangu. Not sure why you lot keep calling him Orbius."

"We could call him by a more accurate name."

"And that would be?"

"Murderer. Tyrant. Dictator. Piece of..."

"I get it, Neprian. You didn't like him."

"Didn't like him? He killed too many of my friends and family to count. He tortured my people. I was glad when I got to see him shot down and the madness stop."

"You saw Duke kill my half-brother?"

"I saw Ja'a—" Po'l began.

Duke interrupted him. "Yes, he saw me do it. He saw me blast a hole in that bastard's chest so wide a three-headed ice wombat would fit through it."

Duke glanced back at Po'l. The Neprian seemed to understand Duke's intention.

"I guess I'll get to complete the circle and you can watch Ot Vangu's half-brother blow a hole through his murderer," LePaco proclaimed, his pulse pistol now aiming directly at Duke.

The Queen stepped forward.

"Enough of this, LePaco. This ends now," she said gently, but with a strong undercurrent of force.

"And you, my lovely Queen, are going to end this?"

"If need be. Tell your men to back down. And I'll take the Shield."

Duke was caught off guard. *So she does know about the Shield?*

LePaco seemed to notice Duke's reaction. "Go ahead, tell your friends about the Shield. About its powers. About how you knew where it was and sent Duke to his likely death to retrieve it."

"That's not true," she countered. "I do know about the Shield. And the shields before it that are forever lost in time.

I did know where it was. But I did not send Duke nor anyone to retrieve it. The last ninety-nine have come and gone without anyone trying to manipulate its power for evil. I had no reason to believe that this one would be any different."

"There wasn't a *me* around for the first ninety-nine," LePaco smirked.

"Why didn't you warn us, at least?" asked Duke.

"I didn't foresee any of this happening."

"Surely you saw Duke's little vacation to Neprius happening, right? You needed him to retrieve your precious Orb?"

"LePaco, you know nothing," the Queen snapped, "about the Shield, the Orb, anything."

"I know about the third piece. The Amplification Key."

Queen Joe paused. Duke couldn't see her, as he had his eyes and Betsy's barrel glued to LePaco, but he could sense her being shaken by that last comment.

"And I know where to find it," LePaco bragged. "What do you think about that, Queen?"

Duke felt a shadow creep over him. He turned, his attention shifting from LePaco and the Four I's soldiers.

Crackles and pops filled the air. The space surrounding Queen Joe turned from hazy gray puffs, to a smoky black cloud, to an obsidian wall of opaque gas that framed her entire body. Her eyes radiated a color Duke had never seen before.

"Admiral LePaco," began the Queen. Her voice had changed. The volume increased, but it became extremely distorted. Light emitted from her mouth as she spoke. "You will not leave here with the Shield."

LePaco was frozen in fear. His infantrymen began to retreat. Duke noticed Lilly and Po'l fall back as well, to avoid the growing ring of onyx gas. Seeing that he was no longer the main target for the admiral's pulse pistol, Duke stepped to one side to stand beside Ishiro'shea.

The admiral fired his pulse pistol directly at the Queen. The gaseous ring closed around her and seemed simply to reject the projectile. The cloud reopened to display an unharmed Queen Joe. The admiral tried the same tactic again, with the same result.

"What are you?" he whimpered.

"Hand me the Shield," she commanded with even more urgency.

LePaco shuffled over to the Shield and picked it up.

The explosion rocked the very ground that they were standing on. Duke looked back to see that the side of the *Deus Ex Machina* had been struck rather violently. And again. The Four I's battle cruiser was attacking.

Mazilda.

Queen Joe's appearance returned to its normal state, or what Duke considered her normal state. The artillery barrage had achieved what Mazilda likely wanted to accomplish: by the time they had collected themselves, Admiral LePaco was nowhere to be seen. Neither was the Shield.

"Let's get back to the ship," screamed Duke. "Before Mazilda turns the cannons on us."

The Four I's soldiers did not engage in a firefight. They fell back to their battle cruiser, providing a barrier to protect LePaco.

"No," replied the Queen. "I can't let him leave with that Shield."

Duke noticed that her eyes were still glowing. The protective gas wall was gone but her hands were still covered in the smoky substance. She raised the gaseous oven mitts, and bolts of electric fury shot out at the soldiers. Three of the men were lifted off the ground and deposited beyond the rows of ships. The remaining infantrymen accelerated in their retreat towards the ramp. The Queen sent another strike to the side of the battle cruiser. Its impact caused as much damage as any cannon that the *Deus* possessed.

"Queen, come back! They're gonna start firing at you," Duke screamed.

"The Shield," the Queen replied. "LePaco can't have the..."

The battle cruiser's cannon blew a small crater in front of the Queen. She was immediately displaced from where she had been standing, but, despite the force, she landed squarely on her feet. She hurled another strike. The battle cruiser rocked and wobbled. The ramp ascended back into the belly of the ship with the remaining Four I's soldiers clinging to it.

"Let them go!" Duke pleaded.

There was another blast from the battle cruiser. The Queen was sent across the loading dock but, again, landed safely on her feet.

Duke turned around and headed towards the *Deus*. As he reached the ship, he heard another explosion shake the Four I's battle cruiser. By the time that he reached the bridge, he could feel the return volley from the ship quake the foundations of the dock.

This isn't stable, thought Duke. *We need to leave now.*

"Buckle up and hold on," Duke advised Lilly, Earl, and Po'l. The *Deus* lifted into the air and hovered over the loading dock, level with the battle cruiser.

Ishiro'shea was already stationed in his usual seat and was nimbly dialing up commands on the control panel.

Phasers sung from the *Deus* and pierced the side of the battle cruiser.

The Queen followed suit with another blast.

"If we aren't leaving," Duke said, "let's at least bring this bastard down!"

Joe and the *Deus* tag-teamed another round of strikes.

"We got 'em," Duke muttered to himself.

Admiral LePaco and Mazilda did not counter with another shot. Instead, the lower hatches opened and a payload of explosives dropped from the innards of the ship.

"Joe!" screamed Duke.

The base of the multitiered dock crumbled immediately. The impact of the bombs caused the entire dock to fall in on itself like a giant sinkhole. It was reduced to a pile of twisted stone and infrastructure within seconds.

"No!" screamed Po'l.

Duke looked up. The battle cruiser was gone.

CHAPTER THIRTY-ONE

RACE TO THE WARP STATION

"I REALLY HOPE WE CAN make up that time," Duke muttered to himself.

"Are you sure it was the right thing to do, leaving Earl and Lilly behind?" Po'l asked. "Shouldn't we have helped them find the Queen? If she's alive."

"Was it the right thing to do?" Duke repeated Po'l's question. "Yes, I think so. Doesn't make it less hard. But it was right. If she survived that blast—and if anyone could, it would be the Queen—they'll find her."

"I hope you're right," Po'l replied.

"Me too," said the bounty hunter in a hopeful tone. "Earl wasn't going to leave the Queen. Even if he saw her scattered across the planet by a photon explosion, he would try and pick up the pieces individually. If he's going to stay, it's only right that we leave someone there to protect him. He's big, but he's a bartender, not a fighter. And you know the Shaman is going to be sending folks in to see why his private loading dock is now a massive pile of rubble."

Ishiro'shea turned away from the control panel and offered a nod of agreement. Duke appreciated the support.

"But why couldn't we stay? All of us?" Po'l asked.

"We have to catch that ship."

"It has a pretty sizeable head start."

"Yes, but the *Deus*, I would bet, is a bit faster, and the battle cruiser took a good deal more damage. I think we can catch up to it before they get to the warp station. Assuming that they used the public warp station."

Po'l thought about this for a moment. He seemed to be struggling with the notion.

"But why the rush? Why do we have to stop them now?"

"I think the universe might depend on it," Duke replied, somewhat cryptically. And dramatically. He turned his attention to Ishiro'shea. "Anything, little buddy?"

He shook his head.

"Damn."

"What do you mean, 'save the universe'?" Po'l said, continuing his line of questioning.

"That Shield that he has..."

"Yeah."

"Well, it's obviously important. Joe risked her life to get it back from LePaco."

"I'll give you that."

"And we know the Orb That Controls Everything and Must Be Respected is somehow connected to it. LePaco is going after it now."

"And Cyborg Joe's is..." Po'l began.

"Defenseless. Empty. Wide open," Duke finished. "I've sent off a few emergency calls for aid and defense to other planets in the system. Surely, Kelt has some friendly neighbors that don't want to see Cyborg Joe's destroyed. It could buy us some more time."

"And?"

"Nothing," replied Duke.

The Neprian sunk down in the co-navigator chair beside Ishiro'shea at the control panel. His dejection was palpable.

"That's why we are going to catch up," Duke said. "And destroy the ship."

"You would destroy the ship?"

"We have to," replied Duke.

"Even with Mazilda on it?" asked Po'l.

Duke paused. He took in lungfuls of air and exhaled slowly. His eyes couldn't meet Po'l's; he kept them firmly fixed on the ground.

"Yes. Even with Mazilda on it," he said solemnly. "She's the reason that we're in this mess. Whether she was truly that greedy or whether she was brainwashed or whatever, it is what it is. She's not more important than the whole universe."

Po'l raised himself up from the control panel and made his way to the circular barrier surrounding the captain's chair. He ducked under it to stand next to Duke. He placed his hand on Duke's back.

"You told me once that you felt that Mazilda was the one that got away. Maybe you *meant* to let her get away. Maybe you know, somehow, that her path was heading in a direction that wasn't right."

"Ya' know, Po'l, I think this is the first time that you've ever given me credit for anything," Duke replied.

"A lot has changed since I first met you in that cave outside of Dre'en. You still might be a bit of an ass for my liking but, as Uu'k called you, you could be my 'small doses friend.'"

Duke cracked a smile.

"Thanks, old friend."

Po'l nodded.

"Maybe I let the wrong one get away," Duke remarked.

"You mean you let her stay on a two-bit primitive rock," added Po'l.

Duke's smile grew as he gazed at the view screen.

Ishiro'shea sprang from his seat. The view screen blinked and beeped.

The battle cruiser.

"We got 'em. We can easily close this gap," Duke said joyously.

Po'l remained beside Duke, grasping the rail as they picked up speed.

"So tell me Duke, how do you know that LePaco's going to head to Joe's? How does he know that Joe has the Orb?"

"It's the same way he knew that it was at Joe's previously, when he sent Korzo-Tapor after me—the residual energy signature."

"It gives it off when it's just sitting there, lying around?"

"Not sure, but it does when it portals, I know that. And when we came back from Neprius, he picked it up. And it hasn't been used since and no other residual signatures were made, so he probably assumes—correctly—that it's still at Joe's. And he knows the Queen isn't there."

"Probably why the Four I's were there when you arrived."

"Seems to make sense," Duke remarked. "Speaking about those Four I's guys, I have a question for you."

"Yeah?"

"How did you get the *Deus* back? Don't get me wrong, I'm extremely happy that you guys did, but how? They seemed to pack a mighty punch. And they had an entire frickin' armada floating around the planet."

Po'l smiled.

"I have no idea."

"What?"

"I have no idea. No idea whatsoever."

"You weren't part of that specific mission?"

"Mission? There wasn't a mission."

"I'm not following you," Duke replied in confusion.

"There wasn't a mission to retrieve the *Deus*. It just started firing and broke free of the Four I's."

"I mean, it has done some interesting things in its day. Remember Vern?"

"We were sitting there—me, Queen Joe, Earl, and Lilly. Might have been a few others. I wouldn't say that we were officially planning or plotting or even scheming, but we were discussing the current situation. After you guys hopped through the portal and Joe sent those soldiers running away—the ones that could still run—we knew they'd be back. And they'd likely be a tad more angry. So we were chatting about how we could drive them away, what types of defenses the planet has, evacuation strategies, et cetera."

"The Queen thought they'd get more aggressive."

"She did. Something changed after you left. She became more and more worried. She didn't shake them off as another trivial nuisance."

"Interesting."

"But, as I was saying, we heard these explosions outside. Loudest thing I'd ever heard—well, until today. We ran out and the *Deus* was up in the air blasting down Four I's tanks, shooting up at the ships hovering close to the ground. It was insane."

"Who was piloting it?" asked Duke eagerly.

"No one. It was doing it alone."

Duke smiled and shook his head. Ishiro'shea turned back as he overheard the recounting of the episode.

Even Ish is shocked.

"Usually there's someone in the *Deus* when these things happen. And a big red button," Duke remarked.

"But after it broke away and sent those goons fleeing, it deposited itself in the field behind Cyborg Joe's. Of course, the Queen went to check it out. She returned sometime later, in a panic. Asked Lilly and I about going into a hostile environment on a rescue mission. I was bored, so I was like, 'I'm in.' Lilly wasn't as eager until she heard that it was on Psitakki."

"She probably thought Yvonne was in danger," Duke replied.

Po'l looked blank.

"Sorry, Po'l, never mind. We met someone that knew Lilly on Psitakki."

"Could be the reason. Not sure. Earl even volunteered to drive. So the Queen whipped up a portal out of thin air and then you know the rest."

"This damn ship," quipped the bounty hunter.

The view screen pulsed again.

"Well, Po'l, get ready. You're about to enjoy your first ever dogfight in space."

"I should probably go sit down, huh?"

CHAPTER THIRTY-TWO

A FEW COINS SHORT

COMPARED TO MOST WARP STATIONS, the one nearest to Psitakki was somewhat pedestrian. Sure, it had a circular portal—commercial-grade—that was half the size of a moon suspended in the vast openness of space, but so did all the others. And the others typically had a much better rest stop with halfway decent eateries and shopping establishments. This one had a moderate-sized snack bar and a few floating kiosks full of bits and bobs of Psitakki-themed merchandise.

However, to Po'l's eyes, the gargantuan disk sitting against its starry backdrop was pretty spectacular. His culture hadn't even made it to the soufflé stage of civilization.

"Quick, Duke, we're going to lose them," screamed Po'l. "They're right near it."

"That's fine. We want them to portal out of here," Duke responded. "We're going to follow them."

"What? What if they're heading back to Kelt?"

"That's the plan."

"Won't we be deposited right in the middle of their armada?"

"Possibly. But it beats us shooting at them, missing, or even hitting them and the explosion cracking the exterior of the warp station's portal. Then, they die..."

"Which is good," said Po'l.

"...and we die. The entire planet of Psitakki dies. Possibly the majority of the system dies."

"Which is not good," Po'l said, correcting himself.

"Nope. But we can tail 'em in there. When we come out, we sneak up on them—when they're out of range of the exit portal, that is—and we attack. We'll just be old memories by the time they clear the portal. There's no chance they'll think we followed them."

Ishiro'shea tapped on the control panel to get Duke's attention. He pointed at the view screen. The Four I's battle cruiser was entering the portal. The *Deus* accelerated to maximum velocity.

"Are you sure this is safe?" asked Po'l. Duke noticed him clenching his stomach.

"What? You've portaled a lot, right? Didn't you go to all of those pleasure planets and on your little 'epic quests'? In fact, you portaled *here*, didn't you?"

"Yes, but those were just door-sized. And coming here happened so quickly; the Queen just kind of pushed us through a slightly larger door, that happened to be in the sky. We didn't race headlong into a flashing hole bigger than a planet."

"It's not that big. But, yeah, you might want to hold on to something. It can get a bit bumpy."

A blue light above the view screen blinked repeatedly. *Click.*

"What was that?" asked the Neprian.

"It's charging us to portal. I just hope that I've got

enough…"

"What's happening?" asked Po'l. "Why are we slowing down?"

"Good question," said Duke. "Ish? What's going on?"

The *Deus* came to a sudden halt, despite Ishiro'shea's attempts to dial up maximum velocity.

An android popped up on the view screen. The robot was a pretty nondescript, standard-issue droid for the Department of Intergalactic Portal Stations. In other words, a titanium toll taker.

"Welcome to the Psitakki Warp Station and Portaling Center, I am Department of Intergalactic Portal Stations representative L43-EE49889. You can call me Wesley. We are very excited that you chose to take our portal directly to Planet Kelt. However, the account balance associated with this craft is not sufficient to fund the travel. Would you like to add funds to your account, Mr. Lafayette LaGrange?"

"Lafayette? No wonder you go by Duke," smirked Po'l.

"Yes, I'll add some cash, my good cybertronic friend," Duke answered.

The bounty hunter gave the robot five different account numbers, but none of them satisfied the monetary requirements.

If mindless procedural robots could appear frustrated, Wesley was at that point. "Mr. LaGrange, it has now been five attempts. I am going to have to ask you to power down your ship and exit the portal queue. You can return when sufficient payment is possible. I'm sorry and we hope to see you soon."

"Wait a second," Duke screamed at the view screen. "We're trying to save the universe. You let Admiral Lothario LePaco through your gate a few moments ago. You know Admiral LePaco, don't you? The most wanted man in the cosmos. And you let him through."

"He had sufficient payment. That is my only require-ment. Other concerns are not in my jurisdiction."

"We have to get through so that we can stop him from destroying the universe," Duke begged.

"If that's the case, I can let you through—" the robot began.

"Thank you," Duke replied.

"—once you have sufficient payment in your account," the robot concluded.

Ishiro'shea hopped up again and signaled out the front window. The portal was closing.

Holy hedgehogs, we must be the last one in the line for Kelt, Duke realized. *They're closing it.*

"We could sure use a nice giant red button right now!" Duke shouted at the ceiling of the *Deus*. "This would be one of those perfect times."

Nothing.

"Mr. LaGrange, please power down your vessel. The ship behind you wants to be on its way."

"Ish, turn on the comm and hail the ship behind us," commanded Duke. "Maybe they'll take an IOU or just help us out from the kindness of their hearts."

The ninja looked back at Duke with a sour expression.

"What?"

The view screen now displayed the ship behind them, which was also trying to leave Psitakki but heading some-where other than Kelt. It was a gorgeous state of the art vessel. Longer than the *Deus* but cylindrical and sleek. It was painted a bright yellow.

"Oh no. Hail him anyways. What can it hurt?"

Ishiro'shea hesitated.

"Yes, I'm sure," Duke groaned. "This is going to be painful."

The screen cut from the nagging robotic toll taker to the

bruised yet still very much handsome face of Maxx Gemstarr, the Universe's Favorite Bounty Hunter.

"Will you get your hunk of garbage out of my way so I can leave this awful system?" screamed Maxx.

"Hello to you, too," replied Duke. "Believe me, I want out of here as much as you do."

"Is that right? People started to turn on you once they found out that you cheated to beat me?"

"Not exactly. I promise I didn't do anything to you."

"My power gauntlets just malfunctioned on their own?"

"I didn't say that either," Duke countered, "I just said I didn't do it. You might have made another enemy on this trip."

Maxx thought about this and appeared to come up blank.

"And that is?"

"Think about it, Maxx. Who else was a tad peeved at you for how you treated them?"

He looked perplexed.

You really can't think of it, you oblivious son of a bitch?

"No idea, LaGrange."

"Mazilda, you idiot."

"Why would she be mad at me?"

"Because you treated her like garbage. Oh, and she was using you to get the Shield."

"You're insane, Duke. Now let me through."

"It's true, Maxx. Don't worry, she used me too. We're trying to track her down and kill her. She's working for Admiral LePaco."

"Now I know you're insane. He's dead. Or hiding. Or something. Why does he want the Shield? Why did Mazilda want it?"

"I don't have time for this. Let's just say that LePaco knows of a few artifacts of extreme power that, if he gets them all, can destroy everything. Mazilda helped him. She used you because you were the tournament's favorite."

"That's for damn sure," Maxx added.

"She sabotaged you because she decided I was easier to manipulate," Duke confessed begrudgingly.

"You're starting to make more sense now."

"I just need to get through the portal, but I'm a few coins short. Would you loan me some? Then I'll track down Mazilda and bring her to the justice that she deserves."

"So, you're admitting that you cheated to beat me, as that was the *only* way in the universe that you could've bested me. Then Mazilda made you look like a bigger fool than me. And now you're broke and need to borrow money from me. If I don't, the universe will likely end because of your gullibility and stupidity. Is that about right?"

The bounty hunter gritted his teeth. He gripped the guardrail around the captain's chair with so much force that he ripped the decorative padding.

I can do this, I can do this, I can do this, he repeated to himself.

"Is that pretty much the gist of it?" Maxx asked again.

"Yes, pretty much," Duke replied.

Gemstarr broke out into hysterical laughter.

"This is better than any Shield," Maxx said in between fits of hilarity. This went on for a few moments, then the screen went black.

"What just happened?" Po'l asked.

"I really don't know. But I didn't like it," Duke replied in the sullen tone of a broken man. "I feel like I've been robbed of my dignity. Not sure how much of that stuff I have left anymore."

The android reappeared on the screen.

"Thank you for your payment, Mr. LaGrange. Enjoy your travels to Kelt."

CHAPTER THIRTY-THREE

COSMIC FLOTSAM

"PRETTY FUNKY, HUH?" ASKED DUKE.

"Different," Po'l replied. "A lot different than when the Queen brought us to Psitakki."

"Oh yeah, her portals are much more pleasant than these D.I.P.S. jobs. You need a ton more oomph to portal ships all day rather than us fleshy hunks of meat with the occasional *Deus* throw in."

The Neprian seemed fine with that explanation.

Ishiro'shea was feverishly tapping the controls. The *Deus Ex Machina* was beeping and blinking as if it was preparing to go to war. And Duke knew that if he didn't nail his plan with precision, they would be.

"Yep, I see 'em, Ish," Duke shouted from his captain's chair. "They're coasting. They don't suspect us at all."

"Which is good, right?" asked Po'l.

"Yes, very. See that massive ship?"

"Yes."

"That's the Armada Titan that the Four I's sent to Kelt. It sits at the very back of the squad. It's basically indestructible. I'm guessing this battle cruiser is going to deposit our good friends LePaco and Mazilda and that Shield right into the Titan's nurturing bosom."

"Which isn't good?"

"It's not going to happen. Because right before they reach the Titan, we're going to blast them out of space. Done. Dead. Gone."

"What about the Titan and the rest of the armada?" asked Po'l.

"The Titan will take a month to turn around—not worried about that. We just have to outrun the other guys. I have a feeling that the fleet will leave once they know LePaco is finished."

"Why's that?"

"Because he's paying them," Duke said bluntly.

"Good call."

"And so we might have to lay low for a while, at least until the news of LePaco's death reaches those cruisers and scout ships that are chasing us. Small price to pay to destroy the Shield and LePaco."

"And Mazilda."

"Yes, and Mazilda," Duke sighed. "Thanks for reminding me, Po'l."

Why couldn't I have left him on Neprius, Duke pondered.

The *Deus* began its final charge to close the gap between itself and the Four I's battle cruiser carrying Admiral LePaco, Mazilda Cloax, and the mystical Psitakki Shield that Queen Joe was so adamant about keeping out of criminal hands.

"Every weapon that we have... Good to go?" asked Duke.

Ever reliable, Ishiro'shea returned a thumbs-up.

"I know this is your first space battle, Po'l," said Duke. "Let's hope that it's not your last."

"Cheers to that," responded Po'l.

He has spent a lot of time at Cyborg Joe's.

The ship was now within striking distance.

"Let loose!" commanded Duke.

The *Deus* fired off a barrage of weaponry that set the celestial backdrop ablaze. The already damaged battle cruiser couldn't get off a single return salvo—it was apparent that the systems had begun to fail. Ishiro'shea guided the *Deus* closer and sent forth a piercing plasma parade that sliced and diced the hull of the Four I's vessel. The lacerations soon became gaping wounds and segments of the ship began to detach amidst a spectacle of explosions. The violent, fiery outburst continued until much of the ship was incinerated beyond recognition. Within mere moments, the battle cruiser was cosmic flotsam.

A handful of rear scout ships peeled off and circled to engage the *Deus*. The Armada Titan sat motionless.

"Coming at us, Ishiro. Looks like four. No, five."

The ninja greeted their new adversaries with some well-placed lasers, clipping two of the ships and sending them spiraling out of control and out of the theater of battle. The other three rattled the *Deus* with concentrated blasts, but the ship's auto-response reciprocated the attack with even more powerful counterattacks. The pulses split two of the ships in half. A lone scout came in for one last approach but was disintegrated by the *Deus* before it could mount any attack.

The battle cruisers that flanked the Armada Titan and some of the accompanying scouts began to shift their focus to the *Deus*. They pulled away from the fleet methodically and moved into intercept courses.

"Time for us to go," ordered Duke.

"Do we try and portal back?" asked Po'l.

"Not sure Maxx gave us that much cash," replied Duke.

"I think we just have to outrun 'em for a bit. I'm thinking we circle back around Kelt and head that way. That puts an entire planet between us and the fleet."

The speed of Ishiro'shea's command inputs increased. Duke hopped over the rail and placed his hand on Ishiro's shoulder.

"I'll drive," he said.

Ishiro'shea quickly vacated his seat. Duke could tell that he was smiling under his mask. The bounty hunter excelled at many things, especially in his own mind, but his piloting skills could never be challenged. Their best bet, no doubt, was to have Duke LaGrange steer the *Deus Ex Machina*.

The Nova Texan took a deep breath. "Hold on."

The ship dipped smoothly, all the while picking up speed, and cut towards the planet. The battle cruiser that was leaving the left flank of the Armada Titan fired an errant shot, missing badly. The scouts pursued closely, the battle cruisers in the rear. Duke began to pull away, out of reach of the scouts' weapons. But not the battle cruisers'.

One of the long-range cannons connected with a glancing blow to the back of the *Deus*. It wobbled but stayed true to its course. Another hit. The *Deus* wavered a bit more, but the impact achieved little more than slowing down the ship momentarily.

"We need to pick it up," Duke muttered to himself, jaws clenched.

Another explosion. But the detonation was a few ships' lengths behind them.

We're putting some space between us now, thought Duke.

"Oh shit."

He gazed up at the view screen. Staring at the *Deus* was the battle cruiser from the other side of the Armada Titan, surrounded by three scout ships.

"What are we going to do?" screamed a panicked Po'l.

The *Deus* jerked again and dove towards the planet's atmosphere. Both battle cruisers and the legion of scout ships continued their pursuit. Duke sped over the uninhabited landmasses of Kelt at low altitude, approaching the more densely populated areas on Kelt's major province, Oldish Kelt. It was older than the seaside metropolis of New Kelt but much younger than the sprawling wastelands on the other side of the planet, dubbed Old Kelt. It was oldish. It was also the home to Cyborg Joe's Grill N' Go & The Why Not Saloon.

"We need to avoid any extended engagements until we're beyond Oldish Kelt," ordered Duke. "We don't need any more casualties."

The *Deus* whizzed over the bar and the surrounding townships that had built up around it.

"We're clear. When those scouts and cruisers are away from the cities, let's see if we can start picking 'em off one at a time."

Ishiro'shea worked furiously next to Duke, organizing a calculated precision attack.

The bridge shook. Po'l lost his balance and hit the floor. Another crash.

"What was that, Ish? Damage report?"

The ninja ran his fingers over the panel. He glanced back at Duke and shrugged.

"What do you mean 'no damage'?"

Another slightly louder noise.

"Check the scanners."

It was clear that Ishiro'shea's excitement was growing. He motioned for Duke to turn the *Deus* around and face their attackers head-on.

"Are you crazy?"

Ishiro'shea's posture straightened.

"Calm down. I trust you."

On the view screen Duke could see that the remaining Four I's ships in pursuit were in various states of destruction. Some were plummeting uncontrollably to the hard Keltian ground. Others were engulfed in some exotic electrical field that seemed to be ravaging the ships' outer hull like termites. It was obvious that the *Deus Ex Machina* was not their primary focus. One of the battle cruisers was relatively unharmed and was now pivoting to engage the ground force that had halted its pursuit of the *Deus*.

"I didn't know the Keltians had that good of a defense," muttered Duke to Ishiro'shea.

Ishiro'shea shook his head in surprise.

"Duke, that's no Keltian army," Po'l remarked.

Ishiro enlarged the view screen.

"She's alive," Duke said. "Son of a bitch, she's alive. And pissed off."

CHAPTER THIRTY-FOUR

THE BATTLE OF OLDISH KELT

"I REALLY NEED TO ASK the Queen about those electric bolt thingies."

"You didn't know she could do that?" inquired Po'l.

"No idea. First I saw of it was back on Psitakki. Crazy stuff. Did you know that she could do that?"

"Nope."

"Any luck hailing Joe's, Ish? Surely Earl or someone will pick up."

The view screen whizzed and blinked.

"Duke, nice to see you."

It was Queen Joe, *sans* black gaseous crowns, glowing eyes, or lightning flowing out of her hands.

"I think it's nicer to see *you*, Queen," Duke replied.

She smiled back. Duke hoped his comment came across as genuine as he intended.

"How did you survive that implosion? We saw you get sucked into that mess."

"What? From that tiny parking garage falling on me? Not even a scratch," she joked. "I'm just glad Earl and Lilly stayed back to help me out of that pile of rubble."

"I know you have a few secrets and I was fine with having to use a little imagination, but these recent events might require some explaining."

"Maybe one day, Duke. Right now, we need to figure out what to do about that Armada Titan and those remaining Four I's ships."

"I'm not worried about them."

"Why is that?"

"We blew up LePaco," Duke paused. "They'll leave now that their funds are gone."

The Queen frowned. It was a melancholy frown, not one of vitriol.

"I'm sorry, Duke. I know you and Mazilda had a history. Even complicated histories are meaningful."

"Can't believe those Four I's ships are still here, to be honest," Duke said, ignoring the urge to dwell on the emotionally-charged moment. "I thought they'd be gone now, especially since we have some ground cover as well."

A ringing sound pierced the bridge of the *Deus*.

"Never mind, Queen. I have a hunch this could be them now. I'll keep you patched in so we can take this surrender together."

The ringing continued.

"Ish, patch them in."

The Queen's image shrank on the screen to allow for a third participant.

"Are you kidding me?" shouted Duke.

"Nice to see you again, too," smirked Admiral LePaco. Mazilda lingered behind him, her gaze fixed on the floor.

"How did you? I saw you..." Duke stammered. "You went... boom."

Not my most articulate line of questioning, thought Duke.

"What? The battle cruiser exploding? We couldn't have

633

survived that. No one could have. Are you crazy? We transferred ships before we portaled back, just in case you gave up on the Queen and tried to chase us down. Sorry about killing her, by the way. This is truly a dark day for drunkards and wastes of space everywhere."

It was Duke's turn to smirk. He nodded in Ishiro'shea's direction. He plugged away on the control panel.

"Hey, Admiral," Joe chirped.

"It can't be. You were crushed!" LePaco shouted as Ishiro patched in the Queen to the conversation. "I saw it collapse on you!"

"I have a few tricks as well," the Queen responded.

"That seems to be true," huffed LePaco. "Oh well."

"Oh well?" repeated Duke.

"Yes, oh well. I guess this just means that I'll have to destroy the *Deus* and Cyborg Joe's today, then," he sighed. "More work, but I'd have to do it someday regardless. Might as well be now."

LePaco cut his communication.

"Stay in the atmosphere," Joe commanded. "Make him come to us. I can help from the bar. Do whatever you can to render that Titan inoperable."

"Any ideas on what that is? I've never had to do anything to an Armada Titan, let alone try and render it inoperable."

"I have no idea. I'm sorry. I'll have Earl and Lilly start evacuating the area. We probably don't have enough time, but whatever we can do will be better than nothing. I can try and portal some of them to other places but I need as much energy as possible to fight LePaco's ships."

"Understood. We'll figure something out."

Duke, Ishiro'shea, and Po'l didn't say a word as they waited for LePaco's legions to break into the Keltian atmosphere. They knew the massive casualties that Kelt was going to suffer, but this was likely unknown to almost every single being on the planet. Duke's stomach turned, tied itself into a knot, untied itself, finished a complex gymnastics routine, and then turned some more.

This was a fight that they couldn't win. The bounty hunter kept peeking around corners to see if a giant red button suddenly appeared. Maybe even the *Deus* gave up on this one.

About twenty Four I's scout ships entered into view. They halted and hovered in the Keltian sky. Three battle cruisers followed suit, and stationed themselves to the left of the squad. Another ship that Duke didn't recognize positioned itself on the right flank. It had an impressive display of weaponry but its model type didn't scream 'Four I's.'

Probably one of LePaco's thugs, thought Duke.

After the other ships had made their way into the skies above Cyborg Joe's, the Armada Titan slowly lowered its bulky country-sized frame into the atmosphere.

The scouts closed in aggressively. Their plan was clear: overwhelm the *Deus* and let the Armada Titan deal with Cyborg Joe's and any ground cover. A single scout, even if it had an hour of free fire on the *Deus*, could accomplish little more than some nasty scarring. However, twenty scouts firing at the same time could cause some major problems.

"You ready, Ish?"

The ninja began to belt out blasts at the approaching Four I's scouts. Duke was still manning the aviation, but even the most skilled pilot would have had a hard time avoiding twenty ships firing from every angle. Po'l stood next to the guardrail, clinging to it for dear life.

Not a good spaceship battle for a newbie.

Ishiro'shea managed to sting a few of the ships, sending them to an early grave in the Keltian countryside. But their offense was relentless.

"A little help, Queen," Duke yelled aloud.

Ishiro'shea tapped him on the shoulder and pointed at the front view screen. A Four I's ship was landing near to Cyborg Joe's. It wasn't firing.

A troop transport.

"Not good, guys—they're sending in a ground force," muttered Duke, as he steered the *Deus* out of the way of enemy fire, as much as he could.

He remained focused on the scene. The Queen was standing at the vanguard of what appeared to be a gathering of the patrons of Cyborg Joe's.

At least some of them have backbones, thought Duke.

The patrons made a circle around the enigmatic bar owner and started to attack the ship transport with a long-range artillery assault. As the troops poured out of the transport carrier, many were dropped by the Cyborg Joe's makeshift militia. However, the Queen's focus was the sky. She hurled electric bolts towards the behemoth Armada Titan. Even from this distance, Duke could see the frustration in the Queen's eyes. The Titan sat motionless and showed no ill effects from the Queen's concentrated assault.

She shifted her stance and set loose a few strikes at the scout ships, dropping two. She shifted again and volleyed more bolts at the transport ship. Even so, the invaders had a clear numbers advantage. The troops pushed on, despite losing numbers to the Queen and Cyborg Joe's makeshift squadron of regulars. They would be on top of Joe's in a matter of moments.

"We have to help them!" screamed Po'l.

"We can't," replied Duke emotionlessly.

"Why? They'll all die," shouted the Neprian.

"If we help them out, these scouts will follow us. They'll pick off the Queen and the entire lot of them without as much as a thought. They have a much better chance against the Four I's soldiers."

Po'l didn't seem satisfied with this answer, but Duke had no time for a thorough debate with the novice spaceman. He continued his elaborate maneuvering, which was designed to give Ishiro'shea as many opportunities as possible to thin out the scout herd.

"Look," shouted Po'l.

Duke fully expected to see the carnage that he hoped he would never have to witness—the destruction of Cyborg Joe's. But it wasn't. Not even close.

The troops were gone. Every last one of them. The transport ship was still docked. The road was littered with a few dead Four I's soldiers, courtesy of the Queen and the bar patrons that had defended their favorite watering hole. But where were the hundreds that had been exiting the transport only moments ago? The entire legion that had been marching towards the bar was no more.

"What happened down there, Po'l?"

"She, uh, sent them somewhere," he stuttered.

"She portaled 'em?" Duke asked.

"Yeah."

"Holy hedgehogs, that's amazing," Duke shouted, finishing on an indistinguishable sound, somewhere between a "woo-hoo" and "yippie."

Duke grinned and slid the *Deus* to one side. Ishiro'shea sprayed an array of lasers that took down four scout ships.

"The tide be a-turnin', little buddy," said Duke.

Queen Joe took out another scout with a bolt of electric death. The *Deus Ex Machina* cleaned up the remainder of the swarm, then Duke turned his attention to the Armada Titan.

"Now what do we do?" Duke asked his team. "I guess we can try to get close and then figure something out?"

Ishiro'shea returned a not-as-enthusiastic-as-it-should-be thumbs-up.

But the *Deus* was rocked unexpectedly. It rolled with such violence that all three aboard were flung across the bridge. As he tumbled and smashed into the walls, Duke noticed the floor was on fire. Thunderous claps echoed throughout the ship. It felt as if the sound waves would crush the ship like a Mega-Troll clutching a commemorative snow globe. Another boom and the ship rolled again. The vessel was out of control—the only way it would stop its current course was either an undesired handshake with the Keltian surface or for someone to get to the control panel.

"We need to stop this!" Duke screamed.

The bounty hunter regained his footing and dove at the panel. He missed entirely and crashed stomach-first into the flooring, which was now located where the wall should have been. Ishiro'shea nimbly made his way to the panel and flew through the air like a Brontortian acrobat. However, he did not account for the ship's roll and he landed on Duke's lap.

At least we'll be buried near Cyborg Joe's, thought Duke.

"Hey guys, I got it."

Duke looked up. Po'l was hanging on to the control panel.

"What do I do now?" he screamed.

"First, you need to push the eleventh lever from the right upwards, then press the silver button next to the teal one... Screw it, just start banging stuff."

Po'l punched the control panel repeatedly. He elbowed it. He even headbutted it. It fizzled and sparked.

The *Deus Ex Machina* came to a grinding halt.

Duke, Ishiro'shea, and Po'l looked at the view screen. Duke had never seen anything this horrific. This one-sided. The Armada Titan was unleashing a wave of unprecedented firepower across Oldish Kelt.

The Queen and the defenders of Joe's were nowhere to be seen.

CHAPTER THIRTY-FIVE

NEW LEPACO CITY

"DUKE, ARE YOU THERE?"

"QUICK, Ish, put her on the view screen," commanded Duke.

An image of Queen Joe appeared, then disappeared, then partially appeared. Static waves distorted the view screen continually.

"You're breaking up, Queen. Are y'all alive?"

"We're back at the bar. But we don't have much... That ship..."

The communication trailed off.

"...we have to take it down," she finished.

"We can't. Did you see it? I don't know what we can do," Duke replied. "I just don't know. It's too powerful."

Duke was a confident being. He knew he was a confident being. During the course of his life, he had been placed in some difficult situations and always found a way to come out of them relatively unscathed, both physically and emotionally. He also knew that many of those situations included invaluable aid from his life-long companion, Ishiro'shea, or his reality-bending ship, the *Deus Ex Machina*.

Both of them were with him now—but even so, he was at a loss, a true loss. The devastation below him around the city centers and neighborhoods of Oldish Kelt was more than he could comprehend. He knew he had played some sort of role in the deaths of the faceless and nameless below him. But the enemy that he faced, the one that he would have to eliminate to save those lucky enough to have survived the Titan's onslaught, was unbeatable.

"Duke, are you there?"

The bounty hunter snapped out of his daze. "I don't know what to do," Duke replied, his voice dripping with a sadness that shocked even him. "I'm sorry."

The *Deus'* view screen started to pulse.

"Answer it, Ish. Sorry, Queen, I have a feeling LePaco's about to ask for a surrender."

"Hold. Don't answer it, Duke. Whatever you do, don't surrender. We can't give up, even if it kills us."

"What do you want me to do? I'm already responsible for the deaths that he caused. I have to end this."

"You aren't responsible for that. LePaco is. The Four I's are. Mazilda Cloax is. Not you. You pulled no trigger that struck down an innocent. They did."

"We have no way to win this. I'm sorry, Queen."

Duke's eyes met Ishiro'shea's. "Patch him in."

"Duke LaGrange, how are you?" squealed Admiral LePaco jovially. "It seems that we can't stop talking to each other as of late."

"I'm elated, of course."

"I won't waste your time. I'm sure you want to try and save some of those poor plebeians down on Kelt that are burning to death. So, please surrender, fly down to help or fly away, I don't really care. I'm going to level Cyborg Joe's now and kill that inter-dimensional bitch."

"And if I say no?" Duke asked.

"Admittedly, you will slow me down. It will take me a bit longer to accomplish what I need to accomplish here but, don't misunderstand me, I will accomplish it. I'm giving you a chance to survive. Or help a few poor folks down below to survive. Like I said, I couldn't care less."

"Why? Why is the honorable Admiral LePaco being so charitable?"

"Let's say it's a favor to a mutual friend."

Duke felt a pain in his chest. It migrated to his stomach. His mouth grew dry. It hurt to swallow. Mazilda's betrayal was as painful to him as the horrors being unleashed upon Oldish Kelt.

Po'l ran over to Duke and whispered in his ear.

"Yes? Your answer, Duke?" the admiral persisted.

Duke looked at the Neprian.

"Are you sure, Po'l?"

He nodded in response.

"Tell Ishiro."

Po'l whispered to the ninja, whose eyes widened immediately, then he glanced towards Duke. A single nod followed.

"Sorry, Admiral. Technical difficulties. We accept your offer. I hope the Queen forgives us."

"She won't be around to hold it against you, LaGrange."

"But we would like to leave now."

"Not going to save the precious citizens of Kelt?"

"We're too insignificant to help. We just want to leave this squabble over some stupid antiques between you and the Queen. No one else needs to die, especially not me. I still have things to do in this universe."

"You're smarter than I thought," replied LePaco.

"Thanks. Good luck. You win."

"I always win," smirked LePaco.

Ishiro'shea cut the view screen.

"There are worse ways to die, I guess."

Duke fidgeted with the controls.

"Next stop, crashing into the Armada Titan."

"They need to name a wing at Cyborg Joe's after us if this works," Duke proclaimed.

Ishiro'shea smiled under his mask. Po'l did not respond but stood before the view screen with his chest puffed out.

He's always loved that honor stuff, thought Duke.

The ringing began again.

"Has to be LePaco again, right?" asked Po'l. "Do we answer?"

"Yes, I think so," replied Duke.

"Are you sure?"

"If we don't, he'll really think something is up. I don't think we can afford to have him question our motives as we try and kamikaze his ship into oblivion."

Ishiro'shea patched in the ruthless fugitive.

"Hello again, Duke. Can I ask you a question?"

"Sure, shoot."

"Why exactly are you heading directly at us? You aren't planning some heroic suicide mission, are you? You aren't a Valkyrie."

"C'mon, Admiral," Duke chuckled, "you know me better than that."

"He loves himself too much," Po'l chimed in.

The admiral smiled apprehensively but seemed to agree with that notion.

"It's true," Mazilda added from behind LePaco. "Duke LaGrange is no hero. He's too vain to be a hero."

"See, Admiral."

"Then why are you coming right at us?"

"I'll peel away right now. We were having some navigational issues. Our system is shot from the damage that we sustained. You had us reeling."

"That I did. Fine, then. Please course correct and exit this sector as quickly as possible before I change my mind."

"Thank you, oh merciful one," Duke said with a slight bow.

LePaco's image vanished. The *Deus* veered away from its direct course into the face of the Armada Titan.

"What are you doing, Duke?"

"Once we're out of his direct vision, we'll approach from the side. As long as we avoid that artillery ship, we'll have a direct shot at him. One ship crashing into the Titan won't do much damage... but flying right into the bridge will take out LePaco and everyone else of consequence."

"Are you sure?"

"Not in the least," replied Duke. "I'm open to suggestions. Even ones that don't involve us dying."

The ship was out of the periphery of the Armada Titan, then the *Deus* about-faced.

"Guys, here we go. Last chance to back out," Duke said.
Silence.

"No takers. Okay then. Maybe we'll get a statue."

The *Deus Ex Machina* sped towards the Armada Titan's forward-facing segment.

"I also hope that this is the right part of the ship. We could have used some schematics to confirm. No wait, I think I can see LePaco's beady eyes from here."

The *Deus* whizzed by the artillery craft and approached the Titan. Then the ship stopped. The abrupt deceleration sent all three men hurtling to the ground.

"That's twice in one day," remarked Duke. "I don't like it. Why'd we stop? What happened?"

The view screen buzzed again.

"Hit it, Ish."

Admiral LePaco appeared again.

"Not cool, LaGrange. Not cool at all. I thought we were becoming friends. Guess not. You had to go and do something stupid like that. I'm lucky that Mazilda clued me in. It helps having someone that knows the complicated mind of Duke LaGrange so intimately."

Duke did not return any response.

"So, if you haven't guessed, you're trapped in one of our close-range tractor beams. We use it to slow down, suspend, and disarm any warheads with the potential of blowing us up. This also includes ships piloted by idiots with death wishes."

"You're a bastard, LePaco," Duke snarled.

"Maybe. But I'm a bastard that has you in a tractor beam. Now I'm going to make you and your friends watch me level Cyborg Joe's, the Queen, and then the rest of Kelt. The Four I's will have fun building up the planet from scratch for me. I think I'll name it New LePaco City."

"But it's a planet. Not a city."

"Whatever, LaGrange."

"And is there an Old LePaco City?"

"Shut up."

"I'm sure the Four I's are going to ask you these questions, Admiral. Just a hunch."

"Regardless, say goodbye to your precious bar and that thick-headed interloper that runs it," LePaco said maniacally.

Ishiro'shea cut off the communication again.

"Thanks, little buddy. I don't want the last thing I ever see to be that guy."

"We failed," said Po'l. "Everyone's going to die because of us."

"Don't forget we're going to die, too," added Duke.

Every single one of the Armada Titan's guns refocused on Cyborg Joe's and the area surrounding the bar.

This is it, thought Duke.

"I'm sorry, Queen," the bounty hunter whispered softly.

On the long-range scanner, Duke could see Joe standing outside of the bar again. She was throwing every bit of lightning she had at the Titan. The damage caused was somewhere between harmless sparks and slightly less harmless sparks.

The Nova Texan left his seat and made his way to the captain's chair. He sunk into its warm embrace. His face dropped into his hands. For the first time, his mind was blank.

This is the end.

Then the entire *Deus Ex Machina* was engulfed in a blinding light. But it didn't shake. It didn't rumble. However, the light was unyielding.

"Is this the afterlife?" asked Po'l.

"If it is, I think it's pretty weak that I'm still in these clothes. I envisioned the afterlife having freshly-washed clothing." Duke murmured.

The ship started to shift slightly.

"Wait, Ish, are we... Hit it!"

The *Deus* broke free of the tractor beam.

"Get us out of here!"

Another wave of illumination permeated the bridge of the ship. But it pressed on. The light dimmed. As they moved away from the light, the explosions became audible. There were so many that it was hard to tell if it was a single, elongated blast or a symphony of detonations. As the *Deus* cleared the chaos, it pivoted to ingest what was happening outside.

Hundreds of ships, all different in size and design, surrounded the Armada Titan. The only thing more varied than the ships was the cacophony of armaments that were pelting the gargantuan vessel. The majority of the attack concentrated on the heavy artillery situated at the front and lower half of the Titan. It didn't get off another shot.

"Who are these guys?" asked Po'l. "I'm guessing they hate the Four I's more than us."

"And they're smarter and chose to bring more than a single ship and a crazy lady with electric fingers," said the bounty hunter.

Ishiro'shea looked back at Duke. They exchanged nods, then the *Deus* readied its guns.

"Let's see if they'll let us join this party!"

The ring of mysterious marauders continued to shell the Four I's flagship. It was clearly injured.

"It's trying to get away!" screamed Duke.

As the Titan slowly exited the Keltian atmosphere and entered space, the attackers moved with it. The constant barrage never ceased. The Titan was not going to escape.

Seems like they've done this before, thought Duke.

The artillery ship and the few ancillary craft that supported the Armada Titan had already been destroyed or had fled at the sight of this new military force. The Titan would not be afforded that luxury. As it approached deeper space, it started to implode. It was dying; the ships picked up their assault. The hull was compromised; a chasm opened up across the underbelly. The Titan started to fold up in a "V" shape. There would be no survivors on board. Escape pods were jettisoned, but the ones that weren't picked off by lasers would likely end up on Kelt, where they would not receive a warm welcome from the locals. The attacking fleet started to back away from the dying vessel so as to not get caught up in the floating fragments that could crush most other ships.

From the fiery wreckage darted a ship like a phoenix. It headed away at unfathomable velocity.

"Damn it!" shouted Duke.

"What?" inquired Po'l. "No one could have survived that, not even LePaco."

"I agree with you. But see that ship, that's him. I know it. It shot out of the Titan."

"You don't know that," snapped Po'l. "That could have been some low-level crew member, a random soldier, or someone inconsequential. It could be one of these new guys."

"Nope, it was the admiral. Probably Mazilda, too."

"What makes you so sure?"

"I doubt a random crew member flies a salmon-colored ship with a license plate that reads 'Mister Macho.'"

"It looked pink," added Po'l.

CHAPTER THIRTY-SIX

THE FLYING ROT

"LET'S ASSUME THESE GUYS ARE hostile," said the bounty hunter cautiously.

"These guys that just brought down the Armada Titan that was about to blow up Kelt, kill the Queen, and dissolve us into goop?" Po'l said. "I think we should be naming our firstborn children after them, rather than assuming they're hostile."

"Po'l, sometimes the enemy of your enemy is your friend," began Duke, "but then your shared enemy dies and they cease being your friend and become your enemy again."

The Neprian shook his head.

"You have *that* many enemies? How do you piss off an entire fleet?"

"I'm not saying they *are* my enemies... but you can never be too sure," said Duke, correcting Po'l. "Anyways, we're about to find out. Ish, I might regret this, but patch them in."

The ninja followed the orders. An elderly lady appeared on the screen. All three of her eyes blinked rapidly, each one focused on a different member of the *Deus Ex Machina*. Her four arms were folded defiantly but her face sported a welcoming grin.

A three-eyed Zylantian female pirate. Only one of those that I'm aware of, concluded Duke.

"I don't think we've had the pleasure of ever meeting face-to-face," Duke began diplomatically, "but your reputation proceeds you, Mama Fong."

Not only did her very noticeable mutation separate her from her kin back home, but she also was the only Zylantian that did not use her given name. For as long as Duke had known, she was simply "Mama Fong."

"As does yours, Duke LaGrange," she replied in a high-pitched whisper. If a voice could be pointy, Mama Fong's would pierce titanium. "I'm happy that you sent me a message. LePaco cannot be taken lightly."

"Excuse me, Mama, but I didn't send you a message."

"You didn't?"

"Nope," replied Duke.

"You didn't send a transmission requesting assistance to save the Kelt and Cyborg Joe's from Admiral LePaco?"

"I did, most definitely, but not to you," Duke clarified.

"That's quite interesting then, Duke," Mama Fong pondered. "I know you're a member in good standing..."

"Hold up, Mama. A member?"

"Yes."

"In good standing?"

"Yes. A member in good standing of the Bounty Hunters Union."

Duke leapt from his chair and hopped over the guardrail. He hugged Ishiro'shea and ran over to Po'l and embraced him.

"Yes! I knew it! I knew it!"

"Excuse me, Duke," Mama Fong chirped. "What's going on? What did you know?"

"Oh, never mind. Let's just say that some folks doubted your existence. Said y'all were a scam!"

"Probably LePaco, huh?"

"Yes, for one."

"He hasn't paid any dues in cycles. That's one of the reasons that we didn't mind blasting him from the sky. That, and the thousands of lives that his treachery has ended," said the BHU representative. "Also, the Union has a firm stance against this Four I's organization and their attempt to outlaw bounty hunting. The fact that they're working in tandem with the admiral is a pleasant coincidence. It made the trip from Daedeaus Purple even more worthwhile."

Daedeaus Purple. I knew it. That's where they are, rejoiced Duke internally.

"We can't thank you enough," said Duke gleefully. "Despite LePaco getting away."

"We noticed that as well. It's hard *not* to notice a ship with the admiral's unique... style. Quite unfortunate, but we have some tracers on his trail. We will know where he is going in short order and, more importantly, why."

"I know where he's going," said Duke. This proclamation shocked both Ishiro'shea and Po'l.

"You do?" said a perplexed Mama Fong.

"Not specifically. But I know he's looking for the third component of an ancient super weapon."

"What is this 'super weapon'?"

"I have no idea. But it has Queen Joe in a tizzy. She put countless Keltians in danger to stop him and get this Shield back, so it has to be something like we've never seen before."

"LePaco cannot be permitted to possess any super weapon," Mama Fong replied.

"There is no denying that statement, my good Mama.

I'm sure the Queen can fill you in. We have more questions for her as well."

"I trust the good Queen. If she's worried then we are worried. And I know she sides with us on the issue of the Four I's. We will pursue the admiral and see if we can slow down his plan. I hope to see you again, Duke LaGrange."

"And I hope it's at LePaco's funeral."

The aged bondswoman and senior official of the Bounty Hunters Union curtsied, then the screen went black.

The interior of Cyborg Joe's Grill N' Go & The Why Not Saloon was decidedly different than the last time Duke had graced the famous watering hole. It was clear that droves of customers had rushed out due to the looming invasion. Barstools were overturned, tables were littered with half-consumed glasses of alcohol, even the band had decided to leave their instruments strewn about the stage. The fiery barrage of the Armada Titan never quite reached the bar, so it was structurally intact. However, the nearby wounded had started to flood the bar's parking lot and front lawn. The Queen was waving them inside for medical attention. She portaled many of them directly to hospitals in the most advanced part of the cosmos, others she took care of herself. She was no medic, but even a powerful being like the Queen wasn't above slapping on a few bandages on some injured citizens.

One constant was Earl. He stood behind the bar. The image of the Glyptodian standing behind the bar at Cyborg Joe's warmed Duke's heart.

Maybe everything will be okay, he thought.

At the bar sat Lilly, the anthropomorphic musk ox from one of the moons of Gartosh. Po'l walked up to her and gave her a hug. There were a few other patrons that Duke recognized but didn't know. He made the rounds and shook each of their hands. There were a lot of questions, but not nearly enough answers.

After the group swapped play-by-play accounts of what had happened, Queen Joe made her way over. Her face was sunken with fatigue and her attire was ripped, shredded, and covered in dirt and blood, likely hers and those of the wounded that were still filing in. She leaned against the bar. All eyes, including Duke's, were on her. She positioned herself directly in front of the Nova Texan.

She said nothing.

"He got away," said Duke, breaking the silence. "His ship was in the Armada Titan. When it was going down, he escaped."

"That's not ideal," she remarked stoically.

"But..."

"Yes, Duke?" asked the Queen.

"The Bounty Hunters Union is following him. They were the ones that brought down the Titan."

The Queen looked at Ishiro'shea. He nodded, corroborating Duke's claim.

"I guess I owe you an apology for not believing," said the Queen.

Duke smiled, but continued the more serious part of the discussion.

"Mama Fong is tracking LePaco. They have a vested interest, with the Four I's trying to outlaw bounty hunting and all."

"That makes sense," the Queen said, again with little emotion.

"So what do we do now?" asked Lilly.

"We have to stop them from getting the Amplification Key," the Queen answered briskly. "They have the Shield, and its power is impressive, even by itself. Much like the Orb, it can cause much damage in the wrong hands. But, if he found a way to get all three, I'm not sure that we'll be able to stop him."

"Could he really take over the universe?" asked one of the patrons, a Sabromm outlaw named Klucky.

"Yes. I have no doubts."

"Luckily, we know that one of the artifacts is safe here," chimed in Po'l.

"For now. If he gets the Key, together with the Shield, he could wield a power that would be too much for me, even with the Orb in my control. Finding the Key is essential."

Duke slammed his fist on the bar. He could feel the dozens of pairs of eyes focusing on him.

I've had enough of this, he thought.

"Do you have something to say, Duke?" asked the Queen.

"I know that these weapons are powerful. I've seen the Orb. I've almost been turned into a burning pile of goo by that damn rock so I have no hesitation in believing that these items can rip apart the very fabric of the universe. But what..." Duke paused. "...what exactly are they?"

"A shield. An orb. A key," Po'l answered.

"I think, my Neprian friend, that Duke wants to know more details about their origins, why they are here..." began the Queen.

"And why I'm always being sucked into portals and landing on strange planets where these doomsday antiques are lying around," interjected Duke.

"I'm not sure that I have a good answer to that question, Duke. I wish that I did."

"How about let's start with what you *can* answer?"

The Queen walked behind the bar and started setting

up a round of drinks. She doused the glasses in Erontian whisky.

"Are you familiar with the story of Grozzel?" she asked.

"The Psitakki Shield guy?"

"Yes, the Psitakki that discovered the stockpile of Shields that saved his planet by forcing out the mysterious shadowy invaders," she confirmed.

"I think I remember something about that," Duke acknowledged.

"Those demon creatures are from another dimension; they're not of this universe. I'm not sure that I could properly communicate their names, but it roughly translates into 'The Flying Rot.'"

"Sounds fitting," Duke added.

"The Rot weren't there to attack the Psitakki," she explained. "In all honesty, they probably didn't even pay them any attention until they started to assemble and impede their chief mission."

"And that was?"

"To find the Shields," the Queen replied bluntly.

"I don't understand," added Po'l.

"As you may have guessed, I'm not from this dimension either," remarked the Queen.

"Yeah, I had a hunch," Duke smirked.

"The Rot are a race that have destroyed more worlds and galaxies than I can count. Their original home, even their original dimension, is unknown. Even to me. After countless ages of constant warfare across my entire universe, my race was able to finally destroy them. We designed weapons that could actually kill the Rot, and kill them we did. We believed that they were entirely eliminated, every last Rot demon."

She set up another round of drinks. Those surrounding the bar were so engrossed in her tale that they almost didn't even notice the free Erontian whisky slid in front of them. Almost. They all downed the liquid and reimmersed themselves in their engaging narrator's yarn.

"As you know from the story of Grozzel, we were wrong. But before we knew of their encroachment into your dimension, our worlds experienced a sustained period of peace. Of course, not every world did—as you know, a universe is a pretty big place—but with my race acting as an overseeing security council, no major conflicts occurred to put our existence in jeopardy. We ruled that the weapons that destroyed the Flying Rot were the only things that could disrupt our universe. If combined in the correct manner with the Amplification Key, these weapons could warp dimensional reality, tear seams in the space-time continuum, and wipe out planets, systems, galaxies, even universes."

"Why didn't *you* destroy them?" asked Po'l.

"We couldn't. They were indestructible," she sighed. "We did the next best thing: disassemble them and stash them away across as many universes as we could go to. Of course, that meant that my race, the only beings that could travel inter-dimensionally, had to leave our home and be scattered for eternity, never to return. I came here with all of the remaining Shields and buried them on a primitive world. That world became Psitakki."

"Man, you're really old," blurted out Po'l. "Millions of cycles old."

"A million more than that," added the Queen with a slight smile.

"So the Rot showed back up again and Grozzel found the Shields before you could get there and save them?" asked Duke.

"Yes. And as the Shaman designated the Shields as trophies for winners of a tournament, I knew it would make my job even more difficult because I would have to keep track of a hundred of these Shields. But I have."

"How?" asked Lilly.

"Indirectly, of course."

"Your portals," said Duke. "You've had patrons bring back key intel without even knowing it."

"Yes. I never put them into danger, just offered a sale on a certain world or accidentally mixed up a portal location. It worked."

"And Ishiro'shea and I were your buffoons for this tournament, huh?"

Queen Joe peered deep into the bounty hunter's eyes. "I chose you to provide updates on this Shield. I had no idea what was going to happen. Had I any indication that LePaco knew of the Shield or the Orb or the Key, I would have gone myself."

Duke crossed his arms and raised an eyebrow.

"Queen Joe," a voice said.

"Yes, Lilly?"

"I still don't quite understand how the other two artifacts made it here," the musk ox said.

"My only guess is that the Rot brought them here when they pursued the Shields."

"And how did they get across the universe?" Lilly continued.

"I don't know."

"The Orb does what it wants," remarked Po'l.

"Very true," Joe began, "and since we don't know where the Key is, it's hard to hypothesize how it got where it is."

Duke rose from the barstool.

"So what you're saying is that if LePaco gets the Amplification Key, he is an Orb away from consuming planets and altering the very foundation of our universe?"

"Yes, I'm afraid so," answered the Queen.

"And this Key, what does it look like?"

The Queen approached a crusty regular sitting at the bar. She extended her hand and he placed his knife hilt-first into it, as if she couldn't have meant anything else by her advance. She stabbed the point of the dagger into the bar, cracking the wood and leaving a sizable divot. She dragged the blade until it formed the outline of an unusual oblong.

"This is what it looks like, though somewhat smaller."

Ishiro'shea dropped his katana on the floor. The high-pitched clank caused the entire room to turn and stare at the ninja.

"What is it little buddy?" asked Duke.

The ninja walked over and picked up the dagger from the bar. He added a circle extending from one end of the drawing of the Key to the other.

A necklace.

Then he began scratching again.

Etched into the bar was a crude rendering of a necklace and the words: *My Father's.*

CHAPTER THIRTY-SEVEN

A STARTING PLACE

THE *DEUS EX MACHINA* DISTANCED itself from Keltian space. Duke LaGrange was firmly planted in his captain's chair. Ishiro'shea worked at the control panel.

"I don't know about you, Ish, but my head hurts thinking about it all. Magic orbs and priests lobbing javelins at us was bad enough, but now we have magic shields and keys. And don't forget about monsters from other dimensions, the Queen being able to shoot lighting from her fingers, LePaco being related to Orbius, and Mazilda, of all people, joining him. Oh, not to mention your parents could have the final piece that determines whether we'll save our universe or doom every known being in it. And we don't have any clue where they are." Duke huffed. "I think that about sums it up."

Ishiro'shea turned around and gave his bounty-hunting companion a friendly thumbs-up.

"Patch me in."

"Hey Duke," said Queen Joe. "Can you hear me fine? I

haven't used one of these comm devices outside of the bar in some time."

"Loud and clear."

"Before we do this, I do hope that, in time, you understand my decision to send you to Psitakki."

"We're ready," Duke replied.

"Of course," said Queen Joe. "I want to get out as far from the bar as I can."

"Just in case you're a bit rusty?"

"Something like that."

The crackle of static permeated throughout the ship.

She must've left the device on, thought Duke.

The Queen's voice could be heard, albeit faintly, through the crackles and buzzes. "Take them to the Father."

The bounty hunters waited in silence, their eyes fixed on the view screen. The stars twinkled against a backdrop of black. It started as flashing sparks, then seemed to double with every blink of an eye. Before a moment had passed, there was a portal looking back at them, an unstable astral anomaly blazing a tantalizing crimson.

"I thought we were done with this damn thing," said Duke.

The *Deus Ex Machina* inched ahead until it breached the threshold of the portal.

"You never get used to that," Duke said as he tried to reorient himself post-portal travel.

He rubbed his eyes and shook his head. "Now where oh where are we, little buddy? Where did this bastard drop us off this time? If we're back near Neprius, I don't know what I'll do."

Ishiro'shea plugged away at the panel. The results

populated on the screen immediately. The ninja swung around in his chair and locked eyes with Duke. His glassy stare was consumed with worry.

"T'ckuvu Prime."

Duke collected himself. "Hey, it's a starting place," he remarked optimistically. "Look, I know it's not a particularly great one, considering T'ckuvu Prime's reputation, but the Key was... is... our best bet. I'm sure your parents are fine."

The ninja gave Duke a half-hearted thumbs-up, then turned around to the control panel.

Yeah, he's not buying that. Come to think of it, neither am I.

THE ADVENTURES OF DUKE LAGRANGE **BOOK III**

HOW TO SAVE THE UNIVERSE WITH A DRUNK SPACE NINJA

JAY KEY

HOW TO SAVE THE
UNIVERSE WITH A DRUNK
SPACE NINJA

BOOK THREE

CHAPTER ONE

T'CKUVU PRIME

THE LIGHTS OF T'CKUVU Prime could be seen from any other planet in the T'ckuvu System; it was a testament and a symbol to the economic boom that the planet had experienced over the last twenty cycles. From orbit, even the keenest observer would be hard pressed to find a solitary patch of rock or grass or water or anything natural. It was an industrial sphere created by business dealings and inflated interest, floating amongst its more imposing but far less colorful brethren. Of course, in Prime's case—"Prime" being the colloquial title used on the planet itself—the business dealings were all shady, the inflated interest was all maliciously manufactured, and the economic boom was another phrase for takeovers by too many criminal syndicates to count. The cloud-piercing structures springing up out of the metallic jungle and neon sea of Prime could not mask the grim reality of the planet's foundation: bloodthirsty, egotistical, megalomaniacal crime lords and gang bosses. It was both a gorgeous visualization of what beings could accomplish with grit, determination, and ingenuity, and a grimy cesspool of malice, cruelty, and greed.

Surprisingly, Duke LaGrange didn't care too much for T'ckuvu Prime. Even he had standards.

The Nova Texan bounty hunter and his Japanese-Irish ninja companion, Ishiro'shea, had been on the planet for roughly a week and were no closer to their goal of locating Ishiro'shea's parents. On the positive side, there had been no major advancements by the universe's most wanted fugitive, Admiral Lothario LePaco, and his following of bureaucratic battalions known as the Four I's—Intergalactic Infrastructure Improvement, Incorporated. During their frequent communications with Queen Joe on Kelt, there had been no evidence of a single sighting of LePaco's salmon-colored spacecraft with the license plate that read "Mister Macho." Nor had there been any sightings of Duke's former lover, the assassin Mazilda Cloax. Nobody had been able to confirm whether she had even survived the Battle of Kelt; but Duke had a hunch that she was still alive. Until it was discovered that she was actually an accomplice of the admiral, this uncertainty would have been a pretty hard pill to swallow; now he was hoping that his hunch was wrong.

Duke and Ishiro'shea had spent their time on T'ckuvu Prime investigating the whereabouts of Ishiro's parents, but they had produced no worthwhile results. They had arrived with no leads and, a week later, they were still without hope. They did their best to avoid attracting the attention of the crime bosses, so brothels and casinos were out of the question, much to Duke's chagrin. The bounty hunters stuck primarily to the establishments that were known throughout the cosmos as the most trusted fountains of knowledge and wisdom and a haven of loose-lipped unknowing informants—the bars.

T'ckuvu Prime's list of bars was lengthy and unrivaled in the sector. There was a drinking establishment for every type of consumer—from dingy and discreet dens to celebrity hangouts to refined lounges for the sophisticated drunkard; and every type of theme or fetish—from a bar that catered to left-handed accountants to one that only served liquids derived from planets that have four moons to a particularly eccentric pub that required its patrons to chase every drink with the Zylantian treat of never-ending mayonnaise. Despite sampling the unique array of alcoholic delicacies of T'ckuvu Prime, it had been an entirely fruitless enterprise. Except for the juice bars.

"Are you sure we haven't been down this one before, Ish?" Duke complained. "These alleys are starting to merge together."

The mute ninja shook his head with certainty.

"I don't see much down this way, little buddy. Anything from the Queen?"

Ishiro'shea shook his head again.

"You know, I still can't believe they found the Four I's main manufacturing planet. Finally a win for us good guys. I was hoping we'd get some more updates on that by now. And, of course, it's in the Tardasio System. You think Sol brokered anything in that deal?"

The ninja didn't respond, his focus solely on the narrow concourse in front of them.

"I bet he did," Duke mumbled to himself.

They traversed the alley, and the deeper they journeyed, the less they were showered with the electric lights of advertisements and marquees that littered this particular district. The corridors grew so dark that it was almost hard to tell that they were still on T'ckuvu Prime, which wasn't an easy effect to achieve.

Ishiro'shea stopped and pointed up at a dilapidated sign

that hung by a single chain from a brick wall. It read "Booze."

Simple yet effective, thought Duke.

Under the sign was a shallow recess, within which was an unremarkable door. The door was beaten up pretty badly but Duke wasn't sure if the dings, dents, and bruises were from the natural wear and tear of time or from the crashing heads of patrons that were no longer welcome at the establishment. There was no handle.

"I guess we just... knock?"

The Nova Texan tapped the door gently with the back of his index finger.

Nothing.

He repeated the action with slightly more force.

Nothing.

He then rapped it with a fist.

A wisp of air grazed Duke's nose, causing the bounty hunter to jump back into the alleyway. Ishiro'shea, equally as close to the falling debris, did not move a single muscle, remaining in place with the poise of a statue. The sign hit the ground and splintered into pieces of various sizes. The chain swung back and forth, continually clinking against the wall.

The door opened slightly, enough for the occupant of the bar to speak without being seen.

"What do you want?"

The voice was aged and gruff, lathered in a lifetime of drink and bad decisions.

"What do you want?" the voice repeated.

"Excuse me, my good man," Duke began, "my colleague and I were in the neighborhood and were looking for a place to enjoy a drink or two. Your fine establishment sprung to mind. We..."

"Nope."

The door shut with a jarring twang.

"That went well," Duke said to Ishiro'shea.

He knocked again. The door opened again, still only slightly ajar.

"Just in case the door being slammed in your faces didn't get the point across... go away!" the voice roared.

"Is this not a bar?" asked Duke.

"It is."

"So why can't we come in and have a drink? That is what typically occurs in a bar," the bounty hunter replied smugly.

"Not this bar. I drink in this bar. A few select folks can drink in this bar. But not you, I'm afraid. Goodbye."

Duke's boot prevented the door from closing.

"Old timer, can we at least chat through this?" pleaded Duke. "We aren't here to cause trouble, we just want a drink."

The man was still not visible despite Duke holding the door open with his foot. There was no sign whatsoever of light within the establishment.

"Your foot being in my door says that you aren't opposed to some trouble," countered the mysterious door-man. "Feel free to go and register a complaint with the authorities if you wish. I'm sure they'll show you a lot of attention for such a heinous act."

"What are you doing in there that's so secretive?"

"Maybe this is an exclusive club of local celebrities and VIPs. And you, as far as I can tell, don't mean anything to anyone of consequence. So, you can go now."

Ishiro'shea tugged Duke's arm and motioned back toward the main drag.

"No, wait a second, Ish. He's lying through his teeth, if he has teeth. Are you a racist? Don't feel like serving drinks to an Earther and a Nova Texan?"

The force on Duke's boots lessened immediately.

"Nova Texan, you say?" the man asked, his tone now inquisitive.

"Yes, Nova Texan."

"Haven't met someone from there in quite some time." The voice softened, as if he was talking to himself. "Earthers, on the other hand, I see them all the time. But Nova Texas. Interesting."

"So can we come in and have a drink?" asked Duke. "It would be an honor. I don't think I've ever had so much trouble getting in to a bar."

The voice didn't reply but the door swung open to reveal a pitch-black hallway.

Duke looked at Ishiro'shea and shrugged. "We've gone into darker places."

"Are you coming or not?" howled the voice behind the door. "If you are, hurry up, and shut the door behind you."

Duke and Ishiro'shea ducked beneath the dangling chain to enter the lightless concourse.

"I wonder if they have any good happy hour specials."

CHAPTER TWO

THE TRUTH, IN MODERATION

THERE WAS A LIGHT AT the end of the tunnel, or in this case, the corridor. It wasn't a particularly nice bar but it had a few places to sit and, as the sign claimed, booze. Duke and Ishiro'shea wiped away stagnant dust that had collected on the barstools and took their seats. The counter was worn and not overly clean, likely one step above failing inspection.

So far, so good, thought Duke.

The doorman walked behind the bar and tied an apron around his waist. He was a burly humanoid, barrel-chested with forearms the size of most Earthers' legs. His face showed his age; cracks made barren tributaries around his nose and mouth. Despite his advanced age, it was clear that he had been a handsome man in his youth. Strands of silver hair covered his head and matching stubble dotted his jawline.

"What'll you have?" he said, his back to his newest patrons.

"Dealer's choice," responded Duke.

The man plucked two bottles from below the bar,

removed their caps, and slid them over to the bounty hunters. His knuckles cracked with every movement.

"Local brews. Good old-fashioned ale. Would rival anything they brew over on Glyptodia, I reckon."

"That's high praise, old timer," Duke responded.

He and Ish inhaled the beer. Duke choked. "Wow. That's... that's different," he coughed. "Are you sure you meant *Glyptodia* Glyptodia?"

"Yeah," the man snarled.

"I think they may have made some advancements in brewing technology since you last ventured out there, my good man."

"Or you're a giant pansy that can't handle a man's beer. Probably prefer a martini, eh?"

Ishiro'shea chuckled under his breath but all Duke could do was think about the Queen's famous martini. Even this calloused throwback would have to admit the tastiness of that concoction. Duke took another sip.

"Better the second time around," he replied, trying to save face.

"Right, stranger."

Duke and Ishiro'shea continued to down the T'ckuvian ale, one cautious sip after the next. Only a few customers were present in the single room: two T'ckuvian locals sat in a dimly-lit corner, a pint-sized Broan occupied the barstool closest to the far wall chomping on snack nuts, and another customer was asleep on the floor. Duke couldn't pinpoint the heritage of the downed drunkard, nor could he confirm that he was just asleep.

Best to let sleeping or possibly deceased unidentified aliens lie, thought Duke.

"So tell me, gents, why were you so eager to visit my humble dive here, even after I made it clear that I didn't want your business?" asked the bartender.

"Yeah, what was that all about?" replied Duke. "Who refuses business? Especially on T'ckuvu Prime."

"I do. And that will suffice for now."

"Anonymity, now that is *very* T'ckuvu Prime," responded Duke.

The bartender leaned in, his forearms resting on the uneven counter. "I repeat, why did you guys want to come in here? I don't think you're food and drink critics for the *Prime Gazette*. I don't owe anyone as much as a single damn T'ckuvian credit. I'm paid up on this place. I'm paid up on taxes. I haven't killed anyone in cycles."

In cycles?

"I'm sure you run a clean operation here," said Duke. "And we damn sure aren't in the bar and restaurant review ring. That racket is beneath even us."

"Then why *are* you here? Why were you so adamant about coming in?"

The incessant nature of the bartender's questioning placed the bounty hunters in a quandary. Duke didn't have a suitable cover and mentioning their true mission was risky. What if this crotchety old drink peddler was aligned with a crime lord? That would essentially guarantee his hatred of bounty hunters and would likely make him a tad curious as to why these two strangers were braving the urban minefield of T'ckuvu Prime to find two missing persons. Or, even worse, what if he had a partnership with LePaco? It was a stretch, admittedly, but LePaco's reach was not only wide but also diverse when it came to associates and accomplices.

The truth it is, then, concluded Duke. *In moderation, of course.*

"We've been on T'ckuvu Prime for some time now," Duke began.

"What's some time? A few cycles?" questioned the bartender.

"No, more like a week."

"Oh." The old man looked unimpressed.

"Hey, it's a dangerous mission that we're on," Duke fired back.

"I'm sure. Did a little girl lose her precious kitty cat? Is it up in a tree?"

"You done, old timer?"

"Go on."

"We're here to find someone. Rather, two people."

"That's not all too uncommon on Prime. People are always looking for someone here. What did these two people do? Murder a family member? Steal some cash?"

"No, we're not after them in *that* manner. We're trying to save them."

"Religious missionaries, then, I presume."

Ishiro'shea entire body pulsated in silent laughter.

"No, definitely not. More likely to be a restaurant critic," Duke replied.

"Then what? What are you saving these two poor souls from?"

"They're on the run and being heavily pursued by a really nasty man."

"This planet has a surplus of nasty people."

"This isn't your ordinary gang thug. This is Admiral LePaco. You know that name?"

The bartender grabbed two more bottles of ale from under the bar. He placed them under Duke and Ishiro'shea's noses.

"Yes, I've heard of Admiral LePaco," he snapped. "Who hasn't? How far from civilized space do you think Prime is?"

"Well, LePaco is back and now has a pretty impressive force at his fingertips. They're causing some major problems and trying to take over the universe."

"So I've heard," the bartender responded.

"You have? Great. Then you understand our situation. We were sent here on good intel from a reliable source, suggesting that the two people that we are trying to locate are somewhere on Prime. They're both from Earth. Probably around your age. Ish, show him the photo."

Ishiro'shea pulled out the photograph of his parents and showed the bartender.

"I'm guessing these are your parents?"

The ninja retracted the photo.

"Why would you say that?" asked Duke. "How could you even say that? He has a mask on."

"He looks just like them. Let me guess, Earthers. She's Japanese. He's Scottish. No wait, Irish. Yeah, definitely Irish. That makes you, well, a very interesting person, huh? Not a lot of Irish and Japanese hugging each other these days, right?"

The bounty hunters looked at each other.

"I'll take it by your silence that I'm right. So why are these two so important?"

"I'm not sure that's any of your business," Duke snapped.

"Fine, fair enough," the bartender replied diplomatically. "I learned a long time ago not to press people on this planet. The majority of the time, ignorance is not only bliss but it's what separates you from a *dead* you."

"We've been to almost every bar on Prime and no one knows anything," said Duke. "We're hoping that you can change that—and I'd say we're off to a promising start."

"Searching the bars first, smart move." The bartender raised a bottle of beer. "But I haven't seen them. I've seen Earthers come through, there's a huge transplant population here. No shock, right? But I haven't seen these two. Are you sure that you can trust your source?"

"It hasn't failed us yet," replied Duke.

"It?"

Duke debated for a moment whether it would be prudent to explain the nature of the astral anomaly produced by the magic orb that the Neprians referred to as the Orb That Controls Everything and Must Be Respected. He decided against it.

"Yeah, 'it.' It's not into gender identification," stammered Duke.

"Right," replied the bartender.

He's not buying that, Duke concluded.

"If you wholeheartedly trust this source of yours—"

"We do," interjected Duke.

"Right, well if you do, then I can only offer my sincere good luck."

"Thanks for the help. And thanks for the local brew. What do I owe you?"

"On the house."

"Really?"

"It's been a while since I talked to a Nova Texan."

"Free beer for being a novelty?"

"I'm sorry if that offends you, stranger."

"Not at all, I wish every place had that policy."

"What's your name, if you don't mind me asking? If I see another Nova Texan in my bar, I'll ask them if they know you."

"Duke LaGrange. Adventurer. Trailblazer. Poet. A true man of the universe. They might not know me, but they'll have heard of me."

Ishiro'shea's eyes rolled back.

"Is that right?"

"And this is Ishiro'shea. Of Earth. But you know that."

"And he doesn't speak?" asked the bartender.

"He can, at least, I think he can. He swore a vow of silence until he's reunited with his parents."

"Honorable. Don't see that much these days," the old man stated. He turned to face the ninja. "I really wish that I could help you, my mute friend."

It was the first time that the grizzly barkeep seemed somewhat likable.

Ishiro'shea placed the photo of his parents on the counter and extended his hand over the bar. The bartender shook it.

"Good luck, Duke LaGrange and Ishiro'shea..." He trailed off as something caught his eye. He picked up the photograph and examined it closely.

"What is it? Do you recognize them after all?" said Duke, his optimism unguarded.

"No."

"Oh."

The bartender sat the photo down and tapped part of the image of Ishiro'shea's father.

"But I know what *this* is."

How did this nameless owner of a ramshackle old bar in an unlit alley on T'ckuvu Prime come to know about Ishiro'shea's father's necklace?

"What *what* is?" asked Duke, feigning ignorance.

"The necklace. Or rather the pendant that he's wearing. Your pops must run with some pretty ritzy crowds, Ishiro'shea."

"I don't understand," replied Duke.

"That flash of jewelry right there is as old as this planet. Maybe older. It was stashed away on Earth. Japan, I'm guessing. It was said to be a magic pendant that helped a brave samurai save his peoples back on ancient Earth. No one knows where he got it, or how he got it. I thought it was locked away in some museum vault. But there it is. Unless it's a replica, of course."

"Probably just a replica," said Duke quickly.

"It's priceless."

At that moment, before the last syllable in "priceless" was finished, the two native T'ckuvians approached and sat on either side of the bounty hunters. They stood as tall as a Jungafallowian, their shoulders extending above where their head rested. It wasn't unreasonable to think that the T'ckuvians evolved to meet the planet's growing need of thugs and street toughs. These guys were big, ugly, and didn't come across as scholastically-minded types.

"'Allo there," the orange T'ckuvian belted. The stench of fermented grain was overwhelming. *Did this guy drink the beer or bathe in it?*

"Yeah, 'allo there from me too," echoed the purple T'ckuvian. "Where are you twos from? Not from here, I see."

"Why do you say that?" asked Duke.

"First off, you don't look like us. Second, I ain't never seen 'ya. Third, and this is the real kicker, you're drinkin' in *this* dump."

The orange T'ckuvian cackled wheezily at the purple brute's joke. The bartender ignored the comment and placed two mugs of ale in front of the locals.

"I need better clientele," said the barman.

"This place isn't that bad," countered Duke. "I prefer a nice local dive bar with a set of esteemed and classy regulars."

He raised his glass. The T'ckuvians did not reciprocate.

"My name's Roller," said the purple T'ckuvian. "This here's Noot."

"'Allo again," added Noot. He scratched the tiny patch of straw yellow hair on the top of his head. "Welcome to Prime."

"Obliged," replied Duke.

"Did we hears you sayin' that you have something priceless that needs findin'?" asked Roller.

"We didn't say anything about anything being priceless. My good man here did," replied Duke, pointing to the bartender.

"He's right," responded the crusty bartender "I did say it. But I'm right. It's quite an artifact. And to think it could be somewhere on T'ckuvu Prime."

The two brutish T'ckuvians exchanged glances and deep-throated laughs.

"Dare I ask what's so funny?" Duke queried hesitantly.

"Artifacts is a fancy word for something that's fancy," answered Noot.

These guys are brilliant.

"And we love findin' fancy things," finished Roller.

"I see. Well, my new friends, I think we have this one under control. No need for any more investigators," replied Duke diplomatically. "But we do appreciate your offer to help."

The two ogres shared another chuckle.

"You ain't hearin' right, stranger," began Roller. "We ain't offerin' to help you find this thing."

"I apologize for the confusion. Boy, do we look silly," said Duke, raising his glass.

"What we are doin', though, is beatin' you senseless and takin' that artifact back to the boss for a payday," finished Roller.

"Is that so?" Duke said.

He stood up and drew his laser revolver, but a sharp pain pierced his hand. Then he didn't feel his gun anymore. The bartender had knocked the pulse pistol out of Duke's clutches with a bottle of the local beer.

Ishiro'shea swung at the bartender, but he dodged the strike. The blade stuck momentarily in the shoddy material of the counter. The barkeep whipped his apron off and wrapped it around Ishiro'shea's head before the ninja could respond. Noot grabbed Ishiro in a vice-like bear hug.

"No point in squirmin'," bellowed Noot. "You ain't goin' nowhere."

Duke turned around and was met with the purple fist of Roller. He hit the floor with a loud crash. Before he could regain his bearings, he felt the pressure of a giant hand grasping the back of his neck. He was whipped up onto his feet in a flash.

"Don't be thinkin' 'bout that other gun neither," threatened Roller. "I won't be pullin' my punch if you do."

That was him pulling his punch?

"Take him to the boss then?" asked Roller.

"I don't care. Do whatever you want," replied the bartender. "This is your show, gents, not mine. But leave their weapons here with me, if you don't mind."

Duke looked up at the grizzled barman through an already swelling eye.

"On second thought, you're an ass and this bar isn't a 'nice local dive,' it's a..." Duke struggled for the right insult, but the pain from being coldcocked and his genuine anger at being deceived by the bartender left little room in his brain for creativity. "...place that serves crap beer."

The bartender smiled. "I'm sorry to hear that, Duke LaGrange of Nova Texas."

CHAPTER THREE

HEFTY AND THE BOOZE MAN

"WE'VE SURE BEEN GETTING CAPTURED a lot, little buddy," Duke noted. "If it's not a bunch of cave-dwelling Neprian rebels, it's Psitakki guards at an imperial gala; if it's not at the Grand Shaman's party, it's at a dumpy bar on T'ckuvu Prime by two moronic goons."

"You're the one with your hands tied. So maybe youse are the moronics," replied Noot.

"Yeah, we're the 'moronics,'" said Duke, rolling his eyes.

"I'm glad you agree with us," remarked Roller.

Two more T'ckuvians entered the room. Both were the same color as Roller.

"These the two guys with the artifacts?" one asked.

"They don't have 'em but they can help us find 'em. It's one of their daddy's necklaces, and daddy is hangin' out somewhere on Prime."

"How'd we know that?" asked one of the new natives.

"Sources," replied Noot. "They've got sources. The Booze Man thinks it's the real deal."

The newcomers looked over Roller and Noot; then they

turned their attention to Duke and Ishiro'shea. They didn't seem all that impressed.

"What'd he say again?"

"Priceless," responded Roller, with a slight twinkle in his eye.

"Good. You follow proper protocol bringin' these guys in?"

"Yeah," began Roller, "we did it like we was told. Bagged their heads 'till we got here. Tied 'em up. Didn't cause any major damage. You can see they're in one piece."

"And you says the Booze Man thought this was a good score?"

"Yeah, we done told you that," replied Roller agitatedly.

"Fine. Let's go see the boss then."

The boss' quarters were as lavish as one would predict a leader of an underground crime syndicate's to be; except this was T'ckuvu Prime and there wasn't anything "underground" about it. At first glance, Duke couldn't tell if this was part of a private residence or part of a multi-floor commercial campus, but then it hit him.

Casino.

Nothing aboveboard happened in the back room of a casino, especially when that casino is located on T'ckuvu Prime. And double-especially when that back room of that casino on T'ckuvu Prime is owned by the extremely wealthy and equally extremely merciless gang boss, Hefty Senchax, leader of the Senchax Crime Syndicate.

"So you're Duke LaGrange? I've heard of you, ya' know," belched the portly crime lord, who was lounging on a burgundy plush velvet sofa. "I thought you'd be bigger."

I thought you'd be smaller, the bounty hunter mused. *Then again, everyone's smaller than you, you obese bastard.*

"I'm sorry to disappoint you, Mr. Senchax," he said

aloud. "It's an honor to meet you, though I'm not exactly sure *why* I'm meeting you."

The rotund Senchax attempted to reposition himself on his velvety throne. It was clear that the overweight criminal wasn't going to fit comfortably in *any* size chair, save for that of a Mega-Troll, and he needed the sofa to account for his excess girth.

"According to my associates Noot and Roller here, you may have a lead on a priceless artifact."

Duke glanced back to see the T'ckuvian thugs grinning. They seemed to be generally proud of themselves.

A servant hoisting up a silver platter passed Hefty's couch. Hefty snatched a few morsels from the carrier, something in a shell. He slurped down most of the contents; the remainder slid over his multiple chins and settled on the front of his dress shirt. Another servant quickly replaced the one hawking the shelled delicacy; this one carried an assortment of skewers sporting a variety of brightly-colored vegetables and fruits from across the galaxy. He picked one of the skewers up with his meaty thumb and index finger and examined it closely. He then tossed it to the side of the room. The server was horrified. Hefty's fist crashed down on the plate, sending it to the floor. The server sprinted to the back of the room. Before the plate ceased its wobbling, another servant was already on all fours cleaning up the mess.

Must be watching his food intake, thought Duke.

Hefty turned his attention back to the bounty hunters. "As I was saying, Noot and Roller claim that you know the whereabouts of something that I might find valuable. And, as much as I trust their infinite wisdom, I also verified this with the Booze Man. It seems that you two may have met him at his fine den of delightful drink."

"Yes, we did. Seemed like a nice enough guy at the time. I guess we were wrong."

"So tell me about this trinket that's supposedly worth more than all of my businesses—every one of them entirely legitimate if anyone asks, by the way—put together and multiplied by seven."

"We aren't looking for any *thing*, we're looking for two people," explained Duke. "And I think your informant might have a drinking problem, because whatever he thinks that necklace is, it's not. No way it's worth that much."

"Is that so?"

"Yes, it's so."

"Why do you think he said that to me, then? Do you think he lied to me?"

"I'm not saying that," Duke stuttered.

"Then what are you saying, Duke LaGrange?" questioned the bulbous boss. "Better yet, how about you tell the Booze Man directly to his face that he's wrong?"

A figure stepped from a dimly-lit recess in the far corner of the room.

"Long time, no see, fellas," he said, acknowledging the bounty hunters. He respectfully bowed to Hefty Senchax.

"These guys here tell me that you're mistaken," said Hefty. "That this necklace isn't worth my time and effort. And I should let them just waltz on out of here."

"Mr. Senchax, it is up to you if you want them to waltz out of here but I can assure you that the necklace is worth as much as I say it is. The pendant that's affixed to it is no ordinary pendant. It's the Heart of Nobunaga."

It was obvious that Hefty Senchax and his menagerie of assorted goons had never heard of the Heart of Nobunaga. It was also clear that Duke LaGrange had never heard of the Heart of Nobunaga. It was even more clear that these facts frustrated the Booze Man.

"Is that good?" asked Hefty.

"Very. It's very good, sir. The Heart of Nobunaga belonged to the man responsible for bringing Japan out of certain despair following one of Earth's great world wars."

"Which one was it?" asked Hefty.

"I'm not sure, I always get numbers thirteen through eighteen confused. Anyways, from the darkness and devastation, Japan rose to prominence, led by a great warrior and leader, Takeo Nobunaga."

I think Ishiro's related to that guy, remembered Duke.

"Nobunaga had an item—an inexplicable and unimaginable item—that helped him defeat his enemies and rebuild his nation in a new image. Over time, the artifact that aided him was lost, found, lost, found, lost, and eventually faded into legend. Scholars just chalked up Japan's rise to charismatic leadership and slightly superior weaponry. The Heart was eventually found again. But, under the assumption that it was just a benign piece of metal, it was displayed in a museum as nothing more than a good luck charm."

"So it's not?" asked the gang leader, repositioning his mounds of blubber.

"I don't know. Not definitively. There's a strong belief that it's more than that. That it really was unimaginable. The legends and tales of Takeo's unbelievable deeds were all a product of the Heart. That's what the Irish believed. You could even say that this pendant laid the foundations for the Nipponese-Gaelic Wars."

"And this little guy's folks jacked it and sped off," Hefty hypothesized.

"That's one possibility," the bartender replied. "I'm not sure. I'm only sure that the pendant in the photograph is the Heart of Nobunaga."

The obese crime lord fiddled with his countless chins

that descended like a waterfall from his jawline. He shut his eyes.

Is he thinking or did he just fall asleep?

"Boss?" asked Roller.

"Shut up, I'm trying to think," Hefty replied.

He opened his eyes. "Here's where I'm at on the matter. These two, aside from being bounty hunters—which is a massive strike against you, by the way—they don't know where this man and woman are. Therefore, they don't know where the Heart of Nobunaga is."

"True," responded the Booze Man.

"And do you think they know anything more than we do at this juncture in time?"

"They likely do not," answered the bartender.

"This is an easy one, then. We kill them. We look for this artifact by ourselves. We get it, sell it, and then turn our attention towards Admiral LePaco."

Duke's attention perked up at the mention of LePaco, particularly the prospect of him being killed by Hefty's men.

"Wait..." Duke began. Then a massive T'ckuvian hand reached around from behind, covering his mouth and transforming his plea to a muddled mess of grunts.

"You're going to die at some point, LaGrange, why not now? Act like a man," said Hefty.

"If I may," the bartender interjected, "could I speak to you privately for a moment?"

"Sure," replied Senchax. "Noot, Roller, you two make sure these bounty hunters don't escape. If they do, you're not going to want to know what'll happen to you."

The Booze Man approached the gang boss, leaned in and started to whisper. Duke couldn't make out any of what he said, but Hefty nodded incessantly and Duke could read his lips. They seemed to mouth "I see," and "Interesting," frequently.

The bartender stepped back with a bow. He returned to the shadowy location from which he had first emerged.

"It seems that I have some new, interesting information. Very interesting, in fact."

So you mouthed, thought Duke.

"Duke LaGrange, his odd sidekick man, you two are safe. For now. It seems that our mutual friend, Admiral Lothario LePaco, has a sizable award posted to anyone that provides intel on your whereabouts. I'm sure that reward will be exponentially increased if I actually have you in my custody."

"Boss," began Noot, "I thought we hated LePaco. Why we helpin' him?"

"My poor, ignorant Noot," Senchax started, "we *do* hate LePaco. More than anyone. His clean-up committee is not exactly friendly to those in charge of operations like that of yours truly, despite everything being legitimate, of course. Myself and my friends need that Four I's crowd eliminated. And we need LePaco eliminated."

"I'm confused," remarked Roller.

"Of course you are, you dumb bastard. What our bartending friend has told me changes everything. We use these two as bait to get LePaco here. We get his reward. We torture him so he tells us the location of the Four I's hub. We off him and then destroy whatever planet they're running their operation from."

"Then we go after that fancy artifact," interjected Noot.

"Yes. We might want to kill these two at some point before that," concluded Hefty.

"What if I could tell you where the Four I's main hub is located?" said Duke.

Hefty Senchax's eyes darted to the Nova Texan.

"Can you?" slurped the husky criminal.

"If you take executing us off the negotiation table."

CHAPTER FOUR

YOU STUPID ORB

"**I**T'S JUST NOT GOING TO happen. Not in a million cycles. With all due respect, of course."

Hefty Senchax pondered Duke's statement for a moment. A few gaseous belches exited the gang boss' mouth. The stench was so putrid that Duke could actually feel the odor stick against his skin.

"And why, pray tell, won't LePaco come down here in person?" asked Hefty. "I'm not some ordinary thug running a two-bit operation on a backwoods planet in a backwoods system, LaGrange."

"Of course not, your worthiness," Duke replied with a bow. "That never crossed my mind and it has nothing to do with anything. He wouldn't come down in person for anyone, especially Ish and me. We just aren't that important, reward notwithstanding."

"You know, the more I think of it," Senchax began, "it wasn't *that* big of a reward."

Should I be offended? thought Duke. "He'll just send some Four I's lackeys to verify it's us and that'll be the end of it. You'll be wired the credits—or he'll turn his ships on you and the rest of Prime."

"He wouldn't dare," gasped the crime lord.

"He would. The Four I's goal is to control the entire universe and, though some might argue the value of Prime's role within the universe, it still is part of it. The Four I's will get here eventually. It might as well be when they take us in. It's the most efficient... and they love efficiency."

"Garbage!" Senchax blurted. "Utter nonsense! They wouldn't dare attack Prime."

"I hate disagreeing with someone as wise and well-thought of..." Duke began.

He was cut off by Senchax. "Stop with the empty praise already, LaGrange! LePaco is smart; he knows not to attack us."

"Oh exalted one..."

"LaGrange!"

"I'm sorry, Mr. Senchax, but he will. They will. It's only a matter of time."

The obese crime lord didn't respond immediately. Once again, he appeared to be in deep thought, analyzing the bounty hunter's line of thinking. It was such deep thought that he allowed two different servants to pass by with trays full of sweets and other delicacies without taking so much as a sniff.

"What do you think?" asked Hefty.

The Booze Man re-emerged from his shadowy corner behind the gang boss.

"It's an interesting choice that has to be made. Use these two as bait and hope that LePaco either comes and we can kill him, or that he sends his goons and the reward, but has no intentions of an attack on Prime. If we do this, we give ourselves more than one outcome that could be considered a win."

"Yes, yes," Senchax blurted, "I knew we should stick to our original plan. They won't attack us."

"But," the Booze Man interjected.

"Oh. What?" Hefty replied dejectedly, as if he knew the Booze Man's next words.

"If this Nova Texan and his friend really do know where the Four I's headquarters is, and if we can destroy it... that would eliminate the biggest threat to your enterprises and render LePaco useless."

Except for the universe-altering mega-weapon he's trying to assemble, Duke thought to himself.

"So you outlined the choices—now what do *you* think I should do?" snapped Senchax.

The Booze Man approached and knelt down before his boss. Duke couldn't hear the conversation, but he didn't have to wait long to learn the Booze Man's recommendation.

"You're a lucky man, LaGrange," began Senchax. "A *really* lucky man."

Noot and Roller both stomped their feet and sighed. It was clear that they wanted to see pain inflicted on their prisoners.

"My colleague seems to think that we should give you a chance to earn your freedom."

"Why thank you, your grace," Duke said, bowing again. "I'm sorry, I mean Mr. Senchax. You won't regret this. I have some ideas on how to take the Four I's out; I've fought them before. Their fleet is impressive. They've constructed a few Armada Titans, dozens of battle cruisers, hundreds of scouts—" He stopped mid-thought. "What type of operation, arms-wise, are we sending out?"

Hefty chuckled to himself.

The Booze Man walked in front of his employer. "Not enough to win a straight-on dogfight, if their fleet is as impressive as you state. We'll signal the top bosses on Prime and in the sector. I'm not sure how many will trust us that this is legit. And for the ones that do come, I'm not sure how many *we* can trust."

"Great."

"Even with a better-than-expected turnout, we will still be overmatched from a numbers standpoint. We will have to use other tactics to get the job done. We have the element of surprise on our side."

"Unless LePaco's already infiltrated some of the other syndicates," Duke countered.

"True. A risk we have no way of avoiding."

"So, best case, how many ships do you think we have?"

The Booze Man looked back at Hefty. The boss shrugged his shoulders, jiggling the rolls of neck that rested on them.

"We have a dozen or so that are battle-ready, including Mr. Senchax's flagship. It won't take down an Armada Titan but it'll leave a few scars to remember us by."

"A dozen? Maybe we should revisit this 'me as bait' plan."

"If some of the other bosses agree, we can probably field a few hundred more."

Still probably outnumbered twenty-to-one and outgunned a thousand-to-one, thought Duke. *Why did I recommend this plan again?*

"The *Deus* packs a punch too."

"The what?" asked Hefty.

"My ship."

"You think I'm going to let you fly your own ship?"

"We need all the firepower that we can get if we're going to—"

"LaGrange, are you an idiot? You think I'm just going to trust you to stand with us—the people that wanted to kill you a few minutes ago—and fight a seemingly insurmountable battle against the Four I's, when you could easily turn your ship around and escape?"

"Kinda. Yeah. We *need* the *Deus*."

"Your ship stays here. You'll be on the flagship. If the base isn't where you say it is, well, let's just say that you'll be hoping that we forked you over to LePaco."

"And if we win, I can trust you to just bring me back to Prime and let me go?"

"The Four I's will be destroyed in that scenario, correct?" asked the Booze Man.

"Yes," answered Duke.

"LePaco will know that we did it, so his readiness to deal with us is going to be null and void."

"You make a good point there."

"So what value will you have to Mr. Senchax?"

Duke didn't want to say it but he knew it was true. His ego would be bruised yet again.

"None."

"That's right, none!" shouted Hefty from behind the bartender. His belly laugh did the size of his belly justice.

Ishiro'shea tugged at Duke's arm. He held up three fingers.

"Three what?" inquired Duke.

The ninja repeated the motion.

"I have no idea what you are talking about?"

Ishiro'shea then took his hand and pointed to the middle of his forehead. He repeated this motion over and over again.

"That's right!" screamed Duke euphorically. "Mr. Senchax, I might have a way to level the playing field a bit. Now, it might not sound logical at first, but it could be just what we need."

"And that is?" asked the crime boss. The Booze Man squinted skeptically.

"I know a group that might help us."

"How much do they cost?" asked Senchax.

"Nothing."

The gang boss' attention perked up.

"They are just as interested in seeing the Four I's removed from the universe. In fact, I've seen them, first-hand, take out an Armada Titan."

"It would take an entire fleet to do that," noted the Booze Man.

"An entire union," replied Duke with a huge smile.

"A union?" asked the bartender.

"The Bounty Hunters Union."

The crime lord's earlier belly laugh was dwarfed by his response to this proclamation. His laughter caused his body to quiver and gyrate until Duke thought his sofa throne might snap.

"You think that exists? It's a legend; a story that criminal mommies tell their delinquent offspring to get them to practice their money laundering exercises. It's not real. LaGrange, you are an idiot."

Duke's fists clenched.

The Booze Man walked back again to advise Senchax. There was a long, drawn-out silence. It was so quiet that Duke could hear Noot and Roller mouth-breathing heavily behind him.

Hefty readjusted himself, wiping away from his top chin rolls pools of saliva that had escaped his mouth during his fit of hilarity.

"Duke," he said with a bit more composure, "even if these mysterious union members did exist, I have no interest in dealing with bounty hunters. Do you realize how much I would be worth to them?"

"I do, actually. And it pales in comparison to what it's worth to destroy the Four I's. They're trying to outlaw bounty hunting."

"The only thing that I agree with them on," replied Hefty.

"They could really help us. At least let me arrange a meeting with Mama Fong."

"Mama Fong? That three-eyed Zylantian hussy! How's she still alive? Every crime boss worth his weight in credits has a hit out on her."

"Just talk to her. If a deal can be reached, then we have a much better chance of taking these guys out."

Hefty looked at the Booze Man, who nodded slightly to his rotund employer. "Fine, fine, fine. What can a quick chat hurt? And you can set this up?"

"Yes, absolutely. Immediately, in fact," replied the Nova Texan.

"Go ahead."

"Thank you, oh most opportunistic one," said Duke with an exaggerated bow.

"What did I say about the groveling, LaGrange?"

"My apologies."

"And of course, Duke will lead this one," commanded Hefty.

"Why thank you, Mr. Senchax," replied Duke. "I'm a little shocked but most honored to receive this newfound trust."

Hefty laughed again, finishing off a triumvirate of belly laughs that would register as small earthquakes on most planets.

"Oh not you, LaGrange. *This* Duke. Duke Dallas."

The Booze Man stepped in front of the gang boss and smirked at the two bounty hunters.

"I just realized that you both have the same first name,"

Hefty chuckled.

The elder Duke nodded.

"Aren't you from Nova Texas, too? Small universe," belched the gang boss.

Ishiro'shea and Duke LaGrange locked eyes. It was clear both were thinking the exact same thing.

Wrong father, you stupid Orb. Wrong flippin' father.

CHAPTER FIVE

SHOCKINGLY SOUND

THE SLIDING DOORS OPENED. LIGHT from the control center that served as the operational nervous system of Hefty Senchax's entire enterprise transformed the dim corridor into something resembling a disco on acid. Duke Dallas, followed by T'ckuvian thugs Noot and Roller, exited with massive grins on their faces. Dallas tipped his Stetson to the younger Duke and Ishiro'shea. The Nova Texan wasn't sure what he thought about Dallas sporting a similar piece of headgear.

"Thanks, LaGrange," he smirked. "Your friend is a shrewd businesswoman."

"So I'm guessing that something was worked out, Booze Man," LaGrange replied with no shortage of snark.

The bartender halted. Noot did too, but Roller wasn't as quick on the uptake and slammed into his partner. The T'ckuvians stumbled toward Dallas but he sidestepped the pair and they crashed into the floor. The two natives guarding Duke and Ishiro'shea helped the bumbling brutes back to their feet.

"Yes. Something was worked out," answered the Booze Man.

"Great."

"But I do think Fong wants a word with you alone."

"Oh, she does?" Duke said with an eye roll.

"What's your deal, LaGrange? I feel like there's something you want to say to me. And if you ask me, the only thing that you *should* be saying to me is 'thank you.' Senchax would've had your head."

"And it would have been the end of all of us. I don't need to thank you for coming to a logical conclusion and doing what's best for everyone, including your own skin."

Duke Dallas shrugged his shoulders as if to admit defeat. He tipped his hat again.

"Well, good luck with your chat regardless."

The Nova Texan didn't return the gesture. He and Ishiro'shea just headed directly into the control center and the awaiting leader of the Bounty Hunters Union.

"She did say alone," remarked Dallas.

"I know," replied Duke LaGrange.

"I'm just relaying what she said. No need to—"

"No, I mean *I know*." The Nova Texan stopped short of the threshold of the control center and turned to face the aging bartender. "I know who you are. I know who you are in relation to me."

There was a long, overly dramatic verbal standstill. Noot and Roller looked confused. The other guards looked disinterested. Duke Dallas looked as if he was trying to articulate his next comment but was coming up empty about how best to proceed.

"Wait, I should explain."

Probably should have thought a bit longer, concluded LaGrange.

Duke LaGrange turned around. The control center

door slid shut, cutting off the four T'ckuvians and Dallas from him and Ishiro'shea.

The walls of the control center were covered in screens of various sizes. Some of the screens were broadcasting what appeared to be security feeds, others appeared to be showing dealings across a wide variety of business associates. There had to be over a hundred screens in the confined control room. Along the perimeter, two parallel rows of desks contained beings from a dozen different systems. They all faced the screens and appeared to be doing their part to keep Hefty's lucrative criminal enterprise afloat.

A subtle tug on his hand diverted Duke's attention to a diminutive alien known as a Broan.

"This way, Mr. LaGrange," he moaned. He was clearly not an enthusiastic little fella.

"We saw you earlier. At the Booze Man's joint."

"His prices are pretty reasonable," replied the Broan in the deadpan cadence typical of his species. "And there's not a lot of small talk. I hate small talk."

"Yeah, I bet," said Duke, sharing a glance with Ishiro'shea.

The trio stepped into a plastic booth. The Broan handed them each a minute earpiece. "See that screen straight ahead of you?"

"Yeah, the big one?"

"Yeah, the big one. That's where I'll broadcast your Zylantian friend. She's pretty aggressive, if you ask me."

"Thank you." Duke paused. "I don't believe I got your name?"

"Fogerly Crasstop."

"Thank you, Fogerly Crasstop."

The Broan closed the door to the cylindrical booth, walked to a panel and tapped away at a few buttons.

Mama Fong's face appeared on the primary screen. Her three eyes focused on Duke.

"It's an honor to talk to you again, Mama Fong."

"And you as well," she reciprocated. Given her manners, Duke had trouble understanding how Mama Fong grew up on such a disgustingly crude planet as Zylantia. "And, I must say, your friend Mr. Dallas, is quite the specimen."

Is she blushing? Is Mama Fong, the grizzled leader of the Bounty Hunters Union, actually blushing?

"I'm not following you?"

"Where have you been hiding him?"

"I just met him, Mama Fong."

"Oh, that's right. I apologize. He's just so charming. And easy on the eyes. That's saying a lot, LaGrange, since I have three. I think I might be a tad out of sorts. It's been a while."

Unbelievable.

"He's apparently a pretty significant part of Hefty Senchax's criminal empire," Duke reminded the Zylantian.

"I have no doubts about that. You know, Duke, if you really think about it..."

"Yes?"

"He's a bit like you."

That's because he's my deadbeat coward of a father that was too full of himself to finish raising an orphaned kid left to die in the heat of the Nova Texan sun.

"I hadn't noticed."

"He's like a slightly more rugged version of you."

Okay, there's that Zylantian congeniality.

"A similar energy, though." She took a breath, gathering herself. "But what do you think? Charm aside, what do you think of this alliance? Is it a trap?"

Duke knew that this potential alliance and his knowledge of the location of the Four I's headquarters were the two things keeping him alive. It was in his best interest to bet on the partnership being on the up-and-up, because anything else would likely find him on the down-and-down. And if he didn't have the partnership, then attacking the Four I's was less of a strategic offensive and more of a suicide mission. The truth was, he wanted to believe Duke Dallas' intentions. He wanted to believe that Hefty Senchax, despite building a multi-planetary empire by double-crossing every person he came across, was capable of seeing that this was the most logical way to take out the oppressive Four I's contingent. He really, really wanted to.

"I don't think it's a trap, no."

"But?" Mama Fong asked.

"I do think that Hefty and any of the crime bosses that decide to join will be quick to turn once the outlook grows the slightest shade of grim."

"Honor amongst thieves?"

"Not with this lot. They give thieves a bad name. A more financially prosperous name, but a bad one, none-theless."

"I see."

"Even so, I do believe that Senchax and his operation are aligned to the fact that a joint attack with the BHU is the best, most plausible way to take out the Four I's. After that, I wouldn't even try and guess his intentions."

"Do you believe this Dallas character?"

"Why does that matter?" Duke snapped.

Mama Fong squinted with all three eyes.

"I'm sorry," the bounty hunter recoiled. "I'm a bit jumpy. It's hasn't been a smooth trip here to Prime."

"Understood, LaGrange."

"Yeah, I believe him. As much as anyone, I guess. What were the terms of the partnership anyways?"

"Pretty standard. We coordinate together as equals. If we can't land on a joint plan, then we don't pursue further. However, assuming that we align on a strategy that both parties feel can win, we do our best to have our teams operate independently."

"I could see how bounty hunters ordering gang bosses around, or vice versa, could be interesting."

"And not productive."

"And if we're successful?"

"We agreed to give them a grace period."

"For what?"

"A grace period of one cycle that we won't pursue those that aided in the battle. In fact, Dallas seemed to think it would be a fairly significant recruiting tool."

"Is that wise?"

"Financially speaking, we will survive. They will be paying us a portion of the fair market value of the bounties on their respective heads. It will be placed into a third party account and distributed over time in equal increments until the cycle has ended."

"Shockingly sound."

"I was surprised too. That Dallas character knows his stuff."

Except how to be a decent father.

"Agreed on plan... Grace period... A fair market fee to leave them alone. Seems pretty airtight."

"Dallas did have one more request."

"What's that?"

The Zylantian's mouth puckered. "He demanded that you remain with him under Hefty's control, at least until the assault is over."

"And?"

"And what? That's why I wanted to talk to you. You're one of the longest-standing members in our ranks. You've never missed a single BHU payment. I won't agree to this without your blessing. Our union is only as strong as our members."

For the first time in what felt like a dozen cycles a warm feeling consumed Duke's body. There was no life-long love selling him out to Admiral LePaco. There was no intergalactic dogfight with an Armada Titan. There was no kidnapped child or swarm of swamp people or power gauntlets. He felt *happy*. Duke searched his memory to remember the last time that he truly felt this way. It was his last night on Neprius. A night with a beautiful, powerful lady.

"Mama Fong, thank you. But it would be selfish—even for me—to deny a chance to take out the Four I's and, possibly, LePaco because of my imprisonment. I'm fine going along with the plan."

Ishiro'shea stepped in front of Duke.

"Ish, you can't go instead of me. I got this."

The ninja pointed to himself adamantly.

"No, you can't join me either. Maybe we can negotiate with Hefty to get the *Deus* back and you can join the BHU fleet."

Ishiro did not yield.

"Guys," Mama Fong interjected, "I think Hefty meant both of you."

Duke noticed Ishiro'shea smiling under his mask.

"I'm not sure when I will be in contact with you again but, on behalf of your brothers and sisters in the Bounty Hunters Union, good luck. Good luck to both of you. I hope we meet again soon."

"In a world without Admiral LePaco and the Four I's."

"That's the plan," Fong replied.

The screen went black. A sharp ringing stung Duke's ears.

"Holy hedgehogs!" Duke screamed.

The ringing smoothed to become the monotone voice of Fogerly Crasstop.

"Sorry about that. But you have another communication coming in," muttered the Broan.

"From who?"

"The boss."

Hefty Senchax appeared on the large screen. His bulbous face extended well beyond the monitor.

"I just talked to Dallas," said the crime lord in between belches that didn't quite escape his mouth, "and it looks like you came through. We might have a chance to take out those bastards after all."

"Looks like," said Duke.

"We start our planning tomorrow with your bounty hunter friends. But tonight we celebrate. I want you and Ishiro'shea to be our honored guests."

"We are definitely honored, Mr. Senchax."

Duke turned to Ishiro'shea and whispered, "I've heard how nuts his parties are; this alone could be worth all that we've been through on this dump of a planet."

"Excellent," said Hefty. "It's going to be one of the biggest events that I've ever thrown, even at this short notice. Many of the other gang bosses are attending. It's going to be epic."

"Sounds fun."

"I even scored the biggest cover band in the sector."

"Congratulations, I'm sure they will add to the marvel of the spectacle."

"The Stampeding Lifeless Androids. You know who they cover?"

"I have an idea, Mr. Senchax."

CHAPTER SIX

A CHAT

HEFTY'S FLAGSHIP WAS IMPRESSIVE. IT was larger than one of the Four I's battle cruisers and appeared to pack as much firepower as an Armada Titan. Clearly, Senchax's bottomless pockets had allowed him to build an intimidating lead vessel. The other gang bosses had impressive ships as well, but Hefty's was something different. Of course, Hefty wasn't *on* the ship. He wasn't about to actually risk his own neck. It was probably a smart decision: Duke assumed that his father was probably more adept in combat than the obese crime lord.

Duke and Ishiro'shea sat on the bridge without any constraints.

Who knew a criminal enterprise could be so trusting? thought Duke.

The bridge was cavernous and followed a similar design to the control center. Screens filled every open space and a litany of races filled the seats, all staring at those screens. Hefty employed the best, regardless of their planet of origin.

The main doors on the back wall slid open. Duke Dallas, trailed by Noot and Roller, stepped over the threshold. The crew all paused and acknowledged the senior officer on the deck with a diverse round of salutes, nods, grunts, and headshakes. Ishiro'shea even extended a thumbs-up.

"Put that down, Ish. He's not *our* captain," said Duke.

"More like cap*tor*," interjected Dallas.

Duke struggled to think of a retort.

"No need for a witty comeback, Duke. I wasn't being serious. You and Ishiro'shea are free men on my ship."

"You are too kind, my liege," Duke replied with a mocking bow. "You are too generous for scum like us."

Duke Dallas sat down in a chair next to the two bounty hunters. He sported a cheerful expression.

"We missed you at Hefty's gala. I hope you're feeling better."

"Much better. Must have been food poisoning," Duke replied.

"You didn't miss much. I wasn't a huge fan of the musical act. I guess I'm not a fan of their source material."

"Yeah, I hear they aren't for everyone," Duke responded, exchanging a quick glance with Ishiro'shea.

A Sabromm approached and handed Duke Dallas a device. He input a few lines of data and handed it back to the thick-skulled crewman. "Thanks, Jerry."

"You're welcome, Captain."

Duke Dallas turned back to the bounty hunters.

"Tardasio System, huh? I should've guessed that. Makes sense. We know the Tardasians aren't going to put up much of a resistance. They're isolated. They have plenty of uninhabited moons and planetoids to set up a nifty little operation."

"Yep, Tardasio," Duke replied, uninterested in the conversation.

"Did you hear about the plans? Surprisingly, the crime syndicates worked well with the BHU," stated Dallas.

"I think bounty hunters and criminal masterminds are probably closer in makeup than one might imagine."

"I don't doubt that," Dallas concurred. "It's a sound strategy. I think we have a chance."

"Possibly."

"And more folks joined up than anticipated. I think news of Oscavia and Erontia falling to the Four I's really hit home. I think they also are close to taking over the entire Ecclox System as well."

"Neat."

The Nova Texan stood up and turned his back on the elder Duke.

Dallas sighed deeply. "Look, I know I owe you a chat."

"You don't owe me anything," Duke snapped back. "As far as I'm concerned, when you left after Trixie was murdered, you were as dead as she was."

"That was a long time ago, Duke."

"I know, so long ago that it's like it never happened. In fact, maybe it didn't. I was young, after all. Maybe it was a figment of my imagination; something to fill the gap after Miss Trixie died. Yeah, I like that story better. I'm going to go with that."

"Duke, please. There *was* a reason."

"Nah, I think I'll stick to my story, if you don't mind."

Duke Dallas plunged his face into his hands. "Look, when Trix died, it hit me hard. The only thing I could think about was revenge. I had to see that son of a bitch mutilated and torn to bits and scattered across the cosmos. It consumed me. I couldn't be a parent. So I left. I had every intention of returning. I thought it would be a few weeks, tops. But the bastard proved to be harder to track. And I just couldn't give up. I knew the girls at Trixie's place would take good care of you."

"You do realize you left me to be raised in a brothel, right?"

"I didn't at the time. I mean, I knew it was a brothel but I didn't consider it 'leaving you.' I thought I'd be right back. But I didn't realize that I'd be so consumed by murderous intent. Death. Killing. But, hey, I couldn't have been all bad, right? You took my name."

The younger Duke shook his head. "First off, you gave me a dumbass name to begin with."

"What? Lafayette? Trix loved that name."

"The reason I was called Duke was only because one of the girls told me you died in battle and you were a hero. When I learned that wasn't the case, it was too late. Everyone knew me as Duke. I even tried to change it but it didn't stick."

"Change it to what?"

"I had a few phases. I went simple. Tom."

"You're not a Tom. You're a Lafayette. You're a Duke," replied Duke Dallas.

"Then I went with Hacksaw LaGrange."

"I'm guessing no luck there either?"

"Have you called me 'Hacksaw LaGrange' yet?"

"Touché."

"I even had a time when I just referred to myself as 'The Jaguar.'"

Duke Dallas did not respond.

"So don't flatter yourself that I go by Duke. It had nothing to do with you, or the real you, at least," said LaGrange.

"Fair enough."

"Did you at least track him down? Did you get your revenge?"

"It took a while."

"What's a while?"

"Fifteen cycles."

"Holy hedgehogs. I'll give you kudos on the dedication."

"I came back to Nova Texas a few times to check in on you. I was too embarrassed. The longer I stayed away and the older you got, the more embarrassed I felt."

"I'm glad a bout with embarrassment was too much to overcome. I know I wasn't your flesh and blood, but you should've told Mom that you weren't interested in a son if something happened to her. She could've made arrangements or sent me back to an orphanage."

"About that—" Dallas began.

"It was almost as bad as my real parents who dumped me on the doorstep of a brothel. Abandoning a kid a second time is pure evil."

He stormed away from Ishiro'shea and his adopted father. *Let's see if I really have freedom on this ship.*

The hall that led from the bridge to a centralized elevator bank was dotted with chairs, benches, and other furniture to accommodate the weary space traveler. Duke plopped down on a resting apparatus designed for a T'cku-vian. He closed his eyes and attempted to collect his thoughts.

After an undeterminable amount of time, he awoke. Sitting next to him was his Irish-Japanese companion.

"Hey, Ish."

The ninja greeted him silently.

"I'm sorry about that. I need to focus on getting out of here. And I hate that the *Deus* is back on Prime collecting dust. I miss her."

Ishiro'shea agreed again.

"I'm worried that this detour with the Four I's is going to put us behind on our real mission. Even if we take out the

Four I's, it doesn't matter if LePaco finds your parents and the Amplification Key."

The ninja placed his hand on Duke's shoulder.

"I hope you're right, Ish. I hope it will all work out. I'm just not so sure with that bastard running the ship. Let's just hope he's a better captain than he was a father. Can you believe that load of garbage he was shoveling at me?"

Ishiro'shea shrugged.

"No, don't tell me that you believed it," cried Duke. "C'mon, Ish."

"Lafayette LaGrange," shouted Duke Dallas.

"Where did you come from? I'm done with your apologies or whatever that was. No more. Let's just try and beat these guys and go on our merry ways."

"Lafayette LaGrange, you weren't adopted. Not by me, at least."

"Is this supposed to make me feel better? Or you?"

"Trixie wasn't your biological mother. But her last name *was* LaGrange."

"Yes, I know this. Should I go get your 'Father of the Cycle' trophy now?"

"We both decided to give you that name so that you weren't dishonored by your biological father. He was a nasty, nasty man that did a lot of nasty things. He was a bounty hunter, back when that wasn't a glamorous gig with unions and fanfare. It was a hard, gritty way of life. It wasn't pretty. It was a different time, especially on a place like Nova Texas."

"And this degenerate was?"

"It was me, you ass. *You* are my flesh and blood. I cared for you, alone, when you were an infant. When I met Trixie, she fell in love with you, as she and I fell in love. We were a family. But knowing my occupation and reputation, I didn't want anyone to know that you were my son. You would've been a target. It was Trixie's idea for us to make up the story that you were orphaned and she adopted you. We thought it would give you a fighting chance to survive."

"So my last name is actually 'Dallas'?"

"Yes."

Duke scratched his chin as he tried to ignore the bowling ball being manufactured in his stomach. "I'm going to stick with LaGrange, if that's okay with you."

"I think that's fair."

"And who's my real mother, then? Who abandoned me at birth to be reared by a notorious, deadbeat bounty hunter with the parenting skills of a soggy hush puppy?"

"That's a different story for a different time, Duke."

Duke stood up and stretched. He was still trying his best to appear unfazed by the news. It was a battle that he knew he couldn't win in the long term.

"Look, I know this is a lot to process," Duke Dallas began. "But I wanted to tell you just in case this is the last time that we see each other."

A T'ckuvian, a Broan, and a Sabromm sprinted down the hall and placed themselves between the father and son.

"Sir," began the Sabromm.

"Yes, Jerry."

"We're at the rendezvous point. The other crime lords are wanting to know when we start the attack on Tardasio."

The elder Duke turned to his son. "I'm sorry that everything turned out how it did. I'm sorry—"

"Sir, we need to go," insisted Jerry.

Duke Dallas turned back and headed towards the bridge.

"Dallas," the younger Duke shouted.

"Yes?"

"Sorry about the 'Father of the Cycle' jab."

CHAPTER SEVEN

AN UNDENIABLE RIGHT

THE PLAN WAS SIMPLE ENOUGH. The bounty hunters would blitz Tardasio 5 with the full strength of their force, hoping to catch the Four I's napping. The expected retaliation would lead to a pitched space battle and, assuming that the BHU could properly feign retreat to draw the Four I's away from their home facility, it would leave the main operations relatively unguarded. At this point, the tenuous allegiance of crime lords, gang bosses, and all-round bad hombres would emerge from the shadows of the uninhabited Tardasio 2 and launch a full-scale assault on the weakened hub of the Four I's. The battle would need to be swift because, as impressive as the BHU-crime lord tandem was, the Four I's could easily send reinforcements from neighboring systems and create a one-sided affair. With the arms manufacturing facility down and a major blow to the Four I's central command achieved, the conquered planets would be able to fight back without having to worry about an endless stream of battle cruisers and soldiers sent to squash any rebellions.

Duke knew the plan could work, barring any creative

ideas from the criminal element of the team. He also knew that it would all amount to nothing if Admiral LePaco retrieved the Amplification Key. Unfortunately, at the present, Duke and Ishiro'shea were stationed on Hefty Senchax's lead battleship at the vanguard of an impending invasion.

All of the crewmen on the bridge were focused on the task at hand. Duke Dallas wasn't sitting in the captain's chair, nor was he even in the captain's area. He moved from crew member to crew member, reviewing every last detail of the strategy.

He locked eyes with his son. He smiled. "Glad you two decided to join us up here for the push."

Duke didn't respond. Ishiro'shea bowed slightly.

"I'm just making sure our preparations are airtight," Dallas began. "I'm not really a 'figure it out as I go' type of guy."

Ishiro'shea chuckled. Duke smirked at his co-conspirator.

"I can make plans and triple-check 'em if I want to," Duke whispered to Ishiro. It was met with an exaggerated eye roll.

"What was that, Duke?" asked Dallas.

"Nothing. Never mind. What's the ETA on the attack?" Duke asked in an attempt to change the subject.

"We're just waiting for the word from Mama Fong. Once she feels that they've pulled the main force away from the planet, we're up."

"And you feel like you can trust these guys?" Duke gestured at the forward screen. "I'm sure Glortos 'Iron Jaw' Reebor isn't super comfortable working with Hefty. Or the Great Poison King of Hyptox, Flaph Goomshoot. Or the Cyclopsian Syndicate. Or—who is that out there? Is that the

Gang of the Mystic Saber? How can you trust those nutjobs?"

Duke Dallas laughed.

"I don't trust them at all. But I trust that they understand what would happen to each of us if the Four I's and Admiral LePaco are allowed to continue doing what they're doing. I don't see an alternative."

You have no idea what LePaco is doing, old man, thought Duke. He bit his tongue.

"And they all signed off on their assignments. The Cyclopsian Syndicate is going to hit the facilities in the Southern Hemisphere. With their fleet and the relative size of the planet, that should be easy for them."

"They like blowing things up," noted Duke.

"Yes, they do."

"Goomshoot and Reebor are focusing on the major plant at the northern pole. It's heavily guarded—too much for one squad, I believe. I figured they have the best chance of working together seeing as they're related."

"And the Sabers?"

"Since they have the greatest number of ships in their fleet, they're going to join the BHU and cut off the Four I's from behind."

"And, let me guess, you'll be leading the run on the Four I's headquarters outside of Pentos City?"

"Yes. With the weapons in our fleet, we have the best chance of crippling it."

"Good plan. Pretty basic. But good," concluded Duke.

Before Dallas could respond, Mama Fong's face filled the screen adjacent to the forward view. Her three eyes were sparkling. "Great news, Dallas. The Four I's took the bait. They sent their entire force out to take us down."

"Are you outnumbered?"

"Oh, considerably," Fong replied, with no less enthusiasm.

I've never seen someone so happy about being over-matched in battle, thought Duke.

"But they're leaving the planet?" asked Dallas.

"In droves. Hold, please." Fong cut communication.

The bridge remained silent as they awaited her return.

Fong's face reappeared. "Sorry, I had a few on my tail. Anyways, the news of us taking down the Armada Titan must've reached Tardasio 5, because they sent the entire cavalry. Right now, it's some battle cruisers and a few random craft that I haven't seen before."

"No Titans?" blurted Duke.

The entire crew turned to look at him. Each being flashed what constituted a scowl or grimace, depending on their physiology.

"Oh, nice to see you again, LaGrange," said Mama Fong. "No, no Titans yet. I thought we'd see a few guarding the planet. But I'm not going to look a gift narwhal in the mouth."

"So are we clear to go?" interjected Duke Dallas anxiously.

"All clear," replied the Zylantian bounty hunter. "And good luck, Duke Dallas. I hope that our union proves beneficial and worthwhile."

"You and me both, Mama."

The Zylantian cut communication.

Duke Dallas turned his back on the view screen image of Tardasio 2. "It's time, everyone. I know you've each made a good living working under Mr. Senchax. And I also know that this mission falls well outside of your ordinary duties for Hefty, excepting those that he hired specifically for this mission. We wouldn't be asking this of you if it wasn't vital to the future of the business. I also thank you for your trust in me to lead this battle. It will get hairy. Dicey. Messy. It might even appear that the desired outcome can, in no way, happen. But even in the bleakest of moments, stick to the game plan. Follow me. Follow our strategy and we will knock these sons of bitches on their asses."

The bridge erupted. Duke turned to see a gleeful Ishiro'shea giving Duke Dallas a thumbs-up.

"For Hefty!"

The bridge returned the chant. Noot and Roller let loose primal screams of excitement.

Sheep, Duke thought. *Nothing but a bunch of sheep.*

Duke Dallas composed himself and began to issue directions. "Jerry, put the others on the screens."

"Everyone, sir?"

"Yes."

The other criminal kingpins appeared on screens of various sizes. They were all there: the Great Poison King of Hyptox; Iron Jaw; the Illustrious Potentate of the Gang of the Mystic Saber; Professor Krob, Chief Executive Officer of the Cyclopsian Syndicate.

"We have the green light from the bounty hunters," Dallas began. "You each know your roles. When we talk again, let's hope it's in a universe in which we can still openly lie, cheat, steal, and blackmail—for that one, undeniable right that should be afforded to all beings..."

Each crime boss leaned in a little closer to the screen, eagerly awaiting the conclusion of Dallas' speech.

"...to get filthy rich," Dallas finished.

This was the solitary connective tissue that held the motley bunch of scum together. Duke Dallas knew that. His son suspected that the crime bosses would follow the plan as it was laid out... as long as it didn't seem like the Four I's were going to win.

CHAPTER EIGHT

THE NORTH POLE

THE CYLINDRICAL VESSEL HOVERED ABOVE the southern continent of Tardasio 5. It looked like nothing more than a floating iron log, drifting in space, as nondescript as an intergalactic spaceship could be. Even the attack squadrons that surrounded it were boring—just miniaturized carbon copies of their prime. But what the vessel lacked in design aesthetics, it made up for in potency —militarily speaking.

The Cyclopsian Syndicate's bombing run was efficient and effective, much like their criminal enterprise. The smaller attack craft laid waste to the few tactical targets—a low-orbit cannon, a few missile stations that housed warheads that could likely reach them, a bit of this and that. Then the main ship let loose a bombing fury like no other. In a flash, the facilities in the southern half of Tardasio 5 were wiped from the face of the planet. Total obliteration. There would be no more ship and weapon construction there.

"The Professor's hailing," screamed Jerry, the Sabromm officer. "I'm putting him through."

The leader of the Cyclopsian Syndicate, Professor Claudius Krob, appeared on the primary screen. His appearance was in total contrast to Hefty Senchax and most other crime lords; he was well-groomed, for starters. His hair was pristine, his teeth a sparkling white, and he sported a specially-designed monocle with temples to simulate an ordinary pair of two-eyed reading glasses.

"The mission has been completed," said the Professor in a soft but commanding tone. Duke noted subtle tones of happiness and appreciation in the Cyclopsian's voice. It was very odd.

"Yes, it appears so," answered Dallas. "We were able to witness most of it. Quite impressive."

"Thank you. It was our pleasure to help in this endeavor. We will now proceed to phase two of our responsibilities and assist the Mystic Saber in their efforts. Please pass along my well-wishes to our brothers, Glortos and Flaph, as they attempt to isolate the forces in the North."

"I'll do that, Professor," replied Dallas.

The transmission ended.

Duke LaGrange and Ishiro'shea sat along the back wall of the bridge.

"You know, Ish, if this raid goes sideways, we're stuck up here. We're going down with this thing."

The ninja nodded.

"I never pictured us going out at as prisoners on a criminal's ship, captained by my biological father, during an attack run on some well-organized middle-management types."

It was clear that the ninja agreed with this statement even more.

"Jerry, patch me through to Reebor and Goomshoot," ordered Duke Dallas.

"Together or individually?"

"Together is fine."

The Sabromm plugged away. Within moments two faces appeared on the screen. Two faces that, despite being related in some form or fashion, looked nothing alike.

Glortos "Iron Jaw" Reebor was familiar to Duke. Before he started his criminal organization, the Glortos Reebor Experience, and was just a lowly thief, Duke and Ishiro'shea had almost brought him in on Oscavia. Unfortunately, Duke let his carnal proclivities cloud his focus, as had many before him on Oscavia, and the weaselly Reebor had slipped off the planet.

"I can't believe that pesky fleabag became so successful," Duke whispered to Ishiro'shea. "To think that we had him in our sights back in the caves."

The Irish-Japanese ninja just rolled his eyes.

"What? You can't hold that one against me. Anyone in my position, literally *that* position..." started Duke, but he trailed off as his memory of the event became clearer... and more graphic.

"What do you want, Dallas?" shrieked the pint-sized Reebor from the view screen. Though he lacked an imposing stature, his voice was amplified enough for him to be mistaken for the hardiest of species. In fact, his nickname of "Iron Jaw" originated from a tale that he took down a Mega-Troll by chomping down on his ankle and not letting go until the behemoth collapsed in exhaustion, pain, and probably a bit of embarrassment. As with many of Reebor's claims, there had been no witnesses.

"I don't have all day, ya' know," Reebor smirked.

"Nice to see you again, Glortos," Dallas responded. "And you, Flaph."

While it was hard for Duke to believe that Reebor had built up a successful organization in spite of his uninspiring physical appearance, it was even harder to believe that Flaph Goomshoot had built up an equally lucrative business in spite of his very limited mental resources. In fact, the menacing moniker that he advertised at every moment possible—the Great Poison King of Hyptox—was rumored to relate less to a strategic dealing of death to a rival and his entire planet of followers, and more to a bit a dumb luck involving a fortuitous missile guidance miscalculation and an unsuspecting ship carrying highly toxic chemicals away from Hyptox's decomposing moon. His Hyptoxian rivals were never heard from again. The event would go down in history as a shrewd tactical maneuver that was both clever and coldhearted. The ironic fact was that Goomshoot was really neither of those things. No one would ever mistake him for a genius and, in Duke's interactions with him and his people, he seemed to be a pretty nice guy.

"Hiya, Dallas. How's my buddy, Hefty? Still fat?" bellowed Flaph. He followed with a hearty laugh of throaty huffs and puffs. Goomshoot, unlike Glortos, was a behemoth. Bigger than a T'ckuvian, smaller than a Mega-Troll, and looked as if he was carved out of an iron boulder. Even with his colossal frame, his overall demeanor was as fluffy as a bunny dipped in fabric softener. Joke attempts notwithstanding.

"Yes, he's still struggling with his weight management," replied the captain. "I'll tell him that you asked after him."

"Oh, is that you, Glortos? How's my favorite relative?"

"Shut up, Flaph," jabbed Reebor. "The quicker Hefty's stooge gives us our directions, the quicker we can kill these bastards and get back to what's important."

"Family?" asked Goomshoot.

Iron Jaw planted his face deeply into his palm. He offered no response to his apparent family member.

"I can tell that you're both busy," interjected Dallas

diplomatically, "and, to be honest, our mission has little room for error. So, I'll get right to it."

"Thank the gods," chimed in Reebor.

"Professor Krob checked in," said Dallas. "The Cyclopsian Syndicate succeeded in knocking out the southern camps. They're off to provide support for the Saber and the BHU. Now it's your turn. Remember the plan?"

"Yeah, yeah, yeah," screamed Reebor.

"Flaph?" asked Dallas.

"I think so. Yeah, no I got it. I remember."

"The pole is heavily guarded but it's their primary mining station for the ore they use to build their ships, including their Armada Titans."

The Nova Texan stood up from the back of the bridge. "And that ore is used as an additive to their fuel supply. We think that's how their craft can travel so far and so long without refueling."

The entire bridge crew looked back at LaGrange.

"What? It's true!" he shouted back.

"Wait a second," began Reebor. "Is that Duke LaGrange? The bounty hunter?"

"Yes, Glortos. It's me."

"You work for Hefty now? Now that's rich. I guess it makes sense."

"And why's that?"

"You were a pretty lousy bounty hunter."

Duke noticed a few giggles amongst the crew.

"You were lucky on Oscavia, pipsqueak. If that masseuse wasn't skilled in... Never mind. Anyways, I don't work for Hefty. It appears that he captured—"

"He's a special advisor for this mission," Dallas interjected. "He has some inside information on LePaco and the Four I's and accepted our generous offer to aid us."

"You're telling me that this mission was based on

LaGrange's knowledge?" said Reebor with a groan. "Oh, we're as good as dead."

"Gnaw on any good ankles lately, Iron Jaw?"

"Stop it, both of you," commanded Dallas. He motioned for Duke to have a seat. "We're running out of time."

"Oh hey, Duke! Hey, Ishiro'shea! Nice to see you two again," chimed in Flaph, oblivious to the last few exchanges.

Duke waved back. Ishiro'shea extended a thumbs-up.

"Flaph, Glortos, are we good to go?" asked Dallas.

"Yeah," they both stated in tandem.

"Keep your visuals open. As soon as we see the mining facility damaged, we're heading in. Get out and join the rest."

"Got it," said Flaph. "When we're done, get some rest."

"No, you moron," barked Reebor, "he said 'join the rest,' got it?"

"Oh, I thought we were gonna blow up the Four I's facilities in the North," muttered the confused crime boss.

"Flaph," began Dallas, "you and Glortos go and blow those facilities at the northern pole to dust. When you're done, just follow Glortos."

"Got it."

Both men faded from the view screen.

Duke Dallas turned around to face his crew.

"Let's hope he knows where the North Pole is."

CHAPTER NINE

A SHUT WINDOW

EXPLOSIONS DOTTED THE NORTHERN CONTINENT of Tardasio 5 like a bad case of acne. Flaph Goomshoot's flagship swung back over the fiery landmass and concentrated one last assault on the main mining facility. It was a direct hit. As his craft exited the lower atmosphere, the plant erupted in a giant blue fireball. A subsequent chain reaction was triggered by the salvo and, moments later, ancillary explosions burst from the mines themselves. Goomshoot and Reebor had successfully knocked out the entire operation in a matter of seconds.

"Good, good," Dallas muttered softly, only just audible enough for Duke to hear. "Now it's our turn."

He stood up and addressed all of his crew members again. *Clearly not his first time in front of a crew.* Stations were manned and attentions were focused on the pending attack.

"So not only is this main hub the most heavily guarded and not only is it situated beside the largest concentration of military outposts in the Tardasio System at Pentos City, but we are the final wave—which means they might actually be prepared for us," Duke said to Ishiro'shea. "Overall, it's a solid plan. Selfishly, I wish we would've been held captive on those Cyclopsian ships. Better life expectancy, I'm afraid."

"Are we ready, Jerry?" asked Duke Dallas.

The Sabromm officer nodded.

"Engage with mission protocol," commanded Dallas.

The imposing ship began to move. It had exited the shadows of Tardasio 2 and acquired a direct sightline to the Four I's planetary base before Duke could even blink.

This plan would really suck if the Tardasio System wasn't so densely packed, thought Duke.

"Forward, direct course to Pentos City. Patch me into our fighters, Jerry," commanded Dallas.

The Sabromm did as instructed.

"Team, Dallas here," he said, speaking into the communications panel, "you have your orders. Follow the course, don't veer off in the slightest. There'll be some anti-aircraft fire from Pentos City. They've had enough time to scramble a pretty salty defense. Ignore it and push through. We *have* to take down those facilities. I'll handle the forces in Pentos, then swing back and finish off the last of those plants... assuming y'all leave me any."

The pilots clearly relished Dallas' optimism. They all replied with a chorus of yips, yells, and sounds that could only be construed as a confident "Heck yeah, boss."

Duke walked over to Dallas. Jerry seemed annoyed that someone would approach the captain's chair without following proper protocol. But the Nova Texan didn't really care what the Sabromm thought.

"Hey, not to be a backseat pilot..." Duke began.

"But you're about to be one," Dallas replied.

"Yeah, kinda."

"Not right now, Duke. We're heading in. This is the proverbial 'it.' Too late for any revisions now."

"You're probably right," the bounty hunter responded. He turned around and walked slowly to join Ishiro'shea at the back of the bridge.

"What is it?" Dallas huffed. "I know you have something to say, so just say it."

Duke spun around gleefully. "You agree that they've had enough time to request some backup, right?"

"Yes. They are nothing if not efficient."

"Right. But none have come through, right?"

"Correct. We have an entire squad guarding the nearest warp station. If they start to come through, we'll blast 'em before they know what hit 'em."

"Wonderful," said Duke. "And have they come through?"

"Nope. What are you getting at, Duke?"

"We're confident that they called for help. We're confident that help will come. We're confident that it hasn't come from the warp station. So..." Duke paused to allow Dallas to finish the thought.

"They're already here," Dallas replied, his tone suddenly solemn. "But we've scanned Tardasio 2. Tardasio 3 and 4 are accounted for as well. Tardasio 6 is so far away that an immediate strike isn't plausible."

"Same with Tardasio 1," added Jerry, obviously having eavesdropped on the conversation.

"The Tardasians aren't known for their facility with numbers," Duke replied.

"What does that even mean?" scowled Jerry.

"It means that—" Duke started.

Dallas cut him off. "Tardasio 7 is closer to us than Tardasio 6. Jerry, tell me we scanned Tardasio 7."

"We did not, sir," the Sabromm replied. "We didn't think that—"

"Full power ahead!" Dallas yelled. "Our window for success just shrank dramatically. We have to hit those targets before we *become* the targets."

"Full power!" echoed Jerry.

Hefty's flagship rattled and began its march towards Tardasio 5.

Then it rattled again—but this time it wasn't due to its engines. This rattling was from fire. Enemy fire. Fire from the ships that were hidden on Tardasio 7.

"Looks like our window might have just shut," Duke whispered to Ishiro'shea.

"Sir," started Jerry, "it might be worse than we feared."

"Go on," replied Dallas.

"They have an Armada Titan."

Murmurs permeated the bridge. Duke sensed the level of confidence dropping quickly. He could almost see it—like water gushing from a bucket with a brand new hole.

Dallas was calm. This was clearly not his first rodeo.

"Return fire. Protect the squadron at all costs. They have to destroy those targets."

The ship was rocked again.

The Titan.

"Hold steady. We have the best weapons in the gods-damn galaxy, let's use 'em!"

"They won't work on something that big!" replied a weapons officer.

"Then take out everything else. That ship can't take out all of our ships. Let them focus on us."

The command was met with some reluctance, though it seemed to Duke that they were following Dallas' orders. The ship was hit hard yet again but kept firing. Hefty had loaded it up with armaments that were neither legal on most planets nor even available in the general—or any—market. Rays and lasers and beams lit up the celestial battlefield. Some were obviously experimental but most proved effective against the Four I's lighter craft. The Titan showed no damage.

"Jerry, patch me in with Mama Fong. And the Saber."

"Done, sir."

Mama Fong, backed by a few other noted bounty hunters, appeared on the screen first. Then at the bottom, an elderly humanoid popped up. His disheveled silver hair was in contrast to his weathered, burnt skin. He sported a conical hat of midnight blue, highlighted by accents the same color as his hair. He wore an eye patch.

"Have you ever seen one of the Mystic Sabers, Ish?" asked Duke.

Ishiro'shea shook his head. In fact, Duke didn't know anyone that had actually met one. They were a powerful criminal organization, but their work was subtle and discreet. They influenced more than coerced, and they were good at it.

"We have a problem," Dallas began. "There was a full reserve force on Tardasio 7. It's been activated."

"How big?" asked the Zylantian.

"Big enough. And they have an Armada Titan."

"I'm sorry, Dallas," Mama Fong continued, "we're in a scrap here. If we disengage, they're just going to follow us back to you."

"I know. How about the Saber?"

The man's expression did not change but his eyes closed. Then his head began to wobble slightly. After a few moments, his eyes opened.

"That's unfortunate," replied Dallas. "Make sure they don't get out of that warp station. Take out the station if you need to. There are other ways that *we* can get back."

He's a telepath, Duke realized. *No wonder the Saber and its members are so quiet.*

"If either of you can spare any support, we need it," Dallas pleaded. "Until then, we'll continue as planned." He cut the communication.

Another huge explosion on the outside of the ship forced a partial roll, throwing many of the officers from their stations. Duke Dallas held steady as if his feet were glued to the floor.

He looked over at Duke and Ishiro'shea. "You two, meet me outside the bridge," he ordered. "Jerry, you're in control until I get back."

"What?"

"Jerry, it's not that hard. Just tell everyone to fire everything they've got. Protect our ships!"

"Yes, sir."

Duke and Ishiro'shea left the bridge. Dallas followed closely behind them.

"Over here," he said, motioning the bounty hunters into a nook in the hallway. The color was drained from his face; his cheeks hollowed. "Good call on the surprise attack, Duke. Very impressive."

"I kinda wish I'd been wrong on that one."

"I know. Look, you both know this isn't likely to end well," Dallas said, biting his lower lip.

"What? We can take 'em."

"No, Duke. I don't see a way that we survive this. I feel like it's my fault that you're here."

"No," began the Nova Texan.

"It is. Don't argue with me, please."

Okay, he's right, thought Duke. *It is.*

"So what do you need from us?"

"I have a feeling that there's more to the Heart of

Nobunaga than you led us to believe. I don't know why. Call it fatherly intuition."

"Let's just call it plain ol' intuition for now," Duke remarked.

"Fine. But in my gut, it's part of all of this. About LePaco. The Four I's. Everything."

"And?"

Duke Dallas handed him an electronic card. "Take this."

"What is it?"

"I have a shuttle craft at the rear. It's not some escape pod; it's one of our attack ships, slightly modified. Fewer weapons but more speed. You and Ishiro'shea head back to T'ckuvu Prime and..."

"Wait. You're letting us bust out of this place?"

"Letting you? I'm giving you a map. Continue on your mission, whatever it is. Destroy LePaco."

"Thanks and all, but how are we going to get through the warp station? It's a war zone."

"This ship can get you far beyond this system, and quickly. I'm sure that you'll find an alternate route to Prime."

"And the card?"

"Go to Hefty's casino. Go to the parking garage and give this to the attendant. No need to say anything. Your ship will be there."

"He parked the *Deus* in his casino's parking garage?"

"Oh, and one more thing."

"Yeah?"

"Your weapons. I brought 'em. I stored them on the shuttle. I had a weird notion that you were going to have to use this craft."

More fatherly intuition? thought Duke.

The ship was hit hard again by the Four I's weaponry.

"Go! Now!" Dallas yelled.

"I don't know what to say. Thank you."

Duke Dallas grabbed his son's hand. He stared directly at him, his eyes unblinking.

"Seeing you again, even under these circumstances, has made me the happiest man in the universe. I now know what my son became—and it's exponentially better than anything that I could've imagined. Or that I deserve."

Dallas' eyes swelled. A steady trickle of tears fell down his cheeks and met his upturned lips. His smile subsided and became the terse expression of a leader facing a challenge that he couldn't win.

"Go, Duke LaGrange. Save the universe."

CHAPTER TEN

THE LUCKIEST MAN ALIVE

V ERY FEW CITIES ESCAPED THE global devastation of World War XVII, and during the hundred cycles since its conclusion, even fewer had managed to rebuild themselves. Kyoto was no different. The once burgeoning metropolis and cultural center of Japan had been reduced to ruins and subsequently abandoned by the survivors in the region. Generations came and went and Kyoto became just an area of dilapidated buildings beyond the mountains in the Yamashiro Basin. The people that sprung up around the deceased city chose to live a more simple lifestyle, feeding off the bounty of the land and the three rivers that called the basin home—the Ujigawa to the south, Kamogawa to the east, and the Katsuragawa to the west. This trio pumped life into the region from Lake Biwa to the northeast, one of the last bodies of water to remain uncorrupted by the war. The lake and its far-reaching tributaries were worshipped as deities.

"It's unusually cold today," said Ayuko Nobunaga as she dipped her finger into the steady current of the Katsuragawa. "I'm hoping that means the fish are extra eager to jump into my net."

"You've never had any problems with them before," replied Takeo. "I still think you trick them somehow. You're like a siren. The Fish Siren. You catch them like you caught me."

Ayuko blushed and splashed some water at her husband. "You're lucky to have me."

"I know, I know. And you're lucky to—"

"Yes? I'm lucky to what?" Lucky to have you?"

"I was going to say, lucky to live near such a beautiful city as Kyoto," Takeo said with a smirk. "Its beauty is only matched by yours, my sweet wife."

"Hey now," she pouted. "That's crossing the line, Takeo."

"You're right, my love. It's not funny to even kid about that smoldering heap of garbage that was once Kyoto."

"When I was a little girl, my grandfather told me about *his* grandfather telling him about it. It sounds like it was once a glorious place," said Ayuko. "Now, it's just a reminder of the war. I just wish the rivers could wash it out to Lake Biwa and we could start over. Build a new Kyoto."

"And the fact that those foreigners are still trying to find something there just makes it worse. The smoke and noise from their machines won't allow us to forget about it."

"What are they even looking for anyway?" asked Ayuko. "There's nothing there but mangled concrete and broken glass."

"I heard from the others in the village that the men are from Oceania—you know, the Coalition."

"Do they still run the world?"

"I think so," answered Takeo. "That's the beauty of being so isolated here—we don't have to worry about that. But the villagers told me that the Oceania Coalition men

734

think there's a stash of active warheads buried below the city."

"From the Seventeenth World War?"

"I guess. Or the sixteenth. No, it's definitely the seventeenth."

"What was that one about again?"

"I don't remember, if I'm being honest. They all run together. I'm no history buff and I didn't really pay attention to Earth history in school."

"I bet it had something to do with those warheads. I doubt they're still active after all these cycles," said Ayuko.

"I don't know, they don't expire, do they? They could still be quite powerful. Maybe more powerful than anything they have now."

"Why do they need *more* powerful weapons? Or weapons at all? Has the planet recovered from the last war?"

"You're a dreamer, wife. A pretty dreamer but a dreamer, nonetheless. It has not recovered. And the recovery periods become longer after each war. Pretty soon, we won't ever recover. There will always be someone or some place that wants to control the rest. It's human nature."

The roar of a once-glorious skyscraper toppling over at the hands of the Oceania Coalition rumbled in the distance. The building must have been quite large as the seismic tremor rippled to the banks of the Katsugawara, sending Takeo into the shallow end rather unceremoniously. His wife giggled uncontrollably at the sight of her drenched husband.

"Hey, stop that! Or I'll throw you in here!" he joked.

"Then who would catch us dinner? I'm the only one that ever catches anything, remember?"

Still submerged in the water but now sitting up, Takeo wrestled with something in the folds of his shirt.

"Oh yeah? What do you call this then?" he asked. In his hands he clutched a wriggling Crucian carp.

"Luck."

"I call it dinner."

"Then *you* can cook it," Ayuko fired back, smiling.

Something else pressed against Takeo's chest. But it wasn't a fish. He reached into his shirt again but his smile turned to a confused frown.

"Did you catch breakfast for tomorrow as well, oh great fisherman of mine?"

"No... but I caught this." He pulled out a bright metallic pendant and showed it to his wife.

She shrugged her shoulders.

"Maybe I caught your birthday present?"

"I think the fact that you caught a fish is birthday present enough," she laughed.

Takeo examined the odd medallion. It looked weathered from countless cycles underwater, the current of the mighty Katsuragawa slowly breaking it down.

"I think it's ancient," he said. "It looks ancient. You know what? I'll apply it to the base my katana. It's not too heavy as to disrupt the balance of the blade."

"Great, junk on junk," said Ayuko, rolling her eyes.

"Antique on antique, you mean?"

"No, I meant junk. Just please don't let go of the—"

The carp squirmed out of Takeo's grasp and bolted down the river as if it had been shot out of a cannon.

"—fish," Ayuko finished.

"I'm sorry."

Ayuko glared at him. Her own fishing rod jolted and then bowed. She yanked on it, the fish bobbing on the river's surface in its fight to survive.

Takeo offered an innocent smile. "I really am the luckiest man alive."

Takeo Nobunaga and his family lived in a cozy wooden house raised above the ground. It was once the grain storehouse for the village, but when storage with double the capacity was erected, Takeo volunteered to move into the old one. The move to the storehouse allowed them to leave their previous and much smaller home to the community as a multipurpose facility. It hosted refugees. It held overflow from the school house. It was a dining hall. However, Takeo made sure to keep the back room off-limits to the public. This was his martial sanctuary. His *bugeikuden*. His dojo.

Not many Japanese adults practiced the martial arts anymore. With bombs and guns and missiles, there wasn't much need for a *gyaku nage* or a *haishu uchi* or a *kocho giri*. However, Takeo's father taught him the ways of a warrior, the ways of a *bujin*. His grandfather had taught his father in the same manner. Takeo's great-grandfather was a *kenshi*, a master swordsman, and his father was a real ninja. When he was alone in the dojo, be it practicing his strikes, meditating, or admiring his favorite possession—his family's katana blade—Takeo felt connected to his past and to his country.

Takeo was trying to perfect his *jiyu hakobuto* technique when his wife rapped on the outside wall of his dojo.

"Come quick, hurry!" Ayuko screamed.

"What's wrong?" Takeo opened the door to see his wife with her eyes wide with fear. "Calm down. What's wrong?"

"Men are here. With guns. They're in the middle of the village demanding to speak to someone in charge."

"There isn't anyone 'in charge.' Didn't someone tell them that?"

"Not exactly."

"What do you mean, 'not exactly'?"

"They all said that *you* were."

"What? Are they crazy? Why me?"

"Can you just come, please? If anyone can talk to them, it's you."

Takeo lowered his eyes and inhaled until he could feel his lungs expanding. He released a rush of air through his nostrils before he raised his head and locked eyes with his wife. "Did they say what they wanted?"

"No, just that they wanted to talk to the person in charge."

Ayuko yanked Takeo from his dojo and onto the stone pathway that led from their old house and between two rows of housing. It was a short walk to the center of the village. In the distance Takeo could see flames from the visitors' torches rising above the straw rooves of the simple dwellings.

The husband and wife entered the circular field that marked the village's plaza, the gathering place for the locals. There were forty or fifty of Takeo's neighbors on one side; on the other were an equal number of foreigners, each decked out in camouflage fatigues. Each of them sported the OC insignia on their uniform or, as seemed to be the case with the grizzlier-looking members, tattooed on their biceps. Until now, Takeo's interactions with outsiders had been minimal, but, based on their skin color, he assumed most of them to be Australians or New Zealanders, the heart of the OC. Interspersed throughout the group were a few "Crazy Islanders," as they were referred to in Japan—known for their decorative tattoos that covered large swaths of real estate on their mahogany bodies. They were typically from Tonga or Samoa and were the muscle of the Coalition. No one messed with them and they were the primary reason that the OC had never lost a ground war.

Over time, the Coalition had conquered many of the other countries in the region, from Thailand to the Korean Peninsula. China had fallen to them thirty cycles ago. Japan, having been plunged into the deepest economic despair, was a Third World non-factor for many decades and avoided the ever-growing roster of Oceania Coalition countries. They didn't offer anything of value to the outside world until the discovery of a stash of potentially active warheads buried under Kyoto. Takeo noticed a pair of husky Mongolians flanking a fidgety Vietnamese soldier, the smallest man in the entire platoon. He was also the only one without an automatic weapon. He snarled and spit at the ground, all the while flashing two rusty knives.

Why is it that he's the one I'm most afraid of? Takeo wondered.

"This is the person in charge of our village," yelled one of the townsfolk. "Talk to him."

A man dressed from head to toe in solid khaki emerged from the gathering of soldiers. He was extremely wiry for such a short figure; his relatively long arms and legs seemed to explode from a truncated torso. His hands and feet were comically large for his frame; his face was long to the point where it was snout-like. Atop a ruddy brown mane sat a slouch hat with the words "Death Wallaby" inscribed across the front.

"My name's Aloysius Kelly. Ya' know me?" he sneered. "Of course ya' do. Everyone knows the Death Wallaby."

Should I tell him I have no idea who he is? Takeo asked himself.

"And who are you? They say you're in charge of this wee village, mate."

Takeo nodded his head and bowed slightly.

"Well great, then," said Kelly. "You and I need to strike up a deal and do it quick."

"What type of deal did you have in mind, Mr. Wallaby?" asked Takeo.

Kelly grinned.

Maybe he doesn't like Mr. Wallaby.

"It's easy, alright. You and the people of this village are going to help us with our excavation of those ruins over there." He pointed to the remnants of the Kyoto skyline in the distance. "And you're goin' to give us your village."

"Why do you need our village?" shouted one of the villagers.

"It's goin' to take us a tick longer than we thought to find the treasures below Kyoto and we're tired of living out of our backpacks. Dining on rations. Drinking recycled urine, when the recycling machine's actually working. This seems like a perfect temporary home for us," Kelly said, one corner of his mouth turning upward. "And you lot seem like a good temporary workforce while we catch up on a little R and R."

"And we give you all of this in exchange for what?" asked Takeo.

"In exchange for us not killing you," said the Death Wallaby smugly. "See that guy over there?"

One of the Mongolians peeled away from the pack. He aimed a cylindrical tube connected to a backpack at one of the buildings surrounding the plaza.

"If you resist," Kelly continued, "he's goin' to do this."

The Mongolian let loose a fiery gust at the wooden structure. In an instant, the entire roof was ablaze. The townspeople gasped, or screamed, or a combination of the two; many fled to their homes. The Death Wallaby and his troops laughed hysterically at this sight.

"Run my little chickies, run," cackled Kelly. He

returned his gaze to Takeo. "So, as the one in charge of this place, are you in agreement with our proposal?"

Takeo felt his wife burrow her face into his left shoulder. In his right hand was his katana. He thought about how many times his ancestors had stood up to enemies, even with odds as long as those that faced him now.

His thoughts halted. He realized that he had extended his sword towards the Oceania Coalition force.

"Takeo, what are you doing?" whispered Ayuko. "Don't pick a fight with these guys."

"I'm sorry, I didn't mean to. The katana just moved itself and—"

Kelly cut him off. "You're going to fight me with that shiny butter knife, are ya'? Fine then, I'll blast a hole in you and your missus. And send this entire village up in flames."

The katana was still extended.

"Put it down, Takeo," pleaded Ayuko.

Villagers began to cry out, "He's not in charge!"

The pendant that Takeo had discovered in the river, which he had fastened above the hilt of his blade, started to pulse. The glow flickered faster and faster.

A fan of radiant silver light shot out of the sword and engulfed the Oceania Coalition forces. There were no cries of pain. There were no shrieks of agony. As the light returned to the mysterious pendant on Takeo's katana, there was no Death Wallaby or Mongolian flame thrower or fidgety Vietnamese soldier. There was no Oceania Coalition.

CHAPTER ELEVEN

THEY'RE GOING WHERE?

"DALLAS WAS RIGHT, THAT SHIP had some giddyup."

Ishiro'shea's wink confirmed that he agreed with the bounty hunter's observation.

"And I'm just glad that they hadn't shut down that portal station outside of the Tardasio System. Otherwise, we might not be here in the nurturing bosom of my love."

The ninja shrugged, but Duke knew that Ishiro was as happy to be back on board the *Deus Ex Machina* as he was. Duke Dallas' card had worked like a charm at the casino; the attendant hadn't even batted an eyelash at the two men asking for their ship. And then they were away from T'ckuvu Prime and heading towards Cyborg Joe's. With Hefty Senchax controlling the portals in and around T'ckuvu System, they made the decision to head to friendlier space before making the jump to Kelt. The gang boss might not believe that his right-hand man had not only let them escape, he had provided the escape pod.

"I mean, I know Hefty's ship was bigger, more modern, had way cooler weapons, a better caterer, and didn't sprout cryptic red buttons when in danger..." Duke paused. "Never mind, lost where I was going with that."

His companion shook his head and went back to plotting the course out of T'ckuvian space.

"Oh hey, look." Duke pointed at a blip on the control panel monitor. "Is that a station? It is. And it's outside of Hefty's reach, I bet... and way closer than trying to head over to the next system. Who knows if the Four I's don't have that guarded, anyway? This could be our ticket, Ish."

Ishiro'shea plotted the course to the wayward station. It was a short trip in the *Deus*; despite her age, she could still move when she wanted to. The ship approached the portal, which appeared to be in working order. The station sported the appropriate DIPS insignia, and off to the side was a toll booth. Duke assumed that the booth housed an unyielding android that had had its customer service programs erased, as was the case with most he'd encountered. The Department of Intergalactic Portal Stations was one of the last vestiges of an attempt to implement an all-powerful cosmic government. Like all of the efforts before and after, it had failed, but the DIPS infrastructure remained. An enterprising businesswoman from Oscavia paid a large sum of money to the collapsing government to buy the network of stations. Her decision to privatize the only easy way to get from one sector of the universe to the other in mere moments rewarded her with a much larger sum of money.

"Before we drop in on what could be a war zone, let's give Queenie a call," Duke suggested.

After some swift movements from Ishiro'shea's dexterous fingers, the control panel buzzed.

Queen Joe appeared on the forward monitor. "Duke, Ishiro'shea, we haven't heard from you in a while."

The window of her office provided a clear view of the bar. As she spoke, Duke's eyes wandered to it as he tried to see if there was anything afoot. It seemed like a normal day at Cyborg Joe's. If they were under attack, they were taking it well.

The Queen noticed Duke's roaming gaze. She turned around to peer at her patrons. "What? You see something?"

"Oh no," Duke said, a bit flustered, "I was just seeing if y'all were burning alive at the hands of the Four I's."

"No, they haven't come back since the BHU bailed us out. It's been pretty quiet, to be honest. Well, except for one thing. I'm glad you reached out, actually."

"Before you get into that—because I'm sure it's just going to make our day—aren't you going to ask us about Ishiro's parents? If we found LePaco?"

The Queen hesitated for a moment. "No. I think I know the answer to that. That's the 'one thing.'"

Duke dreaded what was about to come out of the Queen's mouth.

"You aren't going to like this," she began. "At all."

"Go on. It can't be any worse than what we've been dealing with."

"So, you received a message. More like a messenger. Here at the bar."

"Who?"

"Maxx Gemstarr."

Duke turned to Ishiro'shea. "What does that jackass want?"

The ninja's eyebrows tightened; he looked as confused as Duke.

The Nova Texan turned back to the Queen. "What did that jackass want?"

"He had some information that he wanted to give to you."

"This ought to be good."

"Look, Duke, I know you don't like him, but he was

being sincere. He actually had something that could help us."

"What? An autographed eight-by-ten headshot? A copy of his latest direct-to-home romantic comedy?"

"He knows where LePaco is. Or, rather, where he was heading."

"Bullshit," Duke blurted.

"I believe him," the Queen responded.

"You don't know that buffoon like I know him," countered Duke. "He only thinks about himself. He has an angle, I know it."

"He wanted me to tell you that he's paid his Bounty Hunter Union dues. All of them. Including back payments all the way to when he thought it was just a scam. He heard what happened here and wanted to thank you for opening his eyes."

"It's an angle."

"Let's assume it's not," the Queen replied. "Can you do that for me?"

"Sure, why not?"

"He wanted to tell you that he's been chasing Mazilda Cloax."

"Why?"

"He said he owes her some payback. And that it sounded like you do too. He thought that with both of you on her tail, she wouldn't escape again. He tracked Mazilda and LePaco for some time—but then decided to pause his pursuit and come here to find you."

"And why was that, pray tell?"

"Because they were headed to Earth."

The bounty hunter fell silent. He sat down at the control panel next to Ishiro'shea, utterly perplexed.

"They're going *where*?"

"Earth," Queen Joe repeated.

"Why? What's there?"

"I'd assume Ishiro'shea's parents and the Amplification Key."

"Did he say if they were headed there by their own choosing or if they were being pursued and chased there?"

"Why do you ask?"

"Back on Psitakki," Duke began, "we ran into an Earther that was on their trail. He didn't have all the answers but he was after 'em. I was curious if his bosses actually caught LePaco."

"His bosses?"

"Yeah, he was an Irish gang punk. A heavy hitter in the Nipponese-Gaelic Gang Wars on Earth. Maybe they ran him down."

"I don't think so. It didn't sound like it," said Joe, "but I didn't ask him directly. Anyways, he left shortly after his message. I'm assuming he's headed towards Earth."

"I guess that means that we aren't coming to see ya' after all. We're going to Earth. Fun."

"Good luck, Duke."

"Oh by the way, Queenie," started Duke. "The Orb..."

"Yeah?"

"It took us to the wrong 'father.'"

"What do you mean?"

"It's of no consequence, but—" Duke paused momentarily. "—just be more careful next time."

A sly smirk, equal parts intrigue and confusion, crossed Queen Joe's face. Then she cut the transmission.

"Ready to go home, Ish?" said Duke.

The ninja sat motionless and expressionless.

"Welcome to Warp Station and Portaling Center #808, I am Department of Intergalactic Portal Stations representative L44-RF47249. You can call me Alejandro. We are very excited that you chose to take our portal directly to Earth,

Mr. Lafayette LaGrange. Your funds are sufficient for this jump."

"Thanks."

"Are you sure?" asked Alejandro after a moment's pause. "Like positively positive sure?"

His voice showcased a surprising amount of inflection and personality. For a robot whose entire existence was to perform the most menial of tasks, he seemed oddly concerned about the concept of anyone *choosing* to go to Earth.

"Yes. Earth."

"Good luck to you then," the cybertronic toll taker remarked.

The portal opened and the *Deus* slowly approached.

CHAPTER TWELVE

WHISKY CAKE

THE SPACE AROUND EARTH WAS clear. There were a few transport shuttles entering the atmosphere from neighboring systems, and a fairly long queue from the portal station but, by and large, it was a pretty quiet day around the typically loud blue planet. If Admiral LePaco and Mazilda Cloax really were on Earth, they had arrived without a legion of Four I's ships to protect them. And that seemed odd.

"You don't think Gemstarr was messin' with us, do ya'?" asked Duke. "Sending us to Earth and subjecting us to everything that can happen down there is pretty cruel. Even for him."

Ishiro'shea did not respond.

"Sorry, no offense. I know it's technically your home," added Duke.

The ninja continued to check the scanners silently, without acknowledging his friend.

"It's not like you've lived there in the last decade," Duke said under his breath. Ishiro'shea clearly heard him, however, and shot back a menacing scowl.

"Sorry, sorry," Duke pleaded. "You know Earth and I aren't best friends. Outside of finding you there, it just seems like a big mess to deal with. But I'll keep my thoughts to myself."

After the *Deus* cleared the checkpoints at the portal station alongside the dead planet Mars, it inched out until Earth became visible. The planet glowed bright blue, its massive continents emerging from their oceanic barrier like they were gasping for air. From this vantage point, there was no evidence of the wars that had crippled the planet. *It looks almost peaceful*, thought Duke. And peaceful was a word that hadn't been used to describe Earth in many, many cycles.

Since the time that Ishiro'shea had left, the Nipponese-Gaelic Gang Wars had spread out and consumed most of the planet. The planet's capital—New Tokyo, Ireland—was one of the most dangerous places in the universe. If you weren't killed by the copious amounts of violence from high-grade military installations, you would be murdered by the inhabitants, hardened by countless cycles of unending bloodshed. It wasn't a pretty place.

Both the Irish and the Japanese had a huge presence in New Tokyo; it was the origin point for the conflict and, indeed, one of the roots of it. Both groups declared legitimate claims as the rightful owners of the area and its history —and, most importantly, its resources. From this quibble had been birthed a planet-wide conflict that had consumed nearly every race and government on the planet. Despite being one of the more developed, if not a tad unusual, civilizations during the early advent of space travel, Earth confounded alien outsiders due to its independent network of governments. This country over here believed *this*. This one over there believed *that*.

The situation was considered wildly unorthodox

amongst the other major planetary systems that made up the nexus of advanced civilizations. However, over time, the entire universe began to model itself after Earth's success. The original clamor to have massive governmental bodies to oversee an almost infinite number of planets faded away. The prevailing opinion became: *Everyone do what you want to do and don't encroach on anyone else's turf... and don't get pissy if they're doing something totally different than you.* The only issue was that Earth wasn't a perfect example to use as a prototype. In fact, it had a long history of people not obeying the rules and minding their own business. The small blue planet had more world wars than most galaxies had worlds. Had Earth been introduced to some of these founding races and civilizations during one of their conflicts, the trajectory of the known universe would have been altered. But it hadn't and it wasn't.

Duke, having been reared on a colony of Earth, Nova Texas, had been taught a good amount about its history during his primary school days. He couldn't remember exactly, but there had been around twenty wars that had engulfed the majority of the planet's population. The Nipponese-Gaelic Gang War was number twenty, or perhaps twenty-one. It had left an indelible mark of inexcusable but totally avoidable horror upon the troubled planet.

"Where to, little buddy?" asked Duke. "Where on this mixed-up world should we head?"

Ishiro'shea highlighted an area on the screen. The image zoomed in, to display a smaller area on a tiny island.

It read: *Ireland. New Tokyo. Demilitarized Zone. Aintin Kuniko's Bakery. 4.85 stars out of 5. 3,485 reviews. $$/$$$. Casual. Does not take reservations. Known for whisky cake.*

"This whisky cake better be good," muttered the bounty hunter.

"Quaint," remarked Duke. "They didn't get all those stars from ambience."

The two bounty hunters sat at a circular booth in the center of the café. The wooden table appeared to be hand-crafted. Two large divots graced its top.

"Or the decor," added the Nova Texan.

After a few minutes, Duke stood up and motioned towards a waitress.

"Or the service."

The elderly lady approached. Her skin was gnarled and weather-beaten; it must have been heavy, because she could barely manage a smile when she tried to take their order. Duke assumed that she had eyes but there was no telling on account of the copious amounts of excess wrinkles. Bald spots covered much of her cranium and she had just given up on the follicles that remained.

"What's the order?" she asked through a toothless half-grin.

"We'll just have two whisky cakes for now," replied Duke.

The waitress didn't say anything, but her disgusted look suggested that she could have guessed the request without having asked. She marched to the back of the café. Duke heard her muffled shouting at some poor line cook in the back.

This must be a really damn good cake, thought Duke.

Duke turned his attention to Ishiro'shea, then scanned the establishment.

"And you think we'll find something here? It doesn't seem likely that these old-timers know much—at least, not about what *we* need. We need a source, someone on the inside."

The ninja motioned for his partner to calm down.

"You know I hate being patient," mumbled Duke.

The waitress returned and forcibly slung down two plates. In the middle of each dish was a morsel that looked as if it had leapt off the cover of the *Oscavian Encyclopedia of Culinary Styling and Edible Art*. It sported a dark hazelnut perimeter and a center the color of desert sand. It looked moist. It looked fluffy. It looked delicious.

Duke pinched off a bit and tossed it into his open mouth. He didn't bother to chew.

"Good?" asked the aging server.

"More than good," Duke said, despite having a mouth full of the tasty pastry. "*Life-changing* good."

"Want anything else?" she growled.

"Actually, yeah," Duke began, but Ishiro'shea shot him a piercing glance. He responded with an overly stylized mimicking of Ishiro's earlier calming motion. The ninja's brow knitted together.

"How long have you been here?" Duke asked the waitress.

"At Kuniko's?"

"No, here, in this area. The greater New Tokyo metropolitan area, as they say in these parts."

"We don't say that."

"In New Tokyo then. What, forty, fifty cycles?"

The wrinkles in the woman's face converged in her attempt to convey an expression conveying shock.

"How old do you think I am?" she cackled.

Maybe that expression is "appalled," concluded Duke.

"I didn't intend to be rude," he responded. "There's a reason for my inquiry. I'm looking for someone that can help us figure out a few things around town."

The waitress remained standing, her mouth open. She finally dropped her tray and sprinted to the back.

"What'd I do?" Duke asked Ishiro'shea, who shrugged his shoulders in response.

A short man in a dapper business suit approached their table. He wasn't elderly but it was clear that his youth was far in the rearview mirror.

"Excuse me, friends," he began. "I think that you might have insulted that server."

"I see that," Duke replied, "but I have no idea how. I just asked her how long she's been here. It's a pretty textbook question in the field of small talk."

"Oh yes, no doubt, my friend. But—and I apologize for overhearing your private conversation—that particular young lady is only twenty-five cycles old. And I think you offended her by assuming that she was much older."

"No way," shouted Duke in disbelief. "No way. I don't believe you."

"I know, it is very hard to understand, my friend. But it is true."

"How? Why?"

The gentleman put his hand gently on Duke's shoulder.

"Those that live here have very rough lives, my friends," he said softly. "Those that survive experience more than most entire generations experience. And most of it is bad, very bad, my friends. This place is at the heart of the war. Why people who have the means to leave and choose to stay here is beyond me, my friends." His face grew solemn, his eyes glassy. "Outside of the whisky cake, of course," he said, shrugging off the sadness that had appeared to be consuming him. He chuckled.

Duke reciprocated. "Yeah, it's a pretty damn good cake."

"I'm glad you like it. I've been coming here for as long as I can remember. Do you mind if I join you?" asked the man.

"By all means," said Duke, "we would love some company."

The old man gently slid into the booth next to the Nova Texan. He was glowing.

Clearly doesn't get much company, thought Duke.

"The name's Duke," the bounty hunter said. "This here's..."

He paused. *Oh shit, I can't give us away. What if he knows Ish's name?*

"...Ichabod," he finished, reluctantly.

The ninja shook his head in disbelief.

"Hello, Duke and Ichabod, my new friends," replied the old man. "I'm Eiji. Eiji Otsuka."

"You're Japanese? Like *real* Japanese?" asked Duke.

Ishiro's eyes widened. He then thrust his head into his open palm.

Clearly that could have been a bit more tactful, Duke concluded.

"Yes, Duke. From an old Japanese family. My roots are on that ancient island, near Kyoto, but I came here as a young child. When the war came, I stayed. I was going to wait it out." Eiji chuckled at his obvious misjudgment. "But I was off about how long the conflict would last, my friends. Now I'm too old to leave. For better or worse, this is home."

"At least this demilitarized zone is safe," Duke remarked. "Well, safe-ish."

"Yes, it was always my dream to live in a demilitarized zone," Eiji retorted slyly.

This old codger is pretty spry, thought Duke.

"It's okay, my friend. It's not all that bad. Aintin Kuniko's is here. And the people in this area are tough, if not inspirational. In the epicenter of humanity's worst, they are humanity's best. They are resilient and hopeful; how many can say that they've spent as long as I have living amongst this kind of Earther?"

Duke and Ishiro'shea didn't respond or counter Eiji's statement. How could they? This aging Japanese man saw elegant beauty and found unfindable good in living between two warring factions engaged in one of the bloodiest conflicts in the bloody history of a bloodthirsty planet.

Luckily, Eiji spoke before they were required to reply. "Why are you here visiting our sliver of paradise? Looking for someone?"

"Oh no. Definitely not," blurted Duke. "We're just here..."

"Yes?"

Damnit, we should have come up with a good excuse, Duke realized. "We're just here because we're fans."

"Fans? Of war?" asked the confused geriatric.

"Yeah, well not of war, per se," rambled Duke, "but of history. Of Earth history, to be exact."

"You're researchers? Like from a school? Or writers?"

"Not as such. Just fans of this crazy little planet."

"You two aren't from Earth? He sure looks like a Japanese ninja," Eiji said, pointing at Ishiro'shea.

"Oh no, are you kidding? Him? Ichabod is much too clumsy to be a real ninja. He's just a big fan."

"And he decided to dress up?"

"Yeah. He's really pumped to be here," Duke said. He didn't have the guts to make eye contact with Ishiro.

"I guess a real ninja wouldn't be seen in daylight anyways. And not wearing green," concluded the old man.

"Yeah, I know, right? A green ninja? That's rich." Duke definitely had no plans to look over at Ish now.

"Where are you from, then?" asked Eiji.

"Uh," Duke stammered, "I'm from Nova Texas. Ichy here is from Kelt. Ever heard of it?"

"Everyone has heard of Nova Texas, my friends. Though I'm afraid it doesn't have the best reputation here."

"Understandable," replied Duke. "And Kelt?"

"We only know of it as it pertains to Cyborg Joe's Grill N' Go & The Why Not Saloon."

"Understandable," repeated the bounty hunter. "It's a pretty glorious place. What this place is to whisky cakes, Cyborg Joe's is to most forms of booze."

"Sounds delightful. Do all people on Kelt—and Nova Texas, for that matter—care this much about Earth politics?"

"I think we're in the upper echelon of passionate Earth-ophiles. We're particularly interested in the Father and his wife, Yumi Flaherty. And their role in this conflict, of course."

"You *do* know your history," said Eiji, clearly surprised. "Such a specific interest, too."

"Yeah, we're what you call micro-enthusiasts."

"I know of them both, of course. But we refer to her as Yumi *Nobunaga*-Flaherty."

"In your opinion, as a resident, what happened to them? Do you think that they could still be around?"

Eiji brushed off the question as if it was almost too silly to ask. "Oh no, no chance, my friends. They left early on, when their young son was killed."

Say what?

Duke's jaw hit the ground. Ishiro'shea squirmed uncomfortably in his seat. Beads of sweet streamed from under his mask and rolled off his eyebrows.

"I guess I wasn't aware that they had a son that was—" Duke gulped. "—killed."

"Yes, a young son. Apparently the two sides pressured them both to join the war. Father Flaherty was already a leader amongst the Irish. He was a former military man. I heard he was ruthless. The sweet Yumi was a descendent of the legendary warrior, Takeo Nobunaga. Do you know him?"

"I do. The Heart of Nobunaga and all that stuff," Duke boasted, as if he had been aware of the story from childhood.

"Right, my friend. The Japanese wanted her to support their cause because she was the last symbolic tie to the great hero."

"But both opposed the war."

"Yes, I know Yumi did. Not sure about that Irishman she decided to marry." Eiji now displayed vitriol for the first time. "But, anyways, something happened and their son was killed. My money is on those beer-guzzling thugs. Only they would put an innocent child in harm's way."

He might be a bit biased, realized Duke.

"That's very interesting. So, after their son died, they just vanished."

"Some people think they died. They couldn't believe that these two would abandon their people, even if they disagreed with them. When they left, the war escalated to the level it is now. No one has held the advantage for more than a few days at a time. It's a very evenly-matched contest of murder. It can only end in mutual destruction."

"A 'contest' that now extends to every corner of the planet," added Duke.

"Exactly, my friends. Exactly."

"This is fascinating. Thank you for this firsthand testimony, Eiji. Can we buy you something? Maybe a slice of that whisky cake?"

"No need. You may have guessed, but I don't get to talk to many new people these days. This week has been truly extraordinary."

This week?

"Have there been other Earth history buffs like us visiting Kuniko's?" asked Duke.

"Maybe not as enthusiastic as you two—she wasn't in costume or anything—but she was better looking." The corners of Eiji's mouth shot upward. "I definitely wouldn't kick her out of bed. But she didn't offer to buy me a slice of cake, either. So, we can say you're even."

Mazilda.

"It's funny," the aging diner continued. "She was also interested in Yumi and her husband. I told her that she should try the college on the edge of the zone if she wanted to research them further. The headmaster there is one of their oldest friends. I'm assuming he's still around; he's older than me, if you can believe that."

"The College of Cohorts, Consorts, Co-Conspirators, and Other Assorted Sidekick Types?" asked Duke.

"That's the one. Impressive. You have to be one of the only off-worlders to know of that place."

Before Eiji finished his thought, Ishiro'shea was already sprinting out of Kuniko's.

"Sorry," said Duke. "He's really excited about research."

"I can see that, my friend."

Duke tossed a few bits of currency at the old man. "Enjoy the cake."

CHAPTER THIRTEEN

BACK TO SCHOOL

O N THE EDGE OF THE New Tokyo Demilitarized Zone a cozy grove of trees nestled atop a grassy plateau. To say it was out of place was an understatement. A perimeter fence peeked through behind the first line of trees; behind that, a winding path led to a large red brick structure surrounded by clusters of buildings of various sizes but of a similar style. The property was only a stroll from Aintin Kuniko's, or in Ishiro'shea's case, a frantic sprint.

"Hold up, Ish," Duke shouted between pants. "If she's in there, you'll want backup."

But the ninja kept running until he ran out of real estate. Duke caught up with him at the iron gates. A brick arch rose above the gates; carved into a stone inlay shaped like a setting sun were the words: *College of Cohorts, Consorts, Co-Conspirators, and Other Assorted Sidekick Types.*

Ishiro'shea drew his katana. He raised the blade and brought it down upon the gate in a diagonal strike. The noise was piercing. Sparks exploded from the point of contact. But the gate did not budge. The ninja approached it and examined the strike point. Nothing. Not even a scratch. He repeated the action again, this time adding a battle cry rich with pain and force. The scream contributed nothing. He tried a third time. Duke grimaced: his friend's frustration was palpable. Ishiro tossed aside his katana and charged the gate; he leapt into the air and connected with a *yoko tobi geri* to the padlock. The gate barely rattled.

"Hey, slow down there," Duke said, kneeling beside his visibly shaken partner. "There has to be another way in."

Duke peered around at the seemingly never-ending fence. He felt a gentle tug on his back. He turned around and Ishiro'shea was standing a few paces behind him, holding Ol' Betsy.

"Drop it, Ish," he belted. "Have you ever even fired—"

That unforgettable bellow rang out, echoing around the grove. The blast sent Duke to the ground; debris from the explosion fell from the sky like jagged rain. Ol' Betsy emitted a second boom. The bounty hunter looked up. Ishiro'shea had been knocked to his feet by the unexpected kickback of the sonic shotgun. Duke smiled.

The Nova Texan brushed himself off and turned to see if Ishiro had done any damage to the gate. It remained intact. Betsy hadn't even bent it. However, being a bit of a novice when it came to operating heavy artillery, Ishiro's aim wasn't as precise as his accuracy in wielding a blade. One of the shots had missed the gate entirely and had hit one of the brick pillars that supported the grand archway— and it was now scattered about the lawn. With the column removed, the edges of the impenetrable gate were now exposed, leaving a wide enough gap for Duke and Ishiro'shea to sneak through. The arched sign that sported the college's lengthy name remained intact, miraculously balancing on the damaged support with only a subtle wobble. The bounty hunters hastily made their way through the newly-created doorway and started down the path towards the school.

The campus was eerily tranquil. *Class must not be in session*, surmised Duke. The sun was beginning to set and nightfall had already started to consume the tiny patch of green upon which the school rested.

"Any idea where the headmaster might be? Where his office is?" asked Duke.

Ishiro'shea nodded and pointed to the building closest to their position.

"Main Hall. Headmaster's Office this way," Duke read the sign aloud. "Well, I guess that does make sense."

The ninja repeated his nod.

"Okay, then. Let's be careful. Mazilda could still be here somewhere," Duke said as he opened the unlocked door to the main hall. It opened with an elongated whine, a creaky squeal that could only come from an antiquated door attached to an even more antiquated building. Stealthily, the pair made their way along the darkened corridor.

The next hallway was also dimly lit, but as the two turned the corner, it became apparent that the room at the end was either currently or had recently been occupied. The door was ajar and a light flickered from its depths. They sprinted down the hallway and pushed themselves up against the walls to either side of the opening. Duke motioned to Ishiro'shea that he would take the first glance.

Nothing unusual.

Duke pulled his head back from the entrance, and Ishiro'shea followed suit. The ninja shook his head.

"Yeah, it's pretty dark in there. I can't make out much. We need a closer look."

The Nova Texan entered the room slowly, with his laser revolver drawn. Ishiro'shea entered with even less sound. They both remained low to the ground, trying their best to remain hidden in the shadows as they examined the room in more detail. They dodged and ducked the few flickers of light that twinkled in the room, hiding behind wingback chairs, floor-mounted globes, and tiny liquor cabinets. All typical items in the office of a school administrator. After a few moments, two things were clear. They were alone. And the room had been ransacked.

Duke found the light switch and flipped it on. It was a disaster zone. The bounty hunter knelt down and picked up a gold-plated placard. It read: *Master Ishiro Fukudome, Headmaster.*

We're in the right place, at least, surmised Duke.

Ishiro'shea noticed the nameplate. His eyes welled up.

"Wait a second," said Duke. "Were you named after him? I mean, I'm sure there are millions of people named Ishiro, but it's quite a coincidence."

The ninja nodded slowly.

"Drop it!" a voice said.

The first thing Duke noticed was the voice wasn't female. Or familiar. He also noticed that he and Ishiro didn't have throwing daggers embedded in their backs.

It's not Mazilda.

Duke started to turn to face the newcomer, but then a blazing blue beam whizzed by his face. It crashed down on the table next to him, splitting it in two.

This dude has a laser whip?

"Drop your weapons *now*," the voice shouted. "One move and you're both dead."

"I'm not following you," replied Duke. "How can I drop my weapons and not move? Dropping my weapons, by definition, requires movement."

"Huh?"

"Also, if one of us moves, you're going to kill both of us. That doesn't really seem fair."

"What? Shut up." It was hard to tell if the man was confused or annoyed. Or a little of both.

"Seriously—what if my friend over there moves? You're going to kill me, even though I followed directions perfectly. That's pretty ruthless. Conversely, if Ishiro'shea takes your demands to heart but I'm a tad frisky, he's going to meet that big ninja in the sky. Hardly seems right. You must be quite the coldhearted murderer."

"Did you say Ishiro'shea? As in the Ishiro'shea that attended *this* school? The Ishiro'shea that was the—"

"Salutatorian," Duke interjected. "Yes, the same. But, as you may know, he doesn't talk much."

"Oh yes, a vow of silence. I remember. But I remember his voice from when he first came to the school."

Duke started to slowly rotate. "Is it okay if we turn around now? Or are we going to get sliced and diced by your fancy electric lasso?"

"You can turn around once you drop your weapons," replied the voice. "But slowly. Just because I know who you are doesn't mean I won't kill you."

Duke sighed but placed his pulse pistol and Betsy on the messy floor. Ishiro'shea did the same with his katana.

"Thank you for—kinda—trusting us," said Duke.

The assailant wasn't a large man but he looked as athletic as a gymnast. He wore a blue *shinobi shozoku* but no mask. His face was youthful and his short black hair was matted and unkempt.

Duke looked over at his partner; Ishiro'shea removed the covering over his mouth and smiled.

He does know him.

Ishiro bowed slightly. The man in blue reciprocated the pleasantry.

"It's good to see you again, my old classmate. I would not have thought it would be like this."

Even though the man had addressed Ishiro'shea directly, it was Duke that replied. "We're here to find Master Fukudome. He's in trouble."

The man shifted his gaze to Duke, but then returned it to Ishiro'shea. "What type of trouble?"

No point in lying to this guy.

"There's a very dangerous assassin after him," continued Duke. "A female. Goes by the name of Mazilda Cloax. She thinks the headmaster knows something regarding Ishiro's parents. It's pretty valuable information."

The whip master twisted uneasily.

"An assassin, you say? Would this assassin have purple hair?"

"Yes!" exclaimed Duke. "That's her."

His eyes fell. "Then you are too late. She has already been here. She has already found Ishiro-sama, I'm afraid."

Ishiro'shea collapsed to the ground.

"Do you know where she went?" Duke pleaded. "What she asked him? What he told her?"

"I do not."

"Damnit," the Nova Texan screamed. "Where is he now? Can we speak to him? He has to remember Ish!"

The man returned his attention to Ishiro'shea. "It's not good, Ishiro'shea-san. The master was beaten severely by this treacherous woman. But—"

"Can you take us to him? We need to find out what she knows. The universe is on the line here, kid."

"For Ishiro'shea, I will take you. I know the master was like a father to him, in the absence of his own parents. I know the master would approve."

Duke exhaled. "Thank you."

"But, let me warn you, he is in very critical condition."

"Understood. Thank you again." Duke paused. "Sorry, I didn't catch your name. And we all know Ish isn't going to tell me."

"My name is Yeop."

"I like your lasso, Yeop."

"It's a whip."

CHAPTER FOURTEEN

THE MASTER

YEOP LED DUKE AND ISHIRO'SHEA through a labyrinth of hallways and corridors within the college. There wasn't any damage outside of the master's office; the school was immaculately kept, without a speck of dust or dirt to be found. The trio descended a spiral staircase, traveling farther into the innards of the school.

"So, Yeop, you and Ish were pretty good friends back at school?" asked Duke as he made his way cautiously down the poorly-illuminated stairwell.

"I think so. Or I thought so. I think we were all surprised when he took off like he did. In all honesty, we just assumed we'd hear that he found his parents and he'd return. He was such a good student; we were all jealous of him."

"But not the best, huh?" said Duke jokingly. "I mean, he was *only* Salutatorian."

Duke was taken aback when Yeop didn't laugh.

"What are you talking about? Salutatorian is the highest honor."

"What about Valedictorian? Who won that award?"

Yeop chuckled.

"So who was it?" Duke asked impatiently.

"We are the College of College of Cohorts, Consorts, Co-Conspirators, and Other Assorted Sidekick Types. A sidekick could never have the top billing of Valedictorian. That's just, well, it's just silly."

Should've known that one. Shame on me.

"Down here, to the right. That's the master's secret chamber."

"Secret medical chamber?"

"No, just a regular secret chamber," replied Yeop.

"Who's providing the medical attention?"

"No one. A few of us are trying to make him comfortable but we're just staff here, not medical professionals. Master Fukudome said that he that didn't want to be a burden. If it's his time, it's his time; those were his exact words."

"You said he was in critical condition, though. According to whose diagnosis?"

"His. He said he was dying and didn't want help. I thought that warranted the label of 'critical.'"

"Fair enough."

"Let me go in first and let him know that you're here. I don't want to cause further shock as he's not expecting any visitors. Especially a visitor like Ishiro'shea."

Ishiro'shea bowed appreciatively, and it was Duke's turn to give a thumbs-up.

Yeop disappeared into the chamber, closing the door behind him.

After some time, he re-emerged and signaled for the two to enter.

The chamber was a simple box with blank walls and a single overhead light. There were some uncomfortable-looking chairs in the corner and a raised table in the center, surrounded by smaller ones. Candles, providing ample light and fragrance, sat atop each of these smaller tables. All except for one. Upon that table was a weathered brass bowl; spilling over the top were clumps of blood-soaked rags. On the central platform lay an elderly Japanese man. He was covered in an ornate silk sheet but the tattered ends of bandages hung even lower than the beautiful blanket.

Ishiro'shea approached the dying headmaster. The ninja pulled down the part of his mask that covered his mouth. Duke followed, a step behind his companion. He removed his hat.

The old man slowly turned his head until his eyes fixed on his former pupil.

"Ah, Ishiro'shea," he began quietly, "it has been too long."

The ninja bowed.

"I wish it was under better circumstances," Master Fukudome continued, fighting to speak through coughs, "for you and me both."

His stare shifted to Duke. "And who are you?"

"Duke LaGrange, sir. A friend of Ishiro'shea."

The master squinted intensely as if he was trying to look beyond the bounty hunter's physical being and into his metaphysical interior.

"Nova Texan, I presume?"

"Yes, how'd you know?"

"I'm an old man that's been in this universe for a long time. I've encountered many beings and I've learned that Nova Texans have a certain... well, presence."

"Thank you," Duke replied with a slight bow.

"I didn't say it was a presence that people appreciated," the master added with a smirk.

"You got me, sir," Duke said with another respectful

bow. "Well played. I wish your sense of humor would've rubbed off on Ishiro here."

The ninja playfully pushed Duke away. Master Fukudome gave a subtle giggle. He then turned back to his former student. "I'm guessing you know more about what happened to me than I do, Ishiro'shea."

The ninja nodded.

"Who was that woman who attacked me? She was asking questions that confused me greatly; she was asking about your parents."

"Master Fukudome, sir," Duke interjected, "the woman was Mazilda Cloax. She's an old friend of ours."

"You need to pick your friends more wisely, it seems."

"I don't disagree with you," admitted Duke. "Mazilda is a skilled assassin and is working for a man named Lothario LePaco. He's trying to take over the universe."

"There's always someone," Master Fukudome said.

"But, unlike the others, he has an inside track on how to actually do it. He's discovered a weapon—from another dimension; he has a third of it already—an ancient shield that was on Psitakki. One piece, an orb from a planet called Neprius, is currently under the guard of Queen Joe on Kelt."

"I've heard of this Queen. Some say she is also from another dimension."

"Those people would be right," said Duke. "She is. She's our best hope to keeping the Orb safe. But if LePaco and Mazilda get that third piece—a pendant—then the shift of power might be too much to overcome. LePaco could destroy planets and galaxies with the mere flick of his wrist."

"Fear isn't true power, my friends," said the frail headmaster. "It can only get you so far in the quest for power."

"He also has a massive group that doubles as his army

and his middle management. Just as we used to terraform uninhabited planets, he's taking fully-developed civilizations and reforming them into orderly satellite business units, all cogs in the wheel of this new universe."

"This is troubling. And I'm guessing this pendant of which you speak is the Heart of Nobunaga."

Yeop and the teachers bringing new rags and plumper pillows gasped. Duke and Ishiro'shea both acknowledged the master's correct assumption with simple shakes of the head.

"The Heart of Nobunaga disappeared, Master," cried Yeop. "Many cycles ago."

"It did not disappear, young Yeop. When Ishiro'shea's parents left the war, they took it with them. Its power would have only led to even more death and destruction."

"Can there be more death and destruction than what we have now?" asked Yeop.

"Today, there is still hope. Hope that the wars will end. If the Heart was to be discovered, that hope—no matter how insignificant it may seem—would be completely extinguished. Our world would cease to be."

"So it really is magical? It really did do those things that we've heard about in the legend of Takeo?"

"It did, Yeop. It did. But it wasn't magic. It was just an unidentified science that we never fully understood. It seems that it was from a different dimension. A dimension, I assume, that has different laws of nature, and of physics, and of existence."

Duke leaned over closer to the old man. "Master Fukudome," he whispered, "please tell me that you know where Ishiro's parents are. And that they are safe from Mazilda."

The dying master closed his eyes. He shifted his head back to its natural resting position.

"I know where they *were*, but I'm afraid I don't know

where they are," he replied softly. "They *were* safe. The Heart of Nobunaga *was* safe."

Duke exhaled. "That's good."

"And I did not tell this Mazilda anything."

"That's even better," replied Duke. "Outside of the physical harm that it caused you, of course."

"It's a risk that we take when we are trusted with great secrets, my friends. But, I must tell you, I cannot promise you that they are safe *now*."

"Why is that, Master?" asked Yeop.

"The assassin did beat me badly. And the beating escalated as I remained defiant to her interrogation. But she did not kill me. She departed suddenly."

"Maybe she heard me coming?" Yeop suggested.

Mazilda wouldn't have run from you—even if you do have a really nifty laser lasso, Duke thought.

"Maybe," replied the master. "A more logical assessment could be that she, or someone that she was working with, discovered Yumi's whereabouts. And thus, she knew where Yumi's husband was. And thus, the Heart."

The room said nothing.

The long silence was eventually broken by a middle-aged Earth woman swinging open the chamber door violently. Her face was white with shock.

"We're being invaded, we're being invaded! They're in our atmosphere," she wailed.

Duke turned to Ishiro'shea. "The Four I's. You stay here with Master Fukudome, Ish. I'll go check it out."

The sky was indeed filled with a Four I's fleet. It wasn't large enough to be an invasion force, especially not for a place as rough and tumble as Earth. For starters, there wasn't an Armada Titan. Earth would surely require an Armada Titan. Of course, the Four I's could have made a mistake and sent the bulk of the fleet to a different part of Earth instead of the military epicenter of New Tokyo. But Duke gave them more credit than that.

I guess the Four I's are going to try and reform Earth, Duke concluded. *Good luck with that.*

A black speck moving towards one of the battle cruisers caught the bounty hunter's eye. It disappeared behind the larger spacecraft. Moments later, a handful of the ships departed the atmosphere.

Holy hedgehogs.

"Ish, we gotta go," shouted Duke as he rushed into Master Fukudome's chamber.

There was no response. No one even looked up at the hysterical Nova Texan. They all remained seated, their heads in their hands, peering at the floor.

"This is urgent," screamed Duke. "That force isn't here to invade. It was here to provide safe passage for Mazilda and LePaco. They have your parents, Ish. I know it."

Yeop stood up and grabbed the bounty hunter's shoulders. His face was wet with tears.

"The master is dead."

CHAPTER FIFTEEN

THE TRAVELER

THE *DEUS EX MACHINA* SPED away from the New Tokyo Demilitarized Zone and headed towards the southern part of the planet. Luckily, Duke and Ishiro'shea's intuitions proved correct and the Four I's blockade was solely focused around the visible airspace above Ireland. This also meant that Duke's intuition regarding the Four I's primary mission of extraction was likely correct as well. LePaco and Mazilda probably had Ishiro's parents. Even more problematic was the fact that they likely had the Amplification Key.

As the *Deus* exited the Earth's atmosphere, a new problem presented itself—where were they going to find a warp station that wasn't heavily guarded by LePaco's forces? The *Deus'* scanners whizzed and buzzed but there wasn't a beep to signify an identified portal. Nothing.

Then... something. Not a big something, but a something nonetheless.

"Over there. It's faint but it's the best we got, little buddy," Duke proclaimed.

Ishiro'shea tapped on the control panel and the scanning focused on the planetoid.

Delorme. Rogue Brown Dwarf. Uninhabited. Discovered by Earth scientists during the planetary year of 2012.

"Hey, I know that rock" Duke replied, a bit surprised at his own knowledge. "That's 'The Traveler.' It doesn't orbit any star, it just floats around. It's an ugly booger. I wonder why it's registering up on our portal scan. It's uninhabited."

Ishiro'shea typed even faster, presumably diving deep into the bowels of the *Deus'* databank.

The screen overlay transitioned from the basic details to a two-dimensional, animated timeline, starting with the rogue planet's discovery, then entering a long period of absolute nothing, then a little-known fact that intrigued Duke.

Attempted Jungafallowian Colonization.

Duke read the lengthy entry.

"It seems that the Jungafallowians wanted to always be on the move, and what better way than with a traveling planet? How far did they get on colonizing it?"

The screen changed again, citing that the Jungafallowian efforts were abandoned fairly early on when they discovered they had been unsuccessful at altering the atmospheric composition.

"But," Duke began, "if they made a couple of trips to try it, then they had to set up a means to travel efficiently. Like a private warp station."

Ishiro'shea nodded. He twirled his finger around in a flurry of zigs and zags.

"That's right," Duke acknowledged, "it's 'The Traveler.' So, the portal must be attached to the planet somehow. We gotta try it. It might be our only way to Kelt, even though the detour is through Jungafallow."

The ninja plotted the course and the ship sped away from that crazy blue planet known as Earth.

Delorme was ugly. It was rocky, harsh, barren, but mostly ugly.

This would've been perfect for the Jungafallowians, thought Duke.

"What's the composition? Looks pretty rough."

The computer screen spat out pertinent data: *High metal content. Methane atmosphere. Unsuitable for the biologies of 99.63% of known living species.*

"High metallicity. Maybe the warp portal is anchored to the actual planet; it'd be pretty old school, but then again, the colonization was a long time ago," Duke surmised. "Let's increase the scan to the planet's atmosphere."

The *Deus'* scan intensified yet again. The pulsing beep picked up speed; it then morphed into a constant hum and, finally, into a wailing siren.

"We got it," Duke shouted gleefully. "That has to be it."

Upon further inspection, it was indeed an archaic private portal, built as a bridge to and from a distinct location. Unlike the common warp stations that could be altered to take travelers to multiple destinations, this door and its twin were connected by a single, unyielding tube of space-time.

"Looks like we're going to Jungafallow. Let's just hope it's not Jungafallow III."

It was Jungafallow III.

Thankfully, though, the warp portal was stationed in a

vast expanse of nothing. In fact, it had probably been abandoned many cycles ago by the ruling Jungafallowian party of the time and then forgotten. But it still worked and that was the important thing. Another important thing was that the Four I's had not approached the Jungafallowian System, so all that Duke and Ishiro'shea had to do was find a more modern warp station and head to Kelt. That was the easy part of this whole imbroglio.

The *Deus Ex Machina* cruised along the outskirts of the system and headed for the space outside of Jungafallow IV. The overly conservative residents of Jungafallow IV would have no beef with an alien ship using their portal because it meant that the aliens in question were leaving. The Jungafallowians on IV were much more intelligent, orderly, and civilized than their crude and overly enthusiastic relatives on Jungafallow III, but that didn't mean that they welcomed visitors.

In between the two primary planets in the system, III and IV, there was a sliver of space occupied with a gnarly asteroid belt. It wasn't the most treacherous gathering of space rocks, but it wasn't a picnic to navigate either. Despite the dangers and obstacles presented by the floating chain of unpredictable cosmic debris, the Trampling Death Robots would routinely hold concerts in the belt, much to the delight of their hardcore followers. One of their better-received albums, *Trampling Death Robots LIVE: But Not If These Damn Asteroids Don't Cooperate*, was recorded on this very same asteroid.

Duke looked at his partner. "It's going to be the fastest way back to Kelt. I've driven through worse. I got this," he said confidently.

Duke was correct in this matter: it *was* the fastest way to the warp station.

With the Nova Texan at the wheel, the *Deus* twisted

and dodged, rolled and swayed, as it navigated through the asteroid belt. What should have been a hectic, white knuckle, peek-through-mostly-closed-eyelids moment was rather anticlimactic. It was almost calming.

Duke's focus relaxed once the densely packed portion of the belt was behind them.

"Should be smooth sailing the rest of the way." He removed his hat, sat at the control panel, and let out a sigh of relief.

His attention returned to Ishiro'shea. "I know things have happened kinda fast, but I want you to know that I'm sorry about Master Fukudome."

Ishiro'shea bowed quickly.

"No, Ish, enough with the stoicism and formalities. I know he raised you. It's okay to be angry. It's okay to grieve some," Duke continued. "I know I'm pissed. I still can't believe Mazilda would do something like that."

Ishiro'shea lowered his eyes.

"You're right, I can't keep thinking she's the same person that we knew back then. I just can't believe it. I promise you, little buddy, we'll get her. We'll get LePaco. We'll find your parents. Nothing can stop us."

As the *Deus* exited the last cluster of rogue asteroids, Duke's mouth opened with no intention of shutting anytime soon. Staring back at them was a ship of behemoth proportions. In big block letters, it read: *TRAMPLING DEATH ROBOTS FAN CLUB & ATTACK SQUAD: JUNGAFALLOW III CHAPTER*.

"Not again."

CHAPTER SIXTEEN

KISS MY ASS-TEROID

"DO WE HAVE TO PATCH 'em in? I mean we *should*, right? I'm not really in the mood for Jungafallowians," Duke whined, "but it's not like anyone is ever in the mood for Jungafallowians. I don't even think *Jungafallowians* are ever in the mood for Jungafallowians."

As his thought trailed off, his sidekick did the only reasonable thing: he patched them in.

On the *Deus'* primary screen appeared four faces, four necks, and, of course, two Jungafallowians. These faces, however, Duke and Ishiro'shea immediately recognized. Flakka-Grog and Orbo-Terg.

"Oh hey there, guys," Duke began. "Long time no see. I have to say, I didn't expect to see you again. Ever."

"Because you ran away?" the Flakka head asked.

"And you did everything in your power to hide from our vengeance?" added Grog.

"Big wusses!" shouted both of Orbo-Terg's heads in unison.

"No, because I thought you were dead," Duke replied matter-of-factly.

"Well we ain't," blurted the colossal Orbo-Terg.

"You both look pretty close to it."

Duke shook his arm to simulate injury, then grabbed his chest, grimacing in faux pain. Both Jungafallowians looked down at the bandages that covered much of their upper torso. Orbo-Terg's right arm was in a sling; Flakka-Grog's left arm was cocooned snugly in a hard cast.

"These bruises? It takes more than a few scratches from a Gartoshian sneak attack to stop us from completing our mission," Flakka-Grog said confidently.

"Dare I ask what your mission is?" Duke said reluctantly.

"To avenge the Trampling Death Robots and Sprinkles!"

Orbo-Terg wailed in agreement.

"How is ol' Sprinkles doing these days? Any more katana blades through the eye?"

Flakka-Grog's faces grew red with rage. "Funny, LaGrange. No, your attempts to kill the greatest musician to ever live—"

"Are we classifying a robot as 'alive' these days? Where exactly do you stand on cyber-sentience? For? Against? Undecided?"

"Stop trying to change the subject, bounty hunter," hissed Flakka.

Duke raised his hands in submission. "Continue, please."

"Your attempts were pointless. Despite the hullabaloo that you caused, the Robots only missed one show. In fact, that's where we're headed now."

"Another one of their asteroid belt shows?" asked the Nova Texan. "Aren't those old news nowadays? I mean, get a new trick, Sprinkles."

Clearly, the Jungafallowians did not appreciate Duke's snark. Their eyes grew fiery and their jaws clenched.

"This isn't any concert. This is the 17th Annual Trampling Death Robots 'Kiss My Ass-teroid' Music Festival, honoring the seventeen cycles since the release of their epic album, *Trampling Death Robots LIVE: But Not If These Damn Asteroids Don't Cooperate.*"

"Any good?"

"Only the best ever!" shouted Orbo-Terg from behind his more intelligent friend.

"Yes, the best ever," echoed Flakka. "And now our festival-going experience is going to be kicked up a notch, because we get to kill you and avenge the Robots without so much as a detour."

"That *would* be pretty efficient," joked Duke. "Tell me something, guys—since you're about to kill me anyways, I don't see why it would hurt to provide a little clarity for an old friend."

"What?" sighed Grog.

"How'd you get the Prince's ship?"

The Jungafallowian rambled on regarding something about trivia and losing money and revenge, but Duke was too preoccupied with a discovery that Ishiro'shea had made on the scanner.

"Good eye, Ish," he muttered. "They're coming here?"

The ninja nodded.

"Just one?"

Ishiro'shea nodded again.

"That's not like the Four I's. Maybe they've decided to organize Jungafallow III. If they're trying to 'improve' Earth, why not Jungafallow III?"

Duke returned his attention to the Jungafallowians; Flakka-Grog was still in the midst of his passionate diatribe and, presumably, his explanation about how he had come to captain the ship of the deceased Prince Korzo-Tapor.

"Sorry to cut you off, big guy," Duke interjected, "but it appears that we have company. Both of us. Four I's."

"Moron, we actually *have* four eyes, so it's not an insult," Flakka remarked.

"Intergalactic Infrastructure Improvement, Incorporated," Duke said, enunciating each word deliberately. "Four I's."

"We know about the Four I's. They've been taking over weak-willed planets. But Jungafallow III isn't a pushover. I've heard rumors that we're negotiating an alliance with them, anyways. Supposedly, they signed some deal on Junga-Mini One last week after they took it over. So, I'd wager they're here for you two. You aren't exactly known to have a ton of allies."

"That does make sense. Maybe you should ask, since you're so buddy-buddy with 'em?"

"What?" Flakka said, surprised.

"They're right behind you. Ask 'em."

Immediately, the Jungafallowians cut their transmission to the *Deus*.

The ship that was approaching the Trampling Death Robots Fan Club vessel was definitely a Four I's build. It was larger than their typical scout fighter but nowhere near the size of a cruiser or an Armada Titan. It was clear from its external design that it was built for speed. Its unconcealed weaponry made it equally clear that it was built for war.

"We really don't have time for this, Ish," Duke groaned. "You think we can outrun 'em?"

The ninja shook his head.

"Yeah, maybe the Jungas, but not this ship. Maybe they'll blow up each other? Wishful thinking, I know."

Suddenly, a light show of lasers and explosions cavalcaded across the back half of the Jungafallowian ship. The Four I's unleashed another devastating assault.

I'm guessing Flakka-Grog and Orbo-Terg didn't win these guys over with their magnetic charm and unparalleled wit, surmised Duke.

The Fan Club ship tried to counter, but it was fruitless. Their heavy artillery options were eradicated by the opening barrage from the Four I's. It was clear that the Jungafallowians had one remaining course of action—retreat—and they were trying to do so with all due haste. Their spacecraft dipped and veered to the right; the Four I's vessel did not pursue, but neither did it lessen the assault. Its fire was concentrated on the rear thrusters of the Jungafallowian ship. Before they could have sung the opening lines to *I Want to Smash You, My Binary Baby,* the ship was limping into the asteroid field without the proper propulsion to navigate it safely. Before the Jungafallowians could have sung the second line of the song, the ship was bouncing from asteroid to asteroid like a ping-pong ball hopped up on a sugar high. Before they could have reached the chorus, the spaceship of the Jungafallow III Chapter of the Trampling Death Robots Fan Club was nowhere to be seen.

The Four I's fighter halted its attack. It repositioned to block the *Deus'* escape route.

The control panel blinked furiously.

Why are they hailing us? wondered Duke.

"Patch them in," he said. "But first, get our shields up and every bit of weaponry that we have on this damn ship aimed at that son of a bitch."

Ishiro'shea extended a thumbs-up and began frantically entering weapon sequences.

"Also, Ish," Duke continued, "be on the lookout for a giant red button. We might need it."

The ninja patched in the transmission.

Staring back at them from the primary screen were, once again, two familiar beings. However, these two beings had only two heads between them. It was Sol and his receptionist and better half, Wanda. Okay, maybe only slightly better.

"Duke, baby! How are you?" shouted the overweight Tardasian bondsman. "I recognized the *Deus* on the scanner so I wanted to drop by and say hello. What are the odds? Then I saw that you were in some trouble with those damn Jungafallowians. I'm glad I could be of service."

"You have such a big heart. Were you doing us a favor last time when you set us up? We flew right into a damn Four I's trap. Or when you sold out to those bastards? That base they built on Tardasio 7 almost killed us too. In fact, it might have killed..." Duke trailed off. He didn't want to finish his sentence. Sol didn't need to know about his family issues. And Duke didn't want to think about his biological father's death at the hands of the Four I's.

"What?" replied Sol, dumbstruck.

"They might have killed some friends of mine."

"Look, look, look," Sol stammered, "I made some mistakes. I got into some bad dealings. But it's over now, I promise."

"Sol, you're in one of their damn ships!"

"This thing? I forgot it's one of theirs, to be honest. It was part of my deal with you-know-who. I get him easy access to T7, he gives me a really fast ship."

"LePaco?"

"Like I said, I made some bad deals. But I'm done with that. I mean, c'mon, why would I have saved your sorry behinds if I was trying to weasel my way into a secret life of lavish safety? Makes no sense, LaGrange."

"Yeah, it does," Duke replied swiftly.

"What are you talkin' about?"

"You got rid of those clowns, not because you noticed that we were here, but because you didn't want them to get better seats at the Trampling Death Robots concert."

"What? That's preposterous. That's way outta left field, even for you."

"Is it?"

"Yeah, crazy town. You might need to get yourself checked out, Duke."

"Sol, I can see Wanda from here. I can see the writing on her shirt: 'I'd Dismember Koalas for Sprinkles.'"

"That's a different Sprinkles, Duke," Sol shot back. "Total coincidence."

"She has a souvenir foam hammer in her hand. You know, like Sprinkles."

The bondsman chewed his bottom lip. It was clear he was trying to think of a cover.

"Her hat literally says, 'My Boyfriend is Such a Big TDR Fan that He Would Blow Up a Ship Just to Get Better Seats.'"

"Fine, LaGrange. You got me. I just really hate those guys. They're loud and obnoxious."

"Then why are you going to their concert?"

"Not the Robots, you idiot, those Jungafallowian fan clubs. They ruin it for everyone."

"We agree there, Sol."

"I didn't want to sell out to LePaco and those bastards, but it was either that or he was going to take everything. Or kill me. Either way, no *bueno*."

"It's fine, Sol. I know what type of stuff you're made of. I'm not shocked."

It was clear that the bondsman misinterpreted the bounty hunter's sentiment; he smiled proudly. "Can we call it even, LaGrange?"

"Sure. Enjoy the concert. And you too, Wanda."

The plump secretary blushed and sunk back behind her boyfriend.

"But Sol, just don't go helping any more maniac wannabe overlords anytime soon. Please. I'm begging here."

"Fine, LaGrange. Where are you two heading, anyways?"

"Joe's. We have to stop LePaco."

"You're a bona fide moron, LaGrange. Ishiro'shea, you okay with this nutjob?"

The ninja replied with a thumbs-up.

"You're both morons then."

"Enjoy the concert, Sol," Duke said.

Ishiro'shea cut the transmission.

"That's the closest we're ever going to get to an apology from that fat bastard."

CHAPTER SEVENTEEN

WE ARE ALL BLOP

PASSAGE TO, AND SUBSEQUENTLY THROUGH, the Jungafallow IV Warp Station provided a much needed spell from the constant nuisances that had plagued Duke and Ishiro'shea since they had been captured on T'ckuvu Prime. Duke's biggest lingering uncertainty was whether they would get to Kelt in time to provide any help in repelling Admiral LePaco. The mystery of the relative tranquillity was cleared up as soon as the *Deus Ex Machina* exited the Keltian Warp Station.

"Holy hedgehogs," Duke gasped, "how many ships do you think that is?"

The ninja's dexterous digits fluttered over the control panel. Instantaneously, the screen read: *Armada Titans – 2. Battle Cruisers – 35. Scout Ships, Attack Class – 117. Jungafallowian Fighter Ships – 6. Tardasian Military Ships – 12. Unidentified Spacecraft with Military Capabilities – 23. Unclassified Craft – 37. Recommended strategy – Computing...*

This oughta be good, thought Duke.

...Leave immediately. Don't even say goodbye to loved

ones... Just leave. Now. You have no chance to survive unless you flee.

Duke sighed. *Figures.*

From the formation it was clear that the Four I's fleet was planning on another concentrated assault on Oldish Kelt and, more specifically, Cyborg Joe's. A small portion of the armada covered the exit and entry points on the other side of the planet.

"I'm taking away two things from this situation," began Duke. "Number one... the Bounty Hunters Union and the crime lord partnership did not survive the sneak attack in the Tardasian System—LePaco doesn't seem to care one bit about the Queen receiving reinforcements. We just waltzed through the closest public portal and not a single Four I's ship even raised an eyebrow."

Ishiro'shea nodded in agreement.

"Number two... LePaco has the Key. And this is his big play to get the Orb." Duke scratched his chin. "Which means I forgot the third takeaway: if he gets it, the universe is *done*. Can you try and get ahold of Joe? Maybe she knows something that we don't."

Ishiro plugged away, but the view screen only displayed harsh static. The ninja threw his hands up.

"They've jammed comms, too. Great."

The bounty hunter plopped himself down in the captain's chair. He let out a gasp coated in frustration and wrapped in despair.

"It all ends like this," he moaned. "It's all over, huh? We just got beat, outsmarted, outclassed by that weasel. Not to mention that probably our closest friend that we've ever had killed the man that raised you, will likely kill your parents, and has helped put an end to the universe as we know it. And here we are, with a front row seat to it all. We can't do a damn thing. Not a single damn thing. We couldn't even get through the outer rim of their fleet. There's no way we could get to Cyborg Joe's to try and smuggle the Queen and the Orb out. There won't be a chance to live to fight another day."

Silence reigned aboard the *Deus* for what seemed an eternity. The Four I's fleet was holding steady; it didn't appear that a single shot had been fired. The *Deus* still sat unnoticed—or noticed and ignored.

Ishiro'shea perked up and maximized a scanner on the forward monitor.

The portal had been activated.

"Surely, by now, everyone wanting to avoid seeing a galactic massacre firsthand has been notified to stay away from Keltian space, right?" asked Duke. "So that means our visitor is probably on the ornery side. Let's get our shields up and weapons ready."

The familiar thumbs-up sign was flashed.

Expelled unceremoniously from the portal was a diminutive space vessel the likes of which Duke had never seen. It was no bigger than one of the *Deus'* rear thrusters. It sported no visible markings, had no visible armaments, and, shockingly, didn't appear to have any means of propulsion. One would think something so minute in scale would possess speed and agility, but it showed no signs of these traits either. The metallic ovoid meandered out of the station and approached the *Deus*.

"I know it doesn't look like much, but be on the ready," commanded Duke.

"Hey there, guys."

"What was that?" asked the perplexed Nova Texan.

"Hey there, guys," the voice moaned again.

"Who's talking?" Duke shouted up at the ceiling. "How are you doing this? Who are you?"

He looked at Ishiro'shea, who appeared equally dumbfounded. The ninja's hands were raised but the control panel continued to beep and blink and buzz.

"Oh sorry, wait a second, my apologies," bellowed the mysterious melancholy intruder.

Suddenly, on the forward view screen appeared Blop, a Blop from Blop.

"What... how... why..." stammered Duke.

"Hello there, Duke LaGrange of Nova Texas and Ishiro'shea of Earth," greeted Blop, rather formally.

"You died. Back on Psitakki. How are you—"

The Blop cut him off. "Yes, I did die. Well, one of us died."

Duke just shook his head in disbelief, his mouth hanging open.

"Blop, a Blop from Blop, died on Psitakki," the formless, chewed-bubblegum-esque Blop continued, "and I'm Blop, a Blop from Blop."

"Yeah, you might need to rewind a bit."

"We are all Blop, a Blop from Blop. We all share a single existence. All of us. We are all Blop."

"A Blop from Blop?" added Duke.

"Yes, you got it."

"I *don't* have it," Duke whispered to Ishiro'shea.

"We all share an existence, a being..."

"A hive mind?" asked Duke.

"Something like that. I know what you did back on Psitakki for Blop. That was very kind of you. We don't see a lot of kindness in our collective travels."

"It was nothing," replied Duke, blushing slightly. "But why are you here? I know the Tournament of the Colossal Calamari is tough stuff, but this is on another level. There are two hundred heavily-armed spacecraft out there."

"I know, and that's why I came. We can't let this LePaco get the Orb."

"How do you know—"

"We Blops know a great deal about this dimension, other dimensions, and so on. There are a near-infinite number of Blops, and an infinite number of Blop thoughts. But we happen to like this universe and don't want to see it destroyed. We think that you can help prevent it."

"And how exactly is that, if you don't mind me asking?"

"*You* will have to figure that out. But I can get you to the planet's surface and to the Orb. From there, it's up to you—but you must stop this evil."

Duke had no response. He just stared at the dark, spherical eyes that poked out of the fleshy, fatty, misshapen head of the Blop. It tried to smile.

"Just follow me," the Blop said in a tone that made it impossible for Duke to consider doing anything other than obey the command. "In a few moments, you'll be back with the Orb."

"I trust you," said Duke. "I don't know why, but I do."

"Thank you. Your trust means a great deal to us."

"But I do have one question before we embark on whatever we're about to embark on."

"Go ahead."

"How did you know that we were here and in trouble? Was there another Blop around here, maybe on board one of these Four I's ships? Maybe on Kelt with a really powerful telescope?"

The Blop simulated a human laugh.

"No, Duke LaGrange of Nova Texas. The *Deus* told me."

"Come again?"

"Your ship got in touch with me. All of the Blops."

"How'd it do that? I didn't press any giant red button this time. Did you, Ish?"

"Of course you didn't," answered Blop. "You should really ask your ship."

Blop tried to smile again and, this time, accompanied the action with a slowly developing wink. Duke got what he was going for. Then the transmission ended.

The nondescript, seemingly harmless silver ovoid slipped out in front of the *Deus Ex Machina*. It began to glow. At first, it was a muted yellow. Then a radiant orange. Then it exploded into a sphere of white light, quadruple the size of the ship itself.

In an instant, the fiery ball of Blop tunneled through the heart of the Four I's armada. All vessels in its path were disintegrated. It burrowed through the hull of one of the Armada Titans, setting off a chain reaction of explosions that took down an entire flotilla of scouts, fighters, and battle cruisers.

"I guess we follow that," Duke said to Ishiro'shea.

CHAPTER EIGHTEEN

EVERYWHERE'S A DEATH TRAP

"I WOULD SAY IT'S GOOD to be back but, under these circumstances, well, ya' know, it really isn't."

"Good to see you too, Duke," replied Queen Joe. "We've missed you and Ishiro. As you can see, we've needed every able body and free pair of hands that we can muster."

It wasn't a shock to Duke that Cyborg Joe's hadn't been restored to its usual ambience following the Battle of Oldish Kelt, but it was surprising that after its tenure as a makeshift hospital it had become what appeared to be a war room. There was no mistaking it: Queen Joe was preparing for war.

"Speaking of these able bodies and free hands," began Duke, "you really need to call them off. Send them home. We've come here to help you escape—you and the Orb."

The Queen flashed her perfectly aligned teeth in a wry smile, as if she had been expecting the bounty hunter's plea. "No, Duke. I'm not leaving here. I'm going to fight LePaco and his forces. Here. No running."

Her tone wasn't particularly defiant or harsh. But Joe

wasn't nonchalant either. Her statement was a simple, non-negotiable absolute. She was going to stay and fight.

"You can't."

"I can't?" she shot back.

"No, you *can*. But there's no hope if you do. You're essentially giving LePaco the keys to the universe. We can't hold off an armada of that size."

"I see you helped us out with that."

"What?"

"Reports are that you took out an Armada Titan and some of its supporting cast en route to see us."

"You think *we* did that? I wish. I'd feel better about our prospects if we were capable of something like that."

"I see," replied the Queen coyly. "Then tell our ally 'thanks.'"

"I can't. He's dead. He died so that we could get here and take you away. So we could live to fight another day."

"Blop said that, did he?"

"No, not in those exact... Wait, what? How'd you know about Blop?"

"It's not important. But if I know Blop, I'd suspect that he didn't want you to steal me away; he would—or rather, *they* would—want us to stand up against this evil. Head-on."

"We can't, Queen. Please see reason," begged the Nova Texan. "Please."

"Do you not believe in us? I have certain powers that can be helpful in an attack."

"I've seen the lightning and fire and... whatever that stuff was. I've also seen this planet almost get destroyed by a force that was only a fraction of the size of what's up there now, and without an insane lunatic holding both the Shield and the Key. The odds aren't in our favor."

"We also have the Orb. I'd wager that I can harness the

Orb on a much higher plane than the admiral can wield his two artifacts."

"I guess, Queen," Duke said with a sigh. "I'll have to take your word on that."

"We also have a very tough and respectable ground force."

"A few bar patrons and some homeless Keltian refugees does not an army make," countered Duke.

"No, Duke—we have *thousands* of Keltians. I've positioned them in bunkers below the bar and around this area. The Four I's have a clear advantage in the air, but we know they want one thing—the Orb—and they'll have to come here to get it. Plus, I have Po'l and Lilly getting them into shape and trained up, and leading the ground strategy."

"They *are* going to die, Queen."

Duke felt a powerful hand on his shoulder. The Queen's attention shifted to the being standing behind him. She smiled.

"I'm sorry to interrupt," said a familiar voice. "But I was told that you might need some help."

The bounty hunter turned around and, without thinking, hugged the hairy behemoth. Ishiro'shea joined the embrace.

"Yvonne! So glad to see you," said Duke. "Queen, this is the Furry Mountain of Moon Colony #1. I've seen her knock out a Mega-Troll without breaking a sweat."

"I'm aware of Miss Angerdlarnek's fighting prowess. It's very nice to meet you, Yvonne. Welcome to Joe's and, to answer your question, we can use all the help we can get. As you can see, we are currently losing the numbers game."

"It was only a few days after Lilly contacted me that the Four I's entered our neighbor system," said Yvonne.

"I'm sorry, Yvonne," replied the Queen.

"Don't be. We're a pretty tough race. But instead of

engaging them head-on, we decided to rally our troops and head here. We want to cut off the head of the snake."

"Yvonne, no," began Duke. "Send your people back. This is a death trap."

"Duke, everywhere's a death trap right now. And it'll continue to be until LePaco is dead," replied Yvonne. She returned her attention to Queen Joe. "We have about twenty-five heavy fighters and a few scouts. We also have two transports loaded with ten thousand of the roughest, toughest Gartoshian soldiers that you've ever seen. We landed on the other side of the planet and await your direction."

"How'd you get past the blockade?" asked Joe.

"Easy. When you've been through as many wars as we have on Gartosh, you pick up a few tricks. We sent some scouts through the main Keltian Warp Station. The Four I's paid us no attention."

"They did the same to us," added Duke.

"They paid us no attention because we were in their ships," continued Yvonne. "We borrowed some that happened to be conducting pre-integration analyses on Gartosh and its many moons."

"Excellent."

"Each one carried the components for an extremely crude private warp portal. It had just enough juice to get our entire fleet to the planet. So we are here and ready to help."

"I can't thank you and your leaders enough," said Joe. "In fact, let's open up communication now. I'd love to get their ideas." She motioned for the anthropomorphic musk ox to follow her into the back area of the bar.

"Earl," shouted the Queen over her shoulder, "tell Lilly to come meet us up here. Po'l can handle the training."

The Glyptodian barkeep nodded.

Yvonne grabbed hold of both Duke's and Ishiro'shea's shoulders. "I'm so glad that we got to see each other again. And I'm glad it's not on that awful Psitakki," she chuckled.

"Yvonne," Duke began, "this is suicide."

"No, doing nothing is suicide. We are here to fight. We know we're going to lose some of the bravest Gartoshians in a generation... but we also hope that they save us from losing future generations. This universe cannot have a supreme ruler of any ilk, especially not somebody like LePaco."

She didn't allow a response as she squeezed both bounty hunters tightly.

"I hope to see you again, when this is over."

The underground training bunker below Cyborg Joe's was far larger than Duke could have imagined. In his head, the bounty hunter had pictured a converted wine cellar or beer basement, with Po'l screaming at scrawny Keltians about how to swing a broadsword. In reality, the bunker was more of a compound that stretched the length of a fleet of spacecraft. And the Queen did not exaggerate: thousands upon thousands of beings—mostly but not exclusively Keltian—filled the cavernous structure.

"How are we even going to find him?" Duke asked Ishiro'shea. "Seems to be a lot of training by different trainers going on."

An aged Psitakki conducted hand-to-hand combat drills with some wide-eyed Keltian teens. Beyond this, a group of magenta-skinned Hilterian soldiers were providing a crash course on laser rifle marksmanship. Hilterian snipers were known as the most prolific in the universe, putting even Duke's renowned sharpshooting abilities to shame. In the far corner, a Sabromm was projecting images of Four I's and Tardasian ships, pointing out their perceived weaknesses. The Sabromm followed this with rotating holographic images of Four I's soldiers, demonstrating how they might engage in combat. The Keltians attending the seminar all nodded in unison.

Duke and Ishiro'shea made their way past drills, talks, and exercises to an annex carved into the back wall of the compound. At a wooden circular table stood Po'l, flanked by a Keltian male and female, two athletically-built Psitakki warriors, a female Hilterian, and a Goother Rat. Duke recognized the Goother Rat: it was Gha.

"Po'l!" shouted Duke.

The Neprian looked up and smiled. "It's about damn time, LaGrange," he yelled back. "Everyone, this is Duke LaGrange and Ishiro'shea."

"Yes, I know who he is," said Gha mockingly. "He's the almighty champion of the Tournament of the Shield."

"Good to see you too, Gha," Duke said, extending his hand. Somewhat reluctantly, the Gurlfian shook it. "How 'ya feeling after the Tournament?"

Gha's hands moved to cover up bald patches in his fur, presumably from when he was zapped by Maxx Gemstarr's power gauntlets. It was clear that he was still self-conscious about the blemishes.

"Have the Four I's made their way to Gurlf?" asked Duke.

"No way," snapped the Goother Rat. "I doubt they know that we even exist."

"Then why are you here?"

"I like to fight."

"Fair enough. And who do we have here?" Duke said, extending his hand to the Hilterian female.

"I know who you are as well, Mr. LaGrange," said the Hilterian, batting her eyelashes. "My name is Lutra. I believe that you knew two of my relatives, Turla and Arlut."

Not good, thought Duke. *Whatever I do, don't mention MechaBurgers. Nothing about MechaBurgers.*

"Those names don't ring a bell, I'm sorry," he said. "But it's a pleasure to meet you. And I mean 'meet' as in make your acquaintance. Not 'meat,' like a MechaBurger."

Lutra's eyelashes fluttered at an accelerated velocity.

"Thanks for your service," Duke said hastily. "And these two strapping young bucks?"

The Psitakki duo bowed slightly.

"We know who you are as well," said one of the cephalopodans. "Duke LaGrange—a bounty hunter."

"Oh, were you guys at the Tournament?"

"Yes. And I must say, the way that your bout with Gjrazzel went down wasn't—"

"He's a tough bastard," interjected Duke, knowing full well where this conversation was headed. He turned to the green-skinned Keltians. "And I'm assuming you two know who I am as well?"

They shook their heads and replied, "Nope."

"Wonderful. I'm Duke LaGrange. And this is Ishiro'shea."

"We gathered that," said the male Keltian.

"We really should get back to strategizing," added the female. "It was nice to meet you, Duke LaGrange. Now, if you would excuse us..."

Duke didn't know whether to be insulted or relieved. "Actually, I was hoping to grab Po'l for a minute. We need to chat about a few things."

Before the Neprian had a chance to reply, a slim Keltian interrupted. He was panting heavily. *Must be a scout*, concluded Duke.

"Sorry to barge in, but they're here. They came. An entire warship full of them."

Duke glanced around the room. All faces were frozen, eyes wide and mouths agape.

"I'll be damned," said Gha, breaking the silence.

"This should help our ground defenses substantially," Lutra added.

"Duke, this is huge," Po'l began. "I've never seen one but, from what everyone here has said, we just got a much-needed boost to our force."

"We already know about the Gartoshians," said Duke. "Lilly went up to help the Queen with communications."

"The Gartoshians are here too? On our side?" Gha asked.

"Yeah, ten thousand of them, stationed on the other side of the planet. Even brought a few ships along," replied Duke.

"This just keeps getting better," said the female Keltian.

"But then who are y'all talking about?" said Duke, puzzled.

An erratic clanging noise drew Duke's attention to the back of the compound. The warehouse doors raised, revealing a cave.

That must be the back entrance from the surface, surmised Duke.

Hundreds upon hundreds of armed soldiers marched in perfectly-aligned columns through the entrance. The legion of skeletal warriors stopped their procession and raised their sabers aloft. They let out a collective primal scream that shook the very foundations of Cyborg Joe's.

"To go along with our Gartoshian friends, looks like we have a warship full of Hausen-Ra," stated Lutra.

The eager crowd of amateur soldiers and Keltian refugees rushed around the mysterious Hausen-Ra contingent, showering them with handshakes, hugs, and the occasional kiss.

CHAPTER NINETEEN

THE TREATY

"WELCOME TO MAURITIUS, GENERAL NOBUNAGA," said the security officer outside the hangar. "May I take your belongings?"

Takeo handed the officer his unloaded pistol, a tiny satchel of coins, and his wallet, which only contained photos of his family. The security officer continued staring at him.

"You need my sword as well?"

"There are to be no weapons allowed in the room, General. Even your sword."

"This sword has helped turn the tide of this war, son. You do know that, right? This magnificent and mysterious pendant, see it? It leveled advancing Coalition forces. It repelled invading troops. It restored freedom to areas of this planet that were being mistreated and abused by the OC."

"I have heard the stories, General. They are amazing tales, sir."

"Stories? Tales? Is that what they are, Officer?"

Beads of sweat rushed down the soldier's forehead. "I'm

sorry, sir. I meant they are great..." He struggled to find the words.

"At ease, Officer," said Takeo, placing his hand on the anxious officer's shoulder. "Here you go. Here's my sword."

"Thank you," said the relieved solider. "I promise to return it to you as soon as you exit the room."

"I would expect so," said the general with a wink. He marched through the open door into the hangar bay.

Takeo traversed the hangar, making his way to a room guarded by a dozen heavily-armed soldiers.

I hate guns. So messy, he thought as he bowed and acknowledged each soldier in turn.

The room was a plain metal box with no adornments or decorations, just a table and three chairs. It looked as if they had been shrunken down and locked away in a filing cabinet. An overly dull filing cabinet, at that.

"Please sit, General," instructed a lime-skinned Keltian female.

Takeo sat. Across from him was the Czar of the Oceania Coalition, Arlo Sebastian Northcott. The czar's eyes danced around the general's face but never locked on Takeo's gaze. Northcott had clearly seen better days.

"Czar Arlo Sebastian Northcott," the Keltian moderator began, "representing the Oceania Coalition and all of its subordinate territories. Seconded by the Assistant Czar, Arlo Sebastian Northcott, Jr."

"Present and acknowledged," muttered the elder Northcott.

Interesting spin on a family business, thought Takeo.

"General Takeo Nobunaga of Japan, representing the multinational force of Japan, Ireland, the United States, India, Morocco, Poland, Finland, Mexico, Venezuela, Yemen..."

"Present and acknowledged," said Takeo, politely interrupting the Keltian's reading of the thirty-five partner nations.

"And your second, President Dougal Fionnlagh of the Republic of Ireland."

"That's the *grand* Republic of Ireland, my good woman," added President Fionnlagh.

"Very well," replied the Keltian. "Moving on. As all parties should be aware, much of the treaty has already been discussed independently and agreed upon verbally. These proceedings will finalize all elements of the agreed-upon contract and will, hopefully, usher in a new era of peace to this planet. Because, off the record, Earth is somewhat of a laughingstock in our neighborhood. So, let's not screw this up, okay?"

The Earth representatives looked at each other and nodded.

For the entirety of the meeting, both men signed, initialed, and shook hands on each and every point. With the help of some Keltian ambassadors serving as the chief architects, the Treaty of Nobunaga appeared to be a well-crafted springboard to peace for the war-riddled planet. When the last signature from Northcott was inked on the page, the Oceania Coalition was dissolved and the war was officially over.

Takeo stood up, bowed to the Keltian moderator and to his adversary.

"So what are your plans now, General?" asked Northcott.

The general smiled. "Peace, Arlo, peace. That's what we plan to have."

"And how does one achieve peace, General? Do *you* know? I thought I did at one time."

"Peace by brutality and coercion is not real peace," replied Takeo.

"So how, then? Or are you going to make me wait and find out?"

"First, by removing elements of evil," the general said bluntly.

"I guess that's me," retorted the former czar.

"You know what you've done, Arlo. And once those that are globally recognized as 'bad' are eliminated, we can all be on our merry way. Independence and freedom breeds peace."

"If I may interject," said President Fionnlagh. "What the general is trying to say is that once the allies decide on a strong, fair-minded leader, it will usher in a new era of peace."

"No, President, I didn't mean to say that. I meant to say that every nation can focus on themselves, and figure out what's right for their own people and culture."

"But General, what happens when a great threat like the czar here—"

"*Former* czar," corrected Takeo.

"Yes, like the former czar here, rise up. A bunch of secluded tribes can't stand up against that."

"With all due respect, President, this is not the time nor place to discuss these things."

"Not so easy, is it?" chimed in Northcott. "It all starts with a seemingly insignificant disagreement. And your magic weapon can't help you with this, General. In fact, who's to say that I don't have someone out there trying to steal your precious sword as we speak?"

"That would make me pretty angry," said Takeo. "I love that sword. It's a family heirloom, you know."

"Screw the sword, what about the weapon?" shouted the president. "I'll go look for it. I have my guys out there."

The Irishman dashed to the door, swung it open, and disappeared as it closed with a twang.

"Relax," said Arlo. "I'm not that crazy. How did I lose to you morons?"

"I'm not that stupid, either," replied Takeo with a wink. He tapped his chest, where something made a faint protrusion under his shirt.

"The ol' decoy," smirked Northcott. "Very sneaky."

"Good luck with your exile, Arlo. I hear that where you're going is nice this time of the cycle."

"No, good luck to you, General. Good luck with convincing those power-hungry politicians that are still on a high from winning the war that they should hitch their buggy to your winning horse. That we should all go back to happy, mind-our-own-business pockets of civilization. You're going to love it."

The former czar and his son exited the room.

"He's right, you know," said the Keltian moderator. "I'm not sure that your brethren believe in independence as much as you do, Nobunaga. They have power in their hearts. Not freedom."

"They will see the light and their hearts will be filled to the brim with freedom."

"I hope you are right, General, I do. And I hope that they get it before it's too late."

CHAPTER TWENTY

HOPE

"YA' KNOW, LITTLE BUDDY, I wish I woulda said 'no' to Po'l when he asked to come with us. I feel that we just got him killed."

Ishiro'shea appeared to consider this, but offered no sort of indication as to whether he agreed. Duke was used to this tactic, which forced him to review the words that had just left his mouth. On most occasions, some alteration was required to his initial thought.

"But it was his choice," he added reluctantly. "How could we have predicted this?"

Damnit, he did it again, thought Duke.

They walked back into the main bar area of Cyborg Joe's. The Queen and Earl were in conversation behind the bar. Keltians, Hilterians, and a few Psitakki milled about and appeared to be engaged in "war things." The bounty hunters sat on the two stools closest to the Queen.

Joe looked up and addressed them before Duke could ask a question. "Bigger than you thought, right?"

"What?"

"The force. More people came than you thought, right?"

"I didn't really have a number in mind..."

"The Four I's and LePaco's goals mean an end to everyone that doesn't offer up their resources—their people and their freedom—to their cause. We didn't pay these people. We didn't force them into military servitude. We just asked. In some cases, we didn't even have to ask."

"Queen, I'm not challenging the reason that you're leading this resistance. We're part of that resistance, in the larger sense. I'm just saying that a pitched battle on this already-injured planet, with a makeshift, bandaged-together army against a much larger, fresher, and finely-tuned operation isn't the right way to move our cause forward."

"You still think that I should run?"

"Yes. Legions of Hausen-Ra and Gartoshians aren't going to take out two-hundred-plus spacecraft packing the most advanced life-elimination devices," argued Duke. "The Orb is our most precious resource."

"You're wrong, Duke. Our most precious resource is hope."

The bounty hunter rolled his eyes. "You're too good for tired old clichés and motivational tactics. Hope is good. It doesn't win battles."

"Remember when I told you that if something isn't worth fighting for, it's not worth having?"

"I thought it was 'Anything without a cost isn't worth having,' or something like that."

"Close enough."

"I'm not saying that our freedom isn't worth fighting for... Just not fighting for *right now*."

Queen Joe's face scrunched.

"So, why now?" asked the Nova Texan.

"This is my fault. I let these weapons surface, and two of them fell into the hands of someone as dangerous as any Flying Rot. This *is* our best chance—no, this is *my* best chance—to right the wrong."

"Why?"

"All three items could conceivably be in the same place at the same time."

"Which also means that LePaco has the ability to get ahold of the missing piece to his plan for universal domination."

"It is a risk."

"I can't be part of this," huffed Duke. "This is going to get a lot of good people killed. Did you even ask the others if they agreed with this plan? Did you give them options?"

For the first time in as long as Duke could remember, the Queen seemed to not have a retort. As hard as it was for Duke to believe, she seemed flustered.

Cyborg Joe's began to rumble and shake. A chain of ear-bursting explosions followed. Everyone hit the ground.

"Everyone to the bunker," commanded Queen Joe. "This is it—the assault is on!"

"Ish, think we can make it to the parking lot?" Duke yelled. "We have to get out of here. We can do a lot more damage to LePaco from the *Deus*."

He began to head towards the back door but the ninja grabbed his arm, yanking him almost to the ground. Ishiro'shea shook his head.

"We can make it..."

The barrage escalated until there wasn't a single pocket of dead air, just one long, extended *kaboom*.

Duke sighed. "The bunker it is."

Beyond the training stations, the annex of the main bunker was now filled with more people than just Po'l and his colleagues. Duke didn't recognize the newcomers, save the Queen, Earl, and an anthropomorphic musk ox from one of the moons of Gartosh.

"Ishiro'shea! Duke!" screamed Lilly. "They said that you two were here but I didn't know if I'd get to see you."

"I wish it was for a different reason," responded Duke.

"Don't we all. Yvonne spoke very highly of you two. Sounds like that was quite an adventure on Psitakki."

"Without a doubt. What's going on out there?"

"As predicted, the Four I's have begun an assault on Cyborg Joe's—well, all of Oldish Kelt, really—to try and knock out our ground-to-air defenses."

"The joke's on them," interjected Gha, the Goother Rat, "because we don't have any ground-to-air defenses. They're just wasting energy and ammunition."

"Not exactly a sustainable strategy," replied Duke.

Gha sneered and went back to his conversation with the pair of Keltians.

Duke turned to the Queen. "Will this bunker hold?"

"It will, Duke," she replied. "And the other bunkers will hold, as well. When the battle comes to the surface, we will be ready."

"Why would they ever bring it to the surface? They'll just bomb us until we run out of food, drink, or hope."

It was clear that the Queen didn't appreciate that last jab from the bounty hunter. "You think we'll run out of drinks? This is a bar, isn't it?"

The laughter was proof that the Queen had deflected the query perfectly. Before Duke could respond, she cut him off. "Do you think that our entire strategy, which is built around forcing them to face us in a ground battle, was discussed and agreed upon without us having a way to actually *get* them to the surface?"

"Well, no, but—" the bounty hunter stuttered.

"Lilly?" The Queen gestured to the musk ox.

"Yvonne and the Gartoshian force on the other side of the planet will engage LePaco's fleet," said Lilly.

"And get mauled. Lilly, there's no way that two dozen of your fighters can overcome a ten-to-one disadvantage. Even if you take out half of their fleet, they'll just wait until they overwhelm you and resume bombing us down here. I feel this strategy is still without realistic expectations."

"You should really let your friend finish," said Queen Joe, quite politely.

"After our forces engage the Four I's fleet," continued Lilly, "we hope to capture most of their attention. Then our other fleet can enter through the warp station and attack from their exposed rear. This push should force LePaco's hand. He doesn't want to risk getting blown out of space by a rogue attack; he will come to the surface with what he thinks is a superior force."

That does sound better, thought Duke.

"What other force? More Gartoshians?" he asked.

"No, Duke," answered Lilly. "Most of our entire fleet sits on the other side of the planet."

"Then who?"

"When Yvonne came and told us the good news about the support from Gartosh, she also was working on something through her own personal connections," said Queen Joe with a mischievous grin. "Let's just say that her networking has helped us even the playing field."

The monitor on the annex wall blinked and powered on.

"Can you hear us? Is the transmission going through?" asked Lilly.

The screen fizzled; then coalesced into an image. An image that made Duke LaGrange sick.

"Are you kidding me? Maxx Gemstarr?"

"Hey Duke," Maxx said, waving to his rival. "Didn't expect to see you again."

"You lot think that Maxx Gemstarr is going to turn the tide against that armada?" Duke stared at the rebels gathered around the monitor. "Really, Queen? Lilly? Did y'all go crazy?"

Maxx began to laugh hysterically.

"He *did* find a way to circumnavigate the communications jam," reminded Lilly.

"Duke, you are too funny," Maxx began. "Maxx Gemstarr isn't going to turn the tide singlehandedly."

Great, now he's talking in third person.

"Maxx Gemstarr and a really badass group of pissed-off Earthers are going to turn the tide," said Gemstarr confidently.

"Earth?"

"Yes," replied Lilly. "Yvonne reached out to Maxx about helping the cause. Just about that time, he was heading back to Earth to see if he missed anything on his search for Mazilda, but they were fighting off the Four I's, and successfully. He got in touch with some of the leaders and they agreed to lend some firepower to our cause."

"And they just like to fight," added Maxx. "And I think they were tired of fighting each other. We have about fifty of their best fighter class ships—some Irish, some Japanese, some from places that I've never heard of. I mean what type of name is Ghana?"

Not Ghana be around after this attack, Duke mused.

"And Ishiro'shea, I wanted to tell you that your friend, Yeop, said that he'll meet you at Cyborg Joe's when he's done avenging the master, whatever that means."

Ishiro'shea radiated with happiness. His glance met his longtime friend's.

There goes our "live to fight another day" strategy, concluded Duke.

The bunker shook ferociously as the overhead lighting intermittently blinked and lost power.

CHAPTER TWENTY-ONE

KILL THEM ALL!

EVERYONE IN THE BUNKER REMAINED silent. Whether this was due to the massive surface assault rendering the ability to converse impossible, or the gathering of thoughts before what would likely be their last moments in this life, Duke didn't know. He did know that opening salvo from the Four I's force was lengthier than he would have liked.

LePaco's not leaving anything to chance, he thought.

He turned to Queen Joe. "It's kinda sad. The end of an era."

"What's that, Duke?"

"If—I'm sorry, *when* we go to the surface to fight these cats, Cyborg Joe's is going to be gone. It's gonna be harder to wrap my head around that than I thought."

"The bar will be fine," the Queen replied flippantly. "It's made of pretty stern stuff. Stuff that you or anyone in this universe wouldn't understand."

"I don't know. I've seen it show a bit of wear and tear over these last cycles, and none of that was anything like an all-out barrage by a fully-equipped armada."

"We shall see," she replied calmly.

"What about the portals?"

"The portals are closed. It's not like LePaco can walk in the front door of Joe's and throw them in the back seat of his spaceship. There's nuance to summoning them and even more to controlling them."

"I know he's not going to *take* them. I just wasn't aware if they could be destroyed," Duke explained.

"They'll be okay too."

Earl wedged himself between Duke and Queen Joe. He wasn't being rude—that wasn't in Earl's nature—he just sometimes didn't have the best spatial recognition.

"Our feed is back up, Queen," he said in a throaty baritone. "We have full-range scanning of Kelt and the immediate space outside the planet's atmosphere."

"Great work, Earl. Let's get it up and we can start to plan our counter."

The bombings were still rocking the bunker but the frequency was finally starting to lessen. It was now possible to finish a complete sentence without being knocked over by a detonation. The Queen and those in her makeshift inner circle—Po'l, Lilly, Gha, Lutra, the Keltian couple, an aging Sabromm called Gerald, and a representative of the Hausen-Ra contingent—encircled the large monitor. Earl, with the aid of three Keltians, hooked up four other monitors to create a workable command center.

What appeared on the screens was shocking, though not unexpected. One of the cameras surveyed the immediate area outside of Joe's and panned up to provide intel on the damage to Oldish Kelt, where the bombings were concentrated. It was barren. Forests demolished. Hills flattened. Buildings toppled. The buildings had already been in a bad way following the Battle of Oldish Kelt, but were now simply heaps of rubble. As the feed showed a wider swath of land, it became clear that the Four I's attack force had not only concentrated its firepower around Joe's—it had totally ignored the rest of the planet. This, of course, was good news for the hidden Gartoshians and any bunker outside of the bombing zone.

"Anything on their fleet?"

The Glyptodian barkeep pointed to one of the side monitors. It displayed a clear view of the armada. Other than the results of Blop, the Blop from Blop and his suicide run to allow Duke and Ishiro'shea to reach the planet, the fleet remained intact and unharmed. The two-hundred-plus ships, supported by a massive Armada Titan, hadn't even broken a sweat.

The primary screen scratched and whirled.

"What's going on?" asked the Queen.

"I don't know," replied Earl. "I think someone is hacking our feed."

Ishiro'shea darted past the members of the inner circle to sit beside Earl. After only a handful of taps, pokes, and keystrokes, the erratic noise stopped. The ninja pointed to the primary screen.

"Or someone wants to say 'hello,'" added Duke.

On the screen, in living color, was Admiral Lothario LePaco. In typical LePaco fashion, he was grinning and plucking his wispy mustache. The beautiful, violet-haired assassin, Mazilda Cloax, stood directly behind his left shoulder.

"Good to see you again, Queen," LePaco began. "Always a pleasure. From the lack of dead bodies showing up on my scans, I'm guessing that you and your ragtag bunch of imbeciles are camping out below ground. That might have saved you from the first bombing run, but by bombing run fifty, I'm not so sure."

"We'll take our chances, Admiral," replied Queen Joe decisively.

"And your people there, you speak for them? Those that are supporting this foolish endeavor—all they have to do is convince you to give me the Orb and this will all be over."

"So you can control the universe?"

"I'll admit, I will have a power unmatched by any being in the history of this fair universe and this fair dimension. Yeah. And it might take some time getting used to planets organized by the good people at Intergalactic Infrastructure Improvement, Incorporated... but you'll be alive." He cleared his throat and straightened his posture. "If you can hear me, everyone," he said in a close approximation to a booming voice, "just get the Orb from this charlatan. She has betrayed you. She has lied to you. Bring it to me and this will all be over. Everyone will be safe."

There was little more than a murmur amongst the people that LePaco claimed were being lied to by the Queen.

Clearly, they are loyal, almost to a fault, thought Duke.

Po'l stepped in front of the Queen. With the formality of a politician, he said, "On behalf of the planet of Neprius and our fearless leader, Ja'a of the Southern Land Mass, we reject your offer, Admiral. We reject your offer and we condemn your actions wholeheartedly."

Lutra, the Hilterian representative, made her way to the front. "As a representative of the peaceful planet of Hilteria, I formally denounce the actions of Admiral Lothario LePaco—"

Before she could finish her statement, Gha the Goother Rat cut her off. "The Goother Rats of Gurlf solemnly pledge their allegiance to the cause of capturing or, preferably, killing the heinous murderer and tyrant, Lothario LePaco."

"For his egregious and unforgivable war crimes and the destruction of much of our beloved planet of Kelt," the Keltian duo said in unison, "our leaders have authorized us to declare Admiral Lothario LePaco a being that should be executed upon capture."

A member of every race represented in the bunker stepped before the monitor, looked LePaco directly in his beady eyes, and denounced his aims, actions, and his existence. What the Queen's army lacked in firepower, it made up for in grit.

LePaco interrupted the stream of those declaring their opposition to his rule. "Fine, fine, fine. I get it. You don't like me. You don't want me to rule you. So, unfortunately, that means one thing. You're all going to die. And when I'm done here on Kelt, I'll make sure to personally see to the genocide of each of your races. This universe will go on without Goother Rats—for which, I'm sure I'll win some type of award—Hilterians—though I'll miss those neoprene suits—Sabromms, Neprians—and no one will even notice that one—"

His rambling was cut short by Lilly. The Gartoshian musk ox said, "Admiral LePaco. The government of Gartosh and all of its moon colonies has declared open war on you, your allies from Jungafallow III, the Tardasian System, and the Four I's organization."

"Who cares?" blurted LePaco. "Don't you all get it? I don't care. I'm going to kill you all."

Lilly, undeterred by the screaming madman, continued with her formal decree. "As with any interstellar conflict that befalls the Gartoshian government, we offer the opportunity to discuss a truce prior to conflict."

"You're kidding me? You have to be kidding me," LePaco cackled, eyes rolling. "These declarations, or whatever, don't mean anything. You are all going to—"

Mazilda whispered something into the admiral's ear.

"What?" he shouted in response. "We just lost what? How many?"

Cloax began to whisper again but the admiral pushed her away.

"Never mind. It doesn't matter. A few Gartoshian ships are nothing more than a minor hindrance. A nuisance. Remember that, Gartoshian, your ploy is going to accomplish nothing other than seeing the crews on these ships smashed into stardust at my hands. And I'll make sure to push the button myself when I blow up your crummy planet and all of its crummy moons. Kill them all!"

The admiral ended the communication.

CHAPTER TWENTY-TWO

DUCK AND WEAVE

A S FAR AS DUKE COULD determine from the makeshift command center in the bunker below Cyborg Joe's, the Gartoshian fleet was more than a nuisance for the much larger Four I's armada. The attackers were focusing on thinning the ranks of the Attack Class Scout ships; their strategy was to avoid the heavier hitters like the battle cruisers, leaving those for the reinforcements. It was an intelligent plan, executed properly.

"Earl, patch in Maxx," requested the Queen. "The Gartoshians have done their part."

Duke glanced at Lilly. Her smile radiated pride. Her people had done *more* than their part; indeed, they might have turned the tide.

The screen continued to flash but Maxx Gemstarr's image did not appear. Normally, this would have thrilled Duke but in the circumstances, it was bad. Real bad.

"What's wrong? Where is he?" pleaded the Queen.

Ishiro'shea joined Earl to try and troubleshoot the issue but the screen just kept crackling.

"I think they're jamming us again," said Lutra, the

Hilterian ambassador. "Maybe they figured out Gemstarr's workaround?"

"This complicates things," said Queen Joe.

The Four I's began to recall their scouts, likely sensing that they were losing more dogfights with the Gartoshians than they were winning. The rebel fleet appeared comically minuscule and insignificant drifting around the massive armada like gnats, trying to lure out ships to engage. With every moment that Gemstarr's invasion force remained hidden, LePaco's battle cruisers came closer to encircling the Gartoshians. The proud musk oxen warriors were slowly being trapped.

This isn't good, thought Duke. *Damn, Gemstarr, show yourself!*

Lilly rushed to one of the side monitors. "Can you get ahold of Yvonne?"

The Glyptodian barkeep, now communications specialist, patched in The Furry Mountain of Moon Colony #1.

"Yvonne, we lost contact with Maxx," said Lilly. "You need to abort and retreat."

"I'm not so sure that's going to be possible. They have us surrounded pretty good," Yvonne replied. "No sweat though, we'll hold them off as long as we can. I'm sure Maxx will figure it out."

"I wouldn't hold my breath," Duke smirked.

The Queen flashed him a nasty snarl.

Wait, did I say that out loud?

"Seriously, Yvonne," said Lilly, "get out of there."

"No. Our mission is to cause problems by taking out as many ships as we can. And we're going to do that. Until we have not a single ship operational."

"You mean until you're dead," countered Lilly.

"We promised a service and we're going to deliver. It's for the right cause. We can't let this maniac take over our universe. Whether Maxx comes or not, we're going to try and force these bastards to the surface. When they're there, promise me one thing, Lilly?"

"Yeah?"

"Punch as many of these sons of bitches in the face as you can. Show them what it means to be a Miss Bovine Boxer."

Yvonne winked as she ended the transmission.

The battle cruisers began to unleash a crippling barrage of firepower on the undermanned Gartoshian fleet, but the brave musk oxen charged as if they were the overpowering force. The battle cruisers picked off many of the advancing ships but the Gartoshians were undeterred. Yvonne and the pilots of three other craft collectively incapacitated a cruiser. Then another. The Attack Class Scouts rejoined the ranks. A few of the Tardasian and Jungafallowian Fighters replaced them at the front line.

The Gartoshians, though valiant, could not withstand the closing fist of the Four I's fleet.

Amidst the chaotic scramble, two ships moved beyond the battle cruisers and headed deeper into the heart of the Four I's armada.

"What are they doing?" asked Lutra. "Are they abandoning the fight?"

"They can't be deserting—that's Yvonne," said Lilly. "She wouldn't—"

Duke cut her off. "They aren't running away, they're running *to* the warp station. They're going to go get Maxx's sorry ass."

The two Gartoshian vessels were cruising through a dense concentration of enemy ships, taking some damage, dealing out some, but they appeared to be mostly focused on getting to the warp station. Unfortunately, a massive battle cruiser stood in their way. And behind it, another battle cruiser.

"They're sitting ducks," shouted Gha. "Those cruisers have their route blocked."

The Gartoshian ships maneuvered into single file and kept pushing at a rapid rate.

"No, they aren't," chimed in the bounty hunter. "They're going to get through."

"How?" asked Lilly.

"In the most honorable way possible."

Yvonne's ship charged the first battle cruiser at maximum velocity. She had the forward armaments on full bore but her intention wasn't to shoot down the more powerful Four I's ship.

She was going to ram it. She was going to sacrifice her life.

"Yvonne, don't—" screamed Lilly, hitting the control panel to try and establish a communications link to her fellow Gartoshian.

Ishiro'shea and Duke embraced her simultaneously. They knew what was going to happen.

The explosion lit up the celestial canvas. It was brighter and more magnificent than any of the plasma cannons or lasers. Yvonne's collision ignited the first battle cruiser, which instantly became a fireball the size of a planetoid, obstructing the view of the second battle cruiser. The trailing Gartoshian ship slipped through the carnage and darted directly for the warp station, with the enemy none the wiser.

Duke immediately thought of Blop and his similar gesture that had allowed him and Ishiro'shea to reach Kelt and the resistance. Yvonne's was equally as magnificent and honorable.

Only a few hard-to-capture Gartoshian ships remained.

Their duck and weave tactics were losing their duck and were becoming a tad short on weave. The numerical advantage was now too much. Furthermore, there was no sign that Maxx and his alleged Earth allies had been successfully contacted. As time ticked away, the hopes of forcing LePaco to the surface of Kelt dwindled.

"You don't think that Gemstarr set this whole thing up, do you?" Duke whispered to Ishiro'shea. He looked around to make sure no one had heard him. He didn't want to diminish the already waning morale.

The ninja shook his head violently.

"Okay. If you're that sure, little buddy. I'm with you."

The screen blinked again.

"Maxx!" shouted a Keltian. "It has to be Maxx trying to reach us!"

Earl brought up the visual. Groans echoed around the bunker with as much force as the sounds of the bombing runs.

"Hello again, everybody," chuckled Admiral LePaco. "That was cute. You had me for a second. But, as I was saying before, you are all going to die!"

The image on one of the side view screens caught Duke's eye. He moved in front of Queen Joe to stare directly at LePaco.

"I'll be a monkey's uncle," began the admiral. "Duke LaGrange. I'm surprised that you're still alive, with all the trouble you get into. When I'm done squashing these last few Gartoshians, I'm going to make sure to detonate a few extra special bombs right on top of Cyborg Joe's, in your honor."

The bounty hunter smiled and tipped his hat to the admiral.

The admiral was jolted, crashing to the floor.

CHAPTER TWENTY-THREE

MAXX AND THE EARTHERS

D UKE ALMOST FELT BAD FOR the low regard in which he had held Earth until now. They were an advanced race, technologically-speaking, and had been a key player in the expansion of planetary trade. However, apparently, they weren't advanced enough to exit the pattern of major conflicts that threatened their existence every hundred cycles or so. They were the only known civilization that numbered their "world wars" and even added catchy subtitles for dramatic effect. This began as far back as most Earthers could remember: World War II – *The War to End All Wars*; World War V – *South Pacific Rage*; World War VII – *Kings Versus Presidents*; World War IX – *Super Mega Fight Supreme*; World War XI – *Whose God is the Most Right?* The last of these was a fan favorite within the Andromeda Galaxy.

But the cycles of conflict and turmoil must have infiltrated the very DNA of the Earth human, because they were *good* at it. The Four I's forces had struggled with the flightiness of the Gartoshian attack but they regrouped and used their significant numbers to regain the advantage. The

Earth force was not much larger than the fleet of heroic musk oxen, but now the Four I's fleet was beyond flustered. The humans' patterns of attack were irregular. Some ships worked in tandem, others engaged independently; there was no leader and no coordination. This confused the orderly Four I's greatly.

Ishiro'shea pointed at the monitor, which displayed a ship that was bulky but agile. It had just blasted an Attack Class Scout with a bright green laser and was turning its attention to a Jungafallowian Fighter. The vessel sported a giant shamrock insignia on its flank.

"Irish?" asked Duke.

The ninja nodded.

"And I'm guessing that one's from the Japanese gangs?"

Ishiro'shea nodded again. Onscreen, a trio of sleek, elegant craft executed a synchronized barrage that sliced a Tardasian ship into tattered ribbons.

Having bought some much-needed breathing room, the remaining Gartoshian ships doubled back and resumed hunting the Four I's scouts.

The most unremarkable ship was a saucer-like pod zigging and zagging through the carnage.

"Zoom in on that, Earl," said Duke. "Where's that little guy from?"

The Glyptodian maximized the image just in time for them to witness the tiny ship's hidden ace. Electric blue lasers extended from its flanks and hung limp like a towing cable. The pod began to spin furiously, whipping the lasers to form a deadly circular saw.

Ishiro smiled.

Yeop, surmised Duke.

The vessel spun at a speed that made it unrecognizable as a spacecraft. It clipped a few nearby scout ships en route to its destination: a Four I's battle cruiser. The diminutive saucer approached the hulking cruiser without so much as a warning shot. As the neon saw made contact with the cruiser's hull, it set off a chain reaction of destruction. The battle cruiser tried to belatedly turn its attention to the tiny invader, but its attacks only damaged itself. Yeop's buzzsaw cut through the outer hull and then the tiny craft disappeared. Moments later, it emerged from the other side of the cruiser, ceased spinning, and jetted away to a patch of clear space. The battle cruiser had been cut in two.

Inside the bunker, the mood was becoming ever more positive. The renewed sense of hope was palpable. The Four I's force still maintained a numbers edge on Maxx, Yeop, and the Earthers, but it was now a much more evenly-matched battle. Neither looked to be able to claim a decisive victory. And that played into the Queen and her followers' plan.

"You know what? You guys are really pissing me off!" shouted Admiral LePaco from the screen.

"Did you patch him in?" the Queen asked Earl.

"I think he's found a way to override our comms," replied the furry bartender.

"Yes, I did," smirked LePaco. "It's not that hard, especially with your operation. So you think you're so smart, and that these savage Earthers are going to take out my forces. It doesn't matter. I came to get the Orb, and get it I will. You're about to feel the full might of Admiral LePaco!"

The admiral's eyes were bulging, his nostrils flaring, and Duke could almost feel the tension of his clenched jaw through the transmission.

"This revolt ends now," the maniacal tyrant declared before ending the transmission.

The ancillary monitors showed several sections of the Four I's force breaking off and heading toward the Keltian surface. The plan was working.

That bastard Gemstarr did it, Duke concluded reluctantly. *Maybe he's not such an ass after all.*

Maxx appeared on the primary view screen seconds after LePaco ended his communication.

"I did it, guys. Maxx Gemstarr always delivers," he boasted, flashing his trademark smile, soaked in self-satisfaction.

Never mind.

———

There was an excitement in the bunker. Despite the fact that many of these soldiers wouldn't live to have another drink at Cyborg Joe's, they were all jazzed that their plan had successfully made it to phase two.

"LePaco is likely to provide ground cover with some of his Attack Class Scouts," stated Joe. "We just have to survive this, like we've been doing the entire time. We want him to get those troop transports on the ground. When he does, we'll send out a few of ours around Joe's."

"So he'll think that's the extent of our resistance?" asked the male Keltian.

"Yes. And so he'll concentrate his attack on Joe's," added Lutra.

"Or what's left of Joe's," chimed in Duke. His commentary was ignored.

"Once we engage, then our satellite bunkers will attack from behind the enemy lines," continued the Hilterian ambassador. "When LePaco's troops turn their attention to our surprise squadrons, then our reserves here will make themselves known."

The Hausen-Ra commanders raised their swords in unison.

"Your readiness is not in question" said Lutra, acknowledging the skeletal warriors. "If all goes well, the Gartoshian land force will provide the last bit of offense that we need to win the day."

"And prevent an escape," concluded Queen Joe.

"Yes, Queen. That's the long and short of it, everyone. Any objections?"

The crowd silently nodded affirmation.

"What about if LePaco does turn his ships on the ground forces?" asked the Nova Texan.

Laughter rose around him. The beings around Duke showed disbelief on their faces.

"No, really," Duke added. "What if LePaco—"

"I know he's a crazed maniac, but even the admiral wouldn't turn his guns on his own people."

"If it helped him get the Orb, he would."

The subtle chuckles became hearty belly laughs.

Queen Joe hushed the crowd. "Duke, it's a risk that we're going to have to take." She turned her attention to the greater mass in the bunker. "It is now *our* time. We must continue the efforts of those brave fighters in the sky that gave their lives to give us this chance. Let us all prepare for our final stand. We stand together, Keltian, Hilterian, Hausen-Ra, Psitakki, Sabromm, Neprian, Earther, Gartoshian. Everyone. LePaco's push towards domination ends now."

The group erupted into cheers.

CHAPTER TWENTY-FOUR

PHASE TWO

A S EXPECTED, LEPACO'S FORCES SWEPT over Oldish Kelt, unleashing an impressive load of explosives. However, as none of the Queen's army was on the surface, the bombing wasn't overly effective—unless you were a tree or a rock or a patch of shrubbery that had managed to survive the last few raids. Then it sucked.

"Their transports are landing," said Earl, his voice crackling through the communication device that Queen Joe held. "Our prognostications are holding true. They should be visible from the front steps of the bar."

"Great, Earl. If things go sideways, I just want to thank you for everything."

The Glyptodian did not respond, but Duke thought he heard a subtle whimper from the device.

It would be quite a sight to see a Glyptodian, seven feet of fur-covered mass, reduced to tears.

"We'll make our way through the bar and then fan out as we exit," commanded Joe. "We want them to notice us. Make yourselves big. Fire pulses into the air. You don't need to even hit anything. Just make them aware of us."

"You mean what's left of the bar," interjected Duke. "I don't think it's going to give us much cover after all of these attacks."

The Queen did not acknowledge the bounty hunter and proceeded to give orders to the select squad chosen to draw the attention of the Four I's ground force. Queen Joe was included because she could make the biggest scene. Lightning bolts shooting from her fingertips with giant whirly tornadoes surrounding her arms would be a good start to getting noticed. Duke was included for the same reason: he had Ol' Betsy, and she could make a ton of noise. Ishiro'shea joined them because that was what sidekicks did. Duke had loaned him his laser revolver after making a joke to Ishiro about reflecting the sun from his sword to burn the invading enemies like ants. His partner had not seen the humor. Lutra, the Hilterian, and a host of Keltian volunteer soldiers rounded out the squad. Po'l stayed with the forces in the bunker, including the Hausen-Ra, since he was selected to lead that charge. Lilly remained in the base as well, as she was the point of contact to her brethren on the other side of the planet. Gha stayed back because he was so short that he wasn't likely to get noticed by the Four I's soldiers, even if he had a bazooka strapped to his shoulder.

"Now!" shouted Queen Joe. She motioned the group to make its way through the basement of Cyborg Joe's and up to the main level.

They emerged from the cellar to find the bar pretty much intact. Sure, the rogue neon sign had fallen off the wall. There were some broken martini glasses. A few barstools had toppled over. A grease fire or two burned from the kitchen area. But, all in all, it wasn't too far off from a normal night at Cyborg Joe's.

"How... what... how did..." Duke stammered.

The Queen looked back at the confused bounty hunter. "I told you it was made of some pretty stern stuff."

———

Queen Joe blasted electric charges into the air, lobbing some as far as the transport ships themselves. Duke gave Ol' Betsy the stage and had her belt out a solo that shook the clouds. Lutra, an accomplished sniper—as were most Hilterians—picked off a few unsuspecting Four I's watchmen in the shadows of the largest transport ship. The Keltians screamed. A lot. And it was loud. Louder than the blaster pulses that they fired aimlessly into the air. It was soon apparent that the Four I's forces had noticed the rebels. Troops started to pour out of their ships and head toward the galaxy's loudest bar.

"There has to be fifty thousand of them and counting," commented a Keltian soldier.

"I think more than that," added another.

"Fifty thousand—" began Lutra.

"Or more," interrupted another Keltian.

"Yes, fifty thousand *or more*—to what? A dozen? Those odds aren't the greatest I've encountered," continued the Hilterian.

"But they aren't the worst we've had," added Duke. "Right, Ish?"

The ninja agreed. The Hilterian shook her head.

"Seriously," the bounty hunter continued, "this one time on—what's the name of that planet, Ish?"

His thought was interrupted by an explosion a mere ship's length in front of them.

"Holy hedgehogs, that was close!"

Duke retaliated with a counterblast from Betsy. He

wasn't sure if he killed anything at that distance, but he was pretty confident he at least hurt someone.

The Queen stepped to the front of the configuration. Just as she had done before, she became entrenched in a cosmic trance. Clouds of smoky gas consumed her hands. In a flash, she heaved a flurry of electric bolts into the approaching army. She repeated this over and over.

Though successful, it seemed to prompt the forces to pick up their speed. And it seemed like the stream from the transports was never-ending.

The Four I's sent more long-range projectiles towards the group of rebels. Their aim left something to be desired; the explosions erupted behind Cyborg Joe's.

"Back in the bar, now!" shouted Queen Joe. "Now!"

The group retreated into the confines of the sturdy infrastructure.

Joe grabbed her communications device. "Earl, send them in!"

The sounds of the marching juggernaut were steady, and steadily increasing in volume. But then they stopped. What had been orderly and organized, even amidst the Queen's lightning strikes and blasts from Betsy, became chaotic. This was not like the good folks of Intergalactic Infrastructure Improvement, Incorporated.

They're distracted, thought Duke.

At this realization, he looked at Queen Joe. She returned a wry grin.

"Phase two is on," she said to her team.

Lutra returned from the front steps of Cyborg Joe's.

"They're fully engaged with the troops from the satellite bunkers. Unbelievable. They just assumed that we were the last remaining soldiers," she said.

"Excellent," said Joe. "It's time we make this into a Four I's sandwich."

She raised her communications device. "Earl, tell Po'l that he's up. He can send some up through the basement. The main force can use the back exit, the one the Hausen-Ra used."

"It has been communicated," said the Glyptodian. "Good luck."

"You too, Earl."

Before Earl could sign off, the soldiers flowed from the basement door, through the bar, and out into the skirmish. This squad consisted of Keltians, Sabromms, and Psitakki and were led by the feisty Goother Rat, Gha. Po'l's force, a combined unit of Keltians and Hausen-Ra, was likely exiting through the back of the bunker to meet up with Gha and complete the final clamp on the Four I's contingent. Phase two was in full effect.

"What now?" Duke asked Queen Joe. "What do you want us to do? Join 'em?"

"As much as we'd love to have you out there fighting the Four I's soldiers, I need you, Ishiro'shea, and Lutra to help me get to LePaco. He's here, and we need to either capture him along with the other two artifacts, or kill him."

"You think he's here on the surface?"

"I do. Possibly in the back, near the transports. I have a feeling that he's a let-my-army-clear-me-a-path kinda guy."

"No argument there," replied Duke. "So..."

"So, we blast our way to those transports," she proclaimed.

The Queen's wry grin grew even wryer.

CHAPTER TWENTY-FIVE

A QUEEN AND HER PORTAL

"**H**E HAS TO BE SOMEWHERE by those ships," shouted Queen Joe as she sent a group of Four I's infantrymen into the air with an explosive lightning strike. Another subsequent blast cleared an even wider path for the foursome to advance.

"We still have a long way to go," added Lutra. She rattled off three pulses, knocking down three soldiers with her impeccable marksmanship. "I'm just hoping that he's still there when we make it. He could run if he sees the odds are turning."

Duke knelt down and fired Ol' Betsy, giving the invading quartet even more room.

"Thanks, Duke," said Queen Joe. "I don't think he views this battle here as anything that can be 'won' or 'lost.' I think this is just a necessary mechanism to get me out in the open." She paused and whipped a few more deadly bolts into the Four I's forces. "Or at least in a situation where I can be captured. Or more accurately, the Orb."

Ishiro'shea slashed his katana through a pair of well-armed soldiers.

Though their view was narrowly focused on the forces blocking their path to the transport ships, it was apparent that the Queen's strategy to envelop the Four I's army was working. Duke could even hear and see some of the advancing Keltians from the satellite bunkers making their way to the center of the battle. The Hausen-Ra—noted warriors, especially in close-quarters hand-to-hand combat —were simply overwhelming their opponents. This had the makings for a decisive victory.

"I'm afraid you're right, Queen," screamed Duke, in between blasts from Betsy.

"About what?"

"LePaco. He doesn't care about his soldiers and this fight. No more than he cares about ours. But that brings us to a really big issue."

"And what's that?" asked Joe.

"Yeah, what's that?" added Lutra.

"Those."

Approaching from the sky, barely higher than the tallest building in Oldish Kelt—before the recent bombings, that is —was an attack squad. Ten or so Attack Class Scouts dashed over the battlefield and let loose an artillery barrage, spraying a combination of lasers and short-range missiles across both forces. Explosions overwhelmed large expanses of the battlefield. Duke and Ishiro'shea dove to the ground to avoid the long, erratic reach of the shrapnel. Queen Joe ended up on her stomach next to the bounty hunters.

"I can't believe he—" she began, then corrected herself. "No, I can absolutely believe that he would fire on his own men. It's my fault for only expecting rational tactics from him. This is my fault."

Duke wanted to take credit for considering that this was a possibility, but he knew this was not the time. Barely anything is ideal when one is being shot at by an entire attack squad of spaceships. The frequency of the explosions increased. The casualties on both sides were beginning to mount. Duke fired Betsy into the air, hoping to hit something, but judging by the consistent barrage being unleashed from the air, it was clear that he had not.

"Do we have any air support?" yelled Duke through the hysteria. "Can Lilly send in the Gartoshian troops? Maybe they've got some cannons on that transport."

Joe simply flashed her communication device. It was damaged beyond repair.

Shit.

"We need to do *something*," shouted Lutra. "We can't survive this much longer."

The Queen clambered to her feet. Once again, she entered her trance. The air began to whirl around her, smoke clouding up around her hands. She raised her right hand and flung a series of bolts into the air. One clipped a ship and sent it hurtling into the Keltian soil, where it erupted into a huge fireball. She sent another wave out, knocking out another two ships. The remaining ships in the fleet peeled off and reengaged, focusing their firepower squarely on Queen Joe.

The inter-dimensional bar owner crouched down as the fighters approached, turning her back to the aircraft. A velvet bag hung from her right hip, barely noticeable. In the hectic fury of war, these details are often overlooked, even by the keenest observer. Duke hadn't noticed it until now. But, as the most powerful single entity that he had come across in his many travels turned her back to an airborne onslaught, that's all he *could* notice. Queen Joe reached into the bag and pulled something. She held aloft a glowing violet sphere. The Orb.

The smoky gas that engulfed her ceased. All that remained were the Queen and her Orb. She thrust the sphere in the direction of the attacking ships. Violet beams emerged from the mysterious artifact and fanned out across the Keltian sky. Four of the ships disintegrated immediately. The remaining three circled and regrouped.

The Four I's vessels surrounded Queen Joe and closed in, their pulses targeted squarely on her. The Orb sent out what looked like twisted vines, electrified and radiating bright purple. The vines absorbed the entire round of laser blasts from the Four I's aircraft, knocking out two of the ships in a beautiful explosion. The surviving Keltian vessel swooped away, presumably in order to rejoin the much more predictable battle in space.

The ground forces on both sides were all stunned. They did not resume hand-to-hand warfare. Now both sides understood that they were targets of LePaco's assault.

I'm sure they're questioning what side they're on, thought Duke.

"So did we win?" asked a Keltian solider who had tried to find cover from the attack near Duke and Ishiro'shea. "Did she just win the war?"

Duke started to answer but was distracted. LePaco clearly didn't think anything was over.

Casting a shadow over the entire area around Cyborg Joe's was a fully-equipped battle cruiser. *More* than fully-equipped.

"Holy hedgehogs, they spared no expense on this one. I've seen Titans with less firepower," remarked Duke.

Queen Joe said nothing. She held the Orb in both hands, above her head.

"Concentrate your fire on that ship," ordered Lutra. "Now!"

All rebel soldiers within earshot did as she instructed. Duke rattled off a few puffs of anger from Betsy. The effect of the ground force attack was the equivalent of an ant biting a Mega-Troll. The enhanced battle cruiser pressed on.

The first volley from the advancing ship ripped a crater in the ground, directly in front of the Queen. Soldiers on both sides scattered.

"If that thing hits her, she's dead. The Orb will be destroyed," screamed Lutra. "We have to do something!"

Duke looked at Ishiro'shea quizzically.

He's as empty on ideas as I am, he concluded.

"We played right into his hands, didn't we?" Lutra continued, clearly panicked. "He *wanted* us out here."

"It appears so. LePaco knew we would look for him— and it left us exposed," added the bounty hunter. "Damn."

As the battle cruiser readied another attack, Queen Joe remained motionless, almost tranquil. Her response to LePaco's plan was anything but. The Orb pulsed and shook, now glowing an even brighter shade of purple. Not a single bolt left the spheroid, however. It just vibrated, rose a few inches above her skyward facing palms... then it began to spin. And spin. It spun so fast that it was almost unrecognizable as an orb.

The sky to the right of the battle cruiser sparked, the sparks became a crimson crackle, and that turned into an untamed portal. It looked like the astral anomaly that had sent the *Deus Ex Machina* to Neprius, albeit smaller and less stable. As it formed, it leapt out like an eel emerging from a cave in the sea floor, and consumed the entire front half of the cruiser. It disappeared just as quickly, leaving an inoperable back half of a spacecraft floating uncertainly for a moment in the Keltian sky. Then the posterior of the ship crashed to the ground, just beyond the battlefield.

Everybody around the bar erupted in cheers, rebels and Four I's soliders alike. LePaco's latest ploy was officially foiled.

Queen Joe did not move. The Orb remained slightly above her outstretched hands, still spinning at an unbelievable rate. The unstable portal reappeared above the battlefield. The Queen was locked in a catatonic state, a symbiotic relationship with the magic rock.

"She's doing it without any mustangsen," Duke said to Ishiro'shea. The ninja looked to be as shocked as the Nova Texan. "How's she doing that?"

"And why hasn't she stopped?" Lutra chimed in.

"There must be something else on its way," responded Duke. "Another wave of attacks. She has to sense *something*."

"I would think that they have all they can handle with Maxx, the Earthers, and the Gartoshians," said the Hilterian. "LePaco had a huge fleet but it wasn't infinite."

Cutting through an innocent patch of drifting clouds and heading directly for the entranced Queen Joe was a sleek salmon-colored spaceship. Its license plate read "Mister Macho."

CHAPTER TWENTY-SIX

A QUEEN AND HER EVEN BIGGER PORTAL

D UKE HAD ONLY SEEN LEPACO'S ship from a distance, and at that moment, it had been escaping the fiery remains of an Armada Titan. He hadn't studied it, analyzed it, or even paid that close of attention. Now it was staring down directly at him. And it was an impressive specimen, color scheme and vanity plate notwithstanding. The bounty hunter had never seen anything like it.

Queen Joe's hands dropped to her sides, while the Orb still hovered above her. She flung both hands towards LePaco's ship and rays of electric violence beamed outward from her fingers. The Orb let loose a third bolt. All three struck the forward bow of the ship. It was a crippling blast. The explosion was immense. But LePaco's ship pressed on, unfazed by the strike. In fact, there was almost no visible damage. The Queen repeated her gesture, rocking the ship but not hurting it. LePaco countered with a three-hundred-and-sixty-degree expulsion of bombs, missiles, and lasers. His spray-and-pray tactic took out everything in its path. Those unharmed fled. The Queen, backed by Duke, Ishiro'shea, and Lutra, remained, facing off in a showdown with the awesome ship.

The Orb slowly descended into Joe's hands. The astral anomaly that had been floating harmlessly in the sky was suddenly awake, activated by the Queen. It lunged in the same manner as when it had destroyed the battle cruiser—but LePaco dodged it. Though still in her trance, the Queen flinched in dismay at the miss. It leapt again. Another miss.

"It doesn't even look like he's trying that hard," said Duke aloud. "Is LePaco that good of a pilot?"

A third miss by the rogue portal. The Queen's twitches were become more frequent and more intense.

The portal vanished with a puff and then appeared above the Queen's position, level with the admiral's craft. The crimson glow from the astral anomaly cast a shadow over the entire battlefield; the thing seemed to have doubled in size. The portal crackled and hissed but emitted no heat, and it produced no wind. It was just colored noise.

Queen Joe convulsed. The contortions would have broken the bones of most humanoids, but the Queen appeared to feel nothing. The harder she jerked, the bigger the portal grew. Admiral LePaco's ship did not fire on the portal or at Queen Joe.

What's he up to? thought Duke.

As the portal expanded to the point where its outer rim almost reached the ground, a hatch on the forward bow of LePaco's ship opened. The barrel of a cannon extended out, aimed directly at the portal.

"What's he going to do with that?" Duke said to Ishiro'shea and Lutra, pointing at the gun. "Something that size won't do much damage to a fragile egg, let alone a pissed-off inter-dimensional being with an unhinged portal."

"An unhinged portal that has already taken out a battle cruiser," added the Hilterian.

"Exactly."

The portal's growth spurt finally halted. The Queen's movement came to a stop as well.

Nothing can survive this, Duke thought. *Is this going to be it? The end?*

LePaco's insignificant-looking cannon spat out what appeared to be a pretty insignificant-looking silver beam. The velocity of the beam was just as uninspiring, moving towards the astral anomaly at the pace of a Daedean beach snail.

The portal let out an ear-piercing shriek and rushed towards the ship.

It struck the pedestrian ray and then stopped. The portal began to shake and pulse and then dispersed into billions of particles, splattering a red dust over the Keltian landscape.

"What just happened?" asked an astounded Duke LaGrange, addressing no one in particular. "Did that gun just neutralize the Orb's portals? How...?"

Ishiro'shea tugged on Duke's arm, jolting his attention from the free-falling crimson clouds of portal dust. The ninja raced past even as Duke was still collecting his thoughts as to what just happened. The emerald-clad martial artist hustled to where the Queen had been. She was no longer standing or in her trance; she was sprawled out on the grass, motionless. The bounty hunter and Lutra made their way to her.

"Is she breathing?" asked Lutra. Ishiro'shea nodded. "Good. What was that thing?"

"I have no idea but it totally knocked out the portal," said Duke. "We have to get her back inside."

Ishiro'shea began to lift the Queen to her feet.

"The Key," she mumbled. "He's got the Key."

"What, Queen? What are you saying?" asked Duke.

She cleared her throat.

"LePaco's figured out how to use the Key on its own. That blast was from the Amplification Key... the Key."

"He's learned how to harness it? Already? But, even if he did capture Ish's parents, he's only had it briefly. How did he figure it out so quickly?"

Ishiro'shea squeezed Duke's shoulder. His eyes said everything.

"Your parents told him?" said Duke. "No. I don't believe it."

"I'm sure they were tortured or tricked," suggested Lutra.

The Queen nodded in agreement.

"Well, how would *they* know?"

The ninja lowered his head. He squeezed Duke's shoulder again and pointed to his own heart. It took Duke a second to realize what his partner was trying to say.

He doesn't mean "me." Heart. The Heart of Nobunaga.

Duke's brain continued to race.

"From the accounts—the legends—of Takeo Nobunaga?" Duke guessed.

Ishiro'shea nodded.

"Yes," the injured Queen said faintly.

"I bet that's why she tore up the master's office, not from a scuffle but looking for any of the actual records," added Duke.

"That's great and all, but we gotta go, guys," commanded Lutra. "As in *now*."

LePaco's ship had landed upon the open plain. Troops and special guards poured out of the vessel and surrounded the ship.

"He's in there," Joe added, now on her feet, leaning for support on Duke. "We have to get him."

"Not like this," Duke added. "Plus, they don't have

enough to get through our ground forces, especially without the help of the Four I's ground soldiers. LePaco royally screwed that partnership up."

"Duke," began Lutra in a voice that didn't inspire much confidence, "I think you underestimated his plan to get to us."

The admiral's ship began to transform. Compartments pulled apart to reveal hidden artillery units. Paneling disappeared, and even more weapons emerged. What was once a sleek deep-space fighting vessel was now a stationary war machine with enough firepower to take out a mid-sized moon.

The battle station unleashed a raging fury equal to a thousand rounds from Ol' Betsy. Single blasts toppled buildings. The explosions of light and sound made the chaos even more challenging to navigate.

"Order a retreat," pleaded Joe to Duke and Lutra. "Please."

With no working communication device, the rebels were left with only their voices. And, for once, Duke's voice was wholly inadequate.

The few within a tight enough radius to hear fled for the cover of the bar. But the legions of Keltians and Hausen-Ra followed their original orders honorably. They regrouped and charged at the impenetrable fortress of death.

"They're all going to die," cried the Queen. "LePaco is going to slaughter them. That thing is going to slaughter them."

Another round of chaotic devastation fell upon those in the battlefield.

"We have to go now," shouted Lutra.

"I agree," replied Duke. He hoisted the Queen onto his shoulder. The quartet began to retreat to Cyborg Joe's.

"No, we have to help them," the Queen moaned from atop the bounty hunter.

"LePaco's special guard is on the move. This last spray caused enough confusion that they have a direct path to us and to the bar," screamed Lutra as she attempted to cover their escape with erratic blasts from her sniper rifle. "They'll be on top of us soon. We have to pick it up."

Duke accelerated to a sprint; at least, the best he could do with a passenger aboard.

"We need more cover," screamed the Hilterian.

"Our entire army needs cover from that thing," yelled the bounty hunter.

Rising above the top of Cyborg Joe's was an image that Duke and Ishiro'shea instantly recognized. It was home. It was the *Deus*.

"I thought we lost her," Duke said to Ishiro'shea, only slowing his pace slightly to examine his captainless ship.

But on closer examination he saw that it wasn't captainless at all. Even at that distance, he recognized the tiny silhouette standing next to one of the side windows at the bow of the ship. Po'l.

The *Deus* wobbled a bit.

Easy there. Be gentle to her.

The ship stabilized and then darted towards LePaco's military installation. It wasn't alone. A gargantuan Gartoshian troop transport accompanied by a handful of Gartoshian Fighter ships serving as its escort fanned out behind the *Deus*.

"We have our cover," Duke said, gaining confidence. "Not sure how long it'll last, but if I know my ship, it'll be enough to get us to safety and then some. And, hopefully, it'll give our friends a chance to take out that thing."

"Maybe," said Lutra doubtfully. "Maybe it will. But

we'll still have to deal with the admiral and his officers. They're through the line and closing ground."

The foursome pulled themselves up the steps in front of Cyborg Joe's. Lutra rattled off a few shots. Ishiro'shea did the same with Duke's pulse pistol.

"I'll take Joe down to the bunker," said Duke. "You two hide out in the bar and try to hold the admiral at bay."

"Not much of a plan," said Lutra.

"I'm not the best with plans. I'm more of a 'wing it' type of guy."

"Just do it," snapped Queen Joe, still hanging from Duke's shoulder. "As long as we have the Orb and it's shielded from that cannon, we have a chance. I'll bet that he hasn't mastered the use of either the Shield or the Key without filtering it through his machinery."

"That's a chance we're going to have to take," concluded Duke.

LePaco's special force was in sight now, closing in on Cyborg Joe's. There was no doubt that hidden within that throng of soldiers was Admiral LePaco and, possibly, Mazilda Cloax.

CHAPTER TWENTY-SEVEN

I GAVE YOU THAT KNIFE

I SHIRO'SHEA AND LUTRA ZIPPED BY Duke and into Cyborg Joe's. Duke, still carrying the injured Queen Joe, was gasping for air as he approached the threshold of the popular drinking establishment and temporary headquarters for the ragtag resistance against Admiral LePaco. The Queen wasn't heavy, and he had no shortage of adrenaline considering the circumstances, but he was wearing down. Luckily, safety lay just beyond that swinging door.

In the back of the bar, Duke noticed a friendly face, surrounded by a handful of other friendly faces. Lilly, armed with some sort of Keltian firearm, was flanked by a dozen or so Keltian soldiers and a pair of Hausen-Ra commanders. They all stood behind a makeshift barrier, prepared for one last stand, if need be. And the need *was* be.

Thank the deity of the week! Duke thought. *Lilly! We have a chance.*

The bounty hunter barely had one boot inside Cyborg

Joe's when he felt a stinging pain north of his right hamstring.

I better have not just been shot in the ass, surmised Duke.

The pain sharpened. Then it spread down past his hamstring and into the back of his kneecap. His jog turned into a limp. His limp turned into a tumble. Duke hit the hard floor with a thud, dropping the Queen with an equally cringe-worthy crash.

The bounty hunter looked down through squinted eyes and saw not a mark left by a blaster or rifle, but the pewter hilt of a knife. A throwing dagger, to be exact. Mazilda Cloax's throwing dagger, to be super-duper exact. Luckily for Duke, he recognized this particular dagger, which was one of her shorter blades. If she had connected with one of her favorite throwing daggers, its other end would have ripped through his pelvis and added an extra hole in his belt. But even though it wasn't the most intimidating knife, it hurt. A lot. It was still, after all, a knife that was jabbed into his outer thigh, between his buttock and hip bone.

He looked up and saw Queen Joe struggling to make her way to her feet. He was pleased to see that, at first glance, she appeared to have no knives sticking out of her, and no gunshot wounds.

"Get her! Get Joe!" shouted Duke at Ishiro'shea and Lutra. "Get her behind that wall!"

The pair sprinted to Joe and hoisted her up.

"What about you?" asked the Hilterian.

"I'll be fine. You two take the Queen before she gets shot by these bastards."

Ishiro'shea noticed the dagger. Duke could tell that his partner recognized it immediately.

"Go, Ish. We're all dead if they get her and the Orb. I'll be crawling right behind y'all."

The ninja nodded.

That's why he was Salutatorian.

The sound of the Four I's soldiers' boots rattled the decor in the bar. They were moments away from bull rushing Cyborg Joe's. This was the proverbial "it." Queen Joe's valiant patchwork force would either stop the well-armed Admiral LePaco and his fine-tuned soldiers and save the universe, or else LePaco was about to acquire the final piece in his megalomaniacal puzzle of conquest. And it was going to happen at Cyborg Joe's.

Duke turned onto his side so that he faced the door, resting his weight on the buttock that wasn't impaled by a dagger. He aimed Betsy at the opening.

"Stay back, everyone," he yelled. "I'm going to take out as many as I can. If they walk through that door, Betsy's greeting 'em with her own interpretation of a handshake."

"I'm coming to get you," shouted Lutra over the increasing volume of the invaders. "Just stay there."

"No, stay back. Queen, tell her to stay back."

The bounty hunter didn't look back to see if the Queen held her back or to say a final goodbye to his long-time companion.

Sorry, Ish. Let me be the hero this time.

"Just make sure to keep that Orb away from LePaco, at all costs," yelled Duke as he aimed Betsy at the entrance.

I hope LePaco has the guts to come through first.

"I don't have the Orb. It's gone. Duke, it's gone!"

It was rare to see Queen Joe actually panicking.

Duke lowered Betsy and quickly scanned the ground around him. Splintered tables. Upturned chars. Shattered neon signs. Puddles of booze. Puddles of other stuff that were likely to never be identified properly.

Along the perimeter wall were a handful of half-circle dining booths. Many a MechaBurger 8000 had been consumed in those seats. Many a culinary adventurer had made their final adventure in those seats as well. The first booth was twice the size of the others, as it was reserved for the plus-sized species of traveler. It was also a favorite of those that preferred to walk on four legs, or six. It was spacious. And a glowing purple sphere rested in the shadows beneath its oversized table.

The Orb must have fallen when Duke dropped the Queen. Not only was he the closest to it by a good margin, he was responsible for its current whereabouts.

"I got it," Duke shouted to his cohorts behind the barricade.

The bounty hunter made it onto his knees, balancing his weight on his two hands and one good leg. He pushed off, propelling himself as close to the booth as he could muster. But he was still short. He made his way up again into a similar position.

The sound of the Four I's boots had ceased. In its place was the sound of their guns. They were inside Cyborg Joe's and, as of yet, the Orb was not safe. Duke readied himself for one last lunge. Once he had it, it would be up to his friends to give him enough cover to get back. Or he'd just throw the Orb as far as he could towards them and hope for a miracle. In typical Duke LaGrange fashion, he'd just wing it.

The bounty hunter balanced himself. The firefight had clearly begun, but he could tell by the sound that it was focused around the entrance area.

His jaw cracked. His body hit the floor again. And so did his face.

He turned over to see his worst nightmare; the slightly jaundiced profile of his former love, Mazilda Cloax.

"You punched me," said Duke involuntarily.

"Yeah, and I stabbed you," Cloax added. "How can you be shocked by this?"

"Sorry, habit. I'm used to you being, you know, not a bitch."

Mazilda caught sight of the Orb. She smiled.

Her gaze returned to the Nova Texan. "This time, I am truly sorry, Duke. I never thought I'd be able to kill you but you've forced my hand."

"I wish I could've done something back then that would've prevented you from turning into this."

She unsheathed a blade. The dagger's hilt was pewter, inlaid with sparking red jewels; it was an old knife, but it was meticulously preserved by a true master craftsman. Mazilda was a true master.

"I'm sorry—" she began.

"You can't kill me with that knife," interrupted Duke, "I *gave* you that knife."

She paused and looked at the dagger. "So you did."

As she refocused on the bounty hunter, Duke let loose a primal scream as he ripped the throwing dagger from his backside and slashed Mazilda's forearm. It was little more than a superficial cut, but the assassin dropped her blade. Duke took advantage of her being temporarily stunned, and placed a boot into her stomach, causing her to roll back a few paces from where he lay bleeding on the floor. He scurried backwards, propelled by his three good limbs, to the diner booth.

Mazilda recovered and pounced again. Her knee caught his ribcage flush. A backhanded swipe of her hand hit the bounty hunter's jaw with a thud. She hoisted her dagger in the air, but Duke grabbed her arm, preventing it from crashing down on his skull. He held her wrist with his other hand.

Even when Duke was at full strength and not recovering from a knife wound, Mazilda was the much more accomplished fighter. Though he was physically larger, she was stronger, more athletic. But he scored higher than her when it came to the most important aspect of combat, especially when it's of the mortal variety—somehow he always figured out a way to survive. Whether it was an attack of a three-headed ice wombat, having spears hurled at him from a legion of priest warriors, or fighting in a pit fighting tournament on Psitakki, Duke LaGrange found a way.

He knew he couldn't hold Mazilda at bay for much longer, especially as blood continued to flow from his thigh. Mazilda seemed content on staying the course, knowing that she would eventually overpower the bounty hunter.

"You taught me this one," Duke said through clenched teeth.

He let go of her left wrist; the momentum pulled her body downwards. The trajectory of her upper torso led to a collision between Mazilda's face and Duke's fist. The jab struck her across the bridge of the nose. She rolled to the left until she was completely off of Duke, freeing the bounty hunter to retrieve the Orb.

As the firefight intensified, Duke scrambled to the booth and secured the Orb. Aside from stray blasts and ricochets, the shootout had not made its way to the perimeter. It was a straight shot to safety.

With an earsplitting crack the table shattered into two pieces. Duke clung to the Orb, still not on his feet and still sitting in a pool of his own blood.

Standing over him was Mazilda Cloax, nose crooked and bruising. She did not have her trademark dagger aimed at her former partner. Apparently she was done with daggers. Duke was now staring directly into the barrel of a pulse pistol.

He gripped the Orb tighter.

"I could really use some help right now," he said, his eyes darting to the tattered barrier being bombarded by enemy fire. He didn't see Ishiro'shea or Lilly or Lutra or Queen Joe. But he knew they were behind there somewhere.

"I said I could really use some help right now," he shouted at the top of his lungs.

"You're not getting any help today, my love."

Mazilda squeezed the trigger.

CHAPTER TWENTY-EIGHT

INTER-DIMENSIONAL DOOMSDAY DEVICE

DUKE CLOSED HIS EYES, BRACING himself for a quick descent into lifelessness. There was no way that Mazilda Cloax could miss a point-blank shot.

But she did.

The bounty hunter could feel the heat of the ray above his left shoulder; it warmed his neck and crept down his spine. His grip on the Orb remained firm. He slowly opened his eyes. Mazilda was there, a bewildered expression on her face. She was backlit by a roaring red glow.

"What the—" She turned to face the crackling crimson blob.

Out from the portal stepped a muscular, athletic female with unblemished skin a shade somewhere between bronze and orange. She was taller and leaner than the assassin. In her hand was a golden ceremonial staff that had likely been a gift from a certain Neprian priest.

Duke's eyes widened and his jaw hung open. He looked down at the mustangsen pendant that lay against his chest.

Ja'a.

"Who are you?" screeched Mazilda. Her gun was still

pointed at Duke but her attention was now firmly on the rogue portal opening.

The Neprian glanced at Mazilda, then at Duke, and finally, her eyes landed on the gun being pointed at her friend.

"Who are you?" Mazilda shouted again. She turned to face Duke. "Do you know this woman?"

The strike with the staff was sudden and violent. Mazilda crashed to the bar floor and slid near Duke and the Orb. Her gun flew halfway across the room and landed in the middle of the firefight.

"Are you alright?" Ja'a asked, her eyes darting around as she took in the scene of carnage. "What's going on?"

"I'm fine," Duke lied. "But we need to get over there." He pointed towards the barricade. "We need to get *this* over there."

"The Orb? What's it doing—"

"No time, I'll fill you in later. Let's just say that if those guys over there get it, we're all dead."

Ja'a nodded and helped the bleeding bounty hunter to his feet.

"I don't remember you being this heavy," Ja'a joked as they made their way along the perimeter wall, trying not to attract the Four I's attention or gunfire. "I see you need someone to keep you in shape."

"I'll admit, I haven't had to walk across an entire country in search of a magic rock lately," he said through a grimace.

"But it was good exercise," she replied. "And good times."

Duke couldn't see from his wounded position, but he wanted to believe that Ja'a said that with her magnificent smile.

"Who was that with the gun?"

"An old friend."

"Friend?"

"She *was* an old friend," Duke corrected himself.

"What did I tell you about your particular brand of exploits? I know I'm from a 'backwoods rock' as you like to say, but my assumption is that treating people in the manner *you* treat them is universally unacceptable. You were bound to get in trouble."

"This is not one of those cases. By the way, you're in a good mood for someone that's been deposited in the middle of a war," Duke remarked.

"Let's just say it's good to see you again."

"I'm really glad to see you too. And not just because you saved my ass."

"Looks like I was a bit late on that front," Ja'a commented, playfully patting the bounty hunter's blood-stained hip.

He yelped. "Ouch!"

"Sorry, I didn't—"

Duke felt a force as powerful as a Trampling Death Robots drum solo hit his lower back. The jolt launched him shoulder-first into the wall. He crumpled to the floor. He sighed internally. *Not the floor again.*

Mazilda Cloax leapt to her feet, having tackled the bounty hunter. Ja'a's stumble from the unexpected attack had separated her from Duke and had allowed Mazilda to situate herself between them. The assassin drew her favorite dagger. Ja'a countered with Vernglet Wip's ceremonial rod.

Ja'a blocked Mazilda's first charge, redirecting her out of striking distance. Cloax lunged but, once again, Ja'a was too quick, landing a sharp jab into Mazilda's abdomen with the butt of the staff. Mazilda grimaced but remained focused on the Neprian. Another approach, another denial. Mazilda's face changed from its jaundiced hue to a red equal to that of the portal that brought her opponent here. The struggle raged; Mazilda's anger-fueled advances were all thwarted but Ja'a's fluid combinations with her staff also never found the mark. It was a battle of equals.

A stray blast from one of the Four I's soldiers struck the floor in front of Ja'a, sending fragments into the air and into the face of the Neprian. She closed her eyes and turned her head to avoid the debris.

Mazilda pounced with her dagger aimed at the distracted warrior. Ja'a dodged the death blow with a quick slide to the right, whipped her body around in a full circle, her back now towards her devious counterpart. The momentum of her spin propelled her staff with even more velocity; when it stuck Mazilda, she fell to the floor with a noise louder than the laser strike.

"Get the Orb and go, Duke," barked the still dazed Ja'a.

The bounty hunter pulled himself up, leaning on the wall for support. The Orb was tucked away in the crook of one arm and his other braced against the wall. His hobble grew even more pronounced. But the finish line was in sight.

The dagger embedded itself into the wall an eyelash's length from his face. Duke recoiled with shock, causing him to lose his balance; he caught himself with his right arm before he crashed into the floor yet again. The Orb pried itself loose from his right arm as he hit the ground. Oddly, it didn't bounce: when it connected with the floor, it stopped immediately as if it had been lobbed into a pile of thick sludge. Then, despite having no visible means of locomotion, it began to roll slowly away from Duke. He made one last effort to swipe at it, but it was already out of reach.

He looked up to see the wounded Mazilda. She locked eyes with her former lover and smiled. For the first time,

Duke saw her for who she was, or rather who she had become. It shouldn't have taken him this long, considering the atrocities that she had caused, or stood by and let happen, but for the first time, Duke realized that she was evil. *Very* evil. Admiral LePaco-level evil.

Mazilda's smile lasted only a moment. Ja'a's staff struck her head with a focused force.

If she isn't dead, at the very least she's not going anywhere for a while, thought Duke.

Now Ja'a seemed to notice the rolling Orb. *It wasn't the first time that she'd seen this particular Orb behave this way,* remembered Duke.

"I'll get it," she shouted.

The Orb continued its path; it was directly in the center of the ongoing firefight between the rebel holdouts behind the barricade and the Four I's soldiers.

"No!" Duke screamed with as much power as he could muster. "You'll get shot before you're anywhere near it."

She furled her brow. "I can get it."

"Don't," pleaded the Nova Texan.

He realized that the matrix of lasers and plasma blasts that had crisscrossed the bar had now stopped. Both sides had noticed the glowing violet sphere. It had slowed to a stop and was now nestled comfortably on a shattered floor plank.

"I really can get it now," said the Neprian. She turned to retrieve the Orb, then stopped. Her next steps were backwards towards Duke, not in the direction of the inter-dimensional artifact.

Admiral Lothario LePaco emerged from behind the Four I's lines. He wore his usual garish ensemble, but on his left forearm was draped a shield. *The* Shield. The grand prize of the Tournament of the Shield of the Colossal Calamari. One third of a weapon that could tear apart the fabric of a universe with the nonchalance of somebody brushing their teeth. Furthermore, hanging around his neck was an exceptionally shiny piece of jeweled wire, attached to which was an equally shiny locket. The Amplification Key.

LePaco was followed by a single Four I's commander. He had to be important because he had a lot of medals.

No one fired at either of them. Though the Shield that LePaco carried was one of the most powerful objects in the whole of the universe, his human shield was just as effective. Pressed against him, hands bound behind her back, was Ishiro'shea's mother. The Four I's commander tugged on the chains that held the Father, Ishiro'shea's dad, in check, despite his struggles.

"Shoot him!" boomed the Father. "Forget about us! Shoot him! Now!"

No one fired.

LePaco threw Yumi Nobunaga-Flaherty to the ground. He raised his shielded arm. As the Orb sped towards him, the rebel forces stood motionless in shock. Even Ishiro'shea remained inert.

"Shoot him," echoed Duke. "Now!"

LePaco picked up the Orb. His cackle filled every nook and crevice in Cyborg Joe's.

"You morons," he said, his voice coated in condescension. He held the Orb in the air and examined it.

The recovering Queen Joe peered over the barricade. Duke could see the horror in her eyes.

"Fire! Fire! With everything you've got," she commanded.

The rebels opened fire. Duke scanned the crowd. He didn't see Ishiro'shea.

LePaco lifted his left arm, raising the Shield against the attack. It emitted a blinding light along with a shockwave that sent everyone back a few paces. Duke noted that it wasn't overly painful, more confusing, since light typically didn't move objects. It did provide a distraction, though. He and Ja'a were able to sneak behind the barricade to their allies without being noticed.

The illumination dimmed as the light appeared to be sucked back into the Shield.

Both forces looked around in disbelief. Not a single blast had made its way through. The Four I's were unharmed. As were Ishiro'shea's parents.

Admiral LePaco's cackle escalated in volume and intensity. He rotated his arm so that the Shield faced the ceiling. He slammed down the Orb in the direct center of the Shield. The sound it made was indescribable—it was at once a deep drumming beat and a high-pitched whine; a skull-crushing intensity married with a delicate purr. And yet it wasn't at all any of those things. It was simply indescribable. And it didn't let up. The Orb remained in a stationary position, defying the laws of physics by not rolling off the sloping face of the Shield.

LePaco then yanked the Key from the necklace and jabbed it into the solid Orb. Somehow, the Key cut through its surface like a plastic spork into a tub of never-ending mayonnaise. The noise reached an agonizing climax... then vanished. Silence consumed Cyborg Joe's for the first time in its existence.

The trio of inter-dimensional artifacts had now become a single inter-dimensional doomsday device.

And, despite the efforts of Queen Joe, Duke LaGrange, Ishiro'shea, and countless other brave souls, it was in the hands of Admiral Lothario LePaco.

The universe's days were now numbered.

CHAPTER TWENTY-NINE

NINETY-NINE

T HE NEWLY-FORMED INSTRUMENT OF UNFATHOMABLE destruction glowed upon Admiral LePaco's forearm. The uplighting effect added an extra layer of creepiness to his facial expression. Though Duke believed the Queen regarding the power of this weapon, it was hard not to find it outlandish, looking like the cosmic ray guns in the children's books that his adopted mother would read to him. After all, it was a glowing metallic pendant sticking out of a glowing purple bowling ball adhered, somehow, to a rickety and old glowing shield— like the cherry on top of a scoop of ice cream. And all of this was strapped to the forearm of an outlandishly-dressed super villain. Had the very existence of the universe not depended on the next few moments, there would probably have been comic absurdity to be found in the situation. Then again, what *is* the universe if not comically absurd?

Who had money on the universe ending like this? Duke thought.

The injured Queen Joe raised an eyebrow at the bounty hunter. "You know, Duke," she said, struggling through the pain, "I always knew that you'd be part of the end of the universe."

Duke didn't reply. He just shrugged his shoulders.

A shot was fired from behind the rebels' barricade. It missed LePaco and took out a Four I's infantryman. The admiral looked up and sneered. He thrust his forearm and the unique apparatus attached to it towards the rebel line. A blinding light followed by a shockwave. But LePaco looked displeased.

He wanted to obliterate everyone. That bastard's just winging this, realized Duke. *I can't be out-winged by this dude*.

The admiral repeated the gesture. The same result. A third time, same thing. In frustration, LePaco slapped the Shield. The disc began to twirl; the Orb and the Key levitated a few inches above the Shield as it picked up velocity.

This can't be good, thought Duke.

"Should we shoot it?" barked Lilly. "Queen, what should we do?"

Joe waved her off groggily. "No, we can't harm it. We just have to hope that LePaco hasn't figured out how to use it properly."

The spinning Shield began to hiss and wail. Bulbous droplets of light began to peel off of the whirling disc and scatter across the floor of Cyborg Joe's.

"What's going on, Queen?" asked Duke. "Tell me this is normal and you know what's happening."

All eyes focused on Joe as she replied, "I'm afraid I'm not quite sure. But LePaco seems just as confused."

Abruptly, the spinning stopped. The Orb and Key returned to their stationary positions atop the Shield. The light droplets remained dispersed across the ground as motionless puddles of golden illumination. They were quite beautiful.

The pools of light began to expand, their diameters doubling, then tripling. The light then began to flow upwards, each puddle becoming a different height. The glow intensified, then vanished.

Standing where each of the droplets had landed were numerous beings. No two of them were the same. Some were humanoid. Some were reptiloid. There were a few with wings. More than a few more with horns. One looked like he was made out of molten lava. Another looked like he was made out of notebook paper. Duke swore he saw one that was a pumpkin with fangs and a machete. An eclectic menagerie of alien species with one thing in common—they all appeared to be readying for combat.

"There have to be hundreds of them," a Keltian commented. "Who are they?"

"Do we shoot *them*?" asked Lilly.

"There aren't hundreds of them," replied Joe. "There are ninety-nine."

"Nice party trick, Queen," remarked Duke. "But I don't think the exact number really matters right now. The fact is that there's a lot more of them than us. And they're fully armed."

Ja'a squeezed Duke's wrist.

"Fine, I'll shut up now," he whispered in response.

"It *does* matter, Duke. There's ninety-nine because these are the previous winners of the Tournament of the Shield."

"Wait, what?"

"Apparently, the Shield summoned them."

"How? Some of those dudes have to be a million cycles old."

"Watch it with the ageism," shot back Joe. "I passed that mark a long time ago."

"Sorry."

"I think I know what happened," said the Queen.

"What's the Tournament of the Shield?" asked Ja'a.

"A story for another time," replied Duke.

"When the artifacts were built," began Joe, "the Shield was the only one constructed with a fail-safe in case of abuse. The others should've been; it was a really poor oversight. If a single being stayed in contact with the Shield for an extended period of time, the assumption was that the being in question probably wasn't using it for good. I'm not sure how that time translated to this dimension but my guess is many cycles. Then it would sort of, well, self-implode."

"What does that even mean?" inquired the bounty hunter.

"I'm not entirely sure about that, but I think it would take the abuser and suck them into an inter-dimensional pocket of existence. A purgatory of sorts. After that, I don't know."

"And each of these chumps kept that trophy close by until it gobbled them up, I suppose. Between their press tours, photo ops, and so on and so forth. It probably was a big part of their post-tournament lives."

"That does make sense," said the Queen in between winces.

The newly-appeared collection of beings looked as confused as the rebels. The admiral ordered his men back, some exiting the crowded bar. His eyes were wide and the corners of his mouth reached his ears. He let loose an uncontrolled laugh, teetering on the brink of hysteria.

"Lost warriors of the Shield," the admiral proclaimed, "I am your Shield Master. I have given you all a second chance."

The ninety-nine former champions all turned to face LePaco.

"Unfortunately, it looks like LePaco also figured out who they were," commented Duke.

The admiral continued, "You have waited a long time to return to this universe—"

One of the beings, a gargantuan six-armed combatant, cut him off. "You're telling me, brother," he groaned. "Have you ever been stuck on an island for five hundred thousand cycles without aging?"

"What species is that guy?" Duke asked the Queen in a low voice.

"I think he's a Timorian. Ancient race. They died out thousands of cycles ago. I've only met a few but they've all been pretty good folks."

"I have not, my friend," said the admiral to the horned Timorian. "But you are back now. You and your fellow champions have been brought back to help me rid this planet of these insolent bastards that stand before you."

The former champions didn't rush towards the rebel line. They just stood there. Most just whispered amongst themselves.

"And why should we do that?" said another combatant, who stepped forward to stand mere paces from the admiral and the Shield. He was Psitakki.

"Ah, you must be Grozzel. Grozzel the Great, if I remember correctly."

"Just Grozzel," the Psitakki replied.

"Then as the first champion of the Tournament, you must know that your horde is under my control, as I have the last remaining holy Shield. It is your destiny to do my bidding."

The Psitakki looked back at his colleagues and rolled his eyes, then turned his attention back to LePaco. "I don't think it works that way. At least, I've never heard that. I definitely didn't sign up for that. Where'd you hear that story?"

"You saw that it brought you back from your stasis, didn't you?"

"Yeah, and it was really cool of you to do that."

"So, you are now my servants. I am the Master of the Shield!" LePaco screamed.

"Whoa, whoa. Slow down there, guy. You *did* bring us back. We're all pretty thankful for that. Totally A-OK from this lot, no doubt. But all of us did plenty of fighting in our day and we've kind of enjoyed a more peaceful life. If it's all the same, I think we'll all just head out, let you guys figure out what you need to figure out, and we'll be out of your hair. Sound good?"

LePaco's eyes were ablaze. His temples pounded so hard that Duke imagined they could be heard on the Keltian moons.

"No, my dear Grozzel," the admiral said with a strained formality, "you and your friends *will* do my bidding. And my bidding is to kill every one of these pests... now."

Grozzel looked at the battered barrier. The heads of Keltians and members of other races peered over it to see what was happening.

"What'd they do to you, anyways?" the Psitakki asked.

"They're trying to stop me," LePaco replied.

"From what? Universal domination?"

The Psitakki began to laugh. His comrades joined in. LePaco's face turned scarlet.

"Why yes, my Psitakki friend, universal domination *is* my goal."

"Good one, man. Universal domination—oh, that's a good one." Grozzel wiped tears of laughter from his cheek. "I've been so rude. I never asked your name."

"Admiral Lothario LePaco. And this here is my new

toy." He raised his forearm, once again producing the combination of blinding light followed by a shockwave.

This again? thought Duke.

Most of the beings hit the floor, though some of the sturdier combatants remained upright from the blow of the Shield's shockwave.

"Hey, what was that for?" one of them yelled.

Grozzel returned to his feet. "What gives, Admiral? Just because we won't fight those folks over there, you're going to try and blind us?"

"That's how this whole 'you will do my bidding' arrangement works," answered LePaco.

"These guys don't look too bad. Are you sure you can't work something out? You know how many wars could've been avoided if people just talked things out?"

"Kill them now, slaves!" LePaco shouted, raising the inter-dimensional doomsday device.

"Fine, fine," Grozzel said. He pivoted towards his fellow champions. "Hey, guys, wanna just get this over with and then we can leave and not have to deal with this garbage?"

A wave of "fine's" and "why not's" rippled through the group of tournament winners.

Grozzel turned back to the admiral. "Okay, Admiral. We'll do it. It won't be with a lot of enthusiasm, but we'll do it. Then can we go?"

"Sure," LePaco replied, his grin growing even wider.

The ninety-nine warriors stretched, cracked their necks, and limbered up for the impending assault.

"Alright, let's all get into a formation or something," groaned the Timorian. "These guys don't look like much but neither did Nedrow Ostravok, the Cuddle Monster of Daedeaus Maroon. Little did I know that 'cuddling' on Daedeaus Maroon meant slicing one's enemy into dainty ribbons with a huge sickle that Daedeans excrete from a mucus cell in their stomachs. Ned wasn't cuddly at all."

Duke hobbled to the barricade. With his bleeding having abated a little, he vaulted over. His right leg was still injured from the dagger wound to the thigh and couldn't support him on his landing, which turned into more of a tumble and roll. If anything, it was this that caught the attention of Grozzel and his friends.

CHAPTER THIRTY

SAND

G ROZZEL AND THE WARRIORS SHIFTED into their various battle stances.

"Settle down, fellas, I'm not here to fight you," pleaded Duke.

The entire group began to chuckle again.

"We weren't overly concerned with you and the fight you might bring to us," responded Grozzel.

"Although you might be just like Ned from Daedeaus Maroon," noted the Timorian. "Tell me, do you have a mucus-covered sickle in your belly?"

"I don't, I promise," replied the bounty hunter. "But before you lot try and kill us, I do have two things to say."

"Try?"

"Fine, before you *most undoubtedly* kill us."

"Better. Go on," said the Psitakki graciously.

Duke pointed to Admiral LePaco. "First, and I can't stress this enough, that guy you're helping over there, well, he's a bad dude. He wants to take over the universe. All of it. We may not look like much but we're the best shot of preventing that. The big, funky-looking weapon on his wrist

—that's no joke. Imprisoning you and your friends for a million cycles is nothing compared to what it can do given free reign. We're talking destroy-the-entire-universe level here."

"He speaks the truth," shouted the Father, as he remained in the clutches of LePaco's guards.

Grozzel glanced at the human then began to scratch his chin in contemplation. Duke saw a few of the other champions doing the same, or what he assumed was an equivalent gesture.

The Psitakki's cephalopodan gaze locked on to Duke again. "And your second point?"

"If you kill me, you'd be killing a fellow winner of the Tournament of the Shield of the Colossal Calamari."

A collective gasp rang out amongst the warriors.

"Is that so?" inquired Grozzel.

"Yes, I'm the last winner. And I'm sure there's a rule against murdering another winner."

"Not to state the obvious, 'Mister Winner,' but you don't *have* the Shield, do you? That guy over there does." The Psitakki nodded his head in the general direction of Admiral LePaco.

"And if you are telling the truth," the Timorian began, "the Tournament must be going downhill. No offense."

"None taken," said Duke, trying to ignore the six-armed alien's disrespectful jab. "He stole the Shield. Ask anyone. Make a quick call to the Grand Shaman. Or to one of your ancestors. In fact, a relative of yours named Gjrazzel fought in the event. And did so honorably. He'll tell you the truth."

"Lies! This man is lying!" screamed LePaco.

"And how do we know you're telling the truth?" the Psitakki asked the admiral.

"I have the Shield, don't I?"

"You also tried to kill us with it," countered Grozzel. "So there's that."

"I won the damn tournament! I have the damn Shield. That should be enough proof. Do you think the Psitakki would let some stranger just walk right up and steal it from the champion? Wouldn't a real champion be able to protect a single shield?"

"He has some good points," said the Timorian.

"True, Eux-Auhr-Herx, very true. So, Admiral, tell us about the Tournament. What did it *feel* like to compete?"

LePaco let out a deep sigh. "It was great. I went in there, killed some guys, and claimed my trophy. The Psitakki fans loved me. They said that I reminded them of Grozzel the Great, the first champion of the Tournament of the Shield. There were parades. I don't know... what else... oh yeah, I beat a giant two-headed Jungafallowian that turned out to be a robot."

Grozzel leaned over and said something to Eux-Auhr-Hurx. The Timorian appeared to be in agreement .

"And you, my wounded friend. What did you *feel*?" the Psitakki asked Duke.

Duke closed his eyes. The images from his time on Psitakki raced by, and he tried to pluck out the ones that he thought would be meaningful to the former champions. But the flow of memories was too rapid. He closed his eyes even tighter, trying to tune out the remnants of the battle that surrounded him. He blocked out the images of the ninety-nine warriors staring him down. He blocked out the lingering pain in his thigh from Mazilda's dagger. He did his best to ignore the fact that the most evil being in the known universe was on the other side of the room, wielding a weapon that could send the dimension onto the scrapheap of extinction with the flick of his wrist. Duke let the wave of memories wash over him.

Duke opened his eyes. He looked into the black pupils of the tournament's inaugural champion. He stopped thinking and he simply spoke.

"The sand on the arena floor. I remember the sand. When you walked on it, or pivoted, or dove away from a strike, it was cushioned. But you didn't sink into it, nor did it fight against you. But, when you were thrown from your feet by another's force, it was as solid and painful as any club or rock. It was like it knew if you were deserving of comfort or pain. It had a smell to it too, somewhere between that deep musty smell of wet soil and the sharpness of a salty sea. I felt that it had a mind of its own, it was alive, organic. Somehow it knew the worthiness of the combatants that stood atop it."

The bounty hunter paused to take a deep breath.

"And the crowd. When I was engaged with my opponent, the noise dissipated. It just went away. I knew it was there, somewhere, but I couldn't tell if they were for me or against me. It provided a spark of adrenaline, but also, counter-intuitively, it gave me clarity of mind."

"And your opponents?" asked the Psitakki.

"I hated every second of every fight. I was doing this for what? A Shield? I was hurting other life forms for a trophy? It made me sick. But I kept fighting. The only thing stronger than the illness that the Tournament caused was my desire to win it. For every gut-wrenching moment, there was a smile; for every fleeting instant of joy, there was a sidesplitting sense of agony."

Duke looked up to the ceiling, his eye moistened by tears.

"I see," said Grozzel, his voice cracking.

"You don't believe that garbage," cackled Admiral LePaco. "Really? You can't honestly take that seriously. I have the Shield. I was there. He's just—"

"Admiral, please," interrupted Grozzel. "This man here—"

"Is a liar? A charlatan? An idiot?" interrupted LePaco in turn.

"This man here is a fellow champion. He is a brother."

"And that makes *you* an evil bastard," added the Timorian.

The ninety-nine warrior about-faced to point directly at LePaco and his contingent of Four I's soldiers.

The admiral simply shook his head. "I guess you lot are equally as thick as LaGrange. You could've been my elite guards, my detail; now you'll just be dead."

He tilted his forearm, aiming the device at the champions.

The rebels began to spill over the barricade protecting them from the Four I's assault. They stormed past Duke and joined the ninety-nine warriors, filling in the gaps and creating one sweeping mob, readying themselves for a final charge against LePaco's force. The injured bounty hunter felt a firm, comforting hand on his shoulder.

Thanks, Ish.

Another hand rested on his other shoulder. He turned and exchanged smiles with the beautiful Neprian, Ja'a. Behind her was Lilly, supporting the recovering Queen Joe.

"That was beautiful, what you said, Duke," said Ja'a. "I don't know if I've ever heard you speak like that before."

"I made it up," replied Duke with a smirk. "The sand just felt like... sand."

"You're an ass," said Queen Joe.

"I agree," added Ja'a.

"But I can't think of a better ass to stand beside me at this moment," said Joe.

"I agree with that even more," Ja'a replied.

"That means a lot, don't get me wrong," replied Duke,

"but if LePaco figures out how to fire that thing with anything more than light, none of this matters."

It wasn't the Queen or Duke or Lilly that led the charge. A roar from within the ranks of the ninety-nine warriors signaled the advance. But then it was a collective shriek from the combined force that signaled their sudden stop.

A bolt of green energy shot from LePaco's arm, darted over the heads of the rebels, and blasted through the ceiling of Cyborg Joe's. Constant bombardment from an entire armada of battleships couldn't make a dent on the exterior of the famed watering hole, but one whizzing beam of emerald light from the weapon ripped a hole in the ceiling big enough to survey the entirety of the Keltian sky.

The rebels were mostly sprawled out across the barroom floor, many lying on the ground. Admiral LePaco's eyes bulged. The Key, protruding from the Orb, was radiating the same green as the laser. The color then migrated to the Orb itself. Then the Shield.

Joe looked over at Duke, Ishiro'shea, and Ja'a. Her body was trembling; had she not been held in Gartoshian clutches, she would have collapsed.

"It's powering up."

CHAPTER THIRTY-ONE

OF PENGUINS AND BLENDERS

"I GUESS THIS IS WHERE I would insert my villainous diatribe of power, right?" said Admiral Lothario LePaco. "But we all know how that sort of thing typically ends."

The weapon on his forearm pulsed rapidly, its glow turning Cyborg Joe's interior a rich shade of green. No color was spared. Even greens became, somehow, greener.

"So, without further ado," he continued, "I'm going to blast you all from the very fabric of this existence and into your inter-dimensional graves. I would say it's been a pleasure and that you put up a good fight, but we all know that wouldn't be an honest assessment. LaGrange, you were pretty much as expected but I did think you, Queenie, would provide more resistance. I guess I didn't realize how powerful I really am."

"For someone that wasn't going to start the clichéd, long-winded bad guy speech, you sure are starting a clichéd, long-winded bad guy speech," jabbed the Nova Texan. "You remind me of your half-brother."

"Are you sure pissing him off is the best approach, Duke?" whispered Lilly.

"Probably not but it's just so natural," answered the bounty hunter.

"Fine, LaGrange, I'll hurry up and get on with killing you and your friends. And I bid you all farewell."

The admiral lowered himself, his legs sprawled out to brace himself against the recoil of the weapon.

"Again, LaGrange, I bid you, the Queen, and everyone else fare—"

The blast came from the opening in the ceiling. It wasn't exceptionally loud, or bright, or green. But it was accurate. It struck LePaco's forearm, forcing the maniacal criminal to the ground. He partially released the weapon, but not before he commanded it to serve up another surge of emerald devastation. Once again, the beam entered the Keltian night sky—this time through the preexisting opening. However, LePaco's fall caused the beam to clip the edges of the gaping hole. And the unknown shooter. Ceiling fragments exploded into the air and tumbled down to the floor of Joe's, bringing with it the heroic warrior that had winged the admiral just as he was about to wipe out the last vestiges of hope for the universe's survival.

The marksman hit the ground unceremoniously, coming to rest amongst the debris. He was sprawled out, motionless and clinging to life.

"Dallas."

Even as Duke's brain raced to digest the situation, LePaco was up, appearing to have shaken off any damage caused by Duke Dallas. He made his way to his feet and soon located the weapon, a few paces away. The admiral reached for it but was tackled by a tiny blur. A tiny blur named Yumi Nobunaga-Flaherty. She had broken free. LePaco regained control rather quickly and threw Ishiro's mother to the ground. But was then met with a slightly larger blur, the Father. He wrapped the admiral in a tight bear hug and flung him to the ground. The Father then pounced on the crazed overlord, fists raining down on the turtled LePaco. It wasn't clear how many of the haymakers were connecting solidly but it probably didn't feel good.

Yumi dove on top of the weapon, acting as a human shield between it and the admiral. She was only slightly larger than the device itself.

The Four I's soldiers came to the aid of LePaco, prying the spry Irishman from their leader. He fell to the floor—landing next to his wife, still guarding the weapon. The admiral drew his pulse pistol and aimed it directly at Ishiro'shea's parents.

"I think you have my weapon," he muttered through gritted teeth, his eyes filled with white-hot fire.

A loud crash rang through Cyborg Joe's. It was the sound that a penguin makes when you put it in a blender—then drop it on a landmine.

Oh, that familiar sound.

Duke LaGrange, Nova Texan bounty hunter and playboy, was holding his beloved out-of-date Widowmaker sonic shotgun. It was aimed where the admiral once stood. But Ol' Betsy made sure that the admiral was no longer able to stand. In fact, he was no longer able to do anything that had the prerequisite of being alive. Duke LaGrange had just killed Admiral Lothario LePaco.

Time seemed to stand still; ages seemed to pass.

It was the Hilterian ambassador, Lutra, who broke the silence, shouting, "Let's go!"

Grozzel; Eux-Auhr-Herx; the ninety-seven other past champions of the Tournament of the Shield of the Colossal Calamari; Lilly, the anthropomorphic musk ox from one of the moons of Gartosh; Lutra, the Hilterian sharpshooter;

and Gha, a feisty Goother Rat from Gurlf joined a mix of Keltian freedom fighters and other alien volunteers and charged the disciplined squadron from Intergalactic Infrastructure Improvement, Incorporated.

The Four I's soldiers attempted to flee outside of Cyborg Joe's—but were cut off by even more Keltian defenders, a legion of Hausen-Ra, Gartoshians, Sabromms, and other species that had just taken out the remainder of LePaco's ground force. Hovering in the air above, visible through the gaping hole in the ceiling, was the *Deus Ex Machina*, flanked by the victorious fleet of Earth and Gartoshian ships, led by Maxx Gemstarr.

The Four I's were overwhelmed.

Duke rushed to the pile of debris that covered his father. He began to cast away fragments of wood and stone with the strength of eight T'ckuvians. Ja'a joined him. The amount of debris left in the wake of the weapon's blast was enough to bury an entire colony of three-headed ice wombats. The duo soon cleared away enough to make out a humanoid form.

Duke continued digging until a face looked back at him. And though he'd only seen that face for the first time in adulthood a short while ago, it was part of him. It was his DNA. It was a mirror into his future. It was his father.

"Dad, Dad!" Duke screamed. "Can you hear me?"

"Now you call me Dad?" said Dallas faintly with the slight hint of a grin on his battered face.

"How did you—Why?" the bounty hunter stammered.

"Stop, Lafayette. Stop. I don't have much time."

"We're going to get you out of here," Duke pleaded.

"Stop. Please, stop." He looked to Ja'a. "Pretty lady. Tell him to stop, please."

The Neprian clasped Duke's hand tightly, her other hand gripped his forearm.

"We can get you out—"

"Lafayette, stop and listen to me. I'm dying. So shut up and let me talk."

Duke tried to fight back his emotions. His jaw quivered and his vision grew blurry as salty tears burst from his eyes.

"I'm glad that I sent you back. I know you had a hand in this."

"How'd you survive the attack back on Tardasio 5?"

"Most of us survived. Who knew that BHU and organized crime could work so well together. Maybe a little too well. But we did the opposite of what everyone predicted. When our backs were against the wall after that sneak attack, we fought harder. We laid waste to that entire planet. The Four I's won't be able to produce a construction paper hand turkey with what we left. Then I got a message from a guy claiming to be your best friend. A guy named Maxx."

"Maxx, he's a—Never mind, it doesn't matter."

"He said you'd say something like that."

"However you got here, thank you for saving me. For saving us."

"It's the best that I could do, Duke. I spent my entire life *not* doing the best that I could do, with you in particular. I'll never be able to make that up."

Duke Dallas' voice trembled and he began to cough. A single stream of blood fell from the corner of his mouth. "I never planned on it being like this, but I should tell you about your mother. I owe you that."

"No need, Dad, I knew my mother. She died a long time ago on Nova Texas."

A river of tears cascaded down Dallas' cheek and washed away much of the blood.

"Trix *was* a great woman. I wish you would've had more time with her, Son. I really do." He paused. "But, if you do want to find your *biological* mother, I would start your search on Omarellia. I don't know if she's still there or if she still answers to 'Juni,' or even if she's alive, but that's where I would start. But beware... You probably don't want to know. If it were up to me—and I know it's not—I would leave it alone. But it's not and you deserve the right to make that decision, despite what I say."

"Thank you," replied the bounty hunter. "Thank you."

"And one last thing, Son. I know I don't deserve a last request but if you can find it in your heart, I would appreciate it."

"Yes, anything," stammered Duke.

"Bury me. Bury me on a planet that's—" He stopped, his coughing increasing.

His lungs are filling with blood, concluded Duke.

"Yes, Father."

"A planet that's peaceful. I've only known violence. War. Criminal activity. The death of innocent beings. Bury me on a place that has moved beyond war and death. Or one that wants to. Somewhere untouched by guys like LePaco and criminals like Hefty."

Ja'a strengthened her grip on Duke's arm and rested her head on his shoulder.

"I know the place," Duke said. "You'll love it. Sweeping plains dotted with glass-like ponds. Majestic mountains like you've never seen, protecting vast valleys. And you'll get a kick out of this: they have winged panthers flying around everywhere. There are swamps, full of life and diversity. There are forests, dense forests. And caves... Oh, are there caves."

"What's the name of this paradise?" asked Duke Dallas, his voice reduced to a whisper.

"They call it Neprius."

"It sounds wonderful, Son. It sounds—" Duke Dallas' voice trailed off as his last breath exited his body.

"It's wonderful, Dad. I once thought it was nothing but a primitive, backwards world. But now I know it's the most beautiful place in the whole universe."

As Duke sat motionless on the pile of rubble, he noticed Ishiro'shea race to his parents. The ninja removed the mouth covering on his mask and the recognition was instant. All three burst into tears as they embraced. Despite the emotional ordeal that he had just experienced, Duke smiled.

Just next to the feet of the reunited family, still glowing a radioactive green, were the Key, Orb, and Shield. The hobbled Queen Joe made her way to the trio and extended a firm hand to Ishiro'shea's parents. She hugged the ninja with as much emotion as his own parents did. Ishiro'shea picked up the weapon and handed it to the Queen.

She closed her eyes. From around her hands, the obsidian smoke that typically signified one of her stormy lightning assaults began to fill the air. It formed into winding tubes, weaving around the weapon. The intensity of the artifacts' glow faded until they appeared inert and harmless.

Joe fell to the ground, dropping the weapon. The three artifacts broke apart, scattering to encircle the inter-dimensional being lying on the floor of her bar.

She exhaled deeply, as if she had been holding in her breath for an eon.

CHAPTER THIRTY-TWO

ANOTHER ROUND OF WHISKY

"WE CAUGHT THIS ONE TRYING to escape," said Grozzel the Great, holding up a battered Mazilda Cloax by the neck, her feet dangling in the air. "I think she just woke up. What should we do with her?"

"Just kill me, you bastards," she said through cracked lips matted with dried blood.

A bruise extended from her ear, across the bridge of her nose, and halfway down her opposite cheek. Grozzel poked it with his long cephalopodan finger. The assassin writhed in pain. The Psitakki giggled. "She's feisty."

"Duke, thoughts?" asked Queen Joe. "I feel that this is your call."

"What's your plan, Grozzel? Where are you guys headed now?" asked the bounty hunter.

"We all discussed it and the only place that we'd feel at home is Psitakki. Some of us have been away for a million cycles. Having the arena and the Psitakki people there will help to ease our transition, we think."

"I'm sure we'll be celebrities," added Eux-Auhr-Herx, his chest puffed out and his chin aloft.

"Most definitely," concluded Duke. "How about you guys take her?"

"To Psitakki?" blurted out the Queen.

"Yeah, there's a Chief Interrogator General that will know what to do with her," said the bounty hunter. "Just tell him that Duke LaGrange said to be as creative as possible."

"Sounds fun," replied Grozzel. "We'll do it. And, if I haven't said it already, it was nice meeting you, Duke LaGrange. Now we know all one hundred victors. I don't think we ever thought this day would come. It's provided some much needed closure for us."

Duke removed his hat and placed it against his chest. "I'm humbled to have met all of you. Thank you for your help and for trusting us."

"You made a compelling case with your speech. Very compelling. It sent chills up and down my old spine."

Duke smiled and shook the Psitakki's hand.

He then approached his former love. Mazilda's gaze, even with one eye swollen, was harsh. She opened her mouth but Duke closed it with his finger. She didn't fight back.

"No, you're done talking," he said. "I knew I had bad taste in women. Like really bad. Epically bad. But I thought you were different. I beat myself up, over and over and over for cycles, for letting you go; wondering how different my life would've been with you in it. And I was right to think you were different. You were *worse* than anyone else that I'd ever met. Way worse. Goodbye, Mazilda."

The bounty hunter kissed her on the cheek, putting just enough pressure on the bruise that it caused Mazilda to cringe in pain.

Duke turned to Ja'a, who had been watching the exchange curiously, and flashed her a wink.

"You are awful at picking women, Duke LaGrange," she said.

"What does that say about you?"

Queen Joe was sitting at the bar. The three inter-dimensional artifacts rested on the counter before her.

It's odd seeing the Queen sitting down on one of her own barstools, thought Duke.

Behind the bar, Earl was sorting through the damaged goods, broken bottles, and cracked shelving. The battle had taken its toll on Cyborg Joe's inventory.

The surviving Four I's soldiers that hadn't managed to escape had been rounded up by the Bounty Hunters Union for imprisonment or to be taken to one of the many galactic crime lords for their own unique brand of discipline. And those were the lucky ones. Some were thrown in ships and sent to Earth to be punished as war criminals by the Irish and Japanese.

Many of the Keltians remained at Joe's, sweeping, dusting, and beginning the long road of restoring the bar to its former glory. Po'l and Ja'a joined them, clearing out the bodies of the deceased and other even less savory remnants of combat—reminiscing all the while.

It's good seeing them back together, talking about Neprius, thought Duke. *It has to mean a lot for both of them.*

Duke was helping Ishiro'shea and his parents turn over a booth that had been flipped during the altercation with LePaco's forces when the Queen stood up. She whispered something to Earl, who shot back a perplexed stare. He then turned and started to fumble around behind the bar. In record time, he whipped up a martini. Duke recognized *that* martini. It was the Queen's signature cocktail.

She took a sip and closed her eyes. They opened. She grabbed Earl's furry paw with both of her hands and squeezed. She leaned over and kissed the Glyptodian on the cheek.

Duke could only just make out her words: "That was perfect, Earl. Just like that, every time."

She then said something else to the hulking barkeep and he returned to digging for something under the counter. He resurfaced with two large bottles of Earth whisky. He set a dozen or so glasses on the bar top. They were a hodgepodge of sizes, colors, shapes, and levels of brokenness. He filled them up to their respective brims.

"Everyone, could you please stop for a second?" Joe requested. She wasn't shouting or even talking loudly, but her words seemed to reach everyone's ears as if she was screaming into them from an eyelash's length away.

Everyone stopped, then began to encircle the proprietor of Cyborg Joe's.

The Queen began. "After millions of cycles in this dimension and the last stretch right here on this wonderful planet of Kelt, in this wonderful bar, with the *mostly* wonderful creatures of this universe, it's now time for me to return."

An outburst of shock and defiance poured from her loyal followers and patrons.

"This isn't negotiable, friends," she continued. "I want to stay, but you all know that I can't. Someone has to rid this universe of these things." She gestured at the three artifacts. "And it *has* to be me."

It was an open and shut case. She was the only inter-dimensional being amongst them, the only one capable of securely depositing these weapons somewhere out of the reach of any member of the universe.

"Thank you all for understanding."

"What are you going to do, Queen? *How* are you going to do it?" asked Lilly.

"The portals that I controlled for cycles at the bar—I'm going to channel them all. But I'm going to summon them all simultaneously. They should be able to create a bubble between the realities of two dimensions—I'm not sure which, but two. I will remain there, with these three items, for what you would call eternity."

"You won't be able to leave?" asked Po'l.

"I won't, my Neprian friend," she said, looking down, "but don't fret. I've had enough good company to fill infinite lifetimes. It's not a sacrifice, it's just what has to be done."

"That seems like a pretty heavy cost, Queen," said Lutra.

Joe opened her mouth but stopped as Duke stepped in front of her.

"Anything without a cost isn't worth having, right?" he said.

The Queen chuckled and put her hand on Duke's shoulder.

"Yes, and don't ever forget that, Duke LaGrange."

The bounty hunter yanked her from her barstool and wrapped both arms around her. "Thank you, Queen Joe. Thank you for everything."

Cyborg Joe's was filled with cheers and platitudes regarding the Queen and her bar.

Po'l cleared his throat. "Excuse me, Queen. Not to be insensitive, but what about the bar? Does this mean the end of the bar too?"

Joe looked back at Earl and nodded. "Earl's martinis are virtually indistinguishable from mine," she proclaimed.

The rebels let out a primal cheer in celebration of this good news.

"So you gave it to Earl?" asked Po'l.

"No, Mister Po'l," the Glyptodian bellowed. "I am not the new owner and manager of Cyborg Joe's... However, I have been told that my services as bartender and concierge at Cyborg Joe's will be retained."

"Cheers to that," replied Duke.

"Then who owns it?" asked the Neprian expat.

A head seemed to pop up from behind the bar, an arm's length from Earl. It was a handsome face, youthful and vibrant. His eyes were a twinkling sable, his skin tawny beige. His auburn hair was cut short, but still appeared messy.

No one seemed to immediately recognize this mysterious newcomer. Even Duke was forced to do a double-take.

"You're giving Cyborg Joe's to Ishiro?" asked the bounty hunter.

Queen Joe's smile was so intense that Duke imagined he could fit his entire finger in one of her dimples.

"We just saved the universe with that space ninja right there, so why can't we save Cyborg Joe's with a space ninja?" said Joe.

"Don't you mean a *drunk* space ninja?" asked Ishiro'shea in a rich and honeyed tone. He downed one of the glasses of whisky that Earl had placed on the counter.

The mob let loose a cavalcade of praise upon the new owner as they made their way to the bar to partake in the celebratory liquor.

"So, little buddy," Duke began, "after all these cycles, that's what your voice sounds like?"

"Is it what you thought it would sound like?" asked Ishiro'shea.

"A little underwhelmed, if I'm being honest. Maybe it's an acquired taste," Duke responded, a sly smirk on his face.

"Well, now you know what I've felt like for all this time."

The bounty hunter's grin grew; he nodded to his best friend and partner and tossed the whisky down his throat.

Out of the corner of his eye, in the distance, he saw a flash of crimson light.

She's gone.

CHAPTER THIRTY-THREE

WELCOME TO CYBORG JOE'S... AGAIN

T HE CROWD SLOWLY POURED INTO Cyborg Joe's Grill N' Go & The Why Not Saloon. Given that it had only narrowly escaped destruction, along with the end of the universe, a week earlier, the steady flow of patrons was quite impressive. But the all-new Joe's already had a loyal customer base. Ishiro'shea and team had successfully repaired the ceiling, patching the gaping hole caused by a stray blast from the inter-dimensional doomsday device. Most of the original signs had been rehung, their neon no less vibrant than before they were knocked off the wall during the firefight between the Queen's forces and those of the sinister Admiral LePaco. The floors were even clean—for Cyborg Joe's, that is. The clientele sported a few more locals than normal and, even though the bar's previous main attraction—the Queen's portals—were gone, the atmosphere and buzz remained intact. The kitchen was pumping out MechaBurger 8000s as fast as Earl was mixing *his* famous martinis.

But behind the bar, greeting customers, new and old alike, wasn't an enigmatic inter-dimensional goddess with a sharp wit only matched by her pansophical wisdom. Instead, there was a stout and exuberant man from Earth, a skilled warrior from one of the most violence-riddled planets in the galaxy but who had a caring heart that embraced all. He spoke little, but what he said spoke volumes. In some ways, he was the only one that could have taken over Cyborg Joe's after Queen Joe left the dimension to stow away the three artifacts that almost brought an end to everyone. It was the happiest that Duke had ever seen his long-time friend, Ishiro'shea.

"I still can't believe I'm here," Yeop said to Duke. "One second I'm grieving over Master Ishiro, the next I'm in a space battle, and now I'm at Cyborg Joe's. *The* Cyborg Joe's. No one's going to believe me back home."

"Cheers, Yeop. And thanks again," said Duke, lifting his glass in a toast.

"My fellow Gartoshians spoke very highly of your tactics in the battle, my new tiny Earth friend," said Lilly as she raised her glass of Glytopdian Summer Ale. "Some unorthodox moves that they've never seen before."

Yeop blushed. "Thanks, Lilly. I'm going to miss you guys when I go back to Earth," he said with a frown.

"At least you don't have to go back to Gurlf," replied Po'l.

Gha, the Goother rat, spun around on his stool and sneered at the Neprian. "At least our swamps don't have flesh-eating cannibals," he fired back.

"They have worse. They have *your* relatives," said Po'l.

Liquor was expelled from Gha's nose like flames from a blowtorch. He lost his balance and fell to the floor. "You win this round, Po'l," he chuckled as he climbed back onto his stool. "Well played."

"Indeed," added Lutra in a sultry tone as she draped her arms around Po'l's neck and chest from behind. "And if you keep playing well... Well, who knows." She planted a peck on Po'l's cheek.

"Watch out for her, Po'l," Duke began, "Hilterian women are—"

"They're what?" interjected Ja'a.

"They're to be treated with respect," finished the bounty hunter with a wry grin. "That's all I was going to say."

Ja'a burst into laughter. The rest of the patrons followed suit.

"You've got jokes now?" Duke asked Ja'a. "When did this happen?"

She playfully slapped him on the leg. "You try and run a planetary government. It speeds up the development of one's sense of humor."

"Seriously though, everyone," said the Nova Texan, "if I can make a toast, I would just like to offer cheers to Queen Joe!"

They all raised their glasses to the former owner.

Duke continued, "And to her formidable replacement, a Salutatorian no less, Ishiro'shea Nobunaga-Flaherty!"

They all raised their glasses even higher to the current owner. The ninja blushed.

"You're still paying for those drinks," said Ishiro'shea.

A chorus of playful boos rained down on him.

"So, Ishiro'shea, where are your parents?" asked Lilly. "I haven't seen them the last few days."

"They went back to Earth to try and pick up the broken pieces and start humanity down a different path," replied the bar owner. "It will be difficult, but they were both looking forward to the challenge. They were happy to be going home."

Ishiro dropped down below the bar and pulled out three unique bottles and a short cubical glass. He mixed the liquids quickly but carefully, then slid the glass to the Gartoshian. "Lilly, I wanted you to try this first."

The anthropomorphic musk ox took a hearty sip. Then another.

"This is delicious," she said, taking in another gulp of the creamy beverage. "What's in it?"

"The base is Earth vodka. The Earth ships left some for us before they went back home. I mixed it with Gartoshian Snow Juice. Some of your brethren donated some to the bar before they departed to Gartosh. It's an elegantly sweet liqueur; I can't believe I hadn't discovered it earlier. Lastly, a splash of a secret ingredient."

"Let me taste that," said Duke, swiping the glass from Lilly and finishing off the drink. He swished it around in his mouth, letting the flavorful cocktail touch every taste bud. "Holy hedgehogs, you bastard. I know that 'secret' ingredient. It's the damn icing on Aintin Kuniko's Irish whisky cakes. It has to be. How did you pull that off?"

Ishiro'shea nodded at Yeop.

"Hey, I never leave Earth without stashing away a few boxes in my ship," replied Yeop. "And now I have a reason to come back; Ishiro'shea will need a constant supply if this drink's going to be as popular as I think it'll be."

He's a pretty smart kid, surmised Duke.

"What are you calling this new concoction, Ish?" asked the bounty hunter.

"It's called the Yvonne."

Lilly lowered her head.

I've never seen her like this, thought Duke.

"A worthy name, indeed," said Duke, raising the empty glass to the sky.

"What's a worthy name?"

Not that voice. Please not that voice.

"What'd I miss, guys?" asked Maxx Gemstarr. "It

doesn't matter; what matters is that I'm here now and the partying can begin."

He slapped Duke hard on the back. It hurt.

"How to ruin a moment, courtesy of Maxx Gemstarr, everybody," said Duke.

"C'mon, what's cooking around here—" Maxx paused and turned to Ja'a. "Easy answer: it's you."

He extended his hand to the Neprian. She shook it.

"I'm Maxx Gemstarr, the Universe's Favorite Bounty Hunter. And you are?"

"Ja'a. From Neprius."

"Neprius? Never heard of it. How about a drink?"

"I'm good. Duke keeps me pretty liquored up."

Maxx's brow furrowed. "*That* Duke?"

"Yes, *that* Duke."

"Yes, *this* Duke," said the Nova Texan, pointing to himself.

"I'm sorry, best buddy o' mine, I keep underestimating you. But I do have some good news to share."

"We can't wait," said Duke unenthusiastically.

"I've talked it over with Mama Fong and I'm taking on the role of President of the Bounty Hunters Union. She's retiring to Oscavia."

"What's the good news?" smirked Duke.

"What are you talking about? I—Maxx Gemstarr, the bounty hunter's bounty hunter, Mr. Popular, Everyone's Favorite—am going to be the new BHU president. How awesome is that?"

"I've now officially seen it all. Astral anomalies, magic orbs, and Jungafallowian androids have nothing on this," stated Duke. "But congrats are in order. Ish, pour this man a drink."

Ishiro'shea slid a nearly full glass of Erontian saké to

Maxx. He chugged it, almost gagging on the potent blast of fermented fury.

"It gets even better," Gemstarr said in between coughs. "I'm moving the BHU headquarters from Daedeaus Purple as my first order of business."

"Where to, dare I ask?" inquired Duke.

"Right next door. We're going to be neighbors, Ish."

The ninja slammed down an equally full glass of Erontian saké.

The *Deus Ex Machina* looked as grand as it ever had. Grand in the broad sense of the word, of course. Its shadow engulfed both bounty hunters standing beneath its battle-scarred hull.

"Hard to believe you aren't coming aboard, little buddy," said Duke. "I'm not sure the ship's going to like that. You were always her favorite."

Ishiro'shea didn't say anything, he just embraced his bounty hunting companion.

"If you ever need me, I know you'll find a way to get ahold of me. If anyone can, it's you," said the Nova Texan.

"And if you ever need me—or a well-made martini—I know you'll find a way back here," replied the ninja. He dropped his head and took in a deep breath. "I want to apologize, Duke."

"You? Apologize? For all the crap that *I've* put you through, I don't think *you* need to apologize."

"Seriously. I was selfish for this vow of silence. Think of all of the times that we could have escaped or I could have warned—"

"Ish, shut up. You might not have spoken, but you always said a ton. Don't ever apologize for that again."

Ishiro'shea extended his hand. Duke gripped it tightly and covered both of their hands with his free one.

"It's been beyond a pleasure getting into the scraps we did across this fair universe. We picked up women, we won at pit fighting, and now we saved the universe. And we found your parents. I think that was the most rewarding thing that we've ever done."

"And *your* father too," Ishiro'shea reminded Duke.

"Speaking of my father, I should probably go. I have a deceased father in the ship's deep freeze, waiting to be buried after all. I don't want him to thaw out—and I'm not really sure how long this sliver of Orb will even last. It doesn't look like it has that much juice, but I'm done predicting anything related to magical rocks. The Queen didn't give us any directions, she just said it would be enough to get Ja'a back home."

"That's probably a good idea," replied Ishiro'shea. "When you get to Neprius, say hi to Uu'k for me. Make sure she keeps up with those lessons. She could be a damn good swordswoman if she sticks to it."

"I will," Duke said. He released Ishiro'shea's hand and turned to the *Deus*. After a few steps, he spun around.

"This is just crazy, isn't it? You running Cyborg Joe's... and *talking*. Me carrying back my biological father's frozen body to be buried on Neprius. Ja'a. The Queen. Mazilda. Maxx. I never thought a day like this would ever happen. I never thought we'd be standing here today."

"I did," the ninja said with a wink and a big thumbs-up.

CHAPTER THIRTY-FOUR

THAT PRIMITIVE ROCK

D UKE KNELT AMONGST THE VAST expanse of vegetation in the valley, an endless sea of flax, jade, and white. The rocky cliffs that formed a sky-piercing perimeter around the grassland were as majestic as Duke remembered. He scanned the cloudless sky, his eyes jumping from one to another of the tiny winged silhouettes dancing across the blue tapestry. He closed his eyes and could hear the celebratory purrs of the grundar fighting through the gentle valley breeze. There were no signs of bloodshed or struggle or violence. If Duke had been tasked with explaining what "tranquil" meant to a new species, this vista would be his entry.

He placed a polished stone on a patch of soil, marking the unadorned grave. He pressed and turned it until it was firmly embedded into the soft dirt.

It read: *Here lies Duke H. Dallas. Gunslinger. Ship Captain. Booze Man. Father.*

He stood up and tried his best to soak in all of the beauty that surrounded him. He removed his hat and let the Neprian sun beat down upon him, feeling each ray permeate his skin. The sweet smell of the valley's grass swirled around his nostrils. He inhaled, filling his lungs with its effervescent aroma.

"Hey," said Ja'a, tugging on his arm. "Are you okay?"

Duke turned to look at her. She was still as stunning as the day he had first seen her in the cave. It seemed like so long ago.

"Yes," he replied, "the best I've ever felt."

"Are you sure? You could have stayed with Ishiro'shea and the bar." She stared at the ground. "I would have made sure your father was buried properly."

"Ja'a, I didn't *want* to stay. I want to be here, with you."

He grabbed her chin gently, lifting her head until their eyes met. He kissed her.

"We can always go back," said the Neprian.

"You're kinda in charge of this planet, remember?" Duke jabbed. "I don't think you can just pick up and go on a vacation to Kelt on a whim. Besides, there's not a warp station within a lifetime's voyage that we know about, even in a ship as impressive as the *Deus*."

"True."

"And, in case you forgot, this is all we have left of Queen Joe's present."

Duke extended his hand, his fingers daintily pinching a strand of twine. The twine, in turn, supported a leathery purse no bigger than Duke's fist. He emptied its contents into his other hand, open and facing the sky. Out poured a stream of sand, rocky and metallic, forming a tiny mound in the bounty hunter's palm.

"This is the last of any magic orbs that we'll ever have to see again."

"And your ticket home," Ja'a added.

Duke grinned and, with one massive exhalation, blew

the pile of ground-up Orb into the gentle breeze of the Valley of the Grundar.

"This is my home," he said.

Ja'a gave Duke another kiss.

"We should probably get going if we're going to make it to Sansagon tonight. I know the grundar are fast but I don't want to be late."

Why didn't we take the Deus *again?* thought Duke.

"It would be rude for us to be late," Ja'a continued. "Plus, Vernglet is so eager to hear about your escapades. He won't stop asking me about them. And I'm making soufflés tonight. I think I've mastered them, finally."

Happiness overcame the bounty hunter. *Finally.*

"I'll meet you back at the grundar. Can I have a few more moments with my dad?"

Ja'a squeezed his hand and headed back to the edge of the valley where their winged feline transportation awaited to take them to Sansagon.

Duke looked down at his father's headstone. "I wish you could've been on some of Ish's and my adventures. You woulda loved 'em, Dad. Women, whisky, and weaponry. We had this one trick, it always worked. I would say 'Have you ever seen someone cut off their own head...' Never mind, you had to be there, I guess." The bounty hunter sighed. "We did some good, though. I don't know if I woulda always made you proud but, then again, you weren't exactly perfect either. I know, I know, water under the bridge. You *did* save my life and, kinda, the universe, so I'll give you a pass on the leaving-me-when-I-was-a-kid thing. But, seriously, I wish you woulda been there. You woulda loved Ish too. I had the best friend a degenerate loudmouth bounty hunter could've ever had. And he was the damn Salutatorian. I really hope that I can make it on my own without him. And Queen Joe, for that matter. I don't know how the universe is going to make it without her. But, as long as Cyborg Joe's is around, the universe has a fighting chance."

He looked up into the Neprian sky again. "I finally found someone that makes me think about someone other than myself... and I'm fairly confident that she won't align herself with a maniacal overlord bent on universal domination. At least I hope not. That wouldn't happen twice to the same person, would it? I think you'd approve of Ja'a. And if you didn't, she'd probably beat your ass. She's like no one else I've ever met. And apparently, she's moving her entire race into the 'soufflé stage.' Impressive, right?" Duke took in another breath of fresh Neprian air. "Holy hedgehogs, I nearly forgot. The news of what you did reached Hefty Senchax. He was so moved that he named his ship, a bar, and a casino after you. I think he even petitioned to change the name of T'ckuvu Prime to T'ckuvu Duke. If it happens, I'll make sure to come out here and tell ya'."

The bounty hunter wiped the newly formed tears from his cheeks. "Anyways, I gotta go now. The Shepherd of the Grundar, Fazeek, said that he'd watch over you. You'll be able to rest here for as long as you need." He removed his hat and put it over his heart. "Rest easy, Duke Dallas. Enjoy Neprius. It's a good home."

The bounty hunter walked back to Ja'a and the pair of winged panthers waiting restlessly. Ja'a handed Duke the reins and he vaulted himself onto the back of his grundar. A coordinated combination of the flapping of the creatures' powerful wings and the propulsion from their muscular hindquarters thrust the duo into the sky. After another flap, they had cleared the valley ridge and were high above the northern land mass of Neprius.

"You know, Ja'a, I just had an idea," said Duke.

"What's that?"

"I think I'm going to open up a bar. Cyborg Joe's, Neprius branch. I doubt the franchise fees would be that much. Ish would probably cut me a deal. And you can probably help me fast-track some real estate for it."

Ja'a shook her head with a smile, gave the reins a tug, and her grundar accelerated out in front of Duke and his steed.

"Fine. We can table it for now, honey," he shouted.

Ja'a did not turn around.

The bounty hunter closed his eyes and let the wind splash against his face as he darted through the dimming Neprian sky.

He began humming the Nova Texan Planetary Anthem.

THE END

DELETED SCENE

Everyone loves a deleted scene. It's raw and unpolished; it leaves the reader/viewer with two big questions: "Why was it left out?" and "What impact would it have made if it had been left in?".

As far as set-up goes, the following scene takes place <u>before</u> the very first chapter of How to Pick Up Women with a Drunk Space Ninja. It is really a "Chapter Zero" (or "Chapter 0.5" if you like that better) and helps provide some color to Duke and Ishiro'shea's whereabouts before arriving at Cyborg Joe's on that fateful evening. It is referenced by Duke when he's trying to woo the Hilterian—but this is the real story.

Like most deleted scenes, this is in its full <u>unedited</u> glory. If anything, it goes to show you how much my editors mean to me! Enjoy!

CHAPTER ONE

THE YON-YOR-KAABA FOUR

"Tentacles in the air where I can see 'em," shouted Duke LaGrange. "And drop the quantum particle chainsaw. And the ink blaster. And the tomahawk. And whatever that thing is. Holy hedgehogs, just drop everything. This is your last warning, Yon."

"Last time I checked, LaGrange, there's four of us and only two of you. And by my count, that's twenty-four arms, twenty-four weapons, to your measly four. How about you drop *your* weapons and put your fleshy arm thingies up in the air?" hissed Yon-Yor-Kaaba. His three fellow gang members provided additional hisses for support.

This was not Duke LaGrange's first run-in with the multi-armed reptiloid thug, in fact, Yon-Yor and his notorious speed cycle gang, The Yon-Yor-Kaaba Four, had the distinct honor of being one of the few potential bounties that Duke and Ishiro'shea couldn't bring in. It was a black eye on the duo's relatively sparkling ledger of bounty hunting success. But that was a few cycles ago and in the flatlands of Nomsompton Alpha, where speed trumps all—

including having a ninja. And speed cycles gangs, if anything, were fast.

"Yonny, come on, you know you're outmatched here. I've already turned your precious bikes into rubble. I'll give you your twenty-four shots because, if you don't kill us on that first try, you're all dead," replied Duke.

"We're not valuable to you, dead," responded Yon-Yor.

"True. We won't get any money from Sol for ya' but I'll feel better about that time back on Nomsompton Alpha. That's still bugging me, ya' now. I'll pass on the insultingly pedestrian reward for you lot to get some closure to what was a pretty humiliating ordeal for Ish and I. Right, lil' buddy?"

The emerald clad ninja nodded in agreement without breaking eye contact with the gang.

The four criminals appeared to ponder Duke's threat. Unable to tolerate the silence, Duke broke it.

"Look guys, it's been a good run. You've definitely earned a spot on the 'most successful gangs' list in this sector. Be proud. Depending on the prison you get chunked into, you might be celebrities. You'll never know if you're dead. And do you really want to die on Tardasio 7? In front of, what is it that you're in front of?" Duke paused, looked up and read the entrance sign above the gang members' heads. "In front of the Happy Time Jolly O' Petting Zoo of Tardasio 7? That wouldn't be fitting of goons as sick and twisted and vile as y'all."

The Yon-Yor-Kaaba Four remained silent with weapons drawn.

This is annoying, thought Duke.

Yon-Yor flashed a wry grin. "You know what, LaGrange?"

"What?"

"I think we'll take our...," he began. But Duke knew the

next words out of his mouth and he let loose a rapid collection of pulses from his laser revolver before the gang leader could finish. Seven shots. Six managed to hit the weapons in Yon-Yor's hands, knocking them to the ground. "...chances," finished the reptiloid slowly, his eyes wide and mouth agape. He glanced at all six hands, then at the ground where six smoldering mounds of debris billowed smoke into the Tardasian sky.

The other three gang members did not fire, they were frozen in their attack stances. By the time they refocused their gaze on the bounty hunter, Ishiro'shea was behind them, katana drawn. In one slash, he halved a pair of sonic sniper rifles. He vaulted himself in the air, dodging knife-wielding tentacles, and struck one gang member in the mouth with a powerful kick. He landed without sound, ducked under a poorly aimed pulse, forward rolled and shot up with a debilitating knee strike to another gang member's chin. The third simply raised his tentacles in the air in defeat.

Yon-Yor-Kaaba had pivoted to see Ishiro'shea's attack and, when he turned back around to face Duke LaGrange, he found himself staring down the barrel of an old Widomaker sonic shotgun—Ol' Betsy.

"No receptionist, Sol?" asked Duke.

The obese Tardasian bondsmen grumbled something under his breath.

"Here they are, after all these cycles—The Yon-Yor-Kaaba Four," proclaimed Duke as he led the bound and gagged foursome behind him through the door of Sol's Bail Bonds-O-Rama. "You recognize, Yon-Yor, of course. And this is his little brother, Yawn-Yor, and their two cousins, Yahn-Yor and Yaan-Yor. I'll admit, this one feels good."

"Well, it shouldn't LaGrange," shouted Sol. "You're really putting me in a bind—a financial pinch of epic proportions—by delivering so close to the cut off. I'm going to have to pay extra to express shuttle them to Nomsompton Alpha. That's not cheap. You know how much that costs me these days?"

The bounty hunter shrugged his shoulders.

"In fact," Sol continued, "I should take it out of your cut. Yeah, I *am* taking it out of your cut."

Sol moved towards the bounty hunters and reached for the end of the metallic tube that bound all four gang members together. Duke stepped in front of his grasp.

"Come again, Sol. You're going to charge me for what?"

"Move it, LaGrange, the clock is ticking. Don't make me dock you another month's worth of credits," the bondsman grunted. "Time is money in this trade, you know that."

"I get the full price or *you* don't get these losers," Duke retorted.

"Hey, we're right here," said Yon-Yor. "No need for name calling."

Duke ignored the gang member and remained fixated on the rotund Tardasian. Sol lunged again and Duke stopped his progress with an outstretched arm.

"Sol, we've done a lot of business together over the cycles. Don't get greedy on me," said Duke. "Ish and I brought 'em in before the date and time you told us. We're getting the full compensation."

"Fine, take 'em," Sol said, withdrawing his advance and throwing his arms in the air. "All that work and nothing. Even if I give you eighty percent, it's better than nothing."

He's bluffing, thought Duke.

"True. But at eighty percent, it's not enough to prevent

me from shooting all four of 'em. Just the sheer joy of finally getting rid of these bastards would be worth that amount, no doubt," replied Duke with a smile.

"What if *we* throw in the twenty percent? Just take us to jail," cried Yon-Yor. "Seriously, we'll pay it. Just get us away from this lunatic. I knew you were nuts, LaGrange, but not like this."

"Shut up," yelled Duke and Sol in unison. The gang leader hung his head.

"So, what is it, Sol?" queried Duke. "Original price or we walk."

Sol shook his head and turned his eyes to the ceiling. Silence.

"Fine, then. Be that way. Looks like I can finally get even with these four for outpacing me back on Nomsompton Alpha," said Duke.

The bounty hunter yanked on the tubing, tightening the bonds on all four gang members.

"Let's go," said Duke, signaling for the door.

CRASH!

The front of Sol's Bail-Bonds-O-Rama was ripped away like a powerlifter opening the top of a wet cereal box. The door was thrown in the air, glass and brick and stone shot out across the sidewalk.

Standing in the opening, taking up more than the entire width of what was once the entrance to the most famous bail bonds company in the Tardasian system was a gargantuan three-headed ice wombat.

The explosion caused by the behemoth marsupial threw back all seven men; Duke released the tubing that secured the Yon-Yor-Kaaba Four. Though they were still secured at the wrists, they were no longer bound together or under Duke's control. Even more concerning, Ol' Betsy was tossed across the room and was now resting safely under the drool-dripping snarl of the three-headed ice wombat.

"Kill that thing!" screamed Sol. "Kill it, LaGrange."

The bounty hunter fired his laser revolver. Nothing. The wombat's ferocious roar doubled in volume and it reared up on its hind legs and came down with a thunderous crash. He fired again. The same result.

"Sol," began Duke, "remind me why you live next to a petting zoo? I'm surprised this type of thing doesn't happen more often."

Sol didn't respond as he was darting around the lobby of his office, trying to find a suitable place to hide.

"Why is that thing in a petting zoo?" asked Yon-Yor. "And how'd it get out?"

Damn, that seventh shot must have hit his enclosure. That's what I get for missing.

"It's all relative. Yeah, he can tear *our* heads off with a single swipe of his little wombat paw; but he's a school pet for a Mega-Troll. I mean, he *is* kinda cute, right?"

The center head of the wombat was firmly focused on Duke and Ishiro'shea. The other heads kept their eyes locked on Sol and the huddled gang members respectively.

The beast lumbered forward but he couldn't get all three heads through the brand new wombat-made opening. With each attempt, however, more and more of the façade crumbled. It would only be a matter of minutes before it would be on top of them.

"Can you kill it?" asked Sol. "Tell me you can kill it."

"Don't look at us," Yon-Yor replied. "Our hands are tied. In the literal sense."

Another lunge by the beast. More of the building collapsed.

"I can kill it," said Duke matter-of-factly. "Easy."

"Then kill it," screamed Sol. "Now."

"Okay," Duke answered, "but only if you give me the full bounty."

"What?" yelled Sol. "Why are you thinking about *that* right now? That thing is almost in here. It will kill us all. Chew us up and spit us out."

"Especially you. You do have the most meat on 'ya," joked Duke.

"You are a moron, LaGrange," Sol yelled. "And you're going to kill us all."

"One hundred percent," Duke returned.

"One hundred percent you're going to kill us? Or one hudred percent of the bounty?" asked Sol.

"No wait, one hundred and ten percent of our payment," corrected Duke. "Or I let this thing kill you."

"That's extortion, LaGrange. I won't pay it," responded Sol.

"Fine."

The three-headed ice wombat charged again and was able to get all three heads into the lobby. One more push and his shoulders would be able to squeeze in. There would be nowhere to run.

"Okay, okay, one hundred and ten percent!" acquiesced Sol. "Just do it."

"No matter what happens? If you come out of this alive, I get one hundred and ten percent, correct?" repeated Duke.

"Yes, yes, whatever you want. Just kill it. I don't want to die," screamed Sol.

"Transfer the credits now, please," Duke demanded.

"What? Are you crazy?" shrieked Sol.

"Transfer them."

The Tardasian removed a handheld device, entered some codes, and held it up for Duke to see.

"It's done," shouted Sol. "Kill it!"

Duke placed his revolver in his holster and faced the gang members cowering in the corner.

"First thing that y'all have to do is get to safety, then I can kill it. Luckily, I know a thing or two about three-headed ice wombats from my time tracking down poachers and exotic animal traffickers. When these bastards escape from somewhere, they'll never return to that same place. It's part of their evolution or something like that. Got it?"

"Yeah, I think so," answered Yon-Yor. "You want us to go back to the petting zoo."

"Yes. And hide," added Duke.

"How are we going to get past that thing?" asked one of the gang members.

"He's going to be fully in here in about three seconds. When he breaks the barrier, I'll shoot the far head with my laser revolver and distract it. You four run out."

"Got it," acknowledged Yon-Yor.

"What about me?" asked Sol.

"Same thing. Once they're free, I'll distract them and you'll run to the petting zoo. Okay?"

"Fine, fine," replied Sol, a he ducked behind the receptionist's desk.

Does Sol know how to run? Duke asked himself.

The three-headed ice wombat rushed in and broke through the remaining infrastructure. Its shoulders knocked over the side walls; it was in Sol's lobby, free and clear. It let out three simultaneous growls, exposing fangs as tall as any of the beings in the room.

"Now!" barked Duke as he fired his revolver at the far head. All three heads jerked to face the bounty hunter. "Go!"

The speed cycle gang members jetted for the entrance. They scurried under the four massive legs of the ice wombat and cleared the opening of the building. Duke could see them enter the gate—its doors flung open—that marked the entrance to the petting zoo across the street.

The wombat paused. It withdrew from Sol's lobby. It howled and began a rapid gallop back into the petting zoo. Duke pursued it across the street, stopped short of the opened gate, and shut it. He aimed Ol' Betsy at the massive sign that hung overhead and fired. The sign broke in a dozen pieces and fell to the ground, creating an unmovable pile of wreckage just in front of the gate.

Duke turned around and smiled. "They won't be getting out."

Sol waddled over to him, the color drained from his face, his hair disheveled. Ishiro'shea was behind him, shaking his head and his katana sheathed.

"I thought you said he wouldn't go back there; I thought you said you were an expert on—," Sol began before being cut off by the bounty hunter.

"I was wrong, I guess," Duke chuckled. The screams coming from the petting zoo could have been heard on Tardasio 5. "Okay, I was *really* wrong."

Duke and Ishiro'shea started toward the parking structure down the road a few blocks that housed their ship, the *Deus Ex Machina*.

"Hey wait a minute," screamed Sol. "You tricked me. They aren't going to be worth anything if I have to deliver them as a pile of ice wombat droppings. You get them out of there."

"I don't think so, Sol. But *you* are more than happy to, if it's worth it," replied Duke. He unholstered Ol' Betsy and aimed it at an undamaged part of the petting zoo's perimeter wall. "I'll make you a door right now."

"No, no. Don't. Please. Fine. I'll let this one slide, LaGrange, but no more. Got it?" Sol pleaded.

"Always a pleasure doing business with ya', Sol," Duke replied, tipping the brim of his hat.

Duke turned to Ishiro'shea. It was clear that the ninja wasn't thrilled with his partner's tactics.

"I know, Ish, I know. But those guys were bad news. They had it coming."

Ishiro'shea's expression did not change.

"I'll make it up to you. How about we take these earnings and get a drink?" Ishiro'shea's eyes widened. "How about a trip to Cyborg Joe's?"

Duke could see the ninja's smile under his mask.

I thought that'd cheer him up.

THE OFFICIAL
UNOFFICIAL HISTORY OF
THE ADVENTURES OF
DUKE LAGRANGE

As this is the official unofficial (or is it the unofficial official?) history of The Adventures of Duke LaGrange, I feel obligated to issue the following disclaimer:

1) What follows is accurate to the best of my knowledge; I even consulted a few archived emails to confirm timelines (that's how much I care about you, my cherished and beloved reader);
2) If I made it up, it would be quite a bit more entertaining than this dreck.

If you decided to spend your hard-earned money on this omnibus edition of The Adventures of Duke LaGrange—first off, thank you—then you may actually care or are genuinely curious to know the origins of this little space adventure. And may the gods have mercy on your soul.

CHAPTER ONE

FROM SNOW CRASH TO JURASSIC PARK III

L ike many authors, I showed an interest in writing at an early age. Though I never *loved* school, if a project involved creative writing, I was all in. If I had the chance to write something nonsensical or outright bizarre, I was doubly in. I remember in middle school writing some really outlandish stories; and I pulled from a number of influences at the time—Monty Python, Blackadder, "Weird" Al Yankovic, Ray Stevens, Roger Miller, and more. But, by the time I was in high school, writing morphed from sheer enjoyment to a chore. Assignments or prompts with any level of specificity or guidelines were not my bag. I struggled, often unsuccessfully infusing my irreverent style into more straightforward projects. I became extremely disenfranchised with writing. It ceased to be fun. Despite this being a creative "dark ages", I was lucky enough to be introduced to Neal Stephenson's *Snow Crash* by an amazing professor, Mr. Cy League. In his class, we focused on cyberpunk tomes such as the aforementioned *Snow Crash* as well as William Gibson's *Neuromancer*. While reading the iconic Stephenson sci-fi adventure, I had my first creative epiphany. After being hit over the head by a certain line from *Snow Crash*, I felt a connection to the written word that I hadn't in a long time. Looking back, this could have been the genesis of what would become the foundation of my style and my voice as a writer. In those critical developmental years, you typically Frankenstein together the aspects of your favorite writers that resonate the most. Neal Stephenson was my first building block. "[B]lack chariot of pepperoni fire" gets me every time.

> *"The orange light looks like a gasoline fire. It comes in through people's rear windows, bounces off their rearview mirrors, projects a fiery mask across their eyes, reaches into their subconscious, and unearths terrible fears of being pinned, fully conscious, under a detonating gas tank, makes them want to pull over and let the Deliverator overtake them in his black chariot of pepperoni fire."*

NEAL STEPHENSON, SNOW CRASH

During my freshman year in college, my passion for writing bubbled up to the surface briefly during a creative writing course. But as soon as the class ended, I refocused energy on other subjects. But during the summer months in 2001, I had my second creative epiphany. It was during a screening of *Jurassic Park III*...yes, *that Jurassic Park III*... that I became overwhelmed by a tsunami of emotions. And, since it was *Jurassic Park III* on the screen, we know the film itself wasn't the cause. The feeling was hard to describe but it was akin to a voice inside me saying: *You will never be happy until you create something. Your primary superpower is your imagination, so you use it, dumbass. You can't draw. You can't sing. But you can write. Kinda.*

A week or so later, I had shoved those thoughts to the deepest pits of my mind, seemingly buried forever.

As a professional living in Dallas, Texas, I would spend much of my free time at the flagship Half Price Books (and their wonderful coffee shop) or other local coffee-disseminating establishments. Like a storm without warning, the thoughts from five to six years earlier returned. *Write, you dumbass.* So I wrote. And it was a mess.

I don't still possess those early attempts but they consisted of me describing a scene in rigorous detail. And then adding in some more detail. And then some more. It was obvious that my storytelling abilities were rusty or, more accurately, undeveloped. But, in one of those coffee shops, I started outlining a character named Duke Lafayette. Sound familiar? He was the proto-Duke LaGrange. But he was serious. He was a former foot soldier that turned on his oppressive masters and blossomed into a very John Wayne-esque protagonist. That story centered around the world of Rodiaccia and, within that world, there were names that I would reuse a dozen years later in *The Adventures of Duke LaGrange.*

- San Sagon was an island nation and home of the primary antagonists; it was shortened to **Sansagon**, which became the capital of the northern landmass on Neprius.
- The final battle was to be called the Battle of Mustangson; Mustangson was changed to **mustangsen** and reworked as the metallic substance that could control the Orb in *How to Pick Up Women with a Drunk Space Ninja.*

- San Le Paco was a prominent city in my story; I dropped the "San" and **LePaco** came the last name of the chief baddie, Admiral Lothario LePaco.

Despite the hours spent in the best coffee shops in Dallas (and Starbucks), I just couldn't produce anything resembling a coherent story. I remember telling a friend on a plane to Reykjavik, that I was writing a science fiction story (strategically avoiding the word "novel" because it would have generated a well-deserved eye roll) but kept giving up and deleting it after every few thousand words. I made some sort of claim that it was all therapeutic—which was, of course, a total fabrication; in reality, it was killing me. I simply wasn't good enough. I also didn't want to put in the time or effort to attend workshops or even read a book on writing. It was just supposed to come naturally, right? Wasn't I really talented in seventh grade?

Also, it turned out that "Duke Lafayette" was already being used by an obscure but very real artist. My dreams were dashed.

I gave up again.

CHAPTER TWO

SPIDERS AND DUCKS

Many years later, I was at a book store, probably in 2011, and grabbed this really nifty leather-bound notebook. It had a really Tolkein-esque tree on the cover; if I couldn't be inspired by this to take another crack at writing, I was hopeless. I bought it and hunkered down to write the novel that had always been inside of me. Yeah, a few ideas popped out and made its way onto the page. A few. Bits and bobs about this and that. But unlike the previous attempts, I kept the ideation process alive for months. I'd write an opening paragraph, throw it out, and start again a month or so later. It was all in the spirit of sci-fi adventure, inspired more by 1980s films like *Big Trouble in Little China*, *Krull*, *Spacehunter: Adventures in the Forbidden Zone*, and *Buckaroo Banzai* than any piece of literature. Almost every new false start produced a sillier and more irreverent output. It would have been stuck in this vicious loop had it not been for two things: 1) I started reading Spider Robinson and some other sci-fi comic masters and 2) I began to listen to podcasts about writing and publishing.

I had always loved Douglas Adams and *The Hitchhik-*

er's Guide to the Galaxy but that was the breadth of my humorous sci-fi knowledge base (outside of some books like *Snow Crash* that could be best described as "humorous sci-fi adjacent"). Then I discovered *The Callahan Chronicals* by Spider Robinson. To this day, I still claim Spider Robinson is the greatest writer of the modern era. In the same scene—hell, the same paragraph—he can bust your gut and break your heart. I've never read anything so human, even when the chess pieces that he manipulates are very alien. I don't write like Spider Robinson in style or approach but he will always be that unreachable beacon of quality; an absolute "best" in a world of subjective gradations. But how did this inspire me to get more serious about writing? Simple. I wanted to be part of an industry that could birth and nurture something as rich and complete as Spider's work; I wanted something from my mind, my soul, and my talents to have a chance to live alongside something as important as *The Callahan's Chronicals*. Reading Spider Robinson made me *want* to create. It made *want* to consume more content. And I did. Steven Campbell. A. Lee Martinez. Scott Meyer. John Scalzi. With each word read, my path became less hazy.

During this time, Duke Lafayette morphed into Duke LaGrange. Partly because I liked the ZZ Top song, partly because it sounds a bit like duck à l'orange.

So, then I wrote a few words down and sent it in to an editor. Well, an editor in the sense that it was a somewhat successful author (to remain nameless) that wanted to make a few extra books by examining first chapters for aspiring authors. I paid my money, hit "send", and waited. I knew I would get something back that was heavily redlined; I was excited to learn where I could clean up my chapter and then I would be on my merry way to penning the other 80,000 words. Looking back, the outcome was too predictable. It wasn't just heavily redlined, it was massacred. And rightfully so. I changed tense and POV in the middle of scenes. The dialogue was clunky. The descriptions had descriptions, and they had descriptions. Not enough "showing", lots of "telling". On top of that, the editor didn't particularly care for comic zaniness so some items were just deleted without commentary. For days, I kept re-reading the document. With my ego shot and close to giving up yet again, I emailed her back and asked her if she thought I had any chance of being a writer; if there was a diamond within the pile of muck. Her response was less than flattering. But it was important. The very next day I sat out to improve my craft.

Enter the second critical aspect of getting over the writing hump—podcasts. I searched for the best podcasts on writing craft, storytelling, indie publishing, marketing, etc. The usual suspects of that era popped up—*The Self-Publishing Podcast* with Sean Platt, Johnny B. Truant, and David Wright, Joanna Penn's *The Creative Penn*, *The Sci-Fi and Fantasy Marketing Podcast* with Lindsay Buroker, Joseph Lallo, and Jeffrey M. Poole, and *The Story Grid Podcast* with Tim Grahl and Shawn Coyne. They helped me sharpen my tools. They motivated me to keep pushing.

I revised that same opening chapter that the editor disemboweled less than a year earlier and sent it in to a Writer's Type contest (it was the first writing contest that I found online that was for opening chapters). It placed third. Improvement. From that point on, I never stopped writing; and opportunity reared its beautiful head in late 2014.

CHAPTER THREE

IT'S ALL GEEK TO ME

L iving in Chicago, there was a lot of hype around a new gastropub that would cater to "geek culture". It was written up in every publication one could think of, both locally and nationally (including a piece in Forbes). Geek Bar, the brain child of David Zoltan, was a Kickstarter darling. I was late to the party as the fundraising was completed by the time I had heard of the concept but that didn't stop me from attending a few of their early pre-launch pop-up events. Zoltan was clearly on to something.

Later in 2014, after Geek Bar had landed in Chicago's Wicker Park neighborhood, the bar posted on their various social channels that they were looking for creative types—writers, illustrators, artists, podcasters, filmmakers, musicians, and the like—to be part of a virtual extension of Geek Bar, dubbed Geek Bar DLC. They wanted to go beyond the physical limitations of the bar itself with "geek" news, reviews, and original content. As part of this venture, the original fictional content would all share the same universe —a "Storyverse", if you will. I was intrigued. I signed up and sent in some writing samples for review and crossed my fingers that they would respond.

This leap of faith changed my life. It truly did. I attended the first Storyverse meeting that winter and heard more of the pitch. More importantly, I met some likeminded creative types that would go on to become inspirations, coaches, and friends. People like:

- **Marcus Muller** – comic artist and creator of *King of the Unknown*
- **Frank R. Sjodin** – pulp author, puppeteer, clown, probably the most creative mind that you could meet
- **Ben Nuñez** – amazing illustrator and creator of *The Benerator Robot Factory*
- **Sam Del Rosario** – one of the funniest guys that you will ever meet (and someone that should be writing more!)
- **David Zoltan** – the boss; without him, this never would have existed

The goal (as I understood it) was to have the Storyverse branch out into comics, original fiction, audio dramas, you name it. Each entry could have their own view of the shared universe; comedies could exist alongside horror, surrealism could live in harmony with grit. After a few brain storming sessions, a Storyverse handbook was created so that we would loosely be playing in the same sandbox and then we adjourned for a few months to create.

The skeleton draft of *The Adventures of Duke LaGrange* that I had been working on was retrofitted to align with the Storyverse handbook. I reimagined Duke as more of an unsavory character (a total ass) and was planning to have the arc be his transformation into a more acceptable antihero. Zoltan reviewed the submission and, in the nicest way possible, told me that I had gone too far in one direction and to return it to a form that more resembled my initial sample. Within two days, it was done. And it was approved by the boss man.

At the 2015 Chicago Comic & Entertainment Expo (C2E2), Geek Bar officially announced the launch of Geek Bar DLC and the Storyverse. Approximately two weeks after the announcement, *The Adventures of Duke LaGrange* #1 hit GeekBarDLC.com, the second serial behind Frank R. Sjodin's *Beyond, Beyond*. For the next year, *The Adventures of Duke LaGrange* graced the web every two weeks. For the first time, I had a schedule and I produced meaningful content on a regular basis.

I also began to work on another Geek Bar DLC project, *Of a Mesozoic Mind*. I dreamed up taking a funny but paleobiologically accurate look at some of the more obscure dinosaur-centric media in pop culture. This was a pretty research-intensive endeavor but I thoroughly enjoyed it and it helped me hone my craft. It was well-received critically, as well. From the popularity of the blog and my own site dedicated to the blog, I was given the opportunity to review dinosaur books from Smithsonian Publishing, to become a member of the Society of Vertebrate Paleontology, and to have an email conversation with a childhood hero, Eric Boardman (of *More Dinosaurs* fame). But, make no mistake about it, Duke was my primary passion.

Even though they were not part of Geek Bar, two other close personal friends and talented creatives, Eric Gaydos (photographer) and Nick Bradley (musician, special effects/makeup aficionado), provided a ton of support during this time. I couldn't tell the Duke LaGrange story without them. I will always be thankful of their encouragement.

CHAPTER FOUR

AND NOW THERE'S AN OMNIBUS

About one year into its existence, Geek Bar DLC ceased operations. The creators, myself included, blamed the lack of traction on the non-existent media support (even at the bar itself), that content was pretty sporadic, and some of the desired pillars—namely, a Storyverse comic—never came to fruition (which made the powers that be less excited). What we found out was that the bar was about to cease operations as well—so as the bar went, so did DLC and the Storyverse.

A few weeks after the closing of Geek Bar and Geek Bar DLC, the space was turned into the *Saved by the Bell* pop-up, Saved by the Max. Hey, if something was going to rise from the ashes from something as important to me as Geek Bar, why not this? Full disclosure, I was there on opening night and it was a blast!

Now what for *The Adventures of Duke LaGrange*? It was a story without a home. My first inclination was to turn it into a web serial that I would manage. I was already producing a chapter every other week so the only missing elements were an editor (Geek Bar DLC provided that at no charge), a virtual home, and an investment to get eyeballs to that site. As I pondered the feasibility of this approach, I kept writing. But the best outcome of this period was that I reached out to some amazing artists to develop illustrations and character art for the new site. Marcus Muller had produced a "cover scene" for me previously (it's the one that graces the cover of this omnibus edition) but he was too swamped to produce more. He introduced me to Christian Colbert. I did some research and got in contact with Nathan Anderson. Together, they generated some awe-inspiring character art that added fuel to the creative fire. In fact, this edition contains these drawings as part of *The Art of Duke LaGrange* section. After some time, however, I realized that a bi-weekly serial on a site that had zero traffic was not a viable solution. My only option was to write the damn book.

The two years that followed flew by; I wrote at every free moment that I could muster: on the weekend, during lunch breaks, in bed. I also increased my podcast intake and came to the realization that I needed to complete the trilogy and release in rapid succession. While sitting at the Mudsmith coffee shop in the Lower Greenville area of Dallas, I finished book one. A few months later, I produced book two in a total of six weeks (most of that during a successful NaNoWriMo). Book three was done in less than three months, mostly completed over lunch breaks in late 2017 and early 2018.

The next six months consisted of the boring part of the process (at least from a "describing it to a reader" standpoint)—developmental editing, line editing, proofreading, rewrites, cover design, etc.

After a long journey from the litany of creative crises to

an inspiring leather-bound notebook to a disheartening edit by a successful author to a gastrobup that catered to nerd culture, *The Adventures of Duke LaGrange* hit the market in October 2018.

And now there's an omnibus.

THE ART OF DUKE
LAGRANGE

The following pages showcase some remarkable art from some even more remarkable artists. All five talented illustrators produced work that was instrumental in the creation of The Adventures of Duke LaGrange.

I wanted to say 'thank you' for their inspired efforts and please know that it's my honor to share a bit more of their work with the world.

MARCUS MULLER

Marcus Muller is a comic artist and the creator of *King of the Unknown*, a horror-rock-comedy comic featuring fat Elvis. Marcus has created artwork for DC Comics, Dark Horse Comics, IDW Comics, Locust Moon Press, as well as concept art for video games, beer labels, and any number of random businesses in need of rad art. Has insomnia. Loves pizza and donuts.

Author Notes: This is the earliest concept work of Duke LaGrange. This representation of Duke is still what I consider to be the "true" Duke LaGrange (at least, it's what's in my head when I'm writing the book).

Author Notes: This is an early sketch of the scene that graces the cover of this omnibus. Muller's attention to detail is without equal. If you look closely on the cover, you will see an Easter egg relating to his groundbreaking comic, *King of the Unknown*.

VOJISLAV VASILJEVIĆ

Vojislav Vasiljević is a comic artist from Belgrade, Serbia. He has contributed to publications such as *Bager*, *Strip Mania*, Buddy Wagner's *P.E.R.K.* roleplaying system rulebook, and worked with Alex Banchitta on the comic book series *Captives* for Fright Entertainment. His illustrations can also be seen on the covers of select issues of Croatian SF magazine, *Sirius*, and Serbian SF magazine, *Alef*.

Author Notes: I sent out countless submission requests to find the artist that would bring the world of Duke LaGrange to life on the book's front cover. It was a grueling process...not because I received a ton of bad submissions... but because I received so many good ones! At the end of the day, Vojislav Vasiljević's work stood out. But I almost didn't choose him. A few months prior, I sent out an initial submission request and landed on an artist from Spain. He took the money and ran. After not hearing back from him for a few months, I sent out another request. Luckily, Vojislav answered it.

Above is the first sketch that I received from Vojislav.

Notice that Duke has a beard and Earl has been replaced by an android.

Author Notes: We were getting close at this point. The scene was finalized and we were testing colors and tones. The only major change from this version was that we added more clothing to the female alien (I've dubbed her the "sorta Hilterian") to the right of Duke.

Author Notes: This was Vojislav's first sketch of what would become the cover of *How to Win at Pit Fighting with a Drunk Space Ninja*. I was really wanting to do a scene from the Tournament of the Shield of the Colossal Calamari—but not one of the major scenes. Duke's battle with Glux Xyphormog seemed perfect and could be a great visual. The original drawing showed Glux with four arms—which is cool—but I didn't want there to be any confusion with the many-armed Zylantian race. Other than a few background changes, this is ultimately what went to the press.

Author Notes: I included this version simply because I thought it was really cool to see the characters without the background. Vojislav did an amazing job with the Glux character—it actually looks better than what I had in my head when I wrote his scenes.

Author Notes: This was the original sketch for the cover of *How to Save the Universe with a Drunk Space Ninja*. It was a bit less "polished" than the other early submissions but Vojislav definitely captured the essence of the book in his art.

Author Notes: Vojislav was only a few revisions away from the final cover at this point but this version was so crazy. Duke was in his final form. Ishiro'shea looked like he was straight from a cartoon. The archway appeared as if it was an animation cel. Having no background scene coupled with a Cyborg Joe's neon sign that was in its early stages make this an odd but appealing entry to include in *The Art of Duke LaGrange*.

Christian Colbert was born, raised, and currently resides in Oberlin, Ohio. Christian primarily works digitally, and with traditional pencil, pen and ink. He's inspired by the world around him, music, film, television, and pop culture. Christian has been illustrating and designing for nearly two decades, with such professional credits as *Spider-Man*, *Guardians of the Galaxy*, and *Teenage Mutant Ninja Turtles*. However, Christian is most excited about his own intellectual property, *Lantern Falls,* being optioned for development as a feature film/television series.

Author Notes: After GeekBar DLC shut its virtual doors, I considered launching *The Adventures of Duke LaGrange* as a web serial. As part of that, I wanted to accompany each entry with original character art. Marcus Muller got me in touch with talented artist, Christian Colbert. His interpretation of Ishiro'shea was stunning—it captured the silliness of the world but didn't make the character a cartoon. He looks like he could slice your head off.

Author Notes: I think Colbert had the most fun when I asked him to bring Lilly, the anthropomorphic musk oxen from one of the moons of Gartosh, to life. There's only one word to describe this: perfect. Lilly is one of my favorite characters to write...and I always have *this* image in my head when she's throwing those haymakers! Thanks, Mr. Colbert!

Author Notes: It's easy to see the inspiration behind Colbert's version of the lead singer of The Trampling Death Robots, Sprinkles! By the time that this rendering was complete, I had already moved away from the web serial and decided to go the more traditional novel route.

NATHAN ANDERSON

Nathan Anderson is a Michigan-based illustrator, concept artist and designer. His influences are all over the place, from The Old Masters, 1970s European comics, and colorful arcade games to horror films, classic literature, and retro product design. Nathan is also a huge illustration history buff and loves to collect goofy 1980s action figures.

His credits include work for Wizards of the Coast (via Gale Force Ninja), SyFy (via Laundry LLC), Mayer Hawthorne, Little Caesars, Comedy Central, Hero Complex Gallery, Boxing 247, Kingslayer Game Design, Twisted Indigo, and dozens more.

Author Notes: If I was going to do a web serial, I needed to increase the character art production. So, in August of 2016, I searched for prolific artists that had a similar style as Christian Colbert as he had already finished character art for Ishiro'shea, Lilly, and was working on Sprinkles. Nathan Anderson's work simply popped—and it was close enough to what Christian was doing that I felt it would blend nicely on a site. His first work was Earl, the Glyptodian barkeep. It was perfect right out of the gate! It was also used as a de facto style guide for Earl's likeness on the cover of *How to Pick Up Women with a Drunk Space Ninja* (Vojislav Vasiljević) and *The Adventures of Duke LaGrange Omnibus: Volume One* (Marcus Muller).

Author Notes: I absolutely loved his depiction of Vernglet Wip! It was probably right after seeing this illustration that I was sad that *The Adventures of Duke LaGrange* didn't start out as a comic, graphic novel, or animated show. Vernglet looked better here than anything that I could describe with my words. I hate you, Nathan! Not really.

Author Notes: I remember Nathan turning around General Tsarano Gar in a matter of days. My favorite aspect of this piece was that he shared enough characteristics with his drawing of Vernglet Wip so that you could tell they were from the same race; but, Gar's size and menacing "badassery" is front-and-center.

Author Notes: One of the last items that Nathan worked on for me was the Jungafallowian, Prince Korzo-Tapor. The Jungafallowian trio that he produced was probably the furthest from the book's description but still pretty aligned with what's written on the page—just more fun. I could totally see this lot as the chief baddies on a Saturday morning cartoon (with the Prince leading the charge).

Author Notes: After this depiction of Flakka-Grog was complete, I couldn't help but think of the serpent sidekick from Disney's *Robin Hood* as being one of the heads. I never asked Nathan if that was his inspiration, but, needless to say, I wouldn't want to hang out in Cyborg Joe's with this guy.

Author Notes: Of the three Jungafallowians, Orbo-Terg is my favorite—in both the actual novels and in Nathan's art. He just looks so big and dumb and primal. And that's the point.

Author Notes: I had Christian Colbert create Sprinkles character art but he was unavailable to do the full Trampling Death Robots lineup. So, I had Nathan complete it. It would have been difficult to put them side-by-side as the differences were pretty drastic but I really did like the animation-centric approach and general silliness of this version.

Ben Nuñez, illustrator, draws robots. Lots and lots of robots. He has a series of coloring books featuring his illustrations called the *Benerator Robot Factory*.

You can find all of Ben's amazing work at http://www.instagram.com/benerator.

Author Notes: I met Ben Nuñez as part of the Geek Bar DLC launch. He loaned some of his general "sci-fi" art to the operation and these three images ended up accompanying some of the earliest Duke LaGrange serial entries. Ben is an extremely talented Chicago-based artist and, who knows, had these illustrations not been so appealing, maybe folks would have simply glossed over *The Adventures of Duke LaGrange*!

ACKNOWLEDGMENTS

Writing is, by definition, an isolating enterprise. It's *your* brain. *Your* fingers. *Your* voice. Only *you* are staring back at that unwavering, cold hearted screen (or paper). You are alone.

However, I fully believe that writing is more than keystrokes and words and letters; writing is everything from your first creative idea to the first person that told you that something you created impacted them to your first conversation with an editor. Writing needs support and love and honest critique. To do something as difficult as writing a novel—an endeavor that will take hours of contemplation, ideation, and revision, even more hours of studied concentration converting thoughts and concepts into the written word, and even more hours in an indescribable type of anxiety waiting on peer and reader feedback—you need more than yourself. You need much more. Isolation isn't an option.

Writing is hard.

These are the people that helped lighten the load when

I felt that I was being crushed by my dream or motivated me to push through the ever-present resistance. Without them, *The Adventures of Duke LaGrange* would not exist in any form.

My wife, Shelley—no single person has to tolerate the up and downs of the writing life more than one's partner; and Shelley has been there from the onset to motivate and encourage me through the downs and ground me during the ups.

My daughter, Finley—though it will be years before you can read these books, you are a constant source of joy and inspiration.

Olive—the only one that's been affected by the creation of these books more than my wife is Olive, our French bulldog. She is truly the best writing companion that one could ask for.

My parents, Jack and Linda - growing up in a household that fostered creativity and never stymied independent thought was so very crucial, and for that, my parents deserve all of the credit.

My family—Kyle, Amy, Mia, Georgia, Jacqueline, Kris, Carson, Michael, and Gerrit—thank you for being the world's best support network.

My in-laws—Ann, Kim, Scott, and Annabelle—your unwavering support through the multi-year process of bringing this to fruition was essential and I could never thank you enough.

To all of my friends that were kind enough to give an encouraging word or a pat on the back or a story idea when things were darkest; Eric G., Nick B., J.C., and Donnie M. —thank you.

To those that were responsible for Geek Bar or that I met during that exciting and life-changing time—Marcus

M., Frank S., Sam D., Ben N., David Z., and all of the other creators and editors that brought Geek Bar DLC to life—thank you for creating Duke LaGrange's first home.

My editors, Tim M. and Sasha G.—you help turn something raw into something readable. You two probably know Duke LaGrange as well as anyone and this journey would never have reached the finish line without your hard work and dedication.

The narrator of the audiobooks, Will T.—you literally are the voice of *The Adventures of Duke LaGrange* and one of the most talented voice actors working today. I am honored that you chose my little sci-fi romp to add to your roster of work.

All of the artists and illustrators that touched the series in some capacity—Marcus M., Vojislav V., Christian C., Ben N., and Nathan A.—thank you for providing visuals to this wacky theater of the absurd.

When it comes to inspiration, you can't overlook the educators that helped pave a creative path for you to walk down; I had many but will never forget the impact of such great instructors as Cy League, Norma Wilkerson, the late Karen Giles, the late Dr. Jim Aldridge, Donna Cox, Joan Wood, and Laurie Wash.

To all of the places where the development of these books took place—some are no longer in existence: Crooked Tree Coffee (Dallas, TX), Half Price Books Flagship Store & Black Forest Coffee (Dallas, TX), Union Coffee (Dallas, TX), Mudsmith (Dallas, TX), Buon Giorno (Grapevine, TX), All About Cha (Southlake, TX), Sip (Chicago, IL), Wormhole Coffee (Chicago, IL), Jupiter Outpost (Chicago, IL), Harold Washington Library (Chicago, IL), Nerdvana (Frisco, TX), Hometown Cafe (Colleyville, TX), and Madness Comics & Games (Plano, TX).

I would be leaving a huge gap if I didn't mention those inspirational sources that I've never met (or at least don't have any idea who I am): Spider Robinson, Neal Stephenson, Douglas Adams, Alan Dean Foster, Steven Campbell, John Scalzi, A.Lee Martinez, Scott Meyer.

And, lastly, to the late Ron Warner. We all miss you.

THANK YOU

I hope that you enjoyed *The Adventures of Duke LaGrange Omnibus: Volume I.* If so, I'd love for you to join my newsletter at DukeLaGrange.com.

The fourth book in the series is due out soon:

How to Battle Giant Monsters with a Drunk Space Ninja

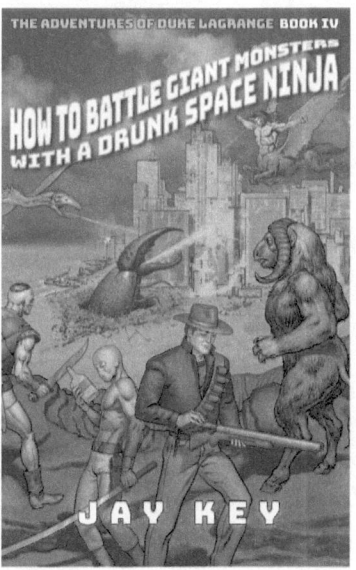

ABOUT THE AUTHOR

©JAY KEY 2019

JAY KEY knew at a young age that he wanted to be the world's first professional wrestler turned fraternity president turned digital media executive turned Society of Vertebrate Paleontology-approved blog writer turned science-fiction comedy author. At various points, Key called Dallas, San Francisco, and Los Angeles home—but it wasn't until a move to Chicago that writing professionally became a reality. Authoring a serialized version of *The Adventures of Duke LaGrange* and a popular blog on the paleobiological accuracy of dinosaurs in pop culture, Key used that momentum to complete *How to Pick Up Women with a Drunk Space Ninja* in 2017. It debuted with Star Wheel Books in 2018. Two sequels followed in 2018.

Jay now lives in a suburb of Dallas-Fort Worth with his wife, Shelley, their daughter, Finley, and their French bulldog, Olive. He is a member of the Science Fiction & Fantasy Writers of America.

 twitter.com/ofamesozoicmind

 instagram.com/jaykkey

 facebook.com/starwheelbooks